blue
rider
press

THE SONG OF THE ORPHANS

THE SILVERS—BOOK TWO

DANIEL PRICE

BLUE RIDER PRESS | NEW YORK

THE SONG OF THE ORPHANS

blue
rider
press

An imprint of Penguin Random House LLC
375 Hudson Street
New York, New York 10014

Grateful acknowledgment is made to reprint lyrics from the following songs:

"Across the Universe." Words and music by John Lennon and Paul
McCartney. Copyright © 1968, 1970 Sony/ATV Music Publishing
LLC. Copyright renewed. All rights administered by Sony/ATV
Music Publishing LLC, 424 Church Street, Suite 1200, Nashville,
TN 37219. International copyright secured. All rights reserved.
Reprinted by permission of Hal Leonard Corporation.

"Wish You Were Here." Words and music by Roger Waters and David
Gilmour. Copyright © 1975 (renewed) Roger Waters Overseas Ltd. and
Pink Floyd Music Publishers Inc. All rights for Roger Waters Overseas
Ltd. in the United States and Canada administered by Warner-Tamerlane
Publishing Corp. All rights reserved. Used by permission of Alfred Music.

ISBN 9780399164996

Printed in the United States of America
10 9 8 7 6 5 4 3 2 1

BOOK DESIGN BY NICOLE LAROCHE

FOR NANCY

A QUICK NOTE FROM THE AUTHOR

The Song of the Orphans is a direct continuation of the story that began in *The Flight of the Silvers*. It goes without saying—though I'll say it anyway—that you'll have a hard time understanding this book if you haven't read the first one.

For those of you who haven't read *The Flight of the Silvers* in a while and have a hazy recollection, fear not. I've set up a special area of my website to let you brush up on the essentials without having to reread it.

Go to **danielprice.info/recap** for a full plot summary, a character guide, and a glossary of temporal and Altamerican terms. You can also sign up to be notified when *The War of the Givens*, the third and final book in the Silvers series, becomes available for pre-order.

I apologize for the crazy long wait between installments. I'm not the world's fastest writer, and these aren't the world's thinnest novels. But I'm working hard on the big finale. Hopefully you won't have to wait too long to see how the story ends for Hannah, Amanda, and company.

PROLOGUE

December had been cruel to New York. The sky sucked its breath on the first of the month, then roared a four-week aria of frost and bitter winds. Aer traffic was shuttered for ten days straight while relentless snow sent Manhattan hiding under tempic cover. Glimmering white panels stretched from building to building, shrouding all the streets at fourth-floor level, turning eighty percent of the island into a lamplit subterrain.

The winter storm ended four days after Christmas. The canopies retracted and generators gorged on the light of the prodigal sun. By the thirty-first, no one cared about the lingering chill. Champagne corks would soon be popping all over.

It was the eve of the Turn and the city smiled in anticipation.

By eleven o'clock, the aerstraunts had taken flight: a hundred giant saucers made of carbon steel and aeris. They drifted like blimps around the Manhattan skyline, offering music and cocktails and rotating vistas. Skyboats from the U.S. Ceremonial Guard hovered steadily at a thousand feet, their projectors primed and ready for the midnight light show.

While the citizenry reveled, twenty-one aerocycles soared east across Newark Bay in a synchronous V. The riders were dressed all in white, from their bleached leather jackboots to their tempis-plated speedsuits to their sleek bresin headshields that looked like welding masks. Their belts were loaded with sidearms that fired everything from gas pellets to stun bolts to good old-fashioned hollow points.

The squadron turned south at Bayonne, then crossed the Kill Van Kull on to Staten Island. The moment they passed the ferry dock of St. George, the riders spotted the first hint of trouble down below. A dozen emergency vehicles had converged outside an art house cinema, a single-screen retroplex with Romanesque trimmings and an electric-bulb marquee that was obsolete to the point to quaintness. Bystanders pooled behind the cordon to rubber-neck, though there wasn't much to see beyond the mob of first responders.

The squadron leader ordered nine of his men to keep their sniper scopes on the theater exits, then sent another eight to do a top-down thermal scan of the building.

"The rest of you are with me," he said through the transcom. "Stay close. Don't speak. Don't do a goddamn thing until I tell you to."

The lone woman in the group knew that Gingold was talking directly to her. She was still new to the unit—so new, in fact, that she didn't have the security clearance to be on this mission. But Cedric Cain had shouted all the right arguments at all the right people, and an emergency exception had been made. No one could deny that Melissa Masaad was a well-tested expert on temporal alien weirdness. If anyone could make sense of this latest strange event, it was her.

Everyone at the crime scene craned their necks as four aerocycles de-shifted above the street. The vehicles descended in graceful unison, as if lowered on wires. Once the wheels touched the pavement, the engines whirred to a stop and the glowing white tires reverted to steel mesh and rubber.

The riders disembarked from their hoppers. A policeman nervously reached for his pistol until an older cop stopped him.

"Stand down. It's all right. They're Integrity."

The police had been warned that federal agents were coming, but nobody said they'd be shades. The National Integrity Commission had been operating behind a shroud of secrecy since its creation in 1913, and had been restructured so many times that even insiders had trouble naming the current director. All the public knew, all they *needed* to know, was that they protected the nation from foreign threats. Seeing Integrity agents on U.S. soil was a rare and disturbing occurrence. No one liked the thought of foreign threats in St. George.

The operatives pulled off their helmets. Melissa, as always, earned her share of curious glances from the crowd. Her cheekbones were overpronounced. Her dark brown eyes were a little bit larger than they had a right to be. And her twelve-inch ropes of dreadlocked hair—a style so uncommon that it didn't even have a name in this country—was simply too exotic for sheltered minds to process.

But for once she wasn't the most conspicuous member of her team. That honor went to her new commander.

Oren Gingold was a formidable figure at six-foot-two, with a lean dancer's build, a sharp-angled jaw, and a fine brush cut of salt-and-pepper hair. In his heyday, before his wayward mission in Palestine, he'd been a conventionally handsome man. Now he only drew stares through the cybernetic cameras that had replaced his eyes. The mirrored black lenses were embedded firmly into his sockets and surrounded by scars, as if a horrible accident had fused a pair of sunglasses to his face.

Sylvester Soo mulled his words carefully as Gingold crossed the police cordon. He had only just recently earned his shield, and he knew as well as anyone that careers were shattered on the frowns of Integrity agents. These people could drop mountains from the sky with a phone call.

Soo peeled off his glove and extended a clammy hand. "Welcome. Hi. I'm—"

"I know who you are," Gingold said, his soft voice marred by a sandpaper rasp. "Any more of you inside?"

"Uh, no, sir. We cleared out on Poe-Chief's orders."

"What's the latest?"

"Well, from what it seems, the whole thing happened 'round forty minutes ago. A strange light—"

"I know all that. I said give me the *latest*."

Soo blinked at him confusedly. "I'm sorry?"

"The intruders," Gingold snapped. "Did any of them leave the building?"

"No, sir. No. I fig none of those folks are in a condition to run."

"You fig or you know?"

"I know," Soo corrected. "Sure as summer. Sir."

Melissa examined the five elderly women being treated under the marquee. Some were bruised. Some were bleeding. One of them had a fractured wrist. The only infirmity they shared, aside from a severe case of shell shock, was a beet-red nose and forehead. Sunburn at the cusp of midnight. That was new.

She crouched beside the nearest casualty, a willowy matron of exquisite attire. Her tight bun had come unraveled, spilling long silver hair over her ears, her brow, her dull, vacant stare.

Gingold photographed the woman through his ocular cameras, then transmitted the image. Two hundred miles away, in a Washington, D.C., office building, analysts ran her facial map through Integrity's databases. The results came back as a murmur in Gingold's earpiece.

"Cassandra Dewalt," he informed Melissa. "Owns the theater. What happened to her face?"

"I have no idea, sir. Permission to ask her?"

Gingold shot her a stony look. "Careful," said a smoky voice in Melissa's earpiece. "He's not keen on sass."

Cedric Cain was the wily old operative who'd recruited Melissa into Integrity, the only person in the agency she even remotely trusted. He'd hacked the image feed from Gingold's optics and now watched from his bedroom in Bethesda, Maryland. Melissa couldn't count the number of encryptions on their private voice link.

"Go ahead," Gingold said to her. Cassandra Dewalt seemed lost to the wind, though Melissa could detect a spark of life behind her hazel eyes.

She deactivated the tempis from her gloves, then touched Cassandra's shoulder. "Ms. Dewalt, can you hear me?"

Cassandra hugged herself anxiously, her gaze still fixed on the ticket booth. "I once sold a seat to Irving Dudley," she creaked. "Long ago, back when he was just a councilman. He smiled at me and asked me my name. I don't . . . I can't remember what film he was seeing . . ."

"Ms. Dewalt, my name's Melissa Masaad. I'm an associate with Integrity. If I could ask you some questions . . ."

Cassandra flinched, as if she'd just woken up from a bad dream. She looked at Melissa with frantic eyes. "Please. This theater's been in my family for three generations. Please don't take it from me."

Melissa shook her head. "We have no cause to do that."

"Yes we do," said Gingold.

"Yes we do," Cain echoed. "The old gal runs a smoke-easy underneath the lobby. She also muds on Mondays."

Melissa sighed. Forty-four years before tobacco was criminalized, the government outlawed the sale and exhibition of foreign films. The act of showing one, even in private, carried a minimum penalty of ten thousand dollars and full asset forfeiture. Melissa was afraid to ask how Integrity knew of Cassandra's crimes. They weren't allowed to spy on U.S. citizens.

She squeezed Cassandra's shoulder. "Ms. Dewalt, we don't care about your other activities. We only want to know about the intruders."

"They came out of the light," Cassandra said. "They came at us so fast. Like they were falling."

"Can you describe this—"

"They came right out of the screen!"

One of Gingold's flying operatives hailed him on the transcom. His voice crackled with wind static. "Thermal scan complete. All clear, sir."

Gingold motioned to his men on the ground, then spoke into his transmitter. "All right. Everyone regroup. Baggers and scanners inside. The rest of you, clear the crowd."

He turned to Detective Soo, his scarred brow arched in suspicion. "How'd you do it?"

"Sir?"

"If these people are the ones we think they are, they're extremely dangerous. How'd you take them down?"

Gingold and Melissa watched Soo closely as he struggled to form an answer. "As much as I'd love to take credit, sir, the truth of the matter's that none of us fired a shot."

He turned his head and took an anxious look at the theater. "Far as we know, those folks showed up dead."

The Dewalt Vintage Filmhouse was a cultural landmark, the oldest standing cinema in the city. The distinction was bittersweet for the owners, as the Cataclysm of 1912 had wiped out most of their competitors. The great white blast had missed Staten Island by a mile, leaving its residents with a deep survivor's guilt that could still be felt today. Commemorative photos of Manhattan, Brooklyn, and Queens lined every wall of the lobby. A brass plaque above the concession stand proudly declared the building to be temporis-free.

Gingold led his team into the main theater, a musty chamber of mahogany and red velvet. Antiquated bulb sconces lit the four hundred seats. Dust swam like minnows in the projector beam.

Melissa barely had a chance to register the scattered bodies in the room before the movie screen stole her attention. A twenty-foot scorch mark scarred the canvas, as if someone had taken a giant cattle brand to it. The fabric was seared in a perfect ring.

Three states away, Cedric Cain sat up in bed and studied the image on his lapbook computer. "Oh, that is interesting. That is very interesting."

Melissa checked her particle scanner. From the dancing gauges, it appeared this was no longer a temporis-free building.

"A teleportal," Cain mused. "Just like the one your friends used last year."

Had Melissa been able to reply without arousing suspicion, she might have reminded Cain that the last portal didn't leave any char residue. It also didn't spit out corpses.

Gingold crouched to inspect the nearest cadaver, a lanky man spread face down in the center aisle. Though his dress shirt and slacks looked perfectly fine, his skin was ashen and covered in frost burns. An icy mist emanated from his wavy brown hair.

Melissa watched from the periphery as Gingold turned the corpse over. The victim's steel-gray eyes were frozen wide, his lips curled in a silent scream.

"Partial recognition," Gingold said. "Central gives it a twenty-two percent match. Masaad?"

A cold grief washed over Melissa as she recognized the deceased, a man who'd been a mystery to her as much as a miscreant. He'd stolen cars, led policemen on chases, rusted the pistols of federal agents. Yet despite his crimes, he'd showed a remarkable concern for the well-being of others. He'd been a good man in a bad situation. He didn't deserve this fate.

"Masaad?"

The voice in her ear grew soft with concern. "Melissa?"

"Yes," she replied to both Gingold and Cain. "That's Zack Trillinger."

She turned her attention to another casualty. This one lay crumpled on his back over two rows of seats, his shaggy blond hair dangling lifelessly over the cushions. Unlike Zack, David Dormer had managed to close his eyes before dying. He looked hauntingly at peace in his current pose, a serene young sleeper on a bed of red velvet.

Gingold raised David's right arm and studied his misshapen hand, the one flaw on an otherwise gorgeous sixteen-year-old. An ill-timed gunshot had robbed the boy of his ring and middle fingers. Melissa had been there when it happened.

"The Australian," Gingold scoffed. "Good riddance."

Melissa wasn't a big fan of David either. The boy had threatened her with her own handgun and then blinded her with lumis. But he'd shown a clear devotion to his friends and had been downright fearless in the face of danger. He might have grown up to be someone truly extraordinary. That alone made his death a tragedy.

Four rows beyond David, a pale arm poked into the aisle. Melissa muttered a curse under her breath. She already knew who it belonged to.

Gingold followed her gaze, then cracked his first smile of the night. "Our little doormaker."

Both Melissa and Integrity believed that Mia Farisi had created the spatial warp at Battery Place, the huge round portal that had enabled her and her people to escape capture back in October. The wormhole was an unprecedented use of temporis, one with staggering implications. The biologists at Sci-Tech practically drooled at the thought of cutting the girl open. For them, Christmas had come fifty-one weeks early.

Cain winced at the dead girl on his computer screen. "Ah, hell. Goddamn it."

Melissa reactivated the tempis on her gloves, then pulled Mia into the aisle. She looked achingly sweet in her beige dress and high heels, an ensemble that might have complemented her olive skin were it not for the frost burns. Trickles of blood ran from her nostrils, marring her cherubic features.

Melissa looked closer. There was something about Mia's arms that bothered her, an incongruity with her visual recollection. The girl had lost at least ten pounds since Melissa last saw her, but that wasn't—

"Found the chinny!"

An armored operative lifted Theo off the floor, brandishing his corpse as if he were a trophy stag. Melissa lowered Mia to the ground, then joined the agent at the back of the theater.

"He's not Chinese," she told him. "If you can't be bothered to read the files, at least show some respect for the dead."

The agent shot her a murderous glare. "I read the files. These people were killers."

"Not this one."

Melissa crouched to examine the late Theo Maranan, the most baffling and enigmatic member of the group. Though his appearance was normally disheveled, he looked shockingly dapper now in a three-piece suit. His face and hair had been groomed to perfection. For a moment, Melissa wondered if Theo had dressed for his own burial, a possibility not entirely far-fetched, as the man had a talent for looking ahead.

She dolefully examined his frost burns. *What happened, Theo? Why didn't you stop this?*

Gingold took a puzzled look around the theater. "Is that it?"

"Is that all the bodies?" Cain asked Melissa. "What about the others?"

Good question, Melissa thought. She scanned the gaps between the seats, her heart pounding with anxious hope. *Maybe they got away. Maybe—*

"Found them," an agent yelled. "Over here."

Melissa moved to the front of the theater, where the Great Sisters Given lay quiet and still.

One was tall and skinny. The other was short and curvy. One had cherry-red hair and sharp green eyes. The other had jet-black tresses and the wide brown stare of a doe. They didn't seem to share a single trait, yet Amanda had assured Melissa that she and Hannah Given were biological siblings. All they truly had in common was their insane predicament, a tale that Melissa still longed to hear.

Melissa's mind flashed back eleven weeks to a windy rooftop in Battery Place. As the sisters dangled over the ledge, Melissa had noticed a matching despair in their expressions, as if everything in the world had suddenly stopped mattering.

"Wouldn't you rather keep living?" Melissa had asked them, genuinely unsure of what they'd say.

"That's all we want," said Hannah.

"That's all we ever wanted," said Amanda.

Now the sisters lay conjoined in a messy heap, their heads pressed together, their hands locked in a frozen clasp. There was a palpable grief on both their faces, a pain that seemed to go far beyond the physical. For all Melissa knew, they'd been looking right at their killer before he or she pulled the final trigger.

The swinging doors flew open. Eight operatives charged in with their stretchers and scanners and black-fiber body bags.

Gingold watched Melissa as she hurried toward the exit. "Where are you going?"

"To canvass the witnesses some more."

"The ghost drills are coming. In twenty minutes, we'll see the whole thing for ourselves."

Melissa shrugged. This place was already teeming with phantoms. If anything, she hoped Cassandra Dewalt would take her to the hidden smoke-easy underneath the lobby. It seemed both women could use a cigarette.

As usual, Cain was one step ahead of her. She could hear the flick of his lighter in her earpiece.

"I'm sorry," he told her. "This isn't how I wanted it to end."

"I know," she said. "I believe you."

She stepped back outside and worked her way through the rabble, until she was just a stone's throw from the marina. Looking up, she saw the Mark of St. George, the illuminated clock tower on the roof of the ferry terminal. Termites had eroded its support beams over the decades, turning a once-proud landmark into a safety hazard. Rather than rebuild, city officials had replaced it with a sixty-foot ghostbox. Now the Mark of St. George existed solely as a hologram, a life-size specter on a twenty-four-hour playback loop. Though it gleamed with sunlight even on the rainiest of days and vexed countless birds with its intangible perches, the clock still kept perfect time.

As the hands reached ten seconds to midnight, the U.S. Ceremonial Guard began their light show. Millions of New Yorkers stopped what they were doing to watch the great celestial countdown in the sky.

10...9...8...

Melissa lowered her head and stuffed her hands in her pockets, her mind venturing deep into next year. Though her case had suffered a tragic setback tonight, there were still blanks to fill. People to find.

7...6...5...

At the top of her list was Peter Pendergen, the getaway driver, the man the fugitives had traveled twenty-five hundred miles to meet. Either Pendergen had betrayed them or he'd simply failed horribly in his mission to protect them. Either way, the man had a lot to answer for.

4...3...2...

Except there was something about the crime scene that continued to plague her, something about Mia Farisi. The girl's arms had become thinner since Melissa last saw them. But more than that—

1 . . .

—they were longer.

The sky erupted in lightworks—starbursts and roses and ethereal balloons, set against the backdrop of a spectral American flag. The Turn was a patriotic rechristening of an old familiar holiday, created by Teddy Roosevelt in 1913 as another venue to promote national exceptionalism. Let the rest of the world blow their noisemakers and call it New Year's Eve. The Eagle, as always, went its own way.

On the roof of the ferry terminal, at the base of the clock tower, a tall and reedy couple watched Melissa with interest. They were an elegant duo in their long English waistcoats and virgin wool slacks, with pulse-heated filament gloves that had yet to be invented on this Earth. While the man's fine white hair stayed perfectly still in the wind, the woman's long brown locks flapped chaotically.

The pair conversed in a foreign tongue, a complex mixture of Asian and European languages that had become the lingua franca of their era.

"This won't last," Esis cautioned. "The woman already creaks with doubt."

Azral scowled at Melissa's distant figure. "Let her. She's no longer a threat."

A portal opened up inside the Mark of St. George. A six-foot man stepped through the surface. Neither Azral nor Esis turned to look as he passed through the illusory wall of the tower. They'd felt him coming from miles away.

The man moved to the ledge, standing snugly between the mother and son. Esis clutched his arm and gave him a crooked smile.

"My heart returns," she cooed. "He teases with his fleeting presence."

Azral regarded him with soft deference. "You didn't need to come, Father."

"There's no risk," the patriarch insisted. "I was careful, as ever."

With his family, Semerjean Pelletier didn't need to wear his many masks. He didn't have to force his words through crude English, or pretend to be interested in the inane prattle of others. Shame he only had a few minutes to enjoy his freedom.

He focused his gaze on Melissa. His sharp blue eyes turned cold, severe. "We should kill that one."

"Not yet," said Azral.

"You underestimate her, *sehgee*. The woman is clever."

"That cleverness will aid us in the future, should these soldiers become a problem again."

Semerjean pursed his lips, frustrated. There was once a time where he could see the strings in all their splendor. Now his foresight had become withered with age, and no amount of temporis could fix it. He had to entrust the long-term planning to his wife and son.

He flipped a hand in surrender. "*Fine,*" he said in unintentional English.

Esis caressed his shoulder. "My poor darling. If you wish to return to us—"

"No," Semerjean insisted. "I'm still needed where I am."

"I just hate to see you suffer so."

Semerjean sighed. It was indeed a chore to live among these ancients, with their stenches and chemicals, their fallacies and histrionics. But they weren't all unbearable. Some were pleasant. Some were amusing. Some even surprised him.

He stood with his family, under the stars and lumic projections, while the locals continued to celebrate another pointless trip around the calendar. Even here, from his high perch, he could smell the flavored poison in their cups. He could hear their discordant warblings of "Auld Lang Syne."

Semerjean felt nothing but pity for the hopeless beasts below, these oblivious cattle. They had four years left until the end of their world, and all they could do was sing.

PART ONE

THE GUITARIST

ONE

Time passed.

January threw one last blizzard at the people of New York before settling in to gentle flurries. February served up a shuffle-deck assortment of sunshine and frigid rain. March brought scattered patches of warmth to the entire country, as well as a few surprises.

On Wednesday the twenty-third, at 6:34 in the morning, an abandoned church in Grandview, Washington, exploded in what witnesses described as a dome of blinding light. The flare ended four seconds after it began, leaving nothing behind but a round, smoking crater. The hole was so smooth and geometrically flawless that a flying reporter for Seattle-9 News briefly lost his composure on live lumivision. "Christ," he'd uttered, from his single-seat Skyro. "There isn't a bomb in the world that can do that."

The bizarre nature of the blast set millions of tongues wagging about miniature Cataclysms and threats of worse to come. Rumors grew so wild, so fast, that the president of the United States had to make an emergency address to the nation.

"We *will* get to the bottom of this," he promised, in his strong and soothing baritone. "In the meantime, I urge you all to stay calm. We're Americans. We don't panic. We persevere."

The story dominated the headlines for four more days, until George Gunther made some startling news of his own. Since 1991, the wealthy industrialist and eminent skeptic had offered twenty million dollars to anyone who could predict five natural disasters in the course of a year. The Gunther Gaia Test had become an annual sweepstakes for the self-proclaimed augurs of America, with thousands mailing their guesses each January. Their continued failure to get even one forecast right served as endless fodder for Gunther, a longtime critic of the billion-dollar prophecy trade.

Then along came Merlin McGee. The aspiring futurist, a coffeehouse poet in Oregon City, had submitted seventeen predictions of natural catastrophes around the world, all of which occurred with pinpoint accuracy. Experts studied his vault-sealed entry for weeks before admitting that there was no earthly way the man could have cheated. Gunther had no choice but to admit that his challenge had been bested. In the course of a day, Merlin McGee became a household name, a multimillionaire, and the world's first certified prophet.

As the cameras snapped at the national press conference, McGee humbly thanked Gunther for his graciousness, then warned the residents of Abilene, Texas, that a Class-3 tornado would strike the town at half past noon the following Sunday. It did.

While America kept chattering about vaporized churches and precognitive poets, the Dewalt Vintage Filmhouse quietly reopened for business.

Cassandra Dewalt tightened her shawl, shivering in the brisk night air as she waited under her new marquee. It had been ninety-four days since a metaphysical mishap brought federal agents to her cinema, as clear a sign as any that she needed to make some changes. She severed ties with her foreign film smugglers, closed the basement smoke-easy, and replaced every sign, seat, and gadget that wasn't up to city code. She'd also found a generous patron to help finance the renovations.

She squinted her gaze as two tall figures in springcoats approached from the east, a rather fetching pair at that. While the younger fellow kept his shy gaze on the pavement, the older one walked with a high head and a cheery gait. Cassandra easily recognized him from his Eaglenet profile. Her financial white knight had arrived right on schedule.

"Mr. Pendergen," she said, extending a hand. "So nice to finally meet you."

He shook her hand warmly. "The pleasure's all mine. And please call me Peter."

Cassandra studied him carefully. He was certainly enticing with his deep blue eyes and chestnut hair, his sturdy build and soft Irish accent. She couldn't even guess the number of blouses his smile had popped open. But behind all his allure, there was something unsettling about Peter, an aura of deceit. The man was a skilled and accomplished liar. Of this Cassandra had no doubt.

She turned to look at Peter's companion, a lithe and lovely teen in an ill-fitting baseball cap. "And what do I call this one?"

Peter clapped the boy's back. "This is Liam, my son. We have some family business after this. Hope you don't mind me bringing him along."

"Well, that depends on what you're—"

"Wow." Peter looked up and marveled at the state-of-the-art marquee, computer-controlled and a hundred percent lumic. The Dewalts would never need their ladder again. "That's wonderful. How's business?"

"Hard to say. We've only been open since Friday."

"No movie tonight?"

"No." Cassandra shifted uneasily on her feet. The theater had been closed on Mondays since 1948. She'd be damned if Peter didn't already know that.

He scanned her expression, his grin deflating to a smirk. "I suppose you're wondering what I'm doing here. Why I sent you that money."

"I have a guess," Cassandra admitted. "I've done my research. When you're not writing sword-and-sorcery novels—"

"Just swords. No sorcery."

"—you write magazine articles about supernatural occurrences."

"Well, yes, but mostly to debunk them. There's usually no sorcery in those tales either."

"You can't debunk mine," she insisted. "It happened."

"I believe you, Cassandra. I didn't curry your favor just to call you a liar."

She shivered again, her mind replaying the awful events in the screening room. "It doesn't matter. My theater's had enough bad press. If you're looking to write an exposé—"

Peter shook his head. "My journalism days are long done. I swear it."

"Then why are you here?"

"I just want to know."

Cassandra puffed a heavy breath, her foot tapping in dilemma. When the universe wasn't throwing portals and corpses at her, she was a powerfully sharp woman. She could sense that Peter was telling the truth about his intentions, yet the man still reeked of deceit.

She sighed with resignation, as if she were about to be probed on an exam table. "Go on, then. Ask your questions."

"That's fine. But—"

"We'd rather look around," said the boy at Peter's side. "Inside. If that's all right with you."

Cassandra studied him closely. This "Liam" wasn't as meek or awkward as he'd first appeared. And though he spoke with a perfect American dialect, there was something unnervingly . . . foreign about him.

"All right," she said, suddenly eager to be done with both men. "Have your look."

Cassandra led them into the lobby, then left them to their business. The moment she closed her office door behind her, Peter glared at his companion.

"I told you to let me do the talking."

"You said 'Don't let her hear your accent.' She didn't."

"You knew what I meant."

David pulled off his baseball cap and fluffed his hair. In the six months since coming to New York, he'd opted to grow it out. Now his golden locks nearly fell to his shoulders. To one smitten housemate, he looked like a rock star. To Peter, he was a throwback to the mid-1980s, when personal grooming had briefly become anathema to the youth of America.

"How'd you do that, anyway?" Peter asked him. "You didn't sound a thing Australian."

David shrugged. "Did some acting in prep school. It's not hard. I can teach you to hide your brogue, if you're interested."

"No thanks. Just warn me before you try something like that again."

"Sure thing, Dad."

The joke didn't sit well with either of them. David knew that Peter missed his real son, just as Peter had heard an earful about David's late father. Neither one of them was in the market for a proxy. Sometimes Mia, who'd grown to adore both men, wondered if they even liked each other.

They stepped into the screening room, which had been thoroughly modernized in recent weeks. A black glass lumiscreen stood in place of the old canvas, while the velvet seats had been swapped for flytex recliners. The upholstery was so new, it still smelled of factory chemicals, a rubbery stench that made Peter wince.

"Oof. Lordy. Let's just get this over with."

David squinted in concentration, his mind traveling back through the room's recent history. He stopped at December thirty-first, then creased his brow at the strange new sights in his head.

"Huh."

"What?" Peter asked. "What do you see?"

"My own corpse."

Peter checked to make sure Cassandra wasn't snooping before turning back to David. "Show me."

With a wave of his hand, David brought the past to life as phantoms. Old wooden armrests poked out from the recliners. A long-dead projector beam lit up the screen. Four government agents in tempic armor moved up and down the aisles—intangible, oblivious to David and Peter.

Peter's eyes shifted gravely around the bodies in the room, the six dead Silvers who lay crumpled in five places. "Well, ain't that a thing."

"Looks disturbingly real," David said. "I'll give them credit for that."

"Give who credit?"

"The Pelletiers."

"What makes you think they did it?"

"Who else could have faked our deaths so convincingly? Who else has motive to throw the Deps off our trail?"

Peter took a nervous look at Oren Gingold. "Those aren't Deps."

"What do you mean? I see Melissa right there."

"Those aren't fake bodies either," Peter said. "I'm afraid that's really you."

The images rippled as David processed the news. His eyes bulged at the spectral screen of old, the large brown ring that had been seared into the fabric.

"You're kidding."

"Nope."

"A *time* portal?"

"The only kind that leaves a scorch."

"You said time travel was impossible."

"Impossible to survive," Peter said. "Easy to do if you don't mind dying."

David blinked at him, flummoxed. "That's insane. You're saying that sometime in the future, my friends and I step into a time portal, knowing full well it'll kill us."

"I doubt it was by choice."

David waved his hand again. The agents and corpses vanished. Now Cassandra Dewalt and four elderly friends sat together in the center seats, sipping wine and chuckling as a black-and-white French comedy played on-screen.

"What are you doing?" Peter asked.

"Jumping back an hour."

"If you're hoping to see the portal, you won't. Those things can't be—"

Before Peter could say "ghosted," a flickering glow appeared in the middle of the movie screen. The tiny bead expanded across the canvas, growing and growing until it became a twenty-foot disc. David had seen Peter and Mia make dozens of portals, but they were never this bright, never this turbulent. The surface churned with stormy waves. The edges danced like a ring of white fire.

Cassandra and her friends shielded their faces, screaming as the light of the portal burned them. A fierce gust of wind pushed the two frailest women over the backs of their chairs.

Peter checked the door for the present-day Cassandra. "For God's sake, boy! Shut it down!"

David muted the noise with a gesture. His eyes remained fixed on the portal.

"I mean stop the whole thing!"

"Not yet," David said. "I want to see."

Peter peeked at the glow through a watery squint. "This is crazy."

"What's crazy?"

"In five generations, none of my people have ever been able to ghost a portal."

"I'm not one of your people."

That was true. Peter was one of the few who knew that David Dormer wasn't born on this world. He was a transplant, a breacher, the orphaned child of a dead sister Earth. Like the rest of the Silvers, he came from a place where time only moved in one speed and direction. Neither man nor machine had the power to bend it.

Now that he had temporis, David wielded it with extraordinary prowess. He wasn't the first of his group to blaze past the limits of Peter's clan. Lord only knew what mighty feats these transdimensional cousins would be pulling a year from now.

If they lived that long.

Suddenly, the Silvers flew through the portal as if a vacuum had pulled them. David froze their ghosts in mid-trajectory and then studied their expressions. Matching looks of pain and surprise had been chiseled onto all their faces, even his own.

"You're right," he said to Peter. "This wasn't voluntary. Someone killed us."

"Well, let's not—"

"I can't get over this. I'm looking at the past and seeing the future."

"*One* future," Peter stressed. "One possible outcome out of trillions."

"It's still the death of everyone I care about."

Peter scoffed. "Thanks."

"I'd mourn you too if you were with us. Why aren't you?"

"How should I know?"

"What if this was your portal?"

Peter's eyes narrowed to slits. "Boy, if you don't trust me by now—"

"I'm not saying it was intentional. Maybe it was an accident. Maybe you were coerced."

"You're getting way ahead of yourself."

"I just witnessed my own murder," David said. "It's made me somewhat speculative."

"Come on. We got what we came for."

Peter moved for the exit, then noticed David wasn't following. His wide blue eyes remained glued on his friends.

"David . . ."

"We're all dressed up, like we're going to a formal event. Any idea what it could be?"

Peter had a guess. "Not a clue. Look, don't try to make sense of it. And don't let it shake you. I'll tell you as many times as you need to hear it: it's just one future out of many."

David vanquished the ghosts and followed Peter up the aisle. He turned around at the exit and took a last lingering look at the screen.

"One more future to avoid."

———————

It happened the same way every time.

By his 115th trip through the God's Eye, Theo had seen the apocalypse from every angle. It clung to its script like a meticulous actor: never improvising, never changing a beat. If any of his friends had asked him (and none of them ever did), he could describe each moment with journalistic detail: a five-stage demise stretched out over three hours.

It begins with the clouds all evaporating at once. In the span of a breath, the sky all over the world gives way to a clear and sickly whiteness, more like an absence than the presence of something new. The air carries a metallic scent and there isn't a hint of wind to be felt anywhere. Living creatures, great and small, become restless. Wary.

With two hours left, the electricity falters. Radios go silent. Fan blades roll to a stop. Every handphone and computer screen on the planet goes dark. The temporic devices, meanwhile, shift into simultaneous overdrive. Tempic walls erupt in spikes. Aeromobiles drift into the sky like lost balloons. Millions of people die in the surge, and the trouble is just beginning.

At the start of the final hour, the temperature drops below freezing. From the sands of the Sahara to the tropics of Oceania, humans huddle together and cry puffs of steam.

Then, with four minutes left, the sky makes a horrific sound—a booming crackle, like a thousand splintering glaciers. The aeric vehicles plummet back to Earth in a hail of flaming wreckage. Those who remain outside, those who still have the strength to crane their necks, see glistening crags far above them, as if the entire upper atmosphere had frosted over with ice.

No, not ice. Something harder. Something worse.

Forty seconds left. The crackling sheet of tempis descends loudly from the heavens, crushing all the tallest mountains, all the highest cities. As the buildings at sea level quickly start to topple, there's not a shred of doubt left in anyone's mind. The sky has fallen.

The end has come for everyone.

For Theo, who'd already survived the death of one Earth, this vision was more than just a prophecy. It was a memory. And now it was his view on the way to work.

He flew through the future as both specter and spectator, a formless observer on a fast-forward dash through time. Here in the God's Eye, in the cold gray space between moments, he had near-total control of his foresight. He could speed up the playback, slow it down, rewind and study a branching string. Not that it ever helped. Every future ended with that same three-hour death rattle. The shrieks. The cries. The god-awful crackling sound.

Furiously, Theo thrust himself forward, through the end of the world and into the hazy void that lay just beyond. At long last, the clamor stopped. His gruesome commute was over.

He took a moment to gather himself, then conjured a floating simulacrum of his body. As always, he dressed himself in his most comforting ensemble: his gray Stanford hoodie with the sun-bleached letters, his loose beige cargo shorts, and ratty old sandals. The clothes reminded him of a simpler time, when he was just a drunken ex-prodigy on the streets of California. When nobody on Earth had expected a damn thing from him.

He turned around and winced at the eyesore in the mist, the great white wall that had become his chore and burden. It stretched endlessly in four directions: a quadrillion points of light, a quadrillion variations of this world's future . . . or lack thereof. Peter believed that somewhere in this sea of severed timelines, a single string extended onward—a blessed chain of events in which humanity somehow dodged its death sentence. The solution was nestled inside that strand, and Theo was the only one who could find it.

He wasn't optimistic.

A tiny gleam suddenly caught his eye, a threadlike protrusion on a distant part of the wall. He swooped toward it like a sparrow, then cursed when he realized his senses had tricked him. It wasn't a full string, just a lone stubborn Earth that managed to live a few weeks longer than the others. The apocalypse refused to commit to a single date on the calendar. It varied from timeline to timeline, bouncing around within a three-month window. The discrepancies littered the wall with an endless array of nooks and nubs.

When Peter had first heard about the variance, four months ago, he became positively giddy.

"You see, Theo? I told you. It wouldn't jump around like that if there wasn't a human factor at work. We have influence over this thing. If it can be moved, it can be stopped."

That was easy for Peter to say. He wasn't the one who had to look for a needle in Nebraska. He didn't have to fly through Armageddon each and every day to see the consequences of his—

"Stop."

—failure.

"Stop it," Theo hissed. "Just shut up and focus."

He continued his search. After a few minutes of dull, fruitless scanning, he heard a familiar crackling noise in the distance. The sound of apocalypse was back in his ears and Theo knew exactly why. His subconscious was torturing him again, wrapping him up in his own insecurities like a straitjacket.

"Stop it."

Despite all his efforts, the crackling got louder, more intense, as if every dying Earth had joined in on the chorus. Theo clenched his teeth, his eyes squinted shut as trillions of skies crystallized into tempis. Billions of screams on each world.

"Stop it!"

It happened the same way every time.

"*Stop!*"

Amanda sat up in her chair with a start.

Until just now, Theo had been sitting quietly on his bed, eyes closed, legs folded neatly beneath him. He'd looked so serene in his meditative state that he might as well have been levitating.

But then his head snapped back, his eyes popped open, and he yelled like a man who'd been thrown from an airplane. Amanda had no idea what was happening. It was usually Hannah or Zack who watched him while he was in the God's Eye. She had no experience augur-sitting.

She dropped her magazine and rushed to his side. "Are you okay?"

Theo rubbed his face with trembling hands. "What . . . what time is it?"

"Nine-thirty."

"Day or night?"

Amanda eyed him worriedly. "Night."

The basement was a windowless den of tumbled stone and cedar, a rather grim place under normal circumstances. Through bright decorations and well-chosen amenities, Zack and Theo managed to turn their room into the brownstone's number one social destination. Rarely an evening passed without the two of them hosting a card game, a movie screening, or a just a breezy late-night gab session. Of course Amanda hadn't been down here much these past few weeks, for reasons that still depressed her.

She kneeled behind Theo and gently rubbed his shoulders, soothing him in accordance with her sister's strict instructions.

"You have to be careful with him," Hannah had told her, ninety minutes before. "Give him warmth, but not too much sympathy. He doesn't like pity."

"I was a cancer nurse," Amanda dryly reminded her. "I know how to comfort people."

Hannah slung her purse over her shoulder, her eyes dark and doleful. "This isn't a patient you're dealing with. This is the whole world's doctor."

Try as she might, Amanda couldn't fault the metaphor. As she kneaded the knobs in Theo's back, she tried for the thousandth time to wrap her mind around the insane scope of his mission. It was a terrible responsibility to drop on anyone, much less a recovering alcoholic. Yet despite all her empathy, a part of her wanted to push him harder. *Just find it, Theo. Find the damn string so we can stop having nightmares.*

Theo looked to his roommate's empty bed. "Where's, uh . . . ?"

"He went to that club with Hannah. Remember?"

"Oh yeah. That was tonight." He chuckled cynically. "After all this time, she's finally meeting her mystery date."

"It's not a date."

"It was implied."

"Well, she doesn't see it that way," Amanda told him. "If she did, she wouldn't have brought Zack."

Theo winced at her painful attempt at massage. The woman had all the finesse of a drunk and angry lobster. It didn't help his mood to think of the power inside Amanda's hands, the same crackling white tempis that was four years away from killing everyone.

"You really don't have to do this," he said.

"It's all right. I don't mind."

Theo sighed in surrender, then studied himself in his hand mirror. He was only twenty-four and already he had flecks of gray in his hair. His bronze skin, a perk of his Filipino heritage, had become hopelessly pallid. He needed sunlight. He needed sleep. He needed to think about something other than the world's goddamn ticking . . .

He adjusted the mirror and did a double-take at Amanda. She caught his stare in the glass.

"What?"

"Nothing. I . . ." Theo censored himself with a headshake. Amanda's reflection had triggered a sudden premonition, a split-second image of her screaming with grief. There was no point warning her about it. Without concrete details, he was just as likely to steer her into the prophecy as out of it.

Amanda clucked her tongue at the tension in his back. "I hate what this is doing to you. I wish there was some way we could help."

He snapped out of his daze. "Sorry. What?"

"I said I wish there was—"

"Hold it." He raised his head toward the ceiling beams.

Amanda followed his gaze. "What?"

"She's waking up."

"Oh."

Amanda climbed off the bed with a loud and weary breath, then scooped up Theo's wastebasket. "I got it."

In a ruddy little bedroom on the second floor, between the generator closet and the hot water shifter, the youngest of the Silvers sat up with a yawn. Sleep had become a fickle commodity in Mia Farisi's life, leaving her pacing around at night and catnapping during the day. She assumed her insomnia was stress related, as she had several good reasons to fret. She was an alien, a fugitive, a chronokinetic freak, a target of Gothams, a girl in love, and the two-time denizen of a dying Earth. On the upside, she'd lost fourteen pounds since coming to Brooklyn, so at least she had that.

Groggy, sightless, Mia reached to remove her blindfold and stubbed her fingers on her hard metal fencing mask. It was a new addition to her sleepwear, one Peter had insisted on after a note from the future dropped into her mouth and nearly choked her to death. The blindfold was an older accessory, the only way to shut out the near-constant glow of tiny portals.

Mia took a cursory look around the room. Rolled-up sticks of paper lay scattered everywhere, from the mattress to the carpet to the folds of her T-shirt—a hundred and sixty-eight notes in total, all delivered over the course of an eighty-minute nap.

This was another reason to worry.

"You're getting stronger," Peter had warned her, five months prior. "Your temporal reach is expanding. Problem is, there are a lot of Mias out there in the future. Until you learn to control your gift, you're going to hear from more of them. God forbid the day should come when you hear from all of them."

Mia thanked her stars every day for Peter Pendergen. The man shared all her portal talents, and had spent decades mastering them. He could draw a door on any flat surface, travel dozens of miles in the blink of an eye. Better still, he had faith that Mia could become a teleporter like him. But first she had to fix her temporal problems.

Under Peter's tutelage, she learned how to consciously refuse deliveries from her future selves, a simple twist of will that was no harder (or easier) than ignoring a ringing phone. Over time, the trick became ingrained into her natural state of being, until she was no longer afflicted by portals in her waking hours. While she slept, however, the Future Mias still had carte blanche to spam her. Even Peter didn't know how to stop them.

"We'll find a way," he'd assured her. "In the meantime, for your sake, there's one thing I need you to do."

Today that "one thing" continued to plague Mia, a daily tug-of-war between her curiosity and her self-control. She untangled a note from her long brown hair, then studied it with tense, busy eyes. *Just one*, her inner self pleaded. *It might be useful. It could save someone's life.*

Guiltily, she unfurled the paper just enough to read the last line.

—genuinely likes you. And she's a great kisser. Give the girl a chance.

Her eyebrows rose. Her mouth fell open. She fumbled to reveal the rest of the dispatch.

"Stop."

Mia gasped and turned her head. She'd been so distracted, she didn't even hear the door open.

Amanda eyed her sternly from the hallway, wastebasket in hand. "You swore you'd stop reading them."

"It's okay. This one's different."

"I don't care. A promise is a promise."

"Wait! Just let me—"

A thin white tendril shot out of Amanda's finger and snatched the note from Mia's grip.

"No!"

Before Mia could move, a pair of large tempic tongs gripped her by the waist and lifted her two feet above the bed. Tiny sticks of paper dropped from her hair and clothes.

"Damn it! Amanda!"

Amanda used her other hand's tempis to sweep the mattress clean. Once all the notes were gathered into a pile, she gently released her captive.

Mia leaned against the headboard, her lips pursed in a seething pout. "This is bullshit."

"It's for your own good."

"Right. Theo can check the future all he wants, but when *I* do it—"

"Theo *sees* the future," Amanda reminded her. "You get secondhand info from a teenage girl who's always biased, sometimes wrong, and often very cruel to you."

Sadly, that was true. The Future Mias had never been kind to her, but lately they'd been downright vicious. Nearly all of the messages Mia had received over the last few months were pure self-abuse. *"You stupid bitch." "Fat dumb bitch." "You're clueless." "You're blind." "You can't even see what's happening right in front of you." "Right under your nose." "It's pathetic." "You're pathetic." "Just do the world a favor and die."*

Though her friends dismissed it as mere insecurity, Mia feared there was more to the situation. Maybe something was coming in the not-too-distant future: a fateful decision, a horrid mistake, a whole new reason for the older Mias to look back at her with disgust. If that was the case, then why didn't they warn her about it? Why were they being so vague?

After a group intervention and a private plea from Amanda, Mia finally agreed to stop reading the portal notes. Her resolve was elastic at best.

She watched Amanda coolly as the last of the papers fell tumbling into the wastebasket. "Has it ever occurred to you that you might be throwing away useful information? Something about the string? Or this guy Hannah's meeting? Or *Zack*?"

A small patch of stress tempis broke out on Amanda's back. It was a low blow to bring her ex-boyfriend into this.

"I know what you're looking for," Amanda said. "You won't find it."

Mia crossed her arms, scowling. Anyone with eyes could see that she was in love with David, though how *he* failed to see it was a mystery of the universe. Was he clueless? Was he shy? Was there any chance at all? Mia's future selves could safely solve the quandary for her. Someday, God willing, one of them would.

She looked up at Amanda defiantly. "You know, the Mias aren't all bad. A few of them still want to help me."

"Yeah, but most of them don't. How can you trust them? How do you know the next note won't be a prank or a nasty trick?"

Amanda had a point. In a universe of branching timelines, the Mias were free to change the past without paradox or consequence. They could ruin her life all they wanted. It would only improve their day.

Mia buried her face in her hands. "God. I'm so screwed up."

"No you're not."

"I get hate mail from myself."

"And I sometimes sneeze tempis," Amanda said. "We're different now. It doesn't mean we're crazy."

She formed a tempic brush and began sweeping the ash from Mia's bed. At least ten percent of the portal messages spontaneously combusted upon arrival. Even Peter couldn't explain it.

Mia grabbed a dust brush from her end table and helped Amanda sweep. "She's telling me that I'm gonna kiss a girl."

Amanda stared at her, blank-faced. "Is that a good thing or a bad thing?"

"I don't know. It's probably nothing. Probably just her weird idea of a joke."

She dumped a handful of ash into the wastebasket, then wiped her palm on her pajamas. "I shouldn't be thinking about this kind of stuff anyway. Not with everything going on."

Amanda's heart sank at Mia's gloom. She was fourteen. She *should* be thinking about boys (or girls). She should be going to school, making friends, getting worked up over silly teenage dramas. Instead she lived in the constant shadow of death, hiding from strangers who wanted to lock her up or worse. Even if all their enemies died, the second apocalypse still loomed over them like a giant sword. Mia had almost no chance of living to see her eighteenth birthday. No wonder her future selves were so angry.

The hallway creaked with footsteps. Theo stepped through the doorframe, a handphone pressed to his ear. He stared at the floor in a gobsmacked stupor, as if his mother had just called him from Heaven.

"Yeah. Okay. I'll tell them. Thanks." He closed the phone, then blinked dazedly at Amanda and Mia. "That was Peter. He, uh . . ."

He pondered his words a moment before chuckling in amazement. "The government has our bodies."

"What?"

Theo told them everything he knew about Peter and David's discovery, the six dead Silvers who had tumbled through time. Though the news was even weirder than Amanda expected, she had no trouble seeing the upside.

"The Deps think we're dead," she exclaimed. "They have no reason to look for us now."

Theo nodded cautiously. He and Amanda had already spent a day in DP-9 custody. They weren't eager to repeat the experience. "Guess not."

"What about Peter?" Mia asked. "Won't they still be looking for him?"

Amanda shook her head. "He's a smart man. He can take care of himself. I'm more worried about us."

"What do you mean?"

Theo understood. "The minute we're caught on camera, or use our powers in public—"

"—they'll know we're alive," Mia said. She looked down at her twitching fingers. "They'll hunt us all over again."

A tense silence filled the room. Amanda rose from the bed with fresh resolve. "We'll be all right. We'll just keep being careful."

The moment she said it, she realized how naïve she sounded. She'd once made national news after Evan Rander drugged her and made her lose control of her tempis. There was careful and there was lucky, and her people weren't lucky.

Shaken, Amanda moved to Mia's window and watched the glimmering streaks of aer traffic. Somewhere in Manhattan, the two most cherished and maddening people in her life were out chasing a prophecy. She squeezed the tiny golden crucifix on her necklace and cast a wish across the river.

Please be careful, she begged Hannah and Zack. *Please be lucky.*

TWO

The Quadrants were playing for one night only. Their performance had been advertised with triple exclamation points, as if the stars had aligned to bring the biggest rock band in history to Teke's Humble Tavern. Hannah could only guess from the half-empty tables that the four men onstage were not, in fact, the Beatles of this world. One song was enough to explain why.

"*You are my shaaaame,*" the lead singer crooned, with the listless mumble of a man cleaning his garage. The instrumentalists followed his lazy cue, flopping each note to the floor like a pound of wet dough. Zack dismissed the group as Nickelback on NyQuil before retreating to the men's room. That was ten minutes ago.

Hannah sat alone at a back corner table, nursing a drink as she scanned her surroundings. From the name, she'd expected Teke's to be a simple American beer joint, all bar stools and dartboards. Instead the place looked more like an alien nightclub. Glass walls danced with psychedelic holograms while a tempic fountain spilled clear blue liquid down an elaborate series of chutes. Even more vexing were the antigravity bar tables, these floating slabs of ashwood and aeris that were completely immovable, despite all logic. Hannah wanted to take a flying leap onto one of them, just to see if she could get it to wobble.

The Quadrants finished their song to withered applause, just as a middle-age man claimed the table next to Hannah's. Like everyone else here, he was dressed in his finest regalia: a three-piece suit, exquisitely tailored and ornamented with gold chains. Hannah wished Peter had briefed her better on Altamerican pub fashion. She felt woefully underdressed in her crepe blouse and blue jeans, her dingy brown sneakers with the Easy-Snap fasteners. Then again, she was a wanted felon with a shitload of enemies. If trouble happened to find her tonight, she'd rather not face it in a dress and high heels.

She studied the gentleman as he took off his jacket. His shirt cuffs were long and ridiculously snug. He couldn't possibly be hiding a thick metal bracelet. This wasn't the guy she was looking for.

The stranger caught her eyeballing him and gave her a curious once-over. "Hello there."

Hannah smiled politely, her mind hissing curses. "Hi."

"You look a bit out of your egg crate, if you don't mind me saying."

She didn't know how to take that, until she remembered her local slang. The man was merely telling her, in his own genteel way, that she stuck out like mud here in Fancyland.

Hannah shrugged, her dark eyes fixed on the Quadrants. "All my gowns are in the laundry."

The gentleman chuckled. "Fair enough. Can I buy you a drink?"

She held up her cherry vim, a fizzy red energy pop that was a staple of all vending machines. "Already have one."

"I mean a real drink."

She shook her head. "I don't have my drinking license."

Her new acquaintance stared at her, dumbstruck. "You came to a tavern without your wet card?"

"What can I say? I really like the band."

At last, the man had enough of Hannah's prickly weirdness. He stood up from his chair and wished her a pleasant evening.

Hannah watched him guiltily as he moved to another table. She didn't want him to take it personally. She just wasn't in a mood to mingle. She was grumpy, she was nervous, and she was increasingly skeptical of the prophecy that had brought her here.

She should have never listened to the girl with two watches.

On the fifth of last October, while the rest of the New York marked the somber anniversary of the Cataclysm, a peculiar young woman had approached Hannah in Union Square. She'd introduced herself as Ioni and then spoke of many things: the nature of time, the perils of foresight, the unfathomable burden that was waiting for Theo. Before taking her leave, she gave Hannah a folded sheet of paper: a flyer for the Quadrants and their one-night-only performance at Teke's. Scribbled in the corner, beneath the tavern's address, was a curious message:

Evan Rander took a good man out of your path. I'm putting one in. Go to this event. Look around. You'll know him when you see him. He's still wearing his bracelet.

Hannah had been tempted many times over the last six months to crumple up the flyer and forget about it. She had little reason to trust Ioni, and even less incentive to go looking for strangers. But the mention of the bracelet was a powerful detail, a clear implication that the man in question was just like the Silvers. If Ioni was right, if this guy was indeed a survivor from Hannah's Earth, then he was worth finding.

But where the hell was he? Hannah had already made four circuits around the tavern, scanning dozens of arms for a Pelletier bracelet. Nothing. Had the guy not arrived yet? Did he already leave? What if this whole thing was just a stupid—

"Any luck?"

Startled, Hannah turned in her seat and saw a tall, unshaven man standing right behind her.

"Christ," she said. "Where the hell have you been?"

"Around."

If there was anyone in the tavern who looked "out of his egg crate," it was Zack. He wore a crimson red Henley shirt, untucked, over a rumpled pair of camouflage pants. His hair was uncombed, his posture was slouched, and he scowled like a man who'd been brought here at gunpoint. Most jarring of all to the strangers around him was his scruffy new goatee, the signature beard style of America's fringe Leninists. If Teke's hadn't been so eager to fill seats tonight, and if Zack hadn't paid double the cover charge, the bouncer might have told him to take his commie ass back to Russia.

Hannah watched Zack sternly as he reclaimed his seat. "You said you were going to the bathroom."

"I did."

"What happened? You get accosted?"

"No. Just texted."

"By who?"

"David."

"Is he okay?"

Zack gripped the edge of their floating table and pushed it as hard as he could. He'd made peace with its resolve to hover thirty-three inches off the ground, but he couldn't understand how the damn thing stayed in place. By all scientific reasoning, it should have slid around the room like an air hockey puck.

"He's fine," he told Hannah. "He and Peter are on their way home."

"They find anything in that movie theater?"

Zack studied her a moment, then tensely shook his head. Hannah was jittery enough already. She didn't need to hear that the U.S. government had her future corpse in a freezer.

"I'll tell you later," he said. "Let's just find this guy."

Frustrated, Hannah looked around the tavern and caught her shadow on the wall. She must have put on at least ten pounds since coming to New York, enough to add a soft new slope to her jawline. The weight gain would have freaked her out in the old days, back when survival was just a matter of paying the rent. But after nine and a half months on a hostile, dying Earth, her perspective had been irrevocably altered. The petty concerns were just white noise in the background. Raindrops on the window.

No one benefitted more from her newfound clarity than Theo, her ex-lover and current messiah. Hannah reveled in her role as his nurse and nurturer, the one who held him together while he searched for the string. She was the savior's savior, and she believed more than anyone that he would heal the world.

But the closer she drew to this mystery meeting, the more she slid back to her old neurotic self. Hannah didn't like the romantic subtext of Ioni's prophecy. The last thing she needed was a new guy clouding up her thoughts. A part of her hoped she wouldn't find him tonight.

As her ears reached their limit on soporific alt-rock, she slouched in her chair and shot a cynical look at Zack. "We've checked every wrist in this place. He's not here."

"I'll take another look around."

"No. Stay. I don't want anyone else hitting on me."

"People are hitting on you?"

"Don't look so surprised."

"I'm not. Not really." He pulled a pen from his pocket and began doodling on a cocktail napkin. "I mean it's dark in here. They can't see your flaws."

Hannah let out a jagged laugh. "I hate you."

"I know."

"Shave your face."

"No."

"You look stupid. You look like your evil twin."

"Well, at least it's consistent with the rule."

"What rule?"

"Original *Star Trek* rule," Zack explained. "If you're from a parallel universe and you have a goatee, you're evil."

"I see." Hannah raised an eyebrow. "Should we be worried about you?"

"Yes, but not for long."

"Why?"

He tugged the hem of his Henley. "Red shirt."

"So?"

Zack eyed her strangely. "Are we even from the same world?"

"Just tell me what it means!"

"Original *Star Trek* rule: on away missions, the guy with the red shirt always dies."

Hannah crossed her arms, frowning. "That's not funny."

"If you truly hated me, you'd find it hilarious."

"I don't hate you. I love you."

"So you don't want me to die?"

"No. I want you to live to reach adulthood."

Zack lowered his head and chuckled, his first real laugh in weeks. Hannah was glad he came out with her tonight. He'd been so miserable in the brownstone, both him and Amanda.

He peeked up and saw Hannah staring at him with big, sad eyes. "Oh, not this again."

"I'm sorry. It just breaks my heart. The two of you should be together."

"Yeah, well, we're not." His head fell forward. He continued his sketch with a bitter scowl. "And we never will be."

Six months prior, on a gray October morning, Amanda joined Zack on the balcony of her bedroom. Only twenty-four hours had passed since Peter brought them to their new home in Brooklyn. Their bodies were still sore from the pre-vious day's battle, a four-way imbroglio in a Battery Park office building. While Zack got away with shrapnel cuts on his neck, Amanda's ankle was broken in two places, leaving her on tempic crutches and a fistful of painkillers.

Amanda vanquished her props and hugged Zack from behind. He stroked her wrists, his gaze flitting anxiously around the rain clouds.

"You bracing me for support or just bad news?"

"A little of both," Amanda admitted.

"Well, if you're going to dump me, at least be funny about it. 'I think we should see better people,' or 'It's not you. It's my opinion of you.'"

"Zack . . ."

"We had a good thing going."

"We did. We do. I *want* to be with you."

"Then why does this feel like a breakup?"

Amanda rested her chin on his shoulder and took a deep, stuttered breath. A short silence passed before she spoke.

"When Esis first gave me my bracelet, she said a lot of weird things. One of them was 'Don't entwine with the funny artist.' That was right before I met you. I had no idea who she was talking about. I didn't even remember she said it until just last week, when you and I . . ."

She closed her eyes. "It was a warning. A threat."

"Against us?"

"Against *you*," said Amanda. "When I saw her again yesterday, she brought it up. She made it very clear that if we 'entwined,' I'd live to regret it and you wouldn't."

Zack leaned against the railing, his eyes darting back and forth in thought. "I don't get it. Why would she have a problem with us?"

"I don't know."

"Why would she even care?"

"I don't know! I just know what she said."

Zack mulled the news for another moment before shaking his head. "Bull-shit. She's bluffing. She and Azral went to a lot of trouble to bring us here. They won't kill us now."

"You haven't met her, Zack. She's crazy. I watched her murder two people without losing her smile. And the way they took Evan . . ."

Amanda pulled her arms back. By the time Zack turned around, she was once again standing on self-made crutches.

"She's a sick, violent woman," Amanda said. "And she doesn't want us together."

"You don't know that for sure."

"Are you willing to bet your life on it?"

"Yes."

"Well, I'm not."

Amanda lowered her head, her crutches rippling like jelly. Her tempis was only as strong as her state of mind.

"I'm sorry, Zack. I've lost too many people already, and you're way too important to me. If I have to keep you at arm's length to keep you alive, I will."

After a month of forced distance and interminable frustration, Amanda gradually began to crack under the weight of Zack's reasoning. Maybe she *was* working off a faulty premise. Maybe Esis had a more stringent definition of "entwine." Surely she wouldn't care if Amanda hugged Zack once in a while, or held his hand on the sofa while they watched a movie. Who knew? Maybe there was a whole world of things they could do without triggering the wrath of that madwoman.

By February, Amanda had convinced herself that sex was the only verboten activity, a limit Zack readily accepted. They spent their days and nights together like young Christian lovers, trading virginal affections under the covers of the attic bed.

For David, the only other Silver to have personal experience with Esis, their romance became an increasing source of concern, like watching nitro dance with glycerin.

"You're making a terrible mistake," he warned Amanda and Zack. "The Pelletiers are alien to us. We have no idea what they want or don't want. For you to assume—"

"You think we haven't thought about that?" said Amanda. "We've agonized over it for months."

"So why take the chance?"

"Because we want to," Zack growled. "It's our decision, hers and mine."

David eyed him skeptically. "Esis might disagree."

"Well, she can explain herself or she can fuck off."

"Or she can kill you," David said. "Just like she warned Amanda. You may not care if you live or die, but some of us do."

He shot a pointed glare at Amanda. "Some of us."

His righteous scorn was enough to bring her full circle. The next day, after a loud and tearful argument, Amanda put a stop to her intimacy with Zack. The two of them had been wretched ever since. They lived together, ate together, forced a pitiful semblance of a friendship. All the while, their thoughts fluttered helplessly around Esis—a single question, posed over and over again. *Why?*

The Quadrants began their next drowsy ballad, their third song in a row about breakups. Zack snatched a blank napkin and began a sketch of the lead singer getting kicked in the groin.

Hannah stroked his arm. "Look, don't give up. You never know what'll happen. Maybe Esis will change her mind or something."

Zack pursed his lips at her wishful thinking, her enviable freedom. She and Theo had spent a whole week banging each other in Indiana and were now the snuggliest ex-lovers Zack had ever seen. Not a peep of warning from the Pelletiers.

"One more hour," he told Hannah. "Then we'll go."

Sighing, she finished her vim and then looked to the entry, where a brand-new arrival caused several heads to turn. She was a petite twentysomething of Asian descent, dressed in a leather jacket and miniskirt, with combat boots that were twice as thick as her ankles. Her eye makeup was so heavy that she looked half insane, yet she carried herself with the poise of a debutante. If she gave even the slightest damn about the sneering eyes around her, it didn't show on her face.

The woman proceeded toward the bar, then gawked at the sight of Hannah. The three nearest tables all wavered in place, as if their aeric lifters were malfunctioning in unison. Before anyone could react, the slabs fell to the floor with a thunderous crash.

Everything came to a screeching halt. The band stopped playing. The patrons stopped talking. As a hundred people gawked at the three fallen tables, Hannah watched the mysterious woman escape through the exit.

Zack looked around, baffled. "What just happened?"

"I don't know," Hannah said. "She just saw me and freaked out."

"Who?"

"No idea. She was Asian and gothy and she looked at me like she knew me. But I didn't recognize her at all."

"Okay . . ." Zack eyeballed the staff as they scrambled to gather the broken tables. "How does it explain that?"

The manager of Teke's, a middle-age redhead in a black taffeta gown, commandeered the microphone and apologized for the disruption. She summoned a strained round of applause for the Quadrants, then announced that their next song would be the last.

Hannah stood up and grabbed her purse. "I don't like this. We should go."

Zack stayed in his seat, his pen tapping anxiously against the table. He had his own reason for wanting to meet Ioni's mystery man. He wasn't ready to give up.

"We've been waiting six months for this. Unless you're absolutely sure—"

"I'm not sure of anything! I don't even know if this guy exists! All I know is I have a bad feeling about this. I really think we should leave."

The Quadrants returned to their places and began their closing number: a soft guitar intro that was far more polished than their other songs.

Hannah moved in front of Zack. "Look, I'd rather be wrong and safe than—"

"Pink Floyd."

"What?"

Zack cocked his head like a puzzled dog, his rapt eyes locked on the musicians. "They're playing Pink Floyd."

Hannah closed her eyes and listened. Zack was right. The opening was a note-for-note match for "Wish You Were Here," one of her mother's all-time favorite songs. Now here it was on the other side of the multiverse. Back from the dead.

She turned around and gawked at the men onstage. "How . . . ?"

"I don't know," Zack said. Though the odds were slim, he couldn't rule out the possibility of a creative coincidence. This world certainly had its share of eerie parallel synchronisms. There was a Hollywood actor named Tom Cruise, a former president named Gerald Ford, and a best-selling horror author who wrote pseudonymously under the name Stephen King. Even more bizarre was the fact that his breakout novel was called *The Stand*. Zack had been disappointed to learn to that the plot revolved strictly around a haunted end table.

After eighty-one seconds of mellow instrumentals, the lead singer opened his mouth and shattered every last possibility of a fluke.

> *So, so you think you can tell*
> *Heaven from Hell,*
> *Blue skies from pain.*
> *Can you tell a green field*
> *From a cold steel rail?*
> *A smile from a veil?*
> *Do you think you can tell?*

Hannah fell back into her seat, gobsmacked. She'd searched every corner of this place for the man she was supposed to meet, but she'd never checked the Quadrants. He'd been standing right in front of her this whole time.

Her heart pounding, she scanned the singer's skinny wrists.

"It's not him," Zack told her. "It's the guy on the right. Look."

Hannah turned her head and took her first good look at the guitarist.

He was the largest of the foursome—six feet tall, with broad and powerful shoulders. Nearly everything about him was walnut brown, from his shlubby clothes to his hooded eyes to the disheveled mop of hair that had been tied into a ponytail. His skin was a sandy shade that Hannah couldn't quite place. All she knew was that he was pretty, in a dull and wooden kind of way. He reminded her of every Keanu Reeves clone who'd tried to woo and "whoa" her in college.

As he continued to strum his electric guitar (the only remotely clean part of his ensemble, Hannah noted), she examined the bulky sweatband around his wrist. Whenever it struck the light the right way, she caught a sharp glint of metal beneath the cotton.

A hint of gold.

Hannah looked to Zack, astonished. "Oh my God. You were right."

Zack had long ago predicted the color of the mystery man's bracelet. Evan Rander once told him that the Pelletiers had rescued ninety-nine people from ten different cities around the world, with each group getting their own colored bangles. For the San Diegans, it was silver. For the New Yorkers . . .

Zack's stomach twisted as he recalled Rebel's teasing boast from October. *Two of the Golds got away from us. Six didn't. Your brother was one of the ones who didn't.*

At long last, Zack had found a living member of the group, someone who could tell him what really happened to Josh Trillinger. He refused to let the matter rest on the word of a psychopath.

Hannah kept her muddled gaze on the guitarist. "How the hell did he end up in a band?"

"I don't know," Zack said. "He's had nine and a half months to adapt. Guess he's better at it than we are."

The guitarist flinched at the sight of the two Silvers. He'd been noticing them all night, this poorly dressed couple who never drank, never smiled, and never stopped snooping on the people around them. Now suddenly their eyes were laser-focused on him. The black-haired woman looked ready to pounce.

Hannah looked away. "Shit. We're freaking him out."

"What?"

"He sees us."

"Great." Zack lowered his head. "He probably thinks we're Rebel's people."

"You think he'll run?"

Zack was more concerned that he'd fight. For all they knew, the guy had all of Amanda's tempis and none of her qualms about using it.

The song ended. The tavern fell into wild applause. The guitarist watched Hannah and Zack intently as they rose from their table. He rushed to unplug his instrument.

"What's the matter?" the bass player asked him.

"I have to go."

"Now? We haven't gotten paid."

"Hold my cut. If you don't see me tomorrow, then keep it. And thanks."

The lead singer gripped his arm. "What is this, man? You breaking us?"

The guitarist saw Zack and Hannah weaving their way toward him. He retreated from the stage, then threw a somber look at his bandmates.

"Sorry."

He bolted through the staff door at the back of the tavern. The drummer called after him. "Trevor, wait!"

"Wait!" Hannah and Zack yelled.

Everyone stopped to watch the pair as they forced their way through the crowd. Hannah fell a step behind Zack, cursing. She was one of the fastest people on Earth, but she couldn't time-shift here. There'd be hell to pay if she went supernatural in front of all these witnesses.

Zack charged into the staff corridor and hooked a sharp left. His target had already reached the back alley exit. Zack only had a moment to shout something. Anything.

"Pink Floyd!"

Stunned, the guitarist stopped in the doorway. Zack took a step forward, his palms raised high. "Look, Trevor—"

The man fled through the exit and vanished into the night.

His name was not Trevor, as his bandmates believed. Nor was it Eric, as he'd told the soup kitchen workers. He was not the "Axel" his slumlord yelled when the rent was overdue, or the "Jimmy" his one-time lover had moaned in the middle of the night. His name was Jonathan Christie, and there was only one person in the world he trusted with that knowledge.

There used to be more.

Jonathan ran through the alley in his thrift store sneakers, a makeshift pair he'd purchased with street coins. He couldn't go home with those people on his tail. He had to lose them.

Guitar in hand, he sprinted across Christopher Street and nearly got clipped by a limousine. Angry honks filled his ears as he dashed to the left, through a twenty-foot archway of tempis and stone.

The West Village Faith Mall had been built in 1989 as an offering of sorts to Pope Clement XV, who'd visited Manhattan the year before and called it a "godless place." The outdoor plaza contained twenty-nine different houses of worship—churches and chapels, synagogues and mosques. All religions were welcome as long as they played nice with each other.

In 1991, after an ecumenical rumble sent three dozen Christians to the hospital, the Faith Mall was broken up into separate properties, each surrounded by a high tempic barrier. The walls made the plaza so complex and confusing that locals took to calling it the Faith Maze.

Jonathan weaved through the corridors without any regard for direction. Left at St. Veronica's, right at St. Michael's, north at the Baptist Center, west at the Temple Chai. After six sharp turns, he slowed down, then rested against a tempic wall. Aside from the traffic and his own wheezing breaths, he couldn't hear anything. He'd lost them. He actually—

"We're not going to hurt you."

He spun a frantic one-eighty. "Jesus!"

Hannah faced him from the other wall, her hands folded behind her back. She looked like she'd been waiting for minutes. She hadn't even broken a sweat.

He fought to speak through winded gasps. "How . . . how the hell . . . ?"

"Doesn't matter," Hannah said, though she knew that wasn't true. Peter would shit a red heifer when he learned about her temporal indiscretions.

Jonathan backed up against the wall, bug-eyed. "You're a Gotham."

"I'm not. I swear. I'm from your world."

"Bullshit."

"Go on. Quiz me. Ask me anything."

"How did you find me?"

Hannah balked. "I meant a trivia question."

"How did you *find* me?"

She fidgeted with the hem of her blouse. "It's complicated. Just trust me when I say we're not your enemy. There are six of us in my group and we're just like you. We can protect you. You don't have to be alone."

Jonathan stared at her expressionlessly before venting a chuckle. "Nice pitch. Needs a jingle."

"You think I'm lying?"

"I *know* you're lying. You think I lived this long by being gullible?"

Hannah crossed her arms. "If I was here to kill you, I would have done it already."

"Except you're not just after me."

"What do you mean?"

Jonathan held his tongue. If she didn't know about Heath, he certainly wasn't going to tell her.

Hannah waved a hand. "Okay, look. Let's start over . . ."

"Let's not." He slung his guitar over his shoulder and started back down the corridor. "I don't know you. I don't trust you. Whatever you're selling, count me out."

Hannah threw her hands up. "I know the song you played!"

He kept walking. "Good for you."

"I've been singing it since I was a little girl. My mother taught it to me."

Jonathan stopped and threw a wary look over his shoulder.

"I never had a feel for the lyrics," Hannah said. "Except for 'two lost souls swimming in a fishbowl.' I love that line. Whenever we sang those words together, I always felt so close to her. My mother and I were the screwballs in our family. It fit us to a T."

Jonathan turned around and saw the tears glistening in her eyes.

"She died with everyone else," Hannah told him. "When the sky came down on our whole goddamn planet. There are so many people that I miss. And there are so few of us left. Whether you like it or not, whether you trust me or not, we have a whole world in common."

Hannah looked down at her shuffling feet. "And I know a lot of songs too."

A fluorescent light washed over the corridor. Jonathan and Hannah looked up to see a flying saucer soar across the sky on glowing struts of aeris. A lumic sign on the undercarriage advertised RICK'S RIVERVIEW BISTRO: YOUR HEAVEN ON THE HUDSON.

The aerstraunt drifted out of view. Hannah snorted bleakly. "Freaks me out every time."

Jonathan's expression softened. "Me too."

"Listen—"

"Did you see it?"

"What?"

"The end of the world," he said. "Did you see the sky come down?"

Hannah bit her lip and nodded. Jonathan pulled off his sweatband and took a long, hard look at his Pelletier bracelet.

"They knocked me out before it happened," he said. "I missed the whole thing."

In the light of the moon, Hannah could see how ragged he was—his clothes, his hair, even his skin.

"I'm Hannah," she said. "Hannah Given. Is your name really Trevor?"

He looked at the ground and grimly shook his head.

"What's your real name?" Hannah asked.

Jonathan took a deep breath and stared up at the night. He stuffed his hands in his pockets. And then he told her.

The Cataclysm had razed Greenwich Village to the ground, giving the architects and city planners the chance to rebuild it with manic flair. Some of the buildings were so oddly shaped that the spaces between them had become works of art. The alley behind Teke's was a particular marvel: a narrow lane that curved north and south in measured arcs. From bird's-eye view, the corridor looked like a sixty-yard sine wave.

Zack waited impatiently at the Christopher Street junction, with Hannah's purse clutched in one hand and her mobile phone in the other. He held the receiver twelve inches away from his ear, the only way to tolerate the howling voice on the other end of the line.

"Goddamn it! What did I tell you two?"

Zack put the phone back to his face. "Peter, calm down."

"The government thinks you're dead! What do you think'll happen when they see a dark-haired woman whizzing around without a speedsuit?"

"She was careful, all right? She didn't shift until she got to the alley."

"That doesn't mean a fly's fart if someone saw her. Christ!"

Zack peeked around the curved wall and saw bouncers guarding the utility door at Teke's. Clearly he and Hannah were no longer welcome there.

He retreated from view. "Peter, if you'd just unclench a moment and focus, you'd see that a taxi isn't our best option."

"I already changed course. We'll be there in ten."

"Okay. Good. The only problem—"

"Call Hannah and tell her to get back to you. *Now*."

"—is that I can't call Hannah," Zack said. "I have her phone."

The line fell silent. Zack could practically hear David face-palming in the background.

"For God's sake," Peter said. "How the hell have you people lived this long?"

"Look, she knows where I am. She'll come back. Just get here as f—"

Something cool and hard pressed the back of Zack's neck. His heartbeat doubled. His hands rose in reflex.

Peter's tinny voice crackled through the receiver. "Zack? You there?"

A hand plucked the phone from his grip and closed it. "Toss the bag."

The voice was a woman's, a very stressed one at that. *A mugger?* Zack wondered. *A junkie?*

He lobbed Hannah's purse across the alley. It fell with a thud atop the lid of a trasher. The square blue bins were scattered all over the city, a way to erase trash through temporal reversal. Zack didn't enjoy sharing the time-bending power of a garbage can, but maybe if he concentrated . . .

The woman pressed her gun into him. "Uh, uh, uh. No temporis. Take five steps forward and turn around."

He did as he was told and saw his assailant in full light. Though she was a complete stranger to Zack, she bore a striking resemblance to the woman Hannah had described earlier, the gothy young woman who'd bolted from the tavern.

His eyes dawdled anxiously around the barrel of her .22. "Who are you?"

"Shut up. I didn't say you could talk."

"You don't look like a Dep."

"Did you not hear me?"

Zack suddenly remembered the three floating tables—all crashing to the ground, as if someone had accidentally sapped the aeris out of them.

He winced in realization. "Shit."

"What?"

"You're a Gotham," Zack said. "You're one of Rebel's goons."

The woman shifted her gun to her other hand. "Don't even think about rifting me, Trillinger."

"I wouldn't."

"You *can't*. I jammed you."

He remembered Amanda telling him about a Gotham she'd fought in Battery Park, a woman who'd blocked her access to tempis. Peter had recognized her description and told them her name. Zack struggled to recall it now. It was something odd. Venus. Mercury.

"Mercy," he blurted. "Your name is Mercy."

Her eyes widened a bit before hardening again. "Enjoy the irony."

Zack didn't. He was too busy calculating. It had been at least six minutes since Mercy fled the tavern, more than enough time for her to call for backup. There was probably a team of Gothams racing toward Hannah right now.

As for him . . .

"Rebel's coming, isn't he? That's why you haven't shot me. He wants to kill me himself."

Mercy avoided his gaze. Her voice fell to a mutter. "I said stop talking."

Zack craned his neck and studied the sliver of night between buildings, a curved belt of stars that looked just like a sneer. He wanted to smack that grin right off the universe, but he couldn't even rust the gun that was holding him here. He was out of options. Out of time.

As his future shrank to flimsy minutes, Zack catalogued a list of regrets. He should have spent every waking moment of the last six months with Amanda. He should have listened to Hannah when she suggested they leave the bar. He should have never let his guard down tonight. He should have never worn the goddamn red shirt.

THREE

The Severson Peregrine was the cheapest aerovan on the market, a squat and boxy eight-seater with all the charm of a cinder block. Like most Severson products, the Peregrine was made with budget parts for budget customers, and it showed. The seats were hard. The engine was weak. The chassis shook at the slightest hint of wind. But it brought the sky to millions of low-income Americans, making it the top-selling van for nine consecutive years.

For Peter Pendergen, fugitive ringleader of the Silvers, there was no better choice of transport. Peregrines were ridiculously easy to acquire on the black market, and had become so damn ubiquitous on the highways and skyways that people barely noticed them. He'd purchased four from a local junker and kept them parked at strategic locations around the brownstone. His companions needed an escape plan that didn't rely on him, should the worst come to pass.

Except now the worst seemed to be happening to two of his people, and Peter wished to God he had a faster ride.

He pursed his lips at the Manhattan skyline, then turned off the Peregrine's altitude lock. "Hang on."

David clutched his seat with a sickly wince as the van lurched upward. It broke away from the traffic of the Staten Island Aerofare and made a diagonal climb toward the heavens. At a thousand feet, Peter coasted to a stop and turned off the lights. The vehicle hovered invisibly above Newark Bay, a lone gray speck in the nightscape.

"Why are you stopping?" David asked. "Zack's—"

"I know."

Peter leaned over and grabbed a wood-handled revolver from the glove box. Like the Peregrines, the .38 was registered under his cover identity: one Arthur King of Avalon, New Jersey.

"We'll never reach him in this thing," he told David. "Not in time."

"You're making a portal."

"Yup."

"I thought you needed a flat surface for those."

"I have one." Peter checked the bullet chamber, then aimed the .38 at the sun roof. "Brace yourself."

David shielded his face as a deafening gunshot shattered the glass. He had to shout over the ringing in his ears.

"You couldn't just open it?"

Peter cleared away the lingering shards. "Doesn't open in flight mode."

It didn't take long for David to see why. The van rocked wildly as Peter climbed through the hatch. He balanced himself with a surfer's grace, then looked down at David.

"You'll have to come with me. Once I'm gone, I can't jump back."

"I don't want to shake you off."

"I'll be fine. Just hurry." Peter crouched down and held his hand out to David. "Son, you have to trust me."

Lack of trust wasn't the issue, as Peter had proven himself over and over again. He was also a ridiculously easy man to read. He roared his opinions with brass trumpet bluster and wore his moods like a quart of cologne. The only time he became cryptic was when he talked about his past. Mia had tried to pry the story of his life, but all she got were the bullet points. Born in Dublin. Orphaned at nine. Discovered by Gothams at thirteen and welcomed into their clandestine community in Quarter Hill, New York. There Peter went on to become many things—a husband, a father, a writer, a widower, a zealous protector of his people's secrets, and one of the greatest teleporters the Gothams had ever known.

He was also their greatest traitor.

His decision to help the Silvers came with consequences, more than Peter was willing to admit. He'd become an exile of the clan, disowned by everyone who'd ever loved him, even his son. Yet Peter remained stubbornly convinced that the troubles would blow over.

"My people are just scared," he'd repeatedly told the Silvers. "The apocalypse has them all turned around. But once they see the light of reason, they'll end their stupid war. We'll all go back to Quarter Hill and we'll work together to stop what's coming."

That right there was David's problem with Peter. He saw everything through rose-colored blinders, as if the universe would bend to his good intentions. Did he really think he could talk sense into his people? He'd spent six months trying to parley with Rebel and Ivy. Nothing had changed. The Gothams still hunted them with mindless obsession. The world was no closer to being saved.

"Please," Peter said. "We can help Zack and Hannah, but you have to do what I say."

Frowning, David took his hand and clambered out of the Peregrine. The chassis swayed from side to side, nearly causing both men to tumble off the roof. Once the van fell still, Peter let go of David and took a careful step forward.

"All right. Don't move. This is the hard part."

He squinted at Lower Manhattan, where the buildings were flecked with bright lumic trimmings of every color. Somewhere deep in that rainbow jungle was the perfect spot. Peter just had to find it.

A traveler has to know where he's going, he'd taught Mia. *If we can't see our destination, we have to remember it. Every wall. Every brick. Every last detail.*

Grunting, he forged a mental link to a ceiling in the West Village, a grocery store not far from Teke's. Peter could only assume that it was empty at this hour. Then again, he hadn't been there in years. For all he knew, the place had become a police station. He had little choice but to take the risk.

Peter waved his hand above the Peregrine. A five-foot-wide portal bloomed across the center of the roof. He lowered himself to his hands and knees and took a quick peek through the surface.

"It's safe," he told David. "I'll go first but you have to be quick. And watch where you jump. You don't want to touch the edges."

Peter leapt forward. The portal swallowed him like thick wet paint.

David watched the sluggish ripples, then took a last anxious look at the city. He hoped Peter knew what the hell he was doing. He hoped Hannah and Zack had the good sense to stay alive.

He took a deep breath and jumped into the portal. The Peregrine rocked four times in his absence, then floated as calmly as the moon and the stars.

———————

Zack stood rigidly in the shadow of the trasher, his tense gaze flitting between Mercy and her .22. She held it steadily enough to suggest that she knew how to use it. If he tried to rush her, he'd get a bullet in the face. If he tried to run, she'd shoot him in the back. He didn't relish the thought of dying in this weird and twisty corridor, this Salvadored alley.

He scrutinized Mercy and saw colorful tattoos through her stockings. One of them was just a single word in artsy script letters.

"'Mercurial,'" he read. "Is that your real name?"

She threw an anxious peek over her shoulder. "I told you to shut up."

"Who names their kid 'Mercurial'?"

Mercy stared at him, astonished. "You don't have a lick of sense, do you?"

"I'm a dead man, anyway. So . . ."

He tucked his hands behind his back and leaned against the trasher. Mercy raised her gun. "Put them back up."

"Fuck you. My arms are tired."

"You think I won't shoot you?"

"I think you're holding me for Rebel," Zack said. "He'll want to know where my friends are. Maybe smack me around. And when he finally sees that I'm not talking, he'll use that big ugly gun of his and finish me. That sound about right?"

"Not even a little." Mercy took another look around. "He doesn't care what you know. He doesn't care who plugs you. He told me to do it."

Zack fought to maintain a cool façade. "So why haven't you?"

"You want me to?"

"No."

"Then *shut the fuck up*."

She swept her hand in a tight circle, filling the alley with an invisible burst of solis. In high doses, the energy hindered all forms of temporal manipulation. Zack's talents were suppressed for another few minutes, while the space around them became impervious to ghost drills. The last thing Mercy needed was Integrity on her trail.

"Augurs," she muttered.

"What?"

"My parents are augurs. They named me Mercurial because they knew that's how I'd be."

Zack crossed his arms with a bitter scowl. "They should've called you Killer."

"I've never killed anyone."

"No. You just take away their powers and let others do the killing."

"Fuck you. You think I'm doing this for fun?"

"I have no idea why you're doing it."

"Don't play dumb," Mercy said. "You know what's coming."

Zack nodded darkly. "The end of the world."

"What? You think I'm lying?"

"No. My best friend's an augur. He sees it every day."

"So do my parents," Mercy said. "They're both wrecks."

"They should be. I already watched it happen to my world. Your future's my past."

"Doesn't matter."

"We have our own plan to stop it, you know. One that doesn't involve murder."

"It doesn't matter!" Mercy yelled. "Every day you people live is another nail in the coffin."

"Who told you that? Rebel?"

Mercy looked away uneasily. Zack snorted. "Yeah. Figured."

"He's the only augur we have who hasn't lost his mind."

"Oh, really? Think again."

"Shut up."

"He's wrong, Mercy. Killing us won't save the world."

"I said *shut up.*" Mercy tightened her grip on her pistol. "Everything was fine till the day you showed up. You and your demon friends."

"My demon *what*?"

"You know damn well who I'm talking about."

Zack blinked at her three times before laughing in astonishment. "The Pelletiers? You think they're our *friends*?"

"They pop up and save you whenever you're in trouble," said Mercy. "They kill us with tempis and tell us to leave you alone. That woman *threatened* me, Trillinger. She looked at me with those black shark eyes and she . . ."

Her mouth trembled. "Don't tell me they're not on your side."

Zack could hear the quaver in her voice. This woman shared every bit of Amanda's fear. When they talked about Esis, they sounded exactly the same.

"Mercy, listen to me. We're not with them. We hate them just as much as you do."

"Bullshit!"

"You're killing innocent people for nothing!"

"Not innocent," said a gravelly voice behind Zack. "And not nothing."

A new figure came around the bend, a man in a stretched black T-shirt and army pants. Though Richard "Rebel" Rosen was every bit the hulking figure that Zack remembered, his appearance had changed. His face was thinner. His once-bald head was covered in fuzz. He wore a matching pair of scars on his cheeks, two pocked brown lines that Semerjean had rifted into his skin like war paint.

Most jarring to Zack was the sight of his right hand, a state-of-the-art prosthetic made of rubber, steel, and wire. Seven months ago, during their first violent encounter, Zack had rifted Rebel's hand to a rotted husk. The temporal damage was irreversible. Permanent.

But if Rebel was angry about it, he hid it very well. He merely greeted Zack with tired eyes, as if they were just passing acquaintances from an old and boring day job.

"Trillinger."

Try as he might, Zack couldn't hide his own contempt. This was the man who'd put a bullet in Mia's chest. He'd bragged to Zack about killing Josh Trillinger—his only brother, the one person in his life who hadn't died in the apocalypse.

"Fuck you," Zack said, his voice a cracked whisper. "I'd rift you again if I could."

"No doubt."

Another Gotham hurried to Rebel's side, a chubby-faced man with blond, curly hair. He took a nervous look around the alley, then closed his eyes in concentration. A pair of illusory screens flanked Zack and his enemies, each one projecting a forced-perspective image of an empty corridor. Mink Rosen had been bending light since he was a child, and was widely considered to be one of the clan's best lumics. The four of them were now completely invisible to prying eyes.

Rebel pulled a long-barreled .44 from his belt holster, then checked the bullets in the chamber. "I told you to kill him."

Mercy leaned against the wall, sulking. "I found him. I kept him here. What do you want from me?"

"I want you to mettle up." He gestured at Zack. "They won't all be as easy as this one."

Zack was too busy thinking to listen. He figured Mercy couldn't use her powers again without disrupting the lumic's illusions. If he could just buy time until her solis wore off, he might have a fighting chance.

He cleared his throat. "Since you're here, Rebel—"

"Won't work."

"What?"

"Stalling," Rebel said. "I see the future. I know your plans before you do."

Ivy hailed him through his transmitter. "Careful. You have company."

Rebel pressed his earpiece. "Who?"

"Peter. He's nearby."

Cursing, Rebel raised his revolver and scanned the upper reaches of the alley. His wife was a traveler like Peter. She could feel his portals from a mile away.

"Where is he?"

"I don't know," Ivy said. "He's covering his tracks. He must know I'm here too."

She was parked a block away in a floating black aerovan, her dark eyes fixed on the computer in her lap. She had camera drones all over the West Village Faith Mall, giving her a perfect view of Hannah and Jonathan as they walked the tempic corridors. Her brother and niece would take care of them soon enough. She was more worried about Rebel.

"Just kill the breacher and get out of there," she told him. "We'll save Peter for another day."

Zack's heart hammered as Rebel raised his weapon again. He struggled to speak with as much dignity as he could muster.

"Four years from now, Rebel, when the end finally comes, you'll see that this all was for nothing. You didn't save the world. You just murdered a whole bunch of innocents."

Rebel looked at him with calm, steady eyes. "You think you know what's going on. You don't. But there's no point arguing."

Mink and Mercy flinched as Rebel aimed his .44 at Zack's head.

"It's time for you to go home."

His head snapped back in sudden alarm. His foresight had many new things to say about the immediate future, none of them good.

Rebel swung his revolver to the left, then the right, then back again. The lumic screens that hid them also kept them blind to the outside world.

Mink eyed Rebel quizzically. A floating word appeared in front of his mouth like a subtitle. PELLETIERS?

Rebel shook his head. "Pendergen."

Bizarrely, his senses were telling him that Peter was coming from the east *and* the west. By the time he realized that they were nothing more than image ghosts, the real Peter jumped through a portal. He grabbed Mercy from behind and pressed his .38 to her temple. Her pistol fell to the ground.

Rebel turned but—

"Stop."

—froze a half second before he was told to.

"One more move and I shoot her," Peter told him. "Look ahead. You know I'm not bluffing."

Rebel's eyes narrowed to slits. "Killing your own now, you piece of shit?"

"Haven't killed her yet." Peter took a quick peek at Zack. "You all right?"

"I'm breathing." He looked to Mercy's fallen gun. "Should I . . ."

"No. Just stay where you are. And let's take it on faith that if I see one flash of lumis or feel a hint of Ivy's portals, I'll put a hole in our girl here." He breathed a whisper through Mercy's hair. "I'm truly sorry, love."

Black mascara tears streamed down her face. "Go to hell."

Rebel raised his hands slowly, his finger still on the trigger. With every inch, he scanned the future for a ricochet path to Peter's skull.

"Uh, uh, uh," said Peter. "No bank shots either. Drop the gun."

Rebel pointed his weapon at Zack again. "I don't think so."

"Goddamn it, Rebel."

"I'm going to count to three . . ."

"Don't make me say it."

"One . . ."

"You need Mercy more than I need Zack!"

Rebel paused, stymied. Sadly, Peter was right. There were only two solics in the clan, and one of them was a child. Without Mercy, Rebel had no hope of killing the Pelletiers.

Grudgingly, he lowered his weapon. Peter glared at him. "I said put it on the ground."

Rebel dropped the gun but kept his foot against it. There was a new wrinkle coming in eighty-five seconds, a final chance to turn the tables. All he had to do was buy the time.

He shifted his gaze between the two illusive screens. "Nice trick you pulled. Guess the Dormer boy's around here somewhere."

"Nowhere close," Peter told Rebel. "I don't put children in harm's way."

"You're putting *all* children in harm's way! How can you even look at yourself?"

"How can *you*?" Zack yelled. "You're murdering people for no reason!"

Peter flashed his palm at Zack. "Let me handle this. And you keep those screens steady, Mink. We don't want the locals seeing our business."

Mink refocused his thoughts until the ghosted blinds stopped rippling.

Rebel sneered at Peter. "Pathetic. Still talking like you're one of us."

"I am one of you." Peter's expression darkened. He lowered his head. "I heard about your sons. You have my sincere condolences. Both of you."

Ivy choked back a cry in the aerovan. Rebel gritted his teeth. Two weeks ago, their twins had been born dead, discolored, as if someone had coated their bodies in metallic paint. Though the doctors were mystified, every Gotham in the village knew what happened. The deaths were a message from the Pelletiers, a vicious warning to leave the Silvers and Golds alone.

Rebel brushed his tears with a finger. "Fuck you."

"Those people are monsters," Peter said. "We have nothing to do with them."

"You have *everything* to do with them! You're guarding their pets!"

Zack clenched his fists. "We are *not* their pets, you goddamn—"

"Zack, shut up." Peter huffed a loud sigh. "Look, no one's gonna change any minds tonight. Let's just call it a draw. It's the only way we're all walking out of here."

Rebel took another peek at the future. Thirty seconds.

"You're still talking to someone in the clan," he mused. "They're feeding you information. Who is it? Olga? Prudent?"

"Look—"

"Can't possibly be Liam," Rebel said. "He's petitioned the elders to renounce his name. He wants to join my crew so he can bring you to justice himself. That's what your son thinks of you."

Mercy suddenly caught an anomaly in her vision, a slightly skewed perspective between the trasher and the wall. Zack followed her gaze and saw exactly what she was looking at. Between the two illusive screens was a third one.

David . . .

Mercy turned to Rebel and opened her mouth. Zack drowned her out with a chuckle aimed at Mink.

"Hey, Harpo. You're new to this unit."

Peter glared at him. "Zack . . ."

"Did Rebel tell you what happened to his other goons? Is that why you're so nervous?"

"Zack, I told you to be quiet."

Mercy's voice was barely a whisper. "Dormer. He's here."

Rebel bent his knees in readiness. *Three . . . two . . . one . . .*

Suddenly a muscular man popped through one of Mink's screens, a bouncer from Teke's Humble Tavern. The moment he stepped through the lumis, five people abruptly turned visible in front of him. Only Rebel knew he was coming.

Everything that happened over the next two seconds was pure reflex. Peter turned his gun toward the bouncer. Rebel grabbed his revolver and aimed it at Peter. David emerged from behind his cover. Mink flinched, then raised a glowing hand at him. Mercy broke free of Peter's grip and reached for the .22 on the ground, just as Zack made a dive for it.

And then chaos.

Between the clamorous gunshot and the multiple flashes of lumis, Zack had no idea what was happening. He opened his eyes in a twitching squint and caught a fleeting glimpse of someone—some*thing*—attacking Rebel. The creature was white from head to toe and moved so fast that he was practically a blur.

By the time Zack's vision fully returned, the stranger was gone. Rebel, Mink, and Mercy lay crumpled on the concrete, their temples dripping with blood, their chests heaving with labored breaths.

Zack stumbled forward. "What just . . . ?"

A hand gripped his shoulder. "Zack? Is that you?"

He spun around to find David in awful condition. His face was drenched in tears. The whites of his eyes were marred with dark red splotches.

Zack held him by the arms. "You okay?"

"I'm not sure. I was hit. I can't see a thing. What happened?"

Zack took another look at the three fallen Gothams. "I don't know. Someone knocked them out."

"Who, Peter?"

"No idea."

"Where is he?"

"I'm here."

Peter stood ten feet behind them, looking no worse than he had before the scuffle. Zack eyed him up and down. "What the hell just happened?"

"God only knows." Peter looked to the street exit. "We have to go."

Zack turned his head and saw the bouncer writhing on his back, clutching his chest with bloody fingers.

"He's hurt."

"Who's hurt?" asked David.

"That bouncer. He . . ." Zack saw a thin wisp of smoke drifting up from Peter's .38. "You shot him."

"He'll live."

"He was innocent."

"He'll *live*," Peter insisted. "The hospitals have revivers. They'll reverse his wounds like they never happened."

He holstered his gun, then opened a portal on the side of the trasher. "Come on."

Zack led David by the arm, his mind struggling to fill the blank spaces. Someone had saved them in the nick of time. Someone fast, faster even than—

"—Hannah." Zack spun around to face Peter. "She's still out there. We have to—"

"We will. Come on."

Peter ushered him and David through the portal, then took a final scan of the alley. Rebel and Ivy weren't entirely fools. They'd likely sent swifters after Hannah, which meant it was already too late to help her. She'd have to get herself out of this mess. Her and her new friend.

FOUR

Hannah paced between two church lots, her anxiety increasing with each hurried step. It had been five minutes and counting since she followed Jonathan into the twisting corridors of the Faith Mall. She had no idea how to get back to Christopher Street. She didn't know if Zack was okay.

Why the hell did you leave your phone with him? said the Amanda in her head. *You could have called him twenty minutes ago.*

She moved along the edge of the Sovereign Grace barrier, her fingers brushing lightly against the tempis. After thirty feet, she reached a T-shaped junction of tempic walls and stopped just short of the corner. "You okay?"

No response. She peeked around the bend. "Jonathan, are you there?"

"Still here," he said. "Still pissing."

"Look, I don't want to rush you, but I'm worried about my friend."

"Who? The guy with the chin fuzz?"

Hannah fought back a laugh. "Zack."

"He's one of us, I take it."

"Yeah." Her smile went flat. "One of the few."

Jonathan zipped his fly, then made his way back to Hannah. Up close, she could see and smell every bit of his squalor. His slacks were patched with withered strips of duct tape. His dark brown button-down hadn't been washed in weeks. She would have expected the Pelletiers to lend him a helping hand—a rescue here, a satchel of cash there—but they seemed perfectly happy to let him twist in the wind.

"So what now?" Jonathan asked her.

"I have to get Zack. He's waiting." Hannah eyed him guardedly. "Will you come back with me?"

Jonathan shuffled his feet a moment before answering. "Okay."

"What's the matter?"

"I'm still not sure what to think about you. I mean, you're obviously not looking to kill us, which is nice, but I don't know if we're better off with you people."

Hannah chewed her lip in contemplation. That was the third time he'd referred to himself in the plural. She hoped to God he wasn't talking about his guitar.

"When you say 'we' . . ."

"That's the other thing," he added. "You told me I don't have to be alone. I never said I was. I have Heath to think about. And he's—"

"Who's Heath?"

"—complex."

"Who is Heath?"

A flying vehicle stopped sixty feet above them, bathing them both in a soft yellow light. Unlike the aerstraunt that had crossed their view earlier, the Dixon Hornet was a tiny rocket darter with one seat and three skinny tires. Its glowing aeric liftplates looked sinister in the darkness, like cat eyes.

Jonathan squinted at the dawdling aero. "What's he doing?"

The pilot was no man. Had Jonathan been able to look through the windshield, he would have seen a pug-faced girl of Indian descent, an eighty-pound child in business wear. Though Gemma Sunder was only ten years old in body and temperament, she continually insisted that she was an adult, and the argument had some merit. Like Evan Rander, she was one of the world's few loopers: a cerebral time traveler who lived a corkscrew life of rewinds and do-overs. She'd been through puberty three times, learned four languages, flown a jet, crashed a car, even killed a man once. She'd seen the start of apocalypse with her very own eyes before fleeing back to pre-adolescence.

Now with four years of space between her and her nightmare, Gemma was determined to help Rebel and Ivy save the world. Her unique ability made her a crucial part of their team. The girl didn't just see the future. She lived it one minute at a time.

As her Hornet idled above the Mall, Gemma smiled at the breachers on her dashboard screen. "Hello, fuckers."

Jonathan turned to Hannah. "Who is that?"

She took a nervous step back, her eyes still raised. "I don't know. Could be Gothams. Could be Deps."

"Deps?"

"Government agents," she explained. "Like the FBI."

"I know what they are. Why do you think it's them?"

Hannah looked at him sheepishly. "We're kinda running from them, too."

Jonathan stared at her, blank-faced. "You're fugitives."

"It's not our fault."

"Federal fugitives."

"It's not our fault!"

"I don't care whose fault it is! That's the last thing Heath and I need!"

"Look—"

Hannah turned her head in alarm. She could feel a pair of smoky auras in the vicinity, two people moving fast—freakishly fast.

Jonathan saw the color drain from her face. "What? What is it?"

"Swifters."

"What?"

"We have to go."

Hannah looked him over in frantic calculation. She'd never shifted a person of his size before. Even if she could fit him in her temporal field, he was way too heavy to carry on her back. It would have to go the other way.

She circled behind him and tugged the guitar on his back. "We can't bring this. You'll have to leave it here."

"Are you insane?"

"I need to shift us."

He pulled away from her. "I have no idea what that means, but my guitar—"

"Jonathan . . ."

"This thing pays the rent."

"There are dangerous people coming for us! We'll die if we stay here!"

Jonathan's eyes bulged. He'd heard similar words seven months ago, in a White Plains research facility. If he hadn't listened to Heath that night, he'd be just as dead as their other friends.

He unslung his guitar and placed it gently against the wall. "Goddamn it. This better not be some sort of trick."

Hannah climbed onto his back, steeling herself for the hard task ahead. If even a small part of Jonathan slipped outside her temporal field, he'd be rifted. Living creatures couldn't exist at two different speeds. It created chaos in the vascular system, triggering everything from gangrene to blood clots to instant, fatal heart attack.

Gemma watched Hannah and Jonathan on her camera screen. She raised her transceiver to her lips. "Speed it up, Bug. They're about to string it."

A deep voice crackled through her headset. "Who do you think you're talking to?"

"Just *listen* to me, Daddy. You have to be careful. You're not the first swifter she's gone up against."

"Doesn't matter," Bug replied. "I'm the last."

Despite his plebeian nickname, a stubborn remnant of his childhood, Deven "Bug" Sunder was a well-respected figure in his clan. He served as one of the three voting heads of the Sunder family and was the longtime primarch of his power guild. There were many reasons why the swifters kept electing him as their leader. His control over temporis was second to none. He could crack the 40x threshold in a heartbeat, shift a room full of people without breaking a sweat. Even more impressive was his unflappable composure. The swifters, by and large, were not known for their emotional stability. Bug proved a shining counterexample. If Hannah had been a Gotham, she might have voted for him too.

She wrapped her legs around Jonathan's waist. "Keep your arms close to me. Keep your balance. And whatever you do, don't bump into anything. You don't want to crash at our speed."

"Our speed? What the hell are you—"

In an instant, everything around him changed. The temperature dropped twenty degrees. The sounds of the city fell to a murmur. His vision took on a deep blue tint, as if someone had wrapped his eyes in cellophane.

Jonathan took a gawking look around the corridor. The windblown litter moved with slow-motion torpor, like objects in space.

"What . . . what is this?"

"It's my weirdness," Hannah said. "Go."

A dark figure popped around the corner, a sturdy-looking man in a black bodysuit and tinted face mask. His outfit glowed with bright blue lines of lumis. *A speedsuit*, Hannah realized. For a moment, she wondered if he was a federal agent, but . . . no, his aura was all natural. Best she could guess, the suit was only there to mask his identity and true nature. The Gothams were still a myth to the public at large. They preferred to keep it that way.

Unlike everything else in the sluggish blue yonder, Bug moved with nimble haste. His arms were nearly a blur as they reached for a wooden weapon on his back. By the time Hannah recognized it as a hunting bow, it was already loaded with an arrow.

"Run!" she yelled.

Panicked, Jonathan turned around and bolted down the tempic corridor. Hannah felt the wind of Bug's arrow as it whizzed past her hip.

Gemma pushed her Hornet into hot pursuit, cursing her father and his vain choice of weapon. Bug had become jealous of Rebel's new prestige and was desperate to outshine him as the clan's epic hero. *Heroes get results, you prancing penis. Next time bring a gun.*

Jonathan hooked a sharp left and threw a frantic look over his shoulder. "Who *is* that guy?"

"I don't know," Hannah said. "I just know who he's with."

"Yeah, no shit." He grunted through clenched teeth. "You led the Gothams right to me."

"I'll get us out of this."

"How?"

"I don't know. Just keep running!"

Hannah glanced up at the liftplates of the Hornet. The vehicle was doing a fine job keeping pace. It must have been shifted as well.

Gemma spoke into her headset. "They're coming your way, Jinn. Get ready."

Her earphone squealed with a half second of incomprehensible shouting. Djinni Godden was moving much faster than the Hornet's 12x limit. Gemma had to wait for the temporal converter to uncompress her garble.

"I know! I can feel them! Just keep a lookout!"

Gemma rolled her eyes. The lovely young swifter had heard the horror stories about the Pelletiers, and was deathly afraid of becoming their next victim. Luckily, Gemma had seen enough of the future to know that Azral and Esis weren't coming tonight. These breachers were on their own.

Jonathan turned a corner and saw a break in the tempis. The Westside exit was just forty yards away. Beyond the arch lay the slow-moving traffic of Riverside Boulevard.

He fought to speak through wheezing breaths. "How do you feel about killing people?"

Hannah opened her eyes. "What?"

"We're about to become open targets. We need a plan."

"How do you expect me to kill him?"

"Not you," Jonathan said. "Me."

"What are you talking about?"

He threw a grim look over his shoulder. "I have a . . . weirdness too."

Hannah flashed back to the Dep she'd pummeled in West Virginia, the Gotham she'd shot at Battery Place. She didn't know if either of them survived and she had no intention of dwelling on it. But she couldn't help fear, in the wake of one doomsday and the shadow of another, that she was losing her perspective. Life was supposed to be a blessed thing, every minute of it sacred. To take it so easily from another person, even an enemy, was a slippery slope to step on. If she and her friends weren't careful, they'd become just like the people they hated the most, the Rebels and Evans and Azrals of this world.

She tightened her grip on Jonathan. "Can't you just, I don't know, hurt him enough to stop him?"

He gravely shook his head. "There's no middle ground. If I hit him, he's dead."

Hannah felt a second energy signature near the exit. They were fast approaching another swifter. And the archer was gaining on them from behind.

"Keep running," she told Jonathan. "All the way to the river."

"What? Hannah—"

"Just trust me!"

She had an idea, though her last working neurons seemed united in doubt. *It won't work! It won't work! You're crazy! You'll die!*

Hannah closed her eyes and floored her inner pedal, pushing her talents to a bold new extreme. The world outside her temporal bubble grew two shades bluer. The air turned cold enough to paint her breath with mist.

Bug turned the corner and felt the aura of his targets. The breacher woman was strong but careless with her temporis. She was burning all her fuel on a wind sprint.

Amateur, he thought. *Your teacher should be ashamed.*

Jonathan burst through the archway and into the bustle of Riverside Boulevard. The pedestrians on the sidewalk were practically statues. The cars moved like boxes on a slow conveyer belt. Jonathan could only assume that he and Hannah were just a misshapen blur to the people around them. He understood now why she told him not to bump into anything. At this speed, even a love tap could—

"Look out!" Hannah yelled.

A swifter in a speedsuit was coming toward them, a smaller one than the man with the bow. Though Jinn Godden had stopped growing at four-foot-ten, she had more marriage offers than anyone else in the clan. She was a certified genius, a classical pianist, a blue-eyed stunner, and one of the rare few Gothams who qualified as a dualer.

"A what?" Hannah asked Peter five weeks ago, when he first mentioned the term.

"A dualer," he'd said. "We've all been blessed. But some of us have been blessed twice."

Djinni Godden was both a swifter and a tempic. She was Hannah and Amanda rolled up into one.

As Jonathan sped past her, Jinn raised her hand. A white spike tore through the palm of her glove and cut through the air like a quarrel. It missed Hannah by inches and hit a parked van with enough force to dent the grille. A second one sailed past Jonathan's head.

"Holy shit!"

"Go to the pier!" Hannah screamed. Her temporal exertions were taking their toll on her—a pain in her skull, like electrified wire. Worse, she could feel her power fading fast. She had thirty seconds of speed left, if that.

Jonathan crossed the expressway, weaving clumsily between cars as Jinn's tempic bolts flew past him. Soon he reached the edge of Hudson Pier 7, a fifty-yard strip of restaurants and gift shops, all closed for the night. As far as escape paths went, the pier was worse than an alley. It was a—

"—dead end. It's a dead end! Hannah, what are we doing?"

"Keep going!"

Bug watched from a distance, shaking his head in amusement. *These are the great breachers that eluded you, Rebel? They don't even have the sense of rabbits.*

Several yards above, Gemma's head dipped forward. Her eyes rapidly fluttered. Her older self had traveled back through time, invading her consciousness with brand-new memories. New information.

She screamed something into her headset. His father had to reduce his velocity to understand her.

"—jump in the water!"

Bug furrowed his brow at the Hornet. "What?"

"I said, *don't let them jump in the water!*"

The moment Jonathan reached the edge of the pier, Hannah de-shifted. The blue tint of their vision washed away. The world around them returned to its normal tempo.

"Turn around!" Hannah said.

With the last ounce of strength in his buckling legs, Jonathan turned and leaned back against the rope rail. He could see the two swifters moving toward him like missiles.

Hannah jerked back with all her weight. As their bodies tumbled over the rope, an arrow nicked the heel of her sneaker. A tempic spike sliced Jonathan's shoulder. They plunged into the river with a towering splash.

Bug and Jinn ran to the railing and aimed their weapons at the rippling water. The Hornet hovered in front of them.

"Goddamn it!" Gemma shrieked. "I told you not to let them get away!"

Bug drank her in through an icy squint. He'd never been particularly fond of the girl, and he had no idea why she was upset now. Everyone knew that swifters weren't exceptional swimmers. The resistance from the water negated most of their speed advantage, and they couldn't hold their breath any longer than a normal person.

"Relax," he told Gemma. "They'll come up."

"No they won't! That's what I'm trying to tell you! They're gone!"

"What are you talking about? Gone how?"

"I don't know! They just disappeared!"

Jinn leaned as far as she could over the rope rail. "That can't be right. Check under the pier."

Gemma palmed her face, groaning. She'd crossed the midnight hour twenty-six times already and had searched the area twenty-six different ways. She'd looked under the pier, over the pier, a yard to the left, an acre to the right. She even kept the Hornet's headlights aimed on the very spot where Hannah and Jonathan submerged, waiting three hours for them to rise as swimmers or corpses.

They didn't show up anywhere. Against all sense and logic, the breachers had vanished.

In the middle of last December, during a relentless blizzard that had brought New York to a standstill, Hannah accidentally learned a new trick.

She lay in her bed in a terry-cloth robe, sneezing and coughing and cursing the virus that had singled her out with malicious glee. It was the Evan Rander of colds, and she hated the fates that inflicted it on her.

Amanda backed through the door with a tray of hot goodies—a cup of herbal tea, a bowl of minestrone, a chocolate chip cookie that had been reversed to oven freshness.

Hannah took a sullen look at her new bounty. "Well, aren't you the happy homemaker."

"Still grumpy, I see."

"It's my second goddamn cold in a month."

Amanda placed the tray on the bedside table. "New world, new viruses. It'll be years before our immune systems catch up."

"So why aren't the rest of you sick?"

Amanda shrugged. "It is what it is."

Hannah bristled at her aphorism, one their mother had used on them all the time. In a worse state of mind, she might have reminded Amanda of that, just to get under her skin. But she was trying to break old habits with her sister, all the nitpicks and microaggressions that came as naturally to them as breathing.

"Theo asked to see you," Amanda said. "Just to say hi."

"Don't let him in."

"Why not?"

"Because if he catches what I have, he'll be too sick to look for the . . . the . . ."

Before she could say "string," she sat up and let out a soul-rattling sneeze, one violent enough to reset all her circuits. By the time she finished blowing her nose, her head was spinning. Her skin burned all over and her vision had turned a hot shade of red.

"God. I'm dying here. I can't . . ."

She looked up and screamed at the sudden presence of all six housemates. They buzzed around her like blurs, holding unintelligible conversations with each other as they repeatedly checked on her. Amanda moved to her bedside sixteen times in the span of a second and flashed a penlight in Hannah's eyes. This was beyond madness. Everyone she knew and loved had suddenly become a swifter.

"What . . . what's happening?"

She peeked down and saw that someone had draped a blanket over her. By the time she looked back up, the lamps were on and the windows had turned black with night. She checked the clock and saw the hours changing like seconds. The minutes flickered in crazy eights. It wasn't just the people around her. The whole world was moving at hyperspeed.

"What the hell's going on?"

The lamps went dark and her burning heat subsided. In the faint glow of the nightlight, she saw Amanda sleeping uncomfortably on the easy chair. The clock had settled on 4:42 A.M.

Hannah rubbed her face. "Oh God. Did it stop?"

Amanda's eyes snapped open. She leapt out of her chair. "Hannah! You're back!"

Within minutes, everyone in the brownstone had gathered in the living room to fill her in on the last sixteen hours.

"You had us all freaked out," Theo said. "You didn't move. You didn't blink. We thought you were paralyzed until you looked down at yourself."

"That took four hours," Mia added.

Hannah turned her rattled gaze onto David. "You're the genius. Explain it."

He hunched his shoulders in a shrug. "Best we can guess, you changed the flow of time a different way. Instead of accelerating, you slowed yourself down. For every second you spent in your temporal bubble, a full hour passed."

"That's crazy. I never . . ." Hannah looked to Peter. "You know a lot of swifters. Has that ever happened to them?"

He shook his head distractedly. "This is brand new."

As soon as Hannah recuperated from her illness, she toyed with her powers until she was able to enter redshift at will. The transition proved to be ridiculously simple, like holding her breath. After losing five mornings in a row to her temporal experiments, she put aside the gimmick and forgot about it. Life was short enough as it was. It was hard to imagine a practical use for super-slowness anyway.

But on the fourth night of April, in the cold, dark waters of the Hudson, she found one.

The moment she dipped below the surface of the river, Hannah wrapped one arm around the pier support and the other one around Jonathan. She hoped she had enough temporis left to redshift both of them. She prayed Peter was right and the Gothams didn't know this trick.

With a twist of thought, she pushed time into fast-forward. The liquid around them turned forty degrees warmer. Their muscles went rigid. Their bodies sank. Their hair and clothes stopped rippling in the current. To Hannah, the sensation was surprisingly pleasant, like finding shade after a long day in the sun.

Jonathan craned his neck and looked up through the water. All he could see was the shimmering moon—a tiny red crescent that, like many new things in his life, moved a hell of a lot faster than it should have. Hannah could only imagine the poor man's anguish. This was their world now. This was the crazy life they shared.

Two lost souls swimming in a fishbowl, she thought.

The Gothams departed. Hannah kept pushing the clock forward. Seventeen feet beneath the surface of the Hudson, the Silver and the Gold embraced like lovers, still holding last night's breath as the sky grew light and the world journeyed on to tomorrow.

FIVE

The rejuvenator stopped with a musical chime. Theo opened the door and retrieved his breakfast: a shrink-wrapped plate of fried bread pockets, all stuffed to the seams with bacon and cheese. Anywhere else, they'd be called "empanadas." But here in Altamerica, where foreign-sounding words gave half the nation the vapors, they were simply known as "morning melts."

Theo brought the platter to the dining room table, then unwrapped it in front of Mia. She looked away from her lapbook, her eyes dancing hungrily around the steaming hot pastries.

"Have some," Theo said. "They're good."

"You know how many chemicals are in those things?"

"That's David talking. Do you really want to eat like him?"

Mia hesitated a moment before shaking her head. "I'm fine."

The mood in the house had been bleak since midnight, when it became painfully clear that Hannah was missing. Amanda, Zack, and Peter were still out looking for her. Mia had spent all night scouring the local newswires. Only David and Theo managed to get some sleep. One was still recovering from his retinal flash burns. The other was afflicted with a rare case of optimism.

Hannah's okay, Theo repeatedly assured his friends. *She'll call us in the morning and she'll be home by ten. Trust me.*

As much as the others wanted to believe him, they knew full well that no futures were certain. Plus, Theo's scenario didn't make sense. If Hannah was all right, she could have easily found a pay phone, borrowed someone's mobile, hailed a cab back to Brooklyn. Yet she'd been out of touch for hours. Where was she?

Theo couldn't answer that. All he knew was what the strings showed him, and the strings showed Hannah, alive and well.

He grabbed a morning meltanada. "Anything in the news?"

"Some people in speedsuits caused trouble at a pier."

"Casualties?"

"No injuries. No arrests."

Mia watched him closely as he bit into the melt. "Just *have* some," Theo said.

She reached for the platter, then pulled her hand back when she heard someone approaching. David entered through the living room, disheveled and groggy. The whites of his eyes were still blotted with red splotches.

Mia pushed the melts away. "Hey. How you feeling?"

"Embalmed." He peeked through the window at the morning sky. "The others back yet?"

Mia shook her head. "They're still looking for her."

David scoffed. "If this keeps up, we'll be looking for them."

He retreated into the kitchen and returned with his breakfast: two red bell peppers and a glass of cold water. The boy had been a vegan for as long as anyone knew him, though he repeatedly insisted that it wasn't a choice. His father had raised him on such a strict hippie diet that he'd developed a natural aversion to most modern foods. By now, the others were used to seeing his disgust at the dining table as they consumed their meatburgers and omelets, their butter-soaked potatoes. Only Mia made an effort to eat healthier around him, or at least less repulsively.

David glanced at Theo's breakfast like it was an unflushed toilet. He took his peppers to the far side of the table. "We're going to have to do something."

"She'll be back," Theo told him.

"I'm not talking about Hannah. I'm talking about the Gothams. We can't just wait for them to change their minds."

"What do you suggest we do?" Theo asked. "Bomb their village? Kill their leaders?"

"Kill them? No, but if we're smart about it, we could apprehend Rebel and Ivy."

Mia shook her head. "Peter says—"

"Peter's approach isn't *working*," David said. "I saw the way they talked to him. They hate him more than they hate us."

"He'll turn them around. He just needs more time."

"I think you might have a little too much faith in him, Mia."

"And you don't have enough."

Theo had to give Mia credit. For such a lovestruck girl, she didn't hesitate to challenge David when she disagreed with him. More than that, she was the only one in the group who could get him to back down from an argument. David obviously adored the girl, enough to make some of their friends wonder if the crush went both ways.

But Theo had yet to see a future where they were romantically involved. Every time he looked at David's strings, he saw a dark-haired girl of staggering beauty, a lumic just like him. But who was she?

David shrugged at Mia, then took a crunchy bite of his bell pepper. "Well, you know Peter better than I do. You certainly have better instincts about people."

Mia responded with a blushing half grin, the same look she got whenever David praised her. Theo had peeked at her future many times and was continually thrown by its inconsistency. She was a trim, athletic blonde in one string and a heavyset goth in another. She carried a Bible in some visions and a crossbow in others. She had boyfriends and girlfriends, tattoos and scars. She was even pregnant in some premonitions. The only unifying trait was the hard look in her eyes, an immutable hatred, like fire. Theo had no idea what the Future Mias were so angry about, but it seemed bigger than heartbreak. Bigger than David.

The neighbors' dogs started barking. Mia rose from her chair and turned toward the front door.

"They're back."

"What?"

A ten-foot portal opened on the wall of the foyer. The brownstone came alive with heavy footsteps and clamorous voices. The louder half of the group had most definitely returned.

"—then let him go alone!" Zack yelled. "He's a ghoster. He'll see what happened."

"I said no."

"You're being stupid, Peter."

"Stupid? You're the one who wants to put David in harm's way."

"He wants to find *Hannah*," Amanda fired back. "We'll do it with or without you."

She shambled into the dining room, her shoulders drooped with fatigue. Her hoodie was riddled with dozens of new holes. She'd clearly had another outbreak of stress tempis.

The Silvers at the table watched quietly as Amanda placed an instrument against the wall: a shiny blue electric guitar.

David ran his finger along the polished wood surface. "Is this, uh . . . ?"

Zack nodded tensely from the living room. "Yeah, it's Trevor's. Or whatever his name is."

"We found it at the Faith Mall," Peter added. "Only trace of them."

Amanda's head lolled to the left. Her tired eyes locked with Theo's. "I'm about to tear this city apart."

"Don't."

"Then *tell* me—"

"She's coming back," Theo insisted again. "I've never been surer of anything in my life."

Sighing, Amanda sat down at the table and rested her head in her hands. While David fetched her a glass of water and Mia scrambled to make her some breakfast, Theo kept a nervous eye on the guitar. From the moment he saw it, he felt a tectonic shift in his foresight: a million new roads opening and a million old ones closing. Hannah was bringing two people home with her—a long-haired man and a dark, nervous boy—and their arrival was already changing the future. The strings of time shook in anticipation of the Golds.

Jonathan poked his head out of the waters of the Hudson, gasping for air as he surveyed his surroundings. When he last drew breath, it had barely been midnight. Now the sky was bright and the river gleamed with ribbons of sunshine. Tomorrow had come way ahead of schedule.

"What? What just . . . ?"

Hannah burst through the surface and hacked a cough. Her mouth tasted awful, like flat beer from an ashtray.

Jonathan swam into the shady underside of the pier and then clutched a wooden strut. His bulging eyes stayed locked on Hannah. "What did you do?"

"Hang on. I can't see."

"It was nighttime a minute ago!"

"Just wait a second!"

She wrapped her arm around a support pillar and brushed the hair from her eyes. She had to spit three times to get the last of the Hudson out of her mouth. "I shifted us the other way."

"What, backward?"

"No. I mean instead of going fast, I slowed us down."

"Wait . . ." Jonathan blinked at her in astonishment, as if she'd just pulled a hat out of a rabbit. "Let me get this straight. We were being chased by super-fast people—"

"Right."

"—and we lost them by going super-*slow*?"

When put that way, it did sound nutty. Hannah had no idea what made her think the stunt would work, yet the Gothams never saw it coming.

Jonathan stared at the horizon, his eyes darting back and forth. "So this . . . holy shit. We were down there all night!"

"Yes, but—"

"Shit. *Shit!*"

Hannah studied him worriedly as he flailed in the water. He'd been so brave when their lives were in danger just a minute before. Now panic washed over him as quickly as the new day.

She noticed an oozing red gash on his shoulder. "Jonathan, you're hurt!"

"I don't care. I have to get home."

"What?"

"He must be freaking out."

"Who?"

"Heath! Heath! I keep telling you about Heath!"

"You only told me his name!"

Jonathan scanned the pier for the nearest ladder. "He's one of us. One of *mine*."

"Okay . . ."

"I was supposed to be back at midnight. He probably thinks I'm dead."

Hannah imagined her people were in a similar tizzy. Hopefully Theo had seen the future and calmed Amanda down. Unless the Gothams gave her another reason to cry.

"Oh no. Zack . . ."

"Who?"

"My friend. I have to make sure he's okay."

"Do what you have to," Jonathan said. "I'm going home."

He found the ladder and swam toward it. Hannah paddled after him. "Wait! How will I reach you?"

"I don't know."

"Jonathan!"

He turned around at the ladder, frantic. "He's just a kid, Hannah. I'm all he has."

Hannah took a quick moment to mull her options. There wasn't anything she could do for Zack at this point. And she sure as hell wasn't going to lose Jonathan now.

"Hang on," she said. "I'm coming with you."

"Okay. Fine. Just . . ."

A delirious chuckle escaped him. *Just hurry up*, he was going to say. *Don't slow me down.* The woman gave mad new meaning to both phrases. Whoever Hannah Given was on the old world, she was something else now. She bent the hours to her will like a wild young goddess. She played the clock like a fine guitar.

Before a great white blast changed the face of Manhattan, the neighborhood had been known as the Meatpacking District. A sprawling industrial park grew from the ashes of the Cataclysm, replacing the slaughterhouses with chemical processing plants. The area was renamed Presin Square in honor of its chief export, a light but durable petroleum resin that, on another world, might have been called "plastic."

In the 1960s, after bio-organic resin (bresin) became the new standard, the area fell to obsolescence. The factories were transformed into warehouses, which were converted into apartment buildings, which degraded into slums. Now Presin Square was the city's most infamous patch of crime and poverty. Jonathan had to offer all the damp blue cash in his pocket to get a cabbie to drop him off at his ramshackle tenement.

As the taxi made its hissing landing, Hannah looked out the window. The buildings were all in horrendous disrepair. Half the windows had been re-placed with sheets or wooden boards. Garbage was strewn everywhere. Only four percent of the trashers in the neighborhood were functional. The rest had been stripped of their temporic components.

"God . . ." Hannah watched a group of grimy, shirtless children chase a stray cat through puddles. "How long have you lived here?"

"About seven months," Jonathan told her. "Best I could do on a street mu-sician's salary."

She spied four ratty thugs on the stoop and understood why Jonathan gave her his button-down. She closed it tight around her still-damp blouse as she stepped out of the cab. Her right foot sank into a curbside puddle, some chunky yellow liquid that would haunt her dreams for days.

Jonathan watched the men warily. "Stay close."

"It's all right. I can smack them twelve times before they even think about touching me."

"Exactly what I'm trying to avoid," he said. "I see now why you're a fugitive."

"Hey, it wasn't easy for us either, okay? We crossed the whole country with Deps and Gothams on our ass, not to mention a psychopath."

Jonathan paused. "Did you lose anyone?"

"No," Hannah said, though that wasn't entirely true. There had once been a Silver named Jury Curado, who was stabbed in an alley before the others had a chance to meet him. *You would have liked him very much,* Evan Rander had teased.

Jonathan's expression hardened as he escorted her into his building. "There used to be eight of us. Now it's just me and Heath."

The lobby reeked of mildew and rat droppings. A scrawny blond teenager nursed her infant on a pile of splintered wood. She did a double-take at Jona-than's soaked undershirt, the thin trickles of blood that dripped from his makeshift bandage.

"Damn, Axel. Someone ripped you up. What tell?"

Jonathan lowered his gaze. "We got mugged."

"Got *what*?"

"Got pouched," he corrected.

"What they pouch you with, a hose? And who's the slice?"

He put an arm around Hannah and walked her to the stairwell. "Mind your own, Hattie."

"Heard. But your boy was thundering all night. Beating the walls and yelling and shit."

Jonathan stopped short. "Is he still there? Did you see him leave?"

"None seen. But you better step light. Bolly heard and he's preffin' to ex you both."

Hannah followed Jonathan up the steps. "Bolly?"

"Landlord."

"And the reason she called you Axel?"

"I use fake names. Makes me feel safer."

"I see. So is Jonathan Christie just another—"

"No," he told her. "You got the real one."

He stopped at apartment 3A, put his ear to the door, and exhaled with relief. He threw a nervous look at Hannah.

"Uh, you might want to hang back."

"Why?"

"Just trust me."

Hannah backstepped a few yards while Jonathan knocked on the door.

"Heath? Buddy, it's me. Are you in there? Are the . . . dogs out?"

The peephole filled with shadow. A high voice filtered through the wood. "Jonathan?"

"It's me, pal. I'm back. If the dogs are out, call them off. It's safe."

The door creaked open. Jonathan looked inside the apartment in slack-faced horror. Hannah had no idea what he was gawking at.

"Oh shit," he uttered. "God, Heath, I'm so sorry."

A child emerged into the hallway, a dark-skinned boy with a frizzy mop of hair. He stood barely an inch taller than Mia, and was so skinny that his golden bracelet would have fallen right through Hannah's old silver one. She recognized his long blue shirt as a New York Giants jersey, a rather crude knockoff at that. The "44" on the front and back were cut from felt and stitched by an amateur hand.

Heath scrutinized Jonathan through large wet eyes, then lowered his gaze to the floor. His left hand flapped frenetically, like he was drying nail polish.

"I waited all night. You told me—"

"Heath . . ."

"You told me you'd be back at midnight."

"I'm sorry, Heath. I ran into trouble. You know I'd never do that on purpose."

"I thought that . . . I thought that maybe . . ."

"No."

"I thought maybe the Gothams got you."

Hannah was surprised to see Jonathan keep his hands to himself. She would have smothered the boy in hugs already.

"They tried," Jonathan told Heath. "They tried their damnedest but we got away. Listen . . ."

The boy looked down the hallway and made eye contact with Hannah. She'd taken him for a pre-adolescent, but now she could see that he was a baby-faced teenager, a rather beautiful one at that. His face was angelic. His lips were femininely divine. His big hazel eyes were utterly captivating. Hannah could have stared at him for hours. But even as she fell in love with him a little, she could tell right away that something was off with him. Something on the inside.

Heath processed her for the briefest of moments before clutching his hair in panic. "No. No no no no . . ."

Jonathan held his arm. "Listen to me, Heath. Listen. She's one of us."

"No she's not!"

He fled into the apartment and slammed the door behind him. Jonathan groaned and raised a finger at Hannah. "One minute."

Hannah waited by the stairwell, her mind plaguing her with grim scenarios. What if the Gothams had killed everyone but her and Mia? Would they have stayed together? Would they have made it to New York? Would they have even lasted a week in this hellhole?

Two minutes later, Jonathan reemerged. Hannah looked him over with awe. "God . . ."

"He's not usually that bad."

"That's not what I meant. I just . . ."

She looked beyond him and saw a fat, bumbling roach on the wall. "You can't live here anymore."

Jonathan leaned against his doorframe. "Yeah, that's just what my land-lord's gonna say. Problem is, Heath doesn't trust you. He thinks you're a Gotham."

"So did you."

"I know. I told him everything, but . . ."

He flipped a hand in surrender. Hannah stroked her jaw. "Is there anything I can do?"

"Yeah, actually. He wants to know why you don't have a bracelet, which is a pretty good question. He'd also like some proof—"

"Name the Beatles!" Heath yelled from inside the apartment.

"—that you're one of us."

"Full names!"

Hannah smiled. She aimed her answer at the door. "John Lennon. Paul McCartney. George Harrison. Ringo Starr. As for the bracelet, I had one in silver. Zack figured out a way to get them off. He can do the same for you."

The hallway fell quiet until Heath muttered something. To Hannah, it sounded an awful lot like "Trillinger."

She furrowed her brow. "Heath, did you just—"

"Name the Beatles' fourth album," he demanded. "Studio, not live."

Hannah froze, stymied. Jonathan frowned at the door. "Not everyone knows that, buddy."

"Yes they do! It's common knowledge."

Jonathan rested against the wall, looking sickly and pale. He was clearly exhausted, and the blood loss wasn't helping.

Hannah examined his shoulder bandage. "You need stitches. My sister's a nurse. She can help you."

"She's lying!" Heath yelled.

Jonathan crouched down and spoke into the keyhole. "We're going to have to trust her, buddy. We can't stay here. When Bolly sees what you did—"

"We'll go somewhere else. We don't need her."

"Heath . . ."

"She's dangerous! She's going to get you killed!"

"Goddamn it, Heath. Will you *listen* to me?"

"No!"

Hannah moved to the door and cleared her throat. Before Jonathan could say anything, her voice filled the hall like a lullaby.

> *Words are flowing out like endless rain into a paper cup*
> *They slither while they pass, they slip away across the universe*

Jonathan stared at her, astonished. Hannah shrugged. It was the only Beatles song she knew by heart. She'd crooned along to the Fiona Apple cover so many times that all the other versions felt like knockoffs.

> *Pools of sorrow, waves of joy are drifting through my opened mind*
> *Possessing and caressing me*

The door creaked open a few inches. Heath looked at Hannah with large, maudlin eyes. His lips moved silently to the refrain.

> *Jai guru deva om*
> *Nothing's gonna change my world*
> *Nothing's gonna change my—*

"Your timing's off."

Hannah stopped. "I'm sorry?"

Heath caught her eye for a fleeting moment before dropping his gaze to her feet. "Your tempo. You were too fast in the opening and too slow in the refrain."

"It's been a while," Hannah admitted with a grin. "You sure know your Beatles."

"I know lots of songs. So does Jonathan. We write them down on music sheets. We're bringing them back one by one."

"That's wonderful, Heath. It's a beautiful thing you're doing. You know, I could help."

He turned away, scowling. Jonathan kneeled in front of him. "Listen to me, buddy. You know I never lie to you, and you know I don't hold back. So when I say we're in deep shit, I really want you to listen. I lost my guitar. We're about to lose our home. The Gothams are closing in on us. We can't beat them on our own."

He jerked his head at Hannah. "Now, she can be a little intense sometimes, and you don't know the half of her timing issues, but she's most definitely a friend. If you won't trust her, then trust me to trust her. Please."

Heath studied Hannah in thorny contemplation. "Where does she live?"

"Brooklyn," Hannah replied.

Heath arched an eyebrow. "House or apartment?"

"Brownstone."

"What color is it?"

"Uh, brown?"

"How did you find Jonathan?"

Hannah pressed her lips and sighed through her fingers. There was no point in lying.

"There's a woman I met. A girl, really. I barely know anything about her except that she wears two watches and she can see the future. She told me six months ago that I'd find Jonathan at that bar. She said he was from my world and that he was a good man, and she was right. I'm pretty sure now that she wanted me to find you too."

The two Golds swapped an inscrutable look. Heath mumbled something under his breath. "Do you like wolves?"

"What?"

He retreated inside the apartment. Jonathan smirked at Hannah. "It's all right. You sold him."

"Are you sure?"

"Yeah. You got the wolf question. You're fine."

Hannah shook her head, baffled. She'd assumed the poor kid had been cracked by the apocalypse. Now she began to wonder if he was a high-functioning autistic. What on earth would the Pelletiers want with this boy?

"Is all that true?" Jonathan asked. "About the girl with two watches?"

She nodded her head, her thoughts still swirling around Azral and company.

"Did she say anything else about me?"

"No," Hannah replied, with a silent asterisk. The girl had certainly *implied* a few things.

Jonathan fished through his pocket and placed three quarters into Hannah's palm. "Pay phone's down the hall. Tell your friends to come quick but don't bring everyone. It'll freak out Heath."

"Don't worry. It'll probably just be Peter and my sister."

Jonathan shook his head in grim wonder. "Can't believe you still have one of those."

"A sister? Yeah. If you think I'm intense, just wait."

"Does she sing like you?"

Hannah eyed him suspiciously. "Depends how you mean it."

"I mean like a goddamn angel."

"Oh." She brushed a lock of hair behind her ear, then forced a casual shrug. "No."

Jonathan glanced down the hall. "Well, I hope Zack got back okay."

"Me too. Let me find out."

"Listen, when you see the—"

Hannah passed the door to Jonathan and Heath's apartment and froze in place. The living room looked like it had been ransacked by savages. Chairs were overturned. Cushions lay in shreds. Broken chunks of plaster littered the floor. Between the cracks and impact fractures, Hannah saw deep lacerations in the walls, diagonal lines in tight groups of three.

Jonathan raised his palms. "Nothing you need to worry about."

"Those look like—"

"They're not," he insisted. "It's not what you think it is. He just had a bad night."

"You asked him before if the dogs were out."

"They're *not* dogs," Heath snapped from inside.

Jonathan ushered Hannah down the hall, his voice an edgy whisper. "Look, it's just me and Heath. I promise. Call your friends. Please. Before Bolly gets here."

Hannah doubled back to the doorway, her thoughts spinning chaotically. She took another look at the claw marks on the wall. Now suddenly she had a wolf question of her own.

SIX

The sky hatch opened on slow metal rollers. A lime-green Peregrine descended through the roof of the brownstone. Mia could hear its arrival from the living room, two floors down. The whole place shook whenever Peter landed his vans in the attic.

She rose from the couch and checked herself in the mirror. She'd swapped her frumpy sweatclothes for a white silk blouse and a knee-length skirt. Was it too formal? Too dainty? There was still time to change.

They won't care how you look, an inner voice insisted. *They have bigger things to worry about, and so do you.*

That was true. Mia had been on pins and needles these last eighty minutes, ever since Hannah called from Presin Square. Two new people were moving into the house today, and nobody knew a thing about them. They could be racists or rapists or undercover Pelletiers. Or maybe they were just obnoxious enough to become a headache for Mia. She got along swimmingly with everyone who lived here. The last thing she needed was a personal conflict.

She opened a twelve-inch portal to the basement and stuck her face into it. David, Zack, and Theo flinched with surprise at her disembodied features.

"They're here," Mia said.

Hannah was the first to reach the second-floor landing. Mia watched her from the base of the stairs, gaping. Her hair was a mess. Her clothes were rumpled. She looked like she'd spent the weekend in the trunk of someone's car, and she had the mood to match it.

Mia met her halfway up the stairs. "Oh my God. Hannah . . ."

"Don't hug me, sweetie. I smell like salted piss."

She descended to the foyer just as the three male Silvers emerged from the cellar. Hannah's stern gaze flitted between Zack and Theo.

"You're lucky I don't smack you both."

"Me?" Theo asked. "What did I do?"

"It's what you *didn't* do, Nostradumbass. You didn't tell me I'd be spending the night in a river." She poked Zack's chest. "And *you*. Next time I say 'I have a bad feeling about this . . .'"

"I know. I'm sorry."

Her expression softened. "Did they hurt you?"

"No." Zack jerked his head at David. "But he got a face full of lumis."

Jonathan and Heath reached the top of the stairwell, their arms filled with knapsacks and duffel bags. They paused at the sight of the small crowd staring up at them.

Hannah beckoned them on. "It's okay."

The foyer fell into awkward silence as the two Golds joined the cluster. Mia was floored by Jonathan's resemblance to her late brother Dominic. They had the same height, the same brawny build, the same long hair and dark, soulful eyes. They looked so alike that Mia once again questioned the choices of the Pelletiers. Why pick this man when they could have picked her brother? Why save two Givens but only one Farisi?

Zack stared at Jonathan's bracelet a moment before forcing himself into eye contact. "Well. Hello again."

Jonathan smiled meekly. "Sorry about last night. I thought you were, uh . . ."

"It's all right," Zack said. "You had every reason not to trust me."

Jonathan slung a bag over his shoulder and extended a hand to David. "Hi. Jonathan Christie."

Hannah jumped in. "Oh, sorry. Jonathan, Heath, this is David. That's Mia. The guy over there is Theo." She clutched Zack's arm. "And you already met this schmuck. This is—"

"Trillinger," Heath muttered.

Six heads turned toward the boy. Jonathan looked at him askance. "What? Why did you say that?"

"Because he's sharp," Zack replied. He gave Heath a shaky smile. "That's pretty impressive. People don't usually see the resemblance."

Heath bit his thumb and lowered his head. Jonathan gawked at Zack. "Wait. Are you . . . ?"

Zack nodded glumly. "I'm Josh's brother."

"Holy shit." Jonathan dropped his bag and gripped Zack's shoulders. "He talked about you all the time. I can't believe . . ."

He pulled away in sudden horror. "Oh God. You probably don't know."

"I know," Zack told him. "I heard."

"Who told you?"

"The piece of shit who killed him."

Amanda followed Peter down the stairs, her heart aching for Zack. He'd been waiting six months for confirmation of Josh's fate. All that time, all that wishing, just to get the worst possible news. His brother had survived the end of the world, but he didn't survive Rebel.

"I'm so sorry," Jonathan said. "Everything happened so fast that night. We couldn't—"

"It's all right." Zack swapped a heavy look with Amanda. "We know what you were up against."

"*We* didn't." Jonathan clenched his teeth. His voice took on a bitter edge. "The Gothams hit us in the middle of the night. We didn't have a chance."

Heath let out a tortured moan. Peter sighed at him from the foot of the stairs. "It's shameful what happened to you and your friends. Words can't express how sorry I am. But you have to know it's not all my people who are doing this. Just a misguided few."

Hannah cringed at Jonathan's surprise. *Goddamn it, Peter. This could have waited.*

"Your people," Jonathan echoed. He shot a burning glare at Hannah. "I thought he was one of us."

"Look—"

"You didn't tell me he was a Gotham!"

Peter shook his head. "We don't call ourselves that."

"I don't care what you call yourself. If you're one of them—"

Heath dropped his bags to the floor. His left hand flapped in a frantic arc. "No no no no . . ."

Hannah rushed to his side. "Heath. Listen to me. Listen! He's not with the people who hurt you. He's working *against* them."

"He gave up everything to help us," Mia stressed. "We'd all be dead if it wasn't for him."

Jonathan drew in a long breath, then rested against a wall. His tired eyes found their way to Zack's. "You vouch for him?"

"I do," Zack responded, with a bit less vigor than Peter would have preferred. "He may not be one of us, but he's on our side."

No one spoke for several moments. Amanda eyed the gash on Jonathan's arm. "I need to take care of that. And Heath needs some rest."

"We set up a room for you in the attic," Mia told Jonathan.

He chuckled darkly. "You mean the garage."

"Next to the garage," Hannah said. "It's a full bedroom. And it's a hell of a lot nicer than that place you were staying."

"Fair point." He turned to his protégé. "All right, buddy. We've come this far. Might as well—"

"No." Heath vehemently shook his head. "I don't like it here. The colors are all wrong. And that guy's missing two fingers."

David self-consciously stuffed his hand in his pocket. Mia stared at Heath indignantly. "Hey!"

Jonathan dropped to a knee in front of Heath. "Look, Amanda's right. You've been up all night. You're falling off your feet. So we're going to show you to your bed—"

"No!"

"—and I'll watch over you." He clutched Heath's shoulders. "I won't let anything happen to you. I swear it."

"Let go of me!"

Heath took a frantic look around the room, his hands and lips quivering. Amanda could tell from the moment she met him that the kid was . . . different. He'd probably spent his whole life feeling like an alien, even among his own. Now here he was on the other side of the multiverse—malnourished, underslept, and trapped on a world he had no hope of understanding.

And that wasn't even the worst of it. Amanda could feel the raw energy coursing beneath his skin. Something cold and hard. Something familiar.

"I'm not a child," Heath declared. "I'm not crazy. Don't judge me."

"No one's judging you," Hannah said.

Zack smiled drolly at his makeshift football jersey. "Well, you're a Giants fan. I'm judging you a little."

Heath giggled, despite himself, then teetered on his feet. Jonathan rushed to steady him. "Whoa. Okay. That does it. Bedtime."

"No . . ."

"Yes. I don't want to hear any more about it. Let's go."

It took another minute of cajoling for Heath to relent. He followed Jonathan up the stairs, then abruptly turned around at the seventh step. His bright hazel eyes homed in on Amanda.

"Do they do what you tell them?" he asked her.

She tilted her head. "I'm sorry?"

"Your wolves."

The Silvers and Peter blinked at him in bafflement. Jonathan traded a dark look with Hannah, then gripped Heath by the hand.

"Come on, buddy."

By noon, the boy was sound asleep in the attic. Jonathan joined the others in the living room and asked, with some embarrassment, if they had a baby monitor on hand. Theo assured him that Heath would remain dead to the world until shortly after sunset. Jonathan had a strong guess as to how he knew.

"You're an augur."

Theo nodded his head. Jonathan matched his glum expression. "Yeah. We had one of those."

He barely had a chance to sit down before his new friends gave him the royal treatment. Amanda cleaned and dressed his shoulder wound while Theo served him a double-size lunch. Peter gave him a mountain of clean clothes. Zack liberated him from his bracelet with a quick flash of temporis. The golden band broke apart on his wrist and fell to the rug in four pieces.

Jonathan was still reeling from their hospitality when Mia presented him with the biggest gift of all.

"My guitar!" He took the instrument from her. "Holy shit. I never thought I'd see it again."

The others watched him quietly as he played the opening chords of "Stairway to Heaven."

"How old are you?" David asked.

"Twenty-six," Jonathan said.

"Are you a native New Yorker?"

"Used to be."

"Christie. That's a Scottish surname, if I recall correctly. Is that your ancestral origin?"

Jonathan looked up from his strings and studied David closely. Clearly Heath wasn't the only peculiar boy in the house.

"Actually, I'm half-Spanish, half-Cherokee."

"Wow." David leaned back in his chair. "That's quite a pedigree."

"You know, you have a pretty good vocabulary for a, uh . . ."

"Australian?"

"I was going to say 'teenager,' but now I'm wondering if you're older."

"He'll be seventeen in July," Amanda said. "How old's Heath?"

"Damned if I know."

He adjusted a tuner, then tested a G-major chord. "Don't bother asking him any personal questions. He keeps that stuff under lock and key. I don't know his age, his birthday, where he lived, what his family was like. Hell, I don't even know his last name."

David tapped his chin in contemplation. "I'm trying to find a delicate way to ask my next question—"

"You want to know what's wrong with him."

"Yes."

Jonathan shrugged. "Can't say for sure. One of our friends, rest her soul, was a psych major. She was convinced that Heath has Asperger's because of the way he fixates on things. Certain colors. Certain music. Certain . . . animals."

Amanda saw Hannah fidgeting on the love seat, an unsettled look in her eyes.

"But he tries to rein it in," Jonathan said. "I mean, if Carina's right, then he must be in his own kind of hell. People like that need structure and stability in their lives. Heath's got a shitload of neither."

He began strumming a tune that only Hannah and Zack recognized, a new-world song he'd played with the Quadrants. It actually sounded pretty good without the lead singer's caterwauling.

"His shirt's homemade," Mia noted. "Did you do that for him?"

Jonathan shook his head. "That was Sebastian, another friend of ours.

When the scientists took us in, they took away our old clothes. Heath was freaking out about his jersey, so Sebastian made him a new one. The kid loves it. He won't wear anything else."

Hannah thought the shirt smelled a little ripe. "I'll sew him a spare."

"Yeah, thanks. Just make sure it's number 44, Ahmad Bradshaw. That's important to him, for some reason. And don't expect him to thank you for it. It's just the way he is."

"Who were the scientists?" Zack asked him.

"They had a weird name. The Azral Foundation, or something like that. They found us right after we arrived. Gave us a big sales pitch and then took us back to their fancy lab."

Zack bristled at his memories of his first six weeks on this world, of Sterling Quint and his ill-fated team of physicists.

"We had the same thing in California," he told Jonathan. "We thought we could trust them, but they were just holding us for the Pelletiers."

"Who?"

Theo motioned to the segmented bracelet on the coffee table. "The people who gave us those."

"Oh." Jonathan frowned at the golden remnants. "We never knew their names."

Amanda squeezed the crucifix on her necklace. She was still recovering from a long and stressful night. She was in no mood to talk about Esis and company.

"Any triggers we should avoid with Heath?" she asked.

Jonathan laughed. "Shit, I could fill a notebook. Don't serve him yellow food. Don't sing off-key. Don't touch him in a way that limits his mobility. And don't, for the love of God, say anything bad or wrong about the Beatles. That's a shortcut to a very bad day."

Mia eyed him worriedly. "What happens? Does he get violent?"

"No. He gets quiet."

He took another bite of his sandwich before playing a slow and pleasant melody, an untitled work of his own creation.

"When we first met Heath, the poor kid was just . . . gone. He wouldn't say a word. Wouldn't look at anyone. He just spent all day in the common room, staring out the window at the pond and the swans."

Hannah cooed with sympathy as Jonathan continued his ballad.

"We took turns sitting with him, feeding him, trying to get him to talk. Guess we all got attached to him. The one time the scientists tried to take him away . . . God, we went batshit. I seriously thought Josh would kill someone." He raised an eyebrow at Zack. "Your brother could be scary."

Zack smiled wanly. "He had anger issues."

"I can't lie. We didn't get along that often. We had a lot of squabbling in the group, us being New Yorkers and all. But when it came to Heath, we were on the same page. It's like he gave us something to fight for, you know? He was a piece of our world."

Amanda understood completely. She'd only known Mia for minutes before she realized she'd kill or die for the girl.

"The scientists tried to win us back with gifts," Jonathan continued. "Josh got a weight set. Sebastian had a whole gourmet kitchen set up for him." He tapped the face of his guitar. "I got this beauty."

He changed his tune to a bright and peppy Beatles song, one that all the Silvers recognized.

"So there I was, playing 'Day Tripper' on my brand-new toy. Suddenly I hear a high voice behind me. 'You're doing it wrong.'"

Hannah covered her mouth. "Oh my God."

Jonathan smiled at her. "I turn around and there's Heath looking me right in the eye, as calm as a Sunday. He says, 'Your timing's off. You're too fast in the opening. You can't rush the opening.' I thought I'd gone nuts. That was right when our powers were starting to . . . let's just say I was questioning a lot at the time."

He stared at the floor, lost in thought, his fingers moving slowly across the fretboard.

"Well, that opened the lid. Heath was talking, but only about certain things. Movies, music, sci-fi, he could go on and on. But when we'd ask him about his parents, he closed up like a clam. So we kept it light. Talked about small stuff. By September, he was like a whole different kid, but . . ."

The music stopped. Jonathan lowered the guitar and tapped a nervous beat on his thigh.

"This one night, at two A.M., he just started screaming and he wouldn't tell us why. We figured he was having a nightmare or something. So I took him to a quiet corner of the building and played some music to calm him down. We were only there a few minutes before he freaked out again. He said, 'We have to go! We have to go! They're coming!'"

Zack tensed up. Mia reached across the sofa and held his hand.

"I don't know how he knew," Jonathan said. "But he did. And while I was trying to convince him that everything was fine, the Gothams were on the other side of the building, killing our friends one by one."

Peter closed his eyes. Jonathan fixed his heavy gaze on Zack. "We were running down the hall when your brother found us. He had Carina in his arms but she was already . . . there was nothing we could do for her. The three of us were about to make a break for it when this big-ass guy with a gun showed up."

Zack nodded mournfully. "Rebel."

"Josh told us to get out of there," Jonathan said. "So I took Heath and ran while your brother went the other way. He took Rebel on, head to head. Faced him like a goddamn warrior."

Amanda could see every crack in Zack's façade. He was fighting like hell to keep from crying. It took every ounce of her willpower not to leap across the table and hold him, Esis be damned.

Jonathan took a deep swig from a soda bottle, then rested his guitar against the side of his chair. "I brought Heath to the city," he continued. "I was born and raised in New York and I thought, 'Hey, how different could it be?' Jesus. It was like a whole 'nother planet. While I was out all day playing songs for nickels, Heath stayed home in our one-room rathole. I don't even know what's holding him together. The poor kid's lost everyone he ever loved. Twice."

"Not everyone," Hannah reminded him.

"Yeah, true. He's constantly afraid that I'll die on him. And he's afraid of making new friends to lose. That's the real reason he's putting up a fight here. You guys have a long road ahead of you."

"We can handle it," Amanda assured him.

"I hope so, because he's worth it. The kid has his issues but he's got a good heart. He's smart as hell."

He smiled softly at Hannah. "And just wait till you hear him sing."

Everyone took a moment to roll their necks and arch their backs. Only Theo remained still in the far corner of the room.

"He knew Rebel was coming," he said to Jonathan. "Does he often see things before they happen?"

"You're asking if he's an augur."

"Yeah."

"He's not."

"He's not," Amanda said simultaneously. "He's tempic."

Jonathan eyed her strangely. "Yeah. How did you . . . what's the deal with you and him? You've been eyeing each other all morning."

"All tempics are connected," Peter explained. "They can sense each other's energy, even from a distance. If Rebel had tempics in his group that night, and I'm almost certain he did, then Heath probably felt them."

Amanda fumbled with her hands. "What did he mean when he asked me about the wolves?"

"That's just . . ." Jonathan stumbled over his words. "It's how his tempis comes out."

Even Peter was thrown by that. "He makes . . . wolves?"

"Afraid so."

"Tempic wolves."

Jonathan threw his hands up. "The first time I saw them, I nearly crapped myself. His wolves look like candle wax, but they move and act just like the real thing. But he has them under control. I swear it. Those things never hurt anyone. They've just done a little . . . property damage."

Hannah took issue with his definition of "little," but she kept quiet.

"And what about you?" David asked Jonathan.

"What do you mean?"

"I assume you have a power of your own."

"Oh. Yeah. I . . ." He paused just long enough to unnerve the others. "Mine is either useless or awful, depending."

"On . . . ?"

"It's hard to describe," he attested. "I'm better off just showing you."

He pointed to the four curved pieces of his bracelet. "Does anyone have any interest in keeping those things? Because once I'm done, they'll be gone forever."

Hannah stared at the glinting metal, her mind flashing back to her last encounter with Azral. "I'm okay with that."

"It's fine," Peter said. He eyed Jonathan anxiously. "Should we . . . move back?"

"No. You're safe."

He flexed his fingers as if he were preparing for another guitar recital, and then brusquely flicked his hand. The golden fragments fell silently through the coffee table. The carpet swallowed them like a cloud.

Theo sat forward, dumbstruck. "Wait. What just happened?"

"They dropped," Jonathan said with a sigh. "That's what I do."

David traced a finger across the glass surface of the table. Not a scratch or crack.

"Intangibility," he said. "You turn solid objects into phantoms."

Jonathan nodded. "Except gravity still gets ahold of them. So down they go. Every time."

"Down where?" Mia asked.

"Through the floor. Through the basement. Through everything, I guess. That bracelet's probably a half mile down by now. For all I know, it's falling all the way to the center of the world."

Zack swept a cautious hand across the carpet. "How is that even possible?"

"How is it *temporal*?" Theo asked.

"There's still a lot we don't know about time and matter," David speculated. "Until tempis came along, scientists believed there were only four physical states. But tempis has proved itself to be a unique fifth, a substance that's neither solid, liquid, gas, or plasma. Maybe Jonathan's talent is a molecular inverse of the process that creates tempis, a chronokinetic phase shift that converts solid matter to an ethereal sixth state."

Jonathan blinked at him. "Who *are* you?"

"The son of a physicist," David humbly replied. "I could be wrong about all of it."

Mia looked at Peter. "Have you ever seen anything like that?"

He sat back in his chair with a pensive expression. "Yeah. We've had some droppers in my clan. It's an extremely rare ability. These days, there's only one person who can do what Jonathan does."

Amanda's eyes widened. "Please don't tell me he works for Rebel."

"No. He's just a boy."

"Oh good. Thank God. No offense, Jonathan, but . . ."

He waved her off. "I get it. Believe me. I told you my power's either useless or awful. On objects, it's useless. On people—"

"That's awful," Hannah said. "They'd fall for miles. They probably wouldn't die until they hit lava."

"Magma," David corrected.

"Yes, thank you."

"And they're much more likely to suffocate," he theorized. "Assuming their bodies even survive the transition."

"Okay, *thank you*, David."

Jonathan gave her a tight smile. "I've dropped some trash and a couple hundred roaches. That's it. The closest I came to killing a person was last night, when you and I were up against the wall. But you found a better way to save us and I'm glad. It's not something I'm eager to try."

"I wasn't worried about you," Hannah assured him.

"Me neither," said Amanda. "If anyone should have a power like that, I'm glad it's you."

"Well, you've only known me an hour."

"Yes, but it's obvious to all of us that you're a good person."

Zack and Mia nodded in agreement. Peter shook a finger at the ceiling. "That boy up there would be dead if it wasn't for you. You carried him for months and you did it with kindness. Now maybe Heath's not the kind to say thank you, but if you believe in Heaven like some of us do, then you know that his loved ones are smiling down on you right now. They're thanking you every day."

A trembling laugh escaped Jonathan. "Wow. That's the nicest thing anyone's ever said to me. Probably nicer than I deserve. I gave you guys the Hollywood version of the story. I left out all the nights I yelled at Heath when I shouldn't have, all those days I almost gave up. Sometimes I got so goddamned tired that all I wanted to do was ditch him at a convent and drink myself stupid."

He turned to Zack. "And there are other times, especially now, that I'm afraid of what I'll do if I see Rebel again. If that son of a bitch ever comes at me or Heath, I won't think twice. I'll drop him straight to Hell."

Zack understood all too well. He too had the power to kill with a thought, and he thought far too often about rifting Rebel dead.

Jonathan took his silence for a rebuke. "I don't know. Maybe I'm not so good after all."

"No. You are. It's just—"

"—complex," Peter finished.

"Complex *how*? We didn't do a thing to your people. What possible reason could they have to kill us?"

The Silvers fell quiet. It had been six months ago in this very room that Peter first told them about the coming apocalypse. In hindsight, they could have happily used another week or two of ignorance.

Peter rose from the couch and cleared the dishes off the table. "Listen, you had a rough night. You lost a whole lot of blood. Why don't you get some rest? Tomorrow, we'll tell you everything we know. You'll hear what we have to say and then you'll decide."

"Decide what?"

Jonathan balked at their matching expressions, an overwhelming look of sorrow and anguish.

"About Heath," Amanda said. "You'll decide what to tell Heath."

SEVEN

As Jonathan and Heath settled into their new life in Brooklyn, a curious death occurred on the other side of the country.

Arnold Hyde Macklin was a staple of Seattle talk radio. The wiry old man had been gracing the airwaves for decades, with his smooth honey baritone and his slow Virginia drawl. *The Arnold Hyde Macklin Hour* was his daily pulpit from which he was free to complain about all the modern things that bothered him: feminists, Leninists, libertarians, pescatarians, men who were too skinny, novels that were too fat. Every morning brought a whole new reason to weep for society.

And nothing infuriated him more than America's increasing dependence on temporal technology.

"Time is cruel for a reason," he told his listeners. "To make us stronger and more resilient. But these days, we bend the clock whenever it strikes our fancy. Got a booboo on your finger? Go to the reviver and erase it from memory. Your precious poodle getting on in years? Goodness, better reverse the creature so you can deny the inevitable. This isn't progress, my friends. Quite the opposite. Temporis is turning us all into dainty little children. Mark my words: these machines will be our literal undoing."

Though nothing could have persuaded him to embrace timebending, he'd eventually opened his heart to tempis. His four-bedroom house on Mercer Island had the most elaborate barrier safeguard system available: tempic gates, tempic safes, tempic doors, and tempic windowshields. His home became a fortress with the flip of a switch. Even Macklin could admit that was kind of cool.

"We live in dangerous times," he'd explained to his listeners. "When it comes to protecting my home and son, I'll take whatever help I can get."

One can only imagine his surprise on the morning of April 6, when he returned from a weeklong hunting trip, deactivated his barriers, and found seven vagrants camped out in his living room.

Macklin barely had a chance to raise his shotgun before one of the intruders, a malnourished teenage girl, hit him square in the chest with a tempic fist. His body flew like a rag doll through the living room window, then struck the front lawn in a shower of glass.

The rest of the morning was a muddled blur for Arnold Macklin, Jr., who'd been standing ten feet from his father when the tempic fist struck. The portly young man leaned forward in a rocking chair, staring vacantly at the rain while Seattle police came in and out of the house. Their investigation lasted fifty-six minutes before Integrity swooped down in a fleet of black aerovans and sent the policemen home.

"Not a word of this," Oren Gingold had told them. "If I see one mention of tempis in the news, I'll wipe my ass with all of you."

The agents moved through the crime scene with quiet diligence—bagging evidence, waving scanners. No one took interest in the victim's son until Melissa found him. She fetched him a glass of milk from the kitchen, then crouched at his side.

"Mr. Macklin, Arnie, is there someone I can call for you? A friend? A relative?"

Arnie examined the milk with dull, glassy eyes. "It was just me and my dad. There's no one else."

Melissa patted his arm with sympathy. She knew from government files that he was of subnormal intelligence, just a few points above the federal disability limit. Maybe she could use her newfound clout to pull a favor from Special Services.

"Arnie, in about five minutes our ghost drills will show a vivid reenactment of your father's death. I don't think you want to be here for that."

"I already saw it."

"I know."

"The girl hit Dad and then they ran. The woman said it was Dad's fault."

"I'm sorry. The woman?"

"Yeah. She was black like you but she had less hair and she wasn't as pretty. She stopped in the doorway and said it was my dad's fault. She said he shouldn't have raised his gun."

Gingold listened intently from the other side of the room, his thoughts swimming with theories. Two weeks before, just six miles away, an empty church had made national news after exploding in a miniature Cataclysm. The proximity hardly seemed a coincidence. More likely than not, there was a new group of chronokinetics causing trouble out here.

An analyst from Central Command hailed him through his earpiece. "Sir, I have an update on the Hudson pier incident. The speedsuit chase."

"What is it?"

"Well, our satellite images were blurry but we managed to form a fairly good composite of the runners. It's a woman riding a man's back. Neither of them are wearing speedsuits."

Gingold wound his finger. "We guessed this already. I want to know *who* they are."

"Well, that's the thing, sir . . ."

"What?"

"Our computers give the woman a thirty percent match for Hannah Given."

Gingold stood in place, expressionless, before retreating to the front porch. His words came out in a hissing whisper. "That's impossible."

"I know."

"That woman's dead. I watched them cut her open."

"I understand, sir. I'm just telling you what the computer said."

Gingold groaned and pressed the bridge of his nose, a small ounce of pressure that caused his vision to go dark. The scientists who'd designed his cybernetic lenses had included the off switch as a comfort. There were times when even a man like Gingold needed to close his eyes and shut out the world.

Twenty-two hundred miles away, in the basement of Integrity's Bethesda headquarters, the analyst balked at Gingold's silence. "Sir, perhaps Agent Masaad would have an idea—"

"She's not an agent. She's an associate. And when I want your advice, I'll ask for it."

"Yes, sir."

"Get me on the next dart to New York," said Gingold. "Have a ghost team ready the minute I arrive. And put a clamp on your findings, you understand me? I don't want anyone else hearing about it."

"Understood, sir."

Melissa watched from the living room as Gingold commandeered an agency Griffin. "You leaving now?" she asked him through the transcom. "The drills are nearly ready."

Gingold met her gaze from the driver's seat. "Something came up."

"Anything I can help with?"

He paused a moment, deliberating. Melissa was not a trusted or welcome presence in Integrity, mostly due to her background in British Intelligence. Some people in the agency feared she was funneling sensitive data across the pond, helping to plant the seeds for a second invasion.

Gingold knew that Melissa bore no allegiance to England. But she did show a troubling amount of regard for the Given sisters and their friends. For all he knew, those corpses in the cinema were part of some clever and elaborate ruse to save them.

He forced a cordial smile through the window. "It's all right. I can handle it myself."

The aerovan launched up into the rain. Gingold glanced down at the home of the late Arnold Hyde Macklin and solemnly shook his head. The freaks were coming out of the woodwork now. He feared the true invasion was only just beginning.

PART TWO

ATROPOS

EIGHT

A cold rain came to Brooklyn on Wednesday, the first of April's showers. The updraft winds and low air temperature prompted the New York Weather Bureau to issue a Level 1 hailstorm alert. All over the city, people doubled back home for their tempic umbrellas. Aeromobile drivers rushed to get to their destinations before flight traffic was grounded.

Jonathan watched the rain from the backyard patio, a red umbrella in his grip. Under normal circumstances, he'd be standing beneath the overhang of the Union Square Skybus Station, playing rock songs for pocket change. Today would have been a real slog. Weather like this made everyone grumpy, stingy. Jonathan would have been lucky to get anything more than nickels in his guitar case.

Thankfully, his scrounging days seemed to be over. Some remarkable strangers had rolled out the red carpet for him on Monday and offered him a better way to live. Now he had all the food, clothing, and shelter he could have ever possibly hoped for, with no strings attached.

Actually, no. There was one string.

Hannah, Amanda, and Peter watched him anxiously from patio chairs, an ominous-looking trio in their hooded black rain slickers. They'd spoken in turns for fifteen minutes, filling him in on the Earth's secret illness. Now, at last, came the Q&A part of the discussion.

Jonathan gazed at the clouds with tense, busy eyes. "Four years," he said. "Shit, that's . . ."

He switched his umbrella to his other hand, then slowly shook his head. "I mean I never expected to grow old on this world. But four years . . ."

"Jonathan—"

"Why does this keep happening?"

Hannah rose from her chair and crouched at his side. "Look, we told you it's not set in stone. We have a chance of stopping it."

"Right. The one string to rule them all."

"It exists," Peter insisted. "I've seen it."

"Even though you're not an augur."

Peter rose from his chair and moved behind Amanda. "I had a bit of a stroke last year. Put me in a coma and sent me to the God's Eye. You don't have to be an augur to go there. You just need the right wires to touch in your brain."

Jonathan took a moment to study Peter and Amanda. He'd thought they were married when he first met them, but apparently they were just friends. They sure did have a vibe to them, though. He wondered what kept them from boffing each other, especially in light of the world's ticking deadline.

"How do you know it wasn't just a dream?" he asked.

Amanda wriggled uncomfortably in her chair. "Because Rebel's seen it too."

Jonathan peeked over his shoulder at the patio door, increasingly nervous that Heath would come looking for him. This wasn't a conversation for his ears. Not yet, anyway.

He turned back to Amanda, skeptical. "So Theo's gonna go to the God's Eye, find the string, prove Rebel to be the asshole that he is, and then save the whole planet."

She shook her head. "He'll tell us what needs to be done."

"It'll be up to all of us to make it happen," Peter said.

A brief white flash filled the eastern half of the sky. Jonathan counted six Mississippis before the thunder came.

"I wasn't exactly a mover and shaker on the old world," he admitted. "This is way beyond my pay grade."

"I was an actress," Hannah said. "Zack was a cartoonist. Theo was a law school dropout. None of us are trained for this."

"We're handling it day by day," Amanda said. "And so will you. Just give it time."

"Time." Jonathan scoffed. "What if Rebel's right? What if killing us 'breachers' is the only way to save everyone?"

The sisters traded a heavy look. Peter cut a slow path toward the brownstone. "I don't believe that's the case."

"And if Theo finds out that it is?"

Peter opened the back door and turned around in the light of the kitchen. Jonathan didn't like the expression on his face. Not one bit.

"Then I guess we're in for another discussion."

Despite all warnings, the hailstorm never came. The rain continued in dribs and drabs throughout the day. By nightfall, the clouds gave way to a bright crescent moon.

At ten o'clock, just minutes after Jonathan and Heath retired to the attic, Peter summoned the Silvers to the basement den. They sat among the beds and chairs, their eyes following Peter as he paced the beaded carpet.

"I'm afraid we have a problem," he began. "A dilemma, actually. Can you stop that?"

Two Davids sat at the foot of Theo's bed: one real, one made entirely out of last night's darkness. He unsummoned his shadow self, then gave Peter his full attention. "Is this about the wolves?"

"It's not Heath's power that worries me. It's Jonathan's." Peter snatched a pencil from Zack's drawing table. "There have been forty-four droppers in the history of my clan, and they've all had the same unfortunate tendency."

"To do what?" asked Amanda.

"To die."

The others paused, blank-faced, while Peter resumed pacing. "When it comes to temporal abilities, my people bloom early and fast. Most of us manifest around the age of two. My son . . ."

He deliberated his words before continuing. "It was God's folly to put such big power in little hands. We've had our share of accidents."

Peter raised Zack's pencil to eye level and dangled it between his fingers.

"The problem with droppers is that their first mistake is always their last. A sudden shock, a bad dream, even an ill-timed thought could trigger their power on themselves. Before anyone can do anything . . ."

He let go of the pencil. It dropped through the air, then disappeared into a twelve-inch portal on the floor.

Hannah covered her mouth. "Oh my God."

"I saw it happen once," Peter said. "Poor girl was playing in the village square. She skinned her knee and next thing we knew, she fell through the grass like a phantom. Didn't even have time to scream."

Theo sat forward, gape-mouthed. "That's horrible."

"Yes. It's the one power we don't consider to be a blessing. It's more like a death sentence."

"How old was the girl when she, uh . . . ?"

"Four," Peter said. "Droppers don't usually live past six."

"But Jonathan's an adult," Mia said. "He has more control than a kid."

"It's not about age, darling. It's experience. And Jonathan's still new to his talent. All things considered, it's a miracle he's still alive."

Amanda flashed back to her early tempic mishaps. If she'd been cursed with Jonathan's power, she would have dropped herself on her very first day.

"There has to be something we can do."

"Maybe," Peter said. "We discovered a while back that tempis is the only thing an intangible object can't fall through. Now our one living dropper spends all his time on it. He has a tempic catcher under his bed, a tempic sheath on his chairs, even tempis on the soles of his shoes. It's not an easy life he lives, but he's twelve years old and still with us."

Zack creased his brow at Peter. "Okay. So we buy a bunch of barriers and line the floors with them. What's the dilemma?"

"It might not be the best choice. There's a force out there even stronger than tempis. It may have been saving Jonathan all along."

Only Amanda caught his gist. "Ignorance."

"Exactly. He doesn't know the danger he's in. We put the fear in his head and it could be self-defeating, like telling a man on a tightrope not to look down. The minute he steps off the tempis, and it's bound to happen sooner or later, his mind could get the better of him. All it takes is a thought."

Theo's heart sank with dread. He'd learned from his many trips through the God's Eye just how cruel the human subconscious could be.

"I have my preference on how to proceed," Peter said. "But we're a group. This should be a group decision."

"It should be *his* decision," Zack countered.

"If we take away his ignorance, the choice is already made."

Mia scratched her neck, agitated. "I don't like this. We shouldn't keep secrets from each other."

"Even if that secret saves his life?" David asked her.

"Ignorance didn't stop me from getting portals in my sleep. It didn't stop you from blinding yourself."

Zack nodded in agreement. "If Jonathan drops in the middle of the night, we'll never forgive ourselves. We'll always know we could have saved him."

"That goes both ways," Amanda said. "If he dies from our meddling—"

"Wouldn't you want us to tell you?"

"I'd want you to do whatever it takes to keep me alive, even if that means lying to me."

Peter puffed a loud breath. "As it stands, I agree with Amanda and David. But if the augur among us has any insight, now's the time to share it."

Theo tapped his leg distractedly. Once again, he caught a prescient glimpse of Amanda screaming with grief, her body erupting in hard spikes of tempis. He didn't think she'd get that hysterical over a man she'd just met. She had to be mourning someone closer to her. Someone in this room.

"I haven't seen a single future where Jonathan drops himself," Theo attested. "That's not to say it can't happen. I just know from experience that some prophecies are self-fulfilling. Some warnings . . ." He took a nervous look at Amanda. "I think telling him will do more harm than good. It won't be great for Heath's state of mind either."

David shook a finger at him. "That's a good point."

"Very good point," Peter said. "We seem to be approaching a quorum."

Mia rose up from her chair. "You can't do this. It's not right!"

"Jonathan put his trust in us," Zack said. "If we keep this from him, we won't deserve it."

Amanda looked to her sister, the lone holdout in the conversation. "Hannah?"

She sat to the side on an inflatable lounger, her finger tracing a slow path across the vinyl. After a moment of thought, she jumped to her feet and fixed her stern brown eyes on Peter.

"There's no dilemma. No debate. First thing tomorrow, I'm telling him."

"Hannah—"

"You don't know him like I do, okay? He's a strong man. A *survivor*. If anyone deserves our respect, it's him."

She gave David a hard look. "And Zack's right. If we start lying to each other, where does it stop?"

The next morning, as a flat gray sky brought another drizzle to Brooklyn, Hannah remembered why she'd spent most of her life avoiding bold decisions.

"Shit."

Jonathan leaned against the rail of her balcony. He rapped the metal with his knuckles, then spun around to face her. "*Shit!* Hannah, why would you tell me that?"

"I don't know! I thought it was something you needed to hear."

"Yeah, well, you thought wrong. This is even worse than your other news."

"How is it worse?"

"Because it is, all right? I just . . ." He rubbed his face with both hands. "You didn't know me on the old world, Hannah. I was a screwup. Anyone who knew me learned real fast not to count on me. Then Heath came along and . . . goddamn it, I *promised* him I'd never leave him. I gave him my word and I meant it."

Hannah shook her head. "It doesn't have to be like that. The tempis—"

"Oh, fuck the tempis. I'm not spending the rest of my life as an invalid. What good does that do anyone?"

"Jonathan . . ."

"Look, I appreciate your concern. I do. But you have to let me handle this my way, okay? Just . . ."

He closed his eyes and let out a pitch-black chuckle. "Just drop it."

Hannah reached out to touch him, then pulled her hand back. She could already feel old patterns reemerging, an insatiable craving for physical distraction. It would be so damn easy for them to screw away the pain, but the relief never lasted. After the intimacy came her fear of intimacy, then the distance, then the fighting. And by this time next week, Hannah Banana (*always needs a man-a*) would have another ex-lover in the house.

No. Not this time. She'd spent the last six months in a state of self-reliance and she had very much come to like it. She would just have to comfort Jonathan as a friend.

"I'm sorry," Hannah said. "Your life was so much simpler before you met us."

"Yeah, well . . ." He looked down at his calloused fingers. "It wasn't exactly a picnic."

Once again, Hannah pondered Ioni's motive for bringing her and Jonathan together. Maybe it was never about sex or romance. Maybe it wasn't about Jonathan at all.

"Heath won't be alone," Hannah told him. "If anything happens to you, and I hope to God it doesn't, we'll take good care of him. I promise."

Jonathan looked at her with a complicated expression, an evincible mixture of fondness and doubt.

"You don't seem convinced," Hannah noted.

"I'm convinced you'll try," he said. "I'm not so sure you'll succeed."

He gripped the railing and blew a hot breath through his nose. "He really doesn't like you people."

The next twelve days passed with slow unease, like sandaled feet on broken glass. Though the Silvers and Peter formed an instant rapport with Jonathan, they had a more difficult time with their other new housemate: a hundred-pound boy of singular name who seemed all but determined not to fit in.

Heath didn't need his tempis to keep the others on edge. He wandered into bedrooms without any sense of propriety, shook dandruff from his hair at the dinner table. He griped to Jonathan about the Silvers while they were in full view and earshot. *"His shirt's torn." "I don't like what she cooked." "Why does he make that sound when he eats?"*

Even worse were his daily outbursts, where he'd flap his arms in shrieking tantrum and run barreling back to his bedroom. No provocation was seemingly too small for him—the wrong word, the wrong sound, the wrong color entrée. The others grew accustomed to hearing his cries from the attic, interrupted by the sound of Jonathan's soft appeasements: *[mumble mumble] "No!" [mumble mumble] "No! I want to leave!"*

By the fifth day, Heath cautiously began to mingle, though the conversations were limited to topics of his choosing. With Zack, the subject was always

Josh Trillinger, a pinch of salt in a suppurating wound. With David, it was his wristwatch. Heath had become fascinated with the antique silver timepiece, the last surviving remnant of David's old life. *"Where did you buy it?" "How often do you wind it?" "Has it ever stopped working?" "Can I have it when you die?"*

With Amanda, Heath only wanted to talk about the power they shared. He was curious to know if she ever killed anyone with her tempis (*"No."*), or hurt someone accidentally (*"Well . . ."*).

"I've never hurt anyone," Heath boasted. He'd found Amanda in the kitchen and watched her closely as she cut up an onion with a self-made knife. "My wolves do what I say, except for Rose."

Amanda looked at him strangely. "Rose?"

"Rose Tyler," he said. "She's the meanest one in the pack and she doesn't always listen to me. She's mad because she wants to kill people and I don't let her."

Amanda's tempic blade rippled with distress. "You have to watch her, Heath."

"I try. But she has her own mind. There's only so much I can do."

He peeked into the pot and scowled at the bubbling sauce. "That smells like puke."

Heath continued to keep his distance from the rest of the group, despite their numerous attempts to be friendly. Whenever Theo and Mia tried to engage him, he simply glanced at them with a skittish side-eye, as if they were ghosts or figments of his imagination.

"Don't take it personally," Jonathan told Mia. "Heath has a weird mental filing system. He's just figuring out where to put you."

It was no mystery how Heath had filed Peter. The man was a Gotham, a rather loud one at that. Amanda could feel Heath's tempic energies spike whenever Peter barged into a room, bellowed with laughter, or invaded Heath's personal space. She feared the day would come when Peter pinched the boy's last nerve and got a formal introduction to Rose Tyler.

As for Hannah, everyone could see that Heath didn't like her, and her servile attempts to please him only made it worse. She followed him around like an anxious new stepmother, offering him every amenity under the sun. She prepared meals to his exact specifications, only to have them pushed away over a smell or color issue. She sewed him a beautiful replica of his football jersey, only to have it languish at the bottom of his dresser. He shrank from her touch. He scowled at her questions. He bristled at the cloying voice she used around him, as if she'd just brought him home from a puppy farm.

On Heath's seventh night with the Silvers, he finally exploded. He threw his dinner plate at the wall, kicked over his chair, and then made a screaming dash for the front door.

Jonathan stumbled after him, but the kid was too damn quick. "Heath, no!"

Hannah jumped into blueshift and passed Heath in the foyer. By the time he registered the hot breeze at his side, she was blocking the door with her body.

"What's your problem with me?" she asked him.

Heath doubled back to the kitchen door, only to find Hannah blocking that too.

"I've been nothing but nice to you."

Howling, Heath ran upstairs to his attic refuge, and barricaded the door with a dresser.

Hannah watched him from the edge of Jonathan's mattress, her legs crossed, her lips curled in a frown.

"I can do this all night."

Heath spun around, bug-eyed. "Leave me alone!"

"Why?"

"Because I don't need you doing that!"

"Doing what? The cooking? The sewing?"

"Pretending to like me!"

Hannah blinked at him, mystified. She'd lived with David so long, she forgot how insecure some teenage boys could be.

"Heath, why would I pretend to like you? What reason could I possibly have?"

Flustered, he began tidying up the bedroom. He hung Jonathan's guitar on a wall hook, then gathered the handwritten song sheets he'd been working on, night and day, for the last eight months. With Jonathan's help, he'd restored sixty-five classic rock songs from memory, and he was just getting started. Heath refused to let the best parts of his world die in some freak cosmic accident. Note by note, lyric by lyric, he would bring them all back.

Hannah's face softened as she watched him scurry around. "I don't know. Maybe I've been trying too hard. I go a little crazy sometimes when I like someone and they don't like me back."

"Why?"

"Because it hurts."

"No. I mean, why do you like me?"

"Oh." She needed a good ten seconds before she could formulate an answer. "Because you remind me of someone."

"Who?"

"Me."

Heath turned around and eyed her skeptically.

"What?" Hannah asked. "You think we don't have anything in common? Music's everything to us. And we didn't just stumble onto it like Jonathan did. There was someone in our lives who passed that love onto us. For me, it was my mother. Who was it for you?"

Her stomach did a cartwheel as she saw Heath's dismay. The last thing she needed was a faceful of wolves.

"You don't have to tell me," she said. "But I see it in you. I recognize it and it makes me . . . I don't know. Ever since I met you, I've had this overwhelming urge to take care of you."

Heath frowned at the floor. "You want to mother me."

"I want to *sister* you," she corrected. "And if you knew me, you'd know how rare that is."

Hannah looked down at her hands and let out a bleak laugh. "I've never been a big sister to anyone."

Over the next few days, she noticed a marked change in Heath's behavior. He didn't grit his teeth when she talked to him. He didn't complain about the meals she cooked. He even managed to find his way into the football jersey she'd made for him. The royal blue fabric practically glistened against his skin.

On the nineteenth of April, a full two weeks after Heath's arrival, Hannah stepped out of her bathroom to find him sitting on her bed. She tightened her towel.

"Uh, sweetie, you should probably knock before you . . ."

She stopped when she noticed the scissors in his hand. They hung loosely between his fingers, the loops pointed awkwardly at Hannah.

"What's going on?" she asked. "What's with the, uh . . ."

Now she could see the pleading look in his eyes, the frustrated way he tugged at his curls.

"Oh." Her eyes widened in revelation. "Oh!"

An hour later, Hannah escorted Heath to the edge of the living room, where five of their housemates had gathered to watch a movie. One by one, they turned away from the lumivision and marveled at Heath's transformation. His unruly afro had been trimmed into a short and tidy wave cut. The style made him look five years older, and stunningly handsome.

Jonathan's mouth fell open. "Holy crap. Who *is* that?"

"You look good," Mia said.

Heath acknowledged her with a twitchy half grin before losing himself in the movie. He sat on the carpet and watched with rapt attention.

Jonathan made room for Hannah on the sofa. He leaned in close for a whisper. "What did you do, drug him?"

"He came to me," she whispered back.

"Well, you've done it this time, sister. He's both of ours now."

Soon Peter and Amanda joined the others in the living room. As the movie progressed to the second act, Theo looked around in the light of the lumivision and studied the faces around him—everyone on this world he cared about. Thankfully, the two new members of the group had a clean and stable future here, at least as far as he could see. Jonathan wasn't dropping out of their lives anytime soon, and Heath had become an all-but-permanent fixture in Theo's visions.

But there was discord in the Silvers' strings, a creeping fog around the future of Theo's closest friends. He'd never seen anything like it before, and nothing he did could penetrate the mist. All he could feel was an impending sense of loss and bereavement. All he could hear was the sound of Amanda's screams.

NINE

Gingold woke up at sunrise, dazed and disturbed. The night had brought such vivid dreams of Palestine that his brain needed a moment to catch up to the present. He wasn't slitting throats in Qalqilya anymore. He was back in the States on a cat-and-mouse mission, chasing a new breed of criminal who redefined the term "foreign threat."

He peeled the battery chargers from his lenses, scanned the sleeping body next to him, then staggered naked across the bedroom carpet. The Atherton Citadel was one of Manhattan's plushest hotels: a fifty-story obelisk of gold-steel and mirrorglass. Gingold's top-floor suite was so ridiculously posh that he couldn't help but feel ambivalent about it. After fourteen years of sleeping in hovels, he was certainly entitled to some luxury at the taxpayers' dime. But then he knew that comfort had a way of dulling the senses. The domestic Integrity agents were the softest bunch of sad sacks he'd ever seen.

By the time he finished relieving himself, his mind was awake and focused on his targets. Zack Trillinger and Hannah Given had recently caused trouble at a Greenwich Village tavern, despite the fact that Integrity had their corpses. That was quite a trick. More impressive, they'd both managed to elude the agency's ghost drills. Zack's spectral trail ended in a haze of solic static while Hannah seemingly dissolved into the dark waters of the Hudson.

Gingold only had one last hope of finding them, a Hail Mary plan that would eat up his entire day. He took another look at his sleeping companion, then crouched at the side of the bed.

"Hey." He poked the man's shoulder, then gave it a shake. "Hey."

His guest came awake with fluttering blinks. Kevin Mando was a lithe and sprightly blond, a drummer in a band called the Quadrants. Though he'd already shared what little he knew about Jonathan Christie ("He was just a hired sub, man. He said his name was Trevor."), Gingold kept coming back to him with questions—again and again, until Kevin finally called him out. *Just ask me back to your place, man.*

Kevin turned over in bed with a drowsy smile. He stroked Gingold's jaw. "Hey yourself, shade."

"No. None of that. I need to work in the other room. You don't have to leave but you can't bother me. I need absolute concentration. You hear me?"

His severity did nothing to dull Kevin's cheer. There were the rare, fleeting souls in Gingold's life who weren't intimidated by his scars and lenses, his steel-wool abrasiveness. Gingold found himself hopelessly drawn to those people, even as they got on his last nerve.

"I'm serious."

"Seen and heard," Kevin teased. "I'm just quilling up a second deal."

"No second deals. You either leave—"

"I'll leave in twenty minutes. And I won't cloud you till you call me, when and if. But . . ."

Gingold raised an eyebrow. "But?"

Kevin ran a hand down Gingold's neck, fingering the four-inch knife scar he'd earned while undermining British interests in Syria.

"It ain't the time, shade. It's all about the smiles."

Twenty minutes and one shower later, Gingold plopped himself down in an easy chair, then activated his laptop image thrower. The lumivision came to life with black-and-white satellite footage, an infrared view of Hudson Pier 7 on the night of Hannah's foot chase. For the hundredth time, Gingold watched Hannah and Jonathan topple backward over the rope rail, plunging deep into the water, never to be seen again.

Unless . . .

Gingold had experienced a minor epiphany last night, a revelation as to why Melissa Masaad had better luck tracking these people than most. It wasn't because she was especially clever (though she was), she was simply willing to take her logic to strange new realms, places rational thinkers didn't dare go. With these freaks, anything was possible. They broke the laws of nature just as easily as the laws of man.

From that perspective, it seemed perfectly reasonable to wonder if Hannah Given, a woman who could move fast without a speedsuit and leave a corpse without dying, was able to stay underwater for unusually long stretches of time. Maybe she could hold her breath all night.

Gingold sat like a statue, watching the satellite video with unblinking focus. One hour passed, then two, then nine. Once daylight broke across the lumivision screen, Gingold feared he'd wasted his time.

But then a cluster of ripples broke the water by the pier. Gingold leaned forward in his seat, slack-jawed. Hannah and Jonathan were treading the Hudson in full sunlight, back among the air-breathers.

Smiling, Gingold reached for his handphone and dialed his second-in-command.

"Get the ghost drills and meet me at Hudson Pier 7," he said. "We have a new trail."

Hannah charged into the dining room in a hazy blur, ruffling every napkin on the table. She de-shifted in her seat and flashed a rattled look at her companions.

"Okay, Heath's coming. I think he's all right but—"

"Whoa, whoa, whoa," said Peter. "What happened?"

Amanda looked across the table at the two empty chairs. Jonathan and Heath were late to dinner and she had a good guess why.

"You told him."

"We told him," Hannah confirmed. "He knows."

Heath was the only one in the group who had yet to learn about the second apocalypse. Jonathan and Hannah had resolved to break the news to him, carefully and at just the right time, but they kept finding excuses to put it off. The others could hardly blame them. No one wanted to play Chicken Little to the boy who cried wolves.

"How did he take it?" Mia asked Hannah.

"Hard to say. He just looked at his feet the whole time. Didn't ask questions. He didn't even make a sound."

Theo processed the news with a furrowed brow. "That seems, uh . . ."

"Out of character," David said. He looked to Hannah. "Are you sure he was listening?"

"I don't know. I mean—"

She paused at the sound of footsteps. Everyone at the table watched Heath nervously as Jonathan escorted him into the dining room. The boy took his seat, served himself, then glanced around suspiciously at his housemates.

Jonathan cleared his throat. "Hey, Amanda, I've been meaning to ask you something."

"Uh-oh."

"No. Nothing bad. I just want to know what Hannah was like as a kid. She says she was a delight. As you can imagine, I'm skeptical."

Hannah smacked his arm. "I never said that, you hair clog. I said I was an entertainer."

"She was definitely an entertainer," Amanda confirmed. "Always singing and dancing, and beautifully, too."

Jonathan frowned at her. "I see. Going for the polite answer, then."

"Afraid so."

"Just give me a hint of the impolite answer. Come on."

Her eyes shifted coyly from Jonathan to Hannah. "Let's just say she had a knack for drama, too."

Heath was the only one who didn't chuckle. Theo peeked up from his plate and saw his thousand-yard stare. *He listened*, Theo thought. *He heard every word.*

Peter gripped Amanda's arm and smiled at Hannah. "And while you were making drama, I imagine this one was cornering the market on precocious maturity."

Hannah rolled her eyes. "You have no idea. She was reading Proust at age ten. She refused to sit at the kids' table at Thanksgiving. And whenever we started to argue about something, she'd throw up her hands and say, 'I don't want to fight with you, Hannah.'"

The laughter rose. Zack noticed Peter's fingers, still firmly wrapped around Amanda's bicep, and lost his sense of humor. *Christ*, he thought. *At least wait till the corpse is cold.*

Mia smiled at Amanda. "It's all right. When I was younger—"

"We had sisters in our group."

All eyes turned to Heath. He combed his rice with a listless fork. "They were twins, but they didn't look alike or act alike. Carina was nice. Deanna . . . had issues."

Jonathan writhed uncomfortably in his chair. "Buddy, let's not—"

"She could see things before they happened. One day she started screaming and crying until they had to sedate her. I went to see her in the infirmary and I asked her what she saw in the future that made her so upset. She just cried and said, 'Nothing.'"

His dreary gaze landed on Theo. "Now I know what she meant."

No one spoke for a full minute. Heath slouched in his seat and twisted his Pelletier bracelet, the very last one in the house. Zack had offered on numerous occasions to remove the damn thing, but Heath stubbornly refused to part ways with it. *It's part of my colors now,* he'd insisted.

Heath turned his attention onto Zack. "When Josh found out that Carina and Deanna were sisters, he was convinced you were still alive. He said that if siblings were getting bracelets, then you must have gotten one in San Diego. We had to talk him out of leaving us."

Jonathan gripped his arm. "Heath—"

"He wanted to go look for you."

Zack pushed his chair back with a loud wooden scrape. His voice trickled out in a quivering whisper. "I'm sorry."

He hurried out of the dining room. Peter leaned toward Mia. "Sweetheart, maybe you should—"

"Yeah."

Before she could get up, a second chair flew back. Amanda jumped to her feet and made a beeline for the basement stairs.

David shot her a grave look. "Amanda . . ."

"Don't," she snapped. "Don't even start."

Zack barely had a chance to register her footsteps before she rushed down the stairs and wrapped him in an ardent hug.

He closed his eyes and held her tight. "I can't stand this."

"I know."

"We weren't even that close. I saw him maybe twice a year."

"It doesn't matter," Amanda said. "He's your brother and you miss him."

Zack pulled back to look at her, his face wet with tears. "I miss us."

"God, me too." She rested her forehead against his. "It's driving me crazy."

"So let's do something about it."

"We *can't.*"

"We're touching right now and there's no fire and brimstone. No cracks in the earth."

"Zack—"

"Yeah. I know. You think Esis will kill me."

"She'll *annihilate* you."

"Except she won't."

"What makes you say that?"

"Because the last time I saw Rebel, he nearly shot me in the face. You know why I'm still breathing?"

Amanda nodded wearily. She'd heard all about the fracas behind Teke's Humble Tavern, the mysterious white stranger who'd swooped in like lightning and clobbered three Gothams. Zack didn't get a good look at his Lone Ranger. He wasn't even sure if it was a man or a woman. But he was convinced of one thing . . .

"A Pelletier saved me," he told Amanda. "They want me alive."

"For *now*."

"For now," Zack admitted. "Maybe they'll kill me the next time we kiss. Or maybe we're misreading the whole situation. You and I could be putting ourselves through hell over nothing."

Amanda broke away and sat on Theo's bed. Her hands fumbled awkwardly in her lap.

"If it was my life in danger, you wouldn't be so reckless."

"Your life *is* in danger," Zack reminded her. "We have four years left until the end of the world, and a one-in-a-trillion chance of stopping it. And that's assuming Peter's even right about the string. If he's not—"

"Don't."

"—if he's *not*, then what the hell are we doing here?"

"Zack . . ."

"We're just killing time before time kills us."

Amanda dipped her head, her hair hanging down in flat red ribbons. She knew Zack Trillinger inside and out, and she could hear every chord being played in his head. He was grieving for his brother, grieving for the world, grieving for himself and his unfulfilled passions. He clearly wasn't thinking straight. So why was she having such a hard time dismissing his arguments?

"I'm still a nurse at heart," she told him. "I was taught to fight for life, no matter what the odds are."

"Yeah, well, I went to art school."

"And?"

"I don't know. I just thought that would impress you."

Amanda laughed and looked away. Zack sat down next to her.

"Look, I want to be with you. Every night and every day and all the little spaces in between. If this was a one-way thing, I could probably get over it. But you feel the same way I do. I can't just let that slide."

He traced a slow finger up her wrist. "If you want to play it safe and go back to the old rules, I can do that. Gladly. It's not sex I need from you, Amanda. It's *this*."

He brushed her hair back and kissed the skin beneath her eye. "This."

Amanda turned to face him, her fingers digging into his shirt. She felt his warm breath on her cheek and, before he could utter his final "this," he pressed his lips against hers.

As she fell into his kiss, her thoughts drifted upward to her lord and creator, the one Zack didn't believe in, the one she loved but only sometimes trusted.

Please, Amanda begged. *Please just let me have this.*

A pair of sneakered feet hit the stairs like punches. Zack and Amanda pulled apart to see David facing them from the seventh step. He bathed them both in his scornful blue glare.

"Idiots."

Amanda jumped to her feet. "Damn it, David!"

"Go away," Zack growled. "This is none of your business."

"If I was dancing at the edge of the cliff, would you mind your own business?"

"I don't know. Go try it!"

Mia hurried down the stairs and stood at David's side. "Don't yell at him. He's only looking out for you."

Amanda shook her head. "We're not doing anything we haven't done a hundred times before."

"More than a hundred," Zack said. "We spent four months together and we didn't get a single warning."

David raised his arms, exasperated. "Has it occurred to you that maybe you're *out* of warnings?"

Their voices carried into the dining room. Hannah and Theo exchanged a weary look, then rose from their chairs.

Jonathan noticed that Peter wasn't joining them. "You're not, uh . . . ?"

"No." He chuckled bleakly. "I don't touch this one."

Soon all the Silvers stood gathered in the basement, four on the stairwell, two by the bed. Zack kept his stony eyes on David. "Since you're the big expert on Pelletiers—"

"I'm not even a small one," David attested. "All I know is that they're powerful, they're vicious, and they *don't* want you and Amanda together. Esis made that abundantly clear."

"No she didn't," Hannah said. "She only used weird words."

David turned around and glared at her. "Would you like her to come by and explain herself?"

"I just don't understand why they can't be together."

"Neither do I," David said. "It doesn't matter."

"Not to you," Zack grumbled.

"Why can't you understand that I'm trying to save you?"

"Because everything about this feels wrong," Zack said. "The Pelletiers have been screwing with us from the minute we got here. All they *do* is play head games."

"Zack . . ."

"You want to keep jumping through their hoops, go ahead. But I, for one—"

"Zack, *stop*."

The warning came from Theo this time. He sat on the stairs with a tortured look, his fingers clenched into his thighs. He hadn't looked this scared in a very long time, not since the Gothams first ambushed them in a Battery Park office building.

"I know you're angry," he told Zack. "You have every right to be. But you have no idea how much trouble you're in. If you won't listen to David, then listen to me."

Amanda's mouth fell open. She took a shaky step toward Theo. "What are you talking about? What do you see?"

Theo didn't see anything. That was the problem. He'd been blind to the strings these past two days, lost in a sea of swirling fog. It wasn't until just now that the mist parted enough to reveal a hint of things to come—a deep black grief that towered over everything. An absence.

There was no hint of Zack in the future. Not a single trace.

The news had put a quick and decisive end to the debate. Amanda looked to Zack with wide, frightened eyes, then swore to never touch him again. They were done. Finished. End of story.

The look on Zack's face was severe enough to make her cry. Hannah followed Amanda up the stairs. She turned around at the last second to face Zack.

"Don't blame her for this. She's already been a widow once."

Zack stared at his feet with hard gray eyes. "I'm not blaming her. I'm not blaming any of you. I just want to be alone, okay?"

A black gloom lingered throughout the house all evening. Amanda and Hannah went to bed early. Jonathan and Heath made a hasty retreat to the attic. Theo and David hunkered down in the living room, their listless gazes locked on the lumivision. Mia was just about to join them when a strong hand gripped her shoulder.

"Uh-uh," said Peter. "You owe me a practice session."

"What, *now*?"

"Now."

Mia sat on the bench by the living room window, her foot tapping impatiently as Peter brought her a smartglobe. The smooth glass ball had a lumic crystal underlay, providing twenty different layers of cartographic information, plus a real-time image of the Earth's cloud patterns. There was a time in Mia's life when she would have killed for a toy like that. Now she just wanted to hurl it out onto the street, along with Peter.

"I don't want to do this," she whined.

"Why not?"

"Because I'm tired and upset." She glanced over at David and Theo, still loosely absorbed in the nine o'clock news. "And the lumivision's distracting me."

"Exactly why we're doing it now," Peter said. "You won't always have optimal conditions. Hell, my teacher used to throw firebangers at me when I was making my portals."

He pushed the globe into her hands. "Come on. Just shoot it up to your room. It'll be easy."

Mia scoffed at him. For all her skill communicating with her past selves, she had a hell of a time ripping portals in the present. Anything wider than eight inches felt painfully unwieldy, like dancing on stilts. If she ever wanted to teleport, she'd have to make bigger doors or become a hell of a lot thinner.

Peter tapped the wood of the window bench. "Don't worry about size. Let the hard, flat surface do the work for you."

"I don't think my weirdness works the way yours does."

"That's not . . ." Peter rubbed his brow. "Okay, first of all, stop calling it a weirdness."

"Why?"

"Because it diminishes you. Call it a power. Call it a blessing. Call it a God-given talent."

"God had nothing to do with it," said a voice from the hallway.

Four heads turned as Zack shuffled into the living room, a sketchbook nestled under his arm. Though his expression remained grim, his face looked almost jarringly clean and youthful. It took Mia four seconds to realize what he'd done.

"Your goatee," she said. "You shaved it."

Shrugging, Zack threw himself onto an easy chair, then began a new doodle.

Mia leapt to her feet and squeezed Peter's arm. "We'll do a double lesson tomorrow."

"You already owe me a double."

"Then we'll make it a triple. I promise."

Peter sighed in surrender, then opened his lapbook. Mia joined her fellow Silvers in front of the lumivision. After a dull and pointless story about a celebrity fad diet, the newscast moved on to one of its favorite new topics: Merlin McGee. The bearded young prophet had only become more popular since his grand debut in January, and continued to stun skeptics with his spot-on weather predictions. Today he'd received a Citizen's Medal for last month's tornado warning, a two-week notice that saved dozens of lives in Texas.

Theo sat up, intrigued. On the surface, there was nothing to dislike about McGee. He was a true and humble augur who used his power for good. Yet Theo couldn't look at him without clenching his teeth. Was it gut instinct? Professional jealousy? Or was his foresight trying to tell him something?

He looked over his shoulder at Peter. "Are you sure there isn't more to that guy?"

Peter had long ago explained the truth about McGee. He was an ex-Gotham named Michael. He'd left the clan years ago to live a quiet life in Oregon, which made his recent decisions all the more baffling. The man was an introvert with an eight-figure trust fund. He didn't need this racket. He certainly didn't need the risks involved with revealing his powers to the world.

"Not sure what else to tell you," Peter said to Theo. "Michael's always been a mystery."

"Maybe he just likes saving lives," Mia mused.

Theo frowned at McGee's image. "If he's an augur, then he knows what's coming. I mean why bother with floods and hurricanes when the real problem—"

Peter and Mia suddenly hollered in pain. They clutched their heads in perfect synch, then doubled over. The smartglobe rolled out of Mia's lap and cracked against the floor.

Zack rushed to Mia's side. "What's happening?"

"I . . ." David studied the travelers from the edge of the room—anxious, helpless. "I don't know."

A piercing noise filled the air, a high-pitched whistle that seemed to come from everywhere and nowhere. Before anyone could speak, a bright bead of light, no larger than a coin, materialized an inch below the ceiling.

All the blood drained out of Theo's face. *Oh no . . .*

The light expanded horizontally, enveloping the ceiling in a twenty-foot disc. The surface churned with violent ripples. The edges danced like fire. Zack had never seen such an angry-looking portal before. Worse, he had a strong hunch who was making it.

"Shit."

Theo screamed over the whistling clamor. "Zack, run!"

"No!" David shouted. "You won't escape them! Listen to me—"

A tendril of tempis shot out of the breach. It reached for Zack with singled-minded focus, snaking around his wrist until it was thoroughly bound.

"*Don't!*" Theo pulled at the tendril. "You don't have to do this! It's over! *They stopped!*"

A second tendril emerged from the portal. It grabbed Theo's head with spindly fingers, then pushed him back with vicious force. His skull collided against the lumivision screen, creating a web of cracks at the center of the glass.

Hannah ran downstairs at shifted speed, then stopped at the edge of the foyer. Theo lay unconscious and bleeding at the far end of the living room. Peter and Mia were suffering the same painful seizure.

And Zack?

Her heart dropped as three more tendrils reached down from the ceiling. They grabbed Zack by the wrists and ankles, dangling him in the air like a broken marionette.

David stopped Hannah before she could reach Zack. "No! Don't!"

Try as she might, Hannah couldn't forget the great tempic hand that had grabbed Evan Rander and pulled him screaming into a portal. It had almost been enough to make her feel sorry for him, and that was a man she hated.

She struggled against David, tears spilling down her face. "*Zack!*"

David cautiously approached him, his brow drenched in sweat. "Zack, listen to me! It's not too late! When you see Esis, apologize and beg for mercy! Convince her you won't be a problem anymore! *Mean* it!"

The tendrils lifted Zack another foot off the ground. They hung him at a slanted angle.

"What are they doing to him?" Hannah screamed. "Why are they just . . . ?"

The answer came stumbling down the stairs. David and Hannah turned around to see Amanda in the entry, her hair tousled, her face slack with disbelief. She'd woken up to the commotion in the living room and tried to convince herself that she was dreaming, or that someone was playing the lumivision too loudly. Or maybe . . .

"No . . ."

The moment she saw Zack, her breath escaped her and her thoughts went white. She thrust her palms at the tempic tentacles.

David lunged. "Wait!"

Her tempis exploded backward, encasing her arms in a craggy shell. It spread across her frame until she was immobilized from the neck down—a creature of rock candy, a geode turned inside out.

While his body writhed and his mind shrieked with terror, Zack found the energy to process Amanda's predicament. *They waited,* he thought. *Those bastards waited for her and now they're going to make her watch.*

Zack opened his mouth to speak but a fifth tempic rope came down through the portal and coiled around his neck. He sucked in air through a croaking rasp.

"Please!" Amanda cried. "Please! You made your point! You made your point!"

Zack's face turned a deep shade of purple. He struggled to speak. "Ah . . . ahlo . . ."

He closed his eyes, his thoughts raging at Esis. *Fuck you. You won't even let me say it.*

"Let him go!" Amanda begged. "I won't touch him! I promise!"

Zack forced his eyes open. He focused every bit of his dwindling consciousness on Amanda, thinking all the words he couldn't say.

Sweetheart, look at me. Look at me.

Amanda held his gaze. "Zack . . ."

I love you.

"Zack!"

The tendrils retracted, pulling him through the portal. The moment he vanished through the turbulent surface, the wormhole shrank to a tiny dot, and then disappeared entirely.

In an instant, the living room became silent. Peter and Mia stopped convulsing. They lay gasping on the floor, their faces moist with sweat and blood. While David tended to Mia and Hannah rushed to Theo's side, the tempic sheath melted away from Amanda's body. She fell to her hands and knees, struggling to remember how to think, how to breathe, how to make simple sounds.

Her eyes drifted over to the smartglobe on the floor. The glass sported a jagged new crack that ran from the horn of Africa to the northern reaches of Canada. From Amanda's angle, the fissure looked evil—a harsh, jagged smile on the face of the world.

She turned her trembling eyes to the ceiling, she thought about Zack, and then she remembered how to scream.

TEN

He woke up on his back, his mind a dark and silent city. As his consciousness returned in scattered patches—a lit window here, a lamppost there—he took a cursory scan of his senses. His limbs were numb. His throat was dry. He felt an unpleasant heaviness in the center of his body, as if all its empty spaces had been filled with wet cement.

He opened his eyes and saw his own splayed image staring down from the ceiling. *What . . . ?*

Wincing, he sat up and scanned his surroundings. Everywhere he looked, another Zack looked back at him. The twelve-by-twelve cell seemed to be composed entirely of mirrors, yet something wasn't right about his reflections. He struggled to pinpoint the discrepancy but became distracted by his attire—a tight, white, short-sleeved garment that covered him from neck to toe.

Zack tugged at the fabric with bristling indignation. *A unitard. They put me in a unitard?*

He caught a glint of silver on the back of his left hand—four nickel-size discs in an even square formation. He pried at them with his fingernails, but he couldn't peel them off. The damn things clung to his skin like warts.

"What . . . ?"

His voice came out in a parched rasp. Zack forced a cough and rose clumsily to his feet. His heart dropped when he noticed a complete lack of doors. He wasn't just a prisoner here. He was entombed.

"Oh God . . ."

He took a deep, calming breath and then reassessed the situation. The air was fresh. There must have been a hidden vent somewhere. The lack of bed and toilet suggested that the Pelletiers weren't planning to keep him here long. Maybe they were sweating him out like TV detectives, waiting for him to crack and confess his crime.

My crime, he thought with a scoffing hiss. *We just wanted to be together.*

He tilted his head at a mirrored wall. Now he realized what looked so strange. None of his reflections had reflections. Wherever he turned—the walls, the floor, or the ceiling above—a lone Zack stared back at him from an empty white room.

"What the . . . ?"

For a moment, he wondered if maybe he was looking at other people through clear glass windows, but no. They were him. They were all him. And they mirrored his every move.

Zack felt another wave of panic coming on. He battled it back and struggled to find a workable strategy.

Apologize, his inner David told him. *It's the only way you're getting out of here.*

Fuck that, said the voice of Josh Trillinger. *You're a dead man and you know it. Are you gonna die on your knees or you gonna go out fighting?*

Zack paced the floor, his mouth running faster than his mind. He cursed Azral and Esis, insulted their mothers, suggested several inappropriate ways for them to interact with farm animals. He crooned Stevie Nicks's "Edge of Seventeen" in a barrage of annoying styles, from an operatic falsetto to a Cookie Monster voice, then expounded at length about the geopolitical structure of the Marvel Universe. By the end of his filibuster, he could only guess that two hours had passed. Somewhere along the way, he'd started to wonder if he was still on Earth.

He smacked his palm against a wall. "You know, this cryptic shit is getting old. If you have something to say, just say it!"

If his captors heard him, they didn't respond. Zack bitterly shook his head.

"Fine. Suit yourselves. Coming up next on Radio Free Trillinger: the many things I love about Amanda Stephanie Giv—"

A portal opened behind him, filling the entirety of a wall. Zack barely had a chance to turn around before a tempic tendril burst through the surface, snaked around his waist, then yanked him howling into the breach.

Zack opened his eyes and found himself being pulled down a long hexagonal tunnel of glimmering gunmetal. Huge tempic panels floated all around him, passing each other but never colliding. The view was an assault on Zack's battered sanity, a living screensaver nestled inside the world's biggest Allen wrench.

Calm down, said the Mia in his thoughts. *They're trying to scare you. Don't let them.*

His stomach flipped when he saw two figures standing side by side at the end of the passage, watching him from a floating metal platform. Once again, Azral cut an intimidating presence with his towering height, his snow-white hair, his fierce blue eyes, and tieless gray business suit. Most unnerving of all was his flawless countenance, a face so calm and eerily symmetrical that Zack wouldn't have been surprised to find circuitry behind it.

Esis, by contrast, looked unmistakably human, despite the tempic tentacle that extended from her arm. She frowned, she blinked, she shuffled impatiently on her feet. Her outfit, a black sleeveless top with a ruffled white skirt and stockings, was discordantly cute for a woman of her stature. For a moment Zack wondered if Amanda had oversold her fearsomeness.

Then he drew closer and saw the unhinged ferocity behind her coal-black eyes. *Shark eyes,* Mercy had called them. Yes. Zack could see that now. He understood exactly why Amanda and the Gothams were terrified of her.

Her tendril retracted to five feet of length, just enough to leave Zack suspended above the edge of the platform. The two Pelletiers studied his dangling form, intrigued, as if he were the most abstract sculpture in their art gallery.

In the silence, Zack's fear turned into something hard and prickly. He thought about all the sins these people had committed—the lies, the threats, the manipulations and murders. Oh, and genocide. If Ioni had told Hannah the truth, then these were the monsters who'd destroyed Zack's world.

He stashed his rage behind a mask of dry humor. "You know, I'm not one to complain—"

Esis extended her tendril with a thrust of her arm, sending Zack all the way back down the length of the corridor. He flew through the portal and tumbled hard across the floor of his prison cell.

"Christ . . ."

Exasperated, he climbed back to his feet and resumed his fitful pacing, determined to keep himself busy. He gnawed and tugged at his clingy outfit, but the fabric refused to tear. He tried drawing on the walls with his breath fog and spit, but the mirrors proved impervious to tampering. He attempted to reverse the silver discs on his hand, only to learn—unsurprisingly—that his power had been nullified.

Time passed invisibly around him, the minutes indistinguishable from hours. After an endless wait, a new portal opened on the opposite wall. Zack flinched at the long white tendril that popped through the surface, but Esis was gentler this time. Her tempis scooped him up in a makeshift chair and carried him leisurely down the corridor.

The Pelletiers watched with cool skepticism as Zack made his second approach. *No jokes this time,* he warned himself. *No back talk.*

Once again, his captors remained silent. Zack stared down at his wringing hands until he found the strength to make eye contact. He stared curiously into Azral's opaline irises. "It wasn't you."

Azral's brow rose in query.

"I got my bracelet from a man in a mask," Zack told him. "I thought it was you but your eyes are different. They're—"

Esis flicked her hand dismissively. Her tempis wrapped around Zack like a python, then whisked him all the way back to his cell.

Zack crashed to the floor and screamed at the shrinking portal. "Goddamn it! What do you want from me? *What do you want?*"

You know what they want, said David. *Fall on your knees and beg for forgiveness.*

Zack's brother scoffed at the notion. *Apologize? After all the shit they've done?*

It's the only way out, David insisted.

Bullshit, said Josh. *Don't listen to him, Zack. Don't let those assholes break you.*

Zack shut out both voices and scrambled back to his feet. He shot a murderous glare at the ceiling.

"You know, if you're going to keep me here, you might want to think about feeding me. Maybe a burger and fries, a nice pasta dish. Or hey, maybe we could split a pizza. You guys like bacon?"

The more he thought about food, the more he realized that he wasn't even remotely hungry. He still had that heavy cement feeling inside of him.

Zack walked the cell in a rapid circle, his fist smacking idly against his palm.

"When Amanda and Hannah were little girls, you saved them from a freeway accident. They said there were three of you but neither of them can remember what the other guy looked like. So who is he? *Where* is he? Who's the man who gave me my bracelet?"

Zack waited for a response, or at least another portal, but the Pelletiers seemed to be done with him for now. That was fine. He had nothing but time.

"No comment, huh? Okay. I'll move on. Why did you give us that van and money last year? If you wanted us to get to Peter so badly, you could have just pushed us through a portal. You're good at that."

He stopped in his tracks, baffled. "Why *did* you want us to get to Peter?"

Soon he found himself juggling more questions than he could handle, everything he'd been pondering for the last several months.

"Why did you give us our powers?"

"Who's Ioni and how does she know you?"

"Why do you go out of your way to save some of us but not others?"

"Why is Rebel still alive after everything he did to you?"

"What the *hell* is your problem with me and Amanda?"

Zack sucked a sharp breath, then tapped his chin in contemplation. "What did you—"

He was cut off by a disembodied laugh: a faint, haunting cackle that filtered in through every wall. By the time Zack stopped to listen, it was already gone. Rattled, he began pacing again.

"What did you do with—"

The cackle returned, louder and more insistent. Either Zack was starting to lose his mind or the Pelletiers were answering his question before he could ask it.

"What did you do with Evan Rander?"

His six mirror images began wavering with distortion, like water reflections. Once the ripples settled, the walls, floor, and ceiling showed the image of an entirely different prisoner: a small and scrawny fellow with ginger-blond hair. He sat in the corner of his stark white prison cube, his head dipped, his arms wrapped around his knees.

Evan lifted his head and looked at Zack. His face lit up in a savage grin. "Well, well, well. Hello, jailbird."

He was the black sheep of the Silvers; the problem child, the outcast. Though his enemies would have never believed it, there was a time in Evan's life—long ago in an alternate past—that he tried to be good. It didn't work out. Mia never warmed up to him, Theo merely tolerated him, and David made it clear in his own inimitable fashion that he was not a friend. Amanda was a hard-eyed nemesis from the moment she and Evan met. She hated his witticisms, his mannerisms, his cynicism and atheism.

And Hannah? She was the best of them before she became the worst.

But Zack had always been a bright spot in Evan's world. In times undone, the two of them were brothers-in-arms, nerds of a feather. It wasn't until Amanda got her talon hooks in him that he began to pull away. *I'm telling you, Zack, there's something wrong with him. The way he looks at Hannah . . .*

But that was all marginalia now, an obsolete draft of the story. In this string of time, Evan Rander was a nemesis of the Silvers. He'd followed them across the nation—taunting them, subverting them, punishing them for slights and transgressions that only he remembered.

Then, in October of last year, he went a little too far, enough to earn the wrath of the Pelletiers. They yanked him away through a portal, then left him to rot in this looking-glass limbo.

But at least now he had company.

"So here we are," Evan chirped. "The Team Supreme. The Dynamic Duo, reunited and doing hard time in the Pelletentiary."

Zack hunkered down against a wall. "Shut up."

"Aw, you must have just gotten here. How long has it been since they took me? What's the date?"

Zack kept quiet. Evan rose from the floor and scowled at him. "Come on, man. I haven't had company in . . . shit, I don't even know. I can only guess we're close to the end."

"We're not," Zack said. "We still have four years left."

Evan howled with laughter, a maniacal sound that broadcast every ounce of his torment. Zack noticed his left hand, the same four silver discs that had been fused to his own skin. The Pelletiers must have been regulating their bodies, eliminating the need for food, sleep, anything that marked the passage of time.

Jesus, Zack thought. *This isn't temporary.*

He rubbed his temples, fighting back the storm of screams that was welling up inside of him.

"What is this place?" he asked.

Evan's laughter died down. He brushed the tears from his eyes. "Do you remember the old research facility in Terra Vista?"

"Yeah. Of course."

"You ever go into Sterling Quint's office?"

"A couple of times. Why?"

"Then you'd remember those ten cages he kept against the wall, that stupid mouse farm of his. He was breeding a special kind for his wife, some researcher at a drug lab. I guess she was hard up for mutants."

Zack glared at him. "What does any of that have to do with—"

"You see, Quint kept an eleventh cage at the foot of his desk, a time-out cube for all the squeakers and biters and other mousy malcontents."

Now Zack got the gist of Evan's metaphor. He didn't like it one bit. "That's all we are to them. Just lab mice."

"Squeak fucking squeak."

Zack clenched his fists. "That's bullshit. You deserve this. I don't."

"Yet here we are in our matching onesies."

"You know what? Don't even talk to me. You're a psychopath."

"Oh, am I?"

"You *tortured* Amanda and Hannah."

"Please. It was just a stun charge."

"They never did anything to you!"

"They did *everything* to me. You have no idea, Zack. You never remember. They . . ."

Evan closed his eyes and collected himself. When he spoke again, his words came out in a grudging mumble.

"No, you're right. I was wrong. I shouldn't have done what I did. I'm sorry."

Zack snorted derisively. "I'm sure the Pelletiers are moved by your sincerity."

"You think I don't regret it? I've been stuck in here forever with nothing but my goddamn reflections. I can't even . . ."

He fluffed his hair with trembling fingers. "Look, I hate the sisters. Nothing's going to change that. But I can change the way I handle it. If I get out of here, I'll never bother them again. I mean it."

He threw his frenzied gaze at the ceiling. "I *mean* it!"

Zack lurched to his feet and paced the floor again. There was nowhere he could turn without seeing Evan. The roof, the floor, the four walls around him, each one had Evan looking back at him from a different angle.

"I don't understand," Zack said. "Why they don't just kill us?"

"Because we're still potentially useful to them."

"And my brother wasn't?"

Evan shrugged. "What can I say? In their eyes, silver's more precious than gold."

Zack rubbed his face, flummoxed. "Jury Curado was a Silver. They let you murder him."

The name drew a hard smile out of Evan. "They didn't just allow it. They thanked me for it."

"Why?"

"Because whenever he lives, he steals the heart of a Given. You should know by now they don't look kindly on that."

"*Why?*"

Evan studied Zack in brief dilemma, then tensely shook his head. "You do this every time, man."

"Do what?"

"Bang your head against Mount Pelletier. You question them, you challenge them, you go out of your way to annoy them. I can't even count the number of times they've stomped you into the ground. There's usually nothing left of you to bury."

"I just want to understand."

"You won't," Evan said. "The Pelletiers don't experience time the way we do. They see all the strings at once—past, present, and future—and it colors every decision they make. When they want a sandwich, they'll buy an umbrella. And while the rest of us are scratching our heads, wondering why the hell they did that, they've started a domino chain of events that ends with them getting the best goddamn sandwich in the universe. They're playing four-dimensional chess and they're a hundred moves ahead of you. How do you expect to understand them, Zack? How do you expect to *beat* them?"

Zack glared at the floor. If the Pelletiers were so omniscient, then how did Rebel once beat the shit out of Esis? How could their mighty plans be threatened by such a cheesy thing as love?

A long silence passed. Evan tapped his fingertips in calculation. "Four years left. So it's been six to eight months since you guys got to Brooklyn. That means . . ."

He laughed with amazement. "Oh wow. She's in the Jonathan Christie era."

Zack cringed at his ominous phrasing. "You enjoy being that?"

"Being what?"

"Hannah's creepy stalker."

Evan's eyes narrowed to slits. "Don't buy the hype. She's the psycho in our little dyad. She stalks me more than I stalk her."

"That's bullshit."

"Oh yeah? Just wait."

Zack glared at him. "You could have been our friend. Shit, with all the things you know, you could have been our guardian angel."

"I tried that," Evan insisted. "You assholes still wouldn't accept me."

"Meaning Hannah still wouldn't sleep with you."

"That's not . . ."

Now it was Evan's turn to bristle. No matter what he did, no matter how many edits he made to Hannah's life, there was always someone else to catch her eye. Jury Curado. Theo Maranan. Even Peter Pendergen had his turn. And now that she'd found her way to Jonathan . . . goddamn it. That one always ended beautifully, with Hannah shattered in a million pieces. Evan hated the thought of missing it. He had to get out of here.

He leaned against a wall and forced a soulful look for all who happened to be watching.

"I never claimed to be a nice guy. God knows I've made mistakes. But you don't know what it's like to have my power. I've been living the same four and a half years for centuries, bouncing back and forth between one apocalypse and the other. I could be the greatest person ever and it wouldn't matter. The sky will come down, the game will start over, and you guys won't remember a thing that I did. I'll just be that weird, skinny geek who rubs most of you the wrong way."

"Then do your own thing," Zack said. "Win some cash. Buy an island. Just leave us alone."

"Oh, I've tried that. I have."

"And?"

Evan sighed at the floor. "What can I say? You people drive me nuts but you're still the closest thing I have to home."

"That's pathetic."

"You think I'm the worst person you know? I'm not even your worst friend."

"Yes. Right. That evil psycho Hannah."

"I'm not talking about Hannah."

Zack turned around. More disturbing than Evan's cryptic comment was his sudden look of horror, as if he'd accidentally opened the gates to Hell. His mirror images became distorted by ripples. He flailed about the cell, his voice fading by the moment.

"Wait! Wait! I wasn't going to . . . look, I wasn't thinking, okay? I'm sorry! Please! Bring him back!"

Zack retreated a step. "Evan, what—"

"Bring him back!"

His howling cries quickly shrank away. As the shimmering walls settled, Zack once again saw his own reflection. He was back to his original status quo, just him and his six doppelgängers.

Zack slid down the wall and sat motionless in the corner. He stared at his knees, pondering everything he'd just heard and witnessed. He didn't move for a very long time.

Eternity.

The word splashed like acid through Zack's troubled consciousness. In the absence of all stimuli, the suppression of all bodily functions, the gears of time came screeching to a halt.

Daunted, but not defeated, he labored to maintain an artificial cycle. He bounced around the cell in busy activity for what felt like sixteen hours, then lay on the floor with his arm draped over his eyes for another estimated eight. At the start of each new "day," he etched a notch on his mental calendar, bid a merry "good morning" to his invisible jailers, then began his first of many exercise routines.

"You're not going to break me," he said between jumping jacks. "I've got a Swiss inner clock and a head full of stories. I've got worlds in here, fuckers. I have—"

Eternity.

"—ideas."

Zack wandered the cell in zigzag patterns, forcing himself down the twisting corridors of his imagination. He envisioned an alternate timeline in which he and his friends made peace with the U.S. government. Under the sage command of Melissa Masaad, they fought crime as an elite team of super-agents (*DP-X*). Zack plotted two full seasons of their television adventures before the series jumped the shark. It then devolved into a hokey silver-age comic book, filled with costumes and code names and cackling supervillains. Zack took vicious glee in casting Azral as the group's haughty archnemesis. He dressed him in a snow-white unitard, then searched for an appropriately ludicrous moniker. Time Tyrant, or Count Tempora, or Doctor—

—Eternity.

No, no. Come on. It has to be something silly. Doctor Dour, or—

"Doctor Douche," he uttered, with hysterical giggles.

On his eleventh day, it occurred to Zack that his cell was probably shifted at an accelerated speed—20x, 40x, 500,000x, who the hell knew? He could languish here in captivity for a thousand years before Amanda's next lunch. The Pelletiers could toss him back in the house by suppertime, a frail and gibbering husk who'd been broken under the weight of—

"No."

—eternity.

"Stay strong. Stay strong. *Stay strong.*"

Despite his resolve, he quickly began to see the strain on his ubiquitous reflections. They met his sideways glances, their brows curled in increasing despair. *Goddamn it. Stop. You're giving them exactly what they want!*

By his twenty-second day, he couldn't bear to look at himself anymore. The existence of his mirror twins plagued him, these sick and twisted freaks. They didn't eat. They didn't sleep. They never grew stubble. Their hairs were unpluckable and their fingernails were too short to chew. They were pathetic, unnatural. And they had to die.

On Day Thirty-Three, Zack punched a reflection, shattering three knuckles against the wall. Just as he delighted in the fresh data of agony, a hazy light filled the cell and he was instantly healed.

"No. *No!*"

Zack screamed and thrashed about the cell. The Pelletiers were trapping him in an endless state of constancy, stretching him out on a rack of time until he begged for forgiveness.

"No no no." He shook his head, his eyes welling with tears. "You owe *me* an apology. You owe *me* an apology."

On the forty-fourth day, he finally stopped counting. His day and night cycles had become a pitiful charade, as messy and erratic as his thoughts. He lay on the floor in a fetal ball and apologized to the Pelletiers over and over. He was sorry for Amanda, sorry for the insults, sorry for not appreciating them and their fine contributions. He promised to be a better team player. He swore to do whatever they wanted him to do.

By the time he gave up apologizing, he could only imagine that years had passed. The second apocalypse had come and gone and the Pelletiers had taken him back to their native era. He wondered if Evan was still alive in a neighboring cell. The last two mice in the farm. Squeak fucking squeak.

"Please," Zack begged his captors. "I just want to talk to him again. Bring him back. Bring him back."

The room went dark. Zack sat up in confusion, then frantically touched his eyeballs. He couldn't remember the last time he'd experienced complete blackness. Was he suffering hysterical blindness, or did something else happen?

He fumbled to his feet. "What's going on? What—"

"Shhhh," said a voice in the darkness. "Calm yourself."

The sound came from all directions, a soft and breathy whisper that swirled around Zack like a breeze. He couldn't tell if his visitor was young or old, male or female, real or imaginary.

"Who . . . who are . . . ?"

"Be quiet. If you wish to leave this awful place, you'll shut your mouth and listen."

Now Zack could tell that the speaker was a man. He detected a hint of a peculiar accent, a highborn cadence that fell far off Zack's registry. Odder still, the man's whispers were garnished with faint aural embellishments—wind chimes and whistles and crackling white noise.

"A final portal will come for you shortly," the stranger informed him. "You'll have one last chance to earn our clemency. I've argued in favor of sparing you but Esis very much wants you dead. If you have a shred of sense left in you, boy, you won't say a thing to provoke her."

Zack shook his head vehemently. "No. I won't. I won't. I just want to go home."

"As ever, the final decision rests with Azral. He'll be watching—"

"Wait. I thought you were—"

"Just listen! As you face him, he'll be watching the strings closely. The only way you'll earn his mercy—the *only* way—is to let Amanda go once and for all. Do you hear me?"

Zack heard plenty. Between the hissing whispers and spectral embellishments, there was something familiar about the man's voice, as if Zack had heard it before in a dream.

"Do you understand?" the stranger asked.

"I hear you," Zack said. "I understand."

A heavy sigh filled his ears. "It baffles me, Trillinger. You're usually one of the more sensible Silvers. Yet when it comes to Amanda—that grating, sanctimonious woman—you lose all sense of reason. Did you think you could evade our wrath on a technicality, a wishful parsing of the word 'entwine'? It was never about sex, you idiot. Amanda has to receive her next lover willingly. She'll never do that as long as you're distracting her."

A dozen questions collided in Zack's head. He sifted through the wreckage, struggling to piece them together. *Is this why . . . What about . . . Breeding mice . . . Peter?*

Don't even bother trying to figure it out, his inner Evan told him. *They're buying another umbrella.*

"So what do I say to Azral?" Zack asked.

"It's not what you say. It's what your future says. Let her go. Stop hindering our work. You do that and you may just find your way back to your friends. They miss you, you know."

Tears streamed down Zack's face. He fought to speak clearly. "How . . . how long have I—"

"You've barely been gone a day."

Zack choked back a cry and palmed his face with both hands. "Who are you?"

"Don't mistake the nature of my aid, boy. We are not friends. I owe you no answers. You, however, owe me your life. Esis would have slaughtered you months ago if it wasn't for me."

The voice seemed to travel now. It trailed around Zack in a slow, menacing loop.

"I think the more pressing question is who are *you?*"

Zack looked around blindly. "What?"

"My son considers you a nuisance. My wife sees you as a dangerous rebel. I disagree with both of them. I believe you're a potential asset, one who could help us achieve great things. Only you can determine which of us is right. Think on it carefully. By now you know full well how we deal with nuisances."

The stranger's voice dropped an octave. "Pray you never learn what we do to rebels."

The lights flickered back on. Zack shielded his eyes and took a twirling scan of the room. He was alone again. Just him and his mirror selves.

His thoughts flashed back to his last day on Earth, his mad encounter with the stranger who gave him his silver bracelet. He was a tall and well-built man whose face was hidden behind a tempic mask. All Zack could see of him were his fierce blue eyes. They'd danced with amusement, even as people burned all around them, even as the whole world crumbled.

Zack had prayed to the gods and fates that he would never meet that man again. Now apparently he had. More disturbing still, it seemed that harsh and faceless stranger was the nicest of the Pelletiers.

———————

The final portal came as promised. Zack stared at the liquid surface, waiting for Esis's tendril. A full minute passed before he realized his mistake. His captors weren't grabbing him this time. They were inviting him.

Zack closed his eyes, sucked a breath, then took his first willful journey through the Pelletiers' portal.

Azral and Esis watched him vacantly as he walked the long corridor. Though he looked every bit the man they'd captured last night, it was clear from his expression and his shambling gait that much had changed with Zack Trillinger. On the inside, he was a gaunt and filthy derelict in ragged hair and tattered cloth. He was broken.

He kept his eyes downward until he reached the Pelletiers. Azral motioned politely to a folding chair in the middle of the platform. *Please.*

Zack took his seat, desperately trying to avoid the hateful gaze of Esis. *Don't provoke,* he told himself. *Don't even look at her.*

Once again, the Pelletiers made no attempt to start a conversation. Zack bit his thumb, racking his brain for the perfect thing to say.

It's not what you say, boy. It's what your future says.

Yes. He knew exactly what he had to do. It was so simple, so basic. Yet he could hear his last shred of pride snarling at him. *Pathetic,* it said. *Giving up the woman you love, just because some assholes locked you in a room. No wonder you can't look at yourself. You're not a man. You're not even a mouse.*

The image of Amanda drifted into his thoughts, her green eyes filled with tears.

He's wrong, Zack. You know me. You know exactly what I want. If you have to cut me out like a tumor in order to live, then do *it, Zack. Live!*

He lowered his head, his jaw clenched with forced composure. A smattering of tears trickled down his cheeks.

Azral and Esis exchanged a meaningful look. Only one of their faces had softened.

"Nyad," Esis hissed. "*L'ua tolla shii hoh-no kiesse!*"

Azral motioned gently at Zack. "*Regaha la-ma.*"

"*Nyad! T'uu makkiné niia hoh-no kiesse!*"

Zack glanced up and saw Azral towering over him. Thankfully, the man still looked serene, though Zack wouldn't go so far as to call his expression friendly.

"You were counseled," Azral surmised.

His accent was different than the whispering stranger's—thicker, more exotic. For a heart-stopping moment, Zack thought he'd said "cancelled."

"My father has some fondness for you," Azral told Zack. "He finds you amusing, unlike us, and he believes you can be redeemed. Admittedly, I do see a shift in the strings. It appears you've had a change of heart."

Esis crossed her arms, skeptical. "Hearts change back."

Azral nodded, his eyes locked on Zack. "That's the trouble with futures. They never settle. Even we're surprised from time to time. You were originally supposed to join your brother in our New York facility. Then circumstances changed. You made a last-minute journey to San Diego, just as we encountered an unexpected vacancy in our group there. So we joined you with the Silvers. In hindsight, it was a mistake."

"It was a mistake to put him anywhere!" Esis insisted.

"Perhaps," Azral said to her. "Yet Father believes he still has potential."

Zack kept his head down as Azral slowly circled him. The man radiated amusement, like a cat toying with its prey.

"You asked why we go out of our way to save some of you but not others. It should be obvious by now that we don't need all of you. We chose ninety-nine people as a safety measure, a pool of redundancies to minimize risk. In the end, all we require is one."

Zack looked up. He couldn't find the nerve to speak the name on his tongue. *Amanda?*

Azral shrugged as if he heard Zack's thoughts. "We can't say for certain who that person will be. As ever, the strings give many answers. But we see patterns in the future. Probabilities. There are those among you who are far more likely to give us what we seek. And so we protect them more zealously."

He looped behind Zack, staying just out of his line of sight. "As you may have guessed by now, you rank very low in our estimations. You have less value to us than any living Silver, including Rander."

"And the little fat girl," Esis said with a roll of her eyes.

Azral frowned. "Yes. Farisi. Another disappointment."

"Another hopeless romantic," Esis teased.

Zack felt his face burn a hot shade of red. His fingers hooked around the edge of his chair. *Just end this already,* he thought. *Let me go or kill me.*

"The sisters stand at the top of our list," Azral said. "The strings favor them both by a significant margin.

"But you *ruin* Amanda!" Esis shouted. "You sully our best hope!"

Azral sighed. "I believe the other one is our best hope, but that's not the issue now. Whatever shall we do with you, Trillinger? I don't believe your mind will withstand much more isolation."

Zack tensely shook his head. *No. No.*

"And yet I fear that if we release you, you'll simply stand in our way again."

"He'll return to *her!*" Esis yelled. "Look and see!"

"I see it, *sehmeer,* and I'm not optimistic. But for the love of my father, I'll give this sad little creature one last chance to prove his worth."

Azral kneeled at Zack's side, his lips hovering an inch from his ear. Zack could hear the dripping condescension in his voice.

"Speak, child. Convince me."

Zack sat forward and pressed his hands to his eyes. It was obvious now that Azral Pelletier was the leader of the pack, the driving force behind all of Zack's sorrows. He was the brutal assassin of one Earth and the cold white death that lingered above another.

He was the archvillain.

And as sure as Zack knew anything, he knew this bastard had no intention of sparing him.

Zack drew a deep breath through his nose. His thoughts died down to a gentle breeze. At the moment he was neither hero nor coward, neither a rebel nor a mouse. He simply reverted back to his default factory settings. He was the smart-mouthed bane of arrogant assholes. He was, once more, a nuisance.

"She's not fat."

The Pelletiers stared at Zack in matching confusion. He raised his head and fixed his steely gaze on Esis.

"Mia," he said. "She's not fat. You'd have to be out of your goddamn mind to think so."

He narrowed his eyes at Azral. "And I liked you better when you were quiet."

Once again, the clock of the universe seemed to grind to a halt. Zack had minutes, *hours* to study the stone-hard expressions of his jailers.

He wasn't surprised to see Esis crack first. She bared her teeth in a silent snarl. Her arms grew thick with tempic spikes.

"*Zhii-tah no-ma!*"

Azral held her back. "Mother, stop."

"You *hear* him!"

"I do."

"He disrespects us again!"

"*Ecouna ma-né,*" he told his mother. "*Ecouna.*"

As the two of them conversed in their complex language, Zack kept a nervous eye on Esis. Though the rage never left her lovely face, she stopped thrashing long enough to listen to Azral. She furrowed her brow. She sputtered in protest. Then, at long last, she turned her back and gave her son a dismissive wave. *Whatever.*

Azral straightened his blazer and approached the prisoner again. Zack flinched in fear when he reached out toward him.

"Calm yourself," Azral said.

He tapped four fingers against the back of Zack's hand, liquefying the discs that had been melded onto his skin. The metal rolled off Zack like quicksilver, then dribbled to the floor.

Zack only had a moment to scan the fresh new divots in his hand before a wave of agonizing hunger overtook him. His body screamed for everything now: food and water, salt and sleep. He was so tired all of a sudden, he could barely see straight.

"Come," Azral said.

"I don't . . . I don't feel . . ."

"The discomfort will pass. Rise, child. Before my mother reconsiders."

Azral helped him to his feet. Zack stumbled forward like a drowsy toddler. A ten-foot portal opened in front of him.

He panicked at the sight of the glimmering disc. "No, no, no, no . . ."

"You're not going back to the holding cell," Azral patiently assured him.

"Then what . . . ?"

"We're releasing you, Trillinger. Must I explain everything?"

"But . . ."

Zack peeked over his shoulder at Esis. Though the madwoman continued to sulk and seethe, there was a glimmering hint of vindication in her eyes. Zack could see that she wasn't entirely displeased.

He looked at the portal, then took a shaky step back. "This doesn't go home."

"Of course not," Azral said. "Did you think you earned our clemency?"

"Wait . . ."

Azral grabbed him by the nape of the neck. "You are nothing, boy. Not even a speck in the larger scheme. But you were chosen, for better or worse. And you will serve our purpose, one way or another."

"Wait!"

Azral pushed Zack through the portal. The world washed away in a sea of burning light.

He stumbled forward into a brand-new environment, a room so dark that he couldn't see a thing. The ground beneath him was smooth and cold. Zack might have thought he was back in his cell if his fingers hadn't brushed a hard line of grout.

Tile, he thought. *Where the hell am I?*

As his eyes adjusted to the darkness, Zack looked up and saw the vague shape of a convection oven. He'd landed in somebody's kitchen in the middle of the night. From what he could see, it was an upscale home, maybe even a mansion. But who—

He gripped the floor in sudden pain. His empty stomach was eating him from the inside. His throat felt like a blistering desert. He was so damn tired that his knees were wobbling, yet all he truly wanted at the moment was warm human contact. He desperately needed to see someone who wasn't a Rander or a—

"Hello?"

—Pelletier.

"Is someone there?"

Zack struggled to see through the dancing spots in his vision and caught a shadowy figure in the glow of the hallway. The woman was as tall and slender as Amanda, with dark, wavy hair that hung down to her hips. Zack could only assume that she was a stranger. But was she the friendly kind, or was he about to suffer a new ordeal?

The woman turned on the kitchen light and gasped at the sight of Zack. "Oh my God! *Richard!*"

Zack scrambled to his knees, struggling to speak through stammering lips. "Wait . . ."

He only had a moment to process the footsteps behind him before a heavy metal fist clubbed the back of his head. He fell to the tile in a soft, messy heap.

Ivy processed Zack through wide, blinking eyes. "Holy shit. That's Trillinger."

"Sure is," said her husband.

"What's he doing here, Richard? What the *hell* is going on?"

Rebel looked down at the hand-delivered enemy, the Silver on a silver platter. All he could do was scratch his head and shrug.

"I have no idea."

ELEVEN

David stood at the window at the end of the hallway, his blond brow creased with confusion. The neighborhood was eerily quiet this morning. There were no children playing in their box yards, no sunbathers and their music spinners. Even the local street traffic, usually a nonstop rumble in the periphery of his hearing, had dried up. It suddenly occurred to David that today was the Sunday after the first full moon after the vernal equinox. The date had a religious significance on this world and the last. It even had a name.

"Easter."

Hannah poked her head out of her bedroom. "Huh?"

"Nothing," he said. "Just thinking out loud."

She stepped into the hallway and closed the door behind her, a breakfast plate in her hand. The food looked like it had barely been touched.

"Still not eating," David noted.

"She's eating a little."

"It's been three days. Maybe she should get up for a bit. Move around."

Hannah looked at him tiredly. "I'll handle Amanda. How's Mia?"

"Sleeping."

"You sure?"

"There are portal notes raining all over her bedroom," David said. "That's a pretty good indicator."

He didn't mean to sound snide about it. He considered apologizing to Hannah, or at least offering to help. Zack's violent departure had shattered the orderly structure of the household, leaving most of the residents in a state of depression, dysfunction, or—in Peter's case—absenteeism. Hannah took it upon herself to become all things to everyone: the cook, the maid, the nurse, the grief counselor. David had expected her own grief to catch up with her by now, but she kept finding new ways to outrun it.

"Look, Hannah—"

"*What the shit?*"

The cursing came from the first floor. David barely managed to turn his head before Hannah sped downstairs, returned the food plate to the kitchen, and joined Jonathan in the laundry closet. His T-shirt and jeans were splattered with soap suds. A tattered wet bra hung from his hand.

"What are you doing?" Hannah asked.

Jonathan jerked his head at the elaborate Vertech machine. "I'm *trying* to wash clothes, but this goddamn thing's from Bizarro World. I mean look at these buttons. Agitate. Pendulate. *Exsiccate?*"

He examined the bra with a baffled expression. "Apparently that last one means 'purée.'"

Hannah threw the garment in the washer, then set the timer for minus-six. "Forget the water features," she told him. "That's for new clothes. For everything else, you want the temporal settings."

"Temporal." Jonathan threw his hands up. "Everything in this house is a time machine."

"You never used one of these?"

"I lived in a slum. We had a sink and a washboard."

Hannah closed the lid and started the Vertech. She brushed some suds from Jonathan's shirt. "You should have told me you were doing this. I would have helped."

"I was doing it to help *you.*"

"You don't have to. I'm all right."

"You're not all right. You've been running around since Friday. You haven't slowed down. You haven't even . . ." He dipped his head and sighed. "Heath's cried more than you have, and he barely knew Zack."

Hannah stepped away from him. "Don't."

"Don't what?"

"Don't talk about him like he's dead."

Jonathan followed her into the kitchen and watched her scrape Amanda's breakfast into juve tins. "Sorry," he said. "After everything that's happened, I guess I've learned to expect the worst."

Hannah surprised him by chuckling. He tilted his head. "What?"

"When I first met Zack, he said something like that. He told me that after twenty-eight years of Jewish conditioning, he'd come to believe that, all things being equal, the darkest explanation is usually the right one." She let out a broken laugh. "He called it Menachem's Razor."

Jonathan smiled until he saw Hannah's lips quiver. She was fighting back tears. Losing.

"Our world had only been gone ten minutes," she said. "And he was able to make jokes. I thought he was crazy but that's just the way he is."

"Hannah . . ."

"He never lets anything break him."

David sat out of view on the stairwell, wincing in misery as he listened to Hannah's cries. He didn't need to look to know that Jonathan was holding her. That was just how it had started with Zack and Amanda.

But would these two learn from the tragic mistakes of others, or would they march blindly over the same cliff? David had no idea. Hindsight was his specialty, not foresight. All he knew was that he'd keep his mouth shut this time. There was nothing to be gained by nagging Jonathan and Hannah. It hadn't done a damn thing to save Zack.

A large portal opened on the wall of the kitchen. Hannah broke away from Jonathan and grabbed a meat cleaver from the counter.

David ran into the kitchen. "Hannah, wait!"

Peter stepped through the surface and jumped at the sight of Hannah's blade. His hands flew up in surrender. "Whoa, whoa, whoa! It's just me! Just me!"

Hannah lowered the cleaver. "Goddamn it. Don't *do* that."

"Sorry."

"Your portals look just like theirs!"

"I know." Peter shrank the gateway out of existence. "I should have called first. I'm sorry."

Everyone in the kitchen took a moment to collect themselves. David looked to Peter's arms and counted twenty-two different bandages. Amanda had become so aggrieved in the wake of Zack's abduction that her body erupted in tempic spikes. She might have brought the whole house down if Peter hadn't subdued her in a chokehold. His quick thinking earned him dozens of puncture wounds.

His handphone vibrated. He pulled it out of his pocket and frowned at the screen. "The others still sleeping?"

David nodded his head. "Pretty much."

"Well, wake them up," said Peter. "I know where Zack is."

No one knew what he'd been up to these past few days. He'd come in and out of the brownstone without a word of explanation, and rarely stayed home for more than an hour at a time. Now Mia, David, Hannah, and Theo watched Peter from the couches as he fiddled with his computer. He jiggled a small black device in the peripheral port, then looked over his shoulder at the lumivision's screen. Whatever he was trying didn't seem to be working.

Mia blinked at him in confusion, her eyes still bloodshot from the Pelletiers' portal attack. "I don't understand. How did he end up—"

"No idea," said Peter. "I'll explain what I know when everyone gets here."

Theo rubbed his bandaged brow, testing his power for the hundredth time. He'd been totally blind to the future since Thursday, and it wasn't because of his concussion. The Pelletiers were clouding his foresight. They were clearly intent on keeping Zack's fate a mystery.

"How do you know that Rebel really has him?" he asked Peter.

"You'll see in a moment."

Jonathan and Heath came down the stairs, the former practically pushing the latter. Heath turned around every fourth step to register his shrill objection.

"You're not listening to me!"

"I heard you, all right? It'll be gone soon enough."

Only Jonathan knew what the boy was upset about: a large yellow truck from the Transpac moving company, parked thirty yards down the street. Heath had been watching it all morning from the attic window, and had yet to see anyone come in or out of it.

"It shouldn't be there," he insisted to Jonathan. "It's Easter. Nobody moves on Easter!"

"Buddy, listen to me. I know you hate yellow—"

"It's not about the color."

"—but we have bigger shit to deal with. Just dial it back, okay?"

Hannah held her hand out to him. "Sweetie, come sit with me."

Heath hurried past her and monitored the truck through a slit in the window blinds.

Jonathan furrowed his brow at Peter. "You're showing us a movie?"

"Not a movie," said Peter. "As soon as—"

Everyone turned their heads toward the stairwell, where the final member of the group made a slow and clumsy descent.

None of the men had seen Amanda since Friday. She'd stayed tucked away in her bedroom, subsisting on liquids and a fistful of sedatives. Her skin was pallid. Her eyes were puffy. Her nightshirt hung off her like a shroud.

Amanda shambled into the living room and fixed her bleary eyes on Peter. "Just tell me he's alive."

"He was as of Friday."

"You've known since *Friday*?"

"I didn't want to tell you until I knew for sure they had him." Peter smacked his computer. "Damn this thing. Why isn't it working?"

David sprang up. "For God's sake . . ."

"What, you fix image throwers now?"

"I *am* one."

David touched the screen with two fingers, then raised his other hand. The room lit up with a giant projection: a still-frame of a tall and elegant Indian woman.

Peter nodded uncomfortably at David. "Thank you. Now—"

"Who's the chick?" Hannah asked.

"Rebel's wife," David said. "I met her last year. She's not pleasant."

"Her name's Ivy Sunder," Peter explained. "She's more than Rebel's wife. She's the other leader of the crusade. I've been bitmailing her these past few months, trying to arrange a parley. She didn't respond until two days ago, when she sent me this spoolie."

Theo crossed his arms indignantly. "Amanda's right. You shouldn't have kept this from us."

"I had good cause. Now, I don't have time to play the whole thing and I'm not going to stop for questions. Just watch and listen."

He tapped his keyboard, unfreezing the playback. The camera followed

Ivy as she walked backward down a lavish hallway. Its marble walls were lined with decorations: paintings and sconces, murals and mirrors. From the length of the corridor alone, it seemed the place was a mansion.

"It breaks my heart that it's come to this, Peter. When I think about you, all I see is that sweet and skinny kid who used to chase me through the warrens. You were the only one who could ever go portal-for-portal with me. I miss those days."

Mia hated herself for finding Ivy attractive. She looked beautiful in her chiffon summer dress, and she spoke with a strong, crisp diction that radiated intelligence. How the hell was she married to a thug like Rebel?

Ivy stared at her audience with soulful brown eyes. "I hate what you're doing now. I hate what *I'm* doing. I think about all the friends I've lost, those six poor strangers who died in White Plains. It kills me what we had to do to those breachers. Their faces still haunt me at night."

Hannah peeked over her shoulder at the two surviving Golds. While Jonathan glowered at Ivy's image, Heath dipped his head with shuddering grief.

"We still don't believe in your plan to save the world," Ivy told Peter. "But now we're starting to wonder if maybe we've been wrong ourselves. God knows these breachers keep surprising us. We thought they were all in league with the Pelletiers."

She gripped the knob of a mahogany door. "But they're clearly no friend of Zack Trillinger. And he's obviously not a fan of them."

Hannah sucked a loud gasp as the door opened to reveal Zack. He sat in an office study, his hands cuffed to the arms of a wooden chair. Tall, humming generators flanked him on all sides, suppressing his power with a solic field.

Zack took a brief, miserable look at the camera before lowering his head. Ivy moved behind him and gripped his shoulders. "He was beaten and half-starved when he found him," she said to the camera. "He told us who tortured him but he won't tell us why."

Amanda leaned forward, her eyes drenched in tears. Though Zack was dressed in clean clothes and showed no visible signs of abuse, she could clearly see the trauma in his eyes. He was barely holding on to his sanity.

"The restraints are just a precaution," Ivy insisted. "As you know, there's bad blood between him and my husband. But the two of them had a good conversation this morning. They hate the Pelletiers more than they hate each other. And they both have a vested interest in seeing the Earth survive."

Ivy crouched down to Zack's level and addressed him in a soft, earnest voice. "If it turns out we were wrong, would you forgive us for our mistakes?"

Zack closed his eyes and nodded. David could feel every ounce of his humiliation. This was pure theater and Zack knew it. But his life depended on playing along.

"And if we're right?" Ivy asked him. "If we offered solid proof that you breachers have to die in order to save this world?"

Zack raised his head with forced dignity, his hooded eyes fixed on the camera. "Well, then I would, in the immortal words of Admiral Ackbar, greet the reaper with a smile."

Theo's and Heath's eyes bulged in synch. "Shit . . ."

Hannah looked at Theo. "What?"

Peter shushed them. "Wait."

Ivy led the cameraman back into the hallway. "He's an interesting one, that Trillinger. I don't believe everything he says, especially about his Earth being egg-shaped, but he has made us question everything we know about the breachers. If it's true that we have a common enemy, and if it's true we have a similar goal, then we might be able to work together after all."

Peter narrowed his eyes at her. "Here it comes."

"Here's what's going to happen now, Peter. On Sunday, I'll text you the address of a meeting location. You'll have two hours to get there. The elders have already sworn us to an oath of armistice. As long as none of you attack us, we can't attack you. We'll return your friend, alive and well, and then we'll see if we can work out a truce. If not, we'll part ways peacefully and save our fight for another day."

Her expression turned severe. "You can understand why, after all your betrayals, we need to be firm with you, Peter. If you're late, or if you leave any of the breachers behind, we'll take that as an act of bad faith. And then we'll have no choice but to respond. I don't have to tell you what that means for Zack."

Mia covered her mouth. Amanda's hands crusted over with tempis. "No . . ."

"I hope you make the right choice," Ivy said to Peter. "For once."

The screen went black. David cleared the lumic projection. Everyone in the room turned their nervous eyes to Peter.

"Before you get your hopes up," he began, "you should know that—"

"It's a trap," Heath blurted.

Theo nodded his head in tense agreement. "He's right. Zack was trying to warn us."

"How?" Amanda asked.

"Admiral Ackbar's a character from *Return of the Jedi*. He barely has any lines but one of them's a classic. It was a running joke on the Internet."

"What's the line?"

"'It's a trap,'" Heath said.

"'It's a trap,'" Theo echoed.

Peter blew a hot breath at the floor. "It's most definitely a trap."

The room went silent. Hannah cocked her head at Peter. "So all that stuff about the truce . . ."

"Malarkey," he said. "I see right through her. She hasn't changed her mind. She wants you all dead. Even if it doesn't save the world, it's a blow to the Pelletiers. That's good enough for her and Rebel."

"So what happens now?" Mia asked. "What do we do when she sends the address?"

"She already sent it," Peter admitted. "I got it ten minutes ago."

Amanda shot to her feet. *"What?"*

"Listen to me—"

"We have to get Zack!"

"Amanda—"

"If we don't go, they'll kill him!"

"Amanda, he might already be dead."

The others paused, horrified. Peter sat down on the sofa, then clutched Amanda's arm. "The trap's been baited. They don't need Zack anymore. Then again, they might keep him alive just to give our augur something to look at. I don't know."

"I don't care," Amanda snapped. "If you're wrong—"

"Just listen to me, okay? There's a better way—"

"No." The objection came from David this time. Peter looked to him, exasperated. "You won't even hear me out?"

"I don't need to. You're about to propose some unilateral rescue effort that risks nobody's life but yours. Ordinarily I'd be fine with that, except I was there the last time you tried to save Zack from Rebel. It didn't go well."

Peter gritted his teeth. "Boy, you don't know half as much as you think you do."

"He knows plenty," Amanda said. "If Zack and I had listened to him, we wouldn't be in this mess. I'm not making that mistake again. And I won't let you throw your life away on some stupid act of chivalry."

"It's not chivalry, it's—"

"Dumb," Hannah said. "You *need* us, Peter. Everyone sees it but you."

He shot to his feet. "Goddamn it! You're playing right into Ivy's hands! This is exactly what she wants."

"What do you expect us to do?" Theo asked. "Let Zack die?"

"*You're* not doing anything," Peter said. "I'll bring the others before I bring you."

"He's my friend!"

"I don't care. Your only job is to stay alive and find that string."

Theo opened his mouth to object, but he could see from the looks on his friends' faces that they were with Peter on this one.

Hannah clasped his hand. "He's right. You're too important."

"And you're all fogged up anyway," Amanda added. "You won't be able to help us."

"I can still help."

Mia shook her head. "If Zack were here, you know what he'd say."

Peter snorted. "Glad you feel that way, darling, because you're not going either."

"What?"

"The others at least have a chance to protect themselves. You can't even make a working portal."

"Then give me a gun!"

David looked at her despondently. "The last time you faced Rebel, he nearly killed you."

"But he *didn't*," Mia said. "Zack saved me. Now you're telling me I can't save him back?"

The heavy faces of her companions told her everything she needed to know. "That's all I am to you. Just dead weight."

"Of course not," said Amanda. "We love you."

"But you don't believe in me."

"Mia . . ."

"Fine. Go." She wiped her eyes, then fled into the foyer. "But you better goddamn save him."

The others stayed silent as she disappeared up the stairwell. Her slammed door echoed through the house.

Peter's gaze shifted gravely between Hannah and David. "I suppose I can't talk either of you out of going."

"No," said David.

"Hell no," said Hannah.

Jonathan fidgeted with his T-shirt, still damp with soapy water. "I'll go."

Heath stared at him in horror. "What? No!"

"You don't have to do this," Hannah said.

"Heath and I would be dead if it wasn't for Josh Trillinger. The least I can do is help save his brother. And as it stands, I like Zack."

Heath tugged his arm. "Don't go! Please."

"You stay here with Theo and Mia. You'll be all right."

"No we won't!"

Amanda looked at the wall clock. "We're wasting time."

Peter nodded. "We leave in ten minutes. Do whatever you need to get ready."

While the others filed out of the living room, Peter asked Amanda to stay behind. She studied the many bandages on his arms, her face racked with guilt.

"I'm sorry about that, Peter. I . . . lost my head."

"I know. That's what worries me. I can't stop you from coming, but you have to pull yourself together. If Zack's dead, or if they kill him in front of us—"

"Don't say that."

"—we can't have any more friendly fire."

Amanda looked down at her fumbling hands. When her emotions ran wild, she was a danger to everyone around her. Even now in the haze of her sedatives, she could feel the tempis waking up. Soon it would be pounding against the bars of its cage, screaming to be released.

"I won't hurt you again," she promised Peter. "Any of you."

"Good to hear." He grabbed a dangling lock of Amanda's hair and tucked it behind her ear. "You realize this is all but a suicide mission. They know our tricks. They're ready for us."

"What choice do we have?"

"You could still let me handle it on my own. Quietly. Diplomatically."

"There's nothing quiet or diplomatic about your people."

"Look—"

"No. Those bastards have hurt us time and time again. It ends today. And I'll tell you something else. If we get there and Zack's dead, or if they kill him in front of us, it won't be my people who need to worry about me."

Amanda brushed past him, then made a hard line up the stairs.

"I'll kill every last Gotham I see."

At eleven o'clock, the rescuers assembled. They looked deceptively normal in their blue jeans and sneakers, their faded gray sweatshirts and bargain-bin windbreakers. They might have passed for Sunday strollers if it wasn't for their more conspicuous adornments. Peter and David each carried a .38 pistol in a belt holster. Hannah had strapped two billy clubs to her legs. Amanda wore a paramedic bag over her shoulder. Jonathan only had himself to bring.

Theo watched from the far side of the garage, his foot tapping a restless beat. Though his foresight remained lost in an impenetrable fog, he couldn't shake his ominous feeling, as if everyone's fate had already been decided. Surely the Pelletiers knew what would happen when they brought to Zack to Rebel. But what did they have to gain by war?

As the sky door opened on rumbling metal wheels, Peter pushed a manila envelope into Theo's hands. "There's thirty thousand dollars in there, plus directions to an apartment in Jersey. If we're not back by sunset, take Heath and Mia and stay there. You remember where the spare van's parked?"

Theo nodded tensely. "I do, but—"

Peter tapped the envelope. "There's something in there for Mia. A note. Don't let her read it till you know I'm dead."

"Jesus. Peter . . ."

"Whatever happens, you keep safe. If you die, we all do. You understand me?"

"I get it. Just be careful."

Jonathan peeked into his bedroom and saw Heath perched on a pair of wooden boxes, his nervous gaze fixed out the window. He turned to Theo.

"He'll be a handful. Just be patient, all right? He's a good kid at heart."

"We'll be okay," Theo assured him.

Amanda checked David's watch. "Fifty minutes."

"Let's go," Peter said.

As her sister and the others climbed into the Peregrine, Hannah hurried over to Theo and gave him a hug. "We'll be back," she promised him. "All of us. Even the funny one."

Theo smiled weakly. "I'm counting on it."

The van doors closed. Peter started the engine. The Peregrine had barely risen a foot off the ground before Mia rushed up the stair ladder and ran to the driver's door. She'd changed into a track top and jogging pants, a knit cap and sneakers. A bookbag dangled in her grip.

Peter rolled down the window, scowling. "Sweetheart, I told you—"

"Bug!"

"What?"

"There'll be a swifter named Bug, a lumic named Mink, a tempic named Jinn, and a solic named Mercy. There'll also be an air brake you have to pull. I'm not sure what that means but I got two different warnings about it. It must be important."

The sisters and Jonathan traded uneasy looks. Mia kept her hard eyes on Peter. "You said I couldn't make a working portal. I just made *two hundred* of them."

She'd spent the last ten minutes opening the floodgates of her mind, filling her bedroom with the portals of Future Mias. She'd only had time to read a fraction of their notes.

Mia opened her bookbag and showed Peter her messy collection of paper scraps. "There's a lot more in here. You can take them all with you, but I'm your best chance at interpreting them."

Peter eyed her skeptically. "Those other Mias hate you. How can you trust them?"

"Because they love Zack. They won't do anything to hurt him."

"Darling . . ."

"You're walking into a trap and you don't even have an augur! You *need* me."

Peter tapped his fingers against the steering wheel, thinking.

"An air brake," he said.

"An air brake," Mia echoed.

Peter muttered a curse, then lowered the Peregrine back to the ground. Mia closed up her bag and ran around to the side door.

"I'll watch over her," David assured Peter. "I won't let anyone hurt her."

Peter didn't know whether to laugh or cry. A sixteen-year-old pledging the safety of a fourteen-year-old. *Lambs to the slaughter,* he thought.

As the Peregrine ascended through the roof of the brownstone, Jonathan peeked down at the street. Heath's dreaded yellow moving truck remained double-parked down the road, its rear gate closed and not a soul in the vicinity. The whole damn street seemed eerily devoid of people.

Hannah caught his troubled expression. "What's the matter?"

Jonathan thought about it a moment, then anxiously shook his head. "Nothing. It's all right."

A hundred feet below them, at the far end of the Transpac trailer, Gingold watched the Peregrine through a surveillance camera. He scowled into his headset.

"I want a shadow on that junker. Don't let it see you and don't let it out of your sight."

He'd been six minutes away from staging a full-blown takedown—twenty-four operatives hiding all around the residence, each one armed with four different kinds of weapons. If that wasn't enough to tip the scales, a solic wasp was coming that would all but guarantee a bloodless victory. These freaks were nothing without their temporis.

But the wasp had yet to arrive, and now the fugitives were leaving. Gingold didn't think for a moment that the timing was coincidence. Someone must have tipped them off. The augur or—

"Sir?"

He turned to look at his imaging analyst. She directed his attention to her thermal scan monitor, at the humanoid orange shapes on the top floor. "They left two behind."

"What?"

Gingold leaned in closer and studied the silhouettes. The boyish figure was unfamiliar to him but he easily recognized the other one. Only one man in the group stood shorter than six feet.

"Maranan."

This was a baffling development. The fugitives were deadly but they weren't callous. They'd never abandon two of their own unless—

—they don't know, said a blithe little voice in Gingold's head. *Even Maranan doesn't know you're here.*

"Sir, how do you want to proceed?" asked Tomlinson, his second-in-command. "Should we—"

"Shut up. Let me think."

Gingold tapped the cleft of his chin, his camera eyes locked on Theo. He didn't like improvising, but a golden opportunity had just presented itself. He figured if Sun Tzu had known about augurs, the old general might have added a tenet to his *Art of War: "Never pass up the chance to take one by surprise."*

He hailed the agents on his network. "All right, folks. We had nine targets. Now we have two. Don't get cocky. Stick to the plan and be ready for anything."

Gingold signaled to Tomlinson. The truck's rear gate opened. Gingold prepped his automatic rifle and took a long, hard look at the brownstone.

"Move in."

TWELVE

The sky hatch closed with an echoing *thud*, throwing the whole garage back into shadow. Theo suddenly felt a vague sense of panic, as if his friends were flying in the wrong direction or had forgotten something crucial. Should he find his phone and call them? Or was he just being—

"Hello, Theo."

—paranoid?

He spun a half turn, puzzled. The voice had come from the edge of his consciousness, an aural premonition that vanished as quickly as it came. Theo closed his eyes and put his ear to the future, listening to the voices in the fog. Though most of the chatter was incomprehensible, he could still draw a few snippets here and there.

". . . we're not raising gods or monsters here . . ."

". . . just saying there's a reason he wears a mask . . ."

". . . never seen David in love before. He looks so . . ."

". . . give us a week. We'll get your message out . . ."

". . . think I like doing this? You think I want Rebel to be right?"

". . . I'm afraid that Peter's done you a great disservice . . ."

"Hello, Theo."

His eyes popped open. There it was again: the low, husky voice of a woman. She sounded close, just minutes away. But who the hell was she?

Theo looked down at his manila envelope, filled with cash and contingency instructions. Peter had told him to wait until sunset, but he wondered if it might be wise to grab Heath now and get out of here.

"No!"

Theo followed the noise to Heath's attic bedroom, where the boy was scrambling around in a tizzy. He threw his sneakers on without tying them, grabbed his song sheets without sorting them, then slung Jonathan's electric guitar over his back.

"Heath, what—"

He rushed out the door. Theo chased him down the stair ladder. "Wait! What are you doing?"

"They're coming!"

"Who's coming?"

Heath turned around at the second floor and stared at Theo inscrutably. Even now, after nineteen days of living together, the two of them had yet to converse in any meaningful way. Theo wasn't equipped to handle Heath's complicated issues, and he was fairly sure the kid felt the same way about him.

He'd barely made it down the steps before Heath bolted again. "Wait!"

Rattled, Theo ran down the hallway and peeked out through the back window. Five men in tempic armor crept side by side across the patio, their rifles aimed at the kitchen door. Their sleek, tight helmets made their faces look creepy, like unfinished mannequins.

A cold fist squeezed Theo's heart. "Oh God."

Heath perched at the top of the second-floor landing, his wide eyes fixed on the front door.

"It's too late," he said. "They're here."

Oren Gingold was a perfectionist at heart, and had taken drastic measures to ensure a flawless operation. At nine A.M., Integrity agents began a systematic evacuation of the neighboring brownstones, escorting residents to a safe zone while jamming all civilian communication channels. Plainclothes operatives stood on every street corner to disinform the public. Even the police had been tricked into thinking there was a toxic spill on Humboldt Street.

By eleven o'clock, the half-mile radius around Peter's house had become a complete blackout zone. There were no reporters or witnesses, no aer traffic or camera drones. There was no law here but Integrity's. As far as Gingold was concerned, this little patch of Brooklyn was now hostile, foreign territory.

Ten snipers trained their crosshairs on the brownstone's main and rear exits, while sixteen gunmen advanced on the property from both sides. Gingold stopped at the front door and fired a small, cone-shaped weapon at the knob. The lock reversed itself with a click.

His thermal analyst hailed him from the Transpac trailer. "Sir, I'm picking up movement on the ground floor. No heat. Just . . . movement."

Gingold stashed his juve gun back in its holster. "Are the targets still upstairs?"

"They are, but I'm getting faint and amorphous readings down below. I'm not entirely sure what I'm looking at."

"Phipps, I don't have time for your nonsense. Is there something down-stairs or not?"

"It . . . might be a sensor error, sir."

Gingold readied his rifle, then pushed the door open a crack. "Follow my lead," he whispered into his headset. "And keep your heads. I don't want to see any . . ."

His face went slack. The foyer was packed with large tempic sculptures, twelve different versions of the same damn thing.

". . . dogs?"

One of the beasts sprang to life and tackled Gingold through the door-way, knocking him to the pavement and cracking one of his lenses.

Heath crouched at the top of the stairwell and wiped the sweat from his face. "They're not dogs."

Nothing could have prepared Theo for the sight of the wolves.

They came into existence as oversize larvae—twelve bean-shaped globs writhing mindlessly in the foyer. They rose from the floor on sprouted legs, then shook themselves until their bodies gained definition—paws and nails, muzzles and tails. Dull, pupilless eyes ballooned inside their sockets. Their white skins rippled with the simulated texture of fur.

All of this happened in the span of three seconds. By the time Theo breathed again, Heath's creatures had gone to war.

They spilled through the front door with coordinated haste, each one moving with a shocking degree of realism. Theo couldn't even imagine the number of nature specials Heath must have watched to capture them so flaw-lessly. Though his wolves looked as fake as giant soap carvings, they were just as nimble as real wolves. But were they just as fierce?

Awful noises drifted in through the front door: shouts and gunfire, a panicked scream. Theo turned to Heath, wide-eyed. "Are they . . . ?"

"No," he replied through a grunt of strain. "We only hurt. We never kill."

Theo didn't care about the fate of the soldiers. He was more worried about Heath. If the government found him dangerous enough, they wouldn't waste time capturing him. They'd shoot him dead on sight.

Theo peeked over his shoulder at the rear hall window. "There are five more coming in from the back."

"Six," said Heath.

"What?"

"Hang on."

Heath closed his eyes and shot six new dollops of tempis into the foyer. By the time Theo looked down the stairwell, the wolves had reached full size and made a synchronized dash for the kitchen.

Theo studied Heath in gobsmacked awe. The boy had eighteen different minions moving independently of each other, all battling government soldiers he couldn't possibly see. How the hell was he doing this? How long could he keep it up?

"We have to get out of here," Theo said. "There's a van three blocks away. The keys are in the kitchen."

He turned to see that Heath wasn't listening. His eyes were shut tight. He flinched and shrieked with invisible pains, as if someone was stabbing a voodoo doll of him.

"Heath! Are you okay?"

He shook his head, crying. "They're *shooting* them!"

Last October, during a particularly bloody battle against the Gothams, Amanda had stopped two bullets with a tempic shield. She later told Theo that each shot was excruciating, like having her brain stabbed with hot knitting needles. Now Heath was taking dozens of rounds.

Theo rubbed his back. "All right. Just hold on. Hang in there."

He scanned the foyer, then pulled Heath to his feet. With his foresight still hobbled, he had no idea if he was leading them into a hail of gunfire. All he knew was that they had to get out of here, and fast.

"Okay," Theo said. *"Now."*

They ran down the stairs and turned toward the kitchen. Theo glanced over his shoulder at the battle on the street. Each wolf had an enemy pinned down or jaw-locked, their paws and teeth hopelessly fused with soldiers' tempic armor.

Theo pulled Heath along. "Come on. We're—"

A wolf leapt from the kitchen and slammed Theo against the wall. Its teeth gnashed dangerously close to his face.

"No!" Heath yelled. "Not him! Not him!"

The wolf shot a peevish look at its creator before rejoining the battle in the backyard. Heath balked at the shallow gash on Theo's chest.

"Sorry. That's Rose. She doesn't always listen to me."

"What?"

"Let's go."

Theo brushed the blood from his wound, then snatched the keys from a wall hook. He looked through the back door and saw a half-dozen agents wrestling Heath's tempic creatures. The kid was right to make six wolves, not five. But how did he know?

It's their tempis, Theo realized. *He can feel the soldiers through their armor.*

A whizzing bullet struck Rose in the head. Heath screamed and dropped his song sheets.

Theo pulled him away from the door, then took a careful look outside. Someone else was shooting at the wolves. The government had snipers on the rooftops, out of sight. Out of reach.

Gingold was the first to catch on to Heath's ethics. The wolf that kept him pinned to the concrete had passed up every opportunity to rip out his throat. The moment Gingold stopped fighting, the creature stopped baring its teeth. It sat lazily on top of him, meeting his cracked black lenses with a dead white stare.

"Everyone stay still," Gingold ordered. "These things aren't lethal. Snipers, hold your fire. Save your shots."

A sharpshooter hailed him through his earpiece. "Sir, what about you?"

"We'll be all right. Just—"

A large shadow washed over him. Gingold looked up to see a remotely piloted aercraft hovering twenty feet above him, a man-size drone that crudely resembled a wasp. It floated through the sky on humming wings of aeris, its long-barreled energy cannon pointing down at the street.

At long last, their solic weapon had arrived.

"Finally," yelled Gingold. "Shoot these goddamn wolves."

Theo rummaged through the cabinets, looking for something—anything—that could help them out of their jam. As long as the snipers were still out there, he and Heath were trapped. They wouldn't even make it to the back-yard fence before getting riddled with bullets.

But there was nothing in the kitchen that was even remotely useful. Their only hope was tempis, which meant their only hope was Heath.

"Listen . . ."

Theo knelt in front of him and swallowed the urge to call him "buddy." "We're all out of moves. We only have one chance to get out of here. We're going to need more wolves. Big ones. As big as elephants."

Heath creased his sweaty brow. "They don't get as big as elephants."

"It's your tempis. They can be whatever you want them to be."

He tensely shook his head. "We can't ride them."

"I'm not talking about riding them. Just trust me. Please."

Heath opened his mouth to say something, then doubled over in pain. The solic wasp was bathing the street in invisible bursts of energy, obliterating every local trace of tempis. The agents' white armor reverted to steel mesh and wire. The wolves in front of the house popped away like cheap balloons.

"They're killing them!" Heath cried.

Theo squeezed his shoulders. "You have no idea how sorry I am. But if these people get us, it's all over. Not just for us. For everyone."

He closed his eyes, then finally spoke the words that had been dominating his life for the last seven months.

"I'm the only one who can save this world."

Theo felt ridiculous for saying it, and even dumber for believing it. All he had to go by was the word of Peter Pendergen, a man who practically flaunted his fallibility. Even if Peter was right, there was no guarantee that they could stop the death that was coming. They had nothing to work with but desperate guesses and wishful thinking.

But the hope had a power all to itself.

Heath looked at Theo, his hazel eyes full of surprise, skepticism, and something else Theo couldn't put his finger on. Was it gratitude? He could only imagine that Heath had spent his whole life being treated like an infirmity, a burden to his family and everyone else around him. Now here he was getting a seat at the big table, the fate of the whole world in his hands. He'd been struggling all this time without a clear sense of purpose. Well, now he had one.

Heath looked out the patio door, his fingers drumming against his hip.

"Okay," he told Theo. "I know what to do."

Gingold stormed into the foyer, his body covered in naked wire mesh. Though the solic wasp had fried his tempic armor, his assault rifle worked just fine. Good thing, too, because he was seriously itching to shoot someone.

He waved his team through the front door, ignoring their uncomfortable stares. Moments ago, he'd peeled away the cracked glass fragments that protected his eye cameras. Now everyone could see the bionic wizardry he'd been hiding: four black-button lenses that advanced and retracted of their own accord. They made him look like something out of a nightmare, an unholy union of man and arachnid.

Gingold was halfway through the living room when he heard a loud *crunch* from the back of the house. By the time he and his crew reached the kitchen, the entire rear wall had been smashed into shards. The soldiers looked beyond the wreckage. Their rifles fell limp at their sides.

"You gotta be fourping kidding me."

Even in Heath's vivid imagination, there was no such thing as giant wolves. It simply wasn't done. If Theo wanted animals that were as big as elephants, there was only one proper way to indulge him.

Four tempic pachyderms charged across the grass in a close diamond formation. Theo crouched in the middle of the cluster, holding Peter's envelope in one hand and Heath's wrist in the other. Though the beasts shielded them from the snipers, as Theo had hoped, there was nothing to protect Heath from his sympathetic bond to his creations. His mind stood exposed in four easy targets.

A sniper shot hit an elephant in the ear. Heath screamed and stumbled. His tempis rippled in distress.

Gingold raised his rifle at the rearmost elephant. "Keep firing!" he ordered. "And get that damn wasp—"

A wolf leapt out from behind the shrubs and sank its teeth into Gingold's wrist. Though Heath had vanquished his tempic hounds, the one named Rose Tyler insisted on staying. She was the bad wolf of the pack, and she was having too much fun.

Theo pulled Heath along. "We have to keep moving."

He swallowed a delirious laugh as he stepped over the fragments of the backyard's wooden fence. He was running through Brooklyn in a herd of tempic elephants, the mighty Snuffleupagi of a boy's creative mind. In a crowded field, this might have seized the trophy as the single most surreal moment of his life.

He heard an odd hum behind him and glanced over his shoulder. A sinister-looking drone rose above the roof of the brownstone, a six-foot hornet made of gunmetal and aeris. He recognized the long, ribbed protrusion that served as its stinger. The Deps had used something similar last year to breach a tempic barrier.

His eyes bulged. "Oh no . . ."

The wasp spun around and aimed its solic cannon at Rose Tyler. It blew her to oblivion with a single shot.

Theo tugged Heath's arm. "Run! Hurry!"

He peeked between elephants and saw a basement hatch at the end of the brownstone block, just fifty yards away. An inner voice urged him on. *It's open. It's unlocked. Go!*

"To the right," he told Heath. "Steer them right."

Theo felt a gust of wind at the back of his ankle. A sharpshooter was aiming at the four human legs that scurried between the elephants.

Heath clutched his brow and stumbled. "Hang on," Theo urged. "We're almost there."

Gingold seethed at the bloody state of his wrist. That last damn wolf must have opened an artery. He tore a tourniquet from his shirt and yelled into his headset. "Snipers, hold your fire! Line up your shot and wait for the wasp."

Theo threw his frenzied gaze between the drone and the basement hatch. They were moments away from losing their cover and they still had thirty yards to go.

"Head shots," Gingold told his snipers. "Don't take any chances."

Twenty yards. Theo shoved the rump of the lead elephant. *Come on. Go. Go!*

At seven and a half yards, the wasp made its final sting. Everything within forty feet of Theo and Heath was doused in solis. A backyard trasher spit a dying hiss of sparks. A four-foot ceramic Jesus, some neighbor's idea of a tasteful Easter decoration, lost its lumic radiance.

The elephants were gone.

"Now!" Gingold shouted.

Theo's heart stopped. *No . . .*

He leapt for the hatch just as the snipers took their shots. Two of the bullets hit the brick of the brownstone. Another two sliced the grass by Theo's feet.

The fifth one hit Heath square in the back.

Had he not been wearing Jonathan's guitar, the bullet would have torn right through him. Instead it shattered the instrument at the wooden base, severing all strings before driving sharp fragments into the small of Heath's back. He stumbled forward with a howl. Theo threw open the hatch, cringing as he dragged Heath down the steps. The snipers were still firing. There was no time to be gentle.

Theo pulled Heath inside the basement, locked the door, then crouched to examine him. The back of Heath's shirt was dripping with blood. His eyes were red and drooped with fatigue.

"Did I . . ."

"It's all right." Theo rubbed his arm. "You're all right."

"Did I do okay?"

Theo squeezed Heath's shoulder and forced a weak smile, while his inner self screamed with fury. He wanted to kill all the bastards who were responsible for Heath's agony, all the soldiers and snipers who'd put this amazing boy through war.

"You did more than okay," Theo told Heath. "You're a goddamn hero."

The basement was as conventional as any Theo had seen, a dusty mausoleum of old boxes and knickknacks. A Vertech washer sang a musical chime. The owner had started a reversal load right before Integrity evacuated him. Now the machine waited patiently for him to return.

Theo looked at the stairs, his instincts howling in panic. It wouldn't be long before the Integrity goons came charging down here. "We have to keep moving. You okay to go?"

Heath cringed at the remnants of Jonathan's guitar, then examined himself in a panic. "My song sheets! I dropped them!"

"It's all right."

"All that music . . ."

"It's still in your head. You can get it all back."

Theo opened the washer and rooted through the clothes. He tossed Heath a baseball cap and an oversize denim jacket, then snagged a newsboy cap for himself. "Come on."

While Humboldt Street had become a veritable ghost town, Jewel Street teemed with life. All the displaced residents had been forcibly gathered here. They hobnobbed on the street, trading nervous gossip with one another while accosting anyone who looked like they had information. *Is it safe to go home? How toxic is this spill? Can I at least go back and get my handphone?*

A policewoman noticed Theo and Heath as they emerged from a brownstone. "Hey!"

Theo kept a tight arm around Heath. *Shit. Shit.*

"Stay out of your home until we tell you it's safe."

"Sorry," Theo said. "I'm sorry."

"If I catch you again, I'm writing you up."

Theo apologized again, and then hurried into the crowd. He feared it'd be moments before Integrity agents burst through the front door and showed a photo of him to the policewoman.

He squeezed Heath's hand. "The van's not far. Hang in there."

The boy let out a miserable moan. They pushed through the bystanders, bowing their heads as Integrity operatives patrolled above on aerocycles. Theo wished to God he'd grabbed his handphone on the way out. He had to warn Hannah and the others that Integrity was on their tail.

After two more blocks, Theo broke away from the crowd and led Heath into a SmartFeast parking lot. Peter's spare white Peregrine rested at the far edge, its windshield covered in dust and ad flyers. Theo hoped he remembered how to pilot the damn thing. It had been four months since he'd practiced.

He unlocked the passenger door and helped Heath inside. The boy let out a sharp cry as he leaned against the seat.

"I'll patch you up as soon as we're safe," Theo promised.

"Where are we going?"

Theo rifled through the contents of Peter's contingency envelope. "Old Tappan. It shouldn't take . . ."

His mouth fell open in sudden realization. If Integrity ran the license plate on Peter's aerovan, they'd know the fake name it was registered under, along with the vehicle IDs of all his other Peregrines. All it would take was one smart agent to run a locational trace—

Heath's eyes went wide. "No!"

Something hard pressed against Theo's back. He raised his hands, his wide eyes locked on the aerovan. He saw a familiar face in the reflection of the window, as sharp and lovely as ever.

Of course, he thought bleakly. *Of course it'd be her.*

Melissa Masaad caught his gaze in the glass. She pressed the gun tighter, then gave him a serene smile. "Hello, Theo."

THIRTEEN

Earlier that morning, as Peter was teleporting home to Brooklyn, his phone lit up with a single-word text message. Ivy knew that her fellow traveler, the love of her youth, wouldn't need a full address to find her. One name was all it took to light a path of torches across the face of New York, to the site of their final battle.

Atropos.

The building stood thirty miles north of the city, in a small and wealthy suburb on the Westchester side of the Hudson. The village had been known as North Tarrytown until 1996, when the name was changed to Sleepy Hollow in honor of the famous Washington Irving story that took place there. By strange coincidence, the same thing had happened on the Silvers' native world in the exact same year. Sometimes the two Earths had moved in perfect rhythm with each other, as if their histories had never split.

Peter broke away from the Pocantico Skyway and flew the Peregrine toward the river. No one in the van had spoken for minutes, not since Mia finished sharing the words and "wisdom" of her future selves. Of a hundred and eighty-six notes, only nine offered intel about the trials ahead of them. The rest were either too vague, too irrelevant, or too noxious to read aloud.

The Peregrine stopped a hundred feet above the edge of Sleepy Hollow. Peter stared out the windshield at the structure in the distance.

"There it is," he said.

His passengers leaned forward and studied their destination, a tortoiseshell complex of glass and steel that looked way too large to be a business office. Hannah figured it was a megamall. Mia assumed it was a stadium of some sort. Only Amanda guessed its true nature from its numerous launching pads. They graced the upper dome like a crown of roses.

"It's an aerport."

Peter nodded. "Atropos National."

Jonathan scanned the empty sky. There were no flights departing or arriving, no cars in the parking lot. Not even the hints of a skeleton crew.

"Dead as hell," he noted. "Is it closed for Easter?"

"Closed for good," Peter said. "Died last year in the cutbacks."

"You've been here before."

"Yeah. Ivy and I used to come here in our younger days, when it was still under construction. At night, we had the whole place to ourselves. It was like a playground for teleporters."

Amanda narrowed her eyes at him. Peter was waxing nostalgic about the woman who may have already slit Zack's throat. "We're wasting time. What's the plan?"

"The plan is we go in."

David eyed him skeptically. "No portals. No tunnels. Just walk right in through the front door."

"Yes."

"Yes," Mia echoed.

The others turned to look at her. She raised a paper scrap in her fingers, the first of nine pertinent notes.

It doesn't matter which way you go in. The Gothams are prepared for every choice you make. They're very, very ready for you.

Peter gestured at the main entrance, the only one that wasn't boarded up with plywood. "She's right. Rebel's an augur. He'll see us coming no matter what we do."

"Then what's to stop him from blowing us out of the sky right now?" Jonathan asked.

"Bigger fish."

"What?"

David understood. "Rebel's not just after us. He wants Azral and Esis too. He's laying a trap for all of us."

Hannah frowned at him. "The Pelletiers got us into this mess. What makes you think they'll show up now?"

"It's not what I think. It's what Rebel and Ivy think."

"I don't care," Amanda said. "Let them come. Let them kill each other. I just want Zack."

"We'll get him," Peter assured her. "But he's still a hostage, so we have to tread carefully. If there's talking to be done, you let me do it. And if it comes down to fighting . . ."

Amanda caught his edgy look. She stared down miserably at her hands. She'd been stressing nonstop about Future Mia's warning, the one that called her out by name:

Watch Amanda closely. She's an atom bomb right now, and the Gothams know just how to set her off.

Peter sighed at the windshield, then shifted the Peregrine back into gear. "Just stay alert," he told everyone. "This is gonna get messy."

Walking into Atropos was like stepping into the throat of a dying dragon. The glass dome turned the entire structure into a hothouse, an unfortunate design choice that had forced the administrators to run the air conditioners eleven months out of the year. Now the fan blades slept beneath a blanket of dust, and the air was thick with heat and mildew. Mia nearly gagged at the fetid taste in her mouth.

You signed up for this, she reminded herself. *You don't get to complain now.*

The entry was lined with bresin sheets and wooden scaffolding, a path of human cobwebs that only grew narrower. Peter asked David to scan the recent past for traps. The boy obliged him with a courteous nod, as if he hadn't been doing that all along.

After sixty feet, the corridor opened up to a huge and dusty mezzanine. The left and right pathways were sealed off with plywood barriers. The only way forward was to go down a dormant escalator, into the shadowy lower concourse.

David squinted suspiciously at the wooden obstructions. "These are less than a day old."

"They're leading us like cattle," Amanda said. "We should make our own path."

Peter shook his head. "Not yet."

"Why not?"

"Because they're leading us to them," he replied. "That's just where Zack will be."

He clutched David's arm and jerked his head at the escalator. "Scan the area below. Just your hindsight. Don't go too far." He turned to the sisters. "Watch his back."

Mia wandered toward a wall mural, a painting of three ancient Greek women toiling on a skein of yarn. Their faces were lovely in a cold, austere way. They were just how Mia imagined Esis to look.

Peter moved behind her and studied the image. "The old governor of New York was a nut for Greek mythology. When he approved the construction of three aerports in Westchester, his only demand was that they be named after the Moirae. You know who they are?"

Mia nodded. "The goddess sisters of Fate."

"That's right. Clotho weaves the threads. Lachesis measures the length of each person's life. And Atropos—"

"—does the cutting," Mia finished.

Peter smiled. "You never fail to impress, darling."

"Then why do you keep things from me?"

"What?"

She retrieved a slip of a paper from her pocket and held it up to him. He plucked it from her fingers.

Merlin McGee's real name is Michael Pendergen. There's a lot Peter's not telling you.

Scowling, he crumpled up the message. Mia kept her stony gaze on the Fates. "You said he was one of your people. You never told us he was family. What is he, your brother?"

Peter sighed over her head. "Not by blood. We're just two Irish street rats who grew up together. When the clan took us in, we chose a new name for ourselves, a variation on Pendragon." He snorted with dark humor. "We do love the Arthurian handles."

Mia wasn't even remotely amused. "So Pendergen isn't even your real name."

"It's the realest name I ever had."

"You've had seven months to let us get to know you."

"You *do* know me," Peter insisted. "I may keep things close to the vest, but I never lied to you and I never will."

He dropped his hands on her shoulders, his eyes fixed on the long shears of Atropos. "We're travelers, sweetheart. You and I are linked. One of these days, when you're strong enough, you'll look inside my head and see exactly what you mean to me."

Mia's expression softened. She supposed she was being a hypocrite. Seven months together and she never told him that her father's name was Peter.

"We found something," Amanda called.

Peter and Mia joined the others at the rail of the mezzanine. David flicked his hand at the shadows down below. A circle of light appeared and formed a twenty-foot ring around the base of the escalator.

"There's some kind of machine down there," David said. "I don't know what it does but they went out of their way to hide it."

Peter clenched his fists. "Son of a bitch."

"What is it?" Jonathan asked.

"A tempic barrier."

Amanda's brow wrinkled. "How is that a problem? It's flat on the floor. It's not even on."

"That's exactly the problem," Peter said. "When you remove all the safety measures, the thing becomes a guillotine. They could've cut us all off at the ankles."

Hannah reeled at the thought of it. "Assholes."

"And cowards," David added. "I expected more from Rebel."

"So did I," said Peter. He raised his voice at the ceiling. "We didn't come here looking for a fight! We just want our friend back. No one has to die today. *Talk* to us."

A hundred yards away, in a boarded-up restaurant on the sunny side of the concourse, Rebel and Ivy listened to Peter through wireless speakers. They could have easily replied through the public address system, but there was no point. The foot trap was just a friendly hello. Their full response was coming.

The command center had once been a four-star kitchen. But the juves were long gone, the refrigerators had been resold, and there was nothing but grime where the ovens used to be. Only the stainless-steel countertops remained, all of them loaded with military-grade computer equipment. Ivy had stolen the devices from a DP-8 armory, along with some weapons and tactical armor. All it took was a pushcart and a portal to rob the Deps of their nicest toys.

Gemma worked her surveillance console from a bar stool, her field armor painstakingly altered to fit her tiny frame. She zoomed in on Amanda and watched with amusement as her tempic fists made short work of Rebel's tempic barrier.

"Smashy smashy," Gemma joked. "The redhead sure loves to break things."

Jinn Godden glowered at her from the neighboring workstation. "You said she's their weak link."

"She is. Patience, girl."

"You know how zizzy you sound when you call me that? I'm twice your age."

"You know how stupid you sound when you use words like 'zizzy'?"

"Quiet," said Deven Sunder, the swifter known as Bug. "Both of you."

He was the only one in the room who looked natural in Dep armor. Between his feathered black hair and his neatly trimmed beard, he might have passed for one of the Bureau's top directors. Only the fear in his eyes revealed how truly out of his element he was.

Bug looked at his twin sister. "I don't get why you're toying with these people. You have the firepower. You could kill them right now."

Ivy leaned against a pantry door, her hand clasping Rebel's. Like the rest of their crew, the two of them had come dressed for war. If everything went according to plan, they wouldn't see a moment of combat. And if things went south . . . well, Rebel and Ivy had prepared for that, too. They'd recorded detailed instructions for their chosen successors. They'd made love an hour ago like it was their very last time.

"We only have one chance to hit the Pelletiers," Ivy told Bug. "We're not going to waste it."

"You don't even know they'll be here."

"They'll be here," Rebel said. "They always come for the Silvers."

Gemma smiled at her father's smoldering indignation. Bug couldn't stand playing second fiddle to his brother-in-law, this ill-bred Jew from the lower houses. But what could he do? Rebel was the clan's big hero, the one who'd thrashed Esis within an inch of her life and exposed the limits of the Pelletiers' power. They weren't all-seeing and they weren't invulnerable. Now they had four solic cannons, three grenade launchers, and six mounted machine guns waiting for them in the concourse. Should those fail, Rebel had installed enough explosive charges to bring half of Atropos down on their heads. The demons weren't getting away this time, and neither were their pets.

Except there was already one of them who got away in advance.

"Where the hell is Maranan?" Rebel asked. "Makes no sense for them to come without their augur."

"Maybe he's guiding them by radio," Jinn offered.

Rebel shook his head. "Can't see the future through someone else's eyes."

"They don't need him," Gemma said. "The Pelletiers are giving them all the guidance they . . ."

Her eyes rolled back. She shuddered on her seat. Though Gemma's twitching spells never failed to unnerve her father, Rebel and Ivy welcomed them. That meant her older self was coming back from the future with fresh new intel.

Her convulsions stopped. Ivy held her by the shoulders. "You okay, sweetie? What did you see?"

Rebel smiled at the girl's savage grin. "The glass," he guessed.

"The glass," Gemma confirmed. "They're about to lose their wonder boy."

David proceeded carefully down a bulb-lit corridor, a rickety enclosure of plywood, tape, and nails. The concourse was teeming with these ramshackle constructions. There was no way across except through the maze. A quick scan of the past revealed its hasty creation: dozens of Gothams working tirelessly over the last forty-eight hours. While tempics hammered and swifters sawed, a team of lumics filled the upper dome with ghostly storm clouds. They were deliberately hiding something far above, as if Rebel had looked to the future and saw David looking back.

Clever, thought David. *He's not a complete idiot.*

Peter reached the corner and watched him nervously. "Don't stray too far, son."

David never failed to bristle whenever Peter called him "son." It was not an affectionate endearment, like the "sweetheart"s and "darling"s he lavished on Mia. It was just a vain man's way of reminding David who was in charge.

He tapped his fist against the roof boards. "We need Amanda to open up the ceiling."

Peter shook his head. "There could be trap triggers."

"Actually, I think the danger's higher."

"I'd rather not chance it."

David spun to face him, his face mottled with sweat. "Would you just *listen* to me for once?"

Amanda turned the corner and splintered the roof with a tempic punch. If recent mistakes had taught her anything, it was to always heed David's warnings. Always.

The Gothams followed their progress on the thermal scanner. While the sisters and Mia were easy to tell apart by silhouette, the men were all six feet tall and athletically built. Ivy could see one of them standing on the digital "X" that Gemma had marked for the glass trap. She squinted at his orange frame. "Is that Dormer?"

Gemma nodded her head, grinning. "Yeah. Just wait."

Rebel's eyes hardened at the image of David. The boy had killed one of his soldiers last year, and then threatened Ivy at gunpoint while she was still pregnant. The kid had earned his own special death.

"Drop it," he ordered Jinn.

"But the others aren't in range."

"I don't care. Do it. And get ready."

Jinn shifted into high speed, pressed a button on her console, and then gripped her weapon triggers. She had six gun turrets and five rocket cannons at her command, plus a lightning-fast reaction time. If the Pelletiers were coming to save David, they were in for a rude awakening.

A hundred small putty charges exploded on the roof of the aerport, each one strong enough to take out a support bolt. The noise was just a rumble to the Silvers down below. Nobody heard it in the din of Peter's and Amanda's shouting.

"Goddamn it! I told you to follow my lead!"

"You're not leading!" Amanda yelled. "*They* are!"

"You want to see Zack again?"

"Of *course* I do."

"Then stop acting rashly and start—"

"Look out!"

Everyone turned to Jonathan, whose wide eyes remained fixed on the ceiling. Mia craned her neck and gasped.

A hexagonal pane of glass had broken off from the dome: twelve feet wide and three inches thick. The explosions that freed it had filed away its edges, leaving sharp, jagged protrusions all around it.

By the time Hannah saw it, it was already halfway down to the concourse. She jumped into blueshift, just as Amanda threw a tempic canopy over everyone around her.

Only Peter caught her mistake. The glass wasn't coming at them. It was falling on the one person outside the shield.

"David!"

Hannah made a fevered dash for him but it was already too late. The glass fell edge-first into David's shoulder blade and then kept on going. Mia screamed in horror, her hands pressed over her mouth. The whole thing played like a slow-motion nightmare. And yet something . . .

"What?"

Something wasn't right. It took three seconds for everyone to realize that David was still alive and standing. The glass had cut right through him, yet he hadn't shed a drop of blood.

Hannah de-shifted in time to watch the last of the pane disappear. It vanished through the floor as if it was nothing but painted air.

While David stood in blinking stupor, the sisters, Mia, and Peter all slowly turned around.

Jonathan crouched motionless behind him, his arm raised high, his face red and sweaty. A trickle of blood dribbled out of his nose.

"Holy shit," he said through panting breaths. "It worked."

The Gothams in the kitchen fell silent. None of them had expected the guitarist to be much of a threat. In fact, they were amazed he still existed. Droppers were rare and tragic beings, children doomed by fate to die falling through the earth. Now here was a full-grown one, walking around without a tempic catchnet, wielding his curse like a superhero.

Ivy screamed and swept a keyboard off a countertop. The Pelletiers would never show up if their minions kept saving themselves.

Gemma shook her head, baffled. "That's not the way it happened. That's not what I saw."

"Just use the damn turrets already," Bug urged his sister. "The Pelletiers obviously aren't coming!"

Ivy grabbed Rebel by the shoulders, her eyes wide and frantic. "He's wrong, Richard. They're here. They're already here and they're *toying* with us. All of them!"

"Honey—"

She looked up at the ceiling, hang-jawed. "All of them."

"Ivy, wait."

She lunged into a portal and emerged two floors above, in a glass-domed terrace that could comfortably seat fifty. In better times, the place had been a scenic dining deck. Now every inch of window was covered by wooden panels. The main light in the room came from six floor lamps around the perimeter. A quartet of solic generators added a sickly blue glow to the center.

Mink Rosen flinched at Ivy's sudden entrance. He rose up from his chair and waved his hand. Radiant blue letters materialized in front of his chest.

WHAT'S HAPPENING? ARE THEY DEAD?

Ivy brushed past him, her eyes fixed on their prisoner. Zack sat on a folding chair between the solic generators, his hands shackled to the floor by long metal chains.

"This was a setup!" Ivy yelled. "You've been working with them all along!"

Zack stared at her, speechless. He'd been a hostage of the Gothams for two and a half days, an experience that served as a polar contrast to his time with the Pelletiers. Here, the seconds moved with fast-ticking fury. He rarely had a moment alone to think. His body churned with needs and discomforts, and he didn't have to worry about silly things like eternity. From the way the winds were blowing, he figured the rest of his life could be measured in minutes.

He forced an insolent sneer at Ivy, his lip still swollen from her last tantrum. Just as he'd learned that it was Azral, not Esis, who was the archvillain of the Pelletiers, it was Ivy, not Rebel, who was the true fanatic of the Gothams.

"'Working with them . . .'" Zack repeated. "If you mean who I think you mean—"

"You know *exactly* who I mean."

"Jesus." He let out a jagged laugh. "You get crazier by the hour."

Mercy Lee winced from the back of the room. She didn't have to be an augur to know that Zack was in for another fat lip. The only mystery was why he insisted on provoking an unhinged woman.

Ivy grabbed his collar. "Don't play games with me. Why did they send you to us? What are they planning?"

"I know therapy may seem like a big step, but with the right doctor—"

She slapped him across the face, then crouched at his side. "We only kept you alive to give the augur hope, but Theo's not here. Peter brought the baby traveler but he didn't bring the augur. Does that make sense to you?"

Try as he might, Zack couldn't hide his anguish. He'd guessed from all the Gothams' chatter that his friends had come to save him. They had no idea what they were walking into.

Ivy pulled her .22 pistol from her belt and ran the barrel down Zack's cheek. "I won't lie, Trillinger. There's nothing you can say that'll stop me from killing you. But if you tell me what Azral's planning—"

"I don't *know* what he's planning!"

"—I can end you quickly. Painlessly. I'll even extend the courtesy to your friends."

Zack dipped his head, scowling. "You won't. You're just as bad as them."

"As bad as your friends?"

"As bad as the Pelletiers!"

Mercy palmed her face. "For God's sake, Trillinger."

The elevator door opened. The eighth and final member of Rebel's team stepped onto the terrace. All Zack could see was his scrawny frame, his messy mop of sandy brown hair. He was a teenager, a stranger to Zack. So then why did he look familiar?

Ivy lowered her pistol. Her expression became soft again. "Honey, what are you doing? I told you to stay downstairs."

Unlike the others, the kid wasn't fully armored. He wore a tactical vest over a T-shirt and jeans. As he moved in closer, Zack noticed his gloves—long and thin and colored to match his skin tone. The kid clearly wasn't wearing them for protection. He was hiding something.

He jerked a nervous shrug. "I heard shouting. I just wanted to help."

"You will, Liam. I promise."

"Liam," Zack echoed. "Shit. Now I know where I've seen you. Your dad carries a photo of you in his wallet."

Liam Pendergen crossed in front of him, livid. Now that he was fully lit, Zack could see his resemblance to Peter. They had the same wide nose, the same sharp blue eyes. But where Peter's face was all hard lines and angles, Liam's features were soft and angelic. Only the rage in his eyes belied his innocence.

"He's not my dad. He stopped being that the minute he turned traitor."

Zack shook his head. "Liam, listen to me. You don't know the whole—"

"Save your breath," Ivy said. "He's too smart for your lies."

She looked to Mercy. "Take him downstairs. Keep him safe."

Mercy took Liam by the arm and walked him to the elevator. "Come on, kid."

They disappeared into the elevator together. Zack glared at Ivy. "You poisoned him against Peter."

"Peter poisoned him against Peter. He abandoned his one and only son for a group of alien strangers. How would you feel?"

"You know damn well why he did it."

"Oh, I know all about his delusions."

Zack laughed. "*His* delusions?"

"All this time, and you still think you're the good guys."

"Compared to you, we're the goddamn Justice League."

Ivy pressed the gun against his face, grinding his teeth through his cheek. "Stop lying and tell me what Azral and Esis are up to." She cocked her pistol. "You're a visual man. Try to imagine what will happen if you shoot your mouth off again."

Zack's heart hammered. "I don't know what they're planning!"

"Yes you do!"

"I hate them as much as you do!"

"Really? Did they kill *your* children? Did they murder *your* babies in the womb?"

"Ivy."

She turned around and saw Rebel at the top of the stairwell. She stumbled toward him. "We have no reason to keep him alive!"

"Yes we do." Rebel approached her and pulled her into his arms. "He's got one more role to play. Just stick to the plan."

Ivy buried her face in his shoulder. "I can't take it anymore."

"Yes, you can. You're the strongest person I know. Don't lose hope, angel. This is it."

Rebel pressed his forehead to hers, his voice choked with emotion. "This is the day we save everyone."

Zack swallowed a scream, torn between his disgust and his pity for these sad fools. He could remember a time, a thousand years ago, when he hugged Amanda in the basement of a Brooklyn brownstone and assured her in similar fashion that everything would be okay. What an idiot he'd been. What a bunch of suckers they all were—the Gothams, the breachers, all the hapless little victims of the Pelletiers. They were all going to war here in Atropos, while the real villains watched them and smiled.

FOURTEEN

The center of the concourse was a veritable oasis, a half-acre clearing in the Gothams' wooden jungle. Sunlight gleamed off a dry stone fountain while long metal benches provided enough seats for dozens. A freestanding partition ran the length of the area, ten inches thick and made entirely of glass. In days of old, before its lumic components were stripped, the wall had served as a giant display board, parading all the day's flight information between hotel ads and public service announcements.

Peter glanced around at the many seats and suggested that everyone take a breather. Amanda looked at him like he'd just proposed an orgy.

"Are you crazy? We have to keep going."

"We will," Peter promised. He leaned in close and lowered his voice. "Just give the boy a minute."

David paced in front of the old display, his fingers tapping his wristwatch. If he was traumatized from having a huge chunk of glass fall through him, it didn't show on his face. But then Amanda knew from hard experience that the David you saw wasn't always the David you got. He could have been dancing on the edge of a nervous breakdown and none of his friends would know.

Amanda acquiesced to Peter, then puttered anxiously by the fountain. She tied her hair back, wiped the sweat from her face, ate half a granola bar just to get something in her stomach. It wasn't until she took a swig from her water bottle that she noticed a patch of stress tempis on her arm. She wished it away, only to feel another one emerge on the small of her back.

You can't hold it in anymore, said the Zack in her head. *It wants to get out and hurt all the people who are hurting me.*

Amanda's face tightened. She closed her eyes and prayed for God to give her strength.

He already did, Zack reminded her. *You have enough power in your hands to tear those Gothams down. You're not a bomb. You're a bazooka.*

Mia looked across the fountain and saw her fidgety discomfort. "Are you okay?"

So point your fingers in the right direction.

"Amanda?"

And fire.

The tempis on her back vanished. Her hands balled into fists. Amanda looked to the wooden maze ahead of her, then extended her arms forward.

"Enough of this bullshit."

Peter eyed her worriedly. "Wait. What are you doing?"

"We are getting him—"

"Amanda . . ."

"—*back!*"

Her hands bloomed open. The tempis shot out of her palms with geyser force, two huge white serpents that barreled their way through the concourse. Plywood shattered. Benches broke off their bolted feet. The skeletal corpse of a hamburger stand was rendered to twisted metal bits.

Amanda's friends watched her from behind, their eyes wide and unblinking. Her command of tempis, like her command of words, had a tendency to collapse whenever she got upset. Her outbursts had broken walls, injured loved ones, even made national news.

But she was in full control of her power now. She could feel every molecule of her tempis working in concert with her thoughts, and it was . . . incredible, as if she'd become a being of pure force. As if the Earth, the moon, and the heavens above all trembled at the might of her righteous fury. *I will suffer no more from you,* Amanda said to the universe. And the universe meekly apologized.

At a hundred feet, the tendrils stopped growing. Amanda waved her hands apart like Moses at the water's edge, toppling three-story scaffolds like they were made of breadsticks.

Jonathan stepped forward and gawked at the devastation. "Holy . . ."

By the time Amanda finished, the eastern half of the concourse had been reduced to wood shards and dust clouds. Winded, she retracted her tempis and rejoined the group, her defiant gaze locked onto Peter's.

"Path cleared."

"That it is," Peter said. "And if they'd put Zack in that tangle of wood—"

"They didn't."

"—we'd have a nice, clear path to his corpse."

"They *didn't*," Amanda stressed. "I felt every inch of that place. There wasn't—"

"There it is!" yelled Mia.

She pointed to the far end of the concourse, where the dust clouds had parted to reveal a large, wooden construct.

Mia's future self had been clear about their final destination:

Zack's being held in a boarded-up restaurant. You can't miss it. It's way over on the sunny side and it's ugly as hell.

She wasn't kidding. Planks were nailed together at messy angles. Loose corners jutted out like cowlicks. The Gothams had enclosed every inch of the structure, with no care at all for aesthetics.

Mia tilted her head at their curious work. "Why would they go through all that trouble just to hide a restaurant?"

"Could be a trick," David said.

Peter shook his head. "They're in there." He turned to Jonathan. "Go get Hannah."

She stood by the restrooms, her body shifted at 20x, her eyes on alert for other falling pieces of Atropos. Jonathan waved his hand in front of her to get her attention.

Hannah fell back to normal speed and blinked at him. "What? What's going on?"

"You missed it," said Jonathan.

"Missed what?"

"Hurricane Amanda."

She turned around and gawked at the sea of splintered wood. "Oh my God."

Amanda wrung her hands, mortified. Her sister was the only one who knew her before the tempis, when she was just a noodle-armed nurse who could barely open a pickle jar. It was Hannah's look more than anything that convinced her of Peter's point. She *had* been reckless. The Gothams could have easily put Zack in her path of destruction.

Hannah crossed the space between them and held Amanda's arm. "Hey . . ."

"I'm okay."

"You're not okay. Your hands are shaking. You're barely—"

"Wait."

Amanda looked back the way they had come and felt a sharp twinge in her senses. There was a whole lot of tempis moving toward them from the aerport's main entrance. She could detect at least thirty different shapes, like hollowed-out people.

Her face went slack. "Oh, no . . ."

"What?"

Gemma Sunder listened through the surveillance mics, then switched the view on Monitor 5. Now she could see what Amanda was feeling.

"Shit. We've got company."

"Who?" Jinn asked. "Pelletiers?"

"No."

Rebel and Ivy looked over Gemma's shoulder as she magnified the picture on-screen. Sleek white figures marched double-file down the escalator—thirty men in tempic armor, their rifle barrels lit with flashlight beams.

At long last, Integrity had come to Atropos.

They'd touched down on the parking lot in a caravan of dropships: thirty-eight soldiers, sixteen pilots, twelve telemetry analysts, four temporal physicists, two reversal medics, and a clergyman. At the helm of the operation was a forty-year veteran of the agency, a silver-haired giant named Noah Butterfield.

He stepped out of the command shuttle in his black metal armor, fifty-four pounds of pure American osplate. It was six times heavier than the standard agency tempic suits, but then osplate didn't flicker when the battery got damaged. Besides, the tempic gear was too constricting for a man like Butterfield, who stood six-foot-eight and weighed 320 pounds. Even Rebel would have looked wispy standing next to him. He could have fit Gemma inside one of his arms.

He walked between the dropships, his head nodding patiently at the voice in his earpiece.

"Use the wasps first," Gingold told him. "And don't take anything for granted. They've got new blood in their group. Even the children are dangerous."

Butterfield wound his finger, waiting for him to finish. He wasn't a fan of that glass-eyed dandy and was glad as hell that he wasn't here. Who was Gingold to be giving pointers, anyway? He'd botched up everything in Brooklyn. Got his arm chewed up by a tempic wolf while his targets ran away on elephants. He was still out there searching for Maranan and the boy.

"Good advice," Butterfield lied. "Don't you fret, Oren. We got all our shoes tied here."

"Whatever you do—"

"Take care of that arm now."

Butterfield terminated the connection, then took a smiling look at Atropos. The fugitives couldn't have picked a better place for a takedown. The aerport was free of civilians, its roof was made of glass, and the whole place was surrounded by an open sea of concrete. There was nowhere to run outside and nowhere to hide inside.

And things were about to get very unpleasant inside.

While a fleet of remote-controlled aercraft moved into position above the complex, Butterfield tossed a nod at the clergyman on his team, a minister of the First American Baptist Church. All the agents in the parking lot bowed their heads respectfully as he spoke a blessing for the good men and women of the National Integrity Commission. Though the prayer wasn't standard procedure, Butterfield insisted on it and nobody dared complain. He wasn't just a big man in the agency, he was the biggest goddamn Baptist any of them had ever seen.

The minister finished. Butterfield thanked him, then turned to his chief weaponeer. "Drop 'em."

The Silvers barely had a chance to register the new shadows on the floor before sixteen drones came crashing through the ceiling. Five of them resembled crude metal wasps. The others looked like kite-size jet fighters.

Glass once again rained down on the concourse. Hannah saw the falling shards, then wrapped her arms around her sister.

"Amanda!"

The Gothams watched on the monitor as Amanda cast a protective dome around her people. Her tempis grew so fast that Rebel could only guess that Hannah had shifted her. *Smart woman*, he thought. The bubble was barely finished before two halves of a broken ceiling pane came crashing down on top of it.

Bug studied the drones on Monitor 1 and let out a shaky laugh. "Well, hell. This just got easy."

He looked around and saw that no one else shared his optimism. "What? It doesn't matter who kills them as long as they're dead, right?"

Gemma scowled at him. "We *told* you, Daddy."

"Told me what?"

Ivy closed her eyes in sorrow. The swifters of the clan rarely lived past fifty, and her brother was already starting to show the first signs of mental degradation. She gave him two more years of time-shifting before he barely remembered his name.

"We can't let the government take them," she explained to Bug. "If even one of the breachers survives, they'll be carted away to some secret facility. We'll never be able to find them, much less kill them."

Bug crossed him arms defensively. "If we stay, they'll get us too."

"No they won't."

The others looked at Rebel, who hadn't budged an inch since Integrity arrived. He wasn't worried about the government thugs. They were hopelessly out of their depth here. But they had enough firepower to legitimately threaten the breachers, which put the Pelletiers in an awkward position. They either had to show up and save their precious Silvers or risk losing them forever.

Come on, Rebel urged them. *Show your faces, you cowards.*

A short distance away, in the middle of the concourse, Amanda struggled to hold her shield dome intact. Her brain was still aching from her last tempic exertion.

David kept the space lit with a slice of old sunshine. He looked to the tempis and saw it wavering with strain. "We can't stay here. We need an exit."

"Working on it," said Peter. He crouched down and swept a patch of floor with his arm. No use. There was too much dirt and sand. Too many grooves and broken tiles.

"Can't do it," he told Amanda. "You'll have to make a wall."

"What?"

"A flat wall," he said. "A portal's our only way out of here."

Amanda looked at him through cracked red eyes. "We're not leaving without Zack!"

"We're not leaving at all. Just trust me!"

Before the tempis enclosed him, Peter had gotten a good look at Integrity's solic wasps. One clean shot was all it would take to pop Amanda's bubble.

"We've got seconds," Peter urged her. "Please."

The tempis quivered like jelly. Amanda gritted her teeth. She didn't have the finesse to make minor adjustments at the moment. She'd have to change the whole structure.

Gemma furrowed her brow at the monitor as Amanda's dome transformed into a large, slanted cube. "What the hell is she doing?"

"It's Peter," Ivy said. "He's making a door."

"He's running?"

"No. He wouldn't d—"

Ivy's senses tingled in sudden awareness. She leaned over Gemma and switched the view on Monitor 3, just in time to see Peter's exit portal open up on a smooth stone wall.

Jinn leaned forward and squinted at the screen. "Where is that?"

"Right here," Gemma said.

"Right next to us," Ivy said. "Bastard."

Rebel chuckled. It was just like Pendergen to spread the risk to everyone. He was deliberately bringing the battle to this side of the aerport, forcing the Gothams to either fight the government or run.

As it stood, Rebel was prepared to do both.

"Get the engines ready," he said to Gemma. "Jinn, take out the drones."

Bug looked at him like he'd gone mad. "Wait. We're *saving* the breachers now?"

"We're saving the mission."

Rebel saw the disappointment on Ivy's face. They were holding their big guns for Azral, Esis, and Semerjean. But now . . .

"They're not coming."

Ivy lowered her head. "I know."

"But we can still take care of the breachers today."

Ivy pinched her lip in tortured thought. The Pelletiers had killed her children. It seemed only fair that she kill theirs.

She turned to Gemma and Jinn. "What are you waiting for? Go!"

Gemma hurried to a laptop on the far side of the kitchen. Jinn jumped back into blueshift and activated her weapons console.

Large wooden boxes suddenly broke apart on the mezzanines, each one exposing a gun turret or rocket cannon. Jinn looked at her targeting screen and smiled at her first victim: a remote-controlled mini-fighter that was appropriately known as a "gunbird." The drone flew through the aerport at sixty miles an hour, but in Jinn's accelerated perceptions, it was nothing. A cardboard rabbit in a carnival game.

She aimed her reticle and squeezed her triggers. The gunbird exploded in a shower of sparks. The Integrity technicians barely had a moment to process its demise before two more gunbirds and a solic wasp fell.

"The *hell* was that?" asked Butterfield. He'd been watching the action from the parking lot, his brown eyes glued to camera drone monitors. He'd expected resistance from the fugitives. He didn't expect artillery fire.

"Find those turrets and take them out!"

"Yes, sir."

He pointed to the image of Amanda's tempic force field. "And break that damn shield already."

Mia and David were the first through Peter's portal. Jonathan moved to follow, then jumped back at the last second. A ripple in Amanda's tempis caused the gateway to flutter out of existence.

"Hold it steady," Peter told her.

"I'm trying!"

She calmed the wavering tempis. Peter re-formed the portal, then nodded at Jonathan. "All right. Go."

"Uh . . ."

"Come on. It's now or never!"

Hannah couldn't blame Jonathan for hesitating. He'd never jumped through a portal before, and this one seemed anything but stable.

She climbed onto his back and shifted them to 40x. The tempis took on a dull gray tint. Amanda and Peter became as still as mannequins.

"It's okay," Hannah told Jonathan. "We'll jump together."

He kept his tense eyes on the portal. "I really don't want to get cut in half."

"You won't," she promised. "*We* won't."

"And if you're wrong?"

"Then I'll buy you a Coke in the next world."

Jonathan looked at her over his shoulder, mystified. "That was strangely profound."

"Just go."

"Okay." He tightened his grip on Hannah, then steeled himself with a breath. "I have deep, crazy feelings for you. Just thought you should know that before we die."

"We're not dying! Go!"

He carried them through the portal at accelerated speed, then stumbled out the exit side. In all their haste, Hannah forgot to warn him that the first portal jump was always the hardest. The body gradually built up a tolerance to the rigors of teleporting. Until then, the experience was agonizing, like being flushed down a toilet of boiling hot water.

Hannah de-shifted them in mid-fall. They crashed to the floor at normal speed, then rolled all the way into the wooden shell of Rebel's base.

David crouched at Hannah's side. "Are you okay?"

"I'm fine."

She dropped to her knees and turned Jonathan over. His skin was a bright shade of pink, as if someone had scrubbed him all over with pumice stones.

He struggled to open his eyes. "Oh Jesus. It *burns.*"

David looked to Hannah, then jerked his head at the restaurant. "We'll need him to drop some of the wood planks. At least enough to get us in there."

"Just give him a minute."

"We may not have one."

Mia kept her anxious gaze to the west, where the turrets and drones continued to wage war on each other. Amanda's tempic cube wiggled precariously in the middle of the battlefield. She and Peter were still stuck out there, and there wasn't a damn thing Mia could do about it.

"C'mon," she muttered. "Come *on* already."

The last solic wasp made a suicide dive toward Amanda's tempis, just as Jinn fired a homing missile at it. They collided together on the floor, creating a loud and massive explosion in the middle of the concourse. Mia covered her mouth as a fist-size chunk of floor tile struck the ground by her feet.

"No!"

Once the fireball dissipated, Mia took a step forward and surveyed the damage. Among the mangled benches and burning wood shards stood Amanda's tempic shield.

Mia gasped with relief. "Oh God. Thank God."

Rebel frowned at the image on the monitor. There was no way Amanda's tempis could have survived a blast like that, not in her current state. Either the woman was a lot stronger than he'd realized or someone else had bolstered her power, a hidden tempic in the margins.

Jinn de-shifted at her console and turned around in her seat. Though her short blond hair was matted with sweat, she grinned like she was having the time of her life.

"All drones down," she told Rebel and Ivy. "We still have four working turrets. Want me to take out the foot soldiers?"

Gemma eyed her worriedly. "Damn, girl."

"Shut up."

"Not yet," Rebel said to Jinn. "Lower the elevator. Tell Mink and the others to strap themselves in."

For once, Bug knew exactly what Rebel was planning. "We're really doing this."

"Yup."

Ivy clasped his hand. "Are you sure, hon? Because once we start, I won't be able to teleport."

"I know."

"We'll be trapped in here with them."

Rebel looked to Monitor 5, where Amanda and Peter were rejoining their companions. He'd had two and a half days to prepare for this fight, and had backup plans for nearly every contingency. Plan F was the most extreme option by far, not to mention the riskiest. But Ivy was looking at it the wrong way. They wouldn't be trapped in here with the breachers. The breachers would be trapped in here with them.

Jonathan squinted at the boarded-up restaurant, his fingers pressed hard against his temples. His skin was still sore from the portal jump, but that wasn't his biggest concern at the moment.

"I'm not used to this," he warned. "Dropping whole objects is easy. Dropping *pieces* . . ."

"You'll be fine," Peter told him, though the croak in his voice was hardly reassuring. The heat of the missile blast had filtered its way into Amanda's tempic shell, nearly cooking them both like clay pots. Now Peter was weak and Amanda looked ready to collapse.

Jonathan took a deep breath and focused on the wooden sheath of the restaurant. The boards at eye level began to teeter and shake, until a large chunk of the wall fell intangibly through the earth.

"Good work," said Mia.

Jonathan blinked dazedly at the eight-foot hole he'd made in the lumber. "Huh."

David peeked inside the opening and shined a light beam from his hand. The restaurant was nearly nonexistent on the ground floor. All he could see were four large support struts and a fat metal column in the center.

"Strange."

He shined his light upward at the underside of the restaurant. The whole thing was covered in duct-taped bedsheets.

"Very strange." He aimed his puzzlement at Mia. "Are you sure this is a restaurant?"

Mia flipped her hands. "It's what the note said."

"Looks more like a trap," Jonathan grumbled. "How are we even supposed to get in?"

"I don't know," said David. "But if Mia's right, then Zack's in there."

Amanda took a nervous look to the west. "There are still soldiers coming. A lot of them."

Peter draped her arm around his shoulder. "Come on."

Two by two, the group crossed the threshold, into the dark underbelly of the restaurant. They'd barely proceeded ten feet before a loud electric *whirr* startled everyone. A sliding door opened on the central support column, revealing the brown leather interior of an elevator car.

"I don't like this," David grumbled. "Not one bit."

Hannah pulled a billy club from her thigh holster and held it defensively. "Jonathan's right. This is a trap." She jerked her head at the lift. "That thing's probably a gas chamber."

"The elevator's fine," Peter said. "They want us inside. That's the part that worries me."

He turned around at the door and faced the others. "I suppose I can't convince you all to wait here while I get Zack."

"No," said Mia.

"Don't be stupid," Hannah said.

"'Stupid' is all of us marching up there." He took an uneasy look at the elevator. "Just stay sharp and keep close to me. If things get choppy, I'm porting us out of here."

They filed into the lift. Peter pressed the button for the main floor. The car had only climbed a couple of feet when Amanda felt a shuddering twinge, like four cold hands being pressed against her spine.

"Wait. Something's happening."

"What do you mean?" David asked.

"I don't know. It feels like tempis, but . . . different."

"Aeris." Peter's eyes bulged in sudden realization. "Oh, you've gotta be kidding me . . ."

"What?"

As the elevator rose, a fluorescent glow spilled in through the door crack. The walls hummed with vibration. Something loud and bright was happening beneath the restaurant.

"What is that?" Mia asked Peter.

"We're going up."

"I know but—"

"No, I don't mean the elevator. I mean this whole thing."

Fifty feet above them, Zack felt the structure rumble. He looked up at the wood beyond the terrace windows. The boards were trembling, breaking apart at the seams.

He watched as Mink scrambled to strap himself into a bucket seat. "What's going on now?"

The tremors reverberated all throughout the concourse. Butterfield gawked at the surveillance monitor as the wooden shroud began to fall apart.

"What the goddamn hell are they doing?"

Soon the entire building rose off the ground. Two feet, four feet, eight feet, twelve. The higher it ascended, the more its plywood shell fell apart. At sixty feet, the last of the boards broke away, revealing an enormous black saucer made of glass and titanium.

"It's an aerstraunt," Butterfield said.

"An aerstraunt," Peter told the Silvers.

AN AERSTRAUNT, Mink informed Zack, in red lumic letters. NOW IT GETS INTERESTING.

FIFTEEN

It had been gathering dust in a New Jersey jet hangar: a two-hundred-ton Douglas Mark VI commercial-class flight carrier. On government records, it was Saucer D-669. But to those who'd experienced the aerstraunt in its heyday, it would forever be known as the *Absence*.

To understand the name, one had to know a little about America after the Cataclysm. The nation had lost two percent of its population on October 5, 1912, an unprecedented tragedy that triggered a spiritual sea change among the survivors. Millions of people found God overnight, while millions more abandoned him in a fit of dismay.

A strange new culture began to form among the ex-believers. By 1920, they could be seen everywhere: angry young nihilists in black clothes and bowler hats, contemptuous of all things cheerful. They were known as the Sinkers and they were mostly despised, though their mantras played like music to the ears of the disaffected:

We're all just flickers in a cold and empty universe. Morality and conformity are merely constructs designed to control us. Free yourselves. Live your lives. The same void awaits us all.

The movement kept growing, despite the scorn and abuse their members received. Hurting the Sinkers merely bolstered their cynicism. Hating them only made them more popular.

Then, in the 1950s, temporis changed everything. Rarely a week went by without a scientist announcing a brand-new way to bend the fabric of time, a chain of discoveries that pushed America into a golden age of prosperity. Suddenly anything seemed possible and bleakness felt . . . passé. The Sinkers hung up their hats and faded into obscurity.

But time has a way of moving in circles. In 2005, an ex-priest named Drew Gavin wrote a seminal essay entitled "Embracing the Absence" that re-explored the philosophy of the Sinkers and updated it for the Temporal Age:

Fifty years of progress and we haven't learned a thing. We still cling to the fantasy of a clockwork universe, where everything has meaning and everyone has a role to play. Perhaps the microbes in my soda bottle suffer the same illusion. I'm sure it comforted them mightily as I threw their world into the trasher and erased it out of existence.

The essay became a viral hit on Eaglenet and embroiled the country in a year-long shouting match between the believers and the cynics. All across the land, millions of people who barely knew about the Sinkers were shocked to learn how much they agreed with them.

By 2007, the movement had returned with a vengeance. Dark clothes and pessimism were suddenly back in vogue, and shrewd investors scrambled to capitalize on the craze.

The most brazen of these cash grabs was the *Absence*, a two-hundred-seat aerstraunt that catered to the rich Manhattan nihilist. It offered ninety-dollar entrées in drab little portions and sailed a nighttime circuit over the Atlantic to showcase the sheer nothingness out there. It was a place to while away the hours until oblivion came, a place for Sinkers to float.

While the *Absence* did well as an eccentric urban novelty, its shtick got old rather quickly. After a hundred and twenty dinner flights and six attempts to sell the business, the owner declared bankruptcy and relinquished the ship to the U.S. government.

It languished on a municipal airfield until just yesterday, when Ivy broke in and rebooted all the systems. Though she was hardly the first person in history to steal a dormant aerstraunt, she was the first to get away with it. By the time security guards noticed the lights inside Hangar 19, the ship had disappeared through a massive portal and had begun its slow descent into Atropos.

Now, after thirty-six hours on the lowest level of the concourse, the *Absence* was taking flight again.

The Integrity agents in the parking lot watched in stupor as a chain of explosions rocked the northern side of the aerport. A huge swath of the dome fell crashing down, and an ebony saucer made a diagonal ascent through the opening. One by one, the duct-taped bedsheets fell away from its underside, exposing four glowing liftplates, each one the size of a swimming pool.

Butterfield gaped at the fleeing aership. "You gotta to be . . ." He waved at his crew. "Everyone back to the shuttles! Now! Now!"

He balked at the expression of his telemetry analyst. "What? What's the problem?"

"They're gone, sir. Every last one of them."

There had been thirty soldiers inside Atropos when Rebel detonated the roof charges. The ones who weren't crushed by falling debris were quickly cut down by Jinn's surviving turrets. Rebel would have gladly left the poor fools alone, but he couldn't have them firing at the *Absence*. The ship had delicate equipment on the underside, flammable hydraulics. A few well-placed shots could bring it falling back to the ground.

"Son of a *bitch*!" yelled Butterfield.

He rushed into his command shuttle, the veins on his temples throbbing. As the *Absence* straightened out to a vertical ascent, he gave his weaponeers full clearance to blow it out of the sky. He didn't care who was on board—hostages, children, his own damn mother. Someone on that bird just killed thirty of his men. They weren't getting away. Not in a goddamn restaurant.

The *Absence* ascended at forty-four miles an hour, the maximum lift speed for pure aeric vehicles. The Integrity ships could rise a bit faster, thanks to their electric fan thrusters, but they were saddled with safeguards that the commercial saucers lacked.

At two thousand feet, the gunships and cannon cycles came to an automatic stop. The drivers were forced to pry open their consoles and manually disable their altitude locks before proceeding. The delay set them back a good eighty seconds, but Butterfield didn't fret. Satellite cameras were already locked on the vessel. There was nowhere in the sky for those people to hide.

At twenty-four hundred feet, an elevator opened inside the *Absence*. Hannah, Amanda, and the rest of their group stepped out onto the main dining floor and took a bewildered look at their surroundings. The floors and walls were made of black marble. Gray velvet partitions bisected the area at random angles. The bolted steel tables were molded into impractical shapes—starbursts and crescents and irregular heptagons. The whole interior seemed to be designed as a protest against symmetry and good cheer. If it wasn't for the blue sky and sunlight shining in the windows, the place would be macabre.

David scanned the past and saw a pale-faced hostess in tight black taffeta, welcoming patrons to the void. "What the hell is this place?"

Peter shook his head. "No idea. It's not like any aerstraunt I've ever seen."

Amanda girded her arms in an uneven coat of tempis. "Why would Rebel do this? What's his strategy?"

"His strategy is to kill us," Peter told her. "It's not so easy to do when some of us can teleport and run a hundred miles an hour. Now we're all boxed in with nowhere to go."

"Why can't you teleport?"

Peter turned to Mia. "Show them what happens."

She cast an eight-inch portal on the nearest partition. It sank through the floor at forty-four miles an hour.

"Travel doors can only exist in a fixed location," Peter explained. "As long as we're moving, we're stuck here."

Jonathan looked out the nearest picture window. The horizon had fallen out of sight. There was nothing but sky as far as the eye could see. "So we have to find a way to stop this thing."

"And get Zack," Amanda added.

"Yeah. Obviously. I'm just saying we can't do one without the—"

"Air brakes," Mia uttered.

The others watched her blankly as she fished four notes from her bookbag.

The air brake's down on the engine level. Find it before they disable it!

There's an emergency brake in the flight bridge. You'll have to hurry if you want to get there.

The next was a pencil sketch of a long metal lever with a rubber grip. The only words on the note were *Air Brake*.

"It's either in the cockpit or the engine room," Mia said. "Maybe both."

"Or maybe neither," Amanda warned. "She's sent you bad notes before."

"Not about this."

Even as she said it, though, she wasn't so sure. Her gaze lingered anxiously around the fourth note, which maddeningly contradicted the other three:

Forget the air brake. Go to the manager's office and look in the closet. The solution's right there.

Peter reread her messages, his brow creased in thought. "Your phones all working?"

The others checked their handphones for signals. Amanda eyed Peter worriedly. "We're splitting up?"

"Afraid so."

"Are you sure that's smart?"

"It's not smart at all, but we have a lot to do in a little time. You and I will look for Zack. David, you find the flight bridge. Should be one floor down on the staff level. Jonathan, go with him but keep your eye out for the manager's office. See if you can dig up that solution Mia's talking about."

He looked to Hannah and Mia. "Go two floors down to the engine level. If there's an air brake anywhere, it'll be there. Just . . ."

Peter closed his eyes in a grimace, stammering as he fumbled for words. "Look, I'm not gonna lie about our chances here, and I won't tell you to be gentle. If you see any of my people coming, you do what you have to. Don't hesitate for a moment, because they won't."

Only Mia had the mind to process Peter's quandary. He'd been straddling the line between two different tribes, trying to minimize losses on both sides. But they were long past the point of handshakes and "sorry"s. Here on the *Absence*, it was kill or be killed.

"But don't get too eager," Peter added. "If we want any hope of ending this war, we'll need one of the leaders alive. That means Rebel or Ivy, preferably both."

He cleared his throat. "The rest are expendable."

A tense silence filled the dining room. Nobody moved until Amanda looked to Peter. "Come on. Time's wasting."

They wished the group luck, then proceeded deeper into the dining room.

Hannah and the others continued along the curved inner wall until they found the employee lift to the lower levels.

As the electric door closed and the motor hummed with power, Jonathan stared at the floor and fidgeted with his sleeve. "Eggs."

Mia turned around. "Huh?"

"What normal people do on Easter," he said. "They color eggs."

Hannah wasn't sure if she'd laugh or cry. Her heart hadn't stopped pounding since the *Absence* took off, and the world never felt bleaker. If she had known about the Sinkers, she would have understood their contempt for humanity and its insatiable need for self-affirming bullshit. *Hard work pays off. Good things come to those who wait. Cheaters never prosper. All you need is love.*

Except Hannah knew of seven billion people whom love hadn't lifted a finger to help. She knew of seven hapless survivors who, like her, had to constantly fight for the right to keep breathing. It was so unfair that she wanted to scream. And yet . . .

Hannah turned her head and took a close look at Jonathan. The guy had all of her problems and then some, but he never once surrendered to despair. More than that, he'd found the time to tell a muddled ex-actress about his deep, crazy feelings for her.

As the *Absence* climbed and the elevator sank, Hannah suddenly felt an overwhelming love for the people in her life—the sister, the savior, and the six other tribemates she couldn't imagine living without. She had more love on this world than she ever had on the old one. But when it came to her fondness for one particular man, she fled for the hills and burned the bridges behind her. Why was she so afraid? What the hell was she running from?

The doors slid open to the staff level. While David and Mia took a cautious peek down the hallway, Hannah gave them a sheepish look. "I'm sorry, you guys."

David looked at her confusedly. "What?"

"This will be awkward."

Hannah cupped the sides of Jonathan's face and kissed him hard on the lips. Their transceivers crackled with soft reverberation. The blood of their shrapnel cuts dotted each other's clothes.

Soon she pulled her head back and drank him in with heavy eyes. "Don't die."

Jonathan stared at her dazedly. "Okay."

"I mean it."

"I wasn't kidding. I really want to do that again."

"Me too." She shook her finger at David. "You play it smart now. No daredevil shit."

"That's not entirely up to me." He took a sullen look at Jonathan. "Come on."

David and Mia shared a quick, heavy glance before the elevator door closed between them. As the two remaining Silvers continued down to the engine level, Hannah pulled a billy club from her holster and clasped her free hand around Mia's. She couldn't tell who was trembling more.

"Why'd you do that?" Mia quietly asked her. "I mean, why now?"

Hannah gazed at the door, the tip of her club tapping frantically against her thigh. "I don't know. Just felt like the right time."

Mia scoffed in self-rebuke. She hadn't even said good luck to David.

The door opened to a long, thin corridor of steam pipes and cables. Hannah sucked in a deep breath, her thoughts overflowing with worries.

"Stay with me," she said to Mia. "Don't leave my side."

They stepped out of the lift together. The doors closed behind them.

The *Absence* was now nine thousand feet above the ruins of Atropos, and rising.

SIXTEEN

Though aerstraunts were designed to cruise at low altitude, the Douglas Corporation built their Mark VI saucers with the same atmospheric protections as the high-flying ships: triple-paned windows, electrothermal de-icers, a cabin pressurization system to prevent passenger hypoxia. The aerstraunt people would probably never need those things but, hey, anything could happen. The motto at Douglas was "Better safe than sued."

At ten thousand feet, the *Absence*'s environmental control system kicked in, blowing reconditioned air into every room and corridor. Zack's ears popped in the pressure readjustment, and he could once again hear the low, ambient noises of the dining terrace. He glanced up from his prisoner's chair and saw clouds breaking left and right against the panoramic sun dome.

"Jesus." Zack looked to Mink, incredulous. "At some point, you people got together and said 'This is a good idea.'"

The lumic glared at him before continuing his work. Zack didn't recognize the long, round device he was setting up on a tripod. He thought it was a spyglass until Mink aimed the lens at him.

"A video camera," Zack guessed. "So that's the plan, Harpo? You're going to slit my throat on Pay-Per-View? How very al-Qaeda of you."

Mink clenched his teeth, fuming. Zack had learned many of his captors' pet peeves over the last two days, and went out of his way to exploit them. Mink was particularly annoyed by his esoteric cultural references.

A tiny green bulb lit up on the camera. "Is it on?" Zack asked. "Can my friends see me?"

"Not yet," said a voice from the stairwell.

Mercy returned to the terrace, looking less comfortable than ever in her black fiber armor. Though Zack wouldn't go so far as to call her a decent woman, she was one of the few Gothams here who actually treated him like a human being.

His eyes lingered on the .22 pistol in her hip holster. "So you're the one."

"The one who what?"

"The one who kills me in front of my people."

Mercy leaned against a wall and gestured at her teammate. "No. That'll be him."

Mink smiled vengefully from behind the lumicam. "Wow," said Zack. "I didn't think he had it in him."

"Me neither. Guess you called him 'shitwad' one too many times."

"Guess so."

Zack closed his eyes, fighting to maintain a semblance of dignity. This was a cruel and humiliating way to die. He didn't want it to be Amanda's last memory of him.

"You know this won't do a thing to stop the end of the world," he told Mercy. "It's just sacrificial bullshit. Lambs on the altar. Virgins in the volcano."

"You telling me you're a virgin?"

"I'm telling you you'll be sorry. When the sky comes down four years from now, you'll hate yourself for wasting all this time. You might even feel bad about the innocent people you killed."

Mercy crossed her arms and looked away. "Just shut up."

Guilt was her sore spot. Zack could see it in her eyes, behind all the dark makeup. She hated everything about this mission, but not enough to tell Rebel and Ivy to go screw themselves.

Mercy took a swig from her water bottle, then paced the floor in a circle. "You think we *like* doing this?"

"I think some of you love it," Zack said.

"Fuck you. I'm an artist."

"So am I."

"Mink's a poet."

"Mink's a shitwad."

Mink turned around, furious. Zack shrugged at him. "Sorry. I keep forgetting you're not deaf."

Two floors down, Ivy glowered at Zack's live image. "Will someone shut him up already?"

"No," Rebel said. "Let him be."

Gemma watched Jonathan and David on a surveillance monitor as they silently parted ways. "They're right outside our door."

"Don't worry," Rebel said. The kitchen had been sealed with tempic barriers. Should those breachers find their way in, Rebel had his .44 ready to drop the dropper and light up the lumic.

His bigger concern was Peter and Amanda. One knew far too much about his team and their weak points. The other was an extremely dangerous tempic, especially when she was angry.

And Amanda was about to become very, very angry.

Zack looked into the camera. "I know you're watching, Rebel. You're standing in the kitchen with Ivy and Bug and that screechy little niece of yours, who I'm pretty sure was Rosemary's Baby."

Gemma threw her hands up. "What does that even mean?"

"I don't have anything left to say to you people—"

"Thank *God*," Ivy groaned.

"—except for Peter's kid."

Liam looked up at the monitor in surprise. Ivy gripped his shoulder. "Don't listen to him."

"He told me a lot about you," Zack said. "That you love comic books and logic puzzles, and those old-fashioned jet planes you only see at stunt shows. He says you're smart as hell, but I don't see it. All I see is an angry brat who's about to learn the hard way that he backed the wrong team. You should have seen right through Rebel and Ivy. You should have never stopped believing in your dad."

The boy bowed his head miserably. Ivy switched on her headset. "Mink, shut him up!"

"He isn't doing this to save the world," Zack told Liam. "He's doing it to save you."

"Mink!"

Furious, Mink crossed into the solic field and wrapped his fingers around Zack's windpipe. Mercy struggled to hold him back, for all the good it did her. She was only half his weight.

"Stop it!" she yelled. "Mink, stop!"

"That's enough," Rebel barked. "Everyone get back to your stations. Now."

He turned his attention to Monitor 8 as Peter and Amanda finally crossed into view. They'd taken their own sweet time making a clockwise sweep around the dining area. Now, at long last, all the enemies were in position.

Rebel nodded at Ivy. She kneeled in front of Liam and brushed the bangs from his eyes. "Hon, I want you to wait in the pantry, all right? Just for a minute."

"Why?"

"Because there's about to be violence, and I promised Mother Olga I wouldn't expose you to that."

"But what about my dad?"

"Liam . . ."

"You said you wouldn't kill him."

Ivy shook her head emphatically. "We don't kill our own. We'll bring him back with us and we'll make him answer for his crimes. I swear it."

Rebel looked at Liam, his voice low and severe. "Go."

Grudgingly, the boy retreated into the pantry. Ivy closed the door behind him, then traded a dark look with Gemma. They had no intention of keeping Peter alive. He was a traitor to his clan, a traitor to the world. The bastard deserved everything that was coming to him.

Rebel studied the swifters on Monitor 10. "All right, you two. You ready?"

Bug and Jinn acknowledged him with a nod. They were crouched in the main stairwell, a quick sprint away from their targets. While Bug held a short-barreled shotgun in his hands, Jinn was armed and ready with her secondary power. Her small fists glimmered with tempis.

"Do it," Rebel told Gemma.

She twisted a knob on a handheld device, a portable snuffer that had been pilfered from DP-8. All wireless phone signals were now thoroughly jammed. The breachers were cut off from each other.

Rebel squeezed his wife's hand. "It's all you, babe."

Ivy activated the ship's public address system, then raised the microphone to her lips. "Everyone *stop*."

Her voice echoed throughout the aerstraunt, freezing all of Zack's friends in place. One by one, they looked up at the ceiling cameras.

Ivy smiled as the last of the breachers met her gaze through the monitor. "You folks came a long way to rescue Zack. Frankly, we don't get it. After two days with him . . ." She closed her eyes in a tortured wince. "He's annoying.

He's very, very annoying. But you all seem to like him. Least we can do is show him to you."

Gemma flipped a switch on her console. A monitor flickered to life in an engine room, inches away from Hannah and Mia. A computer screen came awake on the manager's desk near Jonathan. David saw a lumic projection on the wall outside the control room.

Peter and Amanda got the clearest picture of all. A six-foot image of Zack materialized above a dining booth. Amanda could see fresh welts on his neck, the tears in his eyes as he struggled to catch his breath. Someone had choked him just moments ago.

She gritted her teeth. Sharp spikes of tempis protruded through her shirt. "I swear to God, Ivy . . ."

Her face went white as Mink crossed into the picture and pressed a .38 pistol against Zack's temple. *"No!* Don't you dare!"

"Quiet," said Ivy. "I can see and hear each one of you, and I promise you this: the next one who moves or opens their mouth will be the one who kills Zack Trillinger."

Mia clutched Hannah's arm. Amanda quickly retracted her tempis.

Ivy shook her head condescendingly. "You had to know we'd play this card. I mean, Jesus. You came here without any Pelletier support. You didn't bring your augur. It's like you people *wanted* to lose."

Rebel muttered into his headset. "Get ready, Mink."

"On that note," Ivy continued, "where *is* Maranan? If I hear anything but a true and honest answer, Zack's dead."

Five seconds passed without a peep from the breachers. Ivy nodded understandingly. "Yeah. I probably wouldn't talk either. Maybe the sound of Zack screaming will—"

"No!" Amanda and Mia hollered.

"Don't," Hannah pleaded.

"Kneecap," Rebel ordered Mink. "The left one."

"Hey, Rebel . . ."

"Hold it." Rebel looked between the monitors. One of these men—the Silver, the Gold, or the traitorous ex-kinsman—had decided to call him out.

"Who said that?" Ivy asked through the PA. "Was that you, Peter?"

"That was me," said Jonathan. He stared at the camera from the edge of the manager's office, his eyes cool and defiant. "I know your husband's standing next to you. I can hear him. Are you hiding under her skirt, Rebel, or just behind it?"

Rebel snatched the microphone from Ivy, his slitted eyes locked on Jonathan. "Careful."

"You be careful. I'm not like the others. I barely know Zack."

"Then why are you here?"

"Why do you think?"

Gemma muted the PA system and threw a fearful look at Rebel. "He's not bluffing. He'll drop you the minute he sees you."

Ivy held his arm. "Maybe Jinn—"

"No," said Rebel. "We stick to the plan. Turn it back on."

Gemma reactivated the mic. Rebel sighed at the monitors. Both his foresight and his insight kept insisting that this was pointless. None of them were going to give up Maranan.

"All right, folks. Your mouthy new friend just earned Trillinger a bullet. Mink—"

The overhead lights went dark, along with all the computers and surveillance screens. The only illumination came from the battery-powered laptop that controlled the ship's systems.

"What happened?" Ivy asked.

"What's happening?" Liam yelled through the pantry door.

"No idea." Gemma ran to the laptop and checked the status screen. "Temporics are fine. Electrics are fine. It's just this one circuit."

"*Our* circuit." Ivy scowled at the bank of dead monitors. "Run the pulsers, then get us back up."

"On it." Gemma moved to the wall and pulled a silent alarm. Every ceiling on the *Absence* flashed red with lumis. Bright white arrows pointed passengers to the nearest fire safety rooms.

Rebel looked around in the crimson light, his revolver raised in readiness. "One of them's messing with us."

"Peter," Ivy guessed.

"It's David," said Gemma.

Rebel shook his head. Neither one of them was anywhere near the fuse relay. It had to be someone on the engine level—Farisi or the younger Given. But they'd been standing in front of the camera the whole time. So how the hell did they . . .

His mouth fell open in realization. Ivy followed his line of thought. "Them? *Now?*"

Rebel shut his eyes and scanned the future, though the strings had little to say. If there was a Pelletier on the *Absence*, then he or she was doing a damn good job staying hidden. All Rebel knew for sure was that the breachers were gaining the upper hand. It was time to finish them once and for all.

He reactivated his headset. "All right, showtime. Bug and Jinn, hit your targets. Mink?"

Rebel looked at his wife with a vindictive smile. "Kill the hell out of Trillinger."

The pulsers were barely visible on the dining level. Sunshine gleamed through every window, eclipsing all other light. But clearly something had gone awry in the Gothams' command center. The voices on the speaker had abruptly gone silent. The image of Zack had vanished in a blink.

"What happened?" Amanda asked Peter. "Is this another trick?"

Peter bit his thumb, thinking, worrying. There was a purpose behind Rebel and Ivy's hostage game, and it wasn't just to learn Theo's whereabouts. They were using Zack to keep his friends paralyzed, to hold them perfectly still for the—

"—swifters." He shot a frantic look at Amanda. "Ice up."

"What?"

"Armor! Armor!"

Amanda tried to gird herself in tempis, but her power was still sluggish. She'd barely managed to cover her torso when she heard a rising patter, an eggbeater sound of accelerated footsteps that she'd long come to associate with—

—*Hannah*, she thought, before a hot wind overtook her and a deafening *boom* filled her ears.

Something struck her in the back with agonizing force, like nothing she'd ever felt before. If she'd been looking in the right direction, she might have seen Bug Sunder just in time to watch him empty both barrels of a 12-gauge shotgun into her spine.

Her tempis was all that kept the buckshot from shredding her. The explosion reverberated throughout her body, shattering four ribs and three vertebrae before sending her flying. She crashed against the edge of a bolted steel table, breaking her pelvis in two places.

Amanda crumpled to the floor, her eyes wide open but her senses torn apart. There was a struggle happening somewhere in the periphery of her hearing—a splattering of blood, a man's gurgling death rattle. Her head lolled to the side, but all she could make out in her blurry vision was a mangled corpse on the floor.

"P-Peter . . . ?"

A pair of cold, strong hands gripped her by the shoulders. They flipped her onto her stomach, then tore away at the back of her T-shirt. Her broken bones screamed from a thousand miles away.

"Don't," she said in a tiny voice. "Don't do this."

"Shhhhh."

Amanda flinched as the stranger pressed a cool metal disc to her back. "What . . . what are you . . . ?"

"I'm fixing you," the man replied. "Shut up and stay still."

His voice trickled out in a low, haunting whisper, one that was distorted with impossible sounds: crinkled paper, wind chimes, a humming white noise.

What's happening? Amanda asked herself. *Is this real?*

A liquid warmth filled her body, and she felt a strange sensation inside of her, like ants marching all through her bloodstream. As her broken bones began knitting together, her double vision came into focus, enough to give her a clear view of the casualty on the floor. He was a tall, bearded stranger in tactical armor, an Indian man who was just as striking as Ivy. His throat had been torn wide open. He stared at Amanda through a frozen expression of horror.

She struggled to look at the figure above her, but all she could see was his shadow. "Peter? Is that you?"

The man replied with a mocking chuckle. "Do I sound like Peter?"

The room spun. Amanda's eyelids fluttered. As her consciousness tumbled down a deep, dark well, she took a final moment to ponder her new acquaintance. Though he remained well out of eyeshot, her mind could feel every curve and contour of his skin. That could only mean one thing.

Tempis, she realized. *He's covered in tempis.*

"Mink, stop! Don't do this!"

Zack sat on his chair in the middle of the terrace, his mind lost in the clouds as Mercy pleaded for his life. He was painfully aware of the pistol that was pressed to his temple, and he knew damn well that it wasn't morality or sentiment that kept Mink from pulling the trigger, just squeamishness. Zack had seen him go dizzy at the sight of a bleeding finger. How would he deal with a man's scattered brains?

Sweating, Mink backed up several steps and aimed his .38 at Zack's heart.

"It won't be any cleaner," Mercy warned him. "You're not a killer, Mink. And you don't have to start now. Come on. Think about it. What if Rebel's been wrong this whole time?"

Mink gave her a dirty look, then waved his free hand in a circle. Angry red lumis appeared above his head. HE'S MY COUSIN. WHAT ARE YOU?

"I don't know," Mercy said. "I just know I'm sick of this shit. All of it. I'm done."

FINE. Mink jerked his head at the emergency exit. DOOR'S THAT WAY.

Zack stared at the carpet with busy eyes, torn between the crisis and the whirlwind storm that was happening inside his head. He would die any moment now—horribly, *pointlessly*—yet there was at least one man in the world who saw a function to his suffering.

You were chosen, Azral had told Zack. *For better or worse. And you will serve our purpose, one way or another.*

"An umbrella . . ."

The words spilled out in a listless mutter. Mink and Mercy watched him, expressionless, while he continued to ramble.

"The Pelletiers never move in a straight line. When they want a sandwich, they'll buy an umbrella, because they know it'll start a chain of events that'll get them the best sandwich ever. I thought they sent me to Rebel because they wanted a war. But that's just the umbrella. I think . . ."

He stared at his captors in dark amazement. "I think they want peace."

Zack caught a moving figure in the corner of his eye. He looked to the stairwell and saw a large man hurrying up the steps—bald and muscular and ridiculously pale. It took Zack three blinks to realize that the guy wasn't naked. He was sheathed from head to toe in a molded skin of tempis.

Mercy and Mink spun around and flinched at the formidable presence coming quickly toward them. Only the eyeholes in his mask revealed the man beneath the tempis—bright blue eyes, angry-looking.

And they were locked right on Mink.

"*No!*"

Mink raised his gun in trembling hands, but the stranger was faster. He zipped past Mink in a shifted blur, then doubled back to the stairwell. Zack could see something new in his right hand, a three-foot katana made of pure tempis. The blade was streaked with fresh, wet blood.

Mercy covered her screaming mouth as Mink fell to the carpet in pieces. His legs dropped forward. His torso toppled backward. His round, blond head went rolling under a table. Zack looked just in time to see bright pink organs spill out of his midsection. He turned away, nauseated. *Oh Jesus. Oh God.*

The stranger pivoted on his heels and cast his full attention on Mercy. She stumbled backward, weeping. "No. Please. Please. I'm sorry . . ."

"Don't kill her!" Zack begged. "She won't be a problem. She's done with Rebel. She quit."

His plea for Mercy clearly intrigued the man. He tilted his head at Zack before turning around again. Now Mercy could spot the smile in his eyes, a derisive grin if she ever saw one. He brandished two fingers at her before dashing down the stairs in a hazy white streak.

Mercy fell to her knees, gasping. "Oh my God. Oh my God . . ."

"It's all right," Zack told her. "You're okay."

"Jesus. That was . . . he was a . . ."

"I know." Zack rattled his handcuffs. "Look, we have to get out of here. Can you—"

"Why did he hold up two fingers at me?"

"Mercy . . ."

"What does it *mean*?"

Zack closed his eyes, sighing. He barely knew anything about the third

Pelletier. He was the father of Azral, the husband of Esis, the one who gave Zack his portentous silver bracelet. He was also the only one in the family with a dry sense of humor, as he'd just ably proved.

"It was a symbol on my world," Zack explained to Mercy. He lowered his head and fought the mad urge to laugh. "It means 'peace.'"

SEVENTEEN

The *Absence* was fifteen thousand feet in the air when it finally decided to complain about it. Alarm bulbs flashed all throughout the engine level. Status monitors lit up with bold red text: *Altitude exceeding vehicle capacity. Power consumption at 225%. Engines 1, 3, and 4 at critical risk of malfunction. Proceed toward land immediately or call U.S. Aer Guard for emergency assistance.*

Mia read the display on the south starboard engine, her forehead dripping with sweat. The ship's external de-icers were roaring full blast beneath her, turning the entire chamber into a furnace. More unnerving than the heat was the noise of the engines—a nonstop cacophony of hisses and sighs, like a dozen old men on ventilators. *Shhhhhh. Haaa. Shhhhh. Haaa.*

She looked at the monitor that had recently shown Zack, still dark after a full minute of downtime. God only knew what was happening with the Gothams.

Mia pulled her handphone out of her pocket and tried to call Peter, but she couldn't get a signal. Were they too high up, or was Rebel jamming their connection?

"Shit." She wiped the sweat from her brow, then peeked around the side of the engine. "Hannah."

She was everywhere and nowhere, a hot gust of wind on a clockwise diamond path. The Gothams knew that Hannah and Mia were here, and it was just a matter of time before they came in through one of the room's four entrances. Hannah was determined to spot them early and strike them hard. At 40x, her billy clubs hit like freight trains.

She saw Mia waving, then de-shifted in front of her. "What? Did you find the air brake?"

"Not yet."

"Then keep looking."

"But—"

Hannah jumped back into high speed, then continued her circuit. Mia always found her to be disconcerting in blueshift. Her hummingbird twitches and inability to hear and speak made her an ethereal presence, like a ghost or a mirage. While Mia certainly appreciated Hannah's vigilance, she couldn't help but feel alone down here, just her and the hydraulics. *Shhhhhh. Haaa. Shhhhhh. Haaa.*

She checked the status screen again and saw a brand-new complaint on the ship's list of worries:

Air brake disabled.

"Wait, what?"

Forty feet away, in a small and musty cabin on the other side of the hallway, Jinn Godden crouched behind a steel desk. Killing the manual brake had been easy. The lever was right there in the engineer's office. Killing the swifter, however, would take some finesse. Jinn had skulked through the corridors at unshifted speed to keep Hannah from sensing her aura. Now, at last, she was within striking distance.

Be careful with Given, Rebel had warned her. *She's surprisingly clever.*

Only a man would be surprised that a pretty woman was clever. Jinn had been battling that nonsense half her life. Besides, she already knew not to underestimate Hannah. The breacher had outmaneuvered her back in the Faith Mall, despite the fact that she'd only been swifting for a few months. Hannah was a fast learner, and she had some very unique tricks up her sleeve.

But then so did Jinn.

She raised her finger and extended a thin tendril of tempis across the floor. It hooked a left at the doorway, slithered into the hall, then began a slow, creeping journey toward the engine room. All it would take was a well-placed tripwire to send Hannah tumbling. At that speed, she'd break her neck. The Farisi girl would be an even easier kill, as long as Jinn didn't look at her sweet, adorable face.

Just imagine she's Gemma, she told herself. *The rest will be easy.*

Jinn didn't have to look to know what Hannah was doing. She could feel her temporal signature. The breacher was speeding right toward the tripline, oblivious. Maybe she wasn't so clever after all.

The tendril suddenly retracted, snapping all the way back into Jinn's hand. She stared at her fingers confusedly. Tempis had always been the weaker of her two powers, but it had never revolted against her like this. What the hell was it doing? How—

A brand-new string shot out of her finger. The tempis looped three times around her neck and constricted like a snare.

Bug-eyed, choking, Jinn fell to the floor and struggled against her own creation. She rolled onto her side and saw someone watching her from behind the engineer's desk, a muscular man sheathed entirely in—

No . . .

—tempis.

Djinni Godden had never been humble about her blessings. Even among her own, she was a superior specimen, blessed with brains and beauty, good health, and an abundance of power.

But one look at this creature was enough to reveal her true place in the food chain. The man had all of her talents and then some. He was a swifter, a tempic, a traveler, a lumic.

He was a Pelletier. He came from a world where people like Jinn were considered crippled.

She struggled to speak, to beg for her life, but her throat had completely closed. Her mind defensively threw her into blueshift, but all it did was hasten her demise. She thrashed on the floor at high speed for seven seconds before her body went limp and her head thumped listlessly against the floor.

Hannah came to a stop in the engine room, puzzled. She'd briefly detected another swifter, but it was gone now. Extinguished.

Mia approached her as she de-shifted. "What happened? Are you okay?"

"I'm fine. I just . . ." Hannah followed her senses across the hall, then flinched at the corpse in the engineer's office, a slender young blonde in fiberweave armor. Hannah could see that she'd died violently, but who could have possibly done this to her? Peter? Jonathan? *Amanda?*

"Hey."

She turned around and saw David on the stairwell at the end of the corridor, his pistol clenched in his hand. He hurried down the final steps.

"Are you all right? You look—"

"Did you do that?"

"Do what?"

Mia stepped into the hallway and screamed. *"David! Behind you!"*

David spun around and raised his gun, but it was knocked out of his hand. He fell backward against the wall, giving Hannah and Mia a clear view of his assailant.

The man stood calmly by the stairwell, glistening in his molded tempic armor. At first glance, Mia's mind refused to accept him as real. He was a nonsensical entity—the Superman of mannequins, an unfinished painting come to life.

As David regained his footing, the tempic man slowly approached Mia. He spoke to her in an otherworldly whisper, filled with ancillary noises that no human throat could possibly make.

"Forget the air brakes. They've been disabled, both here and above."

Hannah tightened her grip on her billy clubs. The man's accent was a puzzling mixture of British and God-Knows-What. She had little doubt that he was a Pelletier, though he wasn't quite tall enough to be Azral. Hannah could only guess that he was the other guy in the family, the one she hadn't seen since she was a child. She couldn't remember much about what he'd looked like back then. He certainly hadn't been covered in tempis.

"What do you want with us?" Hannah asked him. "Why do you—"

The stranger walked past her without so much as a glance. "The ship's controls have been diverted to a portable computer," he told Mia. "You'll find it in the kitchen. Stop the ascent and then gather the others. Pendergen will teleport you all to safety."

David stroked his aching arm. "Why should we trust you? If you are who I think you are—"

"Mind your tone, boy."

"You helped kidnap Zack. You delivered him to the Gothams and provoked this whole fight!"

The stranger turned around and cracked a tempic whip at David. The tail cut a one-inch gash on the back of his good hand.

Mia ran to his side. "No!"

"The path to progress is rarely easy," the Pelletier told him. "Sometimes we must walk through dirt. Other times, through fire."

His fierce blue eyes narrowed to slits. "Don't ever raise your voice at me again."

Mia's heart jumped in terror. She struggled to regain herself. "W-what's your name?"

The stranger looked at her with softer eyes, though he hesitated a moment before answering.

"Semerjean."

He flicked his hand in a lazy arc. The ceiling suddenly began to glow. The Silvers watched intently as an eight-foot disc of radiant white energy fell through the hallway. A moving portal.

Semerjean shifted into high speed and dove in headfirst. The gateway swallowed him whole before sinking through the floor grates.

Hannah stared down the empty corridor, stupefied. The man's exit was an act of sheer lunacy, like hooking a ride on a passing comet. Even a swifter like her would have been cut in half.

The engine hissed five more times before David broke the silence. He stared down blankly at his bleeding hand.

"He, uh . . ." He closed his eyes and took a deep, stuttered breath. "He was right about one thing. The air brake upstairs has been disabled. The whole control room's been destroyed."

"So what now?" Hannah asked.

Mia looked into the engineer's office, at the dead Gotham on the floor. She supposed Semerjean could have done worse to David. A lot worse.

"We go to the kitchen," she said, in a small and distant voice. "We do exactly what he says."

The moment Semerjean slipped through the portal, the bulb lights and surveillance monitors came back to life in the kitchen. The screens flickered twice before resuming their clear and steady views of the *Absence*.

Rebel reeled at the sight of the new status quo on the terrace. Zack and Mercy were nowhere to be found, and his cousin had been cut into bloody pieces. Someone had butchered Mink like a goddamn pig.

Ivy moved to Rebel's side, hang-jawed. "Jesus! What happened? Where—"

She turned to Monitor 3 and screamed at the carnage in the dining room.

Her brother lay sprawled on the black tile floor, a gawking corpse with a fist-size hole in his throat. "Deven!"

Gemma looked up. "Daddy?"

Ivy stumbled backward, her head shaking back and forth. "No, no, no, we can fix this." She turned her crying eyes onto Gemma. "*You* can fix this. Go back to the past—"

"No," Rebel said. There was no point and Ivy knew it. Time didn't move in a single path. It wasn't a chalkboard where events could be erased and over-written. The best Gemma could do was save Mink and Bug in a branching string, and even that was futile.

Rebel reached past Gemma and panned the dining room camera. Now his wife and niece could see it clearly. Someone had drawn on the tile with Bug Sunder's blood—a neat little symbol: a smiley face.

Ivy clenched her quivering fists. "Monster . . ."

Rebel lifted his .44 and shot the monitor. The Pelletiers didn't have to sign their work. He knew it by heart. And their savagery was nothing, a kiss and a backrub, compared to what he was going to do to them. They'd have to invent brand-new words for the tortures he was planning.

Ivy ran after him as he rushed toward the waitstaff elevator. "Richard, no!"

He turned around in the lift and met Ivy's gaze. His voice came out in a croaking rasp. "Go."

The door slid closed. Ivy hurried to the other end of the kitchen and typed a password into the command laptop. Gemma could see that she was preparing for an emergency all-stop.

"What are you doing? Are we leaving?"

"Not us," said Ivy. "You."

"What? No! You can't!"

"Our replacements won't stand a chance without you. They need you. You have to guide them."

"But you heard Rebel. He wants you to go!"

"I don't care. If the demons are here, then this is exactly where I need to be."

Gemma threw her arms around Ivy and, for the first time in as long as she could remember, she wept like a child. She was a misfit among her people, a shrill and ugly creature whom few people liked and even fewer understood. But her aunt Ivy was the exception. She never stopped loving Gemma, even after the Pelletiers turned her world upside-down and filled her heart with hatred.

Gemma held her tight. "Please don't leave me."

"We'll be together again in the next world." Ivy kneeled in front of her and gripped her shoulders. "But until then, you need to stay strong. Finish the war. You find every last one of those breachers and you do what needs to be done. You hear me?"

Gemma nodded her head, sniffling. "I will. I promise."

"That's my girl." Ivy moved back to the laptop and summoned the air brake controls. "Get ready."

Gemma looked to the pantry door. "Wait. What about . . . ?"

Ivy shook her head. Trillinger had poisoned Liam's mind. Better the boy should die up here than live to carry his father's legacy. Besides, he still had a function to serve.

She pressed a button on the keyboard. The *Absence* came to a bobbing halt. The moment the ship stabilized, Ivy opened a seven-foot portal on a pantry door.

"Go, love! Now!"

Gemma jumped through the surface. Ivy willed the door shut and resumed the ship's ascent. Nine seconds, and not a single portal to be felt from Peter or his protégé. Perfect.

Ivy pulled the gun from her holster, then shot the laptop twice. The screen exploded in a stream of sparks. No one else was getting off the *Absence*. Not now. Not ever.

She brushed the tears from her eyes and opened the pantry door. Liam crossed his arms impatiently. Ivy couldn't help but marvel at how much the boy looked like Peter when he was angry.

"Can I finally come out?" he asked.

"Yes."

His expression softened. "Are you okay? What happened?"

"Nothing you need to worry about."

"Can I *please* see my dad now?"

"Yes." Ivy eyed her smoking pistol, then smiled weakly at Liam. "Let's go find him."

EIGHTEEN

Zack sat on the floor of a long-forsaken restroom, his body in revolt after two days of captivity. His legs were sore. His wrists were chafed. His spine felt like it had been twisted into a pretzel. But these were minor gripes in light of his current predicament. He was trapped in the sky on a runaway hell-saucer, still separated from his people, with no idea if they were alive or dead. For all he knew, his best friend in the world was now the woman in the nearest stall, an erratic young Gotham named Mercurial Lee.

He caught a glimpse of himself in the bathroom mirror, then anxiously looked away. "I think we should keep moving."

"Fuck you."

Mercy huddled on the toilet in her underwear and socks. She'd been six yards from the restroom when her trauma got the better of her and she puked on her armor. She'd stripped off every piece of it, even the clean ones.

"I knew I shouldn't have come here," she said. "I should have listened to my mother. I . . ."

She covered her face with trembling hands. "God. He cut Mink to pieces."

Zack toyed with a piece of broken floor tile, his heart still pounding from the ordeal on the terrace. Though he was grateful to Mercy for unlocking his chains, his sympathy only went so far. She'd helped Rebel kill six Golds last year, including Zack's brother. The more he thought about it, the more tempted he was to just leave her here.

"I didn't know he could talk," Zack said, out of the blue.

"Who, Mink?"

"Yeah. He screamed something right before he died. I thought he was mute."

Mercy twisted the skull ring on her middle finger. "It wasn't an affliction. It was a choice."

"A choice?"

"We all have to sacrifice something when we turn eighteen. He chose to give up his voice."

Zack shook his head, scoffing. "You people are so goddamn weird."

He heard a faint noise outside the restroom door, a scraping sound, like someone dragging their feet.

"I know it won't mean anything," Mercy said. "But I'm sorry for—"

"Hold it."

Zack stood up on watery legs. Mercy peeked at him through the door crack. "What are you doing?"

"Shhhh."

The bathroom door swung open. Zack's heart skipped a beat at the tall, skinny redhead who stepped inside. "Holy shit . . ."

Amanda blinked at him dazedly. "Zack?"

He had never seen her this shaken up. Her skin was white. Her eyes were glazed. She walked toward him with a slow, shambling gait, as if she'd just been killed and resurrected.

Zack cupped her face. "Are you okay? What happened?"

"I don't know. I . . ."

Her memories came flooding back, until she could recall every painful minute of the last three days. This whole nightmare had started with her and Zack in the basement. It all began with a kiss.

Zack let out a soft, pained chuckle as Amanda yanked her hand away from him. "It's all right," he told her. "You can touch me."

"Are you sure?"

He nodded his head, his gaze lingering anxiously around his reflection. It felt like a hundred years ago that Semerjean visited him in a mirrored room and expounded on his family's objections. *It was never about sex, you idiot. Amanda has to receive her next lover willingly.*

Amanda wrapped Zack in a delirious hug. "God," she cried. "Oh my God. I never thought I'd see you again."

Zack returned the embrace, wincing. She felt so good in his arms that he couldn't help but wonder if maybe he was imagining this. Maybe he'd wake up to learn that he'd never left the mirror room. It was just the Pelletiers screwing with him, teasing him.

He looked into the mirror and saw the state of her back. "Holy shit. Amanda!"

Her jacket and shirt had been torn all the way to her bra strap. Her skin was covered in huge purple bruises. Even more disturbing was the two-inch silver disc that had been embedded at the base of her spine.

"What happened?"

Amanda checked her back in the mirror as best she could. "I don't know. I was standing with Peter when everything went crazy. I don't know where he is."

"What about the others?"

"I don't know." She fished through her pockets. "I can't find my phone. It must have . . ."

She turned her head and saw someone looking at her through a crack in a stall door—an almond-shaped eye, slathered in heavy black makeup. That was all Amanda needed to recognize her.

"You!"

Zack grabbed her arm. "Whoa, whoa! Wait!"

"Wait!" Mercy yelled.

Amanda reached for her with a thick white tendril, just as Mercy fired her solis. The tempis vanished like a popped balloon.

Zack held Amanda back. "Stop! Stop! She's all right."

"All right? I *know* her."

"She's not with them anymore. She's done."

Mercy stepped out of the stall in her faded black skimpies. Amanda studied her through a squint. "You quit the Gothams."

"I quit the mission," Mercy clarified.

"And you're half-naked because . . . ?"

"My clothes are covered in hunkey."

"What the hell is 'hunkey'?"

"You've been here months. Learn the lingo."

"How about I just throw you out a window?"

Zack was about to intervene when the bathroom door creaked open again. Peter leaned in and scowled at the trio inside.

"You're making more noise than the devil in here."

"Peter!" Amanda hurried toward him. "I was worried about you. Where were you?"

He stepped inside and closed the door behind him. The others could see his awful state. His cheek was bruised. His clothes were dusty in some places and shredded in others. A thin trail of blood dribbled down the side of his head.

"Don't rightly know," he told Amanda. "I got knocked out in one place and woke up in another."

He grinned exhaustedly at Zack. "Hello, stranger."

Zack stared at his feet and wrung his hands despondently. "You guys shouldn't have come. I tried to warn you."

"We knew. Didn't stop us." Peter took off his windbreaker and offered it to Mercy. "I know you won't believe me, but I'm glad you're okay."

"Eat shit." She snatched the jacket from him. "Last time I saw you, you put a gun to my head."

"You think you don't deserve it?" Amanda asked her.

"I think it doesn't matter. We're not getting off this ship alive."

"Yes we are," Peter told her. "No one else is dying today."

Mercy threw on the windbreaker and zipped it up to the top. "Big words from a guy who doesn't know what's happening. You don't even know who's here."

"What are you talking about?

"Your son," Zack said. "He's up here with us."

Peter's arms dropped to his sides. He turned to Mercy, red-faced. "Liam's *here*?"

"Wasn't my idea," she said. "Ivy wanted leverage against you, so—"

Peter hollered in rage and tore a paper towel dispenser from the wall. Mercy raised her hands defensively. "I was against it! We all were, even Rebel. But Ivy insisted. She swore she'd only use him as a last resort."

Peter glared at Mercy's reflection. His voice came out in a guttural rasp. "Where is he?"

"Last I knew, down in the kitchen."

"Then that's where we're going."

Mercy recoiled at Peter's approach. Though his temples still throbbed with angry veins, he stuffed his hands in his back pockets. "It's all right," he said. "You're not the one I'm mad at. In fact, I owe you an apology."

"For what? The gun thing?"

"That," Peter said. "And this."

He drew a stun chaser from his pocket and fired it at her. Mercy convulsed on her feet for five long seconds before collapsing to the floor.

Zack gaped at Peter. "Why the hell did you do that?"

"Had to."

"She switched sides!"

"And she could have just as easily switched back," Peter told him. "She's called Mercurial for a reason."

Amanda crouched to the floor and checked Mercy's vitals. "He's right, Zack. We can't trust her."

"If we leave her here, she'll die."

"We won't."

Peter scooped her up and slung her over his back. Though his expression had cooled, his wrath was clearly still bubbling beneath the surface. He had Mercy on his shoulder but murder in his eyes.

"Let's go."

Contrary to public belief, most aerstraunts didn't have a traditional cockpit. There were no uniformed pilots, no navigators, no captains barking orders at a fast-moving crew. The ships were so self-sufficient that all they required was a capable technician. The "bridge" was simply a small, windowed room with a chair and a computer, and even that was unnecessary. Flight conductors could control the saucer from any part of the ship, even the bathroom. They only needed a laptop with the right peripherals, software, and access keys.

The command computer for the *Absence* was currently located in the kitchen, according to Semerjean. David had little reason to doubt his intel. There was, however, an unexpected problem.

He stood outside the kitchen door, his fingers pressed against tempis. The Gothams had erected a portable barrier, one strong enough to stop an elephant. "It won't budge. We're going to need Amanda."

Hannah paced the corridor, her eyes darting back and forth in thought.

She and Mia were both still distracted from their encounter with Semerjean, and David could hardly blame them. Everything about the man had seemed cosmically surreal, as if a curtain had parted to reveal a secret force of the universe, a backstage helper who was never meant to be seen.

But that was a concern for another day. The *Absence* was only getting higher. It was just a matter of time before a crucial system froze and the ship fell to earth like a meteor.

"Hannah . . ."

She stopped in her tracks and threw her arms up. "We can't reach Amanda. The phones are dead."

"Then maybe you and Mia should go look for her while I try to find another way in."

"No," said Hannah.

"No," said Mia. She snapped out of her daze and eyed David sternly. "We've split up enough. Either we all go together or we don't go at all."

David was about to object when the tempic barrier flickered out of existence. A tall man faced him from the other side of the doorway, an unplugged power cord in his hands.

Hannah rushed over and hugged him. "Jonathan! Are you all right?"

"I'm fine," he said. "I was starting to worry about you guys, though. I couldn't find anyone."

"How'd you get in?" David asked him.

"Door on the other side was open."

Jonathan saw their sullen faces, the bleeding cut on David's hand. "Okay. What did I miss?"

"We'll tell you later," Hannah said. "We need to find a laptop."

"A laptop?"

While Hannah explained, David glanced around the kitchen and scanned its recent past. The Gothams had been here just minutes ago, at least some of them. He watched Rebel in retrospect as he fired his revolver at a nearby bank of monitors. It was easy to see what he was angry about.

Mia saw a faint smile bloom on David's face. "What?"

"Three of the Gothams are down. One of them fled. And from everything I can tell, Zack's still alive."

Hannah sighed in hot relief. "Oh, thank God."

"What about Amanda and Peter?" Jonathan asked.

David pursed his lips. When Rebel shot the monitor, he shorted out the whole array. Shame. A camera system would have been very useful right now.

He looked to his right and saw another bullet-cracked screen, a laptop at the far end of the kitchen. "Oh no . . ."

Hannah followed him to the computer. "Wait. Is that it?"

David viewed its final minutes in hindsight. "It *was*." He pushed the device to the floor. "Damn it! That woman's lost her mind."

"Who?"

"Ivy," David said. "She's on a suicide run and she plans to take us with her."

Hannah looked around the kitchen. "There has to be *something*. An escape pod. I don't know."

Mia turned to Jonathan. "Did you find anything in the manager's office?"

He shook a finger at her. "Yeah. I've been waiting to talk to you about that. Your future self has a weird sense of humor."

"What do you mean?"

Jonathan led her to a countertop and showed her the fruits of his search: a fifty-foot cord of nylon rope and a peculiar black device the size of a bread box. The machine was like nothing any of them had ever seen. It had leather straps on one side, as if it was meant to be worn as a backpack. The other side was smooth, white, and utterly featureless.

Hannah furrowed her brow at the mysterious contraption. "This is the big solution you were talking about?"

"Don't ask me," Mia said defensively. "I'm just the messenger."

"But what *is* it?"

"I don't know." Mia turned it over and found a manufacturer code on the side. "If we had Eaglenet access, I could look it up."

David tapped his arm, agitated. "Whatever it is, it won't help us. We need to locate the others and find a way off the ship."

Mia turned her head and did a double-take at a device near Gemma's workstation. "Huh."

"What?" Hannah asked. "You find something?"

"I've seen that thing on the news. Deps use it to jam phone signals."

The others followed her gaze to a box on the floor, a portable machine with seven short antennas. A yellow sticker on the top warned people that this signal duffer was for federal law enforcement purposes. Any other use was prohibited by law and punishable by up to two years in prison.

David squeezed Mia's arm. "You're brilliant."

He located the duffer's power switch. The antennas retracted and the device stopped vibrating.

Mia was the first to check her handphone screen. "Signal's back!"

"So's mine," Jonathan said. "But it's weak as shit."

Hannah opened her phone and was stunned to see that she had twelve new voice mails, all from the same unidentified caller. She played the newest message.

"Goddamn it . . . nah. Call me . . . is number as soon as you . . . this. You're running out . . . time!"

"Who is that?" Mia asked her.

Though the connection was faint and cracking with static, Hannah easily recognized Theo's voice. She pressed the callback button and listened intently. It only rang for a second before he picked up. "Jesus! Finally!"

"Theo! Are you okay?"

"Holy . . . it! I've been . . . to reach you forever!"

Hannah covered her free ear, struggling to understand him. In addition to the connection issues, his voice was curiously muffled, as if he was speaking through a mask.

"I can barely hear you," she said. "Where are you?"

"Right . . . side."

"What?"

"I said I'm right outside!"

Baffled, Hannah looked through the kitchen door, across the hall, and out the window of an employee lounge. A small black object briefly dotted the sky before fluttering out of view.

"What the hell . . . ?"

The others followed Hannah as she hurried into the lounge. Now they could all see it: a sleek black aerovan thirty yards in the distance. It rose in jittery tandem with the *Absence*. The wind knocked it around hard enough to make Mia queasy.

Hannah stared at the vehicle, stupefied. It seemed completely insane, yet entirely appropriate, that Theo had found his way up here. Today was Easter Sunday, a day for saviors to rise.

"What are you doing here?"

Jonathan squinted at the shadowy figures inside. "Is that Heath?"

"Is Heath with you?"

"Heath's with me," Theo said. "He's fine. You're the ones . . . trouble."

Mia pressed against the glass and took a closer look at Theo's ride. She could see two silhouettes in the front seat and one in the middle row. "Who's flying that thing?"

"No idea." Hannah spoke into the phone again. "Theo—"

"I'll explain every . . . later! We have to get you out of there!"

David suddenly caught a glimpse of the driver's silhouette, a slender woman with dreadlocked hair. "You're kidding me."

"What?" Jonathan asked.

"That's Melissa Masaad."

"Who?"

Hannah's mouth dropped open. "Theo, is that *Melissa*?"

Theo traded an uneasy look with the driver, his newfound partner-in-crime. Even if he had the time to explain their new arrangement, he didn't have the words for it.

"Just trust me," he said. "She's on our side."

NINETEEN

She'd been half-asleep in a Seattle hotel room when Cedric Cain called her. Melissa sat up in bed, still fully clothed in her lavender pantsuit and surrounded by notes from her latest investigation. She scanned the bright dawn sky through the crack in the curtains, then switched her phone to her other ear.

"I'm sorry. What did you say?"

"They're alive," Cain repeated. "The orphans are still alive."

Melissa had decided some time ago to coin a universal term for her extraordinary case subjects. "Transdimensional chronokinetics" was a boulder on the tongue, and she refused to call them "freaks" like Gingold did. She'd hoped to make "orphans" the standard agency nomenclature, but only Cain indulged her. To the rest of Integrity, they were benders, mutants, chronnies, blights. Some had even taken to calling them "deadsetters," which especially irked her. It was a racially charged term from the Cataclysm era, a catch-all word for unwelcome immigrants.

In her groggy state, Melissa assumed Cain was talking about the latest group of orphans: the seven fugitives who'd been wreaking havoc in the Pacific Northwest. Melissa had been chasing them for weeks, so why would Cain call to tell her that they were . . .

"Alive." She launched up from the bed, spilling a dozen loose papers to the floor. "You mean *my* orphans. The original six."

"Yes."

"How do you know? Where are they?"

"Brooklyn," Cain told her. "Gingold found them. He's just a few hours away from taking them down. If you hurry—"

Melissa threw on her shoes, raced her Sparrow to the aerport, and used her badge to grab a seat on the next dart to Idlewild. She crossed the country in a transonic blur, her knees bouncing, her eyes dancing in rumination. She *knew* something wasn't right about those corpses in the movie theater, and

Gingold had been excessively cagey these past few weeks. But why did he cut Melissa out of the loop? Did he know what she was planning?

Cain arranged to have an aerovan waiting for her in New York: a black, nine-seat Griffin that had been specially tailored for government use. The shifter could accelerate to twice the legal limit, while a transponder emitted an electronic warning to all policemen in range: *Integrity business. Do not pursue.*

The rocket path that Melissa flew to Brooklyn would have earned anyone else a night in jail. She still didn't get there in time.

"They split up," Cain told her, a mere thirty seconds before she arrived at the siege site. "Most of them fled north in a lime-green Peregrine."

"Who stayed behind?"

"It's too late to save them. Focus on the others."

"*Who* stayed behind?"

Cain sighed in her earpiece. "Theo Maranan and some boy they can't identify. But listen—"

"See if there are other vehicles registered to the owner of that Peregrine."

"What are you doing?"

"I'm intercepting Theo before he gets to his escape car."

"Escape car? Melissa, he's surrounded. He's not getting out of there."

"He'll get out."

"How do you know?"

Melissa looked out her window just in time to see Gingold and his soldiers advancing on the brownstone. "Because I know Theo."

Six minutes later, she greeted him in a SmartFeast parking lot, her pistol pressed firmly against his back. It was lucky for her that Heath was still reeling from the agency's solic wasp. She'd gotten a bird's-eye view of his paranormal talent. The last thing she needed was a tempic animal in her face.

Helpless, Heath shook his head in the back of the Peregrine. "No no no no . . ."

"Calm your friend," Melissa told Theo. "For his sake and yours."

Theo raised a palm at Heath, then looked at Melissa's reflection in the van window. "Let him go. He's just a neighbor's kid."

"Oh? So it was you who made those wolves and elephants?"

"I'm telling you, he's not one of us."

"Then why does he have a Pelletier bracelet on his wrist?"

Theo gaped at her, confounded. "How do you know about those?"

"You know it wounds me, Theo, that the first thing out of your mouth is a lie."

"You have a gun in my back. You're expecting courtesy?"

"I'm expecting foresight." She eyed his reflection with wonder. "You don't see what's coming, do you?"

"You mean the part where scientists cut up my corpse?"

"That already happened. I'm talking about your future."

"And what is my future?"

Melissa leaned in close, smiling. She'd been mourning Theo and his people for months now, tormenting herself with notions of what might have been. Now, through some unholy magic she had yet to understand, they were back. Their second coming gave her a second chance to make everything right.

"*I* am," she said. "I'm the only future you have."

For Theo, the only thing crazier than fleeing the house in a herd of tempic elephants was escaping the government in a government vehicle. He and Heath crouched on the floor of the Griffin until they were five miles away from the battle zone.

Theo leaned forward in the middle row and took a good hard look at Melissa. Though she was just as lovely as he remembered, there was something off about her. Her pantsuit was wrinkled, as if she had slept in it. She looked nervous in a way Theo hadn't seen before. Had she really turned against the U.S. government, or was this whole "rescue" just a complicated con job?

As the Griffin sailed into Manhattan through the Lower East Side, flying high to avoid traffic cameras, Melissa peeked at Heath through the rearview mirror. "Since Theo hasn't seen fit to introduce us, my name's Melissa Masaad. What's yours?"

Heath only gave her the briefest of glances before looking out the window. His left hand rocked back and forth, as if he was shaking an invisible drink.

"Is he . . . all right?" She asked Theo.

"No, he's not all right. Your people nearly killed him."

"They're not my people."

"Bullshit. We know you're with Integrity now."

"Doesn't mean I share their cause. Who told you that, anyway?"

"David. He saw you in that movie theater. You and those armored goons."

"Funny. I saw him too. He was dead, just like the rest of you. Care to explain that one?"

Theo sank in his seat with a look of bitter gloom. "That wasn't us."

"Obviously."

"No, I mean it wasn't our trick. I'm pretty sure the Pelletiers did it."

Melissa sighed out her window. "That's what I was afraid of."

As she flew them over the high-rises of Gramercy, Theo looked down and saw dozens of people enjoying a Sunday barbecue on a rooftop. A pair of teenage boys stood at the railing, laughing as they raced remote control saucers through a series of floating hoops.

That's what Heath should be doing, Theo lamented. *That's the life he should be living.*

He frowned at Melissa. "Last time I saw you, you warned me about Integrity. Kept saying how awful they were."

"I said lawless, not awful. Though some of them are truly foul."

"So why are you working with them?"

"A smarter man might notice that I'm currently working against them."

"Why?"

"Answer my question first."

"Which one?"

Melissa jerked her thumb over her shoulder. "Who *is* he?"

Theo stared out his window for a few quiet seconds before answering. "His name's Heath."

"And I take it he's—"

"Yes," Theo said. "He's from my world."

Melissa took another look at the boy. "Hello, Heath. On behalf of the United States government, I sincerely apologize for your ordeal today. What those men did was inexcusable. In a perfect world, they'd be brought up on charges."

Heath stared down at his hands. Melissa heard him mutter something about a broken guitar.

Two states away, Cain watched her through a bubble cam lens in the dashboard. "Careful. The solis must have worn off by now. You might want to, uh . . ."

Melissa subtly shook her head at the camera. She had a stun chaser in her pocket. She wouldn't use it unless she absolutely had to.

The Griffin broke out of the Manhattan skyline and flew a northern path up the Hudson. "Where are we going?" Theo asked.

"You tell me."

"What?"

"We're ten miles behind your friends," she informed him. "A squadron of gunships are following them. If you have any information—"

"I don't," Theo said. "Peter never, uh . . . he didn't give me an address."

Melissa saw his bewildered distraction. "You all right?"

The fog in his foresight was finally starting to clear. Through the lingering haze, he saw a black metal saucer hanging vertically in the air, like an eclipse. Smoke billowed out of its broken windows. It was plummeting toward the earth—or at least it would be.

"We can save them," Melissa told Theo. "But you have to trust me."

"I'm trying. I am. I just . . . you're committing treason for a bunch of people you barely even know. You seem like the last person on Earth who'd do that."

Melissa stared out the windshield, her fingers tapping against the steering wheel. "When Amanda was in my custody, she was convinced that the government would kill and dissect her. I assured her it wouldn't. Every human being in this nation has rights, even if they're from another Earth, even if they shoot tempis from their hands."

Her expression turned bitter. "But then Integrity took over and . . . let's just say her fears are no longer baseless. I can't abide by what they're doing. They're the ones who've gone rogue. Not me."

Theo eyed her skeptically. "That's your only reason for doing this?"

"Of course not. I haven't slept a full night since I met you people. I want to understand where you came from, how you got here, how you do the things you do. Can you blame me?"

"No. I'm just wondering what your plan is. Even if you save us by some holy miracle, what then?"

"We've set up a safe house in Maine," Melissa told him. "It's in a dense forest, away from the prying eyes of humans and satellites. It's comfortable, secure and, might I add, quite beautiful."

"Back up," said Theo.

"To which part?"

"The part where you said 'we.'"

Melissa threw a brief look at the dashboard camera. "I have an associate. A very resourceful one."

"Careful," Cain muttered in her ear. "No names."

"And you trust this person?" Theo asked.

"I do," Melissa replied, though her assurance came with an asterisk. She knew Cain wanted the orphans alive as much as she did, that he despised what his agency had become. He'd promised her in his own coy way that Integrity was about to undergo a major change in management. Even so, Melissa had no guarantee that the new bosses would be any better than the old ones, or that Cain wouldn't turn on her once he got his beloved Sci-Tech division back.

She looked at Theo pleadingly. "Where are your friends going?"

"I told you—"

"I mean what's their purpose?"

Theo traded a quick, anxious look with Heath. "They're trying to save Zack."

"From who?"

"Gothams."

"Jesus," Cain uttered.

"So they do exist," Melissa said. "Native-born chronokinetics. They're not just a myth."

"Of course not." Theo cocked his head. "You work for the country's biggest intelligence agency. How could you not know?"

"Either it's a classified secret that I'm not privy to, or these Gothams are exceptionally good at staying hidden."

"It's the latter," Cain told her. "Believe me."

"Why would the Gothams take Zack?" Melissa asked Theo.

He hemmed a moment before shaking his head. "We'll be in Canada before I'm done explaining it."

"At least tell me why they left you behind."

He chuckled bleakly. "You definitely don't want the answer to that one."

Melissa thumped the steering wheel. "Damn it. In all your premonitions, haven't you once seen a future where you and I are friends?"

In point of fact, he'd seen futures that went well beyond that. Theo knew the sounds Melissa made in throes of passion, the shape of the mole on her stomach. He'd also seen her shoot him in the rain, chase him down a sewer, and swear more than once that she never meant for things to end this way. The strings extended in all directions, and Theo had every reason to be pessimistic today.

The Griffin flew in testy silence for eight more minutes, until Cain gave Melissa a new instruction. She banked a left toward Sleepy Hollow, then began a sharp descent.

Theo gripped the door handle. "What are you doing?"

"Your friends just landed."

"How do you know?"

"I'm clairvoyant, like all Libras."

Theo scowled at her. "Your friend's feeding you information."

"Why on earth would your people go to Atropos?"

"I don't even know what that is."

"It's an abandoned aerport," Melissa explained. "An awful place to be ambushed by armed federal—"

"They won't be there," Theo blurted.

Melissa and Heath both eyed him intently. Cain leaned in toward his computer.

"What do you mean?" Melissa asked Theo.

"I mean by the time we get there, they'll be someplace else."

"Where?"

His foresight had come back with a vengeance. He couldn't stop seeing that smoldering black saucer, falling through the sky as it quickly fell to pieces. His friends were still on it. He was watching them die—just minutes from now.

"Up," Theo said. "We have to go up."

The Griffin began its climb six minutes before the *Absence* did. Melissa steered them on a 50-degree incline, stopping only to disable the altitude lock.

Unlike the aerstraunt, the van had no atmospheric protections. At sixteen thousand feet, Melissa sent Theo to the back for emergency supplies. He found four breathing masks but only two oxygen bottles.

"Give one to Heath," she told him. "You and I can share."

Theo sat hip-to-hip with Melissa in the front seat, their air tubes connected to the canister's twin ports.

He jerked his head at the dashboard's blinking red gauges. "Will this thing hold up?"

"I'm not sure," Melissa said. "The heaters and stabilizers have gone into overdrive. It's eating up the battery charge."

"How long do we have?"

She checked the power meter. "We'll have to start our descent in nine minutes. After that, there'll be no hope for a soft landing."

At twenty thousand feet, the *Absence* burst through a cloud and continued its wayward climb. Melissa straightened the Griffin to a vertical ascent, struggling to keep pace with the saucer.

"This is a bad idea," Cain told Melissa. "I've known Noah Butterfield for thirty years. He's as mean as they come. You get in his way, he won't hesitate to kill you."

Melissa's gut twisted. She looked to Theo, still frantically punching numbers into her handphone. "You *need* to reach them."

"I'm trying!"

He'd left his own phone in Brooklyn, along with all his friends' contact information. Luckily, Heath had changed and tested Hannah's ringtone enough to know her number by heart. Theo dialed it again, only to get her voice mail a seventh time.

"Goddamn it, Hannah. Call me at this number as soon as you get this. You're running out of time!"

Cain sighed into his headset. "Melissa, I'm begging you. Cut your losses and get out of there. Two is better than none. And personally speaking, I like you better when you're alive."

"That's how I feel about them," she murmured.

Theo looked up. "What?"

"Nothing. Just keep trying."

At twenty-five thousand feet, Hannah finally answered her phone. She and Theo spoke back and forth for a minute before he explained Melissa's escape plan.

"We'll have to dock with the ship," Theo said. "There's a delivery hatch on the staff level, not far from you. It's locked in flight but it should have an emergency override."

"Where?" Hannah asked.

"Where's the override?" Theo asked Melissa.

"Not sure." She took a closer look at the aerstraunt. "It's a Douglas ship. Anything could be anywhere."

"They don't have time to go looking!"

Hannah's voice crackled through the phone. "Jonathan says he can drop the door."

"Is he sure?"

"Yeah. He's dropped bigger things today. I just don't know if it's safe."

"It's not safe at all," Theo said. "Your ship's pressurized, so when you open that thing—"

"It'll suck," Hannah guessed.

"A lot. Can he drop it from a distance?"

"He goddamn better."

"What do you mean 'drop it'?" Melissa asked Theo.

"We have a guy who does that."

"Does what?"

"Drops things. Just wait."

Heath gripped Theo's shoulder. "Tell him to be careful!"

Melissa scanned the ship's lower levels, then pointed to a large metal hatch. "There it is."

"Okay, we see the delivery door," Theo told Hannah. "We'll line up the van as best we can but this'll be tricky. Amanda will have to use her tempis to tether us."

"Shit!"

"What?"

"She's not here," Hannah said. "She and Peter are still looking for Zack."

"Shit." Theo covered the receiver and looked to Melissa. "They're still split up."

Hundreds of miles away, in the suburbs of central Maryland, Cain leaned back in his office chair and watched Melissa and Theo on his monitor. A message popped up near the top of the screen, an encrypted bitmail from one of his informants.

> **Butterfield's crew almost caught up with aerstraunt. ETA 90 seconds.**

Cain deleted the message, cursing. It was already too late. Even if Melissa fled right this second, the gunships would catch her and blow her out of the sky. She had gambled everything to save these orphans, and lost. There was nowhere left for any of them to go but down.

TWENTY

The dining level of the *Absence* was all glass on the outside, a sixty-five-piece window wall that wrapped around the ship like a waist belt. The only thing that kept passengers from having a full 360-degree view was the circle of conveniences in the middle of the deck—two stairwells, three elevators, four restrooms, and a lumivision lounge.

Somewhere in that cluster was the lift to the kitchen, but Amanda had no idea where. All she could do was lead Zack and Peter on a clockwise path along the curved inner wall. Had she gone the other way, she would have seen Melissa's Griffin through the far window. Instead, she backtracked through the dining partitions, to the awful place where Bug Sunder had shot her. His body remained spread-eagled on the floor, next to a smiley face that had been painted in his blood.

Peter grimaced at Semerjean's artwork. "That's just depraved."

Zack nodded in dark agreement. "You should see what he did to Mink."

"For a group of evolved beings, they're pretty damn savage."

Amanda frowned at Peter. "I could say the same about your people."

"I told you—"

"'They're not all like Ivy and Rebel,'" Amanda said. "I know. But your clan still supports them. They're cheering them on from the sidelines, rooting for them to kill us."

Peter slung Mercy off his shoulder and carried her in his arms. "They're just scared."

"And ignorant," Zack added.

"That can be fixed."

"You still think you can change their minds."

"We just have to change Rebel and Ivy's," Peter said. "The rest will follow."

While Zack and Amanda traded a cynical look, Peter noticed the waitstaff elevator nestled snugly between stairwells. "There it is."

Amanda pressed the call button, then waited restlessly by the door. She felt ridiculously spry for someone who'd just been shot in the back with a 12-gauge. God only knew what insane nanowizardry that Pelletier had put into her body. What if the disc on her spine did more than heal her? What if it gave Esis direct control over her mind, her body, her *tempis*?

Zack peeked around the stairwell and saw the bobbing black aerovan in the distance. "Uh . . ."

"What?"

"There's someone outside."

"Outside."

"I'm not kidding. Come look. It's right—"

A gunshot echoed through the dining room. Zack's throat opened in a gush of blood. He clutched his neck with both hands, gurgling.

Amanda screamed as he toppled to the floor. *"Zack!"*

Rebel hid behind a partition, his face drenched in sweat. He'd been stalking Zack and the others since they first left the restroom, waiting for the right moment to strike. He knew he had one free shot before he was attacked.

So who do I hit? Rebel had asked the future, and the future said, *"Trillinger."* His girlfriend would drop to the ground in a hysterical effort to save him, leaving Pendergen as the only threat. But his portals were useless here, and he couldn't reach his pistol with Mercy in his arms. Once Zack fell, Amanda and Peter would be easy kills.

Unfortunately for Rebel, human beings were less predictable than bullets. They moved in erratic paths, making split-second turns based on chemical impulses and irrational whims. Rebel looked around the partition only to see his expectations reversed. It was Peter who'd dropped to the ground to save Zack.

It was Amanda who went to war.

Hard, jagged tempis covered every inch of her skin, stretching her clothes in some places and tearing it in others. Her face became a rocky mask. White lips parted to reveal clenched teeth.

Rebel looked down at her huge spiked fists. Suddenly the future had a grim new tale to tell.

Shit . . .

He fired his .44 at Amanda's left eye, only to watch her block it with her hand. He shot two more bullets at her chest. The impact alone should have brought her to her knees, but she just kept coming.

Amanda grabbed the partition and tossed it to the side. Her voice came out in a guttural rasp.

"That's the last person you hurt."

Rebel stumbled backward and raised his revolver again. Amanda knocked it out of his hand with enough force to break two of his fingers. He howled in pain, then reached for a grenade with his mechanical arm.

Amanda gripped him by the neck and raised him off his feet.

"That's the last person you hurt," she repeated.

She threw him against a window. His body slammed against the tempered glass before crumpling to the floor. He made a feeble attempt to crawl away, but Amanda grabbed him by the back of his vest.

"That is—"

She shoved Rebel into a partition. His front teeth cracked against the metal edge.

"—the last person—"

She drove him down onto the surface of a table, breaking his nose.

"—*you hurt!*"

At last, Amanda slammed his body down onto the floor, lacerating his liver and bruising his spleen.

Peter kneeled at Zack's side and pressed the wound on his neck. Hot blood coursed through his fingers. Zack writhed beneath him, gasping in shock.

"Hold still," Peter said. "For God's sake."

He knew his efforts were only buying Zack moments at best. He was losing too much blood, too fast. Someone had to clamp the artery.

"Amanda . . ."

Amanda watched Rebel with idle curiosity as he writhed across the tile. He struggled to reach his gun.

"I don't think you heard me, Richard . . ."

She smashed a tempic hammer down on his fingers, reducing his prosthetic to scrap metal and wires. She clutched his head with a tempic prong and raised him back up to eye level.

"Let me say it again."

Rebel coughed up blood, then bared his broken teeth at her. "I heard you the first time. And I know just who you sound like."

"Shut up."

"You are Esis through and through."

Peter looked up, wide-eyed. "Amanda!"

"*Stop!*"

The second voice came from the top of the stairwell—a high, piercing shout that turned everyone's heads.

Ivy stepped into the dining room, her arm wrapped tightly around Liam's neck. Sweat dripped down the sides of her face as she pressed her pistol against the boy's temple.

"No!" Peter yelled. "Don't you dare!"

Liam looked up, his face streaked with tears. "Dad . . ."

"Shut up! All of you!" Ivy gritted her teeth at Amanda. "Get your goddamn hands off Richard. Now."

Amanda hesitated, conflicted. She had Ivy's husband at her mercy. A well-placed threat might get her to back down.

But one look into Ivy's deep brown eyes was enough to see her mental state. She was unstable. Dangerous. Amanda wasn't about to gamble with the life of Peter's only child.

She retracted all her tempis, then let go of Rebel. He fell to the floor and shot a tortured look at Ivy. "I told you to leave . . ."

"We're in this together, love. All the way to the bitter end."

"Let my son go," Peter pleaded. "He's innocent. You know that."

"I said *shut up.*" She scanned the area suspiciously. "And *you*! I know you're here. Show yourself!"

Amanda and Peter took a puzzled glance around the dining room. Ivy was yelling at empty air.

"What, you killed my brother and now you don't even have the guts to face me? Come on, Semerjean! Be a man!"

Peter shook his head at her. "He's gone, Ivy."

"One more word out of you, and I swear to God . . ."

Amanda stepped toward Zack for a clearer view. Peter was doing an awful job stemming his blood loss. He was too shaken, too distracted. "No!"

Ivy pulled Liam back and repositioned the gun. "Stay where you are!"

"Go to hell."

"I mean it!"

"Ivy . . ." Rebel coughed more blood. "Let her help him. She's not . . . she's not going anywhere."

Ivy saw his expression and knew exactly what he was planning. He had one last trick up his sleeve. But he needed time to prepare it. She had to keep their enemies distracted.

She flicked a dismissive hand at Amanda. "Fine. Go tend to your boy-friend."

Amanda kneeled at Zack's side and took over for Peter. Tiny threads of tempis snaked out of her fingertips, gripping Zack's severed artery and clamping it shut. But she could see that he'd lost too much blood already. He was on the slow, greasy slide to oblivion, and even her tempis couldn't save him.

She cradled him in her arms, her voice choked with tears. "Just hang on, Zack. Stay with me."

Peter climbed to his feet and raised his bloody hands at Ivy. "Look, there's been enough death today."

"Oh, really? Who have you lost? Last I checked, the breachers were still alive."

"Not all of them," Peter reminded her.

"Right, yes, the Golds." Ivy laughed. "Funny how the Pelletiers didn't lift a finger to save them. But they didn't like what we did that night. Oh boy, were they mad. You know how I know?"

Peter closed his eyes. "Ivy . . ."

"Shut up." She turned to face Amanda. "He never told you what happened, did he? What your demon masters did."

Amanda glared at her. "What the hell are you talking about?"

"I was pregnant with twins," Ivy said. "Two big, healthy boys. You should have seen the echosounds. They were gorgeous. They were *perfect.*"

Her eyes glistened with tears. Her gun quivered against Liam. "But then my due date came and I couldn't stop bleeding. Something had gone wrong. Richard rushed me to the hospital but it was already too late. When they pulled my sons out of me . . ."

She let out a cracked, delirious laugh. "They were shiny all over, as if their bodies had been dipped in metallic paint. Can you picture it, Amanda? Can you guess the colors of my sons' corpses?"

"Look—"

"Silver and gold!" Ivy cried. "Gold and silver! Do you get it now? It was a message from the Pelletiers. They killed my children and desecrated their bodies while *they were still inside me.*"

"We have nothing to do with them," Peter said.

"Bullshit!" She gestured at Bug. "My brother's dead! Semerjean ripped his throat out, all to save *this* woman."

Amanda had to fight to keep her tempis from screaming out of her. "We never asked them to help us. We didn't ask for *any* of this! We hate them as much as you do!"

"Well, they love you," Ivy said. "They love you Silvers like their very own children. So you can see what a delicious opportunity this presents for me. I only wish I had some metallic paint for your corpse. That would really make it poetic."

Peter caught a gleam in the corner of his eye. He turned and saw Rebel fumbling with something, a small, metallic device with a radio antenna.

A detonator.

"No!"

There were three rooms in the *Absence* that none of the Silvers got to see: a closet on the engine level, a pantry in the kitchen, and the lumivision lounge on the dining deck. Inside each one was a hundred-pound block of cyclo-trimethylene putty, a powerful explosive more commonly known as Wild-9.

Rebel had installed enough of the stuff to vaporize the *Absence*. He'd been saving his present for the Pelletiers, but this seemed a good enough time to use it. If he was lucky, maybe Semerjean was still on the ship somewhere.

Panicked, Peter made a fevered dash toward Rebel. Ivy aimed her gun at him and fired. The bullet cut a path through his shoulder blade. His chest exploded in a fist-size spray of blood.

Liam's eyes went wide. He broke away from Ivy. *"Dad!"*

The moment Ivy lost her hostage, Amanda attacked. A tendril of tempis crashed down on Ivy's forearm, breaking its bones and throwing the gun out of her hand. It skidded across the tile and came to a stop between the unconscious bodies of Zack and Mercy.

Rebel gripped the detonator with his last three working fingers. He flipped the lid with his teeth, closed his teary eyes, then slammed the button against his chest.

And then . . . everything stopped.

Rebel was so wrapped up in his expectations that it took him three full seconds to realize that the Wild-9 hadn't exploded. The ship was still in one piece, but something had changed. All the partitions had toppled to the floor. The floors and walls stopped vibrating.

The *Absence* had come to a complete and abrupt halt.

A hundred yards away, the struggling black Griffin shot several yards above the saucer. Theo looked at Melissa, frantic. "What are you doing?"

"It's not us." She slammed the air brake, then peered out her window. "It's them. They stopped."

"What?" Theo raised Melissa's phone to his mouth. "Hannah, are you there?"

Hannah sat up in the kitchen and rubbed her throbbing skull. Everything had gone topsy-turvy. All the people in the room, all the Gothams' fancy equipment, they'd all been thrown to the floor.

She saw her phone on the tile and picked it up. "Jesus. What happened?"

"I don't know," Theo said. "I don't like this."

Heath peeked out of his window, then sucked a loud gasp. Melissa followed his gaze and saw exactly what he was looking at.

"Mother of God . . ."

A dark new shadow filled the dining room. Amanda and the Gothams turned their heads to the east. Two enormous faces peeked in through the nearest windows—a white-haired man with fierce blue eyes, a brown-haired woman with irises as black as tar.

Esis looked down at Amanda, her huge lips curled in a smile. "Hello, child."

TWENTY-ONE

Melissa Masaad had seen enough supernatural mayhem in the last eight months to fundamentally alter her reasoning. She'd moved mountains to make room for the existence of chronokinetics, unhinged her jaw to swallow the notion of parallel Earths. She'd made peace with the fact that were no givens left in her universe, only Givens.

But nothing could have prepared her for the sight of the Pelletiers.

They floated thirty thousand feet above the ruins of Atropos, standing shoulder to shoulder on a floor of pure sky. Azral wore a sharp gray business suit with a casual open collar. Esis sported a Russian leather waistcoat over a white blouse and slacks. They both looked perfectly comfortable in the upper troposphere, despite the subzero temperature and the unbreathable air. The wind blew all around them without ruffling a hair.

Most jarring of all was their impossible size. Theo had once told Melissa that the Pelletiers were abnormally tall, but he'd undersold them by at least two hundred feet. The *Absence* looked like a beach umbrella next to them. The Griffin was just a hummingbird in the backdrop.

"That . . ." Melissa tried to form words, but her brain was still trying to process the situation. Like Jack on the beanstalk, she'd climbed beyond the clouds and was now facing giants.

Her paralysis broke. She gripped Theo's wrist. "Tell me those are lumic projections."

He shared her thunderstruck expression. "Those are lumic projections."

"Are you sure?"

"No."

Melissa snatched a wireless transceiver from the glove box and set it to Integrity's main frequency.

Cain watched her through the dashboard camera. "Wait. What are you doing?"

"What are you doing?" Theo asked her.

"There are two people out there whom I feel very comfortable calling 'aliens,'" she said. "If these are indeed the Pelletiers you warned me about—"

"They are," Theo said.

"—then we have a whole new problem. All of us."

The radio crackled with chatter. She raised the handset to her mouth. "This is Melissa Masaad, Integrity Associate 42144. Authorization rider: 6-Athena-26."

She closed her eyes and took a deep breath. "I need to speak to Noah Butterfield. Now."

If Mink Rosen had still been alive, he would have been the only one on the ship to see the real Azral and Esis. They stood together under the glass dome of the terrace, their attention fixed on a small, floating hologram of the *Absence*. Through its ethereal windows, they watched live, tiny replicas of the people in the main dining room: the living, the dead, and the two men caught in between.

Esis assessed Zack's and Peter's conditions before focusing on Rebel. He continued to clutch the Wild-9 detonator, slamming the button over and over.

"Richard . . ."

Every move she made was matched in real time by her giant lumic doppelgänger. Every sound was amplified to a thunderous degree. When the big Esis spoke, the windows shook. Teeth rattled. Even the Silvers in the kitchen could hear her, like a neighbor's TV that had been turned to top volume.

Ivy cradled her broken arm and fixed her crying eyes on Rebel. "Do it, love! Do it!"

Rebel was trying, but the detonation signal was jammed. Nothing he did could set off the explosives.

Esis rolled her eyes. "Oh, for heaven's sake . . ."

"*Ga'helgen la-ïl*," Azral muttered to her.

"Yes. Of course."

She made a quick, twirling gesture with her finger. A horizontal portal, no larger than a tea saucer, opened ten inches above Peter's dying body.

Liam kneeled at his side, distraught and confused. "What—"

A silver disc dropped through the opening and landed on Peter's chest. The survivors in the room watched intently as the metal burned through his T-shirt and affixed itself to his skin.

Liam shook him in panic. "No! Dad!"

"Calm yourself," Esis said. "He heals."

Peter thrashed on the floor, his body coated in a sickly yellow glow. After four seconds, the light faded and his convulsions stopped. His eyelids fluttered chaotically.

Liam checked his wrist pulse, then lifted his shirt. Though his skin was drenched in sweat and blood, his exit wound had already sealed. Only a thick, jagged scar remained, and even that was starting to shrink.

Amanda stayed at Zack's side, her tempis still clamped around his severed neck artery. His vital signs were getting weaker, but no new portals were opening. Azral and Esis didn't seem to have any interest in healing him.

"Goddamn you . . ."

A tempic knife popped out of Amanda's fist like a switchblade. She moved it to the healing disc on her back.

"Stop."

She looked up to see Esis's huge black eyes fixed squarely on her.

"Those devices are disposable," Esis warned her. "They only work once. You won't heal him. You'll simply harm yourself."

Amanda met her gaze with trembling fury. "Save him."

"Why? So you can defy me yet again?"

"We were done! We broke up!"

Esis pursed her lips skeptically. "A lie that only you believe."

"Don't let him die. Please!"

"We'll deal with you in a moment," Azral told her. "If you have any sense, you'll keep your mouth shut and wait."

He turned back to Rebel, sneering. "It must ail you, Richard, to see your careful plans fall to dust. These elaborate traps you set for us."

Rebel looked away from the window. "Fuck you."

"Ever the poet," Esis quipped.

"And the fool," Azral said. "I almost pity him. But then I remember all the atrocities he's committed—"

"*Atrocities?*" Ivy rose to her feet, red-faced. "Look at yourselves!"

The Pelletiers viewed her with matching scorn. "I blame this one," Azral said. "The fanatical voice in his ear."

"Oh, she's awful," said Esis. "Like a lesion in the midbrain. She stimulates aggression."

"Shut up!" Ivy cried. "You killed my sons!"

"*You* killed your sons. You could have seen the light of reason. You could have listened to Pendergen when he tried to make peace."

Azral shook his head reproachfully. "And yet you persisted with your violent crusade, forcing us all down a harder path. My family has been inconvenienced but *you*, Ilavarasi, have lost friends, children, siblings. How many more must fall before you finally learn?"

Ivy wept into the crook of her arm. "I'll kill you . . ."

"And still she swears violence," Azral said to Esis. "She is beyond hope."

Rebel spat blood at them. "Just get it over with already, you shitcocks. I'm sick of looking at you."

Azral scoffed. "Did you think we came here to kill you? Is that what you see in your future?"

"He sees nothing," Esis said. "He's no true augur."

"Nor a martyr," Azral added. "Death is a far better fate than he deserves. No, *sehmeer*, I believe he should be exposed for the false prophet he is. Let him live to bear the condemnation of his people."

Screaming, Ivy searched the area for her fallen gun. "Monsters! Demons!"

Azral looked to his mother with weary eyes. "*Mortula shi-la ma'tin.*"

"With pleasure."

Esis pinched two fingers together. A two-inch portal materialized in the dining room, a meter away from Ivy's head. She didn't see it. Her attention was on the shotgun by her brother's corpse.

She rushed toward the weapon, babbling incoherently with rage. Once upon a time, she'd been a princess among her people, the most gifted daughter of the clan's most powerful family. But now even Amanda felt pity for the creature Ivy Sunder had become. She wondered how many more losses it would take before she became just as broken and twisted as the woman in front of her.

Ivy seized the shotgun and spun around to face the Pelletiers. "I'll kill you! I'll—"

A fast-moving projectile flew out of the Pelletiers' portal, piercing the back of Ivy's skull. Her head snapped back. She sucked a sharp breath.

Rebel struggled to crawl to her. "Baby?"

Ivy touched her scalp with a trembling hand, saw the blood on her fingers, then stared in astonishment at her husband. "I . . ."

Her eyes rolled back. She fell face-first over Bug, then lay gravely still on his chest.

"*Ivy!*"

Esis smiled vindictively. "When last we met, Richard, you fired your noisy weapon at me. I captured the bullet in a temporal portal and promised you it would return one day."

She leaned in closer, her nose almost touching the window. "You sealed her fate seven months ago. She died by your hand."

Rebel dragged himself toward Ivy, his cracked voice wavering between a whimper and a scream.

"Do you think he heard us?" Esis asked Azral.

"Doesn't matter. Already I see a change in the strings."

"Oh yes," said Esis. "A new day dawns. Only one question remains . . ."

She narrowed her eyes at Amanda and Zack. "What are we to do with this pair?"

Hannah looked down the hallway, her fingers clenched like steel hooks. She had too many reasons to be nervous at the moment. The Pelletiers were upstairs, along with half her group. Integrity gunships were approaching quickly from below. And she wasn't entirely sure that the ship was free of its Gotham problem.

But her biggest concern was twenty yards in front of her, in a shallow nook at the end of the corridor. A man she'd kissed just minutes ago was about to do something stupid, and very likely fatal.

"I don't like this," Hannah yelled down the hall. "I think we should try something else."

"There's no time," Jonathan said. "We need an exit."

His alcove was just ten feet away from the delivery hatch, far closer than

Hannah would have liked. Once the big door dropped, the entire hallway would become a vacuum, a rather strong one at that. Hannah had once seen an episode of *MythBusters* where the hosts simulated an explosive decompression on an airplane. It didn't end well for the test dummy.

"At least use the rope you found," she urged Jonathan.

"I told you, there's nothing to tie it to."

"I can anchor you. I'm heavy as shit."

Twelve feet behind her, Mia and David toiled frantically in the kitchen. While one scrambled to get Gemma's surveillance station back online, the other fiddled with the ship's public address system.

Mia pressed a green button on the console and spoke into the microphone. "Hello? Can anyone hear me? Peter?"

Not a squeak from the ceiling speakers. Cursing, Mia scanned the console screen. "It says 'Remote Locked.' But who's locking it? Integrity?"

"No idea," David said. "It's obviously not working. Look for something else."

Once again, Mia pondered the strange black device that Jonathan had found in the manager's office, the cryptic "solution" her future self had told her about.

She picked it up by its cloth straps and studied it from every angle. There was a sliding compartment on the lower left side, one she'd never noticed before. Opening it revealed a pair of thick sport goggles, plus a yellow slip of paper with bold-faced warning text:

Always make sure your aerochute is fully charged before jumping. Do not jump anywhere near a solic generator tower.

"Aerochute . . ."

Sixty feet away, Jonathan took a deep breath, then squinted his eyes at the delivery hatch.

"Okay, get ready," he told Hannah. "It's too heavy to drop all at once. I'm just gonna drop the edges."

"Just be careful," Hannah yelled. "You and I have unfinished business."

"You make it sound like you're gonna whack me."

He peeked out of the nook and eyed Hannah awkwardly. "That was a mob joke, not a—"

"Just do it already!"

He focused his thoughts and dropped a one-inch sliver from the base of the door. The sky took a hissing breath through the slit. All the dust bunnies in the corridor began rolling toward the opening.

Mia ran to Hannah and brandished the aerochute. "Wait! Tell him to put this on!"

"What?"

"It's for skydivers! It—"

Jonathan's next drop blew the hatch wide open. It hurtled away from the *Absence*, taking half the doorjamb with it. The hallway filled with sunlight and shrieking wind. Hannah could feel the draft from the kitchen.

"Jonathan!"

He retreated into the nook as far as he could. "I'm all right! I'm okay!"

"Hang in there!" Hannah yelled. "The van's coming!"

She pulled her phone from her pocket and saw that her connection had been terminated. She redialed Melissa's number. "Come on, Theo . . ."

The phone lit up silently on Theo's lap, far outside his notice. His eyes were locked on the giant Pelletiers while he listened intently to Melissa's radio conversation.

"Sir, if you'd just hear me out—"

"Oh, I'm listening," Butterfield told her. "All I hear is you dodging my questions."

The Integrity fleet hovered four hundred feet below her—twelve gunships and ten cannon cycles, all loaded with enough firepower to level a city block. Though Butterfield was relieved that the *Absence* had finally stopped moving, the satellite images of Azral and Esis gave him cold pause. Nothing, not even his worst nightmares, could have prepared him for the sight of two building-size Eurotrashers.

He paced the aisle of the command shuttle, his armored fist smacking into his palm. "I'll ask again, Masaad. How did a woman who's not even part of this operation get here before us? Who's your source?"

"There's no time to explain," Melissa said. "You and your people are in imminent danger."

Butterfield frowned. "If you're talking about those big floating yahoos, I bet they're nothing but ghosts. The Dormer boy probably hung them up like scarecrows."

"The illusions go far beyond David's capabilities," Melissa assured him. "The Pelletiers are here, and they're extremely lethal. If you read my report—"

"I read your report. I know your whole damn history. And I'm wondering why the hell I should trust you when your own damn boss looks at you cockeyed."

A thermal scan analyst muttered into Butterfield's ear. His bushy eyebrows rose.

"Well, I'll be damned," he told Melissa. "These *Pelleh-teers* aren't giving off a scrap of heat. You, however, have two passengers with you, a man and a boy. Funny how Gingold's missing one of each."

Theo and Cain winced in unison. Melissa raised her handset. "If you want to interrogate me when this is over—"

"Oh, I'd say there's a good chance of that."

"—I'll cooperate. But I'm begging you, sir, for the sake of your people—"

Butterfield cut off the transmission, then addressed his crew through the radio. "All right. Enough of this threep. Weapons ready. Everyone in position. I want a clock formation around that saucer. Nobody fire till I give you the signal."

The ships rose. Butterfield clasped the arm of his chief weaponeer, then pointed to Melissa's van on the targeting screen.

"That tub moves an inch, you blow it to hell."

Amanda crouched on steel-hard tendons, only half aware of the chatter around her. Her heartbeat hammered loudly in her ears, and her mind wouldn't stop screaming the obvious. Zack would be dead in a matter of seconds. There was nothing she could do about it.

"Are you listening, child?"

Though Amanda knew she should make eye contact with Esis, she couldn't stop looking at Rebel. He wept in a corner with Ivy in his arms, a broken man in every way imaginable. For a moment, Amanda forgot that she was the one who'd smashed his nose, cracked his ribs, snapped his fingers of bone and metal. She would have run her tempis right through him if Ivy hadn't stopped her.

Esis scowled. "We're short on time, girl. If you seek our forgiveness—"

"Your what?"

Amanda looked up with hot green eyes. Her lips stammered with disbelief. "You took Zack from me. You tortured him and then handed him off to lunatics. He's dying right now because of you."

"You're responsible for his every—"

"*You* did this!" Amanda yelled. "Nobody forced you! No one made you kill Ivy or murder her unborn children. That was all you!"

Azral scoffed. "You would have died as a child were it not for us."

"Only because you need me for something. You need all of us, even Zack."

"You overstate his importance," said Esis.

"And understate his stubbornness," Azral added. "We were fully prepared to release him. He had but to ask. Instead he chose to mock and obstruct us, as he's done before. As he would no doubt do again."

"It's simply his nature," Esis insisted. "There is no saving him."

The blood rushed louder in Amanda's ears, and she understood every bit of Ivy's mania. These weren't evolved creatures. They were small-minded and petty and utterly self-absorbed. They couldn't be reasoned with, only threatened.

Amanda cast a tempic tendril at the .38 on the floor, the one that had blown a hole in Peter's chest, the one that Amanda had knocked out of Ivy's hand.

Azral watched her with a crinkled brow. "If you think you can hurt us—"

The gun retracted into Amanda's hand. She pressed the muzzle against her temple.

Esis's eyes opened wide. "No!"

"Don't be foolish," Azral snapped. Amanda could hear the new tension in his voice.

"Heal him," she demanded.

As Amanda committed to her desperate ploy, she spared a thought for her other loved ones, especially Hannah and Mia. Should the worst come to pass, she could only pray they'd forgive her someday. God certainly wouldn't.

"You see the future," Amanda told them. "You know I'm not bluffing. You heal Zack *right now* or I swear to you . . ."

She saw new movement behind the Pelletiers, a smattering of black shapes. A fleet of armed vehicles rose around the *Absence* in a halo. A deep, gritty voice addressed them through the ship's commandeered PA system.

"This is Noah Butterfield, Senior Commander of the National Integrity Commission. We have you surrounded, with enough ordnance here to tear you all to shreds. On behalf of the United States government, I order all survivors to get to the escape lift and surrender yourselves immediately. You have two minutes to comply."

Rebel bared his teeth in a savage grin. Seems he didn't need the Wild-9 after all.

"You know what?" Butterfield said. "Chuck that. You killed a bunch of my men back at Atropos and I'm still mad. So you all have *thirty seconds* to surrender yourselves. And I truly hope you don't."

One floor down, Hannah shared a fretful look with Mia and David. Even if they were foolish enough to throw themselves at the mercy of Integrity, there was no way they could get Jonathan in time.

Heath launched forward from the middle seat of the Griffin and shook Melissa's shoulder. "We have to save them!"

Theo shook his head. "We can't."

"We can't," Melissa confirmed. While every other gunship aimed its weapons at the aerstraunt, the command shuttle had its turret locked on the van. It was obvious what would happen if they moved.

Melissa looked at the Pelletiers, the only wild cards left in the equation. Their attention remained hopelessly fixed on the *Absence*. Someone or something was making them nervous.

Azral held Esis's arm and addressed her through their neural link. They spoke in a lightning-quick exchange of thoughts and images that were only loosely translatable.

<She is too [foolish/angry/unstable] to live,> Azral said of Amanda. *<Even if we disarm her, she is lost to us.>*

<No.>

<We have to save the viable Silvers.>

<She's the most viable of them all [I decreasingly believe]!>
<It's her sister. You see it now.>
<I will not give up on [my favorite]!>

Semerjean broke into the discussion, his consciousness filled with strain. *<If [valued] Zack dies, you'll lose all the Silvers. Amanda will never cooperate. [My favorite] will never cooperate.>*

"Twenty seconds," Butterfield announced.

Zack convulsed in Amanda's lap. His breathing had stopped. He wouldn't even last the countdown.

"Goddamn you, Esis! *Heal him!*"

"Mother—"

Esis vanished with a scream, leaving Azral alone in the sky and the terrace. She charged down the stairs in a hot, angry blur and stopped inches in front of Amanda.

"You threaten our life's work? You threaten *me*?"

Amanda's skin burned. Her heart felt close to bursting. The six-foot Esis was even more terrifying than the giant one, but Amanda could still see the fear in her eyes.

"Heal him."

"Ten seconds."

Azral hailed Esis again. *<Mother, I need you.>*

Esis yanked a silver disc from her pocket and hurled it at Zack. It burned through his shirt, attaching itself to his chest. He twitched on the floor like a man possessed. His skin glowed yellow, just as the veins in his neck turned a dark shade of gray.

Amanda kept the .38 against her head, her whole body trembling in anticipation. She half expected Zack to wither or burn or harden to stone, as punishment for her unmitigated gall. But the bruises on his face began to fade. The gash on his throat closed like a zipper.

She's doing it, Amanda thought. *She's really doing it.*

Esis pointed a long finger at her. "Do not try that a second time. You won't like my reaction."

Butterfield began the three-second countdown over the speakers. Azral vanquished his great lumic doppelgänger.

<Mother!>

"I come!"

Esis re-shifted and fled back up the stairs, just as Butterfield reached the end of his timer.

"Okay then," he said. "All weapons—"

"Sir!"

His pilot pointed out the windshield, at the spherical glow in the sky. Esis emerged from the light on glowing wings of aeris. Azral floated out on a paper-thin disc of gold.

Butterfield lowered his radio, stymied by this smaller, weirder version of the Pelletiers. "You got to be shitting me."

Azral grinned at Esis. "They do not fear us. Shall we educate them?"

His mother didn't smile back. She leveled a glare at Butterfield's ship. Her fists grew thick and hard with tempis.

"Yes," she said. "Let us."

No one who saw it would ever dare call it a battle. Though the witnesses in the sky only managed to catch a fraction of the violence, the tiny bit they saw was enough. This wasn't a fight. It was a massacre. Forty-four seconds was all it took for Azral and Esis to annihilate Integrity's forces.

Butterfield unwittingly did most of the work himself. On his command, every gunship and cannon cycle fired thermobaric missiles. The projectiles corkscrewed toward the Pelletiers before vanishing into a network of portals. A half second later, the missiles reappeared and returned on their senders. Sixteen vessels perished immediately in the backfire. The rest were spared through dumb luck or Esis's deliberate miscalculations. Her confrontation with Amanda had left her in the foulest of moods. She was determined to vent every ounce of her aggression.

She grabbed two cycles in giant claws of tempis and clapped them together like chalkboard erasers. Their payloads detonated in her grip.

As the charred remains drizzled from her palms, a gunship lined her up in its sights. Esis soared past it in a blur, her aeric wings slicing a razor path through the hull. The ship plummeted in two pieces, as did every soldier inside.

Azral de-shifted behind a gunship and aged it four centuries in the span of a breath. The vehicle came apart in a rain of rusty debris.

Butterfield watched the slaughter from the command ship, bug-eyed, quivering. These devils had torn through his unit like paper dolls. His few remaining soldiers were scattering in panic.

"Hold your positions," he ordered. "Hold the line!"

Azral doused two ships in solis, sending them both spiraling back toward Earth. Esis threw long tempic vines around a fleeing aerocycle and then slung it in an underhanded arc. The vehicle hurled toward the *Absence* in a clumsy spin, then crashed against the underside.

The explosion rocked the entire saucer, toppling everyone who remained standing. By the time the ship righted itself, one of the liftplates had gone permanently dark.

Azral glared at his mother. <*Careful,*> he warned though the neural link. <*You jeopardize the Silvers.*>

<*And me!*> Semerjean added.

Esis impaled the last remaining cycle pilot on a tempic spike, then hurled his body toward Earth.

<*I grow weary of this,*> she sent. <*These brutal men, these fickle children, this whole backward era!*>

Semerjean sighed in her thoughts. <*We go where the strings take us, beloved.*>

<*And they will lead us to our prize,*> Azral added. <*Everything you've worked for—*>

Esis looked over his shoulder and pointed in alarm. "*Sehnsenn!*"

Azral turned around to see a thermobaric missile flying at him. He aged it to a rusted husk, then shattered it with a burst of heat. A spinning piece of shrapnel nicked a shallow gash in his chin.

Esis flew to his side. "Love! Are you hurt?"

Azral touched the wound, then curiously examined his fingers. While his parents had both suffered brutal injuries on this world, he had yet to bleed until now. The pain was both fascinating and infuriating.

Butterfield watched them on the monitor. "Solic cannon! Now! Now!"

Four soldiers and a minister fell screaming through the bottom of the command ship. They passed through the floor like ghosts, and would continue to plummet long after they reached the ground.

Azral and Esis hovered in front of the windshield, their hard eyes fixed on their last remaining enemy. Butterfield reached for his sidearm, then immediately thought better of it. Instead, he took off his armored gauntlets and raised his huge pink hands in surrender.

"You made your point, all right? You win. Just let me go and I'll keep the agency off your back. I-I'll make up a cover story. We won't give you any more trouble."

The Pelletiers smiled mockingly. Their voices filtered into Butterfield's ear as if they were standing right next to him.

"Trouble?" Esis asked. "Do we *look* troubled?"

Though no one on the *Absence* could see the Pelletiers from their vantage, the trio in the Griffin had an unobstructed view. Theo and Melissa watched from the front seat, their sweaty hands clasped together. Heath leaned forward far enough to form a third head on their shoulders.

"Something's happening," he said.

Theo looked at him. "What?"

He pointed at Esis. "Something's happening with her tempis."

Esis thrust her hands at Butterfield's gunship. A black and inky substance spewed out of her fingertips, adhering to the hull in thick, gooey strands. Inch by inch, it spread across the surface of the vehicle, until every last part of it was covered.

"My God," Melissa uttered. The gunship looked like an oily shadow, and the shape of it was changing right before her eyes. It was becoming smoother, rounder.

Smaller.

Heath screamed and looked away. Theo and Melissa twisted in their seats. "What—"

"It's *eating* him!"

By the time they looked again, both the gunship and Butterfield had been completely dissolved.

Melissa gawked at Esis as she retracted the black tempis into her hands. "What *was* that stuff?"

Theo shook his head. He'd never seen it before in his life, though its name was dancing at the edge of his prescience. He could hear it in the future like a whisper in the wind.

Mortis.

"I don't know," he said. "I . . ."

Theo looked to the distance and suddenly realized that Esis was alone. What happened to the other one? Where was—

"Look out!" yelled Heath.

Azral punched through the driver's side window and gripped his hand around Melissa's throat. Her oxygen mask fell off her face.

"No!" Theo yelled. "Not her!"

"Be quiet."

Azral pulled Melissa toward him and spoke directly into her ear. "I have a message for your superiors in the United States government. Will you relay it?"

Wincing, gasping, Melissa nodded her head. The freezing air rushed in through the window, stinging every inch of her skin.

"Inform them that these 'orphans,' as you call them, are no longer their province," Azral said. "Should any of them come to harm at the hands of your agency, we'll slaughter your people by the hundreds. We won't waste our time on expendable foot soldiers. Our hostility will be aimed at the highest-ranking members of your organization, as well as their families."

Esis flew over to the passenger side of the van and gave Heath a crooked smile. He shrank away from her, cringing.

Azral pulled Melissa closer, until her cheek was touching the broken glass. "If your government needs an enemy, they're perfectly free to come after us."

His lip curled in a sardonic grin. "It's no trouble at all."

"Let her go!" Theo shouted. "Enough!"

Azral released his grip. Melissa lurched forward, red-faced and coughing. Theo slipped her oxygen mask back over her mouth.

"You didn't have to hurt her," he growled. "She—"

He glanced up to empty windows. Both Azral and Esis had disappeared in a blink.

Theo held Melissa's arm. "You okay?"

She hacked a violent cough, then took a worried look at the *Absence*. It hadn't fared well in the Pelletiers' battle. Smoke billowed out from the underside. The three surviving liftplates flickered with strain. It wouldn't stay afloat much longer, and neither would the Griffin. The engine battery was almost depleted.

"We need . . ." Melissa winced at the rough new scrape in her throat. "We need to get your friends."

TWENTY-TWO

The monitors in the kitchen flickered back to life. A hard restart was all it took for David to wake up the surveillance console and get most of the screens working again. He scanned the view of the upstairs dining room and found six survivors: Zack and Amanda, Peter and Rebel, a young Asian Gotham who lay unconscious by the elevator, and a teenage boy who he could only assume was Peter's son. Only Amanda and Liam looked healthy enough to move quickly. The other four were bloody wrecks.

"Damn it." David grabbed Hannah's handphone, his scowling eyes locked on the monitor. "They'll never make it down here. You'll have to pick them up from the main level."

Theo eyed the dining room from the front seat of the Griffin. He could barely see inside with all the sunlight gleaming off the windows. "Okay. We'll try. Can you guys meet us there?"

"Not yet. Jonathan's stuck by the delivery hatch."

"Well, get him unstuck and then get upstairs. We're running out of time."

A liftplate flickered. The *Absence* tilted ten degrees before awkwardly righting itself.

"That's not good." David looked to Mia. "Any luck with the—"

The public address system finally finished rebooting. The ship's speakers came to life with a loud, crackling hiss.

"I think that did it," she said.

"Good." David passed her the microphone. "Get Amanda up to speed. They'll need her to secure the van."

Mia watched him anxiously as he grabbed the aerochute and rope coil that had been found in the manager's office. "What are you doing?"

He turned around at the kitchen door, his handsome face racked with doubt. "Getting Jonathan."

Ninety seconds later, Amanda's tempic fist shattered a picture window in the dining room. A cold, sucking wind blew all around her, lashing her skin with a thousand whips. Grimacing, she wrapped a tempic cord around a table and held on for dear life.

"Hang in there," Mia told her through the speakers. *"They're coming."*

Melissa tried to line up the Griffin with the broken window, but the sky was determined to knock her around. Worse, the *Absence*'s liftplate troubles sent it lurching at random intervals. This would be an insanely tricky maneuver, like threading a needle on horseback.

Amanda watched the struggle from inside the ship. *It's not going to work*, she thought. *We're never getting off this thing.*

Yes you are, an inner voice insisted. *The Pelletiers need you. They won't let you die here.*

Amanda wasn't so sure about that. After that stunt she pulled on Azral and Esis, they were probably watching her now with smiles and popcorn.

A dark shape filled the window. The Griffin thumped against the hull. Theo slid the side hatch open, his fingers gripped tightly around the doorholds. "Now!"

Amanda cast a tendril from each hand. Eight giant white fingers hooked inside the van and held it firmly against the *Absence*. She expanded the tempis to cover the remaining gaps in the window, until the vacuum wind finally stopped.

Theo boarded the aerstraunt and took a baffled look around. "What *is* this place?"

"Just get the others," Amanda said. "I can't hold this forever."

"Where are they?"

"Other side."

"Other side," Mia said. *"Right around that middle section."*

As Theo disappeared around the curved wall of restrooms, Heath climbed out of the van and examined Amanda's tempis. The back of his shirt was just as tattered as hers. Bloodstains marred the royal blue fabric.

"You're hurt," Amanda said. "What happened?"

Heath kept his sullen gaze on her tempis. "They shot the guitar."

"What?"

"We have to get Jonathan."

"We will," Melissa promised. "We're not leaving anyone behind."

Amanda moved to the left and got a clear look inside the Griffin. She hadn't seen Melissa since October of last year, when she chased Amanda and Hannah to the roof of an office building. Their day would have ended on a much darker note if their friends hadn't arrived in the nick of time.

"Why are you helping us?"

Melissa turned in her seat, huddling herself for warmth. The air was forty degrees below zero outside, and she had a broken window. "I'm just trying to do what's right."

"What's *right*? Your people just threatened to shoot us down!"

"They're not my people," Melissa said. "It's safe to say I'm no longer employed with them."

Amanda readjusted her tempic clamps, her face twitching with strain. "So what now?"

"I take you and your people off this wretched aership."

"And then?"

Melissa had no idea. Her mind was still reeling from the massacre she'd witnessed. All she knew was that the Griffin had to start descending within the next three minutes. After that, it wouldn't matter which ship they were on. They'd all come raining down on Westchester—the orphans, the Gothams, and the ex–federal agent who'd failed to save any of them.

For Theo, the scene on the other side of the dining room was like something out of a horror movie. Blood was splattered everywhere—on the floors, on the windows, on the tables and partitions. There were two people here who had clearly died terribly. The rest were either dazed, unconscious, or catatonic with grief.

Theo kneeled at the side of the most familiar casualty, a sharp-witted cartoonist who'd become his best friend and roommate. "Oh God . . ."

Zack had never looked worse. His neck and shirt were drenched in blood. He twitched on the floor like he was lost in a nightmare. Theo might have thought he was dying if he hadn't looked to the strings and seen the healthy state of his future. Zack would survive this day and a whole lot more, as long as he got off this saucer.

Theo scooped him into his arms and noticed a shiny silver disc on his chest. "What is this?"

"A gift," said a croaking voice behind him.

Peter sat by the window, looking just as awful as Zack. His shirt had been torn wide open, revealing a mess of caked blood and the same silver disc that Zack sported. The Pelletiers must have brought them both back from the edge of oblivion. Apparently they healed as well as they hurt.

Peter's head doddered weakly as he struggled to process Theo. "What the hell are you doing here?"

"Long story. You think you can make a portal?"

"None that I'd trust."

"Well, then you'll have to get up."

Peter clambered to his feet on wobbly legs. Liam rushed to brace him. "Dad, slow down. You're hurt."

"No time," said Theo. "We need to go. Can you carry someone?"

"Mister, I don't even know who you are."

"He's all right," Peter told Liam. "Go get Mercy."

Theo looked to the unconscious Gotham and was thrown by his prescient glimpses. This Mercy woman was all over Zack's future. Their strings were entwined as far as the eye could see.

Liam crouched at her side, then gestured at the last survivor. "What about him?"

Rebel ignored all the chatter around him. He merely cradled Ivy's corpse, his face wet with tears as he gently stroked her hair.

Peter sighed at him. "Rebel . . ."

"Shut up," he creaked. "Just take your damn breachers and go."

"I can't let you die here."

"Why not?" Liam asked. "He's a sham and a liar, just like Ivy."

Rebel shot him a seething glare. "Boy . . ."

"Don't 'boy' me. You *lied* to me! You lied about everything!"

"It doesn't matter," Peter said. "He's coming with us."

Rebel scoffed. "The hell I am."

Peter drew his stun chaser from his pocket. Rebel laughed at his weak, faltering aim. "Pathetic. You can't even—"

Liam yanked the chaser from Peter's hand and fired it at Rebel. His body thrashed for seven seconds before collapsing on top of Ivy.

"Shut up," Liam growled. "Just shut up."

Peter gripped his shoulder. "Son . . ."

"Don't touch me." He shoved the chaser back at Peter, his voice choked with grief. "Let's just go."

As Liam scooped up Mercy, Theo turned around and eyed Rebel worriedly. No one here had the arms or strength to carry him, and there wasn't time for a second trip. Theo certainly wasn't going to risk the lives of Hannah and the others just to save this vicious thug.

"Peter, I hate to say it but—"

A large glob of tempis suddenly smacked against the tile. Long, hairy limbs sprouted out of the surface. The Pendergens and Theo watched in dull-eyed stupor as the tempis took on an unexpected shape: a silverback gorilla, six feet tall and rippling with musculature.

The creature sprang to life and moved across the dining room, shuffling its limbs with unnerving realism. It snatched up Rebel in its massive arms, threw him over its shoulder, then carted him off in the direction of the Griffin.

Theo turned around to see Heath by the restrooms, his skinny arms crossed in a knot. Did he even recognize the man he was saving, the bastard who'd murdered six of his friends? Yes, of course he knew. The boy had a mind like a steel trap. That, and a heart of pure gold.

Heath lowered his head and dawdled anxiously on his feet. "Come on. Jonathan's waiting."

Hannah stood at the edge of the kitchen, a rope in her hands, her body planted against the doorframe. She wasn't a fan of David's latest brainstorm, not even a little. But they had to get Jonathan before gravity got him, and there weren't any better ideas.

"More slack," David yelled from the middle of the corridor.

The other end of the rope had been tied around his waist in a bowline, a knot that Hannah had learned while playing Calamity Jane in a college musical. She hoped to God she did it right, because the closer David got to the ship's open hatch, the more the hungry sky pulled at him. She wasn't even sure there was enough rope to get him all the way to Jonathan.

Mia peeked over Hannah's shoulder, her tense eyes lingering around David's new adornments—a pair of skydiver's goggles and a dusty black aerochute. They didn't even know if the damn thing worked.

"God. I wish I'd never told him about that."

"It's just a backup," Hannah said. "If we're lucky, he won't need it."

She leaned into the doorway and shouted into the wind. "Do you see him?"

"I see him," David yelled back. "Just ten more feet."

"How is he?"

Jonathan remained tucked away at the end of the hallway, his body squeezed into a tight and shallow nook. The cold, thin air hadn't been kind to him. His face was red and chapped all over. His breath came out in shallow puffs of steam.

"He's barely conscious," David told Hannah. "He needs oxygen."

Mia ran to the kitchen's emergency cabinet, only to find dust and a dead cockroach inside.

"Goddamn it," she said. "You'd think Rebel would at least—"

A hydraulic pipe exploded on the underside of the *Absence*, sending the entire engine system into chaos. The three remaining liftplates went dark for four-fifths of a second, a brief but total propulsion failure that caused the saucer to drop thirty feet.

For a moment, everything became weightless. Then the liftplates returned to maximum power and the ship came to a violent halt. Windows cracked. Water pipes burst. A power cable dropped from the roof of the engine level, its live end swinging heedlessly around a closet. Directly beneath it was a large gray cube of putty explosive, one of Rebel's three deposits of Wild-9.

For the four beleaguered orphans on the kitchen level, the drop felt like doomsday all over again. Mia thumped her head against the edge of a counter. Hannah fell hard enough to lose hold of the rope. Jonathan and David both crashed to the floor of the corridor. Their bodies tumbled helplessly toward the open sky.

Hannah looked up from the doorway. *"No!"*

She jumped into blueshift and caught the end of David's rope. He fumbled for Jonathan, but he was inches out of reach. While David stopped, Jonathan kept rolling. He tumbled out of the delivery hatch, then dropped out of view.

Hannah screamed into the wind. *"Jonathan!"*

The Griffin suddenly rose up in front of the opening, its nine seats filled with passengers. Peter joined Theo and Melissa in the front. Zack, Rebel, and Mercy had been buckled into the back. Liam and Heath sat in the center row, shivering as Amanda held the side door open. She'd clamped herself to the Griffin with one hand's tempis and formed a giant white tendril with the other.

Hannah watched from the kitchen door, breathless, as the rest of Amanda's creation came into view. At the end of her tendril was a massive hand, and in the middle of the hand was—

"Jonathan!" Hannah covered her mouth, her teary eyes locked on her sister. "You did it! You d—"

One floor down and sixty feet to the north, the electrical cable swung into Rebel's Wild-9. The putty exploded, obliterating a liftplate and pitching the ship at a 60-degree angle. Hannah toppled backwards into the kitchen.

The concussive force of the blast sent the Griffin into a barrel roll. Amanda reinforced her hold on the van while she fought to keep Jonathan in her grip. Her tempis held, but there was something going on behind her. An unbuckled passenger was pressing against her back, and then her hip, and then—

"Help!"

It wasn't until the Griffin leveled out that Amanda realized what had happened. She'd kept her hold on Jonathan, but she'd let someone else fall out of the van.

Peter was the first to register the missing face in the center row. "Liam?" He looked out his window. *"Liam!"*

Amanda pulled Jonathan into the Griffin, then took a frantic peek out the door. There was nothing she could do. The boy had fallen out of reach.

"Oh God, Peter . . ."

"No!"

Peter struggled to open the passenger door. Theo held him back. "Peter, stop. Stop!"

"Close that door!" Melissa yelled at Amanda.

Amanda shut the side hatch, then took a worried look at the *Absence*. "God. They're still on there. Hannah and Mia. David . . ."

"Not David," said a high voice next to her.

Everyone turned to look at Heath. He cradled Jonathan's head in his lap, his hazel eyes locked on the aerstraunt. He'd been the only one on the van who caught what happened, the only one to see David jump.

Four and a half miles above the ruins of Atropos, two teenage boys tumbled past the smoking remains of the *Absence*. David's rope flapped behind him as he fell through the troposphere, his numb fingers wrapped around the straps of his aerochute. He had no idea how to operate the device, but he had at least ninety more seconds to figure it out.

His bigger concern at the moment was the kid he was trying to save, a shadowy wisp in the distance. Liam had a sixty-foot lead on the race to the ground. Catching up to him would take some effort.

David straightened out to a jackknife plummet, his skin bristling in the frigid sky. He was fifty percent sure he could reach Liam and still have time to make a soft landing, but it would be close. He'd be lucky to survive all this without getting frostbite. The last thing he needed was to lose more fingers.

He dove after Liam, the cold wind whistling in his ears. Somewhere in the back of his addled thoughts, he remembered that two people he cared about were still on the aerstraunt. He could have used his aerochute to help him. Yet here he was, saving some damn fool Gotham.

Stupid boy, David chided himself. *Stupid, stupid boy.*

There was no system in place to keep the *Absence* flying on half engine power, nor was there a loophole in physics that allowed a saucer to remain level on two liftplates.

The ship swung like a hinge on its functional lifters, then dropped vertically through the air. Floors became walls. Hallways became pits. Every loose object tumbled to the port side of the vessel. Hannah slid down the delivery corridor, scrambling to grab hold of something. *Anything.*

"Hannah!"

Mia extended her arm out the kitchen door. Hannah de-shifted and grabbed it with all her strength.

Wincing, Mia struggled to help Hannah climb back into the room. They perched together on the doorframe, hugging each other as they both gasped for air.

Hannah pulled back and saw a thick stream of blood on the side of Mia's face. "You okay?"

"I'm fine. Where are the others?"

"They caught Jonathan," Hannah said. "I don't know where David is."

"Oh God."

"He has the chute. He'll be okay. Do you still have my phone?"

"Yeah." Mia fished it out of her pocket and handed it to her. Hannah re-dialed Melissa's number.

The phone vibrated in Theo's hand. He pressed it to his ear. "Hannah? Are you okay?"

"I'm here with Mia. We're okay, but we're stuck in the kitchen. Can you still get us?"

Theo looked at Melissa and was disheartened by her expression. From the moment the Griffin straightened out, she'd pushed it into full descent. It wasn't nearly enough.

She covered the receiver. "We can't reach them in time. The van has a drop speed limit of forty miles an hour. It's a safety measure. I can't undo it."

The *Absence* was falling at least twice that velocity. The two surviving liftplates provided just enough drag force to make it a casual plummet.

Amanda reached for the side door. "Let me jump! If I can reach them—"

"You won't reach them," Melissa told her. "You'll only die."

Peter dabbed his crying eyes, then seized the handset from Theo. "Hannah, put Mia on."

"Peter?"

"Just put her on. Quickly!"

Hannah passed the phone to Mia. Peter looked out the window at the smoldering saucer. "Listen, sweetheart, is there a long wall near you?"

Mia peeked down the forty-foot shaft that was, until recently, a hallway. "Yeah. Why?"

"You won't like this, darling, but it's your only way out."

"What are you talking about?"

He took a deep breath, then aimed his heavy gaze out the window. "You're going to have to make a portal."

By the time Mia finished registering her objections, the *Absence* had dropped another thousand feet. She'd studied under Peter for months now, struggling to turn her dime-size portals into full-fledged travel doors. No matter how hard she tried, she couldn't do it. And even if it *was* possible . . .

"It won't help," Mia told Peter. "Portals can only exist in a fixed location."

"Look—"

"It'll fly right past us. There won't be time!"

Peter shook his head. "You've got a swifter right next to you. She'll *make* the time."

Mia thought back to Semerjean's exit, the way he threw himself at high speed through a rapidly falling portal. The maneuver seemed tricky even for a Pelletier. Now Hannah was supposed to catch a portal going twice as fast in the other direction.

"I don't know, Peter . . ."

Her voice crackled and faded. The *Absence* was dropping out of transmission range.

"We don't have time to argue!" Peter shouted. "I already lost . . ."

He covered his face with a quivering hand. Theo muted the handset. "Your son will be okay. David's saving him right now."

"You don't know that."

"You don't know David."

Melissa was starting to realize that *she* didn't know David. After everything he'd pulled, all his pragmatic violence, she'd written him off as a sociopath. Clearly she had him all wrong.

Amanda clutched Peter's shoulder. "Please. You're their only chance."

He raised the handset again. "Okay, listen, Mia. No more back talk. I *know* you, darling. I know you can do this."

"But where are we supposed to go? Home?"

Peter looked to Theo. "The brownstone. Is it—"

"No!" Heath yelled.

"It's compromised," Theo told him. "Heath and I barely got out of there."

Peter tapped his leg in dilemma. If Mia couldn't draw a door to Brooklyn, then it had to be someplace else she knew by memory, somewhere fresh in her thoughts.

"You remember that painting we saw back at Atropos?" he asked her. "The mural of the Fates?"

"Yeah . . ."

"That's your exit point. You have to recall every detail of it. The colors. The texture. *Visualize* it."

Mia swapped a fretful look with Hannah. "Okay. I'll try."

"That's my girl," Peter said. "Tell Hannah the plan and then hold her tight. The moment she sees that portal coming, she has to shift as fast as she can. It's got to be a clean jump. You can't hit the edges."

The saucer made an unholy sound, a metallic squeal that echoed off of every wall. The last two liftplates were breaking free of their moorings. Soon the *Absence* would be nothing but two hundred tons of falling glass and metal.

Peter heard the noise over the phone. "You're out of time, Mia. Hurry!"

After a rushed and frantic explanation, Mia climbed onto Hannah's back and focused all her thoughts on the mural of the Moirae. She pictured the faces of the ancient Greek sisters, the way the dust and grime made them look almost sinister. But what if the portal didn't work? What if she couldn't—

No. Mia shut out all her worries and rechanneled her thoughts, until she managed to form a spatial link with the mural wall. She could feel it in her thoughts like a cool metal coin beneath her toe.

Hannah looked down the shaft and saw a bright white circle rising up the farthest wall. She jumped into blueshift, but everything felt wrong. The portal was too far away. Too—

"—small. It's too small. Mia . . ."

The disc of light sailed straight past them, then disappeared in a blink. Hannah de-shifted.

Peter's voice came in through crackling static. "Did you do it?"

Mia lowered her head. "No."

"You have to concentrate!"

"I'm *trying!*"

Another creak tore through the *Absence*. The ship was coming apart fast.

"This is your last chance," Peter told Mia. "If you don't—"

His voice fizzled out. The connection was gone.

Mia wrapped her arms around Hannah and pressed her forehead to the back of her skull. "I'm so sorry."

Hannah squeezed her wrists. "It's not your fault. It's Rebel's and Azral's and every other asshole who got us here." She bowed her head miserably. "I don't want to die in a stupid aerstraunt."

"Me neither," Mia said. "Let me try something different."

"What do you mean?"

"Just get ready."

Though Mia couldn't have asked for a better teacher than Peter, the man had his stubborn blind spots. He remained steadfast in his belief that no traveler could draw a door in midair, any more than Zack could draw a sketch on a pool of water. *You need a hard surface*, Peter insisted. *It's the backbone of our power.*

But Mia believed more and more that her talent worked differently. Her portals were only hindered by walls. They needed air to breathe. They needed to *float*.

Mia drew a new link to the mural of the Fates, then cut a freestanding portal in the middle of the shaft. Already, she could feel a visceral comfort in her thoughts, as if she was all the way back in her natural element.

Hannah re-shifted at the sight of the second portal, then squinted her eyes at the moving target.

Slow down, you bastard. Just give me one chance.

Her vision turned four shades bluer. The temperature dropped thirty degrees. The portal now rose with a slow, lazy drift, like a child's balloon.

And it was expanding.

It's bigger, Hannah thought. *She's doing it. Oh, Mia . . .*

One of the last two liftplates finally broke free from the hull. It dangled on its power cords like a giant gouged eye before separating itself from the ship.

The *Absence* dropped faster. Hannah saw the portal speed up. "No!"

She held Mia tight and leapt from the kitchen. The portal swallowed them whole, just as an electrical surge coursed throughout the ship and set off Rebel's last two charges of Wild-9.

The *Absence* burst apart with fiery vengeance, as if colliding against an invisible mountain. A hundred thousand fragments rained down on Sleepy Hollow—splashing in water, crashing through windshields. Four thousand pieces found their way back to Atropos, shattering what little remained of its curved glass shell.

By the time the Griffin made its rough return to land, the aerport was littered with smoldering debris. There was nothing left in the sky but two teenage boys fluttering down to earth on a sputtering aerochute. They flopped into the grass on the shore of the Hudson, then lay perfectly still.

TWENTY-THREE

Zack came awake on a floor of concrete, his memories a hazy blur. Last he recalled, he'd been miles up in the sky, gurgling on blood while everyone screamed around him. Now he was back on the ground in a quiet, sunny parking lot. His skin was warm. His mouth was dry. His insides throbbed as if he'd just come out of surgery. What the hell had happened?

"Hello, Zack."

Melissa sat ten feet away, her body slouched against the grille of her Griffin. She'd touched down at Atropos with nine seconds of power left in the battery, a landing had that shattered every last window and cracked the engine in half. The van was in such wretched condition that even a full-body reversal wouldn't get it working again. It was the day's final casualty, or so Melissa hoped.

Zack sat up with a wince, then chortled with black humor. Melissa looked at him askance. "That's not the reaction I was expecting."

"Only sane reaction left," Zack said. "Every time I wake up, I'm someone else's prisoner."

"You're not my prisoner. Far from it."

He scanned his bright surroundings. "Where are the others?"

"Half your friends are gathering the other half," Melissa said. "We had some troubles on the way down."

"Where are *your* others?"

Melissa looked away with a heavy expression. "You don't have to worry about them."

Zack looked over his shoulder and saw the Golds sitting on a nearby bench. Heath tended to Jonathan dutifully as he shivered under a blanket, his shoulders hunched, his head drooped miserably.

"Is he okay?" Zack asked Melissa.

"He's hypothermic. He'll be all right as long as he keeps warm." She studied Jonathan and Heath in wonder. "The orphans are coming out of the woodwork, aren't they?"

"Orphans," Zack echoed.

"My term for your people. Hope you don't mind it."

"We've been called worse."

Zack looked down and noticed the silver disc on his chest. God only knew what Amanda had to do to get Azral and Esis to heal him. They would have never done it on their own.

He glanced up at Melissa. "You saw them, didn't you? The Pelletiers."

She nodded her head, her neck still aching from Azral's cold fingers. "I have many questions about those two."

"Three," Zack corrected. "There are three of them."

"That's . . . disheartening to hear."

A portal swirled to life on the stone wall of the terminal. Peter burst through the surface with Liam in his arms. Theo and David emerged next, the former propping up the latter.

"Any more blankets in the van?" Peter asked Melissa.

She shook her head, her wide eyes locked on the spatial breach behind him.

Peter laid his son out on a bus bench, then disappeared through a new portal. He returned ten seconds later with a pair of thick comforters in his arms.

"My God," said Melissa. "We always thought Mia created that escape portal last year. It was you. You're a native-born chronokinetic."

Her mouth went slack. "You're a Gotham."

Peter shot her a tense look before wrapping up Liam. Theo pulled the other comforter around David. Though the future was looking better and better for him and his friends, he could see storm clouds gathering over Melissa's strings.

Careful, Theo thought. *He's very protective about his people's secrets.*

David lifted his head and flashed a wry, shivering smile at Zack. "H-hey, I know you."

"God. What happened?"

"Took the scenic route back. D-don't recommend it."

Peter stared at him with awe. "That was miraculous what you did."

"It was foolish," David insisted. "It was m-miraculous that we lived."

Amanda stumbled out the aerport's main entrance, her arms draped around Hannah and Mia. She had to plow through seven tons of wreckage to get to their landing spot, and had nearly been crushed by a collapsing mezzanine. Now the three of them were covered in white plaster dust. They looked like ghosts of themselves, the pale and mortal reflections of the three sister Fates.

The Silvers reunited at the Griffin, too tired and traumatized to even embrace. Only Peter had the strength to wrap his arms around Mia. He hugged her tight, his voice strained with emotion.

"I knew you could do it," he told her. "I never doubted you for a second."

Mia looked over Peter's shoulder and saw Liam watching them confusedly. "Wait. Is that—"

"Yes," Peter said. "I'll explain later."

Theo looked around at the dozen different smoke plumes rising into the sky. "Guys, we have about five minutes before this place is crawling with cops and firemen."

"It's all right," Peter told him. "We'll be far away by the time they get here."

Hannah frowned at his implication. She was still recovering from the last portal jump.

Amanda gestured at the Gothams in the back of the Griffin. "What about them?"

Though Rebel remained deeply unconscious, Mercy was beginning to stir. Peter lifted her out of the van and carried her through a portal on the wall. He came back almost immediately. Alone.

"Where'd you drop her?" Zack asked him.

"She'll be fine."

Liam eyed the portal anxiously. "Don't send me back, Dad. I don't want to go back."

"No, no, no." Peter squeezed his shoulder. "I'm not leaving you again. You're coming with us."

Melissa climbed to her feet and took a closer look at Rebel. "This man needs medical attention."

"We'll take care of him," Amanda promised.

"That's what worries me."

Peter shook his head. "It's not like that. We want him to live."

"Speak for yourself," Jonathan grumbled.

"I put myself at great risk for you people," Melissa said. "Because I believe you're all decent at heart. I hope you don't prove me wrong."

David chuckled at her. "That's rich coming from you."

"She saved us," Theo reminded David. "We'd all be dead if it wasn't for her."

"Same could be said for the Pelletiers. That doesn't make them our friends."

Peter raised his palms. "All right. All right. There's no need to argue. You did us a good turn, Melissa, and we thank you for it. But this is where we part ways."

Theo shook his head. "We can't just leave her. Integrity knows she helped us. They'll hunt her down and lock her up."

Hannah stared at him incredulously. "You want her to come with us."

"I want us to go with her," he countered. "She has a place in Maine. A safe house."

"No," said David.

"Absolutely not," said Peter.

"Would you just *listen* to me?"

"It's out of the question," Peter said. "You know what's at stake here. I'm not putting our fates in the hands of a government agent."

Theo threw his hands up. "So what's your plan, then? We can't go home."

"I've got another place."

"Oh, really? Because if it's as safe as the last one—"

A soft, choking cry cut him off. Everyone looked to Mia. After all her trials and tribulations, all the near-death experiences, her emotions had finally caught up with her. They'd come all this way to save Zack. Now he was just sitting there, unacknowledged.

She crossed the space between them and wrapped her arms around him. Zack squeezed her back with a tired half grin. "Hey, you."

"Hi, Zack."

Their hug sent a shock wave of emotion through the others, all the weary combatants who'd climbed halfway to heaven today and somehow found their way back. They were alive. They were alive and reunited, and it was nothing short of a miracle.

Melissa sighed defeatedly. There was no hope of selling Peter on her plan. She didn't even have time to try.

"Will you be okay?" Amanda asked her.

"I appreciate your concern, but my situation isn't as dire as Theo believes. I have options."

"I'm sorry," said Peter.

"So am I. I just hope that one day soon—"

"No, you don't understand." Peter looked away with an uncomfortable expression. "I can't let you leave with the information you have."

The Silvers and Golds stared at him in disbelief. Even David was stunned. "You can't be serious."

Amanda shot to her feet. "Don't even think about it."

Liam eyed her strangely. "What are you people going on about?"

"If he's talking about killing her—"

"He's *not*."

"He isn't," Melissa said. "I've been sitting here wondering how his people managed to stay hidden for so long without leaving a trail of witnesses. Now I get it. He intends to erase my memory through reversal."

The orphans looked to Peter for confirmation. He turned his attention onto Zack. "You up to it?"

"What, you want *me* to do it?"

"You're the only one here with the power."

"The only human," Melissa clarified. "If you can't do it, then Peter will have to wound me badly enough to warrant the use of a medical reviver. All told, my chances will be better with you."

Theo looked at the .38 in Peter's holster. "Is this really necessary?"

"I'm just trying to protect us," Peter said. "Your people and mine."

"Just let me talk to her a second. Alone."

Peter took a nervous scan of the parking lot. "Make it quick."

Theo led Melissa to the other side of the Griffin. He threw a furtive peek at his friends, then leaned in for a whisper. "I was right, wasn't I?"

"About what?"

"You've been transmitting to your associate this whole time."

While Cain listened intently from his home office in Maryland, Melissa reached into her blouse and peeled a small communication device from her chest. She pressed it into Theo's palm.

"You should tell Peter," he urged her. "He'll back off. He'll know there's no point reversing you."

"There's still a point. The agency will interrogate me about my role in this disaster. A memory wipe will give me plausible deniability. It's a smart move for all of us."

Theo studied her incredulously. "You're really willing to give up all this knowledge you gained?"

"I'll still have the audio recording," Melissa reminded him. "And a fair bit of camera footage."

"You're a little bit crazy. You know that, right?"

She gave him a glum shrug. "It's a delicate game I'm playing, Theo. I believe Integrity can become a powerful ally to you and your friends, but not in its current state."

Melissa looked to the smoking remains of an agency dropship. "The situation will get worse before it gets better, so stay safe. Stay hidden."

Theo gripped her arm. "Just look out for yourself. Please."

Hannah watched them through the van's broken windows. She knew enough about Theo's body language to know that he was smitten. *Jesus*, she thought. *He really does love a challenge.*

Soon Theo and Melissa rejoined the others. Zack cleared a ten-foot space around her.

"I don't like doing this," he said. "If it goes wrong . . ."

She grinned at him. "You're a good man to worry but I assure you that reversal's quite safe on healthy people." Her humor quickly faded. "Just don't overdo it. I'd rather not relive puberty."

"I'm only setting you back six hours."

"That'll work," she said.

Amanda looked at her, guiltily. "We won't forget what you did for us."

"I wish I could say the same," Melissa joked. "In any case, I'm glad you're all—" Her eyes went wide in sudden recollection. "Wait!"

Zack stopped his preparations. The others looked at Melissa in puzzlement.

"There are seven people at large in the Seattle area," she told them. "Chronokinetics, just like you. They destroyed an abandoned church back in March. One of them recently killed a civilian with her tempis."

Mia rose to her feet, fascinated. "Wait. That mini-Cataclysm that was all over the news . . ."

"That was them," Melissa said. "I've been chasing them for weeks. They're very elusive. All I've managed to capture of them is a hazy ghost image. They each wear a bracelet that closely resembles Heath's, except not gold. Their bands look more like brass. Or copper."

Zack was flabbergasted by her news. She wasn't kidding when she said the orphans were coming out of the woodwork. "Why are you telling us this?"

"Because despite their crimes, I suspect they're good people in a bad situation, much like you. It's in their best interest that you find them before Integrity does."

"That's . . . incredibly decent of you," David said.

"We still have a lot to learn about each other. Maybe someday we'll get the chance."

Sirens blared in the distance. Melissa turned to Zack. "You better get on with it."

Zack steeled himself with a breath, then engulfed her in a sheath of bright white temporis. Melissa's eyes rolled back. Her muscles froze. Her hair and clothes rippled. By the time the process finished, her pantsuit was clean and the bruises on her neck had vanished.

Melissa teetered on her feet, dazed and disoriented. Amanda caught her before she could collapse. She kneeled on the ground beside her and checked her vital signs.

"She's all right."

Theo whispered at his hand, into the wafer-thin transmitter that Melissa had given him.

"You keep her safe now, Cedric. I'll be watching you."

He threw the device to the concrete and crushed it under his shoe.

A piercing squeal filled Cain's earphones. Grimacing, he pulled them off his head. It took him ten long seconds to realize that Melissa had never told Theo his name.

All around the aerport, the sirens grew louder. Peter drew one last portal in the wall before tossing a nod at Heath. "Uh, son, if you don't mind . . ."

Heath conjured another tempic gorilla and sent it to retrieve Rebel from the van. Even Jonathan was thrown by the sight of it. "Apes? When the hell did you start making apes?"

Hannah took his arm. "Come on."

Two by two, the survivors moved toward the portal—six Silvers, two Golds, two Pendergens, and their prisoner-of-war, the only man who could put an end to the Gothams' bloody conflict.

This, Peter knew, would be the hardest part.

As the last of his people disappeared through the portal, Peter stopped at the edge and took a final look at the wreckage. He drew a deep breath, stepped into the breach, and then left Atropos behind by miles.

TWENTY-FOUR

At the northern edge of New Jersey, in the genteel suburb of Old Tappan, a cylindrical tower loomed hundreds of feet above its neighbors. It was a frequent source of scorn among the locals, a bubbly glass eyesore that stuck out from the landscape like a giant cob of corn.

It was famously known as the Aerie.

The building debuted at the peak of America's antigravity craze, the nation's first and only aerial apartment complex. Beyond the space-age premise of modular flying housepods, the Aerie promised unprecedented freedom for its residents. Tired of your view? Trade docks with a neighbor. Tired of your neighbor? Pick up your apartment and move to another side of the building.

Though its developers billed the Aerie as the future of American living, its tenants quickly learned the downsides of their new mobile lifestyle. A lift-plate hiccup broke half the windows in one unit. A woman nearly drowned after a piloting error sent her apartment into Lake Tappan. Two neighbors came to blows in the wake of a fender-bender home collision. The final straw broke when hooligans made off with the building owner's penthouse. It was recovered in Hackensack, freed of all valuables and soiled in unmentionable ways.

One year after its christening, the hundred and sixty-two housepods were fused to the framework, never to fly again. Today the Aerie was just another static high-rise, though the developers continued to tout its futuristic design and modular plumbing system.

Peter didn't care about any of that. He only came to the Aerie for its easy cash leases. He'd secured a twelfth-floor unit six months ago under the name Lance Percival, then kept it as an emergency backup residence. Of course, if he'd known he'd be housing eleven people, he would have sprung for something larger than a one-level, three-bedroom box unit.

"It's only temporary," he assured his companions. "A few days at the most."

Mia woke up at dawn on the floor of a closet, the only space in the apartment she could rightfully claim for herself. She didn't want anyone else to suffer the near-constant glow of her sleep portals. More than that, she just wanted a place of her own to be miserable. Like everyone else, she was still recovering from the ordeal at Atropos. Between her altitude sickness and her thundering head cold, her body felt like it was hanging upside-down in a moving meat truck.

Groaning, Mia switched on the closet light and studied her latest sleep notes: a hundred and twelve paper scraps, all rolled into sticks and delivered by portal. She didn't have the strength to clean them up at the moment. That would have to be a job for her future self.

She stepped out of the closet and walked a sleepy path toward the bathroom. The door was closed, but someone was talking in there. Mia pressed her ear to the wood and heard Hannah embroiled in a tense conversation.

"—just worried we're making the same mistake as Zack and Amanda."

"Says who?" Jonathan argued. "Did anyone ever warn you about entwining with me?"

"No."

"And wasn't it an augur who brought us together?"

"Yeah . . ."

"Okay then. So if the Pelletiers aren't bitching about us, and if this Ioni woman thinks we have a future together, then what the hell are we talking about?"

Good point, Mia conceded.

"I don't know," Hannah said. "When you fell out of that ship yesterday, my heart just—"

Mia pulled away from the door, embarrassed. She shouldn't have been eavesdropping on them. She knew how the conversation would end, anyway. More kisses. More groping. At least someone in this apartment was having a good time.

A door creaked open. David shambled into the hallway, looking worse than Mia had ever seen him. His hair was limp. His eyes were puffy. He moved like a man five times his age. His body clearly didn't enjoy his four-mile skydive. It was a wonder he was still in one piece.

David blew his nose into a tissue and read Mia's expression. "That bad, huh?"

"You look fine."

"I feel wretched."

"Serves you right for the stunt you pulled. What the hell were you thinking?"

David shrugged and sniffled. "Liam fell. Someone had to save him."

Mia's heartbeat doubled, and she once again found herself in a fluttering state of awe. David was just three months shy of seventeen, and he was already a superhero. She didn't think his parents made him that way, or even fate. At some point, he simply chose to be the incredible person that he was.

David backstepped at her approach. "I don't want you to get sick."

"I'm already sick."

She took his hand and studied the scabrous wound on the back of it, the one-inch gash that Semerjean had inflicted. "God."

"It's all right. Could have been worse."

"Yeah. He could have killed you. You should have never talked back to him." She dropped his hand with a stern expression. "One of these days, your bravery's gonna backfire on you."

"Look—"

"I just hope you think twice next time, because there are people on this world who love you and need you."

"Mia . . ."

"*I* love you."

Mia sucked a sharp breath, as if she'd suddenly become naked, as if she'd leapt through a portal into a strange and dangerous realm. Her immediate instinct was to backtrack, to insist that she didn't mean it like *that*. Of course I didn't. Don't be silly.

But after a hard day at Atropos, in which the universe once again went out of its way to remind her that life was short, Mia was out of excuses. She was out of anxieties, out of time, out of patience with the status quo. And she couldn't forget the way that Hannah had kissed Jonathan. She'd thrown herself at him while they were a mile in the sky. And he caught her.

As her stomach lurched and blood rushed furiously in her ears, Mia closed her eyes. She drew a deep breath. And then she jumped.

"I love you," she echoed, her voice barely a whisper. "I'm in love with you."

In an instant, time seemed to come to a skidding halt. Mia had minutes, hours, days to analyze David's reaction. She watched his brow curl in painful slow motion, saw the corners of his lips twist with a tectonic grind. His expression was going the wrong way. Everything was going the wrong way.

She looked down at her trembling fingers. "It's okay. You don't . . . you don't . . ."

"Mia . . ."

"You don't have to say it back."

David held her by the shoulders. "Mia, look at me."

She could only manage a half second of eye contact. The look on his face—solemn, pitying—made her want to run back to her closet and lock the door forever.

"We can't be together," he told her. "Not in that way."

"I'm only two years younger than you."

"It's not about age."

"I know I'm not pretty—"

"Of course you are. That's not even remotely the issue."

"Then *why*?"

"You *know* why."

She could hear the impatience in his voice now, enough to make her wonder. All this time, she thought he'd been oblivious to her feelings. But what if he'd known all along?

"The Pelletiers don't want us together," David said. "Any of us. Zack and Amanda didn't listen and they paid the price. Jonathan and Hannah aren't listening, and they'll pay the price. If I thought I could dissuade them—"

Mia shook her head. "Bullshit."

"You think I'm lying?"

"I think you're wrong. More than that, I think you're using the whole Pelletier thing as an excuse. If you don't feel that way about me, just tell me. Say the words."

"Why?"

"Because I need to know!"

David looked away, exasperated. It suddenly dawned on Mia, with no pleasant amount of irony, that Hannah and Jonathan were probably eaves-dropping on her from the bathroom.

"We shouldn't have had this conversation," David grumbled. "She should have told you the truth a long time ago."

"Who?"

"Your future self."

A bedroom door creaked open a few inches, but no one stepped outside. Mia could only guess that Amanda was awake. The door was her gentle way of warning Mia that everyone could hear them. Everyone.

Mia rushed back into her closet refuge and slammed the door behind her. Her bare feet crunched over dozens of notes, all the latest words and "wisdom" of the Future Mias.

She opened her bookbag, ripped a scrap of paper from her journal, and then began writing a message of her own.

It's never going to happen with you and David. Nobody ever told me, so I'm telling you now. He doesn't feel that way about you. He never did.

By the time Mia finished, her face was drenched in tears. She opened a half-inch portal to December of last year, then hesitated. Why save a younger Mia from this horrible pain she was feeling? The stupid girl deserved every bit of it. The signs had been there all along. She was just too stupid to see them.

Mia closed the portal with a brusque hand gesture, then crumpled up her note. To hell with her other selves. Let them all learn the hard way. Let them all suffer.

The living room was a twenty-foot box at the front of the apartment, all slate and bare plaster. Peter had only done a minimal amount of furnishing, with no decoration whatsoever. The only thing that saved the room from dreariness was the panoramic window on the north side. Sadly, Peter insisted on keeping the blinds closed at all hours, just in case Integrity got lucky with their camera drones.

Nestled among the folding seats and inflatable sofas was a squeaky metal wheelchair. Bicycle chains held Rebel to the frame, though he was hardly a threat with his injuries. Amanda had gone through four medkits trying to treat the damage that she herself had inflicted, for all the good it did. Rebel's abdomen was rock hard and purple, which suggested internal bleeding.

Theo's prognosis was even less encouraging. "He'll be dead before sunrise."

He'd followed Peter into the kitchen, speaking in a mutter while they dumped bowl fragments into the trasher. Rebel wasn't keen to be spoon-fed by anyone, least of all Peter. He'd bucked at just the right moment to send corn chowder everywhere.

"How sure are you?" he asked Theo.

"It's the only future I see."

Peter closed the trasher, scowling. "Then he sees it, too."

Rebel hadn't been coy about his desire to die. He resisted all nourishment, thrashed violently in his chair to aggravate his wounds. He provoked Zack and Jonathan, his two most vocal enemies, in the hope that one of them would snap. He didn't care if he was rifted or dropped as long as it did the job.

"We're running out of time," Theo said. "Look, I talked to Zack. He's willing to heal him."

Peter shook his head. "Can't."

"Why not?"

"Because if we reverse Rebel, he'll forget everything that happened yesterday. The Pelletiers, Ivy, all of it. He needs those memories fresh in his head if we want any chance of turning him."

Theo rubbed his face, exasperated. They could be recuperating in a nice, secluded house in Maine. But no, Peter thought it was a much better plan to pin all their hopes on a psychopath.

"You're not going to turn Rebel," Theo told him. "Not in twelve hours. Not in twelve *weeks*."

Peter pulled off his soup-stained shirt and reversed it in the juve. Theo couldn't help but marvel at the pristine state of his chest. His Pelletier healing disc had crumbled to dust in the middle of the night, its work well completed. The gunshot wound that had nearly killed him yesterday was just a faint red line today.

"We don't have a choice," Peter said. "Rebel built this war to outlast him. If he dies, his replacements will take over and we'll all be back at square one. We have to turn him. There's no other way."

"Peter, *look* at him. His apocalypse already happened. He doesn't give a shit."

Though Rebel couldn't make out what Peter and Theo were saying, their hushed, angry whispers brought a smile to his face. There was a pleasure to be had in aggravating one's captors. If anyone knew that, it was the breacher in the room.

Zack sprawled on a sofa, sketching *Bloom County* characters on scrap paper. Rebel found it funny, in a jaw-clenching way, that the man he shot yesterday was one of the healthiest people in the apartment.

"You must be loving this," Rebel growled. "Tables turned. Now I'm the one in the chair."

Zack continued his Opus with inscrutable aloofness. "It's not without its irony."

"I'm sitting right here, the man who killed Josh Trillinger. And you're just drawing horseflakes."

"Horseflakes?"

"Nonsense," Rebel explained. "Things that don't exist."

"Oh." Zack creased his brow. "Never heard that one."

Rebel shook his head. "Pathetic. If your brother could see you now—"

"Oh, shut up already." Zack finally made eye contact with him. "You can goad me all you want. I'm not going to kill you."

"You'd rather I suffer."

"Yup."

"That's what Azral wants, too. You like carrying his water?"

Zack wagged a finger. "See, that was a better attempt at provoking me. I'll give it a C-plus."

Rebel scoffed. "You're no man."

"D-minus."

"Fuck you. There was a time I thought we actually understood each other."

Zack sat up, his pencil twirling furiously in his hand. He and Rebel had had some disturbingly agreeable conversations over the last few days. And the man had been a surprisingly honorable jailer. He'd never once hit Zack or starved him or taunted him with threats. He'd even arranged for him to take a shower between his solic generators, the only time during the whole ordeal that Zack had felt like a human being. There was clearly *some* goodness tucked away in that battered soul, which made his crimes all the more tragic.

"I hate what the Pelletiers did to me," Zack said. "I hate what Amanda had to do to save me. I hate the fact that every time I close my eyes, I see what Semerjean did to Mink."

Rebel winced in sorrow. He'd been so busy mourning Ivy that he'd barely spared a thought for his cousin.

"It makes no sense," he said. "Azral and Esis hate you, but Semerjean keeps saving your life."

Zack hunched his shoulders in a nervous shrug. "They don't always see eye to eye."

"Why does he keep sparing Mercy's life?"

"I've been asking myself that same question."

"And why the goddamn mask?"

"That's the big one," Zack admitted. "That's the one that keeps me up at night."

Theo and Peter flanked the kitchen door, surprised by the increasingly civil discussion Zack and Rebel were having.

"He masks his voice, too," Zack noted. "He only talks in whispers and—"

"—wind chimes," said Rebel.

Zack nodded uncomfortably. "Like he doesn't want us to recognize him."

"You think he's someone we know?"

"It's possible," Zack said. "Or maybe he's someone we'll meet in the future. The Pelletiers always plan a hundred moves ahead."

Rebel chewed his lip in thought. "Our cameras went out right before Semerjean arrived."

"So?"

"It wasn't coincidence. There was something about his entrance that he didn't want us to see. I'd assumed he came by portal, but now I'm wondering if maybe he showed up earlier. Maybe he'd boarded the ship with your friends."

Zack looked up with a cynical sneer. "I see where you're going with this."

"Maybe beneath all that tempis—"

"Uh-uh."

"—he *is* one of your friends."

Zack laughed off the theory. "Bullshit. Pure and utter horseflakes."

"Is it?" Rebel asked. "The more I think about it—"

"—the more you're wrong. If the Pelletiers put a spy anywhere, it's with your people."

"I've known my people my whole life. How long have you known yours?"

Zack dipped his head. "Oh, for God's sake . . ."

"Did anyone see David while Semerjean was running around the ship?"

"Yes!"

"Did anyone see Jonathan?"

Zack paused a moment before chuckling again. "I think your mental hamster just died in the wheel."

"Hey, you opened the door to this."

"And I'm glad I did, Rebel, because I find it very illuminating to see how your mind 'works,' that razor-sharp sense of deduction that made you kill my brother for no reason."

"I had every reason in the world, just like you have every reason to kill me now. But you won't. And it's not because you're clever or ethical. You're just a coward."

Theo moved to intervene. Peter held him back. "Wait."

Zack rose to his feet. "*I'm* the coward?"

"You heard me."

"The people who killed your wife and children are out there right now. They're *laughing* at you, Rebel. And what are you doing? You're praying for death. You're begging me to kill you because you just can't take it anymore."

Rebel gritted his teeth. "Fuck you."

"If you were half the man you pretend to be, you'd open your eyes and *think*. You want to stop what's coming? You want the Pelletiers gone? Well, guess what? So do we."

Amanda and Hannah opened the door of their bedroom. Mia listened breathlessly from the closet.

"We're not the people you think we are," Zack told Rebel. "What will it take for you to finally see that?"

"You're their children. Their pets!"

"That was Ivy's psychosis, not yours."

"Fuck you. You people wouldn't last a day without the Pelletiers. You wouldn't last a *minute* as their enemy."

"Oh yeah? Esis wanted me dead yesterday. Amanda didn't. Guess who won."

Rebel pursed his lips and looked away. Zack leaned in close. "You've had allies right in front of you this whole time, but you refuse to see it. You've gone about this all wrong and it has cost you *everything*. If there's an ounce of sense left in you, Richard, you'll swallow your pride and ask yourself if maybe, just maybe, there's a better way to save the world."

Zack pressed his finger against Rebel's temple. *"Think."*

He grabbed his sketch and disappeared down the hallway, just as Peter and Theo stepped in from the kitchen. Though Rebel wasted no time hurling curses at them, Theo could feel a shift in the strings. Zack had just opened the door to an interesting new future. Maybe there was hope after all.

TWENTY-FIVE

As evening fell on Old Tappan, a portal opened on the wall of the Aerie. Peter and Liam returned to the apartment with bottled drinks and a stack of take-out boxes from Italian Eddie's Speedery.

Liam looked at the seven orphans in the room and saw the same cringing expression. "What's the matter? You don't like cheese pies?"

"We do," Theo said.

"We *did*," Hannah amended.

One of the more baffling aspects of this parallel culture was its perversion of the American pizza. Instead of mozzarella, they were baked with a colorless goo that looked like snot and tasted like old mayonnaise. The crust had the appearance, flavor, and consistency of saltines. Even more disturbing were the toppings, a mindboggling selection that included boiled beef, fried leeks, mashed potatoes, and apples. Hannah couldn't even begin to fathom the historical deviations that led a nation to accept apples on its pizza.

Peter dropped the boxes on the coffee table. "Sorry, guys. It was the only place without a line."

"There's a reason for that," Zack grumbled.

"You of all people should be grateful for real food." He passed a bag of bell peppers to David. "Here. You can juve them if they're not fresh enough."

"They're fine," David listlessly replied. No one had to guess why he was sullen today, or why Mia remained tucked away in her closet refuge. They both got testy whenever anyone tried to talk to them about it.

Amanda opened the door to the apartment's half bathroom, where their belligerent captive had been stashed for the evening. "I suppose I can't convince you to eat something."

Rebel glared at her from his wheelchair. "You should have shot yourself when you had the chance."

"I'll take that as a no."

She closed the door again. Jonathan shot a wrathful look at Peter. "Just give me the word."

"No."

"He's gonna die anyway."

"Just eat, all right?"

The orphans and Pendergens sat around the coffee table, dining in silence as they stared down at their plates.

Heath studied Liam's hands with idle fascination. "Why does he wear gloves?" he asked Jonathan.

"I told you—"

"Why do you wear gloves?" he asked Liam.

The boy recoiled as if he'd been slapped. He looked at his father in hot surprise. "You didn't tell them?"

Peter shook his head. "I was leaving the choice to you."

Liam put down his plate and fidgeted with his gloves. He started and stopped himself three times before speaking.

"I'm a thermic," he said. "I burn things. When I was two years old, I . . . uh, I had an accident with my power. A bad one. If you saw my scars, you'd probably never eat again."

"That's not true," Peter said.

"It's true enough."

Rebel chuckled from behind the bathroom door. "It's not the worst part of the story," he teased. "Go on, kid. Tell 'em."

"Shut up!"

"Tell him what it did to your mom."

Peter held back Liam, while Hannah and Zack struggled to keep Jonathan in his chair. Amidst all the clamor, Mia finally joined the others in the living room. She grabbed a small device from an end table and then disappeared into Rebel's bathroom.

One by one, her companions stopped what they were doing and listened to the sharp, buzzing sound coming from behind the wooden door.

"What's happening?" asked Hannah.

Eight seconds after she entered, Mia re-emerged. Though her eyes were red and cracked with grief, her expression was as hard as stone. She put Peter's stun chaser back where she found it, sat down at the coffee table, and took a drippy slice of cheese pie for herself.

"He'll be quiet for a while," she matter-of-factly informed the others. Her heavy eyes lingered on Liam. "Sorry about your mom."

Rebel woke up two hours later, his head full of cobwebs, his whole body throbbing with pain. He scanned his surroundings with bleary eyes and saw that he was back in the living room. His captors had wheeled him into a circle of seats. Everywhere he looked, a Silver or Gold looked back at him.

Zack faced him from the other side of the coffee table, his hands folded serenely in his lap. "Hello, Rebel. I think it's time we talked."

With the exception of Heath, who was fiddling with a lumic puzzle sphere, the breachers made a point of maintaining eye contact with Rebel. He shot a dirty look at each and every one of them.

"No Pendergens," he noted. He chuckled at Theo. "This is your doing."

"It is," Theo admitted.

"Hide the two people I have history with. Face me as a group. Stay calm. Stay focused. Let Trillinger do the talking. Is that the big plan?"

"More or less," said Zack. "Except we're hoping you'll do most of the talking."

"Me?" Rebel laughed. "That's not gonna get me to change my mind."

"Then change ours," Amanda challenged. "Convince us why we have to die."

Rebel lost his smile. There was a cold new wind blowing in from the future, an ominous hint of grief to come. He couldn't see the shape of it. All he knew was that he'd be weeping like a child before this was over.

"I'm not playing your bullshit game."

"What game?" David asked him. "We just want to know your reasoning."

Hannah nodded. "You've shot half the people in this room. Killed six of our kind, including Zack's brother."

"And for what?" said Zack. "I've been asking you the same question for the last three days, and you won't answer me."

"Fuck you."

"What makes you think that killing us will save the world?"

Rebel heard harsh whispering in the kitchen. Of course Peter and Liam would be hiding in earshot. They wouldn't want to miss a word.

"What's the matter, Pendergen? Too scared to face me yourself?"

"Answer the question," Mia said.

He narrowed his eyes at her. "You're the one who zapped me."

"And you're the one who put a bullet in my chest. I almost died last year."

"I wish you had."

"Tell me why."

"You goddamn know why!"

"You think we're the death of this world."

"I *know* you are."

"How?" Theo threw his hands up. "You're an augur, just like me. You must have seen something to make you so sure. What was it?"

"Why can't you just tell us?" Zack asked.

Rebel wriggled in his chair. The grief was getting ever closer. *Stay strong,* his inner Ivy told him. *Don't you dare let them break you.*

"I'll answer your question," he promised. He jerked his head at Jonathan. "If he answers one first."

Jonathan sat up in his easy chair, suspicious. "If you're just trying to piss me off—"

"Where were you when Semerjean was running around yesterday?"

A cold, hard silence overtook the living room. Heath looked up from his puzzle sphere, baffled.

Jonathan squinted at Rebel. "What the hell are you getting at?"

"You're the only one on the ship who didn't run into him. I find that mighty interesting."

Hannah scoffed. "You're an idiot."

"You're also wrong," said a voice from the kitchen. Liam stood in the doorway and eyed Rebel sternly. "I didn't see one bit of this Semerjean. Maybe I'm the man beneath the tempis."

Rebel laughed. "You're no man at all."

"Neither are you," Liam said. "The more you stall, the more I think you made up this whole tale about the breachers."

"Watch it now."

"Your wife, your cousins, your unborn sons. All dead because of your lie."

"It's no lie!"

"Then *tell* us," Theo yelled. "Tell us what you saw!"

"I never said I saw anything! I said I got my information from the future."

At long last, David and Mia made eye contact with each other. They traded a confused look before turning back to Rebel.

"Meaning what?" asked David.

"A future self?" asked Mia.

Theo suddenly caught a hint of the revelation to come, the real reason why Rebel was dodging the question.

"It was someone else," he mused. "You got your information from another augur."

Rebel lowered his head. "She's never steered me wrong."

"Who?" Liam asked. "Gemma? Prudent?"

"No. She's not anyone in the clan. She . . ."

Peter stood in the doorway and stared at Rebel intently. "Who?"

"She's been popping in and out of my life ever since I was a kid. A young woman, never aging, always filled with knowledge. Every single thing she's told me about the future has come true. She's never missed a beat. She told me the Pelletiers were coming a month before they arrived. She knew all three of them by name."

He chuckled darkly at the orphans. "She told me the names of all you bastards."

Only Hannah knew what to do with the information. She walked around the coffee table and crouched at Rebel's side.

"This woman. Describe her."

"I don't know. She's young, short, pretty. Her hairstyle changes every time I see her, but the rest of her stays the same."

"And she wears two watches," Hannah guessed.

Rebel stared at her, dumbstruck. "How the hell did you know that?"

"Because we know her too," Theo said. He covered his face with his hands. "Shit."

Jonathan blinked at him. "Wait, Ioni? He's talking about *Ioni*?"

"Who's Ioni?" Liam asked.

"We're not entirely sure," Mia admitted. "She visited me and Theo once, and met Hannah a month later. She's always given us good information. She even saved Theo's life."

David tapped his leg in edgy thought. "She's been playing us this whole time."

"All of us," Zack stressed. "We got conned, Rebel."

"No . . ."

"*You* got conned."

"No!" Rebel shook his head. "It doesn't make sense. She's been nothing but a saint to me. Why would she—"

"—help your mortal enemies?" Amanda asked. Her eyes narrowed to slits. "Take a wild guess."

"She's *not* a Pelletier!"

"I don't think so either," Theo said. "But she's obviously playing some kind of game."

Mia caught Hannah and Jonathan exchanging a worried look. Ioni was the one who'd brought them together, but why? What was her angle?

Peter crossed into the living room. "Look, I never met this Ioni woman. But if she's your only source of information—"

"Bullshit," Rebel hissed. "I still trust her more than I trust you."

"What exactly did she say about us?" Theo asked. "Did she *specifically* tell you to kill us?"

"Of course she did! She . . ." Rebel closed his eyes. It felt like a hundred years since their last encounter. Ioni's words had become lost in a fog of grief, twisted by desire and his wife's interpretations. *Of course she wants us to kill them, Richard! Why else would she say it?*

"Answer us, Rebel. What were her exact words?"

"She said this world couldn't live as long as you people were on it!"

The room went quiet again. Zack's hands clenched into fists. "And that's all it took, huh? No questions. No 'show me the proof.' Just point the way and pass the ammo."

"The world is *dying*. That's a fact!"

"My friends died faster," Jonathan fired back. "You killed them all on a goddamned rumor. *That's* a fact."

"You made my dad a pariah," Liam added. "He tried to warn you, but you turned everyone against him. Even me."

"Shut up! All of you!"

Amanda gripped Rebel's chair by the armrests, her face mere inches from his. Though her sharp green eyes were as intense as ever, her voice was calm, even sympathetic.

"I never in my life thought I'd say this, Rebel, but I understand where you're coming from. I get it. You saw the end of the world and you were desperate to stop it. A woman you trusted gave you the answer, and you believed her. If I had to kill a few dozen people to save billions, I'd do it. I might not even wait for proof."

She grabbed a napkin from the table and dabbed the sweat on Rebel's brow.

"Except it's all gone wrong," she continued. "You've lost so many people that you cared about that you don't even know how to handle it. There's no one on Earth who understands that feeling more than we do. We lived your worst nightmare, Rebel. Our world's already gone."

Rebel looked away, quivering. Mia confronted him from his left side.

"Look at me." Mia clasped his cheek and turned his gaze back onto her. "You put a bullet in my chest and I forgive you. More than that, I'll work with you to stop what's coming. This may not be my world but I'll lay down my life to save it. I can't think of a better reason to die."

Liam studied her in admiration and then nodded at Rebel. "If she can forgive you, so can I."

"Me too," Heath said from the sofa.

"Me too," said David.

"Not me," Jonathan said. "I'll never forgive you for what you did and I hope you die painfully. But I'm all aboard the 'save the world' train. If that means teaming up with you, then I'll do it. I'm a musician. I know how to work with assholes."

Zack wagged a finger at Jonathan. "Yeah. What he said. You fucked up bad and you're not done paying for it. But I'll work with you. I'll fight by your side."

He moved in closer. His voice dropped an octave. "And if you're looking to hurt the Pelletiers, you most definitely have a partner."

Amanda closed her eyes, livid. Zack had already learned the folly of enraging Azral and Esis. Now here he was, leaping at the chance to become their victim again.

It's simply his nature, Esis had told her yesterday. *There is no saving him.*

Rebel shrank away from the people around him, using every last ounce of his willpower to keep his composure. But then the levees broke, and he blubbered exactly in the way he'd predicted.

The orphans watched him jadedly as he wept in his chair. Even the most charitable among them didn't think he was wailing over the strangers he'd murdered, or the awful things he'd done to the people in this room. Amanda wasn't even sure he was sorry about the soldiers he'd lost, at least a dozen dead Gothams by her count. It was his dear, beloved wife he was crying over. It was all about Ivy.

Peter dropped a box of tissues onto Rebel's lap, then unwrapped the bicycle chains around his arms. There was no point restraining him anymore. Let the poor fool dab his own eyes.

The others watched in confusion as Peter pushed Rebel's chair down the hallway.

"What are you doing?" Theo asked.

"We have some final matters to discuss," Peter said. "Best we do it alone."

He wheeled Rebel into his little green bedroom, and shut the door behind them.

The orphans and Liam fell back in their seats, their shoulders slumped, their faces racked with gloom. Only Heath had the will to keep himself busy. He picked up his lumic puzzle sphere and continued to twist the glowing rings.

Forty minutes later, the bedroom door reopened and Peter came out alone. He fetched a glass of water from the kitchen and drank the whole thing before addressing his companions. From the exhausted half grin on his face, no one had to ask how his final parley went.

"We did it," Peter announced. "War's over."

Peter spent the next ten minutes explaining what came next. He and Liam would take Rebel back to their village and get him the medical help he needed. Once he was well enough to face the clan elders, Rebel would reveal the faulty intelligence behind his crusade, and then publicly admit that he'd been wrong about the breachers. Peter would then ask the elders to swear the entire village to an oath of armistice, ensuring a lasting peace between the Gothams and the orphans.

"And then?" Jonathan asked.

"Then you all come back with me to Quarter Hill," Peter said. "Our home becomes your home. My people become your people."

The faces all around him went slack with astonishment.

Holy shit, Hannah thought. *We're going to be Gothams.*

By midnight, Peter and Liam were fully dressed and ready to go. Rebel walked between them on wobbly legs, his arms slung over their shoulders. He avoided the gazes of the Silvers and Golds until he was halfway across the living room.

"Stop," Rebel said to the Pendergens. "Give me a second."

He leveled his tired gaze at the orphans on the sofas. "I don't know what to think anymore. If Ioni was lying . . ." He dipped his head. "There's nothing I can say. I hurt innocent people and I lost everyone who ever mattered to me. Everyone."

He could see the impatience on everyone's faces. His audience, his handlers, they all just wanted him to leave.

"You won't have to worry about me anymore," he promised. "Even if it turns out Ioni was right, I don't care. I don't care if this world lives or dies. I only have one thing left to do."

Rebel looked to Zack, a fresh rage in his eyes.

"I hope you meant what you said, Trillinger, because I'll need all the help I can get with the Pelletiers. I also believe with all my heart that Semerjean's disguised as one of you. I think he's been pulling your strings from day one."

Rebel scanned the different reactions on their faces—skepticism and anger, confusion and distrust. Only Zack met his gaze with calm, thoughtful eyes.

"If I'm right," Rebel continued, "then Semerjean's in this room right now. I've got a message for him."

He waved a splinted finger at the orphans, his aim bouncing stubbornly between Jonathan and David. "I'm coming for you. You and your wife and that chalk-headed son of yours. I will not rest until I find you all and kill you. That's a promise."

A testy silence filled the apartment. Peter waved a portal onto the wall. "Come on."

All eyes followed Rebel as he hobbled toward the exit—the brown ones, the blue ones, the vengeful, and the weary. Only one man's face showed a glimmer of amusement. He stared at Rebel mockingly and cast a thought in an arcane language. *Noted.*

PART THREE

UNDERLAND

May arrived in a veil of mist, an impenetrable haze that rolled in from the east and blanketed fifty square miles of New York. At sunrise, the state Transit Authority issued a Level 4 fog alert, grounding all civilian aer traffic in the metro region and its suburbs. From Staten Island to Haverstraw, the streets were clogged with automobiles and aeromobiles.

Peter sat at the wheel of his rental van and scowled at the congestion on the freeway. What should have been a breezy Sunday drive through Rockland County had become an eighty-minute fit of stops and starts. His fault, he supposed, for being delicate. He didn't want to teleport the orphans to their brand-new home in Quarter Hill. The village was best introduced slowly, one cold splash at a time.

As he pushed his way into the exit lane, Peter looked in the rearview and scanned the faces of his eight passengers. If they were glad to leave the Aerie after a week of cramped quarters, they didn't show it. Even Hannah, the sunniest of the bunch, gazed out the window with vacant gloom.

Peter focused the mirror on Jonathan and Heath. "The Cataclysm started in Brooklyn, just a few blocks north of the old brownstone. In the blink of an eye, it spread five miles in every direction, a dome of light that stretched from Hoboken to Queens."

The two Golds stared at Peter, blank-faced, as he continued to answer a question they never asked.

"Everyone inside the blast radius died, but there were thousands of people caught on the edge, in a narrow ring of space that became known as the Halo of Gotham. Aside from some trauma, those folks were just fine. The only ones who had trouble were women in the early stages of pregnancy. Most of their babies came out dead or deformed. Some were just born . . . different."

Jonathan finally got his point. "So that's how your people came to be."

"That's how we were born. You want to know how we came to be, you have to jump ahead twenty years."

Mia breathed with relief when Peter finally got off the freeway. This trip was taking forever. She just wanted to get to Gotham City (or whatever they called it) and get all the awkwardness out of the way.

"Those timebending children were scattered all over the world," Peter explained. "The Cataclysm threw everything into chaos. Thousands of families left New York, willingly and otherwise. Some, like my great-grandparents, were rounded up and sent back to Ireland."

Hannah looked at him askance. "They blamed the Cataclysm on the *Irish*?"

"They blamed all foreigners," Peter told her. "That's why Integrity was originally formed. To flush out all the no-good, dirty immigrants."

David scoffed from the backseat. "How far they've come."

"It wasn't a good time to be different," Peter said. "The first of my people grew up scared and alone. But as they got older and ventured out into the world, the travelers began to sense each other. The tempics felt each other's energy. By 1930, there were more than three dozen mini-groups. Some of the couples already had kids together, the first of the second generation."

Amanda sat forward. A huge mass of tempis loomed ahead of them, invisible in the fog but prevalent in her senses. She could tell from the way Heath writhed in his seat that he felt it too.

Peter reached into his tote bag and grabbed a remote control clicker. "It was Ashwin Sunder, Ivy's great-grandfather, who brought the founding members of the clan together. He was one of the world's first augurs, a powerful one at that. He didn't just see the faces of his future kinsmen, he envisioned a safe haven for all of them, a place where they could live together and look out for each other."

Now everyone could see the tempis up ahead: a tall, curved barrier that stretched deep into the mist. The surface was lined with cameras and trespass warnings.

"This is it," Peter said. "Well, the start of it."

Theo studied the barrier with a cocked eyebrow. "That's how your people stayed hidden all this time? A big fat wall and a 'Keep Out' sign?"

Peter chuckled. "There's a little more to it than that."

As he continued toward the barrier, he explained that Quarter Hill was a gated village of twenty-two hundred people. Only half the residents were members of the clan. The other half had no idea they were living among chronokinetics. Even the local police were oblivious.

"And your people never had a mishap?" David asked. "No tempic hands or ill-timed portals?"

"We've had to erase a few memories," Peter admitted. "It's been at least twenty years since the last incident."

"Wow. That's disciplined."

"That's fear." Peter stopped at the wall and pressed his clicker. A single-lane tunnel opened in the tempis. "We all know what the government would do to us."

As the van crossed the threshold, the orphans sat up in their seats and took a wary scan of the neighborhood. The houses near the barrier were all humble colonials but with each passing block, they became larger, more elaborate, with rolling front yards encased in ornate iron fences.

Hannah marveled at the palatial estates. "Just how rich are you people?"

"Filthy," Peter said. "Augurs make good investors."

Zack was more thrown by the innocuousness of Quarter Hill, a molecular clone of every posh suburb he'd ever seen. "You Gothams sure are good at playing normal."

Peter scowled at him through the rearview. "I told you to stop using that word."

"Normal?"

"Gothams. We don't call ourselves that, any more than you call yourselves 'breachers.'"

"So what do you call yourselves?" Jonathan asked.

"We don't."

"No name?"

"We know who we are," Peter said. "We don't need a letterhead."

Jonathan eyed him curiously. "So how did you get saddled with the G-word, then?"

Hannah nodded. "Yeah. I mean if you guys are so careful, why does the whole country have a nickname for you?"

Peter blew a hot breath through his nose. "Hold that thought."

He pulled into the parking lot of a blond brick complex, a three-story high school that looked as posh as a hotel. The campus was empty on this gray Sunday morning. Only a lone woman jogged with her sheepdog in tow. The moment she left, Peter parked the van in the faculty lot, then escorted his passengers to a utility door on the far side of the building.

Amanda watched him closely as he opened the lock with a black metal key. "Peter, what exactly are we doing here?"

"Just bear with me. We're almost there."

He led the procession down a long, tiled corridor, its walls lined with lockers as far as the eye could see. Mia reeled at the overwhelming familiarity of the school. She could remember a time, long ago on another Earth, when her entire life revolved around being a student.

"Is this place real?" she asked Peter.

"Of course it is."

"I don't know. I thought maybe it was a front."

Peter shook his head. "Everything in town is exactly what it's supposed to be."

He summoned an elevator and motioned everyone inside. As the doors closed and the group squeezed together, Peter stuck an electronic card key into the control console, then punched the floor buttons in an elaborate sequence of ones, twos, and threes.

Hannah crossed her arms, skeptical. "Is there a secret wall that's supposed to—"

The lift came to life with a lurch. The motor hummed, and the car began descending, fast.

Peter turned to his puzzled companions. "About forty years ago, a Dep named Alexander Wingo came to town on a murder investigation. He was a peculiar little man, a hell of a lot smarter than anyone expected him to be. He learned a bunch of stuff he shouldn't have and he got away before anyone could reverse his memory."

"So he started the whole Gotham thing," Jonathan said.

Peter nodded. "He wrote a best-selling 'exposé' about us, mostly lies and exaggerations. But the myth persisted. We still get conspiracy loons sniffing around the village, hoping to catch a glimpse."

"Why don't you just move?" Theo asked him.

"We did. After that whole Wingo flap, we spent two years building a brand-new base for ourselves. Someplace more secure and out of the way."

"I'll say." Zack touched the vibrating wall. "We must be eighty floors down by now."

"No floors," Peter said. "Just a thousand feet of bedrock."

"And then?"

The elevator came to a stop. The orphans were shocked to see sunshine spilling into the lift.

Peter motioned to the door. "See for yourself."

Two by two, they walked into the light. Amanda thought she'd stepped outside again until she saw giant air vents in the clouds. The "sky" was just a lumic projection on a dome-shaped ceiling, a rather massive one at that. This underground cavern looked large enough to fit a small town.

And in point of fact, it did.

The Silvers and Golds looked around in wonder at the trees and small buildings, all nestled together in a perfect grid. Gothams drove up and down the streets in golf carts, past churches and parlors and lush green parks. At least fifty pedestrians stood within eyeshot, each one going about their day. At first glance, the village looked like a replica of Everytown USA, a snow-globe dream of suburbia at its finest.

At second glance, the dream turned weird.

Everywhere the orphans looked, someone was using temporis. Swifter children chased each other in streaking blurs. A pair of tempics carried groceries in self-generated baskets. A portly man in overalls unwilted several begonias with a flick of his finger. A family of four emerged from a portal on the side of a firehouse. No one batted an eye at them.

Peter smiled at his companions. "Welcome to the underland."

Theo staggered forward, his mouth hanging open. "Jesus Christ. It's just—"

"—crazy," Heath finished. He hadn't spoken a word since he'd left Old Tappan, but now his anxiousness had been supplanted with a bright, mystic awe.

He craned his neck, then tugged at Jonathan's sleeve. The others followed their slack, upward gazes.

A trio of Gothams soared high above them on white wings of aeris, swooping and turning in perfect synchronicity. One of them caught sight of the breachers down below and smacked his wing against the illusive sky. He might have fallen all the way into the ground if his partners hadn't caught him with long tempic arms.

Soon everyone in view stopped what they were doing to stare at the newcomers. The swifter boys came to a screeching halt. A tempic woman dropped her groceries.

Amanda looked at Peter nervously. "You said they were expecting us."

"They are," Peter assured her. "Give them time."

The last seven days had been tumultuous for the clan. They'd barely had a chance to mourn their latest casualties when everything they knew was turned upside down. Their hero Rebel Rosen had been nothing but a dupe, while the traitor Peter Pendergen had been right about everything.

Four days ago, the council of elders absolved Peter of all crimes, then issued a startling decree. There would be no more violence against these alien breachers, on penalty of expulsion. More than that, the otherworlders would be welcomed into their society, with all the rights and protections of native kinsmen.

Gemma Sunder took the news with such shrieking protest that she had to be dragged out of the assembly. The moment she got home, she wrote a furious bitmail to her people:

> **Ivy died for you and this is how you repay her? Shame on you!**
> **Don't be fooled by Rebel's surrender. These breachers can't be**
> **trusted. They walk hand in hand with Pelletiers.**

Only Semerjean knew how right she was. While the locals glowered at him and his friends, he looked around with a disapproving scowl. What a ridiculous little burrow these Gothams had dug for themselves, as crude and flimsy as their ethics. All it would take was an earthquake or a government invasion to bring their fake sky crashing down on their heads.

Esis hailed him through their neural link. *<Careful, my love. There are those in the clan who would still do harm to the Silvers.>*

<No kidding,> Semerjean replied in cheeky English. *<I'll be sleeping lightly for a while.>*

Peter beamed at the sight of a familiar figure weaving his way through the crowd. "There he is."

Liam had recovered nicely in the seven days since Atropos. His skin had reclaimed its healthy pink color and he once again moved with the spry, springy steps of a fourteen-year-old.

He joined his father's side and smiled at the others. Hannah caught his bashful gaze lingering on Mia. "Nice to see you all again."

"Nice to be welcomed," Zack griped.

"Give them time. They've spent months listening to Rebel and Ivy's scare talk. Half of them still think you have horns."

A shrill honking noise filled the air. The onlookers parted to make room for a white-haired gentleman in a wheelless, floating golf cart.

Peter sighed as the man disembarked. "Our first greeter," he warned the others. "Have patience. He means well."

He was a short, rotund fellow in an exquisitely tailored business suit, with a hearty white mustache that drooped an inch below his jowls. Hannah could see from his walrus gut and effortless smile that life had been good to him. She couldn't remember the last time she saw someone that contented.

The man shook Peter's hand, then greeted the others with a comical bow. "Welcome, my friends. Welcome! I'm Daniel Whitten: house lord of the Whittens, primarch of the lumics, and Primary Executive in Charge of Underland Operations."

The orphans nodded blankly, more puzzled than dazzled by the man's many titles.

"You can just call him Mayor," Peter said. "We all do."

"A pet name," the Mayor insisted. "Not a formal rank of office. In any case, it's a thrill and an honor to meet you. I never thought I'd see the day when . . ." He cut himself off with a chortle. "Let's just say these are interesting times."

The Mayor clutched his lapels and rocked merrily on his feet. "You'll be pleased to know that your houses have been cleaned and fully—"

"Houses?" Theo asked.

"Yes. You'll have five homes to share. If you need more . . ."

The group shook their heads, gobsmacked. After nine months of close-quarter living, the Mayor's news was a windfall, like inheriting Texas.

"I hope we're not pushing anyone out," Amanda said.

"No, no. Not at all. Very few of us sleep down here. We'd give you one of our surface homes but in light of your, ah, legal troubles . . ."

Peter smiled knowingly. "We're not going topside for a good long while."

Zack fought the urge to challenge him, as they still had to go to Seattle and look for the seven wayward Coppers that Melissa had told them about. He made a note to bug Peter about it later.

The Mayor clapped his hands together. A flash of rainbow light escaped his palms. "Now which one of you is David Dormer?"

David sheepishly waved at him. "Uh, that would be me."

The Mayor shook his hand. "Ah, there you are. My goodness, what a handsome boy. I hear you're a lumic of extraordinary talent. The power of light runs strong in the Whitten family. I've been running the guild for seventeen years."

"Guild?"

"Oh, yes, yes. There are ninety-six lumics like us in the clan. We're a very tight community. If you're free tonight, you can meet some of them. I know my daughter Yvonne's dying to meet you. She's your age and already one of our best illusionists. I think the two of you—"

"All right," Peter said. He patted the Mayor's back. "Let's give him a chance to get settled."

"Of course. Of course. Let me know if there's anything you need. And welcome again. This is truly a momentous day."

The Mayor gave David one last smile before gliding away in his aerocart.

"What the hell was that about?" Hannah asked Peter.

He exchanged a weary look with Liam before answering. "There are forty-four families in the clan. Most of them are locked in endless competition with each other. They're always quibbling over who has the strongest bloodline, the most powerful children."

David balked at his news. "So all that talk about his daughter was—"

"Setup," Peter said. "He's already plotting the next generation of Whittens."

Theo blinked at him. "Is he in denial or just optimistic?"

"A little of both. He thinks this whole end-of-the-world business will solve itself somehow. It's a disturbingly common attitude around here."

A large black shadow washed over the group. They all looked up to see a flying tempic descending on them, a gaunt and stringy blonde of late middle age. She made a graceful landing on the grass, then retracted her wings into her shoulder blades. While half the Silvers flinched at the backless white leotard that left little to the imagination, the other half saw her eyes locked firmly on one of their own.

"Amanda Given," said the tempic. "It's a pleasure to finally meet you."

Amanda awkwardly returned the handshake. "I'm afraid you have me at a, uh . . ."

The woman squinted at Peter. "You didn't tell her about me?"

He met her frown with a glower. "We've been busy."

"I'm Victoria Chisholm," she said to Amanda. "Voting head of the Chisholm family and primarch of the tempics. I'm told you're a woman of substantial power. If that's true, then I would gladly welcome you to join our clan's largest guild."

"How large?" Zack inquired.

"There are three hundred and sixty-three of us," Victoria proudly replied. "Tempis is by far the most prevalent blessing among our kind. Mastery, however, is—"

"How many of you can fly?" David asked.

Victoria directed her answer at Amanda. "Only ten percent of us can generate aeris, and only half that number have mastered the art of wing flight. Perhaps one day you'll join us in the sky." She glowered at the ceiling. "Or what passes for sky here."

Hannah gripped Heath's shoulder. "You know, he's a tempic too. A really good one."

Victoria looked Heath up and down before throwing a scornful look at Peter. "Don't you think that one's better with the Majee?"

"No," Peter growled. "And if I hear that talk again, there'll be trouble."

"Watch yourself," Victoria snapped. "Oathbreaker."

She tossed a cordial nod at Amanda before spreading her wings and launching back into the air.

Jonathan watched her fly away. "I liked the fat guy better."

"She won't be a problem," Peter promised.

"What was all that stuff about Heath and the Magi?"

"Majee," Peter corrected. "It's complicated."

David scanned the local populace. "Actually, I'd say it's quite simple."

The others looked around and quickly caught his gist. Though there were a few tan faces among the Gothams, Heath was the only African-American in sight.

Hannah glared at Peter. "What kind of country club shit is this?"

"It's not what you think."

"What's 'Majee'? A racial slur?"

"Of course not," Liam said. "It's their chosen name."

"Who?"

Peter closed his eyes, sighing. "There are nine black families down south in Atlanta. They have their own clan, their own laws, their own *skyscraper*, for God's sake. They're doing just fine without us."

"Did they leave willingly?" Theo asked. "Or were they forced out?"

Amanda could guess the answer from Peter's expression. "They were never invited."

Peter rubbed his face. For all its oil-powered engines and nontemporic devices, the world of the Silvers was clearly more evolved on certain fronts. There was no good way to spin this.

Jonathan clutched Heath's arm. "If he's not welcome, we're out of here."

"All of us," Hannah stressed.

"No one's going anywhere." Peter dropped to a knee in front of Heath. "Look, I don't need to tell you that there are small-minded people out there. I'm sorry to say there are some in here. But I promise you, son, I *promise* you—"

"Our people will adapt," said a soft voice behind them.

No one had noticed her approach—a small, weathered Asian woman in a handsome dress and shawl. Peter smiled at her warmly. "Everyone, this is Prudent Lee, the primarch of the augurs. Rest easy. She's one of the good ones."

Amanda wanted to believe it, but there was something about Prudent's expression that bothered her, a glazed and sluggish dolor that strongly suggested she was on tranquilizers. If Prudent was an augur, then she had every reason in the world to sedate herself. Still, it was unnerving. Amanda also didn't like the way she kept looking at Zack out of the corner of her eye.

"I'm so glad to finally meet you," Prudent said to Theo. She spoke in a slow, stammering cadence, as if she kept losing her train of thought. "I . . . cannot apologize enough for the harm my people have caused you. Rebel was my student. I should have . . . taught him better. I should have challenged him openly, as Peter did."

Liam shook his head. "He had us all fooled, Matron. And you had your own problems to deal with."

"Thank you. This has been a most difficult time. I . . ."

She sneaked another peek at Zack before focusing on Theo. "Last year at this time, there were sixty-six augurs in the guild. Now we are half that."

Prudent lowered her head. "The visions have not been kind."

Theo winced. He could only imagine how the other augurs died: gunshots and nooses and chemical overdoses, all to shut out the images of apocalypse. "I'm sorry."

"Those of us who remain are eager to help," Prudent said. "We . . . lack your ability to enter the God's Eye willingly, though perhaps there is knowledge you have that will help us overcome this. In return, I hope that some of us can assist you in the search for the string."

Theo stared at her, dumbstruck. After meeting Victoria and the Mayor, he wasn't expecting good news from any of these Gothams. But if his burden could be shared . . .

"God, yeah, of course. Just tell me what you need."

"Come to my house at seven o'clock. We'll discuss it over dinner."

Prudent turned to Zack. "I invite you as well."

He balked at her offer. "I'm no augur."

"No, but you're well acquainted with my daughter, Mercy."

"Oh. I didn't know she was, uh . . . how's she doing?"

"Not well," Prudent admitted. "She believed in Rebel and did terrible things for him. Now that she knows his cause was . . . flawed, she's beside herself with grief. If you could speak to her, maybe find it in your heart to forgive her, it would . . . bring her out of her dark place. I've lost too many loved ones to despair. I can't lose her, too."

Zack traded a heavy look with Theo before shrugging in acquiescence. "Yeah. Okay."

Prudent squeezed his wrist. "Thank you. You've suffered much in recent days, but there is happiness in your future. I've seen it."

Amanda watched her suspiciously as she said her good-byes and left.

Mia frowned at Peter. "So when do I meet the head of the travelers?"

"You won't."

"Why not?"

"Because Esis killed her last Sunday."

"Oh." Mia stuffed her hands in her pockets and stared down at the grass. She didn't know that Ivy Sunder had been primarch, but it made perfect sense. Her replacement probably wouldn't be extending any courtesies to Mia anytime soon. There was still so much bad blood between the Gothams and breachers. Now they were all expected to live together in this underground pressure cooker.

Peter looked to the clock tower in the center of the village. "Come on. Let's keep going."

They walked down the street in a tight, anxious cluster. Though the locals went back to their normal Sunday business, the orphans felt the heat of a hundred glares as Peter escorted them through town.

Along the way, he drowned them all in idle trivia. The underland occupied 22.4 million cubic feet of space and was powered by four hundred solic generators. It was connected to the surface by thirty elevators, ten stairwells, one sloping tunnel, and a volunteer team of travelers who remained on call, like a taxi service. Below their feet lay the land beneath the underland: a vast network of tunnels containing survival bunkers and emergency supplies, enough to sustain a thousand people for years. The Gothams were prepared to withstand almost any calamity the good Lord threw at them, everything short of apocalypse. In a better mood, Zack would have almost found that funny.

As the procession continued toward the village square, David saw a young mother clutch her toddler defensively, as if the forces of Sauron had invaded the Shire. A creepy-looking man stared intently at Amanda. Mia couldn't tell if he wanted to kill her or kiss her.

Hannah shot a surly look at Peter. "This isn't the Brigadoon you sold us on."

"I never promised a confetti welcome," he said. "Just safety."

"Then why do I feel like setting bear traps around my bed tonight?"

"I told you, everyone here's sworn an oath of armistice. They can't lay a finger on you."

Soon the group reached the square at the base of the clock tower, one of the nicest parks that Theo had ever seen. Among the fountains and flowers and the wrought-iron benches stood a pair of black stone walls, each one chiseled with hundreds of markings.

Zack took a closer look at the wall on the left, a visual directory of the clan's forty-four families. They were all linked to each other through a twisting array of dotted lines.

"Marriages," he guessed. He turned to Peter. "You only shack up with your own kind."

"Have to. It's the law."

"And how many of these things are, uh . . . ?"

"Arranged?" Peter smiled wanly. "Only some families do that. The rest of us pick who we like."

As long as they're a Gotham, Zack thought bitterly. It seemed these people, like the Pelletiers, had their own arbitrary rules about who could entwine with whom.

Mia was intrigued by the other wall, an extensive list of all the talent guilds and their members. Some of the classifications were utterly foreign.

"What's a turner?" she asked Liam.

"The temporal reversers, like Zack and Mother Olga."

"Mother Olga?"

"Their primarch," Liam explained. "Best healer we have. You'll meet her soon enough. She's a good woman."

David stood behind them and squinted at the directory. "What's a sub-thermic?"

"They're like me," Liam said. "Except instead of burning things, they freeze them."

"Huh." David looked to Mia. "Like that woman we fought at Terra Vista."

Mia scowled and moved away from him. He knew damn well what a subthermic was. He was just trying to wheedle his way back into her good graces. *Remember that time I saved your life? Remember?*

Heath looked up at the huge roster of tempics. Some of the names, like Victoria Chisholm's, featured a bird-wing icon. All of them were followed by a number.

Liam tapped the 98 next to Victoria's name. "Everyone takes a power test once a year. They're graded on a hundred-point scale."

"Why?"

"Good question," said Liam. "For some parents, a kid's power score is more important than their school grades. It's good for bragging. Good for marrying your son or daughter into a more powerful family, like the Whittens or the Sunders."

Heath lowered his head. "I don't like this place."

Mia frowned at him. "Heath . . ."

"It's okay," Liam said. "We deserve it after everything we did to you. Lord knows, you folks have seen the worst of us."

"But you haven't seen the best," Peter added. He approached the guild directory and pointed to a stately engraving at the top.

HUMANITY. HUMILITY. TEMPERANCE.

"We're good people at heart," he said. "We look out for each other. We teach our kids to use their gifts responsibly, with compassion. We're not raising gods or monsters here. We just want to live our lives, like the rest of the world."

He gripped Liam's shoulders. "We just want to live."

Amanda took a solemn look at the strangers around her, all grim-faced and nervous. She'd been given only four minutes to prepare for the death of her world. These people had four years. Four years to fret, four years to cry, four years to clench their fists and scream at their gods.

"We'll give them a chance," she promised Peter. "We'll work with your people, but they have to work with us. They have to realize once and for all that we're not the cause of their problem."

Zack nodded his fervent agreement. "And that we're not Pelletiers."

"You got us this far," Hannah said to Peter. "Make them understand."

He flipped his hands in surrender. "I've been telling them all week. I'll be telling them again. All I'm saying now is be patient. We've only just come together."

He looked up at the highest window of the clock tower and saw a young face looking back at him. At first glance, she looked like the vengeful ghost of Ivy. But no, it was just her baby niece. Still bitter. Still angry.

Peter turned back to the orphans and sighed. "It'll just take time."

Gemma retreated from the window, her heart pounding. She'd been watching Peter and the breachers from the moment they stepped off the elevator, confident that they wouldn't see her up here. But the Irish prick had sharp eyes. She'd have to set up a camera system if she wanted to keep tabs on them.

Five children and a figment watched her gingerly from the other side of the clock chamber. "This is crazy," the figment growled. "You'll get us all in trouble."

Gemma found it both ironic and irksome that a fluorescent blue tiger was questioning her sanity. The creature was made entirely of light, conjured from the mind of a twelve-year-old lumic. The boy was Harold Herrick. The tiger's name was Bo.

"We won't get in trouble," she told Harold, a chubby blond in Coke-bottle glasses. "As long as we're careful—"

"Why are you talking to him?" Bo asked. "That fat fuck is useless. Talk to me."

The other kids bristled as Harold recoiled at his own abuse. The boy had more psychological issues than his family knew what to do with, but he was a prodigy with lumis. He tested so far off the charts that the Mayor had to fudge his test results just to save face for the rest of the guild. Gemma needed Harold, which meant she had to put up with his baffling quirks.

She grudgingly faced the tiger. "As long as we're careful, we won't get caught. I've seen the future. I've *lived* it."

"How do we *know* that?" asked Suki Godden. "You may not be as crazy as Harold but you're sure as hell not stable."

Gemma turned to face her. Suki was eleven years old and, like all Goddens, she was achingly pretty. But everyone in the clan knew that her long blond hair was just a wig. Her eyebrows were glue-ons. Suki's solic-electric powers rendered her completely hairless. The bizarre, incomprehensible nature of her blessing made her the embarrassment of her family. Gemma could certainly relate.

"You came here, Suki, because you know that I'm a veteran. I fought the Silvers in Terra Vista. I helped kill six Golds in White Plains. I stood with Ivy at Battery Park. And I survived Atropos, unlike your bitch sister."

Suki flicked her thumb, throwing crackling blue sparks. She clearly wasn't offended by Gemma's harsh words for Jinn. She'd never much liked her either.

"Calm down," said Suki. "I'm just asking questions."

"What about Rebel?" asked a thin and handsome twelve-year-old. "Can't he help us?"

Until Heath came along, Miguel "Squid" Tam was the darkest boy in the village. His caramel skin came from four generations of cross-breeding—an exotic blend of Spanish, Indian, and Chinese DNA. His chronokinetic pedigree, however, was much purer. All of his forebears were tempic.

Unfortunately for Squid, Victoria Chisholm refused to let him into the esteemed tempics' guild, as the corrosive black goo that spewed from his fingers bore little relation to tempis. Another misfit. Another black sheep for Gemma's flock.

"Forget about Rebel," she said. "He's broken. He can't help anyone."

"And what makes you think we'll do any better?" Squid pressed.

"Because I learned from his mistakes." Her face lit up in a confident smile. "And I picked better people."

Gemma's praise drew reluctant grins from the children, none of whom were accustomed to compliments. Naomi Byers listened through her temporal converter, then clapped her hands with excitement. The girl was to swifters what Harold was to lumics—a wunderkind, a chart-breaking oddity. She came into the world at 30x speed, cut from the womb of her dead, rifted mother. That was six months ago.

Now Naomi stood five-foot-three, a wild-haired brunette in torn, mismatched clothes. She typed with blurry haste into her wrist keyboard. The lumic projector on her back beamed bright yellow letters above her head:

WEN DO I GET 2 KILL SOME1?

The kids around her all shuddered with revulsion. Clearly Naomi was missing more than a brake pedal. Though the Byers had tried their best to raise a civilized girl under mad circumstances, it hadn't worked. Bug had often said that the savage little freak should be euthanized.

"Soon," Gemma promised her. "Patience."

Naomi accelerated Gemma's response for comprehension, then crossed her arms in annoyance. She was a cheetah in a world of snails. Patience was all she knew.

OK, she typed. S'LONG AS I GET 2 UZE KNIFE.

Bo narrowed his bright tiger eyes. "That bitch is crazy."

"Cut it out," Gemma snapped. "We get enough shit from the others. Let's be the team that works together."

Squid snorted. "Yeah, and we can all get exiled together."

Gemma shook her head. "Even if the worst happens—and it *won't*—the elders will never kick us out. We're kids."

"That won't matter to the Pelletiers," Suki reminded her. "They've killed unborn babies."

Gemma took a deep breath. She'd had this conversation more than once today. Each time she failed to convince the others, she jumped back a few minutes and tried a new approach. Now, after fifteen do-overs, she finally had it.

"I can't tell you what I have planned for them," she whispered. "They have ears everywhere. Just trust me when I say that they'll be my problem, not yours. While you're off fighting the breachers, I'll be somewhere else. Fighting them."

The others drank her in with awe. Even Bo was thunderstruck. Gemma felt guilty for the lie, but they couldn't know her real plan. They'd turn against her in a heartbeat.

"This'll work," she assured them. "The breachers will be gone. The world will be saved. And everyone will know that it was the six of us—the outcasts, the *disparates*—who finished the job that Ivy started."

Gemma studied the faces of her teammates. "So can I count on you?"

One by one, the children nodded. Only one last holdout—a twelve-year-old redhead with a sweet freckled face—remained hunched in uncertainty.

Gemma looked to him. "Please tell me you're with us, Dunk. We can't do this without you."

No one who knew Duncan Rall would have ever expected to find him among this odious group. He was a good-natured boy who brought no shame to his family, only sympathy. Dunk had been terminal from the moment he was born, destined for a death that even criminals didn't deserve. Though he'd managed his curse with remarkable aplomb, he was tired of tongue clucks, tired of pity, tired of being a victim of his own power. Better he should accomplish something with his life before he fell into darkness.

He walked across the room on thick tempic boots, then studied the Silvers and Golds through the window.

"Yeah," he said faintly. "I'm in."

He locked his gaze on Jonathan Christie, the only person on Earth who shared his affliction. Shame that the man had to die, but if that's what it took to save the world, then Dunk was ready. He'd drop each and every one of these breachers to Hell.

TWENTY-SEVEN

For the thirty-three flying tempics of the clan, the underland was both freedom and oppression. It was the only place on Earth where they could spread their wings and enjoy their natural blessings. But the dome was confining and the view was downright tedious. By now, the aerial map of the village had become scorched onto their retinas: a crosshatch square of sixteen streets, each one paved to the exact same length and capped with a bed of pink and white oleander.

A seventeenth street ruined the symmetry of the grid: a tree-lined cul-de-sac on the southwest corner of town. It had no name, no curb, no developments at all except for six wooden cottages at the end. They flanked the crest in a tight semicircle, each house boasting a slightly different architecture.

The orphans and Pendergens stood clustered on the cobblestone, surveying their homes with dull poker faces. The cottages had a loose and shoddy look to them, as if they'd been built from a kit with vague instructions or ordered online from a not-so-reputable reseller.

Jonathan focused on a half-rotted window shutter. "Huh."

"The insides are nicer," Peter assured him.

"Hey, don't get me wrong. I've lived in worse places. I'm just confused. I mean you're a Marvin Gardens kind of people, and these are all—"

"Baltic," Zack said.

Jonathan nodded at Peter. "We're just wondering why any of you would live here when you have all those mansions up above."

Liam smiled softly. "No one chooses to live here. They're redemption houses."

"They're what?"

"Halfway homes," Peter clarified. "For our troublemakers."

That surprised Theo. "I thought you kicked out the troublemakers."

"Very rarely. We prefer to work with them, figure out what's making them angry."

Mia studied the villas suspiciously. "The Mayor said we have five houses. There are six."

Peter pointed to the rightmost cottage. "That one's occupied."

"By who?"

"No one you know," Peter said. "You don't have to worry about her. She's a good kid at heart—"

Liam cut him off with a sharp, bitter laugh.

"—and she'll keep to herself," Peter finished.

He gripped his son's shoulder, then took a sweeping glance at the others. "All right. Pick a house, pick your housemates, and then get real comfortable."

Peter looked up at the illusive clouds. "This isn't temporary."

They spent the rest of the day settling into their new homes. To everyone's relief, Peter had been right. The cottages were much nicer on the inside. The walls and floors were all polished mahogany, with furniture that could have been lifted from a five-star ski resort. The amenities and appliances were brand-spanking-new, and every house was well stocked with fresh food and linens. It seemed even the troublemakers lived well here in Gotham Country. Hannah still felt compelled to check for traps and hidden cameras.

She rejoined her sister in their new living room and tested the feel of the sofa cushions. "I hate to admit it, but I could get real comfortable here."

Amanda rummaged through the drawers of a cedar credenza. "I don't like it."

"Too small?"

"Too separate. I don't like us all living under different roofs."

David stepped out of the cozy second bedroom, his eyes flitting anxiously between the Givens. "You sure you're okay with me staying here?"

"Of course we are," Hannah said.

In choosing their homes, the group had split along predictable lines— Peter and Liam, Jonathan and Heath, Zack and Theo. The sisters were hurt but hardly shocked when Mia opted to live with the Silver men. She had a low tolerance for Amanda and Hannah's microsquabbles, and her brother-heavy upbringing made her more comfortable with guys.

The real surprise was David. Everyone had expected him to claim the final cottage for himself and then bask in his newfound privacy. Yet he meekly asked Amanda and Hannah if he could live with them, at least until he felt more settled.

David took a furtive peek out the window before joining Hannah on the sofa. "I'm not a fan of this split-living arrangement. It makes us more vulnerable."

Amanda pointed at him. "See? That's *exactly* why I don't like it."

"We should probably set up a night watch," David suggested. "If the Gothams attack us, it'll be—"

"Jesus."

Hannah rose to her feet. David and Amanda watched her as she hurried to the door.

"Where are you going?" Amanda asked her.

"To check on Heath."

"Why?"

"Because if you two are this freaked out, then he must be climbing the walls."

"Hannah—"

She closed the door behind her. David slouched in his seat, brooding. "She can't possibly fault us for being nervous."

"She doesn't," Amanda said. "She just has her own way of coping."

Amanda watched through the window as Hannah dashed across the cul-de-sac. "She's been sneaking kisses with Jonathan all week. She thinks I don't know."

"We *all* know," David said.

"She saw what the Pelletiers did to Zack. What the hell is she thinking?"

David shrugged from the couch. "No idea. I just know I'm staying out of it. Every time I meddle, I only make things worse."

Amanda stared down at her wringing hands. "I'm sorry we didn't listen to you."

"Do you think Hannah will listen to *you*?"

She grimly shook her head. "It'd only push her away."

Amanda hunkered down in an easy chair and grew a small tempic tree out of her hand. "I'd like to think that there's a timeline out there where we make all the right decisions. Where we save the world, beat our enemies, and live happily ever after with the people we want to be with."

David watched solemnly as her tree bloomed branches and leaves. "Could still happen."

"You really believe that?"

"No," he admitted. "I don't expect to grow old on this world."

The tempic tree wilted. Amanda vanquished it with a sigh. God gave her the power to break things, but not the power to fix them. She couldn't be with Zack, she couldn't help Theo, she couldn't heal the rift between Mia and David. And she couldn't prevent her sister from making the same mistake she did.

But she could do something about these goddamned Gothams.

"The night watch is a good idea," she said. "I also think you should get to know the Mayor. Have some coffee. Meet his daughter. I'll try to become friendly with Victoria Chisholm, as unpleasant as she seems."

"What's your reasoning?" David asked.

"If we're going to live with these people, we need to understand them. I don't want to wait for Peter to explain things. And if trouble's coming, I want to see it early. No more surprises. No more mistakes."

David smiled approvingly. "You've come a long way from the woman I met in San Diego."

"Not really," she said. "You just met me on a bad day."

Amanda stood up and stared out the window again. In the afternoon light, the houses didn't look so bad. They just needed a few touch-ups. Maybe a fresh coat of paint. Who knew? If the stars aligned and the Gothams played nice, she might finally be able to relax here. She might even like it.

While a gray and cloudy dusk fell over Quarter Hill, the residents of the underland got a much nicer sunset. The sky above the village turned a luminous shade of red, as clear and warm as a Wyoming summer. Mia didn't know if there was some kind of machine projecting all this fakery, or if the lumics were merely working in shifts. She made a note to ask Liam the next time she saw him.

She sat up in bed with a creaky yawn, then scanned her new environment.

Her wood-paneled bedroom was tiny, even smaller than her glorified closet in Brooklyn. But this one had a cozy elegance to it, plus a goose-down mattress that was the most comfortable thing she'd ever slept on.

Mia walked across the room, paper scraps crunching under her feet. As always, her cat nap had brought a downpour of messages from the future, along with the usual scattered patches of ash. More and more of her notes were combusting upon delivery, and she still didn't know why. If this kept up, she'd need a fireproof blanket.

To her surprise, the cottage was silent. No footsteps, no lumivision, no jocular chatter. She checked Zack and Theo's bedroom, then the oversize living room. Empty. They must have left to have dinner with that freaky augur woman. Mia could only hope that Theo—

"I said *no!*"

The sound had come from a neighbor's yard, a shrill and angry voice that Mia didn't recognize. She crept onto the backyard patio and peeked around the corner. Two houses away, a teenage blonde in a tank top and shorts was flailing in rage at a large, bearded man. Mia could barely hear him, though it was clear from his gestures that he was trying to calm her down.

"I swear to God I'm gonna slit my wrists if you don't fly the hell off!"

"Carrie—"

"Just leave me alone, Daddy! Go!"

Flustered, the father glanced around. Mia ducked out of view. By the time she dared to look again, he'd pulled off his sweatshirt and sprouted large wings of aeris from his back. He launched into the air with a jiggly leap.

The daughter noticed Mia gawking at him. She crossed her arms with sullen gloom. "Hey."

Mia blinked at her, red-faced. "I'm sorry. I didn't—"

"It's all right. I'm sorry you had to see my dad's fat belly."

The girl tilted her head and studied Mia with intrigue. "Wow. I thought you breachers would be all scarred and angry-looking, but you're like . . . huh."

She crossed the empty yard between them, her ponytail swinging with each step. She was a small and skinny thing, barely an inch taller than Mia. She couldn't have been a day over fourteen.

The girl stopped at the edge of the patio and shined a wide, cheery smile.

"Hi. I'm Carrie Bloom, scourge of the thermics and all-around nutbird. What's your kit, cat?"

"Huh?"

"Your *name*."

"Oh. I'm Mia. Mia Farisi."

"Mia Farisi. I *like* that. It has a real chime to it."

Mia studied her new friend in puzzlement. Her name had a certain ring of its own. *Bloom. Bloom. Why does that sound so familiar?*

Carrie saw her wary expression. "Oh no. Did Liam already shitmouth me? Whatever he said—"

"No. He didn't say anything."

"Oh. Well . . . good, because I've got tales on that burny twerper." Carrie processed Mia before smiling again. "Hey, you want to come by for a blender?"

Mia paused to remember her local slang. On this world, a blender was a frozen drink, not the machine that made it.

"Uh, yeah. Okay."

She followed Carrie into her cottage, struggling to make heads or tails of the girl. Peter said these houses were for troublemakers, but Carrie looked more like the queen of the pep squad—perky and pretty and effortlessly nice. She fluttered around the kitchen, speaking a mile a minute as she griped about her father.

"He's such a tempic. Always stubborn, never listening. Even now, he thinks everything's business as usual. But *I* can't pretend. And I'm not just gonna stand there while Rebel Fucking Rosen walks around the village, all forgiven and shit."

"What?"

Carrie cringed at Mia's expression. "Sorry. Like my problems even compare to yours. Has anyone even apologized for what Rebel and Ivy did to you people? Because if they don't, I will. It's sickening."

Mia couldn't help but grin. After all the Gothams she'd met this morning, it was almost jarring to find a good one.

Carrie looked her over with heavy blue eyes. "Holy hell, you're really from another world. There are so many questions I want to ask you, but that's probably the last thing you need. We'll go Q-for-Q when you're more settled. I can tell you things about this place. Boy, can I."

She mixed strawberries and cream in an electric whirlet, until it all became a lukewarm goop. Mia watched Carrie confusedly as she poured the liquid into two drinking cups.

"Uh, shouldn't you—"

Carrie waved her hand over the counter. A frigid blast of air filled the kitchen. Mia peeked inside the cups and marveled at their new slushy state.

"You're a subthermic."

"Yup. One of many reasons why Liam and I hate each other. The burners and coolers are like cats and dogs. We can't help it. It's our nature."

Carrie raised an eyebrow at Mia's expression. "Are you okay?"

She wasn't. David had recently reminded her of the very first Gotham they fought, a thirty-something blonde in thick winter clothes. She'd frozen the door of Mia's hideout, then broken the wood like it was peanut brittle. Mia had never forgotten the eyes behind her ski mask: blue and wet and filled with remorse.

I'm sorry, she'd said to Mia. *I don't want to do this. But I have a daughter your age. She has to live.*

Mia would have never known the woman's name if her future self hadn't sent it to her. "Bloom," she uttered. "Krista Bloom. Is she your . . . ?"

Carrie's arms fell to her sides. She plopped down on a stool. "She was my mother. I wasn't sure you met her. I was kind of hoping you didn't."

She dabbed her eyes with a dish towel. "You must hate me now."

"Of course not. It's not your fault. I don't even think it was her fault."

"She and Ivy were like sisters," Carrie said. "I begged her not to go, but she said she had to. Ivy needed her. That's all there was to it."

She gritted her teeth. The temperature in the room dropped twenty degrees. "But they *left* her there. The moment the Pelletiers showed up, Ivy and Rebel just teleported away. My mom didn't last a minute against Esis."

Mia gripped her arm. "I'm so sorry."

Carrie sniffled. "Ivy got what was coming to her, but Rebel's still walking around. Barely got a slap on the wrist. I saw him in the vivery last week and . . . I don't know. I guess I tried to freeze him."

"Wow," Mia said. "Is he, uh . . . ?"

"Oh, he's fine. Just a little bit of frostbite. But the elders weren't happy with me. It'll be at least six months before they let me back on the surface."

She looked down at her feet. A dark laugh escaped her. "I'll be long gone by then."

"What do you mean?"

"I've got some savings," Carrie told her. "I'm just waiting for the right chance to hop. There's a whole wide world out there. I'd like to see it before it goes."

"Don't leave," Mia urged her. "Please."

"Why not?"

"Because you're the first person I met here that I like."

Carrie scrutinized her a moment before laughing again. "You know the sad thing? I could probably say the same about you."

The girls picked up their blenders, then took a deep sip through the straws. The drink was just as cold and delicious as Mia hoped it would be. It was absolutely perfect.

The dining room was large enough to hold a cottage of its own. Roman columns stood thirty feet high, each one carved from the finest Italian marble. There seemed to be no limit to the Lees' decorating budget. Zack and Theo's first sight upon stepping off the elevator was *The Blue Boy*, the iconic 1770 painting by Thomas Gainsborough. Their host informed them, in her slow and wobbly cadence, that it wasn't a reproduction.

Theo and Zack sat stiffly at the table while Prudent and Jun Lee watched them from the far ends. The primarch of the augurs was a verbal dynamo compared to her husband, a short and balding prophet who merely sat and smiled dazedly. Theo couldn't even guess the number of tranquilizers that were coursing through Jun's system, fogging his view of apocalypse.

Zack studied the ham steak on his plate, a meat only slightly less glazed than the people who'd served it. "Looks delicious."

"Thank you," Prudent said. "My daughter will be here shortly."

Theo studied her features. "Forgive me for asking, but—"

"We're Chinese and Korean," she told him. "As well as Japanese and Thai. Our family is the last pure Asian bloodline in the clan."

"Yay us," said a voice from the hallway.

Prudent scowled at Mercy as she entered the dining room. "You're late."

Unlike the others, who had all dressed nicely, Mercy came to dinner in tattered jeans and a paint-flecked T-shirt. Though her eyes were dark with mascara and gloom, she didn't strike Zack as the emotional train wreck her mother had made her out to be.

She returned his curious stare. "I know why Theo's here. What brings you?"

"Free ham," he joked. "It's my kryptonite."

"What the hell is kryptonite?"

"You're kryptonite."

Mercy frowned at him. "You don't give a fuck if anyone understands you."

"Mind your language," Prudent told her. "And sit."

Mercy pressed a hand to Jun's forehead and doused him in solis. Theo watched with fascination as the man sighed with relief. It seemed Mercy really was kryptonite to chronokinetics. She could even stop augurs from seeing the future.

The meal began on a dark note, as Prudent invoked a prayer for her missing son. Peter had already briefed Zack and Theo on the matter of Sage Lee, the sixteen-year-old augur who'd been abducted by portal nine months ago, along with thirty other Gothams. The Pelletiers had all but signed their work as the kidnappers, though they had yet to explain their reasoning or offer any demands for their release.

Prudent finished the prayer and gave her guests a gentle smile. "There's no need for grief. My son will return to us, healthy and whole. I've seen it. We merely pray that he is comfortable."

Zack cut his ham with nervous distraction. If Sage was locked in a mirror room, then the poor kid was better off dead.

Theo threw a quizzical look at Prudent. "Do you have any idea why they took your son in particular? Does he have anything in common with those other missing people?"

"Yeah," said Mercy. "They're all—"

"We do not speculate," Prudent snapped, with enough emphasis to kill the discussion.

After an awkward silence, Prudent told Zack about his fellow turners. There were eighty-one other people in the clan who could reverse and advance the flow of time. Most of them worked as healers. Some were content to use their powers for gardening. Without natural sunlight, all the plants in the underland were doomed to die. Only frequent reversals kept them healthy and lush.

"And what about solics?" Zack asked Mercy. "How many of them are there?"

"Just me and Suki."

"Who?"

"Suki Godden, Jinn's little sister. She's not as strong with the solis, but she can do other things, like shoot lightning from her hands."

"Wow," said Theo. "I hope she's well-adjusted."

Mercy shook her head. "She's a disparate."

"What does that mean?"

"It means her powers are unique and untestable, which makes her the freak of her family." Mercy glared at her mother. "That doesn't do wonders for a girl's self-esteem."

After a few more minutes of small talk, Theo tossed a stone into deeper waters. "What's the deal with Merlin McGee?"

By now, nearly everyone in the world knew of the amazing American augur who'd gained wealth and acclaim through his natural disaster predictions. Peter had already told the Silvers that McGee was an ex-Gotham named Michael. It wasn't until Mia pressed him that he confessed that his full name was Michael Pendergen, and that he'd been a brother of sorts to Peter.

"He was my best student," Prudent admitted. "But he was never happy here. Our ways conflicted with his . . . lifestyle choice."

Mercy rolled her eyes. "It's not a choice, Mom."

"All behavior is a choice."

"His only choice was to be true to himself. He didn't want to play in the clan's stupid breeding games and they hated him for it. We forgive murderers and thieves, but not that. Oh no."

Zack swirled his water glass. "Peter may not be the most progressive guy, but he's certainly not a homophobe."

"No," Mercy said. "I'll give him credit for that. He stuck by Michael, thick and thin."

"So how come Peter never talks about him?"

"Because Michael didn't stick by him," Theo mused.

He took a final bite of his ham steak, then pushed the plate away. "When the big trouble started, Peter must have gone to him for help. I mean, the guy's a powerful augur. He could have shed some light on the string that Peter saw. Hell, he could've been the world's savior."

He cast a bitter stare at the tablecloth. "Instead he becomes Merlin McGee, a glorified weatherman and celebrity prophet. That's why Peter doesn't talk about him. I wouldn't either."

Prudent poked the remains of her dinner. "Michael has always been selfish."

"Michael has always been *right*," Mercy said. "If he's living it up like there's no tomorrow, then you damn well better believe there's no tomorrow."

Prudent closed her eyes. "Mercy . . ."

"No! I fell for Rebel's bullshit. I'm not falling for Peter's. This whole world's fucked. Get used to it."

Jun's soft smile faded. He shuddered miserably in his chair. Mercy looked at him with a hangdog expression. "I'm sorry, Daddy."

"Why don't you show Zack your paintings?" Prudent suggested. "I'm sure he'd appreciate—"

"Yeah, yeah. I get it." Mercy rose from her seat. "Come on, Trillinger. Let's let the augurs talk their business."

Zack looked to Theo worriedly. "If you'd rather I stay—"

"I'll be fine," Theo said, though that was a lie. His insight and foresight had come together in a swirl of grim tidings. He just figured out why Prudent had really arranged this dinner. It had nothing to do with the string.

Prudent watched Theo closely as Zack and Mercy left the room together. "You see it now."

He lowered his head. "I saw it a week ago."

"They're like-minded artists, spirited and defiant. They'll be happy together. Why are you troubled?"

"Because he's in love with someone else."

"He can't have her."

"What do you know about that?"

"I know these are dire times, Theo. We must all make . . . concessions."

Theo narrowed his eyes. "You know more about the Pelletiers than you're letting on."

Prudent set up a chair next to her husband and wiped flecks of food from his mouth. Theo could see the nervousness in her eyes.

"They destroyed a whole world to bring us here," he said. "Everything that's happened to us, everything that's been happening with you and your people, revolves around them. I can't read them for shit. They put something in my head that keeps me from seeing all the stuff they don't want me to see. But you have a clear view. If there's something you know, then *tell* me."

Prudent looked away, her voice a trembling mutter. "I will not risk their wrath. Not while they have my son."

Theo's mouth went slack in revelation. "That's what they have in common, those missing people. They're all the loved ones of augurs. That's how they're keeping your guild under control."

Jun let out a tortured moan. Prudent brushed a tear from his eye. "If you had children, you would understand."

"If I had children, they'd be dead. My world ended. This one's next. Four years from now, it won't matter that you kept your son alive. He'll be just as dead as the—"

"Stop."

Prudent threw a furtive look around the room before sitting next to Theo. She leaned in and spoke in a conspiratorial whisper. "The fate of this world . . . does not concern them. It's irrelevant to their plans."

"So?"

"If we *work* with the Pelletiers, give them everything they want—"

"You think they'll save the world for us? Are you kidding me?"

"If not them, then who else?"

"Me," Theo insisted. "Help me find the string—"

"There *is* no string."

Theo turned in his chair, his wide eyes locked on Prudent's. She shrank from his gaze and twisted the diamond ring on her finger.

"I'm afraid that Peter's done you a great disservice," she said.

"He's not lying."

"Lying?" Prudent chuckled. "Perhaps not. Perhaps he did glimpse something in the God's Eye. But what he fails to accept, what Michael tried to tell him, is that our perceptions there are influenced by our desires. If Peter saw a string of hope, it's because—"

"—he wanted to see it," Theo finished.

He stood up and paced the length of the table, a chain of screams welling up in his throat. It was so obvious now. He could wear any clothes he wanted in the God's Eye, play any song from the annals of memory. A man with Peter's stubborn will could have turned the place into his own personal wish factory. And yet Theo had repeatedly failed to see the signs. He'd wasted months chasing rainbows, all because he wanted to play messiah.

"You can't tell the others," Prudent warned him. "Not even your closest friends. They don't see the strings like we do. They would cause untold—"

"Shut up."

"I'm trying to help you."

"Yeah? Well, you don't know shit if you think the Pelletiers are our best hope."

"I know they're a hair's-breadth away from killing Zack and Mercy," Prudent said. "The promise of their coupling is all that saves them."

"Why?"

"They . . . do not want you to know yet. It jeopardizes their plans. And should my daughter and Zack get wind of their desire—"

"I know," Theo muttered. He knew damn well how Zack would react if he learned the Pelletiers were meddling in his love life again. He would fight and rage against them. And then he would die.

Theo threw down his napkin and made a hasty path for the door. "They'll be talking awhile. Tell Zack I went home."

"Theo . . ."

He turned around in the doorway, his eyes cold and severe. "Don't worry. I won't do anything to jeopardize your son or daughter."

Prudent exhaled with relief. "Oh, thank you. Thank you."

"But you and I are done, you hear me? I'm not even going to pretend I like you. And the next time you see the Pelletiers—"

"Just one."

"What?"

"There's only one of them who speaks with me," Prudent informed him.

"Yeah? Well, tell him I said 'fuck you.'"

He stormed out of the room, toward the family's secret elevator. Prudent pushed her chair back and stared down at her trembling hands.

"You'll see him before I do," she muttered.

By the time he returned to the depths of the underland, the town had gone eerily quiet. The dome was a nightscape of twinkling lights, a perfect map of the constellations. Only a handful of embellishments ruined the naturalism: a streaking comet, an aurora borealis, a moon twice as large as it should have been. Theo had barely been here a day and already he could see a pattern emerging. The Gothams liked to embrace illusion over reality. They happily pulled the wool over their own eyes.

He returned to the cul-de-sac and found Heath sitting alone on the porch of the empty cottage. The boy was hunched over a card table, drawing ruler lines onto a sheet of paper in tight groups of five—new music sheets.

Heath barely gave him a glance as Theo sat down in the other seat. "You're back early."

"Short dinner," Theo said. "What are you doing outside?"

"We're not outside. It's all fake. Even the crickets."

"Well, what are you doing *here*?"

Heath shrugged. "Jonathan's with Hannah. They're trying not to make noise but—"

"Oh." Theo pursed his lips. At least someone was having a good time tonight.

"Are the other augurs going to help you?" Heath asked.

Theo slouched in his chair and sighed. "Doesn't seem likely."

"Why not?"

For a moment, Theo almost told him. But he knew Prudent was right. People did desperate things when all hope was lost. Dangerous things. Theo was having a hard enough time keeping his own head together.

"Doesn't matter," he replied. He propped his chin on his fist and studied Heath sorrowfully. "I think I owe you an apology."

"For what?"

"When Integrity attacked us, I . . . said things to you. I pressured you into saving my life like I was more important than other people."

Heath furrowed his brow. "But you are more important."

"That's what Peter says."

"That's what you told me. You said the whole world depended on saving you. So I did."

Theo smiled weakly. "You most definitely did."

"Now when you find the string, I'll know I helped save the world because I saved you."

Theo rubbed his eyes, fighting to keep his despair inside of him. "But what if I'm not the messiah that everyone thinks I am? What if it was all just a stupid misunderstanding?"

Heath went back to drawing his staves. "You're not sure you're the savior?"

"No."

"But you're not sure you're *not*."

Theo balked at his query. "Well, no. Not a hundred percent but—"

"Then you have to keep trying," Heath said. "You can't ever stop. If you stumble, you start again. If one way's blocked, you find another."

Theo suppressed a delirious laugh. He wasn't sure if Heath was quoting lyrics or merely platitudes. In either case, the boy certainly practiced what he preached. He'd lost all his music in the Integrity raid, yet he remained dauntless in his desire to resurrect the songs of his world. He was starting over from scratch, line by line, note by note.

Nearly a minute passed in silence. Theo listened to the crickets and realized Heath was wrong about one thing. The loud little critters had somehow made their way down here. They were real.

"Give me some paper," he said. "I'll help you."

Expressionless, Heath split up his paper stack, and then gave Theo rigid instructions on how to make a proper music sheet.

Theo sat with him under the fake moon and stars, drawing ruler lines on paper until his inner winds settled. Soon a semblance of reason returned to him. The solution to the world's greatest problem wouldn't be found in the God's Eye. Nor would it come from the Pelletiers.

No. There was another way to stop what was coming. Theo just had to find it.

TWENTY-EIGHT

On their fifth day in the village, as the pink light of dawn pricked the edges of the undersky, the orphans received some unwelcome visitors. A pair of masked swifters moved back and forth between the cottages, a paint sprayer in each hand. They left forty seconds later in a gust of hot wind.

Heath was the first to step outside and see the fruits of their labor: a barrage of red graffiti, spread carelessly across all six houses. The messages ranged from the predictable (*"Go home, breachers!"*) to the despicable (*"Pelliteer whores"*) to the downright odd (*"Freak Street"*).

The defacement was undone by a team of Mother Olga's turners. The Mayor sent his top ghosters to find and track the vandals. At sunset, Fleeta Byers, acting primarch of the swifters, brought the culprits back to the scene of the crime and forced them to apologize. They were just boys, no older than Mia. It was clear from the smoldering resentment in their eyes that they weren't even remotely sorry.

"Why 'Freak Street'?" Hannah asked them. "Aren't we all freaks here?"

The boys shrugged at the ground and mumbled incoherently. Semerjean considered paying them a visit later, maybe disfigure their faces as a warning to others. No, that would only make the Silvers look more entrenched with his family. The Gothams had to get over their mistrust. They needed to embrace these "breachers" as part of the clan.

At high noon the next day, the Mayor led a small army up the cobblestones of Freak Street. Twenty sprightly young lumics walked behind him in lockstep, the best and brightest of their guild. They set up four tables on the loop of the cul-de-sac, then covered them all in gourmet lunch foods.

"An apology gift," the Mayor told the orphans. "Come, come! Feast!"

Soon David found himself surrounded by a dozen teenage lumics, each one trying to impress him. One boy turned himself into the semblance of sand. Another built a scale-model Manhattan out of ambient light. A sixteen-year-old girl combusted into flames, then vanished. She emerged five seconds later from behind an illusive wall, to David's applause. More impressive than her trick was the patience involved in setting it up. She'd been hiding in the margins, invisible, for nearly twenty minutes. David had been talking with her ghost this whole time.

Carrie Bloom watched from her porch swing, a sandwich in her hand and a sneer on her lip. "That's Yvonne Whitten, the Mayor's daughter. In case you were wondering."

Mia chewed her lunch with forced aloofness. "I wasn't."

That was a lie. Mia had noticed Yvonne as soon as she'd arrived: a raven-haired stunner with the height of an Amazon, the face of a teen model, and an elegant spring dress that flattered her figure without flaunting it. Worst of all, she looked smart. She carried herself with the same precocious maturity that David did.

"The grownups love her," Carrie said. "The kids can't stand her. She's boring and patronizing, and her ego pokes the moon. She struts around like she's queen of the village, all because of her double-O's."

"Her what?"

"Her power score. She got a perfect hundred on her last four tests."

Mia scoffed. "And that matters *why*?"

"It's just how they are in the upper houses. The Whittens, the Sunders, the Goddens, the Rubineks. They all think they're the *shit de la shit*, and they think the numbers prove it."

Carrie took another bite of her sandwich. "We'll see how special they feel four years from now, when the boot comes down on all of us."

Mia looked up and saw the lingering eyelock between Yvonne and David. He certainly didn't seem to find her boring.

Carrie looked at Mia disappointedly. "Aw, don't tell me you're sweet on him."

"I was," she admitted. "Not anymore."

"Good. He's too cold for you. Hell, he's too cold for me and I'm a subthermic."

Carrie rocked the swing, her bright eyes fixed on Yvonne. "But he's perfect for Wondersnoot over there. They'll probably hump like old British nobles."

Mia choked on her drink, convulsing with laughter. Carrie had been a godsend to her these past six days, an endlessly entertaining companion who provided crucial intel about the Gothams. Better still, she gave Mia space from her fellow Silvers. They'd been fused at the hip for so long that she forgot what it was like to be her own person.

Only David made an effort to mingle with the lumics. Hannah and Amanda stood off to the side. Jonathan sat on his porch and tuned his new guitar. Theo and Heath played video games with Liam. Peter was away on some cryptic clan business.

Amanda looked between houses and saw Zack in his backyard, dabbing colorful strokes on a canvas while Mercy guided his arm. She had dared him to put away his pencils and try oil painting for a week. Zack double-dared Mercy to go the other way. They spent hours each day on their clumsy new artforms, teaching and teasing each other at every turn.

Hannah glared at Mercy. "She was there in White Plains the night Jonathan's friends died. She took away their powers when they needed them the most. Made them all sitting ducks for Rebel."

Amanda shook her head glumly. "It's in the past now."

"Yeah, so's Zack's brother. Does he even know what she did?"

"Of course he knows."

"Then how can he be friends with her?"

Amanda looked down at her shuffling feet. "The Pelletiers did something to him. He won't talk about it, but I can see it in his eyes. They scarred him."

She kicked a small stone. "I guess he's saving all his anger for them."

The party ended an hour after it began. While the lumics gathered their tables and dishes, Yvonne pulled David aside. She daintily adjusted his collar, her dark eyes heavy with concern.

"Listen, you're a perceptive guy. You must know by now that my father's hoping for us to, uh . . ."

"Get better acquainted," David said. "I assume that was the real motive behind this lunch."

Yvonne rolled her eyes. "He's stuck in the old ways, but I don't give a flip about marriage or children. Not at this age. Not with everything going on."

David beamed with bright surprise. At first glance, he'd taken Yvonne to be a vapid thing, a storefront mannequin designed only to impress people.

But the more he talked to her, the more she teased her hidden layers. There was a smart, weird, and very interesting girl behind the makeup, and she was almost afraid to show it.

Yvonne saw his expression and smiled. "Okay, good. So the pressure's off. We can be friends or guildmates or whatever makes you comfortable. I just hope we have another conversation soon."

"We can have one now," David said. "If you feel like staying."

He balked at her stammering reaction. "I'm sorry. I don't know the etiquette here. If that was too—"

"No. It's fine." Yvonne threw a quick glance at her people. "I'll tell them to go without me."

Ninety minutes later, Peter returned to the cul-de-sac and gathered everyone up for a backyard meeting. Eight orphans and three kinsmen watched him curiously from folding chairs, all clueless to his agenda. Peter wasn't pleased that Zack and David invited their new ladyfriends into the circle, but at least Mercy would be discreet. The real problem was Yvonne. Anything she heard would get back to the Mayor, which would then get to everyone.

Peter snatched a pen from his shirt pocket and twirled it in his fingers. "So I just met with the elders."

Mercy scoffed at her sketchbook. "Those dried-up milksacks. What do they want now?"

"The good news is that they finally heard me on the matter of the Coppers. If Melissa Masaad wasn't lying about those people—"

"She wasn't," Theo insisted.

"—then it's in everyone's best interest that we go to Seattle and find them."

"Finally," Mia said. "When do we leave?"

Peter shook his head. "The elders are putting together a team, but they don't want us on it. We're still fugitives, and the Coppers have that city crawling with federal agents."

"Those are our people," Zack reminded him. "We should be the ones reaching out to them."

"I made that very argument. They've agreed to let me go on the mission, and I can bring two of you with me. *Only* two."

Mia, Zack, and David all quickly volunteered.

"We'll work it out," Peter said. "We're not leaving for a couple of days."

Theo got a prescient wind of Peter's next bit of business. "Are you *kidding* me?"

"Now hang on . . ."

"That's bullshit!"

Jonathan fanned a puzzled look between Theo and Peter. "What did I just miss?"

"Our augur's getting ahead of us," Peter said. He flashed his palms at Theo. "Just hear me out, all right? It's not what you think."

The others watched him closely as he deliberated over his words. "Our people are big on rituals. You name it, we have a ceremony for it. The whole thing can get a little, uh—"

"Soul-crushing," Liam grumbled.

"—tedious. The thing is, we don't have a ritual for welcoming full-grown adults into the clan. Until now, we never needed one. So instead of coming up with a whole new deal, the elders want to induct you through a rite we hold when a kinsman turns eighteen. It's called a Testament."

Liam closed his eyes and groaned. Mercy let out a cynical laugh. "Those assholes."

Yvonne frowned at her. "What? It's a beautiful service."

"It's bullshit." Mercy gestured at the Silvers. "For these people, it's cruel."

Amanda tossed up her hands. "Will someone please explain it already?"

"It's a sacrament of initiation," Peter told her. "You'll declare your loyalty to the clan and its core tenets of humanity, humility, and temperance. The only sticking point, and I fought them tooth and nail on this, is the humility part. Traditionally, a Testament involves a sacrifice."

The Silvers and Golds traded baffled looks. David stared at Peter, deadpan. "What, like a goat?"

"A *personal* sacrifice. You have to give up something of value."

Now the others caught up with Theo's outrage. Hannah vehemently shook her head. "Uh-uh. No way. We already lost our world."

"We lost *everything*," Zack stressed. "What the hell do they expect us to give up?"

"You two are the easy ones," Peter said. "One of you draws. The other one sings."

Hannah gaped. "Are you high?"

"No way," Zack growled. "No goddamn way."

Peter rubbed his face. They were all getting worked up over nothing, but he couldn't tell them why as long as Yvonne was here.

Mercy smiled at Zack. "You can give up painting. You suck at it anyway."

His eyes bulged. "Holy shit. That's brilliant. Can I do that?"

"Of course not," said Yvonne. "The sacrifice has to be genuine."

Zack turned to her, mystified. He'd just met her ten minutes ago, this teenage clone of Esis. He hoped for David's sake that the resemblance was only skin-deep.

"So what did you give up?" he asked her.

"I'm sixteen. I haven't had my Testament yet."

"It's just for the adults," Peter told him. "You and Amanda and Theo and Hannah. The rest of you don't have to worry."

Jonathan eyed him strangely. "You do know I'm a grownup, right?"

"Yes, but you're also a dropper. As far as the elders are concerned, your sacrifice has already been made."

Nobody in the circle appreciated the sentiment, least of all Hannah and Heath.

"It's no big deal," Mercy told them. "I broke my oath years ago. So did Peter. There's no consequence. You'll just get some dirty looks from the zealots."

"That's not true," said Yvonne.

"Well, no, not for bootlickers like you. But for the rest of us—"

"Mind your mouth," David snapped. "It's taking a lot of effort for some of us to be polite to you."

Mercy recoiled at his vitriol. "I never asked for politeness."

"You never asked for forgiveness either."

"Yes she did," said Zack.

"Yes I did." Mercy jerked her head at Zack. "I asked him. But whatever."

She closed her sketchbook, rose from her chair, and then clutched Zack's shoulder. Everyone could see her fighting back tears.

"Don't give up a goddamn thing."

The group sat in grim silence as Mercy left the yard. Peter leaned forward and pressed his folded hands to his lips.

"She's a good woman at heart. If Zack can forgive her, so can the rest of you. That said, she's wrong about the Testament. The day I broke my oath is the day I lost my credibility. If I'd had it when I first challenged Rebel, who knows? I could have stopped this war before it started. That's no small consequence."

Mia swallowed a scream when she saw Yvonne nodding in agreement. The girl had done nothing to stop Rebel's violence. She'd probably been an early supporter.

"The ceremony's a crucial step in healing the damage between us," Peter said. "I'd very much like to get it right."

Amanda shrugged helplessly. "I don't want to make light of it. I just don't know what to sacrifice."

Peter narrowed his eyes at Yvonne before looking away. In truth, he shared all of Mercy's contempt for the elders and their rituals. But while Mercy confronted them with screams of rebellion, Peter had learned a more artful game. He knew how to face the council with a smile and a pair of crossed fingers behind his back. And soon so would the Silvers.

The amphitheater graced the northern edge of the underland: fifty rows of gray velvet seats, all sloping and funneling toward a giant clamshell stage. The place was used twice a month for town hall meetings. On special occasions, there were creative performances. The lumics staged a patriotic light show every Fourth of July. The White Hand Groove, the all-tempic jazz band, held their annual concert in March.

On this Tuesday night, the tenth of May, the clan once again filed into the amphitheater. Mia looked around from the thirtieth row. It was downright surreal to see so many Gothams in one place. The tribe had grown so large that the seating pool wasn't even big enough to hold them anymore. Mia glanced over her shoulder and saw a hundred young Gothams standing at the gate of the upper mezzanine, looking thoroughly miserable in their formal suits and dresses. She could certainly relate. She was decked to the nines in a navy-blue wrap gown, liberated from the closet of the late Krista Bloom. For

Mia, the only thing worse than wearing a dress was wearing the dress of a dead enemy.

Carrie sat to her left, her hand clasped firmly around Mia's. "Don't worry. I've been to a hundred of these things. Your biggest threat is boredom."

Mia couldn't stop marveling at Carrie's transformation. She'd taken off her ponytail band and let her golden hair flow. Her face was made up flawlessly, and she wore a one-sleeve dress that looked absolutely stunning on her. She could have been the Barbie to David's Ken, a thought that came with a slew of discomforts. Mia never forgot the partial note she'd once glimpsed from her future self.

—genuinely likes you. And she's a great kisser. Give the girl a chance.

She leaned forward and peeked down at her fellow Silvers. Four tall wooden chairs had been set at the base of the seating pool, an exclusive front row for the ceremony's inductees. Mia felt guilty for not sitting near Amanda and the others, but Carrie assured her that she was better off here in the cheap seats.

The elders sat onstage behind a curved stone table, all looking majestic in their long ivory vestments. Mia had expected the council to be a gaggle of Gandalfs, but three of them were women of late middle age. The two men only had flecks of gray in their beards. According to Liam, these people were indeed some of the clan's oldest members, as few of the Gothams ever lived past sixty. When Mia asked him why, Liam had merely shrugged. "I don't know. Guess time always hurts the ones it loves."

A muddled hush coursed through the audience as a late arrival walked down the aisle. Rebel was the last person anyone expected to see here tonight. He'd been keeping to himself these past ten days, wallowing in grief as he recovered from his injuries. Though his loose black suit was formal enough for the occasion, his cheeks were covered in beard scruff. His eyes were hidden behind aviator shades. He passed by Mia without so much as a glance, then claimed a seat in the twelfth row, just spitting distance from David.

Yvonne whispered into David's ear. "We can move."

"I'm fine," he insisted. Like Mia, he'd opted to sit with new friends over old ones. He figured this farce would be more tolerable at a distance, in pleasant company.

Yvonne caressed the stumps of his missing fingers. "Did Rebel do that to you?"

David shook his head. "Federal agent."

She tapped the thin red scar on the back of his other hand. "And that one?"

"Semerjean. That's a fairly new one."

Yvonne stared at him, awestruck. "God. The hells you've suffered. They would have broken a lesser man."

David smiled humbly. "I'm not technically a man yet."

"Oh, yes you are." She clutched his arm. "More than that, you're one of us now. Whatever happens from this point forward, you have eleven hundred people on your side."

David turned to his right and swapped a frosty look with Rebel. "Give or take."

By eight o'clock, everyone was seated. The lumicands were extinguished. All the light in the amphitheater now came from the stage.

The council rose. The elder in the middle—a distinguished-looking man of Indian heritage—raised his hands in the air. Peter had warned the Silvers that he was the only one they had to watch out for. He was an ornery bastard even on the best of days, and these were not good days for Irwin Sunder. His favorite son and only daughter had recently died on a runaway aerstraunt. And he was angry about it.

"Let us begin," said Sunder.

The sermon seemed to go on forever, an endless invocation of *blessed* this and *sacred* that. Amanda was surprised by the flexibility of the Gothams' dogma, the way their faith stretched to cover all existing religions. The Christians, Jews, and Hindus of the tribe had no trouble working chronokinesis into their orthodoxies. In their minds, their powers were merely proof that they were all the favored children of their gods.

Hannah sat to her left, her knees bouncing uneasily. This whole damn liturgy was just a big circle jerk, a vainglorious ode to the greatness of time-benders. She might have tolerated the tedium if she hadn't been forced into the most uncomfortable dress ever—a white, frilly number that made her look like a doily and feel like the bride of Frankenstein.

Even more distracting, she kept sensing the aura of a nearby swifter, a pint-size girl who dashed through the village at impossible speeds. If Hannah had known about Naomi Byers, she would have understood why the child couldn't sit still for ceremonies, why she delighted in having the whole town to herself. There was something very, very wrong about her energies.

"Hannah?"

She snapped out of her daze. "Huh?"

"They just called you," Theo whispered. "You're up."

Hannah looked around and saw everyone staring at her expectantly. Alma Rubinek, the oldest and largest of the elders, beckoned her with a wrinkled hand. "Come."

Shaken, Hannah stood up, straightened her dress, then climbed the ramp to the stage. Though she could barely see the crowd with all the floodlights on her, she could easily feel their rigidness. The Gothams were as cold as her worst theater audiences—a thousand critics and only a couple of fans.

Rubinek plucked a microphone from its stand and passed it to her. Hannah suddenly had the daft urge to belt out a song. Some Leonard Cohen, maybe. Or Madonna.

"State your full name," Rubinek said.

Hannah cleared her throat and spoke into the mic. "Hannah Marie Given."

"Hannah Marie Given. You are one of time's sacred children. Do you accept your blessing with grace and humility?"

"Stupid-ass question," Mia muttered under her breath. Carrie giggled and shushed her.

"I do," Hannah said.

"And what is your sacrifice?"

Hannah squinted at the front row and saw Jonathan and Heath sitting snugly between the Pendergens. They looked just as embittered as she felt.

"I sacrifice my singing."

A wave of grumbles swept through the theater. The elders traded incredulous looks.

"That is insufficient," Irwin Sunder insisted. "There are those among us who relinquish their voice entirely. Your offering insults them."

Jonathan shot to his feet. "Hey!"

Peter pulled him down, just as another member of the audience stood up. Olga Varnov was a thick-bodied woman with flowing white hair, a venerated figure in the village. She was the primarch of the turners, the matron of the vivery, the beloved nanny to all the clan's children.

Her strong voice echoed throughout the hall. "We discussed this, Elder. I implored you to show lenience in light of the circumstances."

"We heard you, Mother Olga—"

"Clearly you didn't." She gestured at Hannah. "This woman has bled at our hands and now you scold her for not sacrificing enough. Where's *your* humility?"

The crowd fell into high-strung chatter. Peter smiled behind his hand. Only his godmother could speak to the elders like that and get away with it.

The council converged in hasty conference. Hannah dawdled onstage, her dark eyes locked on Amanda's.

This doesn't mean a damn thing, her sister had told her. *You can still sing behind closed doors.*

Even so, Hannah was livid. All she had left of her old life was her voice and her sibling. Now she had to hide one of them like a criminal, just to please these fanatics.

The elders finished their debate. It was clear from Sunder's pouting expression that he'd been outvoted.

"I still believe that this is a meager offering," he attested. "But Mother Olga makes a compelling point. We reluctantly accept your sacrifice."

As the crowd kept mumbling, Sunder raised his finger at Hannah. "But I advise you to keep your oath with stringent honor, and to seek other avenues of humility."

"But—"

"Be seated."

Hannah descended the ramp, red-faced, seething. The moment she sat down, Jonathan leaned forward and gave her shoulder an affectionate squeeze. A smaller, darker hand reached out and patted her other arm. Hannah wasn't sure if she'd laugh or cry. She could have leapt over her seat and hugged Jonathan and Heath for hours. Her treasures. Her Golds.

The council called Theo up to the stage next. As Rubinek passed the microphone into his hand, he looked to the front row and shot a skeptical glance at Peter. The man had made a bizarre suggestion about what Theo should sacrifice.

"*Guitar?*" Theo had asked him, three nights before. "I don't even play."

"The elders don't know that," Peter had assured him. "Nobody knows but us."

"But what if they see through it? What if they ask for a demonstration?"

Peter shook his head. "If they'll go easy on anyone, it'll be you."

"State your name," Elder Rubinek said flatly.

He spoke into the mic. "Uh, Theo. Theo Maranan. I don't have a middle name."

"Theo Maranan. You are one of time's sacred children. Do you accept your blessing with grace and humility?"

"I do."

"Are you prepared to save us all from the death that comes?"

Theo was a hair's-breadth away from saying "guitar" when he suddenly realized the question. He turned to Rubinek, wide-eyed. "What?"

"Does this string exist?" Elder Howell asked from the table. "Can you find it?"

Theo's stomach dropped. He found Prudent Lee in the second row and watched her shrink away from his gaze.

"Yes," he lied. "I believe I can."

A wind of a thousand breaths passed through the theater. Some of the Gothams began to applaud. Sunder silenced them with a gesture.

"You are exempt from making a sacrifice," he told Theo. "You may be seated."

Theo returned to his chair, desperately avoiding the smiles of his friends. They all saw this as a minor victory when it was really just a con job. He was conning every living soul in this theater, even his own people.

Amanda approached the stage next, her lower back covered in stress tempis. She hated public speaking. She hated the creepy doll dress she was wearing. She especially hated having hundreds of tempics in her vicinity. She could feel them all in the periphery of her senses. Each one was like a bee on her skin.

"State your name," said Rubinek.

Amanda leaned into the microphone, her hands folded over her fluttering stomach. "Amanda Stephanie Given."

"Amanda Stephanie Given. You are one of time's sacred children. Do you—"

"Yes."

Rubinek narrowed her eyes. "Do you accept your blessing with grace and humility?"

"I do."

"What is your sacrifice?"

"Cuisine," Amanda declared. "I take the whitefood vow."

The audience grumbled with skepticism. No Gotham had ever adhered to the whitefood diet for more than a year. There was only so long a person could subsist on water, rice, and vitamins before losing their mind. In recent times, it had become the go-to choice for those who had no intention of honoring their oath. Mercy Lee had taken the whitefood vow with a candy bar in her pocket, and then wolfed it down in front of the whole clan. Amanda planned to be more discreet with her cheating.

"You've chosen a difficult path," Sunder warned her. "Do you truly plan to commit to it, or are you merely offering lip service?"

Amanda glared at him. "I watched my whole world die, Elder. Everyone I ever loved. The path ahead is nothing compared to the one I've traveled."

"That's not an answer."

"That's the answer you get."

Amanda could feel the angry white energy beneath Sunder's skin. The man had been primarch of the tempics for twenty years before becoming an elder. By all accounts, his power was legendary.

"Your offering is accepted," Sunder declared, with a dismissive gesture. "Take your seat."

A mutter escaped Amanda's lips. Sunder turned to her. "Excuse me?"

"I said you had no right to talk to my sister like that. Singing was her life."

Peter winced at the startled gasps behind him. Sunder stood up at the table, his knuckles white with tempis. "Your sister still *has* her life, unlike my son and daughter."

"Your son and daughter were murderers."

The hall erupted in shouts of protest. Peter urgently motioned to Amanda while the elders struggled to calm Sunder down.

The Mayor stood up in the third row and used his power to amplify himself. *"Kinsmen."*

His booming voice echoed all throughout the village. To those in the theater, it sounded as if God himself was speaking. Everyone stopped to look at him.

"We have enough troubles," the Mayor reminded them. "All of us. So let's show our new friends the breadth of our temperance, and finish this ceremony in peace."

One by one, the audience settled back into their seats. David nodded approvingly. "Okay, that was impressive."

Yvonne smiled. "My dad has his moments."

It took another thirty seconds for the chatter to die down. Elder Tam instructed everyone to remain quiet for the fourth and final pledge.

Peter sat forward and studied Zack warily. "Don't you dare."

"Don't I dare what?"

"I know that look. You're up to no good."

Amanda shuffled in her seat, her skin still flush from her confrontation with Sunder. She saw the acerbic gleam in Zack's eyes and immediately knew that Peter was right. He was about to go Bugs Bunny on some very serious people.

"I screwed up," Amanda told him. "Don't make the same mistake I did."

Peter nodded. "Just tell him what they want to hear and be done with it. Please."

Elder Rubinek called Zack to the stage. He rose from his seat and leaned into Amanda. Her heartbeat doubled as she felt his warm breath on her ear.

"You were beautiful up there," he whispered. "I'll never stop loving you."

Amanda fought back tears and squeezed Zack's wrist, just as Rubinek summoned him again. He climbed the ramp, approached the microphone, and then loosened his tie.

"State your full name," said the elder.

"Zarack Obama Trillinger." He smiled into the mic. "I live on Freak Street."

A hundred low chuckles rolled through the audience. Mia and Carrie doubled over in laughter. Peter shook his head, grimacing.

None of the elders were particularly amused. "Mr. Trillinger, if you won't take this seriously—"

"I take this very seriously," Zack insisted. "I was fully prepared to stand here and pretend to give up my drawing. But now I have something better to give you. Something real."

Elder Tam eyed him dubiously. "So you accept your—"

"Yes," Zack said. "I'm one of time's sacred children and I accept my blessing with grace and humility."

Rubinek crossed her heavy arms. "And what is your sacrifice?"

Zack held the mic in both hands, his head bowed and his eyes closed. Most of the audience assumed he was praying.

"Fury," Zack said at last. "I sacrifice my anger at each and every one of you."

The theater churned with agitated voices. Zack moved downstage before Rubinek could take the microphone from him.

"I had a brother," he reminded everyone. "The one thing in my life the Pelletiers didn't take from me. Yet I lost him all the same, and why? Because ten months ago, you listened to the wrong guy."

Elder Kohl thumped the table. "Mr. Trillinger—"

"Please. Call me Zarack."

"You're playing a very dangerous game here."

"It's no game, Elder. My only brother died for no reason. So far, only one of you has had the decency to apologize."

Mercy watched him from the back row, her lip quivering with emotion.

"I'm not trying to guilt you," Zack said. "I'm just offering to let go of my anger. Believe me, that's no small—"

"Enough!" Sunder yelled. "You're making a mockery of this ceremony!"

The shouting intensified. The Mayor, Peter, and Mother Olga all rose to speak. They were drowned out by a gravelly voice from the tenth row.

"Elders."

Rebel rose to his feet and walked toward the stage. "I seek private word with the council."

Sunder nodded at his son-in-law, then shot a baleful look at Zack. "Return to your seat."

Zack descended the ramp just as Rebel climbed it. "What the hell are you doing?"

Rebel took off his shades and folded them into his pocket. "You give any more thought to the Semerjean thing?"

"No."

"Then we got nothing to talk about."

Soon Rebel and the elders disappeared behind the curtain. The audience resumed their anxious blather.

Amanda turned in her chair to face Peter. "What's going on?"

"No idea," he confessed. "This whole thing just went off the rails."

Three minutes after the conference started, Rebel and the council re-emerged. The elders took their seats at the table. Sunder looked down at the front row and kept his inscrutable gaze on Zack.

"You are exempt."

"What?"

"*What?*" Liam exclaimed.

Peter stared at Rebel, hang-jawed. "Well, I'll be damned."

"What just happened?" Jonathan asked.

"He took on a sacrifice for Zack."

"Who, *Rebel*?"

"It would seem so."

"I didn't even know you could do that."

"In rare cases," Peter said. "When one kinsman has gravely wronged another."

Theo turned his astonished gaze onto Zack. "I think you just got your apology."

A thousand eyes followed Rebel as he exited the amphitheater. Zack watched him the whole way, speechless.

Soon Elder Howell summoned all the Silvers and Golds onto the stage. They stood side by side in fidgety unease while Elder Tam repeated the same liturgy for each of them. By the eighth and final go-round, the audience had fallen back into docile boredom.

At long last, Elder Rubinek proclaimed the orphans to be members of the clan. For a moment, the Gothams forgot all their grievances and fell into the spirit of the ceremony. The lumics threw lightworks. The tempics cast winding white streamers. Carrie blew a shrieking whistle through her fingers.

Only Gemma Sunder withheld her applause. She stood in the mezzanine with the other children, brushing bitter tears from her eyes. She could only imagine that her beloved aunt Ivy was weeping from Heaven at the sorry spectacle down here.

Don't cry, Gemma told her. *Don't you cry, Ivy. I'll take care of all of them for you.*

Mia woke up at the crack of dawn on Saturday, a fog in her head and a familiar presence sleeping next to her. She and Carrie had been talking late into the night when fatigue finally got the better of them. They conked out in Carrie's bed and now . . .

"Oh no."

Mia had expected to find the bedroom covered in portal notes, but there were barely any to be seen. A few on the floor. A dozen on the bed. One of them had found its way into Carrie's hair. But still, this was a shockingly light load. Had Carrie woken up and read some of the notes already? Or were the Mias being gentle for once?

It's Carrie, an inner voice suggested. *She made your life better. Now she's healing your future.*

Mia felt a tingling sensation at the base of her thoughts, a man-size portal in another part of the cottage. The traveler's signature was strong but pleasant, like warm apple cider. Mia knew it all too well.

She peeked into Carrie's living room and saw Peter standing at the front door, fully dressed but half awake.

"What are you doing?" she whispered.

"Came to get you," he whispered back. "You weren't home."

Mia closed the bedroom door behind her. "We were talking. We fell asleep."

"You don't need to explain it. You're your own girl."

She checked the clock in the kitchen. "It's six A.M. What—"

"Seattle," he told her.

"What, *now*?"

"The dart leaves in thirty minutes. Get dressed, pack a bag, and then meet me back at my place."

Mia looked to the bedroom. She still had those notes to gather. "But—"

"No buts. The plane goes with or without you."

Peter disappeared into the portal and emerged forty yards away, in the living room of the street's uninhabited cottage. Mia wasn't the only one who hadn't slept at home last night. A large heap of blankets covered the mattress in the main bedroom. A pair of bare white feet stuck out from the bottom.

"Zack . . ."

A bearish grumble rose up from the bed. Peter poked at the blankets. "Zack, wake up."

Zack peeked out from under the covers and registered Peter through his one open eye. "Huh?"

"You still want to find those Coppers of yours?"

"Yeah. Of course . . ."

"Good. We leave in a half hour."

"*What?* Why the short notice?"

"Not my doing. I just got the call." He looked to the writhing mass at Zack's side. "You too, darling. You're coming with us."

Mercy's head popped out of the blankets. She shot a crusty glare at Peter. "Fuck you. I'm done playing soldier."

"Doesn't matter. We need a solic in case these strangers get ornery."

"Peter . . ."

"Get dressed, both of you."

While Mercy spat a string of profanities, Zack flashed a shaky look at Peter. There were painfully few secrets in the group, and there was no hiding what had happened between him and Mercy last night. Still, he didn't want Amanda to hear about it secondhand. He could only imagine his reaction if someone else told him that she was sleeping with Peter.

"Uh, listen—"

"I won't say a word," Peter promised.

"Thank you."

"Just be ready."

He waved a portal in the wall and was gone in an instant. Mercy traded a bemused look with Zack.

"Shit," she said. "I never thought we'd be doing that together."

"What? Screwing?"

"No." Mercy leaned over and reached for her shirt. "Hunting breachers."

At half past six, all the residents of Freak Street gathered to say good-bye to the splinter group. They stood outside in their bathrobes and sweatclothes, too sleepy to do anything more than wish Peter, Zack, and Mia good luck.

"We'll be gone three days," Peter told them. "Four at the most."

While most of the others went back to sleep, Amanda puttered around her living room, agitated. She'd resolved days ago to get to know some Gothams, but she still couldn't work up the stomach to become friendly with Victoria Chisholm. It was a moot point, anyway, as the primarch of the tempics was also the leader of the Seattle mission. She was already halfway across the country.

Amanda knew she couldn't just lounge around the house forever, but what else could she do? Maybe the vivery needed a volunteer nurse. Or maybe Theo could use someone to talk to. He'd seemed tense and distracted these past two weeks, ever since his dinner with Prudent Lee.

A knock on the door made Amanda jump. She opened it to find a flustered Carrie Bloom.

"Hi, what—"

Carrie forced her way inside and slammed the door behind her. Her hair was a mess and her skin was sweaty, as if wild tigers had chased her here.

"I'm so sorry to bother you," Carrie said. "I didn't know where else to go. I've never been in this shitpot before and it's making me all zizzy!"

"Okay, okay." Amanda led her to the sofa and sat down next to her. "Just calm down. Breathe."

It took several deep breaths and a long swig of water before Carrie was able to speak coherently. She stared down at her bouncing knees.

"Mia dashed my house in a hurry," she began. "Leaving all these notes in my bedroom. I told her I'd clean them up. No big deal. I mean I knew all about her future-self problems. I told her I wouldn't . . . oh God."

Amanda feared where this was going. "You read her notes."

"Only a few. I couldn't help it! I was just so . . . look, I *love* Mia. Like *scary* love her. I just wanted to understand how a girl so sweet could be so nasty in the future."

Amanda shook her head. "Forget them. Whatever you saw—"

"I can't. I mean, I can brush aside the awful things she said to herself. But *this* one . . ." She plucked a paper scrap from her shirt pocket and brandished it like a live grenade. "This one scared the hell out of me. If this thing's true, then you people are in a lot of trouble, Hannah most of all."

"What?" Amanda peeked out the window. Her sister was sleeping in the other house, as usual. By now, she had practically moved in with the Golds.

Carrie held the note out. "I really think you should read this."

Amanda felt her instincts tugging at her, the same way she used to tug Mia away from her portal messages: *Just walk away. Ignore them. Nothing good will come of it.*

But if Hannah's life was really in danger . . .

Amanda took the crinkled paper from Carrie's hand. She sucked a deep breath, then unfurled it.

Don't trust Jonathan. He's not who he says he is.

TWENTY-NINE

The Douglas M-9 was the crème de la crème of the dart-class aerships: a high-end, short-winged, double-engined twenty-seater that looked like a cross between a limousine and a missile. Despite its aerodynamic chassis and electric turbine thrusters, the ship couldn't fly much faster than an old-world seaplane, at least not without help. A 20x shifter accelerated it to four times the speed of sound, allowing it to travel from New York to Washington State in thirty-eight minutes, external time. The passengers inside the temporal field had twelve and a half hours to kill.

Mia sat up in her seat and took a nervous look around the cabin. Sixteen Gothams were accompanying her and Zack, a hand-picked roster of all-stars and primarchs from most of the major power guilds. Mia was particularly vexed by Shauna and Angela Ryder, a pair of twentysomething bottle blondes who shared her teleporting talent, yet practically snarled at the sight of her.

Peter told her not to mind the Ryder twins. The travelers were an insular group, and were wary of all newcomers to their neurospatial network. It didn't help that they'd all worshipped Ivy and hated anyone even tangentially involved with her death.

Mia crossed her arms, brooding. "Great. So we're both on their shit list."

"We don't need them," Peter told her. "You and I are a guild of our own."

"Can I be primarch?"

"No."

He reclined his seat and settled in for a long nap. Mia scowled out the window. Unlike him, she was forced to stay awake for the duration of the flight. At this speed, her sleep portals would tear through the plane like bullets.

She unbuckled her safety belt and wandered up the aisle. The cockpit was surprisingly basic for a transonic aerojet, more Winnebago than Cessna. Victoria Chisholm leaned back in the pilot's chair and filed her nails with a tempic emery board. Mia found it odd and a little bit funny that a woman with wings had her own private aerplane. From the frown on her face, this wasn't her favorite way to fly.

The Mayor rode the shotgun seat and took an admiring look at the dashboard. "I should buy a dart of my own. This is marvelous."

"My husband's toy," Victoria said. "He barely used it."

The Mayor's grin deflated. "He was a good man."

"He was a coward." She pursed her lips at the three-dimensional flight map. The M-9 was just a blip above the Porcupine Mountains of Michigan. "I don't even know why we're doing this."

The Mayor shrugged. "If there are more of our kind out there—"

"*Our* kind?"

"They may be alien, but they're blessed in all the same ways we are. And they need us."

Mia listened from the periphery, surprised and impressed. She'd thought the Mayor's geniality was just an act, but it seemed the man was genuinely nice.

Victoria stared out the window at the indigo sky. "There's still so much we don't know about these breachers. It's not like we can check their pasts. They could all be lying about who they are. Or *what* they are."

Mia rolled her eyes. The Mayor merely smiled. "We would have never survived this long if we didn't have instincts."

"Yes, well, my instincts are screaming about that black boy of theirs. There's something very different about his temporal energy."

"Can't attest to Heath," the Mayor said. "I just know David's a good lad. He and my daughter have become inseparable these days. I've never seen her so happy."

Mia winced and backed away. She didn't need to hear any more on that topic.

She moved down the aisle, past row upon row of slumbering passengers. Zack and Mercy slept on the plane's one sofa, their bodies spooned, their arms locked together. It seemed David wasn't the only one to find love among the Gothams.

Oh, like you haven't, her inner Carrie teased.

The rear curtain parted and a hulking figure emerged from the kitchenette.

It wasn't until they'd arrived at the aerplane hangar that Peter warned Mia about the augur on the team, a man she knew all too well.

Rebel placed his meal on the tiny conference table. He looked at Mia through his ever-present sunglasses.

"Can't tell if you're gonna run away or hit me."

Mia sat down at the table, if only to confound his expectations. "I don't care that you shot me. I'm over that."

"*Over* that." Rebel smiled at her alien slang. "You don't look over it."

"It's what you did to Carrie's mom that pisses me off."

His smile flattened. He reached into his pocket and pulled out a bottle of vitamins. "I didn't kill her. Esis did."

"You left her behind for Esis to kill. She was your friend—"

"She was *Ivy's* friend."

"—and you abandoned her."

Rebel stared out the window at the ever-changing colors. At 20x, the sky took on a tenuous hue. It was royal blue one moment, indigo the next. The afternoon hours brought a warmer spectrum, everything from saffron yellow to burnt orange.

"One of these days, you'll find yourself on the wrong side of the Pelletiers," he warned Mia. "You'll get their sword, not their shield. Then you'll know what it's like to make hard decisions."

"Doesn't change what you did."

"Nothing does," Rebel said. "And nothing will."

Mia looked at his meal and saw that it was just a bowl of plain, boiled rice. "The whitefood diet," she guessed. "That was the sacrifice you made for Zack."

She checked Zack's sleeping form, then spoke to Rebel in a hushed voice. "So you *do* feel guilty."

Rebel eyed her cynically. "Maybe I just like rice."

"Whatever." Mia stood up from the table. "I can't believe they picked you for this mission."

"Me neither," Rebel admitted. "Guess I'm the only good augur they have."

"You're the *worst* augur they have. You've been wrong about everything."

"Not everything."

"Shut up."

"There's a Pelletier among you. He's been right under your nose this whole time."

"You are so . . ." Mia closed her eyes and shook her head. "You know what? Forget it. You're not even worth it."

She returned to her seat, her thoughts bubbling like lava. Though she tried to lose herself in her electronic novel, Rebel's vague and nasty warning kept circling through her head. Her future selves kept excoriating her for being so stupid, so blind. What if they were all angry about the same thing? What if that thing was Semerjean?

No. She flushed the thought and then lost herself in the novel. Eight hours later, the M-9 de-shifted with a lurch. As Victoria announced their impending arrival, Mia focused on the mission ahead. The Coppers were from her world, but that didn't necessarily make them good people. She could only hope, when and if they were found, that they were less like Evan Rander and more like Jonathan Christie.

The Seattle of this world was a much different city than the one Zack remembered. In place of skyscrapers and space needles stood a four-mile strip of hotel-casinos, each one flamboyantly lit and capped with giant holograms: a chest-beating ape, an overendowed cowgirl, a fifty-foot wizard with dollar signs for eyes. After the Cataclysm of 1912 wiped out half the New York underworld, a criminal empire arose on the other side of the country. It was Gerry "Midas" Goldberg, the youngest and sharpest of the New Pacific gangsters, who turned this damp little town into a bustling neon Gomorrah.

Today, while Las Vegas served as a tiny desert commune for artisans, Seattle had become immortalized as the "City of Chance." Every legal vice in the country could be indulged here. A more determined sinner could book passage on one of the many drugships and aerdellos that hovered high among the clouds. The skies above the city were virtually lawless. To find the seedy underbelly of Seattle, all one had to do was look up.

Zack had no interest in sampling the local debauchery. He had only one purpose here. Unfortunately, Victoria insisted on keeping him and Mia out of sight until they were needed. They spent their first three days sequestered inside the Poseidon, a thirty-story hotel that took its undersea gimmick to ridiculous extremes. The hallways were lined with aquatic animations, while hidden speakers pushed the intermittent sound of whale songs. Every suite had at least three lumiquariums, each one featuring the same holographic fish. Zack had watched them long enough to know exactly when the animation looped—every forty-nine minutes, right when the red mosaic guppy kissed the green neon tetra.

Even more grating than the accommodations were the disguises. In order to thwart the government cameras, the Ryder sisters fitted everyone on the team with face-altering prosthetics. Mia was glad that Carrie couldn't see her with her fat putty chin, the bulbous nose that made her look like an aardvark. She and Zack were ordered to stay in their disguises at all times, even in the privacy of their rooms.

Mercy assured them that the away team had it worse. "It's bullshit," she griped. "All we do is stand around and keep watch while the Mayor plays detective."

The hunt for the Coppers began in Grandview, a small and affluent suburb on the lip of the bay. The town had made national news back in March when an abandoned church exploded in what witnesses described as a miniature Cataclysm. Though the incident remained a public mystery, the Mayor scanned the past and saw exactly what happened. The Coppers had been using the church as a refuge when a passing patrolman caught sight of them through a window. As he parked his cruiser, the group leader—a short-haired black woman—waved her arms in a panic. The church was engulfed in a dome of light, leaving nothing behind of the building or its inhabitants.

By all appearances, the Coppers had been vaporized. Yet two weeks later, in the nearby town of Gatewood, an elderly radio host came home to find them looting his valuables. He pulled a shotgun on them, only to be punched through a wall by a teenage girl and her tempic fist.

This time, Integrity arrived quickly enough to keep the incident out of the news. This time, they had a trail to follow.

The Mayor spent the next two days ghosting the chase, a path that took him all around the outskirts of Seattle. The Coppers seemed to grow savvier by the minute, thanks to their adaptive leader and their ever-improving augur. Once their solic learned how to hinder all temporal scrying efforts, that was it. The group was nothing but static in Integrity's ghost drills. The Mayor stopped seeing them in his hindsight.

On the fourth night of the search mission, Victoria gathered the team for an emergency meeting. Fifteen Gothams and two Silvers clustered together in her hotel suite, their weary eyes following her as she paced in front of a lumi-quarium. By now Zack was sure that he despised Victoria, though Peter told him not to judge her too harshly. Her husband was one of the three dozen augurs who'd killed themselves last year, while her son had died violently in Rebel and Ivy's service.

But despite her grief, Victoria never buckled for a moment. She remained as cool and unyielding as the tempis inside of her.

She studied the ghostfish with dark, somber eyes before turning to address her crew.

"We gave it our best try, but these breachers have eluded us. For all we know, they're thousands of miles away by now. I believe, and the elders agree, that we've run our course here."

Peter leaned against a dresser and popped a lemon candy. He was one of the few people on the team to retain a modicum of handsomeness with his disguise. Zack and Mia agreed that he looked like Liam Neeson after some anaphylactic swelling.

"Give it one more day," he urged. "We might catch a break tomorrow."

Victoria shook her head. "It's too dangerous."

Zack rose to his feet. "If we don't find these people, the government will."

"And if we stay any longer, Integrity will find *us*. We're putting the whole clan at risk."

The Mayor looked to Zack with sympathy. "I understand your frustration, but there's nothing more we can do."

"Bullshit." Zack turned to Rebel. "You're the big breacher hunter. How did you keep finding us?"

Rebel stared at the floor with a dour expression. "You know how."

"Ioni." Zack chuckled bleakly. "That's just great."

Mercy held his arm. "I hate to say it, but Victoria's right. If they left the city—"

"They didn't." Zack moved toward the door. "If you guys want to go, then go. Mia and I will keep looking."

Peter sighed. "Zack . . ."

"We're *all* leaving," Victoria insisted. "That's an order."

"You seem to have me confused with one of your flying monkeys."

"You're part of our clan now, Trillinger. That means you follow our rules."

"Or what? You'll kill me?"

"No. We'll just never let you back in the underland."

Zack looked to Peter, whose dark expression confirmed the veracity of the threat. He opened the door and bathed the Gothams in a seething glare. "I see. When it comes to killing my people, the sky's the limit. But when we need to be saved, it's 'so long and fuck you.'"

He slammed the door behind him. Victoria sighed at her underling. "Call Aer Control. Get us the next available flight slot."

Mia gave Mercy a few seconds to chase after Zack, and was only mildly surprised when she didn't. The two of them made a curiously aloof couple, all shrugs and *whatevers.* Mia hoped it was just a skittish early phase of their relationship. What was the point of having someone if you didn't love them with all your heart?

She followed Zack to his room and found him staring out at the city. His window faced the Via Fortuna, a six-level skyway that cut through the heart of the casino district. The aeromobiles all glowed in the night, trailing gorgeous streaks of color as they passed at high speed.

Zack peeked at Mia over his shoulder, then looked back at the skyway. "They'll never understand. Even Peter doesn't get it."

Mia hugged him from behind, her cheek pressed to his shoulder blade. "I get it."

He gripped her wrists. "Ninety-nine people out of seven billion. God only knows how many of us are left. Evan killed one. Rebel got six. We keep dropping like this . . ."

"Zack . . ."

He sighed at the window. "A world only dies when there's no one left to remember it."

Mia held him tight. She knew that Zack wasn't just grieving for the late great Earth. He was grieving for his brother, for Amanda, for the pieces of himself he lost in the Pelletiers' torture room. The Coppers were his best chance to snatch a small victory from the universe. Now they were slipping through his fingers, too.

The room phone rang in a high, piercing tweedle. Zack and Mia ignored it until it stopped. The only people who had their number were the Gothams down the hall. They could damn well wait.

"I'll open up some portals," Mia offered. "See if the other Mias know anything."

Zack turned around to face her. "You sure?"

"No, but what else can we do?"

"You don't have to read them. I will."

"I'm not worried about the insults. I just—"

The phone rang again. Mia rushed to the nightstand and yanked the handset from the cradle. *"What?"*

A sharp laugh filled her ear. "Whoa. Easy there, Snappy."

She couldn't recognize the voice at all. He sounded youthful and vibrant, but not in any pleasant way. He was most definitely not one of Victoria's crew.

"I think you have the wrong number," Mia said.

"Au contraire, ma chère. The number I have is seven. Seven Coppers, hiding out on a pier at the far end of the Wallows. Ask Peter. He'll know where it is."

Zack eyed Mia quizzically. "Who is that?"

"Who are you?"

"Who's to say?" the caller teased. "I could be a friend. I could be an enemy. It's getting hard to tell which are which these days."

"Why should I trust you?"

The stranger laughed again. "It's the City of Chance, girl. Take a gamble."

The line went dead. Mia hung up the phone.

"You all right?" Zack asked her.

"No." She looked beyond the Via Fortuna, at the dark and distant sky. "Get Peter."

The aeric revolution did a number on the maritime shipping industry. As old iron barges were replaced with low-flying cargolifts, a slew of cheaper, more convenient docks sprouted up across the inland. Year by year, pier by pier, the port of Seattle withered away to an antiquity. After several failed attempts to lease the harbor to commercial developers, the city surrendered it to the bums and seagulls. Soon the place became a haven for all of Seattle's downtrodden—the addicts and erratics, the castoffs and casualties.

To keep the homeless from wandering back into the city proper, the government converted a thousand old boats and shipping containers into habitable shelters. Food drops were made on a daily basis while volunteer health workers roamed the piers with medkits. The port had its own bathhouse, its own economy, even its own justice system. All it took was a scream to bring a dozen people down on the head of a predator.

Still, there was a reason the place was called the Wallows. On this wet black evening, Mia couldn't imagine a more wretched hell. Families huddled together in rusty metal boxes, scraping meat out of tins with filthy fingers. A burn-scarred man screamed the Gospel of Jesus while a frantic woman accosted everyone she saw with a photo of a teenage girl. "Have you seen her? Please. She's my daughter. I have to find her."

Mia and Peter walked the perimeter of the entry plaza, a chaotic bazaar of charity stations and barter stalls. Between a tetanus shot kiosk and a purveyor of dry blankets sat a sickly old oracle who traded prophecies for cigarettes.

Peter winced at his loud, hacking cough. "Christ, man. There are at least three doctors floating around here. Go see one of them."

"Fuck off, Irish."

"Lovely." Peter plunked a twenty-dollar bill into the man's cup and took Mia's hand. "Come on."

Mia looked to the distance and saw the Ryder sisters grimacing at the local sights and smells. None of the Gothams were particularly happy to be here. Even Zack seemed dubious about her anonymous caller's information. What if it was just a Pelletier trick? What if Integrity was luring them into a trap?

Ten yards away, Victoria did a double-take at one of the locals. She gripped the Mayor's arm. "Over there. That girl."

He followed her gaze to a petite figure in a rain slicker and germ mask. She was haggling with a trader twice her size, demanding six solic batteries for the fresh-caught salmon in her hands.

The Mayor squinted. "Can't make spit of her. What are you seeing?"

"Not seeing," Victoria said. "Feeling."

He stared at her, surprised. "She's a tempic?"

"A strong one."

The girl left the bazaar with four batteries and a scowl. The Mayor motioned to his nephew, a lumic named Flynn. He nodded in acknowledgment, disappeared behind an illusive screen, then followed the tempic with chameleon stealth.

Ten minutes later, the team joined Flynn at the western edge of the harbor, where three metal shanties flanked the end of a pier. It seemed Mia's tipster hadn't lied. The Coppers had claimed a desolate corner of the Wallows, their own little Freak Street.

Zack peeked around the edge of a shipping can and studied the hovels. "So what now?"

"We neutralize their powers," Victoria said. "It's the only way to be safe."

Mercy scoffed. "I can't sap seven people at once."

"It's also a bad way to earn their trust," Peter said.

Victoria frowned at him. "We can't just walk up to these breachers. They're fugitives. They're skittish."

"And one of them makes Cataclysms," the Mayor anxiously reminded everyone.

"Let us do it," Mia proposed. "Me and Zack. We're from their world. We speak their language."

Zack nodded in agreement. "This is why you brought us."

Peter traded a heavy look with Victoria before shrugging at Mia. "We'll give it a shot, but stay in view. If we see *one* hint of trouble—"

"You won't," said Rebel. "They'll be fine."

Even his fellow Gothams looked skeptical. Half of them couldn't seem to decide if he was incompetent or lying. If his dear, beloved Ivy had seen the looks on their faces, she would have given them all an earful. *Bastards! He fought and bled for you! He lost everything, and this is how you treat him?*

It's all right, Rebel thought. *They're in for a surprise.*

The downpour stopped. Zack and Mia closed their umbrellas and cautiously emerged from cover. Without the pattering rain, the pier was eerily quiet. They couldn't hear a hint of noise from the shanties.

Mia glanced over her shoulder and saw all sixteen Gothams gathering at the base of the pier. She figured it was Peter's idea to stand out in the open, as a good-faith gesture and a warning to the Coppers. Still, she wished they'd stayed hidden. They were an ornery-looking bunch. Their presence would only make these people more nervous.

"Don't worry," Zack told her. "If their augur's worth a damn, she'll—"

A metallic squeal filled the air. A speeding figure burst out of a hovel and screeched to a halt in front of them. He was a gangly boy of Korean descent, not a day older than thirteen. Zack and Mia had already learned from the Mayor's divinations that the Coppers had a swifter among them, a severely injured one at that. His wheelchair didn't seem to slow him down a bit.

Peter blanched at the sight of the sawed-off shotgun in the boy's hands. The barrel moved between Zack and Mia with the whizzing speed of a fan blade.

Rebel held Peter back before he could intervene. "Wait."

"Wait!" Zack raised his hands at the swifter. "We're friends!"

"He can't hear you," said a voice from the shanties. "Not in that state."

Four more Coppers emerged from the hovels and formed an orderly wall behind the swifter. They were all dressed in rain slickers, with overstuffed duffels strapped securely to their backs. They were obviously prepared for company tonight. They all looked ready to flee or fight at a moment's notice.

They also had something else in common.

"Jesus," Mercy uttered. "They really are kids."

The Mayor had revealed the unique makeup of the Coppers three days ago, after his first hindsight scan. The Pelletiers had filled the group with adolescents—all Mias, Heaths, and Davids—with one glaring exception.

At last, the leader stepped out of her hovel. She was a tall, black woman of powerful build, with close-cropped hair and a bright yellow dress that brazenly clashed with her surroundings. Zack assumed the garb was pure strategy, a way to keep enemy eyes on her. The Mayor had seen for himself the obsessive, protective love this woman had for her young ones. She was their teacher, their sergeant, their nursemaid, their nun. She'd rechristened them all with brand-new names and demanded they adapt to their circumstances.

The Coppers listened. They adapted. And now they called her Mother.

Zack jerked his head at the gun-wielding swifter. "Look, tell your boy—"

"No boy."

"What?"

Mother crossed her arms. "He's seen unimaginable horrors. He suffers constant pain, yet still he fights. Sweep is many things, but he is no boy."

She spoke with a thick Haitian accent, and sounded much younger than she looked. At first glance, Zack had taken her for a woman in her mid-to-late thirties. Now he had to wonder if she was even older than Hannah.

Mother beckoned to Sweep. He wheeled past her and took his place in the formation. Mia locked eyes with the small brunette next to him, the Copper's lone tempic. She sneered at Zack and Mia menacingly, just daring them to try something.

"Look, we're not here to make trouble. My name's—"

"—Mia Farisi," said Mother. "The man is Zack Trillinger. We know who you are. We've been expecting you for two days."

The seventh and final Copper emerged from her hut. She was a twelve-year-old girl with light brown skin, as tense and pretty as Heath. Clearly Mother had yet to hone this one into a soldier. Zack had a good guess why.

Their augur, he realized. *Oh God. That poor kid.*

The girl called See stepped into the moonlight and daintily clutched Mother's waist. She bounced her muddled glare between the two Silvers.

"That's not how they look. They're wearing disguises."

"We have no choice," Zack said. "We're fugitives, just like you. We have all the same problems you have. Same enemies. Same history."

"Same powers," Mia added. From the moment she'd stepped within twenty feet of Mother, she felt a shocking twinge of intimacy, as if their naked hips were touching. The woman was most definitely a traveler. They were linked in ways that neither of them understood.

Mother processed her with an uncomfortable expression. "Show us your true faces."

Zack and Mia swapped a hesitant look, then peeled off their putty adornments. Peter muttered a curse from the distance. He'd have to teleport them out of here. The docks were filled with civic cameras.

Mother studied them intently while stroking See's hair. "This one has been cursed with terrible visions, but her foresight keeps us alive. She told us on Sunday that you were coming—a man and girl just like us, offering safe haven from the soldiers who hunt us. But all See knows are the words you bring. She doesn't know if they're true."

Zack opened his mouth to speak, but Mother cut him off. "I wanted the chance to judge you for myself, and I do believe now that you're everything you say you are. I believe you come to us with good intentions."

She motioned to the Gothams at the base of the pier. "But I do not trust these people you bring."

Ninety feet away, in a cracked glass booth that had once been a gatehouse, a woman in rags crouched against the wall and watched the meeting on a laptop screen. Gingold had sent her here a week ago to keep an eye out for temporal weirdness. All she'd gotten so far was a rash and a newfound empathy for the underclass.

Still, there was something awfully shady about these new visitors. They stood out like diamonds here in the Wallows, and they moved about the docks with suspicious purpose.

The agent scanned the Gothams through her remote-control camera, but none of them registered in the agency's database. She sent the spy-eye up the pier, toward the Silvers and Coppers.

Only Rebel noticed the plum-size drone flying ten feet above the water. He gripped the revolver beneath his raincoat. *Here we go.*

Mother kept her dark eyes on the Gothams, oblivious to See's growing discomfort.

"We put our trust in strangers once," she told Zack and Mia. "Long ago, when we first came to this world. I had my doubts, but I didn't listen."

She dipped her head in sorrow. "There were nine of us then."

Zack's heart sank at her news. Every orphan death was like a genocide to his people. Now there two more names on the casualty list.

Mia looked at Mother. "These people you're talking about, they were scientists, right? They had a weird name and a fancy building and they told you everything would be okay. Except it wasn't."

A ripple of unease crossed Mother's face. "What does it matter?"

"Because it happened to us," Zack said. "I told you, we have the same history."

"But you didn't learn the same lessons." Mother glared at the Gothams. "Can you truly tell me that you trust those people with your lives?"

While Zack and Mia hemmed, the camera drone scanned their faces. A computer in Maryland processed the images. Within moments, a hundred different handphones lit up with a Priority-1 notice.

See caught the new future, then shrieked at the sky. *"They're coming!"*

Mother turned to the Silvers, her eyes wide with betrayal. Zack raised his palms. "Wait—"

The tempic saw his hands and attacked. She was a fourteen-year-old girl of explosive temperament, a killer on two Earths. Under the loving care of Mother, she'd learned to control her violent impulses . . . to an extent.

She'd been born Olivia Bassin. Her only name now was Stitch.

A fist of white force extended from her arm. It struck Zack in the chest, breaking six ribs and throwing him fifty feet off the side of the pier.

Mia watched in horror as he skidded into the ocean. *"Zack!"*

Peter ran up the pier, panicked. Even worse than Zack's predicament was the ominous change he felt inside Mother—a swirling vortex of energy, like a breath before a roar.

"Kounya!" Mother yelled. She closed her eyes and grabbed onto See. Her children braced each other for support.

Streaks of light burst from her skin, until she and See were encased in a glowing white dome. It ballooned in size. Five feet. Ten feet. Twenty-five. Forty.

All over the Wallows, people looked to the west with squinting eyes. Something bizarre was happening on the horizon—an unexpected radiance, like a second moon rising up from the ocean. The bubble flared for three more seconds, then disappeared in a blink.

Red spots danced in Peter's vision as he struggled to survey the damage. The pier was half as long as it used to be, ending in a smooth, curved line at his feet. There was nothing beyond him now but black sky and water.

The Coppers were gone, and so was Mia.

Seventeen miles to the east, two identical portals bloomed on the wall of a private jet hangar. The Ryder sisters emerged in synch, each one trailed by a stumbling queue of Gothams.

Angela Ryder waved them in. "Hurry! Hurry!"

Victoria popped out of the wall, her hands encased in a floating tempic gurney. As the group had made their frantic escape from the Wallows, the Integrity agent in the gatehouse fired a Hail Mary shot from her service pistol. The bullet struck the Mayor in the small of his back.

He lay cheek-down on the tempis, his white lips stammering. "Please. Don't let me die. My daughters . . ."

"You won't die," Victoria told him. "You won't even remember this. I promise you."

She looked to Sean Howell, the team's handsome young turner. He'd learned the art of healing from Mother Olga herself, though he admitted that the Mayor posed a unique challenge. Between his age, his girth, and his artificial heart, Sean gave the man a fifty percent chance of surviving reversal.

Victoria tapped her foot in anxious thought. "Can Olga heal him?"

"Olga can heal anyone," Sean said.

"Then keep him stable. We'll bring him to her."

Rebel was the last to emerge from the portal. He'd lingered behind at the dock to return fire on the Integrity agent. His first shot nicked her thigh. The second one cut every string of her future.

He pulled off his raincoat and holstered his gun. "We have to go before they ground all flights."

Mercy looked at the shrinking portals. "Wait! What about—"

A third portal opened on the nearby wall, gushing a torrent of seawater. Peter and Zack spilled out through the opening. The water carried them twenty feet before Peter was able to wave the gate shut.

He scrambled to Zack's side and listened for breath. Mercy watched him frantically as he began to resuscitate him. "Oh, don't you dare. Don't you *dare*, Trillinger . . ."

Zack spit up water and coughed. Peter motioned for Mercy and two of Victoria's tempics.

"Get him on the plane. Carefully. He's got broken bones and probably internal damage."

As the tempics laid Zack out on a platform, Peter stormed across the wet floor of the hangar. His disguise had come off in the ocean. He aimed his naked rage at one kinsman in particular.

Rebel sighed at his approach. "Look—"

Peter clocked him in the jaw. He hit the wall with an echoing *thud*.

Victoria rushed to Peter's side. "What are you doing?"

"You happy now?" he asked Rebel. "You like how that went?"

"Peter, stop!"

He looked to Victoria and jerked his thumb at Rebel. "He saw what was coming. That son of a bitch knew exactly what we were in for."

Rebel struggled to his feet and wiped the blood from his mouth. Victoria shook her head in disbelief. "No. He wouldn't risk our lives like that. Not for a couple of breachers."

"The breachers weren't his target."

Peter clamped Rebel's chin and forced him into eye contact. "He figured if Mia and Zack got in enough trouble, the Pelletiers would show up to save them. Maybe he'd get lucky and put a bullet in one of them. Was that it? Was that the big plan?"

Rebel shoved him away. "They killed my family!"

"And you risked mine! Mia's in a world of trouble right now because of you. If she gets hurt, I swear to Christ I'll kill you myself."

Rebel flinched at Peter's expression. There was a savagery in his deep blue eyes that was both brand-new and shockingly familiar.

Peter turned to Victoria. "You guys go. I'll find Mia."

"Look, Peter, I'm sorry, but are you sure she's even—"

"She's alive."

He drew a portal in the wall. Victoria ordered everyone onto the M-9, then pointed a stern finger at Rebel.

"There'll be hell to pay when we get home. If you have any sense left in you, you'll shut your mouth and do what you're told. Are we clear?"

Her words were nothing but static in Rebel's ears. His every thought was fixed on Peter. All this time, he'd thought Semerjean was posing as one of the breachers. But what if he'd been looking in the wrong place? What if a demon had been hiding among his people for years?

"Are we clear?" Victoria repeated.

Rebel watched Peter as he disappeared through the portal. He narrowed his eyes, then spit a gob of blood at the floor. "Crystal."

For eighty-one creatures in the woods of northern Washington, the apocalypse came four years early. A rabbit stopped to sniff the strange smell of ozone. An owl shrieked at a high-pitched whine. Then everything in a fifty-foot radius was obliterated in a bubble of bright temporis.

By the time the light dissipated, the environment had changed. The forest now had a perfectly round clearing with a floor of broken concrete, plus three aluminum shanties that leaned at odd angles. Displaced salmon flopped helplessly around the perimeter.

In the center of the circle, seven orphans fell to their hand and knees. An eighth one slumped in his wheelchair.

Mia ran a trembling hand down the side of her face. Mother's three-dimensional portals were worse than anything she'd ever experienced—a sickening journey, like being passed through a giant's loose bowels.

She turned her head and saw Mother crouched on the concrete, caressing See's back while the girl loudly retched. The others had managed to keep their dinners inside them, but just barely.

"It's a terrible power," Mother said to Mia. "I don't like using it. But you gave me no choice."

Mia fought the urge to hit her. "We came here to *help* you!"

"Help?" said Sweep. "You led the feds right to us!"

"We could have gotten you out! We have travelers too. *Better* ones."

"You shut your mouth," said Stitch.

"You shut yours. If you killed Zack, I swear to God—"

"Enough," Mother snapped. "*Leve kanpe.*"

Stitch rose to her feet on wobbly legs and formed a large tempic square on the ground. Two of the Coppers carried Sweep's wheelchair onto the surface. The rest followed them aboard.

Soon a freckled redhead named Sky pressed her temples in concentration. The tempis glowed on the underside before rising into the air like a flying carpet.

Mother took a somber look at Mia. "Under better circumstances, I'd invite you to join us. You'd fit in well with our family."

Mia closed her eyes. Even worse than the physical discomfort of the portal jaunt was the psychic intimacy she'd shared with Mother. She could feel the sickness behind the woman's devotion, a fear of abandonment that colored her every thought. Mother would lay down her life for her beloved children. She'd also kill the first one who tried to leave her.

The platform continued its slow ascent. Mia looked up at Mother. "We can still help you. It's not too late."

"I think we've had quite enough of your help."

"You can't keep running. You have to trust someone!"

"Perhaps," said Mother. "But not today."

As the Coppers rose above the canopy of trees, Sweep enveloped them all in a temporal shift field. Shade shrouded them in a black lumic haze. The group fled the scene in a near-invisible blur, a fleeting smudge in the night.

Mia sat down on the tattered remains of the pier, her palms pressed against her face. She had no money, no handphone, not a damn thing to work with except a gauzy patch of moonlight. She could be anywhere in the world right now, or even anywhere in time.

Her inner Peter scoffed at her. *Oh, come on. Only the Pelletiers can survive time travel. And only they can jump more than a hundred miles at a stretch.*

Mia frowned at the thought. Clearly Mother was an entirely different breed of teleporter. Who knew what her limits were?

Rules are rules, hon. And what's the first rule of traveling?

She sighed. "Know your bearings."

That's my girl.

She cast her thoughts across the landscape, following the fetid aura of Mother's jump trail. It arched like a rainbow back toward the Wallows, a ten-mile trip at best. She was just a quick hop away from Peter and the others, but the docks were still foreign to her. She didn't know them well enough to make a memory leap. It probably wasn't wise to go back there anyway. By now, the place would be crawling with—

Harsh white spotlights drenched the clearing from above. Mia shielded her eyes and saw dozens of liftplates in rapid descent. A whole squadron of aerships had de-shifted right above her.

Her throat closed. *Oh no . . .*

She ran for the trees, cursing herself for dawdling. Integrity had known about Mother for two months now, and were just waiting for her to make another "Cataclysm." They probably saw her dome of light from miles away.

The Integrity squad leader watched Mia on his infrared monitor. "Got the girl. She's alone out here. Orders?"

Gingold paced the floor of his Bethesda apartment, tapping his headset in contemplation. Like Rebel, he'd developed a white whale vendetta against the Pelletiers. These other freaks were little fish. Farisi was barely a minnow.

"Juice her," he ordered. "Juice the whole area."

"Yes, sir."

Six solic cannons took aim at the clearing. Mia lined up her jump with nervous precision. A shrieking voice inside her told her to screw the formalities. *Just go to the hotel! Go!*

She waved a six-foot portal into the air and leapt through it, just as the cannons fired their solis. The gateway closed on the tail of her raincoat, shearing nine inches off in a molecularly even line.

Mia moved her way through the folds of space, all the way to the floor of a dimly lit corridor. She had barely tumbled to a stop before she frantically checked her limbs. Mercifully, nothing got severed when the portal closed on her, but something still wasn't right. She looked up and saw two dozen men staring back at her incredulously. Behind them, three fish-tailed showgirls screamed silent bubbles from their water tank.

"Oh no . . ."

She'd been hoping to jump back to her private suite at the Poseidon, but panic had warped her aim. Instead, she landed twelve floors down in the Mermaid Walk, the hotel's 24-hour girlquarium. Mia had come here six times during her short stay, if only to figure out how the performers managed to stay underwater so long. At some point during the end of her fifth visit, she'd opened herself to possibility that maybe, just maybe, the mermaids turned her on a little.

The exhibit had just begun its midnight "natural hour," where admission was restricted, the seashell cups came off, and the showgirls earned double-wage. The men in the corridor had paid good money to see nipples, but now their eyes were fixed on a fully clothed teenager, one who'd popped into the walk through a glowing hole in the air.

Twenty-four hundred miles away, an Integrity analyst blinked in disbelief at his monitor readings.

"Uh, sir . . . the cameras found Farisi at the Poseidon Hotel. It's no mistake. I'm looking right at her."

Gingold spat a string of curses. Integrity's files on Mia were hopelessly incomplete. Melissa had speculated that the girl was an augur of some sort. But augurs didn't jump twenty miles in a blink.

"Jensen, get your squad to the Poseidon *now*. Rossi, patch their cameras. I want eyes on that kid every second. You hear me?"

"Yes, sir. Should I notify the—"

"No," said Gingold. "Let them at her. See if they slow her down."

Few forces on Earth operated with more ruthless efficiency than casino security. The moment Mia disrupted the Mermaid Walk, a manager brought a metal gate down on both entrances and sent three men after her. They burst into the passageway through a hidden tunnel door.

Mia's stomach dropped at the sight of the security guards. They were covered from head to toe in glossy black latex, these reverse-Semerjeans that moved on her like cheetahs. Clearly they were all wearing speedsuits. They would have reached her already if there wasn't a gaggle of bystanders in their path.

Frantic, Mia waved two portals into existence, one on each side of the aquarium glass. A thousand gallons of water splashed onto the security guards, knocking them down and shorting out their shifters. A mermaid poured screaming out of the portal and flopped helplessly on top of them.

Mia fled down the corridor and teleported through the northern gate. She reached the edge of the main casino and gasped at the sight of five more guards speeding toward her. Everyone on the floor, from the servers to the dealers to the wild-eyed gamblers, stopped what they were doing to watch the men advance on Mia.

Her heart thundered as she pondered her options. She didn't have the time or strength to make a memory jump. Her only hope was to look through the glass of the lobby entrance, then prepare herself for a line-of-sight teleport.

She had just finished willing her portals into the air when a fast-moving guard caught her from behind. Mia thrashed and kicked in his grip. "No! Get off me! Get off!"

Just then, a stranger's hand popped out of the portal and pressed a .44 revolver to the guard's face mask. "Wha—"

The gun went off with an ear-splitting *boom*, covering three people in gore and sending two hundred others into a state of screaming panic.

Patrons shoved and tripped over each other on the way to the exits. A cocktail waitress got knocked to the ground. The remaining security guards drew their pistols, but the killer's hand had already retreated.

Mia stood in a trembling daze, her face and hair peppered with blood. The gunshot had robbed her of everything she had left—her hearing, her thoughts, her hold on reality. She existed in a mad new continuum, an alternate-alternate reality where time didn't move and everything shrieked in a piercing whistle.

The gunman reached back through Mia's portal and took a firm hold of her wrist. She barely had time to notice the *SS* tattoo on his hand before he yanked her through the gateway and pulled her out onto the street. He steadied her before she could fall.

"Whoa there, partner."

Mia couldn't hear him through the ringing in her ears. She looked up and studied him with round, vacant eyes. He was a scrawny young guy in a newsboy cap and leather jacket. He looked eerily chipper for a man who'd just killed someone.

Mia blinked at him stupidly. "Who—"

He raised a computer tablet in front of her face. Huge, black letters filled the screen. Close your portals.

She waved her floating discs shut. The stranger took her by the hand and led her to the open front door of an aerocab. Mia got into the passenger seat with glazed obedience, stopping only to pluck a bloody piece of face mask from her hair.

At long last, she was able to form a coherent thought. *He shot that guy. He shot that guy right in the face. Why am I going with him? Why—*

The cabbie passed her his tablet, then closed the passenger door. Mia looked down at the fresh new text on the screen.

Integrity will be here in 41 seconds. If they catch you, you're dead. That makes me your Lone Ranger.

So buckle up. And smile. ☺

By the time she finished reading, her rescuer had run around to the driver's seat. He closed the door and started the ignition.

"Who are you?" Mia asked.

Smirking, he tapped the tablet in her hands. The screen advanced to a third message.

Think it through. It'll come to you.

She looked again at the *SS* tattoo on his hand. On closer inspection, they weren't letters, they were numbers. Her future self had long ago warned her about the owner of such a brand.

If you see a small and creepy guy with a 55 on his hand, run. That's Evan Rander. He's bad news.

"No . . ."

Mia reached for the exit just as the door locks clicked and the cab lifted off the ground.

"Relax," Evan told her. "I'm not gonna hurt you. Sorry about the Coppers, by the way. I should have warned you when I called you. They're a little nutty."

"What?"

"*I said the Coppers are—*" He waved her off. "I'll tell you later."

As the taxi rose, Mia caught a flash of light through the windshield. A fleet of Integrity dropships had de-shifted in the sky and were descending fast on the Poseidon.

Evan clucked his tongue at the squadron. "Right on cue. Boy, did I show up in the nick of time."

"Get us out of here."

He teasingly cupped his ear. "I'm sorry. I couldn't hear that."

"*Go!*"

"Yes, ma'am!" Evan's face lit up in a devilish grin. "Hi-yo Silver."

They rose to the taxi level of the skyway, then shot off like a missile. By the time the Integrity shuttles landed, Evan's cab had blended into the traffic, just another streak of light on the Via Fortuna.

THIRTY

The midnight hour brought a soothing hush to the underland. Most of the Gothams retired to their surface homes, leaving a scattered few to enjoy their cigarettes, their solitude, their secret affairs and eccentric club gatherings. The naturalists took their nightly "free walk" around the perimeter park. The mystics met in the village square to eat psychedelic mushrooms and commune with their ancestors. The fantasists convened in the alley behind the library to shoot the next scene of their film project: a quasi-erotic horror thriller that was tentatively called *The Torment*.

By two A.M., the last of the locals went topside and the village fell into mechanical white noise. David loved being awake at this hour. He'd been living in cramped, loud spaces from the day he arrived on this world. Now he and Yvonne had a whole town to themselves.

They kissed on the grass of the Memorial Garden, their bodies lit with spectral incandescence. Yvonne had furnished everything they needed for their tryst: a goose-down blanket, an orange-jasmine scentstick, a high-fidelity spinner loaded with sensual (but not overly erotic) pop music, and the *pièce de résistance*: a ten-ounce bowl of Lambert cherries, fresh from the market and one hundred percent unjuvenated. Yvonne had gone out of her way to please David without giving up her sweeter fruits, and he had no intention of pressing her on the matter. He liked what he had with Yvonne already. Why muddy it up with hormonal demands?

Yvonne fed him another cherry, giggling as she plucked the stem from his lips. "Tell me another one."

David chuckled. The girl was endlessly amused by alt-Earth slang. She'd already cried with laughter over *booboo*, *dork*, and *wedgie*, and those were just the American terms. David feared she'd asphyxiate if he started teaching her the Australian lingo.

"What kind of word are you looking for?" he asked. "Crude? Insulting?"

"Complimentary." Yvonne rolled onto her side and traced a finger across his chest. "What do you call a man who's exceedingly sexy?"

"Hunky."

She laughed. "Liar."

"It's true."

"That's what we call our vomit."

"I have no control over that."

"Fine." She squinted at him. "What do you call a man who's exceedingly brave?"

"Ballsy."

Yvonne buried her face in his shoulder and shook with laughter. David particularly enjoyed her in the wee hours, when fatigue made her goofy and effortlessly sincere. In the light of day, she put too much work into the semblance of perfection, always striving to say the right thing, wear the right thing, be the right thing at all times. David blamed the Mayor for her neurosis. Like most of these Gothams, he was all about appearances. He'd turned his poor daughter's life into a never-ending pageant.

Her giggles subsided. She brushed the bangs from David's brow. "Your compliments are disgusting. I'll just call you brave and sexy."

"I'm not as brave as you think I am."

"Oh, puff."

"I'm really not."

"David, look at that."

She drew his gaze to the Requiem Wall, an ornately chiseled list of every deceased Gotham. Yvonne shined a lumic spotlight on thirty recent names.

"Those were our augurs," she said. "The mere thought of apocalypse drove them to suicide. But you lived through it. You watched your whole world fall and it didn't break you. Don't tell me you're not brave."

David wriggled uncomfortably on the blanket. "Then why do I live in constant fear of dying?"

"Because you're sane." Yvonne sat up and hugged herself. "Because you're sixteen and you have everything to live for."

David felt an unpleasant tickle at the base of his throat. He coughed into his hand, then turned off the music. "Come here."

Yvonne fell back into his embrace. He caressed her arm distractedly. His instincts were growling for reasons he couldn't pinpoint. Something felt . . . off.

"Our two worlds were siblings," he reminded Yvonne. "Until 1912, they were perfect twins. But there are countless other Earths out there: cousins, neighbors, distant strangers. I don't believe they share our malady. No matter what happens here, I believe life will go on for trillions of people."

Yvonne didn't draw much comfort from that. She looked up at the night-scape with dark, doleful eyes. "Gumbled."

"What?"

"Slang word. It means 'born in the wrong place at the wrong—'"

"*Yvonne!*"

The voice hit them from the distance: a high, girlish cry that rattled every window in the village.

David sat up with a start. "What was that?"

"My sister." Yvonne hurriedly buttoned her blouse. "Get dressed."

Winnifred Whitten was one of the clan's rare dualers, a twelve-year-old swifter/lumic. Though her light-bending skills were average at best, her control over sound was unparalleled. She could steer a whisper through the warrens, drown half the village in silence. When the right or wrong mood struck her, she could project her voice like a mighty goddess.

"*Yvonne, where are you?*"

Cursing, Yvonne flicked her hand and cast a giant white arrow above her. David heard the accelerated patter of footsteps in the darkness.

Winnie rushed into the garden and de-shifted in front of her sister. Her chubby cheeks were streaked with tears.

"Daddy's been shot!"

Yvonne jumped to her feet. "*What?*"

"They just got back. He's at the vivery. Come on!"

David's head spun with dizziness as he rose from the blanket. "Are the others okay? Zack? Mia?"

Winnie saw his open shirt and bashfully looked away. "I don't know. I think one of them's hurt."

"Come with us," Yvonne said.

David shook his head. "I'll meet you there. I have to . . ."

He broke away for a second cough, a throaty hack that made his eyes water.

Yvonne touched his back. "Are you okay?"

Winnie tugged her arm. "Come *on!*"

David waved her on, then ran to the other exit.

A hundred yards away, the residents of Freak Street stumbled out of their cottages, groggy and bewildered. Only Carrie knew the voice that had woken them all up.

"Winnie Whitten. Has to be."

Jonathan looked around. "Jesus. The lungs on her."

"I know. We're all dreading the day she gets a boyfriend."

Theo turned to his left and saw a familiar figure staggering up the street. "Oh my God . . ."

Even from a distance, David looked terrible. His skin was pale and glistening with sweat. He weaved on his feet like a drunkard.

Hannah sped to his side. "David! What happened?"

He opened his mouth to speak, then doubled over and retched. Hannah barely had a chance to see the blood in his vomit before his eyes rolled back and he fell unconscious to the cobblestone.

A thousand feet above the village, in the bedroom wing of a Quarter Hill mansion, Gemma Sunder watched David on her computer screen. She'd lived through this day nine times already, and knew just the right moment to sneak into Yvonne's kitchen, just the right cherry to poison. Now the smartest of the breachers had been knocked off the chessboard. And that was just her opening move.

Gemma raised a microphone to her smiling lips. "You're up, Harold."

Unbearable images rushed through Amanda's head as she checked David's vitals. His pulse was weak. His breathing was labored. He needed far more help than an ex-nurse could offer him. Of all the nights to be without their healer and teleporters.

She looked to Carrie. "What do you people do in emergencies?"

"We, uh . . ."

Carrie stared at David's bloody mouth and lost her train of thought. She'd been living among the orphans for two weeks now, but she had yet to see their struggles firsthand.

"Carrie!"

"We call the vivery! That's where the turners are."

"Good," Amanda said. "*Call* them."

"Wait!"

The shout came from behind them. In all the commotion, no one had noticed Liam on the lawn. They didn't even know he was back in the underland. He'd been staying topside with the Varnovs while Peter was away.

He raised a gloved finger at the others, then continued his phone call. "Yeah, I don't know. He looks bad." Liam listened and nodded. "All right. We'll get him there."

He closed the handphone and pocketed it. "That was Mother Olga. She's waiting for us."

"Can't she come here?" Hannah asked.

"She moves slowly these days. It'll be easier to go to her. It's not far. Come on."

Amanda crouched to pick up David. Jonathan swooped in from the other side. "I got him."

"It's all right. I can—"

"Amanda, I got him."

Carrie and Amanda watched him guardedly as he hoisted David in his arms. They'd been thinking about him a lot these past few days, ever since Carrie found that ominous message from Future Mia: *Don't trust Jonathan. He's not who he says he is.*

Though Amanda was all but certain that the note was a lie, she didn't want to dismiss it completely. She decided to bottle the issue until Mia returned from Seattle. If anyone could untangle that mess, it was her.

Except now Mia could be coming home to much worse news.

"Come on!" Liam shouted. He dashed down the street as if on springs. Only Heath noticed the soles of his sneakers. They weren't just treadless, they were completely blank.

"That's not . . ." Heath rushed to Theo's side. "Something's not right."

Theo looked at him distractedly. He assumed that Heath was talking about David. "He'll be okay."

"You sure?"

"Yeah. I see it."

Gemma listened to their chatter through directional mics and laughed. Just minutes before, while Theo slept, Suki Godden had crept outside his cottage and flooded him with solis. The man wasn't seeing anything but his own wishful thoughts.

Liam led the others to the village square, then pointed to the top of the clock tower. "She's up there. Come on."

"Up there?" Carrie eyed him suspiciously. "It's nothing but gears and old boxes. Why would Olga—"

"I don't know." Liam opened the front door of the municipal building. "I didn't ask."

"Look, maybe we should just go to the vivery."

"It's on the other side of town," Liam snapped. "You want David to die? You want to be the one who tells Mia?"

Carrie recoiled. "Of course not."

"Then stop wasting time."

Gemma watched their exchange with delight. *Oh Harold. I'd kiss you if you weren't so gross.*

The municipal building was the underland's largest structure: a two-story palace of polished white marble. Every elder, primarch, and head-of-house had an office here, with designated chambers for each government function. For the Gothams, it was the White House, the Capitol, and the Pentagon combined.

Liam escorted the others through the ornate lobby, up the marble steps, and to a spiral staircase at the end of the second floor. The wooden steps twisted all the way up the clock tower, to a cavernous chamber of drywall and brick. One look at the place was enough to confirm Carrie's description. The room contained nothing but junk: withered old boxes in haphazard stacks, inscrutable tools, and long-abandoned gewgaws.

The orphans had to crane their necks to see the tower's true attraction: a massive array of cogs and pinions, all turning in harmony to keep the four clocks running. Catwalk bridges provided easy access to every part of the mechanism.

Olga Varnov stood at the western clock face, her large frame striped in the shadows of gearworks. She wore a fire-red sweatshirt under white denim overalls, an ensemble that Hannah thought made her look vaguely surreal, like an alt-world Santa Claus. If the primarch of the turners had a reason to be up here at two-thirty in the morning, there were no clues to show it.

Mother Olga blanched at the sight of David. "Bring him in. Bring him in. My goodness. What happened?"

Amanda guided him forward on a platform of tempis. "I don't know. I think he was poisoned."

Olga leaned forward and sniffed his lips. "Does he have a taste for the spirits?"

"What?"

"Alcohol," Olga said. "Is he an excessive drinker?"

"*Him?* No. He's a health-obsessed vegan."

"What does it matter?" Hannah asked. "Can't you just heal him?"

Olga scoffed at her. "Reversal isn't magic. It's a complicated process. The more I know about David's sickness, the better chance he'll have."

At last, the stragglers arrived. Theo and Carrie emerged through the stair hatch while Heath shot Olga a leery look from the top steps.

Gemma narrowed her eyes at Heath's pixelated image. "Come on, you weirdo. Get in."

"Come in," Olga told him. "It's okay, child. I don't bite."

He retreated a step, his fists clenched at his sides. "You're not real."

Gemma spat a string of curses. She'd been counting on David's illness to keep the others distracted, but the little Gold was sharp. Now the curtain was falling, the wolves were coming, and the swifter among them was about to get wise.

Hannah looked to a distant corner of the room. While her eyes registered nothing but dim and empty space, her mind detected a highly shifted presence—one she'd felt once before.

"Wait . . ."

Gemma gripped the mic. "*Now!*"

The orphans watched, stupefied, as Liam and Olga melted before their eyes. Their ethereal forms merged into something even more surreal: a spectral blue tiger with a neon-yellow stare. It roared triumphantly at its enemies before exploding into a cloud of mist. The fog quickly expanded to fill every inch of the chamber.

Gemma switched her monitor to thermal view, her knees bouncing with excitement. Harold Herrick had done a man's job. Now it was time for the other kids to play.

Hannah shifted into velocity and took a frantic glance around the room. At 40x, Harold's illusions took on a flickering transparency. She could see five small figures through the mist, all scattered around the periphery. Their eyes glowed in cool blue squares.

Thermal goggles, Hannah guessed. *They can see us.*

Her heart jumped when one of the children moved. The swifter girl was advancing quickly, but not on her.

Oh no . . .

Naomi Byers raced across the room, an eight-inch hunting knife in her grip. Her goggles brought some interesting new colors into her monochromatic world. The walls were beige. Her friends were green. Her enemies were all a ghastly shade of orange. Her best friend, Gemma, had shown her the silhouettes of a tall, skinny woman named Amenada (*was that right?*) and a small, frizzy boy named Heef. Gemma told her to stab those two first because they were tempics and they were dangerous and they had to die.

But Naomi was never good at following directions, and there was an orange girl right in front of her. She had such thin and pretty arms. It'd be a shame not to cut them.

Hannah ran through the fog and got her first look at Naomi: a feral-looking brunette in tattered, mismatched clothes. The child looped around Carrie, then slit both her wrists.

"No!"

If Hannah had been friendly with her fellow swifters, they would have told her that there was no catching Naomi. The child lived in the red upper limits, beyond the reach of even the guild's fastest runners. They had as much luck chasing her as they did raising her.

By the time Hannah reached Carrie, Naomi had moved on to her next victim. She stabbed Jonathan once through the hand, then twice in the stomach. Blood gushed out of him in slow, messy arcs.

Hannah's thoughts went white with rage, and she lost all sense of place.

She could have been anywhere in the universe now. She could have been any-one. She was a floating, nameless entity, and she only had one mission: to stop this twisted little horror before she hurt anyone else.

Screaming, Hannah floored her inner pedal and lunged at Naomi. The girl saw her coming and easily dodged, but now Hannah had her attention. This new orange woman was a soft and clumsy thing, yet she moved faster than the others. Was she one of the slowquicks? Was she a relative?

No matter. The woman was no threat, and Naomi still had a job to do.

Hannah sucked a sharp gasp when the girl raised her knife at Amanda. There was no time to reach her. There was only time to yell.

"You *bitch*! You sick and ugly freak!"

Naomi stopped in place as her temporal converter accelerated Hannah's words. She sounded just like her relatives, the ones who shouted at her and screamed at her and tried to make her slow. Sometimes they drugged Naomi's food and tied her up while she slept. Sometimes they kept her chained for days.

Hannah backstepped toward the stairwell. "Come on, you weasel. *Come at me!*"

Gemma couldn't comprehend her in her accelerated state. But she'd been to the future and back, and she knew exactly what Hannah was planning. Worse, she knew that it would work.

"Don't listen to her," Gemma urged Naomi. "She's trying to draw you out of the room."

Naomi lifted her goggles and squinted at Hannah. In the haze, she looked like her aunt, Fleeta Byers, the worst relative of them all. She'd once caught Naomi in a net trap and beat her bloody with a broomstick. *You butchered my dog, you monster! That dog was sweet and it was loved! What are you?*

"You're nothing," Hannah hissed. "You're less than nothing. You should have slit your own wrists. The world would be better off."

Naomi's face quivered. Her knuckles went white around the hilt of her knife.

Gemma raised her microphone. "No! Kill her sister! Kill the—"

Naomi shrieked and charged after Hannah. The two of them bolted down the wooden steps, past Heath's half-frozen form. His face was contorted in a scream. Larval globs of tempis flew slowly from his fingertips. Hannah prayed that his creatures were strong enough to protect Jonathan and the others. With everyone else either blind or dying, Heath was all that stood against the other four children. This was his war now.

"Here come the wolves," Gemma warned her teammates. "Stay sharp. Act fast. You know what to do."

She leaned back in her chair, fuming. This was her ninth attempt to kill the breachers tonight. With each failed attack, she jumped back in time and readjusted her strategy. Most of the lessons were obvious in retrospect: take out David early, neutralize Theo's foresight, keep the enemies in a blind, tight space, *and don't let the tempics attack.*

"Goddamn it, Naomi . . ."

Gemma was tempted to rewind and start over, but screw it. Let the battle play out. The Pelletiers obviously weren't coming, for one reason or another, which meant that she had all the time in the world to test different strategies. She was curious to see how Heath held up against the lovers on her team, her two strongest fighters.

She leaned forward in her chair. "Come on, Squid and Suki. You can take him."

"*You* come down here and try!" Suki yelled back.

The pretty young blonde had already obliterated four of Heath's wolves with her solic lightning, but it certainly wasn't easy. The beasts were faint blue shapes in her thermal vision, and they had no trouble finding her in the fog. She'd made the mistake of wearing tempic boots as a safeguard against Jonathan's power. Heath could feel them from the other side of the room.

Another wolf jumped at her. Squid cast a fat black tendril and caught the beast in midair.

"Ha! Gotcha!"

None of the Gothams knew what to make of Miguel Xavier Tam, the boy that all the children called Squid. His mortis was like nothing any of them had seen before: a dark, oily substance that corroded everything it touched. In a matter of seconds, it could reduce wood to dust, steel to rust, cats to bone. Tempis was especially vulnerable to the effect. The wolf crumpled in Squid's grip like a hollow egg. Its death filled Heath with greasy nausea.

Together, Squid and Suki made short work of Heath's remaining minions. The moment they finished, they looked up to see more wolves charging at them. A new pack of fourteen.

"Oh *come on*," Squid griped.

Gemma rolled her eyes. "Hit the *boy*."

"We're trying! We can't get close enough!"

"Then wear him down. He can't make those things forever."

Gemma checked on the other breachers, still lost and separated in the fog. Harold was keeping them on edge with a barrage of menacing noises—a roar here, a growl there, a hiss here, a chitter there.

Theo lifted David with a grunt. He realized now—too little, too late—that his precognition had been hobbled. His third eye was just as blind as the other two.

He twirled around in the fog. "Can anyone hear me? Amanda? Hannah?"

A high voice called out to him. "Theo?"

He turned to the left. "Carrie? Is that you?"

"It's me! I'm hurt! Someone cut me!"

"Where are you?"

"I don't know. I can barely see. Oh God, I'm *bleeding*."

Theo's forehead dripped with sweat. He carried David in the direction of her voice. "Okay, I'm coming. Keep talking to me!"

Harold crouched in a corner, with Bo at his side. As Theo shuffled toward them, they had to bite their lips to keep from laughing.

"I'm here!" the tiger yelled in Carrie's voice. "Hurry!"

Gemma shook her head in dark wonder. All it took was a little bit of solis to expose the great "messiah" for the sucker that he was.

"He's coming, Dunk. You better be ready."

Duncan Rall crouched behind a box, his freckled face filled with unease. He hated the vicious glee that Gemma took in these murders. He hated working with nutters like Harold and Naomi. Most of all, he hated the fact that Carrie Bloom got caught up in the violence. She was a kinsman, not a breacher. This whole mission felt wrong.

"They're worldkillers," Gemma impatiently reminded him. "If even one of them lives, we die."

Dunk peered through the mist at Theo. "But what if we're wrong? What if he really is the savior?"

"*Listen* to me. My aunt gave her *life* to save people like you. You think she would have done that if she was only half sure?"

Dunk lowered his head guiltily. "No."

"If you're not man enough to help me—"

"I didn't say that."

"Then do your job and *drop them.*"

Twelve feet away, Amanda was lost in her own quandary. She kneeled on the floor between Jonathan and Carrie, struggling to tear her sweatpants into tourniquets. Even in the fog, she could see the severity of their wounds, the blood that gushed from multiple cuts. They didn't have time for old-school triage. If Amanda wanted to save them both, she'd have to get creative.

She closed her eyes in concentration. Four spindly white arms grew out of her rib cage and ripped through the cloth of her T-shirt. She guided them over Jonathan and Carrie, then pressed down on their skin. Her two patients winced as cool tempis oozed into their wounds, clamping veins, sealing gashes.

Carrie writhed on the floor. A jet of blood sprayed Amanda's arm. She held her down with a fifth tempic appendage. "Carrie, listen to me. *Listen.* You're going to be okay but you have to stay still."

"It *hurts.*"

"I know."

"Please! I don't want to die!"

"You won't die. I won't let you."

A loud, eerie clacking sound filled the area, like the mandibles of a giant insect. Carrie raised her head. "What is that?"

Amanda held her still. "It's just an illusion. It can't hurt us."

"It's cover," Jonathan said. He took a feeble grip of Amanda's wrist. "Get out of here."

His voice came out in a raspy croak. Amanda could feel the weakness of his pulse. Carrie had every chance of surviving her wounds, but Jonathan was slipping fast. Even with the tempis, he had minutes at best before his organs shut down.

"I'll hold them off," he told Amanda. "Just take Carrie and go. Save the others."

Amanda bandaged his hand, her mind hissing curses at Future Mia. She had no idea why the girl had sent that warning about Jonathan. It couldn't have been more wrong.

"Forget it," she told him. "I'm not leaving you behind."

"But Heath—"

"Heath's fine. I can feel his wolves. They're protecting him."

"And Hannah?"

Amanda's heart skipped. Just moments before, she'd caught a lightning-quick glimpse of her sister confronting someone. Hannah was battling another speedster, the most vicious one yet.

"She'll make it," Amanda assured Jonathan. "She always finds a way."

Far above in the Sunder house, Gemma switched her view to the stairwell cameras. The swifter chase had ended four seconds after it started. The results were horrific.

For Hannah, the downward spiral began on a string of ugly truths. They hit her like punches as she fled down the wooden steps.

She's faster than you.

You can't outrun her.

You can't disarm her.

She'll cut you open before you can touch her.

Then she'll run right back upstairs and—

For the twentieth time, her mind replayed the image of Naomi stabbing Jonathan, the fat beads of blood that flew out of him in slow motion. They split apart in mid-trajectory, like the liquid globs in those retro novelty lamps. What were those things called again?

She's faster than you.

Lava lamps. That was it. His death looked like a lava lamp.

He's not dead, a calmer voice insisted. *Amanda will find him. She'll find him and she'll save him. Because she's Amanda and that's what she does.*

Hannah jumped the last step, then hurried onto the marble staircase.

Naomi's aura was getting hotter. The girl was closing the gap with each fractured second.

You can't outrun her. You won't make it to the bottom.

THEN WHAT DO I DO? her inner self screamed. Hannah was a neophyte swifter in bare feet, at least fifty pounds heavier than the sleek young cheetah behind her. But if she had just one second to overpower the girl, one second to—

(kill her)

—snap her leg, then she wouldn't be a threat to anyone.

Yes. That was it. There was a reason Hannah kept beating the more experienced swifters who came after her. It wasn't because she was smarter or more powerful than them. She simply did things they didn't expect.

And what was the last thing that little beast expected?

For me to get behind her.

As Hannah neared the second floor, she prepared for the most dangerous trick of her life. Ten months of swifting had taught her a lot about the mechanics of her talent. She knew that if she pushed her temporis to the limit, she'd have one second of speed advantage over Naomi, one second before her engine died and threw her out of blueshift. She'd have to use that second just right or she was dead.

The moment the pair reached the landing, Hannah opened the floodgates of her power. Her vision turned a muddy gray. Icicles of pain stabbed her skin, her eyes, her every thought. Was this the world that horrid girl lived in? Was this all she knew?

The clock was ticking. Hannah positioned herself for a 150-degree hook spin. It was a move she'd learned in college, under the tutelage of a particularly mean dance instructor. *You'll never get it right,* he'd said after her fifth flub. *You're too fleshy. Too imbalanced.*

Though she nearly broke her ankle doing it, Hannah eventually proved him wrong. She went on to use the maneuver as Velma Kelly in a community production of *Chicago.* Even now, she couldn't plot her steps without hearing the music.

First I'd . . .

She threw all her weight onto her right foot, then made a rubber-band reversal on the landing. She bounced past Naomi in a windy dash.

Then she'd . . .

Naomi looked over her shoulder, her eyes round with surprise. From out of nowhere, this soft, clumsy woman got quick. Hannah had just been in front of her. How did she get behind her?

Then we'd . . .

Hannah paused for the briefest of moments as Naomi skidded to a halt. The girl flailed awkwardly at the edge of the landing. Hannah could tell in an instant that she'd regain her balance. Gravity wanted her to fall so badly. *But I can't do it alone.*

A cold, sick dread washed over Hannah. She knew exactly what would happen if she pushed Naomi, and what would happen if she didn't.

Hannah thought of Jonathan. She charged at Naomi with her last gasp of speed.

And she pushed.

The child flew down the steps at an external velocity of 119 miles an hour. Her first impact broke her hip. Her second one snapped her arm in two places. Her third one cracked her head and drove a skull fragment into her frontal lobe. Everything after that was immaterial, just meat and bone in limp kinesis. She crashed into the wall at the base of the steps, then lay eerily still.

Winded, Hannah joined her on the ground floor and studied the mangled body at her feet. A small eternity seemed to pass before an inner voice dared to state the obvious.

She's dead. You killed her.

A hysterical scream lodged itself in Hannah's throat. She swallowed it down to the deepest depths of her psyche, her nether Neverland. That scream would never, never see the light of day. And it would never, never die.

Hannah straightened her shirt with trembling fingers. She took a last look at Naomi, then started her long, slow journey back up the stairs.

Theo's shoulders throbbed with pain as he carried David across the clock chamber. The boy was a lot heavier than he looked. He also looked worse than he did two minutes ago. Theo could guess now why their enemies took him out first. David would have seen right through the fake Liam and Olga. He could have cleared this fog in a—

Stop.

—heartbeat.

The solis was wearing off. Theo's foresight pricked at him from the corners of his consciousness. He caught a glimpse of the whole tower toppling from his perspective. It was spinning and spinning and . . .

No, not the tower. Him. He was about to fall a very long distance if he didn't—

STOP!

He froze where he stood. The illusive Carrie called at him through the mist. "Theo, where *are* you? I need help!"

His thoughts churned in frantic dilemma. He'd never forgive himself if he let Carrie die, but he couldn't shake his sense of dread. He and David would both fall to their deaths if he took another step.

Gemma squinted at his image on her monitor. "What are you waiting for? Do it!"

Dunk shook his head, quivering. "I-I can't, Gemma. I just . . ."

"Fucking coward! You're no good to anyone!"

She heard a high cry through her speakers. At long last, Heath was succumbing to strain. His tempic wolves had become crude, primitive objects, like tribal carvings. Squid and Suki were able to swat them away with ease. With each victory, they closed the gap on Heath, until they had him backed against a wall.

Suki raised her goggles and sneered at him. "He's finally out of doggies."

"About time," Squid said. "You want to do the honors?"

"No, babe. We should do it together."

Gemma palmed her face. "For the love of God, will somebody please kill someone?"

"On three," said Suki. "One—"

Heath thrust his arm and shot four snowball-size globs at her. She was right about Heath being all out of wolves. Unfortunately for her, he had just enough tempis left for a more intimate attack.

Suki looked down to find four large rats clinging tightly to her body, their eyes as white as their teeth. They climbed her shirt on hooked claws. One of them bit her hard enough to draw blood.

The girl shrieked and flailed in mindless panic. Squid reach out to help her. "Suki!"

They'd only been a couple for nine days, though one could hardly tell from their gooey devotion to each other. On hindsight, Gemma should have seen it coming. No other girl wanted to touch Squid and his icky mortis. No other boy wanted to risk an electric kiss from Suki. The two of them had come to believe, in the drippy way of children, that their love was pure destiny.

But if Squid had known Suki better, he would have realized that approaching her during a power tantrum was the worst possible thing to do. He'd just reached her side when her body erupted in a six-foot globe of crackling electricity. Residual solis spilled in all directions, killing the nearest lumic cameras and clearing the local fog.

While half the people in the clock chamber got their vision back, Gemma lost her view of Suki and Squid. She shook her computer screen. "No, no, no. What's happening? Talk to me!"

The lightning storm subsided. Suki checked her body for rats, then shot a murderous glare at Heath.

"You little bastard! You . . ."

Her left foot brushed against something soft. She looked down to see Squid sprawled on the floor, his eyes wide and unblinking. His handsome face was charred with electrical burns. The tips of his hair still smoldered.

Suki uttered a noise that fell somewhere between a gasp and a scream. "M-Miguel?"

Heath processed the boy's demise, then began a creeping retreat along the wall. Suki turned her crying eyes on him. *"You!"*

A sizzling bolt shot out of her palm and struck Heath in the stomach. He fell to the floor with a cry.

"You killed him!" She shocked Heath again. *"You killed him!"*

In the diminished haze, Jonathan had a clear view of Suki. He raised his bleeding hand at the catwalk bridge, then dropped it at both edges. A pair of one-inch slivers passed intangibly through the floor. Everything in between came down as hard, solid steel.

By the time Suki looked up, it was already too late. The catwalk drove her down to the floor with enough force to shatter half her bones. Only Heath could see her face beneath the wreckage. The impact had torn off her wig and one of her synthetic eyebrows. In death, the girl had become something different—a broken doll, a bad dream, a Martian crashed to Earth.

Amanda looked to the debris. "Jonathan, what—"

A beam of light struck her eyes, burning her corneas. Before Jonathan could react, his head was engulfed in an orb of screaming noise. His eardrums ruptured. He fell unconscious to the floor.

Now it was Harold Herrick's turn to throw a power tantrum. He'd been promised glory and honor, a once-in-a-lifetime chance to prove his worth to the clan.

But Gemma was wrong. She lied. Everything was coming undone.

As always, Bo was there to voice the boy's cruelest thoughts. The tiger circled Harold, its ethereal nails clacking against the floorboards.

"Stupid bastard. This is all your fault. You should've made a better Olga. You should've thrown them all in darkness, not fog."

Harold buried his face in his hands. "I did my best."

"'I did my best,'" Bo mocked. "Your best is shit. When Dad finds out what you did—"

"*No!*"

The walls grew loud with howling white faces. Storm clouds filled the upper chamber and rained tigers down on everyone. They enveloped the room, tormenting friend and foe alike with their mighty roars.

Theo lowered David to the floor. He'd had more than enough of this lunacy. The man behind the tigers was in here somewhere. No, not a man. A *boy*. A very sick and imaginative child. Every Hobbes had a Calvin. Theo just had to find him.

He fumbled for the nearest loose object, a twelve-ounce jar of clock oil, then raised it in his hand. When he'd first met Rebel, the man had shot him without even looking. He'd used his foresight to guide his aim, a trick that Theo had yet to learn.

It's easy, Rebel had explained in more than one prophecy. Theo had glimpsed a surprising number of futures in which the two augurs became allies. In his visions, Rebel took him deep into the warrens and set him up with a pistol, a blindfold, and a wall target.

Clear your head, he'd tell Theo. *Don't let the future ramble. You gotta grab it by the throat and force it down to two answers: hit or miss.*

Theo turned in a slow circle, prodding his foresight every three or four degrees. Rebel's trick was almost brilliant in its simplicity. With each new increment, he felt a prescient twinge of disappointment.

Miss. He turned a tick. *Miss.* He turned again. *Miss.*

The Bos continued their relentless assault. Amanda struggled to hold her tempis while a dozen tiny tigers tore at her concentration. They circled her head on wasp wings, roaring in her face and ears.

Theo turned faster. *Miss. Miss. Miss. Wait!*

He stopped and reversed himself. *Here?*

Just a . . . little . . . bit . . .

He raised his arm an inch, then felt a wave of preemptive satisfaction. *Hit.*

Theo hurled the jar. It arced through fifteen tigers before cracking against Harold's head. His glasses flew off his face. His illusions flickered but persisted.

Furious, Theo yanked a lug wrench from the floor and made a beeline for Harold. The boy cried from the corner, his scalp dripping blood and oil.

"No! Get away!"

He flicked his hand, throwing Theo's senses into chaos. Everything around him swirled in a vortex. His ears were filled with the Doppler sounds of whooshing objects. Theo wobbled on his feet, nauseated and disoriented. He covered his eyes with one hand and raised the wrench with the other.

"Stop it!" he urged Harold. "Don't make me do this!"

The whirlwind continued. Theo clenched his jaw, then let the future guide him one last time.

Hit.

He brought the wrench down on Harold's head. The boy toppled against a stack of old boxes, bringing the whole pile down on him. His illusions vanished in a blink.

Theo, Amanda, and Heath all struggled to get their bearings. Their vision danced with spots. Their ears rang with tinnitus. Only Heath was close enough to the stairwell to see someone approaching.

Hannah returned to the clock chamber and took an anxious look around. She barely had a chance to process the carnage before she noticed the last enemy standing. The red-haired boy was in the peak of health, and he was right behind—

"Theo!"

Theo turned around. If he hadn't been so rattled, he might have seen the fear on Duncan Rall's face. He might have realized that the kid's only plan was surrender. But after six long minutes of bedlam and anguish, Theo's nerves were worn to the barest of threads.

He raised his wrench in reflex. Dunk waved his hand in panic.

Theo dropped through the floorboards, then began his long fall.

THIRTY-ONE

Hannah screamed herself into a new velocity. The clock gears slowed to a six-tieth of their usual speed, turning minute hands to hour hands and hour hands to statues. Dust mites stalled in mid-trajectory. The survivors in the room came to the same doddering standstill.

Only one man moved through the languor, though "moved" wasn't the word on Hannah's mind.

Dropped. He's dropping. Oh my God.

From the moment she first learned about Jonathan's power, she'd lived in constant fear of his death. It could happen at any moment. He could be taking a shower, playing guitar, or simply walking across a room when the wrong wires touched and he fell through the earth for miles. To Hannah, his fatal plunge was more than a nightmare, it was an inevitability, a Chekhov's gun just waiting to be fired.

Except now that death was happening to someone else she loved. Someone the whole world needed.

"Theo!"

She hadn't realized until now that she'd jumped into blueshift. She thought her power had burned out after the fight with Naomi, yet here she was at the cusp of 60x. She was fast enough to catch the surprise in Theo's eyes as they sank through the floor. The wood was swallowing him inch by inch, like quicksand.

Hannah wrung her hands, her mind lost in frantic calculation. She had time, time, time, and speed. She had the time and speed to race him down the tower. But how she could catch him if he was intangible? How could she break his fall without—

Tempis.

Yes. Of course. Tempis was the only force in the universe that could stop a dropped object. Peter had told her about the one Gotham with Jonathan's power, a twelve-year-old boy who'd spent every minute of his life on safety barriers. He walked in tempic boots and slept on tempic beds and . . .

Hannah did a double-take at Dunk. *Holy shit. That's him.*

She sped across the room and shoved him. His body hit the wall with a loud, sickening *crack*. Hannah had no idea what she broke in him. She didn't care. She didn't care if he lived or died as long as no one else got dropped.

Oh God. Theo.

His last tufts of hair disappeared through the floorboards. Hannah bounced her gaze between Amanda and Heath. One of them would have to come downstairs with her, but neither of them looked like they were in any condition to help. Amanda's eyes were squinted and full of tears, as if someone had poked them both with sticks. Worse, her tempis was keeping pressure on Jonathan's and Carrie's wounds. There was no way to move her without risking their lives.

It had to be Heath.

Hannah rushed toward him, her arms curled into hooks. She had to pick him up in a way that didn't break his bones or rift him, and she had to do it fast.

She de-shifted three feet in front of Heath, scooped him up, then triggered her power again. The maneuver went far less smoothly than she'd hoped. In her haste, she'd kneed his thigh and scraped his neck. Worse, she'd taken too long to get a stable grip on him. Theo must have dropped halfway to hell by now.

No. It's not too late.

Heath bucked in Hannah's arms as she carried him down the stairwell. She hoisted him by the buttocks, his head forced over her shoulder.

"What are you doing? Put me down!"

"Just hold on," Hannah said. "Keep your arms and legs close to me."

Her heart pounded as she carried Heath down the steps. If she tripped and fell at this speed, they were both goners. She didn't have to wonder what their corpses would look like. The ghastly image of Naomi had been seared onto her psyche like a cattle brand.

From the desperate way he clung to Hannah, Heath clearly understood the risks as well. "Why are you doing this?"

"You didn't see it?"

"See what?"

"Theo. He got dropped."

Heath's muscles turned to stone. He pulled back to look at Hannah. "He can't die. He's the savior."

"I know. That's why I need you. You have to make something to catch him. A wolf, an ape, *anything*."

"I . . . can't."

"What?"

"I can't! That girl, she hit me with her lightning. Her lightning kills tempis."

"What are you talking about?"

Heath bowed his head. "She killed the tempis in me."

Hannah's stomach twisted. Oily thoughts spilled over her landscape, gumming her works, painting her whole world black.

It's over. I failed.

She racked her mind, searching for some trick, cheat, or miracle that would help her save Theo. Maybe there was a way to jumpstart Heath's tempis. Or maybe—

Hannah . . .

Tears rolled her down her cheeks. She clutched Heath's shirt in bunches. *No. No.*

He's gone.

A boyfriend once told her that a shark could keep swimming even after it died. Their reflexes could carry them through the water, sometimes for miles. Skeptical, Hannah had bet him a steak dinner that he couldn't find scientific evidence to back up his claim. He couldn't.

Now, a lifetime later, she'd become a living embodiment of the myth. She was a dead thing in motion, an empty husk running purely on impulse. She could barely feel the stairs under her feet. She couldn't hear Heath, even with his mouth at her ear.

"Hannah?"

A cold, empty bleakness overtook her, ballooning from her thoughts until it swallowed all of creation. She didn't know why she was surprised to find life so cruel. People died. Worlds died. Children fell down stairwells.

"Hannah, what do we do?"

And good men plunged screaming into darkness, along with all hope for the future.

At long last, Hannah understood the sickness inside Evan Rander, the black and festering nihilism that kept him swimming long after he lost the will to live.

She had no idea that at that very moment, on the other side of the country, Evan was discussing the sickness inside her.

"I can sum up her problem in two words: willful ignorance."

Mia crossed her arms, her thorny gaze aimed out the passenger window. Though Evan insisted that she wasn't his prisoner, he'd already flown the cab five times around the Via Fortuna skyway, past the same five-mile loop of casinos. He was keeping her in motion so she couldn't escape by portal, but what did he want with her? All he'd done so far was make small talk and complain about their fellow Silvers.

"It's not entirely Hannah's fault," Evan said. "Her mom taught her to believe that she's the center of the universe, and she had guy after guy eating out of her hand. Life's nothing but a breeze for the fair of face and large of rack. They don't want us to know that, but it's true."

Mia glowered at him. Her brother Bobby had spouted the same caveman bullshit until a very smart girlfriend made him read a few books. Clearly Evan had yet to find such a partner.

"But now Hannah has real problems," he continued. "The universe has made it damn clear that she's just a bit player in this show, barely an extra. And she's in for the same bad ending as the rest of us."

He raised a dramatic finger. "But she *believes*, oh yes! She still believes that everything will work out for her. And she'll grasp at any straw, no matter how flimsy, to give herself hope. Willful ignorance. She's got it in spades. Not that you and the others are much better."

A truck swooped down from the upper lane, forcing Evan to brake. He honked his horn. The driver replied with an obscene gesture.

Mia watched Evan anxiously as he memorized the license plate number. She feared the trucker would be dead by the end of the week, or maybe even the end of *last* week. Evan wasn't limited by the normal constraints of time. He bounced up and down the strings like a yo-yo, and he carried his grudges with him.

"You know how frustrating it is to watch you people do the same things over and over again?" he asked Mia. "Go there, fight that, save him, fetch that. You jump from one pointless drama to another. You don't even stop to question the script."

Mia might have challenged Evan if she wasn't so afraid of him. Her ears still rang from his point-blank gunshot. The blood of his victim was still drying in her hair.

"There's a Silver you don't know," he told her. "Natalie Tipton-Elder. She was with us in San Diego when everything went cuckoo. Came crashing into this world, just like us. The reason I know her and you don't—"

—*is because you killed her,* Mia guessed.

"—is because she panicked and ran up the stairs of her building. Why the Pelletiers didn't warn her, I don't know. She must have been ten floors up when the big switcheroo happened. Poor girl dropped like a stone."

Mia became lost in bad memories. She'd suffered the opposite problem that day. She went to the basement of her house and got buried alive.

"Whenever I start over, I make a point of seeing her," Evan said. "First person I visit. She's always laying flat on the same patch of park, this cute little blonde with a broken back and a freaked-out look. 'Oh God. Where am I? What happened? Call an ambulance! Please!'"

Mia looked at Evan suspiciously. "She's alive?"

"She is when I find her. She hangs on for a good five minutes. Well, not a *good* five minutes."

"But you never call for help."

"Oh, I've tried. Lots of times. Believe me, I'd love to save her, just to mix things up." He shrugged. "But she's a small woman in a big park. The ambulance never finds her in time."

A shiver ran up Mia's back. Talking to Evan was like seeing the ugly side of existence. There was no light, no hope. Worst of all, he seemed to thrive in the darkness.

"But at least she never dies alone," he said. "I chat her up just to pass the time. Got her whole life story in pieces. Of course she always has the same questions for me. 'Where am I? What happened? Why is this happening to me?'"

He clucked his tongue. "Ah, Natalie, Natalie. She never even has time for the short answer."

Mia closed her eyes in a sickened wince. "Why are you telling me this?"

"Because that's all you guys are, just a drawn-out version of her. You flail, you cry, you ask the same questions. You spend your whole life waiting for an ambulance that never comes."

The cab fell silent. Evan shook a finger at Mia. "It's all right. You'll catch on. The others won't, but you will. That's what I like about you."

He gave her a teasing smile. "Well, Future You."

Mia flinched when Evan reached over her thigh and pulled a small bag of candies from the glove box.

"But Hannah? She never stops believing. Never stops to think it through. And why would she? She has everything she needs here. Romance and action and drama galore. You've heard that kick in her voice whenever something exciting happens. 'Oh no! The Deps took Amanda! We have to save her!' 'Oh no! Ioni wants me to meet a tall, handsome stranger! I mustn't fall in love!'"

Evan unwrapped a hard caramel. "Don't let her fool you. She's living the life she always wanted."

He stuffed the candy into his mouth, then crunched it to shards. "This world was made for Hannah Given."

A spark of life returned to her thoughts, a strange new notion that flickered in the darkness. As she continued down the stairs with Heath in her arms, Hannah replayed the last words she heard from him.

That girl, she hit me with her lightning. Her lightning kills tempis.

Except that wasn't true.

She killed the tempis in me.

No. Lightning didn't kill tempis. Solis did. If Heath was hit by solis—

"There he is!" he yelled.

Hannah snapped out of her daze and looked around. "What?"

"Down there!"

She peered over the railing and gasped at the sight of Theo. He was falling back-first through the lowest flight of stairs, toward a sloped and shady alcove. That nook would be the last place to catch him. After that . . .

A queasy dread washed over Hannah. She couldn't bear the thought of Theo drowning in stone, dying alone and afraid in the bowels of the earth.

But something had changed. When Hannah first jumped into blueshift, Theo had been falling at the pace of a creaky old elevator. Now he was a mere trifle in gravity's hand—a feather, a spore, a half-filled balloon. Hannah must have been shifted at 100x, but that was impossible. She should have been in agony. How the hell was she doing this?

Maybe she wasn't. The more Hannah thought about it, the more she felt an external sense of momentum, as if a giant invisible hand was pushing from behind. Someone powerful was giving her speed.

Giving her *time*.

Hannah slowed down to a trot. "What are you doing?" Heath asked.

Her chalkboard filled with new equations. Her foot speed didn't matter anymore. She could walk to the bottom and still beat Theo.

No, the real race was happening elsewhere now. It was happening inside Heath.

"You'll get it back," Hannah told him. "I've never been hit with lightning but I've been hit with solis. It only lasts a couple of minutes. You'll get the tempis back."

Heath nervously checked on Theo. "We don't have time."

"I'll make the time," Hannah said. "You just make the tempis."

She drew a deep breath, then pushed her power to a dangerous extreme. Hot needles of pain pricked every corner of her mind as the environment around her shed its final flecks of color. She peeked one eye open and saw Theo sinking through the air with all the speed of a sunset.

Heath marveled at his changed surroundings. The world around him swirled with visual artifacts—dots and lines and hazy lights, all the peculiar things one sees on the inside of their eyelids.

"How are you doing this?"

His voice echoed off invisible walls. Hannah reeled to think that it was the sound barrier.

"I don't know," she lied. She had little doubt that there was a Pelletier on the other side of that question, but she didn't care. To save Theo, she'd kiss the devil himself.

Hannah stepped off the final stair, carefully leaping over Naomi's body. The girl's blood-flecked knife had slid across the floor, all the way to the alcove where Theo's fate would be decided. Even at this speed, Hannah guessed that they had less than forty seconds. There was nothing else she could do. This was as far as time would bend.

"Heath . . ."

"I'm trying," he insisted. "I've been trying."

"Just let me know when you're ready."

Heath looked over Hannah's shoulder and studied the savage, ugly girl on the floor. "Rose Tyler."

Hannah turned her head. "What? Is that her name?"

"It's the name of my wolf, the bad one who doesn't listen to me."

He kept his somber eyes on Naomi. "If Rose was a girl, she'd look just like that."

Hannah stayed quiet. She didn't have the strength to hate Naomi anymore. She only hated the people who made her, the ones who didn't love her enough.

"What happened?" Heath asked.

Hannah puffed a loud sigh before answering. "I pushed her."

If Heath had any reaction, he hid it deep inside of him. Eight seconds passed before he spoke again.

"I made the lightning girl kill a friend of hers. I didn't mean for it to happen."

Tears welled up in Hannah's eyes. "It's not your fault."

"I just didn't want to die."

Hannah squeezed him tight, her face buried in his shoulder. She could have hugged him like this for hours, with the whole world hushed and her thoughts crystal clear. For once in her life, the voices in her head had fallen into perfect harmony. They sang like a choir—a song of hope, a song of pain, a song of rage and determination. She knew she was powerless to stop the universe from taking the people she loved, but there was one thing she refused to accept. Good people like Theo don't die like this. They don't die like this. They don't—

"—go to hell."

Heath looked up. "What?"

She studied the shrinking gap between Theo and the floor. They weren't going to make it. They didn't have enough time.

"Good people don't go to hell," Hannah said. "That's not the way it works. If Amanda was here . . ."

Her teeth clenched. She pushed against the wall of her power. It resisted with savage ferocity, as if every force of nature had banded together against her.

"If Amanda was here, she would not . . ."

Hannah's mind screamed with pain. Blood trickled from her ears.

". . . let it . . ."

Heath could feel Hannah's heartbeat against his chest. It was speeding up.

". . . *happen!*"

The lobby rippled all around them as time once again slowed down. Hannah watched Theo through bloodshot eyes. He had all but stopped in midair, a frozen scream on his face. From Theo's perspective, he'd only been falling for two and a half seconds, more than enough time for him to realize what was happening, enough for a thousand frightened thoughts.

"He sees us," Hannah said. "He knows we're here."

Heath studied him anxiously. "You think he sees what'll happen?"

"I don't know, sweetie. All I can tell you is that I lived seventeen minutes on this world without knowing him, and they weren't good ones. I don't even care that the whole planet needs him."

She closed her eyes and bowed her head. "I need him."

Heath looked up and saw a small, glassy orb affixed to the wall. A camera. The mastermind behind the attack was still watching them from a distance. Heath glared at her through the lens.

"Turn me around," he said. "I'm ready."

THIRTY-TWO

Gemma tore up her bedroom in a shrieking tantrum. Lamps crashed. Chairs toppled. Knickknacks went flying in every direction. Her Lakshmi idol crashed straight through the wall of her aquarium, drenching her feet and sending seventeen fish to an early death. For all of Gemma's hard-earned experience, the dozens of years she'd lived and relived, a child's heart still beat inside of her. She still cried like a ten-year-old, sulked like a ten-year-old, railed and wailed and flailed like a ten-year-old.

Now she was starting to fear that she waged her wars like a ten-year-old. Moments before her screaming fit, her camera system had come back online and revealed the sorry state of affairs in the clock tower. All of her soldiers were either dead or dying, yet the breachers still clung to life. Even the one who got dropped managed to beat the reaper, with some last-second help from his friends.

Gemma had watched Theo remotely as he crashed onto the backs of six decumbent wolves. The impact alone should have been enough to kill him, yet Gemma could see him writhing on the tempis—broken, but very much alive.

"Fuck! Fuck! *Fuck!*"

By the time the last doomed fish stopped flopping on the carpet, Gemma had become calm enough to ponder her next steps. She couldn't stand this timeline one second longer, but she couldn't bear the thought of another defeat. No, it was time to change things up, jump back two weeks and build a whole new army. No scatterbrains like Naomi. No cowards like Dunk. Next time, she'd have a stronger team and a smarter plan. And she'd be sure as hell to kill Heath first.

She steadied herself with a deep, cleansing breath, then prepared her mind for travel. All it took was an ounce of thought to turn the wheels of time the other way and send her consciousness to the past—a tingly sensation, like swimming upstream in a river of soda.

Except Gemma didn't feel any bubbles this time. Baffled, she opened her eyes to find herself right where she was before—same room, same mess, same fish on the rug. Something had kept her rooted in the present.

"What—"

She turned her head and jumped at the intruder in the room: a tall, willowy brunette in a black-pattern shift dress. She sat on the edge of Gemma's bed, her red lips curled in a scowl.

"You."

Gemma screamed and ran for the door. She'd never had the displeasure of meeting Esis before, but she'd seen enough of her on camera. The woman was a maniac, a *butcher*. And now she was here.

A tempic hand blocked the door before Gemma could reach it. She barely had a chance to turn around before a cool white tendril looped around her, again and again, until every inch of her was wrapped like spider's prey.

Esis pulled Gemma into her arms and caressed her squealing, wriggling form. "Shhhhh. Hush, girl."

She pressed a silver coin to the tempis, sending Gemma's body into a shockingly pleasant stasis. Her muscles relaxed. Her breathing and heartbeat stabilized. Her eyes fell half closed, even while her thoughts kept screaming in terror.

Esis dissolved the tempis and cradled Gemma on her lap. "There. Much nicer. And much safer for you, I'd wager. I'm very, very angry with you, child. A wrong word, a wrong gesture . . . I cringe to think what I might do."

The blood drained from Gemma's face. Esis raked her hair with slow, gentle fingers.

"You've caused extraordinary damage tonight. More than you realize. I can't tell if it was skill, luck, or something more sinister. Tell me, were you counseled? Perhaps visited in the night by the Lady Deschane?"

Gemma's brow creased. She had no idea who Esis was talking about.

"You acted alone," Esis mused. "Remarkable. Such a clever girl, yet so blind. Even if your plan had merit, and I assure you it doesn't, you fail to account for our many other subjects. We have dozens of these so-called 'breachers' around the planet. How do you expect to kill them if you can't find them? There are even Silvers you don't know about."

Esis studied a framed photo on the desk, a smiling portrait of Gemma and Ivy. "But then I suppose this isn't about saving the world anymore, is it?"

Tears spilled from Gemma's eyes. Esis wiped them clean. Her voice became soft and tender, as if she was reading a bedtime story.

"I'm well aware of the harm my family has caused. If we could tread this world lightly, without a ripple of consequence, we would. But we have no choice but to go where the strings take us. Our work is too important to fail."

Her black eyes dawdled around the fish on the floor, all the helpless victims of Gemma's rage.

"Death is a scourge, even in my era. We've conquered illness, mastered time, yet the beast always finds a way to take us. It tortures us with slow and painful degradations."

She narrowed her eyes at her quivering fingers. "But I've seen the future. I know the victory that awaits. This world will be death's final feast, I assure you of that."

Gemma struggled to force a plea up her throat. Esis saw her concern and waved it off.

"Calm yourself, little one. I've lost all desire to kill you. You see what silence buys you? If only Trillinger would learn."

Esis chewed her lip in contemplation. "Still, we can't have you causing more trouble now, can we?"

She pressed a finger to Gemma's brow. "*Zhu'anté.*"

Gemma convulsed in Esis's lap. Her skin tingled with the kiss of a billion bubbles. She could feel her consciousness moving with dizzying speed, backward and backward, until everything went white.

By the time Gemma opened her eyes again, she felt like she'd been asleep for years. Her thoughts were hazy, her limbs were numb. She could barely remember her own name.

Where . . . who . . . ?

She looked around but couldn't see much beyond a low curtain barrier. The fabric curved all around her, as if she were laid out flat in an open casket. She spied patches of light on an off-white ceiling. It was all so blurry. Everything looked so far away.

"Wuh?"

Esis suddenly eclipsed her view from above, looking exactly the same as she did before. No, not the same. She was bigger now. She looked big enough to wear Gemma as a hat.

"Don't speak," said Esis. "Your neural pathways are unformed. But you'll learn in time, as you've done before. Soon, you'll find all of this quite familiar."

Gemma turned her head. A naked brown arm was flopping clumsily on a cotton blanket. She was looking at her own hand, except it was so short, so stubby, so . . .

Her eyes bulged. *No. Oh God, no.*

"You've been given a fresh start," Esis told her. "Use it wisely. Reflect on your mistakes and choose better paths. Perhaps you'll find some happiness this time."

She gripped the edge of Gemma's bassinet and flashed her a crooked smile. "Perhaps not."

Esis waved a temporal portal into the air, creating a sucking wind that ruffled the drapes and sent the loose papers in the room flying. She summoned a coat of yellow light around her body, then stepped into the rift.

Soon the portal closed and the wind quickly dissipated, leaving no one the wiser to Esis's visit. There in the nursery—ten years, nine months, and seventeen days ago—three newborn Gothams dawdled in their cribs. One of them slept. One of them gurgled. And one of them screamed.

Theo paced the floor of the lobby, his sandals smacking against the tile with loud, echoing *clop*s. Though he had at least a dozen bigger concerns at the moment, he couldn't help but wonder why his shoes were making noise. Here in the God's Eye, in the space between moments, his body was just a psychic visualization. He could appear as anything he wanted—a lobster, a Shriner, Amanda in a sombrero. But as always, he came as Just Plain Theo, in his Just Plain Theo clothes. Apparently his subconscious had added some realism for effect. His sandals clopped. His feet kicked up dust. His body even cast a shadow.

He turned around and checked the clock on the wall, still stuck at 2:34 and 28 seconds. Everything around him was suspended in still-frame, including his real body. The other Theo lay face-up beneath a stairwell, his broken frame sprawled on a bed of tempic wolves. His arms were bent at unnatural angles. His left ankle was snapped so badly that Theo could see the bone. God only knew the internal damage he was suffering. From the way things looked, he probably wouldn't live to see 2:35.

"Shit. *Shit!*"

Hannah and Heath crouched near his body, their expressions frozen in fear. Clearly they had a dim view of Theo's prospects as well. And why wouldn't they? That freckle-faced kid had gotten him good. He would have dropped Theo all the way to Hades if Hannah and Heath hadn't acted quickly.

But was he truly saved?

"Okay . . ." He took a deep breath through nonexistent lungs, then resumed his fitful pacing. "This isn't over. I'm not dead. Think. *Think . . .*"

He looked around the lobby. Every wall and surface was covered in a sheath of mist, the usual God's Eye dressings. Normally there would be twinkling lights in the fringes, each one the start of a different future. But Theo couldn't see a single one now. That wasn't a good sign.

The fog on the northern wall darkened. Tendrils of mist swirled in a stormy vortex. Theo had seen that effect once before, when a certain Pelletier came to visit him in the God's Eye. He couldn't think of anyone he wanted to see less right now.

Theo took a nervous step forward. "Azral?"

To his surprise, a woman emerged from the mist, a petite young blonde in a lily-white sundress. If she was a Gotham, then Theo had never seen her before. And if she was a Pelletier . . . no, she was far too cute to be part of that brood. But who knew? Maybe Azral had a bubbly niece with an equally weird name. Jezral. Or Sepsis.

It wasn't until she smiled at Theo that he finally recognized her. Of course. He should have known her right away, even with the new hairstyle. He should have checked her wrist and counted the watches.

"You."

Ioni stopped in her tracks, stone-faced. "That's one way to greet me."

"You think I'd be happy to see you?"

"Hang on."

"You're the one who—"

"I said *hang on*."

Ioni crouched in the alcove, her lower half disappearing inside Heath's tempic wolves. She leaned in close to Hannah and stared intently into her eyes.

"What are you doing?" Theo asked.

"Diagnosing." She rose to her feet again. "Shit on ice."

"What?"

"What do you mean 'what'? Did you even look at her?"

Theo approached Hannah and studied her more closely. Her eyes were red with burst vessels. A trickle of blood escaped her left ear.

"Jesus. What happened to her?"

"Power strain," Ioni said. "I pushed her too hard."

"What are you talking about?"

"When you got dropped, she didn't have an ounce of temporis left in her. She shot her wad fighting that little monster."

Ioni pointed to the corpse at the base of the stairwell, a ferocious-looking girl who'd taken a nasty spill. Theo had been so wrapped up in his own crisis that he hadn't even noticed Naomi.

"Hannah couldn't save you," Ioni explained to him. "Not on her own. So I gave her a boost and she used it beautifully."

"But?"

"But she's still a first-generation swifter. Her body can't . . ." Ioni closed her eyes and sighed. "There'll be damage."

"What kind of damage?"

"Headaches. Bad ones. Whenever she goes into blueshift."

"How long before it gets better?"

"It won't."

Theo retreated from the stairwell. "Goddamn you."

"It's a small price to save you. Hannah would agree."

"*Save* me? This is your fault. You're the one who told Rebel to kill us." He gestured at Naomi. "You're the reason any of these people want us dead!"

Ioni followed him across the lobby, her high heels clacking against the marble floor. Theo didn't know if it was her subconscious or his that was adding the noise. They were both specters here.

She waved her arm and summoned a red felt pool table. The balls were already racked in a triangle.

Theo eyed her strangely. "What are you doing now?"

"Making trouble."

"Trouble?"

"Right here in River City."

Ioni saw his bemusement and pouted. "Hannah would have gotten that."

"I got the reference." He narrowed his eyes at her. "You're from my world."

"If you mean Earth—"

"You know what I mean."

"I'm from your timeline," Ioni admitted. "But not your time."

She crossed to the other side of the pool table. "And I never told Rebel to kill you. Not in those words."

"So what did you tell him?"

Ioni materialized a cue stick in each hand. She held one out to Theo. "Come on. Eight ball. Old-world rules. We're going to be here a while. Might as well have some fun."

"Go to hell."

"Fine. I'll play myself."

She threw a cue stick across the table. A second Ioni appeared out of nowhere and caught it. The clone had copper-red hair and wore a crimson sundress. While the blonde lined up her breaking shot, the redhead blew a childish raspberry at Theo.

He kept his surly gaze on the original Ioni. "What exactly did you say to Rebel?"

She hit the cue ball at the 1 and sent all the others scattering. Only the 4 ball rolled into a pocket.

Ioni smiled at her doppelgänger. "Guess I'm solids."

The redhead jerked her thumb at Theo. "He asked you a question."

"You're taking *his* side?"

"I'm a ginger. We're complex."

Ioni lined up her shot at the 3 ball. Her expression turned grim. "I told Rebel this world couldn't live as long as you breachers were on it."

Theo blinked at her, dumbfounded. "How did you expect him to take that?"

"Exactly the way he took it."

"Why?"

"Aren't you going to ask me if it's true?"

"I wouldn't trust your answer."

"Then why would you trust my 'why'?"

The 3 ball stopped just shy of a side pocket. As Red Ioni began her turn, White Ioni leaned on her cue stick and cast a jaded look at Theo.

"Let me ask you something. Last year, when you and your friends first got to New York, you guys had a really shitty day. The Gothams, the Deps, the Pelletiers, Evan Rander, they all converged on you in the same office building. You remember that?"

Theo narrowed his eyes. "Of course I do. What about it?"

"Four of you escaped through an old steam tunnel. Hannah and Amanda got left behind. Zack didn't want to leave without them, but you made him. You insisted on it."

"I had no choice."

"You knew damn well that the sisters were suffering."

"We *had* to go."

"Why?"

"It was the only way to save them," Theo said. "I knew they'd die if we didn't get to Peter."

"Zack didn't see it that way."

"Zack didn't see the strings."

Theo stopped in his tracks. He looked to Ioni in horror. "Wait a second. You can't possibly . . ."

She crossed her arms with a vindictive sneer. "Now you're getting it."

"You're drawing a parallel?"

"I'm explaining the 'why.'"

Theo plopped down on a couch, stammering. "You sent Rebel to kill us in order to *save* us? Is that what you're telling me?"

"She's telling you what you already know," said Red Ioni. "The future's a tricky business. It's never a straight line. It's always—"

She knocked the cue ball to the far side of the table. It cut a triangular path around a tight cluster of solids, then deftly sank the 10.

"—bank shots."

Theo stared at Ioni in disbelief. She jerked a lazy shrug. "Sometimes you have to make things worse to make them better. You know this. You're not new to the game."

"The game."

Ioni frowned. "Figuratively speaking."

"No, no." Theo leapt to his feet and approached the table. His voice dripped with venom. "A game. That's perfect. Now I really understand."

"Look—"

"Since you're such a big fan of visual aids, let me show you something."

He picked up the 6 ball and chucked it over his shoulder. "That was Zack's brother, the one Rebel killed."

He moved down the table and tossed five more balls. "Those were the rest of Heath and Jonathan's friends. All dead now, thanks to you."

The Ionis sighed in unison. "Theo . . ."

He swept the remaining billiards to the floor. "That was Ivy Sunder and every other Gotham who got killed in your war."

"Theo!"

He pointed at Naomi. "That was a *child* who died in your game!"

The pool table vanished, along with both Ionis. Theo threw his puzzled gaze around the lobby. "Hello?"

After ten seconds of silence, he waved her off and stretched out on the sofa. *Good riddance.*

Theo supposed he had all the time in the world to figure out his next move. He certainly wasn't eager to jump back into that mangled wreck of a body. Maybe if he held on long enough, his friends could get him to the vivery and have the real Mother Olga reverse him back to full health. She'd certainly have her work cut out for her tonight, between David and Carrie and Jonathan and—

"You think I'm doing this for fun?"

Theo sat up and looked around. Ioni had complained right in his ear but he couldn't see her. She was nothing but a disembodied voice.

"You think I like seeing good people die?"

He once again heard the *clip-clop* of wooden heels. The sound seemed to be coming from everywhere and nowhere.

"I love Rebel. He's one of my favorite people on this world, and I betrayed

him. I set him on a path that cost him everything. You think that makes me feel good?"

The footsteps stopped. A heavy sigh filled the lobby.

"The worst part is that he won't even live to see the fruits of his sacrifice. He'll die without knowing why he suffered."

"Why *did* he suffer?" Theo asked her. "Why did we have to suffer him?"

"You still don't see it."

"See what?"

"Me."

She appeared out of nothingness and straddled him on the couch, a new Ioni. This one had jet-black hair and a charcoal-colored sundress. Her eyes were slathered in shadowy cosmetics, making her wrath all the more fearsome. This Ioni was clearly in no mood for games.

Theo struggled beneath her, but he couldn't move. Ioni pressed him down with the weight of an elephant.

"You piss me off, Theo. You're the strongest augur of your age, but you're so damn myopic. You think this is all about you and your friends."

"Then tell me! Tell me what it's about!"

"Oh, I'll do better than that. Brace yourself."

"For what?"

A smile teased the corners of her lips. "A visual aid."

She arched her back and exploded into a million glowing spores. They swarmed inside Theo, invading him through his mouth and nostrils, his ears, even his pupils. His eyeballs flared like tiny suns. He screamed with affliction as thousands of images flooded his consciousness at once. The sensation was overwhelming, *nauseating*. He felt like he'd been dropped all over again.

Once the initial shock passed, Theo found himself back on an old, familiar voyage. He was flying forward through time, toward the great white void at the end of all strings. The journey felt the same as it ever did—same sights, same sounds, same sickening dread.

But then the path abruptly curved and Theo found himself in strange territory. He saw new faces mixed in with the old: orphans and Gothams and government agents, a strong-looking clan of dark-skinned timebenders. They were all fighting together on the streets of an abandoned city, against a fast-moving army that Theo could barely see. There was a massive explosion. A Cataclysm.

And then everything changed.

The new world looked almost suspiciously like the old one. No flying traffic, no lumic billboards, no tempic barriers as far as the eye could see. Food lines stretched for city blocks, past decrepit buildings and long-shuttered stores. The country was suffering a new Great Depression, but how did it happen?

Theo watched in fast-forward as the situation improved. The cities looked cleaner. The suburbs looked greener. The land was almost beginning to resemble Altamerica again, yet Theo didn't see a single face he recognized. There was no one even remotely familiar to him except—

Oh my God.

—one woman. Her skin was wrinkled and her hair was white, but Theo knew those eyes anywhere.

Melissa Masaad was as beautiful as ever. And she was very, very old.

He had no idea how far he'd traveled. He must have shot decades past the four-year mark, miles beyond the apocalypse. Except there had been no apocalypse. The danger was gone, and the strings of time stretched out to infinity. This world had more future than Theo had ever—

"Stop."

He snapped out of his travels and found himself back in the lobby, back on the couch, still pressed beneath the weight of Ioni. She'd reverted to her bleached blond state, and had become so light that Theo could have pushed her to the floor. Instead he gripped her arms and shook them desperately.

"Bring it back! Bring it back!"

"I can't."

"Please! I need to see more!"

Ioni shook her head softly. "It's still a fragile string. I can't show you more without breaking it."

She pulled a handkerchief out of thin air and dabbed the tears from his eyes. "This is the game I'm playing, Theo. These are the stakes I'm playing for. Billions of people with infinite futures. We're the only hope they have."

Theo ran his fingers down the side of her face, awestruck, oblivious to propriety. Ioni smiled patiently as his hands moved down her arms, her ribs, her narrow hips. There was nothing rude about the way he explored her. He touched her like a boy who had just discovered his birth mother.

"Who are you?" he asked, his voice a trembling whisper.

"I'm Ioni Anata T'llari Deschane. I have forty-four titles and not a damn one would make sense to you. I'm not from this Earth, but I've lived here a long time. This is my home, and I intend to save it."

She climbed off his lap and joined him on the sofa. They sat shoulder to shoulder, their ethereal legs propped up on an ottoman.

"It hasn't been easy," Ioni said. "I'm making a thousand-point bank shot on a very busy table, and there are consequences at every turn. A lot more lives will be ruined before this is over, Theo. A lot more people will die."

"Why didn't you just tell us what you were doing?"

"Why didn't you tell Zack that Evan was torturing Amanda?"

Theo nodded knowingly. "Because he would have gone back for her."

"And he would have died," Ioni said. "It's a lonely road we travel, my dear. We lie to the people we love. We manipulate them. And sometimes, when there's no other choice, we throw them to the wolves. We do horrible things for the greater good. It doesn't make it any easier."

Theo looked at Naomi's corpse. "But why set us against the Gothams? How does that serve the greater good?"

Ioni waved two swords into the air. One was a broad blade, as thick and rugged as iron. The other was a rapier—sleek and shiny, like silver.

"Human will is a stubborn force," she explained. "Sometimes dense, often inflexible. I needed your people and Rebel's people to come together as one, but I knew that words wouldn't do it. Your alliance would never last on promises and handshakes. You needed something stronger."

The two blades melted, then merged together, resolidifying into a formidable-looking scimitar.

"You needed fire."

Theo scowled at her. "You think we're happily bonded now?"

"Happily? No. But you are bonded. It may not seem like it, but this was your very last fight with the Gothams. They'll be your allies now till the bitter end."

She vanquished the scimitar, then folded her hands on her stomach. "The string just got a whole lot stronger tonight."

Theo studied Hannah from a distance. He could barely imagine the hell she had gone through, all the quick and stressful decisions she'd been forced to make. The Hannah of last year would have never survived this battle. The Hannah of next year wouldn't have broken a sweat. Like everyone else in the group, she was a blade forged in fire, folded and folded into an increasingly powerful weapon. Maybe that was also by Ioni's design.

"It's bullshit," he muttered at the floor.

"What is?"

"All that talk about me being the messiah." He looked to Ioni. "It's been you all along."

Her hair and dress turned red before his eyes. She straddled Theo and grabbed him by the collar. "I don't ever want to hear that word from you again. You understand me?"

Theo struggled in her grip. "What are you doing?"

"'Messiah' is a stupid term that only stupid people use. Ask me why."

"Why?"

"Causality," she said. "Everything we do, everything we say, even the things we *think* make ripples in time. Just look at all the stuff that happened in the last six minutes. Hannah saved Amanda, Amanda saved Jonathan, Jonathan saved Heath, and Heath saved you. You remove any one of those links and you'd be dead now. So tell me, Theo, who was your messiah tonight? Which one person will you single out for that honor?"

Theo couldn't form a coherent response. His glimpse of the string had left him thoroughly discombobulated. He couldn't even chart his many different feelings for Ioni. A part of him still hated her and a part of him had fallen in love.

"We're all connected," she told him. "Our friends, our enemies, the people we know and the ones we don't. It doesn't matter who we are. We're all messiahs, or none of us are."

She let go of Theo and stared at him for what felt like a small eternity. "You're having quite a night, aren't you?"

He nodded weakly. "There's been some stress."

"Want to do something about it?"

"What do you mean?"

"What do you think I mean?"

"Uh . . ."

Ioni scrutinized him for a moment before rolling her eyes. "Christ. I've got three men working for me, and none of them want to . . ." She threw her hands up. "Am I really that intimidating?"

"What? No. I just—"

"Fine. We'll keep it professional."

She stood up, spun around, and clapped her hands together. By the time she faced Theo again, her dress had become an executive pantsuit. She willed a floating recliner into existence, then dropped it on the other side of the ottoman.

"Guess there's nothing left to do but talk business."

"Business?"

Ioni sat down, crossed her legs, and stared at Theo with calm blue eyes.

"The future," she said. "We need to talk about the future."

Hannah struggled to hold herself together. Her exertions had left her with a blinding headache, while her whole body teetered on the verge of collapse. She could have passed out right here if it wasn't for the pressing matter of Theo. Her first instinct was to run to the vivery and get one of the night-shift turners. But her powers were as tapped out as the rest of her. She couldn't move faster than anyone else.

Heath glanced around, then noticed a lime-green phone on the eastern wall of the lobby. The receiver had been painted with a heart in a clock face, the Altamerican symbol for medical reversal.

Hannah watched him nervously as he made a beeline for the phone. "What are you doing?"

She didn't know how far Heath could be from his creations before they started disappearing. The wolves were the only things keeping Theo alive.

"Heath, wait! What about—"

Theo woke up on the tempis with a howl of pain. Ioni had warned him that his return would be . . . unpleasant. If anything, she'd undersold it. His spine had been shattered in two places, leaving him paralyzed and numb below the neck. Everything above it was concentrated agony. He felt like a severed head on a plate of broken glass.

Hannah reached for him, then pulled her hand back. The last thing they needed was for him to solidify with her fingers inside him.

"Don't try to move."

"Hannah, listen to me . . ."

"You took a bad fall but—"

"Hannah, *listen!*" He closed his eyes and spoke through shallow breaths. "I only have eighty-one seconds before I pass out. The turners are coming, and they'll heal me just fine. But I'll forget everything I learned tonight. You have to remember *exactly* what I tell you now. You need to give me the message when I wake up."

Hannah wrung her hands in tense dilemma. She had no idea what Theo could have possibly learned during his three-second fall, but who knew how augurs worked? She could already see Heath talking to someone on the emergency phone. Maybe Theo was right. Maybe the turners *were* coming.

She gathered herself and nodded at him. "Okay. I'm ready."

"We have to find our people," Theo told her. "All of them. The Coppers of Seattle, the Platinums of Tampa, the Irons of Austin. They split into two."

"What?"

"There are a bunch of us in other countries too," he said. "The Netherlands, Japan, England, Canada. We have to find out exactly where these people are and get them. Every one of us who lived. Even . . ."

Theo censored himself. He didn't have the heart to tell Hannah what he learned about Evan Rander, the pivotal role he'd play in events to come.

He could feel himself slipping. He fought to stay lucid. "We're gonna need every timebender on Earth, no matter who they are or where they come from. There's no hope for this world unless we all work together."

Hannah took a skeptical look at Naomi. After a fight like this, she couldn't imagine any future where the Gothams and her people got along.

"Are you sure about this, Theo? I mean—"

"I've never been surer of anything in my life."

He thought of Melissa, so old and so lovely. His eyes welled up just thinking about it.

"It exists, Hannah. I've seen it."

"What?"

"I've seen the string."

His eyelids fluttered. His head rolled to the side. Hannah leaned forward. "Theo?"

A ten-foot portal opened up on the wall. Sean Howell stepped out and ushered in a team of turners in lime-green jackets. Hannah watched in confusion as they hurried up the stairs.

"Wait! Stop! What about . . . ?"

A final figure emerged from the portal, a heavyset woman that Hannah had no trouble recognizing. She hurried into the stairwell and fixed her wide blue eyes on Theo.

"My goodness."

As Hannah processed the real Mother Olga, she realized what a crude forgery Harold Herrick had made. That Olga had scoffed at her like a bratty teenager. This one carried years of wisdom in her eyes.

Olga kneeled at Theo's side. Hannah flinched when she reached for his arm. "No, wait! He's not—"

Shockingly, Olga was able to touch his wrist with no trouble at all. The drop effect must have worn off.

Heath dashed back into the stairwell and looked to Mother Olga. "Can you save him?"

Hannah was almost terrified to hear the answer. It seemed crazy to have hope on this awful night, but she needed something to hold on to. She had to believe that all her struggles were for something. Otherwise, what was the point?

Olga put her ear to Theo's mouth and listened to his breaths for a long, quiet moment.

"Oh yes," she told Heath. "I absolutely can."

THIRTY-THREE

Mia looked out the window and saw the devil yet again. He grinned at her from the top of a twenty-story building, a colossal red demon with flaming horns and swordlike teeth. By now the taxi had flown forty-four circuits around the Via Fortuna skyway, enough for Mia to memorize all the casinos by their rooftop holograms. The Midas had a golden bull. The Infernal had a big red Satan. The Magellan had a ship that sailed repeatedly over the same five waves. It seemed the whole damn world was stuck in a playback loop. If Evan was trying to give her a taste of his madness, he was succeeding.

She turned a cold eye on her driver. After bending Mia's ear with a litany of monologues—"The Sickness in Hannah," "The Hypocrisy of Amanda," "The Short, Sad Life of Natalie Tipton-Elder"—Evan tried to engage her in friendly chitchat. He asked about her personal life with a disturbing amount of detail. He knew all about her sleep portals, the angry Mias, the increasing number of messages that spontaneously combusted upon delivery.

"Burning notes." Evan shook his head, tsking. "What's *that* about?"

Mia could tell from his mocking tone that he already knew the answer. He'd probably dangle it over her head until she begged him to tell her. Screw that. She wasn't going to play his stupid games. She got enough psychological torment from her future selves.

Evan scanned her surly expression. "Well, aren't you the Chatty Cathy. You know, this isn't a dream date for me either. I really wanted Zack to be here."

Mia's heart dropped. Last she saw Zack, a tempic had knocked him fifty feet into dark waters.

She looked at Evan, cringing. "Is he dead?"

"Who, Zack? I hope not."

"You don't know?"

"How would I?"

"I thought you knew everything."

Evan laughed. "I only know what I've seen, and I've never seen the Coppers kill Zack. It's always Esis who does him in."

Blood pounded in Mia's veins. She would have sold her soul to be back in the underland, drinking strawberry blenders with Carrie. Anything but this.

Evan snapped his fingers. "Oh, hey. I almost forgot."

He reached into the backseat and dropped a bag onto Mia's lap—the white leather shoulder pack that she had brought with her to Seattle.

"Got it from your hotel room," Evan explained. "Integrity's gonna be all over that place. You don't want them thumbing through your notebooks. Trust me."

Mia opened the bag and examined her two journals, the one she used as a personal diary and the one she reserved for the words and wisdom of her future selves. She hadn't updated the latter book in months, not since the Mias went toxic on her.

Evan tapped the hardbound cover. "You have some bad information in there."

"You read it?"

"Skimmed it." He snorted derisively. "You got me all wrong."

"I didn't write them."

"*She* got me wrong. I'm not a bad guy. And before you say—"

"You tortured Hannah and Amanda!"

Evan palmed his face. "Sweet Holy Jesus."

"Are you saying you didn't hurt them?"

"I'm saying they've done far worse to me."

"When?"

"You wouldn't remember."

"Because it happened in another timeline."

"It happened to *me*."

Mia flinched at the change in his expression. At long last she could see the man behind the glib veneer, the first-draft Evan who screamed and raged at the universe. Now she knew exactly why Hannah and Amanda had nightmares about him. He was broken on a level she could barely comprehend.

As Evan cut into a faster lane, Mia studied the markings on the back of his left hand: four nickel-size divots in a perfect square.

"Zack has the same scars," she noted.

"Wow. Imagine the odds."

"What did the Pelletiers do to you?"

"Zack didn't tell you?"

"Zack won't talk about it."

"Then why the hell would I?"

He unwrapped another hard candy and popped it into his mouth. Mia could see from the packaging that they were Calmamels: the "Relaxing Candy." Each one contained twenty milligrams of apasticine, an alkaloid opiate that was nearly indistinguishable from nicotine. Mia had already watched Evan go through a bag and a half of the stuff. He gulped them down like popcorn.

"I know your next question," he said.

"I don't have a next question."

"I have no idea why they let me go. There was no parole hearing. No threats or warnings. Not even a slap on the ass. They just opened up a portal and *boom*, I was free."

He let out a shaky laugh. "Guess they looked to the future and knew I'd be a good boy. No more messing with their precious Silvers."

Mia glared at him. "You're messing with me."

"You're not one of their precious ones," he told her. "You're down at the bottom with me and Zack."

The cab flew on in frosty silence. Mia could see the Infernal's red devil on the horizon again. Their forty-fifth loop was about to begin.

"I love this city," Evan said. "Most honest place in America. You won't find any of that *Leave It to Beaver* 'yes, ma'am,' 'sure, ma'am,' 'everything's fine and dandy, ma'am' bullshit. Seattle caters to the people we are, not the ones we pretend to be."

Mia groaned and rubbed her face. "How much longer are we going to do this?"

"What, you're not enjoying yourself?"

"No!"

"Well, shit, hon. You should have said something sooner."

He dipped down to the exit level, then pulled the taxi into a chargery. The station was tucked beneath a highway overpass, far removed from the garish spectacle of the casinos. The only hologram in view was the temporal ghost of a service attendant. He tipped his cap at Evan and thanked him for choosing MerryBolt.

Mia watched Evan carefully as he fed a ten-dollar bill into the spark hydrant. "What are you doing?"

He plugged a cable into the cab's charging port. "Filling up. What does it look like?"

"You know I could just make a portal and leave."

"All right." Evan gave her a sardonic wave. "See ya."

Mia looked around and weighed her options. The underland was far out of teleport range, and she sure as hell couldn't go back to the Poseidon. She supposed she could try a memory jump to the Wallows, but that place would also be crawling with Integrity agents. She had no good escape route, and Evan damn well knew it.

But maybe . . .

She drew a deep breath, then opened a six-inch portal behind her back. She could only hope that Peter was out there looking for her. Maybe he'd feel her presence in the network, a tiny, flashing blip on his radar.

Mia leaned against the taxi and looked across the roof at Evan. "Why did you save me?"

"Why wouldn't I?"

"Because you hate us."

"I hate the sisters," Evan countered. "I'm not particularly fond of David. Theo I just feel sorry for. And Zack's one of my favorite people on Earth."

"And where do I fit in all this?"

"I don't know," he admitted. "That's why I appreciate you."

He walked around the vehicle and leaned on the trunk. Mia turned to hide the portal behind her.

"I've played this game a whole bunch of times," Evan said. "Round and round the mulberry bush. I've watched your friends follow the same damn script over and over again, like clockwork."

He shook a finger at her. "But you, you're a wild card. You're a bouncing ball on the roulette wheel. I can barely count the different Mias I've seen you become. The wristcutter, the asskicker, the chain-smoking nihilist, the born-again Catholic—"

"What?"

"I know, right? As if the group needed another one of those."

"You're lying."

"I'm not lying. I'm not even finished. There's Celibate Mia, Lesbian Mia, Pansexual Orgy Mia—"

"*What?*"

"Hell, there's even a Mama Mia," Evan proclaimed. "I've seen you have a baby."

"Bullshit!"

Evan shrugged. "You don't have to believe me, but it's true. You keep on changing and I love you for it. There's only one thing you do the same way every time."

"I don't want to h—"

"You get angry," Evan told her. "You get very, very angry."

Mia felt a soft twinge in the back of her mind. Peter's voice brushed against her thoughts like a tinny radio signal.

Hang on, darling. I feel you. I'm coming.

Evan's head snapped back as if he just remembered something. He scanned the wooden fence at the edge of the chargery, then yanked the power cable from the taxi.

"Well, that's my cue. It's been real, my dear."

"Wait. Why do I get angry?"

"Tell Hannah she doesn't have to worry about me anymore. The Pelletiers got their point across. I won't bother her again."

"*Why do I get angry?*"

Evan opened the driver's door and gave her one last look. There was something in his eyes that rattled her to the core—a brand-new sincerity, a *sympathy.*

"You'll find out very soon."

He hurried into the cab and started the ignition. The vehicle lifted off the pavement with a loud, airy hiss before the wheels folded inward and the liftplates roared to life.

Evan had just risen out of view when a portal bloomed open on the fence. Peter burst through the surface and took a frantic look around.

Mia ran to meet him. "Peter!"

He hugged her tight. "Oh, thank God. Are you all right?"

She nodded weakly. "I'm okay."

"What *happened* to you?"

Mia wasn't sure how to explain it. She didn't even know what to think. She'd been so determined to keep Evan from messing with her head, but now he towered over every thought, a huge grinning devil. In her mind, he still had her flying in circles.

"Just get me out of here," she said to Peter. "Take me home."

THIRTY-FOUR

The vivery was a uniquely American establishment, a product of loopholes in temporal technology regulations. While hospital revivers were restricted to the treatment of life-threatening injuries, private clinics were free to offer twenty-four-hour rewinds to anyone who could afford one, for any reason they wished. Broke your arm but don't want to spend weeks in a cast? Go to a vivery. Want to undo that new tattoo? Unscrew the cad you met last night? Go to a vivery. Regret was the lifeblood of the chronoregression industry. In 2006, a famous young actress confessed to *Gab* magazine that she'd had her virginity restored 115 times. She died of an aneurysm the following year, a grim reminder to everyone that time was not a toy.

No one knew that better than Olga Varnov, the primarch of the turners and the matron of the Gothams' sole vivery. Her clinic was unique on several fronts, not the least of which was its lack of reviver technology. All temporal manipulations were performed by human beings, cost-free, and with every bit of prudence that the hospitals used. Anyone who wasn't facing death or dismemberment would have to heal the old-fashioned way. There were no papercut reversals on Mother Olga's watch.

The calamitous events of late Tuesday night left her with more medical emergencies than she had ever seen—nine injured souls from the battle in the clock tower, two from the wayward mission in Seattle.

Only four of the wounded were healthy enough for traditional care. Amanda was given eye drops for her corneal flash burns. Carrie received stitches and a blood transfusion. Heath was treated for electrical shock. Hannah got the standard Gotham remedy for power strain: an aspirin, a sedative, and sixteen hours of uninterrupted sleep.

The remaining seven patients—Theo, David, Jonathan, Zack, Harold Herrick, Duncan Rall, and the Mayor—were clear-cut cases for reversal. Only one of them died in the process. While Dunk's young body moved backward in time, an electrical surge in his brain caused his power to activate. He dropped through the floor and was gone before anyone could even scream.

Ironically, it was Jonathan, the other dropper, who had the smoothest recovery. He emerged from the temporis in perfect health, with little to show for his trouble but a four-hour memory gap. The others were saddled with reversal sickness of one kind or another. Harold was delirious. The Mayor was blind. Zack couldn't move or bend his fingers. Theo couldn't keep his meals down. Their maladies would heal over the next few days, though Zack would never again draw as quickly as he used to.

The real concern was David.

He came out of reversal looking sicker than ever. His body twitched in restless slumber while his vital signs diminished by the hour. Though Olga assured his friends that he'd pull through, the other turners didn't share her optimism. They feared David would be the first of the breachers to have his name carved on the Requiem Wall.

Then, in the middle of the night, his health took a miraculous turn. By sunrise, all the color had returned to his skin. By eight A.M., he was sitting up in bed and eating breakfast with savage zeal. Yvonne had never seen anyone make such a feast of water and bell peppers.

She sat with him in the recovery room, stroking his hair as she filled him in on everything he'd missed.

"Amanda and Hannah barely left your side," she said. "Zack and Theo kept coming in to check on you. Olga threatened to chain them to their beds."

"They still here?"

"No. They were discharged. It's just you and my dad now."

David crunched into another pepper, his thoughts smoldering with self-rebuke. After everything he'd been through, all the dire perils he'd survived, he'd nearly let himself get killed by a psychotic ten-year-old. It was shameful. *Humiliating.* How could he have been so foolish?

Yvonne saw his expression and sighed. "You have every reason to be angry. *I'm* angry. That horrid girl was in my kitchen. She poisoned you with *my* food."

"Where is she now?"

Yvonne looked away. "You don't have to worry about Gemma."

The previous morning, as dawn rose over Quarter Hill, Irwin Sunder barged into his granddaughter's bedroom and found her lying face-up on the carpet, catatonic. A brain scan revealed the full extent of the damage. Gemma had been stripped of all cerebral function, a jet without a pilot. The doctors gave it a month before her body shut down as well.

David had a good guess what had happened to her . . . or *who* had happened to her, specifically. He couldn't decide if the girl got more or less punishment than she deserved.

He threw his pepper stems into the trash. Yvonne squeezed his arm and rested her head against his. "You won't remember it, but we were having a very nice date before the trouble started."

He forced a wavering smile. "You'll have to tell me all about it."

"Oh, I'll do more than tell you," Yvonne said. "When you get better . . ."

She and David peeked up and saw Mia standing in the doorway, looking every bit as exhausted as she felt. Her hair was limp. Her shoulders were drooped. She had yet to change out of the sweater, jeans, and sneakers she'd been wearing for two days straight.

"Hi." She backstepped into the hall. "If this is a bad time—"

"No, no." David stared at her, gobsmacked. She'd been a ghost in his life for three weeks running. Now here she was, looking right at him.

Yvonne jumped to her feet with a courteous smile. "I'll let you two catch up."

She clutched Mia's shoulder on the way out the door. "My cousin says you were amazing in Seattle. Totally fearless in the face of danger."

"Oh. I don't know about that."

"Well, in any case, I'm glad you're back. If there's anything you need, just ask."

"Thank you. That's very nice of you."

Mia didn't mean to sound as surprised as she did. She'd let jealousy and Carrie color her opinion of Yvonne. Clearly that was a mistake. She should have known that David wouldn't fall for just a pretty face.

"When did you get back?" he asked Mia.

"A half hour ago. I just found out about all of this. Jesus."

"You're not too far behind me."

Mia stepped inside and took a closer look at his pulse monitor. His heart seemed to be beating just fine. "How are you feeling?"

"Embalmed. You?"

"Same." She settled into a folding chair. "I just saw Hannah. She looks . . . different somehow. Older."

"She's one of the few people who remembers the fight."

"I'm sorry I wasn't here to help."

"I'm sorry we couldn't help you," David said. "I've only heard bits and pieces about the mission. What happened?"

Mia dragged her chair closer and filled him in on her misadventures. Though she'd only planned to give him a broad-strokes summary, she ended up walking him through every beat of the story, from the bright casino holograms to the hard, desperate look in the eyes of the Coppers. David fell into hysterics when she told him about the half-naked showgirl she accidentally teleported at the Poseidon.

It was only when she got to the Evan Rander part of the story that Mia censored herself. She skipped ahead to the long trek home, one of the most unique and fascinating experiences of her life.

David blinked at her in deadpan stupor. "You teleported."

"Yup."

"Across the whole United States."

Mia grinned immodestly. "It's not as easy as it sounds."

Her journey with Peter had taken twenty-nine hours, a dotted trail across the northern half of the nation. Most of their progress was made through line-of-sight portal jumps to the distant horizon. When they moved within range of a place Peter knew, he carried them through a memory leap. Whenever he got tired, he let Mia draw the shortcuts.

Though the trip was exhausting, Mia couldn't remember the last time she'd had so much fun. The weather was nice, the scenery was gorgeous, and Peter's portals were as pleasant as a warm water slide. With each teleport, Mia could feel his strong, fatherly love for her. And when she took the reins . . . oh, the power. The *freedom*. She'd never felt so dominant in her life. At Peter's side, she was a true force of nature. The world was a tiny thing at her feet.

She tried to explain her joy to David but his smiling expression made her feel self-conscious.

"Is it wrong?" Mia asked him.

"Is what wrong?"

"I don't know. I mean my family's gone, the whole world's dying, but I couldn't stop thinking how incredible my life's become. It just seems so—"

"—wonderful," he said.

"—selfish," she said.

David shook his head. "You're anything but selfish."

Mia twitched in discomfort. Even now after all this time, David still had a ridiculous amount of power over her. She remembered why she hated his smile, always warm but never hot, always admiring but never desiring. Even worse was the fact that she'd punished him for it. She froze him out of her life, all because he loved her like a sibling.

She looked away. Her voice shook with sorrow. "I'm sorry."

"You have nothing to apologize for."

"I shouldn't have left things the way I did. If you had died—"

"I didn't."

"It wasn't fair of me."

"It doesn't matter," David said. "You're here, I'm here, and you've never looked so . . ." He chuckled in wonder. "It's unreal. You could almost be her mother."

"Who?"

"Her."

He created a life-size hologram on the other side of the room, a memory ghost of the Mia who'd first arrived on this world. She sat on a chair in an oversize bathrobe, her hair still wet from the shower. She was so meek and dainty that she looked like a stiff breeze could knock her over, like a harsh word could shatter her to pieces.

Mia closed her eyes, disgusted. "Put it away."

"Just showing you how far you've come."

"Please."

David vanquished the image. "I'm sorry. I wasn't trying to upset you."

"It's not you. I just . . ."

Mia stared at the floor, her thoughts teeming with memories of Evan. She should have never let the bastard get to her. Not even for a moment.

She rose from her chair and made for the exit. "I should let you rest."

"Mia . . ."

She turned around in the doorway. David looked at her with a complicated expression, one she couldn't even begin to untangle.

"It's good to see you again. I've missed you."

Mia stared at the floor with dark, guilty eyes. "I missed you too."

She walked down the hall in a state of fidgety unrest. After ten months on this world, she'd become used to a life of near-constant turmoil. But there was something about this latest upheaval that left her utterly terrified. Things were changing faster than normal. *She* was changing. But where would she land when all the spinning stopped? What would she be?

Angry, Evan had teased. *You get very, very angry.*

"Mia!"

She doubled back a few steps and saw Carrie sitting on an exam table. Her hair was unwashed. Her skin was shockingly pale. She looked like she'd been freed after a long and torturous kidnapping.

"Oh my God . . ."

Mia stepped into the exam room, then jumped at the sight of a large, bearded man in the corner. He glowered at the sight of her.

Carrie sighed. "Daddy, give us a minute. Please."

Stan Bloom mulled her request a moment, his frosty eyes never leaving Mia.

"*One* minute," he growled, before stepping out of the room. Carrie closed the door behind him and spoke to Mia in a furtive mutter.

"I have to be careful. He's *this* close to pulling me out of Freak Street."

"What? No!"

"He doesn't think I'm safe around you people." She showed Mia her wrists, each one laced with ten ugly stitches. "Can't entirely blame him."

"Oh my God. Carrie . . ." Mia wrapped her in a tight embrace. "I'm so sorry."

"It's not your fault. Even my dad knows that."

"I don't want you to leave."

"I'm not going anywhere." Carrie held her hands. "And you, my love, are staying right here with me. No more Copper hunts. I heard what happened to you."

Mia grimly shook her head. "I'm done with those people."

"Good. Then I have you all to myself again. As soon as Dad goes topside, we'll meet in the house and, uh . . ."

Mia could see the strain on Carrie's face, as if she'd just remembered something terrible. "What? What's the matter?"

Carrie squeezed Mia's fingers and gave her a shaky grin. "Let me just enjoy this for a second, okay? Before you get mad at me."

"Why would I get mad?"

A long moment passed before Carrie looked up again. Her bright blue eyes danced back and forth in thought.

"We have a problem."

THIRTY-FIVE

Of all the celestial projectors on the market, none were more powerful than the Heavensend Elite. The two-ton, glass-eyed, million-dollar lumicaster could throw a photorealistic sky over any indoor environment, no matter how large. The console offered a wide variety of day and night modules, everything from sunshine to storm clouds to an aurora borealis with meteors.

Every Friday morning, the elders convened in the council chamber and chose the following week's weather for the underland. Elder Sunder preferred an eternally pleasant climate. Elder Howell insisted on variety. Elder Rubinek was adamant that the climate stay true to the seasonal calendar. Elders Kohl and Tam didn't give a flying fig, and traded their votes for political favors.

At two P.M. on Thursday, thirty-six hours after the battle in the clock tower, Sunder convened an emergency conference and demanded the cheeriest sky imaginable. The clan had just lost five of its children, and the people needed sunshine. Not next week. *Now.*

An hour later, Amanda cracked her blinds and winced at the overbearing brightness. White light gleamed off every stone and window, pricking her through her tinted glasses. Her corneas were still recovering from Harold Herrick's flash attack. She didn't need this now.

Squinting, she peeked across the street and saw Heath on the porch of the vacant cottage, his studious attention focused on his song sheets. He only worked outside when Hannah and Jonathan were . . . occupied. That was good. Amanda didn't want them getting wind of what she was doing. She'd quietly brought four people to her house, and it wasn't to talk about the weather.

Her guests watched her solemnly as she sat down to join them. They all looked miserable in their own little ways. Carrie was meek. Mia was livid. Theo was downright morose. Zack was the most distracting of all. He sat forward in a love seat, struggling to shuffle a deck of cards. Every time they spilled from his stiff and palsied fingers, he'd mutter a curse and scoop them up again. Though Amanda sympathized with his plight, she still wanted to throttle him. She was mad at him for reasons that had nothing to do with the playing cards.

She took off her sunglasses and sighed. "Well, I guess we can start."

The others looked to the crumpled scrap of paper on the coffee table, the reason for their secret meeting. By now everyone in the room was familiar with its incendiary message:

Don't trust Jonathan. He's not who he says he is.

"For the record, I don't buy it," Amanda said. "If you had seen him in that clock tower—"

Carrie clucked her tongue. "Awful."

"He'd been stabbed three times. He was on the verge of organ failure, yet all he cared about was getting others to safety. Even the best liar in the world couldn't act in that condition. He's a genuinely good man. I believe he's exactly who he says he is."

"Of *course* he is," Mia snapped.

She'd come to the meeting in a bathrobe and slippers, her hair still wet from the tub. The long hot soak had done little to relax her. She looked ready to maul someone.

"The whole thing is bullshit. I could have told you that from the start." She turned her scornful gaze onto Carrie. "This is *exactly* why I asked you not to read those notes."

Carrie shrank away. "I'm sorry, okay? I'm really, really sorry."

The playing cards spilled out of Zack's hands again. Amanda closed her eyes and took a deep breath.

"The message still bothers me. If it's right and I'm wrong, then we're in a lot of trouble. I just want to make absolutely sure—"

"I'm sure," Mia said. "I'm telling you, the note's a lie. All she does is lie."

"You *are* her," Amanda countered. "If she's lying, then you're the one I'm worried about."

Mia covered her eyes, groaning. She couldn't handle one more conversation about the girl she was, would be, might be, or shouldn't be.

Carrie touched her arm. "Look, we're only concerned because the Mia we
know would never play a trick like that."

Amanda shook her head. "Worse than a trick. It was an attack. It was
designed to hurt Jonathan and everyone who cares for him. Why would she
do that?"

"I don't know!" Mia looked to Theo. "Who are you worried about, me or
Jonathan?"

He shifted his legs on the coffee table, his brow creased distractedly.
Amanda hated dragging him into this mess, as he had much bigger things to
worry about. Everyone in the village was talking about his epiphany in the
God's Eye, the earth-shaking vision that he could no longer remember. All
he knew was what he'd told Hannah to tell him: *Find the orphans. All of them.*

He shrugged at Mia. "I don't know. I think Amanda's right about Jonathan
and I think Carrie's right about you. That's a harsh note, even for the
Mianati."

Zack laughed. "Mianati?"

"What, too cheesy?"

"Too sinister. You make it sound like they rule the world."

"What would you call them?"

"The Mianut Gallery."

Theo glared at him. Zack threw his hand up. "Fine. The Mialstrom."

"No."

"Miasma?"

"Yes." Theo shook a finger at him. "That's the one."

Amanda felt the flesh on the back of her neck tighten. Mia rose from her
chair. "Well, this was fun. Thanks for having me."

"Wait," Zack said. "Aren't you going to ask me who I'm worried about?"

Mia narrowed her eyes, steeling herself for another bad pun. "Who are
you worried about?"

"Semerjean."

The others stared at him, expressionless. Zack jerked his head at the note.
"Come on. I can't be the only one who read that and thought 'Pelletier.'"

"You're not," Amanda said. "But if you think Jonathan is secretly—"

"Forget Jonathan. Let's look at this from the other side. We know Semerjean wears a mask and disguises his voice. He wouldn't do that if he didn't want us recognizing him. I think it's time we started asking why."

Mia sat back down with a cynical sneer. "You're saying you believe Rebel now."

"Believe him? No. But when it comes to the Pelletiers, I'm willing to listen. He hates them just as much as we do, and he's given them a lot of thought. He actually made a few good points to me."

"When was this?" Theo asked.

"Yesterday. He, uh . . ." Zack tossed a nervous look at Amanda. "He visited me."

Everyone felt the cold new air around Amanda, though only she and Zack knew the cause of it. She'd gone to the vivery last night to check on him, only to find him in deep conversation with two former enemies. While Rebel was content to lean against the wall, Mercy had crawled into bed with Zack. She lay at his hip like a conjoined twin, massaging his fingers with the loving care of a wife. A nurse.

Amanda had never felt as foolish as she did at that moment, standing in the doorway with her mouth hanging open. She figured she was the last person in the underland to learn about their romance. If Zack wanted to shack up with an old foe, a woman who'd once tried to kill Amanda, that was his choice. But he could have at least told her. He could have shown her that respect.

Theo looked between them. "Uh, do you two need a minute to—"

"Yes," said Zack.

"No," said Amanda. "What did Rebel say?"

Zack sank in his seat. "He used to think that Semerjean was posing as one of us." He motioned to everyone but Carrie. "I mean *us*. The orphans. The ones who know who Batman is."

Amanda wound her finger. "But then?"

"But then he realized it doesn't make sense. The Pelletiers are playing a bigger game. It's not just us they're trying to manipulate, it's the Gothams."

He sheepishly looked at Carrie. "Sorry. Does that word bother you?"

"No. I'm still stuck on Batman."

"I'll tell you later. The thing is, Rebel's right. If the Pelletiers were going to plant a mole, they'd put him in a position of maximum influence, a place where he could manipulate both us *and* the Gothams."

Theo balked at the implication. "You just narrowed it down to one guy."

"Peter." Amanda stared at Zack in disbelief. "You think Semerjean is *Peter*?"

"*I* don't. I'm just telling you what Rebel thinks."

Zack took a nervous peek at Mia, who remained perfectly still in her seat. Droplets of water dawdled down long hair strands. Her dark eyes never left his.

Carrie chuckled. "Come on. Peter's no Pelletier. He's lived here my whole life."

"But not *his* whole life," Zack said. "He came here as an orphan with no traceable history."

"He has a brother," Amanda reminded him. "A son."

"Adopted brother. As for Liam, I have no idea. I just know the Pelletiers play head games, and I don't mean 'tap your shoulder from the other side.' They're four-dimensional mindfuckers. They have temporal tricks we don't even know about."

Zack frowned at Theo's laughter. "Look, even if you don't take the long view, remember that Esis is a surgeon from the year Whatever. She could have the tools to make anyone look like anyone. Who knows? Maybe there really was a Peter and the Pelletiers killed him. Maybe the one we have now is . . . not who he says he is."

Amanda shook her head, horrified. "Do you have any idea how crazy you sound?"

"Our baseline for crazy got moved a long time ago. It's not like we haven't been fooled by a fake Peter before."

Carrie gestured at Theo. "You have an augur right here. If Peter was tugging you, wouldn't—"

"No," said Zack.

"No," said Theo. He tapped his temple. "The Pelletiers put a ring in my brain. Some kind of selective fogger. I can't see crap when it comes to them."

He turned a hard eye on Zack. "Doesn't mean I believe you."

"I'm not the one saying it! I'm just playing—"

"—Rebel's Advocate," Amanda said.

Zack laid his cards on the coffee table. "Call it what you like, but there are four ugly truths I can't get around. Number one is the fact that the Pelletiers wanted us to get to Peter. They gave us a van and a whole lot of money to reach him. Do you deny that?"

"No," Theo said. "It's still not proof."

"No, but it's troubling. Fact number two is that nobody saw Peter on that aerstraunt when Semerjean was running around."

"*I* did," Amanda said. "I was right there with him when Semerjean killed Ivy's brother."

"You were shot in the back with a twelve-gauge," Zack reminded her. "You were barely conscious. Did you actually *see* Semerjean kill Bug? Did you see him save Peter?"

Amanda scowled at him. "You're still reaching."

"Three: Rebel tried every trick in the book to draw Azral and Esis out of hiding that day. He'd set a ton of traps, but they wouldn't take the bait. It wasn't until Ivy shot Peter that they showed up with a vengeance. And the first thing they did, the *very* first thing—"

Mia closed her eyes. "Goddamn it, Zack . . ."

"—was heal him."

"Enough!"

She hurled her teacup, shattering it against the fireplace. Zack barely had a chance to view the bouncing shards before a furious Mia eclipsed his view.

"What is *wrong* with you?"

"Look—"

"He's saved your life over and over again! He saved your life in Seattle!"

"I'm not saying—"

"You *are* saying it! Don't hide behind weasel words. You're trusting the man who killed your brother over the man who saved your life. That's *pathetic*, Zack. You should be ashamed of yourself!"

Zack's steel-gray eyes held Mia like chains. "You don't even remember, do you?"

"Remember what?"

He snatched her note from the coffee table and brandished it in front of her.

"Fact number four," he said. "You got this exact same message about Peter."

Mia's eyes bulged. Her righteous wrath fled her in an instant. Zack was right. It had been one of the very first notes her future self had sent her, a vague and cryptic warning about a man she had yet to meet.

Don't trust Peter. He's not who he says he is.

She waved a portal into the air and vanished. Carrie shot to her feet. "Mia, wait!"

"It's okay," Theo told her. "She'll be back."

Zack flicked his hand at the teacup fragments. The pieces jittered on the floor until, one by one, they all snapped together and the cracks melted away.

While Carrie returned the cup to the kitchen, Amanda and Theo kept their cool eyes on Zack. He scooped up his playing cards and resumed his clumsy shuffling.

"You think I like doing this? You think I want Rebel to be right?"

"What *do* you want?" Amanda asked.

A grim chuckle escaped him. Amanda knew the sound all too well. It was the noise he made when he was censoring a joke, one of his patented funny-but-truisms that exposed his rawest feelings.

"The Pelletiers have been screwing with us for months on end," he said. "They've been messing with your life since you were a little girl. I don't know about you, but I'm sick of their bullshit. For once, I'd like to know the punchline before they spring it on us."

He stared at her defiantly. "And if you were seeing someone, I wouldn't want to know."

Amanda put on her glasses and looked out the window again. She had at least six retorts lined up, half of them profane, but she suppressed every one of them. She didn't even have the strength to be angry with him anymore. She feared the Pelletiers broke him even more than she realized.

"Maybe this is all part of their game," Theo mused. "They want us to suspect each other, mistrust each other."

Carrie returned from the kitchen, nodding. "Maybe these notes aren't even Mia's."

A portal opened by the front door. Mia returned to the living room with her prophecy journal in hand. She sat back in her seat and began flipping through the pages.

"I got two notes about Peter that day," she said. "The first one told me not to trust him. The second one said just the opposite. I don't remember the exact words but . . . wait . . ."

She found the message she was looking for on the second page of her journal.

Disregard that first note. I was just testing something. Peter's good. He's great, actually.

Mia stared at the message, her heart pounding wildly. She'd assumed those contradictory notes were nonsense, just another prank from her future self. But now two words leapt out at her with fresh new context. *Testing something. Testing something . . .*

Her mouth fell open. She let out the breath she'd been holding. "Oh my God . . ."

The others watched in rapt attention as two long-standing mysteries converged in her head. They fit together like a lock and key, solving each other with a simple click.

She looked to her friends in stammering wonder. "I know what she's doing."

Mia needed a minute and a full glass of water before she could explain herself. Her mood had become bubbly, loopy, as if she could break out in giggles at any moment. She paced in front of the fireplace, only occasionally stopping to check the confounded expressions of her audience.

"Okay, let's pretend for a minute that Rebel's right, that someone we know is Semerjean. And let's say Future Mia found out who it is beyond a shadow of a doubt. What's the first thing she'd do?"

"Warn you," Theo said.

"Right." Mia snatched the paper scrap with Jonathan's name on it. "But she wouldn't write this vague shit. She'd spell it out for me in big letters. 'Don't trust Jonathan! He's Semerjean Pelletier!' And she wouldn't just write it once. I'd be getting that note dozens of times. *Hundreds*. Trust me. I know her."

Carrie laughed, perplexed. "We trust you."

"But the Pelletiers don't. If they have a spy, the last thing they'd want is for Future Me to blow his cover. And if they have a way to stop Theo from learning the truth, they must have a way to stop me."

Amanda saw where she was going with this. She'd spent many a morning helping Mia clean up her portal refuse—all the colorful little paper sticks, all the countless flakes of ash.

"The burning notes . . ."

Mia pointed at her. "The burning notes. I never understood why some of the papers caught fire before I could read them. Now I'm thinking it's—"

"—censorship," Zack said. He blinked at her, astonished. "They're reading your mail."

Mia nodded. She pictured Azral and Esis sitting at a kitchen table, sorting through her dispatches, laughing at the silliest ones. No, it wouldn't be that simple. They probably had some automated system that scanned her notes in transit and burned the ones with forbidden information.

But the news came with an upside. Carrie was the first of Mia's friends to see it.

"Peter and Jonathan are both innocent," she said. "If either one of them was Semerjean—"

"—their notes would have burned," Theo said. He gawked at Mia. "That's exactly why she sent those notes. She was testing the filter."

Mia fought a maniacal cackle. All these months, she thought her future selves were nothing but a gaggle of loons. But some of them still had their wits about them. Some were even clever enough to use the Pelletiers' trick against them.

Zack tapped his leg in contemplation. "She must have sent a note like that for everyone she knows. Theo, Amanda, David, me."

"And the one that catches fire . . ." Carrie recoiled. "You think that would work?"

Theo was skeptical. The stunt seemed almost embarrassingly obvious, like reverse psychology. Then again, he knew from painful experience that smart people weren't immune to dumb tricks. It was easy to kick a man's shin when his head was in the clouds.

"I don't know," he said. "Seems worth a try, if only for peace of mind."

Mia scoffed at his choice of words. Evan had recently told her that she was one of the Pelletiers' least favorite Silvers. Now she was about to challenge them in a way that no one had before. Even if she managed to beat their system, all she'd get for her trouble was some devastating news about someone she loved and trusted. This was a sucker's game from the start to finish. There would certainly be no peace of mind.

At midnight, Mia ran out of excuses to stall. She sequestered herself in her bedroom with a pad, a pen, and a strawberry blender. And then she got to work.

By the time she finished, an hour later, she was ready to cry. She didn't want to face Zack or Theo or anyone else in her circle. There was only one person in the world she wanted to see.

Carrie leapt up from the sofa as Mia teleported into her living room. She had no trouble reading the anguish in her eyes and lips, her drooped posture, her everything.

"Oh shit," Carrie said. "Is it David? It's David, isn't it."

Mia shook her head. "His note didn't burn."

She dropped onto the couch, exhausted. "None of them burned."

Mia had sent thirty-three messages to the past, each one a warning about someone in her life. *"Don't trust Hannah. She's not who she says she is." "Don't trust Liam. He's not who he says he is." "Don't trust Mercy . . ." "Don't trust the Mayor . . ."* One fake warning for everyone she knew. She even gave Peter and Jonathan a second chance to incriminate themselves. Nothing. The papers traveled through time without a spark of interference.

Carrie cocked her head. "Okay, well, isn't that good news?"

"It's no news," Mia said. "All it proves is that the Pelletiers are too smart for me."

"Yeah, or maybe all this Semerjean stuff is horseflakes. Maybe he just wears a mask because he's ugly."

On a better night, Mia might have laughed, but her emotions were still too raw. With every fake note, she'd imagined a world in which the warning proved true. What if the Peter she loved was just an elaborately crafted cover identity? What if David had been sneering at her behind her back this whole time? What if the real Zack Trillinger was still rotting away in a Pelletier dungeon? What if the one they rescued was . . . not who he said he was?

But none of those scenarios hurt as much as the one right in front of her. Carrie had piercing blue eyes, just like Semerjean's. All it would take was a little illusion and a whole lot of tempis to make her look like a formidable man. The thought had been horrific enough to make Mia's fingers quiver. She could barely push Carrie's note into the temporal portal.

Carrie sat down next to her and held her by the hands. "Aw, sweetie, don't feel bad. That could have gone much, much worse."

"I know. I'm just . . ." She closed her eyes, stuck for words. "I don't want to deal with it anymore. The notes, the warnings, the Past Mias, the Future Mias. I never asked for that power and I never wanted it. I wish I could just . . ."

"What?"

"I wish I could just travel."

Carrie tucked her legs beneath her and turned her whole body toward Mia. "Hey. Look at me."

Mia twisted in her seat and matched her lotus pose, until they were both sitting kneecap to kneecap. She saw the gorgeous expression on Carrie's face—a soft, slanted grin that made her look ten years older.

Carrie raised her injured wrists. "I got a taste of the life you guys live and it nearly killed me. I mean I knew you had it rough but . . . God, Mia. You've been fighting for your life from the minute you got to this world. You've barely had a chance to catch your breath."

Mia lowered her head. Carrie cupped her cheeks and raised her back into eye contact. "You want to be a traveler, then be a traveler. Go around the world, see all the things you never got to see. If anyone's entitled to live the life they want, it's you. There's only one thing I ask."

"What's that?"

"Take me with you," Carrie said. "Wherever you go, for the rest of your life, just bring me along and keep me close. Because that, my dear . . ."

She brushed a warm hand down the side of the Mia's face. "That's the only life I want."

They sat together in perfect silence, hands clasped, their bodies locked in a delicate stasis. Mia found it ironic that two girls who'd dreamed of traveling the world together couldn't seem to venture beyond the confines of the sofa, as if a fragile thing would shatter if they spoke or moved a muscle.

After a long, breathless moment, Mia reached her arm through a portal and turned off the overhead lights. In the darkness, hands clasped, they leaned forward into each other. Their lips touched, and then suddenly Mia's world became perfect. There were no past or future selves to be found in the shadows, no friends, no fears, no Semerjeans or Evan Randers. Her universe had become a small and cozy thing, and it was beautiful. If there had been any doubt left about what she wanted from life and Carrie Bloom, it died right there on the couch.

As the village clock rang the two A.M. hour, the girls stopped kissing and fell back onto the cushions. They traded soft, tender words for another forty minutes—secret thoughts, secret fears, all the things they'd never dared tell each other—until fatigue finally got the better of them.

Soon the darkness was pierced by a twinkling coin of light, then another, then another, then a hundred others. Within moments, Mia's portals filled the room like stars. Rolled-up scraps of paper flittered in from a hundred different futures. Every one of them carried the same dire message. Every one of them burned.

THIRTY-SIX

The sixteenth floor of the Poseidon Hotel had functionally ceased to exist. The rooms had been cleared of all guests and staff. The windows were shuttered with tempic blinds. Any hapless soul who wandered off the elevator was quickly turned away by goons in white armor. Integrity had become host to Seattle's most exclusive event: a temporal investigation. Ghost teams moved through fourteen suites, scouring the past for intel. Some very interesting people had stayed here recently. Gingold was determined to learn their deepest secrets.

He walked between the holograms of the Executive Suite, his mechanical eyes recording every detail. The drills had captured a curious meeting that occurred here Tuesday night. Eighteen adults and one minor gathered around the sofas while a stern-faced woman addressed them. The minor of course was Mia Farisi, whose teleporting shenanigans had already become the stuff of folklore. Retinal scanners recognized Zack Trillinger and Peter Pendergen through their putty disguises.

None of the other people had criminal records, which made them harder to identify. Luckily, they'd left a bounty of clues. Victoria Chisholm had a vehicle registry code on the fob of her aerplane key. Mercy Lee sported several distinct tattoos. Rebel Rosen wore a Gelinger Mark V prosthetic hand, a device so expensive that only nine people in the country owned one. A few hours of detective work uncovered their true identities. They were all trust fund millionaires, all from the posh little enclave of Quarter Hill, New York.

The news baffled Gingold. The town had been famous since 1971, when Alexander Wingo published a breathless "exposé" about a secret society of chronokinetics. But if Wingo was right, if Quarter Hill really was filled with these so-called Gothams, then why hadn't anyone found proof yet? How could they have stayed hidden in plain sight for four goddamn decades?

"Sir?"

Gingold turned around to see a diminutive blonde in a jumpsuit, one of the many young analysts from the Tacoma office. A pop-up on his visual feed informed him that her name was Kenja Purkey.

"What, Purkey? What is it?"

The agent threw a furtive glance around the room. "I don't mean to stir up trouble, sir, but I think your lipper made a mistake on one of the transcripts."

Gingold eyed her suspiciously. Even the most advanced ghost drills couldn't replicate sound. All dialogue had to be gleaned from lip-readers. Purkey, however, was a forensic technician. This was far out of her playing field.

"What do you know about lipping?" he asked her.

She pulled back her hair and showed him the elaborate devices on the back of her ears. "I spent the first half of my life as a deaf woman, sir. I guess modern technology's been good for both of us."

Purkey could see Gingold's patience withering away. She held up her computer tablet. "Sir, if I could just show you the problem . . ."

Gingold noticed a familiar presence in the corner of his vision, a silver-haired man in a black fedora and trench coat. He stood just outside the doorway, chatting amicably with two senior agents.

"Damn it. *Tomlinson.*"

A tall, burly operative rushed to Gingold's side. "Sir?"

"What the hell is he doing here?"

Tomlinson looked at the man in the hallway, then shrugged helplessly at Gingold. "He has clearance, sir."

Cedric Cain had been making a lot of people nervous these days. The old man didn't hide his frustration with Integrity's leadership, and he had powerful friends in the White House. Rumor had it that he and his pals were planning a full management takeover, a forced return to the agency's "good old days." Gingold knew how eager Cain was to get the Sci-Tech division back in his hands, especially now with timebending aliens running wild.

Gingold turned to Tomlinson. "Shadow him. I want to know everything he says and does."

"Yes, sir."

While Tomlinson inched his way into Cain's earshot, Gingold turned back to Purkey. "You still here?"

"Yes, sir. I was waiting to show you—"

"Right." He snatched the tablet from her hands and read the screen. Purkey had highlighted a snippet of a transcript, a testy exchange between Victoria Chisholm and Zack.

> CHISHOLM: You're part of our clan now, Trillinger. That means you follow our rules.
>
> TRILLINGER: Or what? You'll kill me?
>
> CHISHOLM: No. We'll just never let you back in the wonderland.

Purkey tapped the screen. "It's that last word I have a problem with. The phoneme for 'W' sounds is very distinct." She gestured at Victoria's image. "I watched her three times. I didn't see it on her lips."

"So then what the hell was she—"

"*Oren Gingold.*"

Cain's booming voice stopped every conversation in the room. Seven agents watched blankly as he cut a path through the ghost field. It was hard not to stare at him. He stood six-foot-nine with his hat on. His clothes were outdated to the point of anachronism. He could have stepped straight out of a 1940s crime flick, the mysterious rogue who leads the hero on a back-alley foot chase. If Zack had seen him, he would have stopped wondering what became of The Shadow.

Cain extended his hand. "You old warhorse. How the hell are you?"

Gingold returned the handshake. His voice could have wilted flowers. "Long time no see."

"Funny words coming from you." He smiled at Purkey. "I built his eyes. First of their kind. Could've sold the patent and lived like a king. Yet here I am doing government work."

Purkey indulged him with a polite half smile. Gingold remained stone-faced. "What exactly brings you here?"

Cain laughed and jerked a thumb over his shoulder. "Are you kidding? How could I miss the chance to look at Gothams? Real live no-foolin' Gothams."

Everyone around him cringed at his word choice. They had barely wrapped their minds around the notion of extradimensional visitors. Now they were forced to accept an old crackpot myth about superpowered suburbanites. The world was becoming an increasingly hard place for skeptics.

Cain took a wistful look at the ghosted Gothams. "You know when Xander Wingo first talked about these people, the Deps laughed him out of the Bureau. Integrity wrote him off as a nutter. But I knew the guy. Best damn detective I ever met. I asked my bosses to let me go to Quarter Hill and investigate, just to make sure."

"But you didn't find anything," Gingold said.

"Oh, I found something. A week into my visit, I woke up in an alley with a headache and a twelve-hour memory gap. Mind you, this was back when reversal was just a theory. I had no idea it happened to me. So I brushed it off and kept digging. Two days later, it happened again. And then again the following week. Every time I got within clocking distance of these people, they counterclocked me."

The other agents gave Cain their full attention. He kept his sharp blue eyes on Gingold.

"After the third time, I got the message. I knew damn well that Wingo was right about the Gothams but I kept my mouth shut."

"Why?" Gingold asked. "Because they got the better of you?"

"It's not what they did, Oren. It's what they didn't do. These people weren't killers. They just wanted to be left alone."

Cain turned around and addressed the others. "We're in the threat management business. Always have been, always will be. The problem these days is that we see everything as a threat. And we only have one way to manage them."

Gingold glowered at him. "We lost sixty-three agents at Atropos."

"We lost them to the Pelletiers."

"Who were protecting *these* people."

"From us," Cain reminded him. "I wonder what might have happened if we'd done things Melissa's way."

Gingold chuckled bitterly. The last time he tried diplomacy, he lost both eyes. "How *is* Masaad?"

"Your guess is as good as mine."

Gingold had wanted Melissa executed for her treasonous actions at

Atropos, but Cain convinced the Bureau to let her off with a pink slip. He argued that it was much more prudent to let her go and follow her. If anyone could find a way to reconnect with the orphans, it was Melissa.

Unfortunately, she flew her aerocycle into the Holland Tunnel five days ago and never came out, a disappearing act worthy of Houdini. No one could figure out her trick, though Gingold was sure as hell that Cain had a hand in it. The crafty old fox was up to something.

Cain clapped his hands together. "Well, I've taken enough of your time. Whatever happens, Oren, I hope you play it smart. There are a lot of lives riding on what you do next."

"You don't say."

Cain beckoned to Tomlinson. "Come on. I have two more people to see."

Tomlinson threw a confused look at his boss. Gingold nodded curtly. *Do it.*

Purkey watched Cain with both humor and bemusement. "Interesting guy. Reminds me of my grandpa."

Gingold frowned at her. "What is it you keep trying to tell me?"

"Underland."

"What?"

"That's the word Chisholm said to Trillinger. She was talking about some kind of underland."

Gingold's face went slack. His hands dropped to his sides. He took the tablet out of Purkey's hands and gave it his full attention.

THIRTY-SEVEN

The Gothams laid their fallen souls to rest on Friday. Eleven hundred people gathered in the amphitheater in their darkest suits and dresses, their bleakest expressions. Barely three weeks had passed since their last quadruple funeral, when the clan said good-bye to Ivy, Djinni, Bug, and Mink. Now they sat and watched while tempics carried four more coffins onto the stage. The casualties were all children this time, not a single one older than twelve. They were the disparates, the misfits, the quiet shames of their families. Though everyone in the theater mourned them, only a handful would miss them. A few dared to wonder if maybe, just maybe, the clan should have treated them better.

As the organist played and the choral club sang, the caskets were lowered by ropes into a temporal portal—first Squid's, then Suki's, then Naomi's, and then Dunk's empty coffin. Even the travelers didn't know where the bodies were going. The past, the future, it didn't matter. Time would embrace its blessed children. Time would hold them to its loving breast and give them the comfort and peace they never knew on this world. Time would heal all broken hearts and mend the threatening cracks in the walls of the universe.

Time would go on.

The Gothams believed these things because they had to, because the alternative was despair and despair was a dangerous thing for powerful people to have.

The portal closed and the elders began their long-winded eulogies. Not a word was said about Gemma Sunder, who continued to languish in a vegetative state, or about Harold Herrick, who remained locked away in a solic cell until the council could figure out what to do with him. The elders also avoided any mention of the breachers, none of whom were in attendance. Mother Olga had advised them to stay home, as if they didn't know any better, as if they were clamoring to meet the families of the sad, twisted children they had killed.

The mood on Freak Street remained edgy all weekend. The Silvers and Golds kept to their houses, only occasionally emerging to socialize. On Sunday night, Peter went door to door to collect the weekly supply requisitions. He couldn't take a list without getting an earful from an anxious orphan.

"I already have a bag packed," Jonathan warned him. "If I get so much as a cross-eyed look from your people, I'm pulling Heath out of here."

"You need to keep a closer watch on your malcontents," David told him. "That mess with Gemma should have never happened."

"Do we even have a plan if Integrity finds this place?" Zack asked.

"I just want an escape plan," Mia said. "I need to know there's a place we can go if everything falls apart here."

By the time Peter finished, he was spiritually drained. He kicked back on his living room sofa, a scowl on his face and a beer in his hand.

Amanda watched him from the easy chair, her finger tracing a slow path around the rim of her wineglass. "You can't blame us for being nervous."

"I'm only blaming myself." He sat up straight and vented a mighty sigh. "David's right. I should have kept a closer watch on Gemma."

Amanda bristled at the mention of her housemate. Ever since he got back from the vivery, he'd ditched every last shred of his emotional restraint and became a boy in love. He canoodled with Yvonne in the living room, the kitchen, seemingly everywhere but his bedroom. Amanda couldn't walk through her home without getting caught in their cloying little nuzzlesphere.

David was just as insufferable without Yvonne. When he wasn't talking about her at maddening length, he conspired to make Amanda as happy as he was. "I met a turner at the vivery. He's your age. He's very nice." "Yvonne has a cousin you might like." "Did you know the tempics guild has a group devoted entirely to young singles?"

When Amanda finally snapped and told him to ease up, he'd stared at her woundedly. "I'm sorry. You just seem lonely. I figure if Zack can move on, so can you."

That had been enough to send her out the door. She went to Peter's house with a trivial addendum to her shopping list and stared at him expectantly until he invited her inside.

She swallowed down the rest of her wine, then peeked into Liam's bedroom. "Where did you say he was again?"

"At his guild precursory."

He saw her blank-faced reaction and chuckled. "It's an informal competition between thermics. Helps the kids prepare for their power finals."

"So, what? They put him in a ring and make him fight Carrie?"

"It's just dummy targets. Carrie's not even there."

"But she's a thermic."

"She's a subthermic," Peter said. "The freezers don't compete till tomorrow."

Amanda shook her head, confounded. "I used to have a normal life."

She moved toward the wall and examined a collage, all photos of Liam that extended back to his infancy. Only one included the boy's mother, a heavyset woman with surprisingly plain features. Amanda didn't know why she'd expected Jenny Varnov-Pendergen to be some lyrical beauty. Maybe she'd assumed that Peter, like most handsome men, would demand a wife of equal allure. Clearly she'd underestimated him again.

"You never talk about your wife," she noted.

"You never talk about your husband," Peter countered.

Amanda kept her somber eyes on the collage. "He was a mostly good man."

"That sounds mostly awful."

"It could have been worse. How was your marriage?"

"It was fine for what it was."

"What was it?"

"An arrangement."

Amanda turned around and looked at him in surprise. "I thought only the snooty families did that."

Peter shrugged. "We couldn't have the people we wanted, and the elders were pressuring us to pick someone, so we came to an agreement. It worked out better than we could have hoped. She was a real saint."

"It was Ivy, wasn't it?"

"What?"

"The woman you loved," Amanda mused. "The one you couldn't marry."

Peter's expression hardened. He swallowed the last of his beer. "That's all ancient history."

Amanda wasn't encouraged by the bitterness in his voice. She knew exactly what it was like to have a lover yanked away. She had hoped the anger would diminish over time. Apparently it didn't.

Peter joined her at the collage. "It's all right. It all turned out for the best." He tapped a photo of Liam. "The strings pulled me in a different direction and look at what they gave me."

Amanda held his arm. "He's a wonderful kid. You should be proud of him."

"Every minute of the day."

"And he should be proud of you."

"Well, that's a taller order."

"He's still mad at you for leaving him?"

"Wouldn't you be?"

Amanda took his hand and stroked it, her thoughts swimming with guilt. Nobody had worked harder to bring the orphans and Gothams together, yet all Peter got was grief from both sides. He should have been a hero to everyone in the village. Instead there were some who believed that he shouldn't be trusted at all.

Peter saw her agitated expression and gave her hand an affectionate squeeze. "Thank you, by the way."

"For what?"

"For not believing it."

"Believing what?"

Peter eyed her cynically. "Come on. I'm not dumb. There's been chatter about me being a certain Pelletier. It started with Rebel. Now I've got people in my own circle looking at me cockeyed."

Amanda lowered her head. "I'm sorry. I should have told you."

"I'm just glad you don't buy it."

"*None* of us buy it."

"Not even Zack?"

Amanda rubbed her brow. She wished to God she could go one day without having to think about him. "He has his own issues."

"I would have hoped I earned his faith by now."

"It's not about you. It's about them. The Pelletiers have got him all turned around and he's just . . . he'll see his way through this. Just give him time."

Peter's fists unclenched. He fingered the crucifix on Amanda's collarbone. "It's been a long, bad week for all of us."

"Yes it has."

Amanda pulled him into a hug, a paltry little gesture that made her body seethe with frustration. It reminded her of all her unfulfilled needs, all of *his* needs, all the many different ways they could comfort each other. They wouldn't have to make a whole big production out of it. They could just . . . be.

Peter returned the embrace and stroked her back with both hands. From the way his fingers moved down the bumps of her spine, Amanda gave it even odds that she'd be sleeping with him tonight. She blamed the wine. She blamed David.

She hugged Peter tighter and breathed a soft whisper into his ear. "This week will be better," she promised him. "It all gets better from here."

At midnight, Yvonne gave David a goodnight kiss before sneaking back to her surface house. Amanda and Peter retreated into his bedroom and fumbled at each other's shirt buttons. Mia and Carrie traded kisses in the dark. Hannah, Heath, and Jonathan fell asleep on a sofa. Zack lounged in bed with Mercy, bellowing with laughter as she tinkered on a lapbook. She'd hacked into the Heavensend and had added her own special touches to tomorrow's sky. The weather promised to be cloudy with a chance of butt photos.

At 1:55 A.M., the last light on Freak Street went out. The only glow came from the forty-inch lumivision in Theo's bedroom. He lay on his mattress in a fetal position, clicking the remote with glazed perplexity. The local airwaves became utterly daft after midnight. A googly-eyed sock puppet yelled all the day's news. A clown in lingerie hosted a contentious talk show. A man dressed like Teddy Roosevelt spent an hour playing practical jokes on animals. Theo couldn't watch any of it without wondering if humanity sensed, somewhere deep in its lizard brain, that the world was doomed and there was no point left to anything. Maybe these freaks were the true prophets. Maybe the only real fools were down here in the underland, the ones who'd placed their faith in Theo.

He nodded off a moment, then sat up in confusion. The lumivision had switched itself off. The room was pitch-black. Soft, mellow music drifted into his ears like a lullaby. Someone in the vicinity was playing guitar. Even in his groggy state, Theo could recognize it as the opening riff to "Come Together." But who in their right mind would be strumming the Beatles at this hour? And why did they sound so close?

"*Shoop.*"

The intro repeated. Mystified, Theo rose from the bed and followed the song to his bathroom. He pushed the door open, half expecting to find Jonathan in a musical fugue state. Instead he was doused in a flood of sunshine. His bathroom had become a gateway to a bright, grassy meadow. It stretched as far as his squinting eyes could see.

Theo felt reasonably certain now that he was dreaming.

He crossed over the threshold and was stunned by sensory pleasures—the warm wind, the soft grass, the enchanting smell of wildflowers. Theo prayed that his subconscious would stay nice to him for once. He'd be lucky to get through this without seeing his dead naked parents.

"*Shoop.*"

The song continued to beckon him from the distance. Theo knew, in the inexplicable way of dreamers, that the guitarist was waiting for him at the top of a hill, just slightly out of view.

He climbed the slope until he reached the edge of a cliff. A stunning city loomed in the distance, with the most eclectic skyline Theo had ever seen. Gothic buildings stood side by side with modern glass spires. One skyscraper was shaped like a pair of crossed scimitars. Another resembled an inverted chandelier. Theo couldn't see a trace of human life anywhere. No cars. No trains. No hovering aerstraunts. He might have wondered if he was looking at a still frame if it wasn't for the scattered flocks of birds.

"This place is real," he mumbled to himself. "I've seen it before."

"You're seeing it now."

Theo flinched at the stranger lounging next to him, a thirtysomething blond in a turtleneck and jeans. He faced the edge of the cliff in a patio chair, his legs propped up on a speaker. The electric guitar in his hands looked just like the cherry-red replacement that Peter had bought for Jonathan. For all Theo knew, it was the exact same instrument.

The guitarist continued to pluck the opening notes of "Come Together," punctuating each riff with a soft, hissing "*shoop.*"

"Why don't you play the rest of it?" Theo asked.

"Because then I'd have to sing it, and I don't know the words. I'm really just in it for the *shoop*."

Theo scrutinized the man. Though he seemed comfortable enough in his own skin, he spoke in a shy, reticent tone. He also had a faint but unmistakable accent.

"You're Irish."

"You're Korean," the stranger fired back. "Any other business you want to get out of the way?"

"Yeah. I'm Filipino. And there's no *shoop*."

"What?"

"The *shoop*. It's wrong. John Lennon never sang that. He sang 'shoot me.'"

The guitarist stared at him in blinking thought. "Huh. Well I don't know this Lennon fellow but I'd bet my life savings that someone ended up shooting him."

Theo nodded. "That's how he died."

"Of course it is." The stranger chortled. "The strings thrive on irony. You always have to be careful."

He replayed the intro with a defiant smirk. "*Shoop*."

Theo took a closer look at his new acquaintance. His hair and beard were thoroughly unkempt, but he had a handsome face. A *smart* face. He could have been David in twenty years, a rumpled ex-professor traveling from coffeehouse to coffeehouse, sharing his cynical wisdom with anyone willing to listen.

He was also, like the city and guitar, a maddeningly familiar presence.

"I know you," Theo said. "We've met before, haven't we?"

"Not that I'm aware of."

"I must have seen you in visions, then."

"Lumivisions, maybe."

Theo snapped his fingers. "That's it! You're Merlin McGee! You're that big, famous weather prophet."

Merlin scoffed. "Weather prophet. I predict natural disasters. Saved more than a few lives doing it."

"I don't care. You're an asshole."

"How am I an asshole?"

"You were the strongest augur in the clan," Theo said. "Peter begged you to help him, but you couldn't be bothered. Now you're off making millions while the whole world's dying. And I'm the one stuck with your burden."

Merlin shook his head bitterly. "There's so much wrong with that, I don't even know where to start."

"Okay. Enlighten me. Tell me—" Theo stopped himself, puzzled. "Wait. How do you know this song? You're not from my world."

"Everyone knows this song."

"That makes no sense."

Theo looked to the skyline and finally saw movement. A speck of an aero-van circled the top of a skyscraper. Just one vehicle in the whole damn city.

"This isn't a vision," Theo realized. "It's not even a prophetic dream. It's just nonsense."

Merlin shrugged. "Sometimes a guitar is just a guitar. Then again, you once had a dream where you were floating in front of a great white wall. Was that nonsense?"

He played through the song intro again. "*Shoop.*"

Theo crouched on the grass and took in the view. An ominous sense of finality plagued him, as if he'd skipped ahead to the very last page of his story. He couldn't shake the feeling that he would die in that city, that he was *meant* to die there.

"I hate this power," he said. "I hate everything about it."

"You and me both, brother."

"You seem to have made the most of it."

Merlin glared at him. "You think I like being famous? I've got everyone and their mother hounding me for predictions. I'm always looking over my shoulder for government scientists. You just know they're aching to get my brain in a jar."

"So why'd you do it, then?"

"*She* made me."

"Who did?"

"Who do you think? My boss. Your boss. Ioni Anata T'llari Deschane."

Merlin laughed at Theo's surprise. "What, you haven't figured it out? We're her augurs, her soldiers, her three horsemen of the anti-apocalypse."

"Three?"

"I'm including Rebel," Merlin said. "I probably shouldn't. The man's all done. Ioni used him up like a soapsheet."

Theo felt the push of invisible fingers on his shoulder. Someone was jostling him in the real world. Waking him.

"Theo?"

Wait.

"Wait." He looked to Merlin. "*Who's* Ioni? I mean who is she really?"

"If you have to ask, you're not ready to know."

"But what is this city? Why is it so—"

"—ominous?" Merlin chuckled. "I know, right? I get butterflies just looking at it."

"Why?"

Merlin jerked his head at the skyline. "That's where all the roads converge, brother. Where it all gets decided. It's either the end of the world or the end of the world as we know it."

The jostling persisted. Theo heard Zack calling him like a howl in the wind.

"The city's falling either way," Merlin said. "And so are we."

He looked down at his guitar with somber eyes, then took a final pluck at the strings. "*Shoop.*"

"Theo!"

Theo sat up with a gasp. Zack leapt back from the bed. "Whoa. That did it."

"God . . ."

Wincing, Theo looked around the bedroom. Sunlight filtered in through the half-open blinds, painting the walls in radiant stripes. His head pounded. His heart raced. The images of the dream were already beginning to fade.

Zack sat on the edge of his bed. "Look, I'm sorry but Peter—"

"Wait!"

Theo yanked his notepad off the dresser and furiously scribbled in shorthand. He couldn't let the dream slip away. There was prophetic significance to the things he'd witnessed, and not just about the city. Something about Merlin. Something about that song.

Zack tapped his thigh patiently as Theo scrawled his final notes. "You got it?"

He dropped the pad and rubbed his eyes. "I think so."

"Good vision or bad vision?"

"I don't know. It was different. Strange." He glanced up at Zack. "Why'd you wake me?"

"The meeting's in an hour. Peter wants you fresh and ready."

Theo looked at the clock and groaned. The elders had given everyone the weekend to lick their wounds and gather their wits. Now the clan was officially back to business. It was time to talk about Theo's other vision, the one that had everyone chattering. Theo wasn't even remotely ready to deal with it.

He fluffed his hair, then wiped the sandy grit from his eyes. "All right. I'm coming."

Hannah could have strangled Peter. When he'd first told her and the others about the council meeting, he billed it as a small affair. *Just the leaders*, he'd assured them. *None of the rabble.*

What he failed to mention was that the conference room was the size of a gymnasium and that the leaders were a mob unto themselves. They presided around a massive ring of tables—five elders, eight primarchs, two acting primarchs, and the voting heads of all forty-four families. They were all casually dressed and calm in demeanor, despite the gravity of the agenda. Hannah was stunned by the warm looks some of them threw her way. She'd expected them to hate her for killing Naomi Byers, yet she didn't get a single glare. If anything, they seemed ashamed and embarrassed over what their children had done.

She sat off to the side in the visitor seats, along with most of her people—Amanda and Mia, David and Zack, Jonathan and Heath, Liam and Carrie. None of them were required to be here, nor were they particularly enthused. They only came as a show of support for Theo, who sat trapped in the center of the ring. He faced the elders from the testimony table, looking dapper but grim in a black shirt and slacks. Peter sat at his side like a vigilant attorney. Hannah noticed a bloody bandage on his right palm, as if he'd come down with a sudden and unfortunate case of stigmata.

She leaned in toward Mia, whispering. "What happened to him?"

"Who?"

"Peter. Look at his hand."

Mia studied his bandage from a distance. "Oh. I don't know."

Amanda sank in her seat, a hot blush in her cheeks. She had gotten a little . . . spiky in the throes of passion last night. Peter had a few other tempis wounds they couldn't see.

The Mayor quieted the room with a flashing strobe of lumis, then called the meeting to order. He began with an apology for this morning's unfortunate incident with the Heavensend. The early-rising Gothams had to shield their eyes from the huge, naked ass pictures that flared down at them from the undersky, a dozen moons around the sun. The elders thanked the Mayor for fixing the problem so quickly and urged him to change the password on the Heavensend.

Carrie caught the juvenile smirk on Zack's face. "Really?"

"I admit nothing."

"Just tell me that wasn't your splitter I saw up there."

"You'll never prove it in court."

While the opening business continued, Theo leaned over and muttered to Peter, "Can I tell you one more time how very much I hate you?"

"You'll be fine," Peter whispered. "Just follow my lead and stay sunny. All they want are assurances."

Theo studied him distractedly. "You have a different accent than your brother."

"What?"

"I thought you were both Dubliners."

"He's from Belfast. Why are you bringing this up?"

"I had a dream about him," Theo said. "But now I'm thinking it wasn't a dream."

"What?"

"Is everything all right?" Elder Howell asked them.

Peter nodded. "Yes, sir. We're just eager to start so we can get to work."

"We understand. We'll keep this brief."

The council did anything but. For the next forty minutes, they walked Peter and Theo through an exhaustive rehash of recent events, just to confirm the details. On Tuesday night, while his body lay dying on the floor of a stairwell, Theo had slipped into the God's Eye and caught a glimpse of the vaunted string. The solution to Earth's greatest problem had flashed before his eyes and now he had . . . something—a hunch, a hint, a *revelation*. The story had grown through gossip and wishful thinking, until half the clan believed that Theo had all the answers. He'd been given step-by-step instructions on how to stop the apocalypse, bow-wrapped and blessed by God Himself.

In truth, he didn't remember a thing about his conversation with Ioni. All he had was the scattered, fumbling message he gave to Hannah before his reversal.

We have to find our people. All of them.

No one was particularly pleased by that hitch, least of all the elders. Once they finally caught up on the backstory, Peter began his formal presentation. He stood up and activated a lumic display board. The screen came to life with a projection of his handwriting.

THE PLATINUMS—TAMPA, FL

THE IRONS—AUSTIN, TX (SPLIT INTO TWO)

THE COPPERS—SEATTLE, WA (?)

EVAN RANDER (??)

"This is what we have on the orphans at large," Peter explained. "We know there are at least five other groups in foreign countries."

"But you don't know which countries," Elder Rubinek stressed.

"Between Theo and our other augurs, I'm sure we'll fill in the gaps."

Victoria Chisholm shot him a skeptical look. "It's not the gaps that worry me, it's the danger. The Seattle mission was a disaster on every level. Do you deny this?"

"It could have gone better," Peter admitted.

"Now you want to try the exact same thing in other cities."

Peter nodded. "And Seattle again."

A wave of grumbles filled the chamber. Irwin Sunder fumed from the elders' table. "You're asking us to risk our lives and freedom over the vision of an amateur augur."

"A vision he can't even *remember*," Elder Tam added. "You have to realize how crazy that sounds."

Peter shook his head. "Crazy is thinking the world will fix itself. Crazy is doing nothing while our children are dying."

"My children are already dead!" Sunder yelled. "I lost my son, my daughter, and my granddaughter, all because we trusted the wrong augur."

Mia rose to her feet. "He warned you! Peter warned you about Rebel and you didn't listen!"

"*Sit down*," snapped Elder Howell. "This isn't an open forum."

Mother Olga gestured at Mia. "But she's right. If we had all listened to Peter—"

"One reckless act doesn't fix another," said Elder Rubinek. "If anything, it's all the more reason to be cautious."

"Bullshit."

All eyes fell on Zack. Sunder glowered at him. "We *told* you—"

"I don't care. Throw me out. It doesn't change the facts. You guys have been begging Theo to show you the way. Now he's saying, 'Okay, here's the way,' and you're all crapping kittens. Did you think saving the world would be easy? Did you think it wouldn't involve risk?"

Hannah pointed to Jonathan and Heath. "An augur once told us where to find these two. We didn't know her and we didn't trust her, but we took a chance anyway and it was the best decision we ever made."

David nodded in agreement. "Unlike you, we see the value in strangers. For all we know, there are orphans out there who've seen even more of the string than Theo has."

"We *need* to find these people," Amanda said. "If you're not going to help us, then get out of our way."

Elder Kohl turned her jaded eyes on Theo. "We seem to be hearing from everyone but the augur in question. Why is that?"

Theo looked up in blinking distraction. Truth be told, he was barely listening. His mind was still stuck on Merlin McGee. How could a Gotham know a Beatles song? Why did he insist that everyone knew it? The mystery vexed Theo like a seed in his teeth. The answer was right there. He just had to pry it loose.

He shrugged at Elder Kohl. "I don't know what to tell you. You're looking for assurances and I can't give you any. All I have are hunches based on glimpses, and frankly, they're not very encouraging."

Peter winced. "Look, I think we're getting off the—"

"No. I want to hear this," Kohl said. She looked to Theo again. "What do you know?"

"I know the woman who gave me my information is the same one who misled Rebel. I know that some of the people we need to find aren't very nice." He motioned to Evan's name on the display board. "One of them's a psychopath."

Anxious murmurs filled the room. Theo stood up and paced the floor. "And I know it's not just our missing people we need, it's yours. All the chronokinetics who never found their way here. All the ones you exiled. Those nine black families you willfully excluded. What are they called again?"

Sunder's voice dropped an octave. "The Majee."

"Yeah. We're going to need them too."

The Mayor had to douse the room in flashing light in order to quell the ruckus. Theo cut him off before he could speak.

"But none of this matters as long as the Pelletiers are around. They're the ones who started this mess. If we want any chance of surviving, we're going to have to deal with them."

"*Deal* with them?" Elder Rubinek asked.

"I mean send them home or kill them," Theo said. "I don't think there's any other way."

A loud din swept through the chamber. Semerjean sat off to the side and solemnly shook his head. *Oh, Theo.*

"Zack's right," Theo continued. "No one said this would be easy. If it was, there'd be more than one string. But as long as we *have* one, as long as there's a single . . ."

He stopped in place with an astonished expression. A hissing word escaped his lips. Only Peter was close enough to hear it. It sounded an awful lot like *shoop.*

All eyes followed Theo as he rushed to the edge of the table ring. He fixed his urgent gaze on Jonathan and Heath.

"Your music sheets, those songs you've been working on. Is one of them 'Come Together'?"

The two Golds traded a confused look. "Yeah," Jonathan said. "Why?"

"You have the whole thing. The notes, the lyrics."

Heath crossed his arms indignantly. "It's the Beatles. Of course we have it."

"Holy shit . . ."

Peter gripped Theo's arm. "Listen—"

"Your brother. I didn't see him. I saw a *future* him. That's why I was confused."

"What?"

"That's how he'll know the song. We teach it to him. We teach everyone!"

Theo ran to the display board and scanned the names of the three missing groups—the Coppers, the Platinums, the Irons. All the American breachers.

Come together, right now . . .

"Oh my God."

Seventy-two people watched him with the same befuddled expression. Even his friends seemed to be questioning his state of mind. Theo didn't care. He'd never felt saner in his life.

He tapped the display board, his face lit up in a daffy grin.

"I know how to find these people," he said. "All of them."

THIRTY-EIGHT

A vast network of tunnels stretched out beneath the village, an under-underland that only a handful of Gothams ever visited. Amidst all the store-rooms and bunkers and junk-cluttered passages lay a few buried secrets. Journey Tam kept a psilocybin mushroom farm. Rebel Rosen had his own private shooting range. Frank Godden had stashed an entire pornography theater behind a wall of emergency rations—six seats, one projector, and no judgments.

More benign and well known was the half-million-dollar recording studio at the north end of the tunnels, directly beneath the amphitheater. The Gothams had used it to produce fourteen albums over the last eight years, all demo tracks and vanity spins from the clan's avid musicians. The White Hand Groove, the all-tempic jazz band, recorded a new compilation disc every December. They handed them out as stocking stuffers.

On Tuesday morning, the twenty-fourth of May, the studio was opened once again. Jonathan had recruited a bassist, a drummer, and a rhythm guitarist from The White Hand Groove and spent two days rehearsing with them. Playing "Come Together" was easy. Playing it the *right* way, the Heath and Beatles way, was a nightmare. The boy ruled the group with tyrannical exactitude, shrieking with rage whenever one of them strayed from the song sheet. The tempics were so fed up with him that Hannah began fearing for his safety. Luckily Jonathan, no stranger to band friction, was able to keep the peace.

By Friday morning, the musicians were ready to cut their single. Heath took his place in the recording booth and cast a doleful look at Hannah.

"You should be doing this," he said. "You have the better voice."

It had been seventeen days since Hannah sacrificed her singing, and she had yet to croon a single note. Though she'd never intended to take her testament seriously, Irwin Sunder's scornful tone had pushed a button deep inside of her. Hannah was fiercely determined to shatter his misconceptions. She'd keep her word like a goddamn champion and show that prick the true meaning of willpower.

Hannah smiled at Heath from the control room. "You got this, sweetie. Nobody knows the song better than you."

That was certainly true. Hannah couldn't even guess the number of times Heath had listened to *Abbey Road* on the old world. He channeled John Lennon with supernatural precision—every note, every cadence, every split-second pause. This was more than a cover. It was a resurrection.

Heath raised his mic to mouth level, then nodded anxiously at the producer. "Okay. I'm ready."

"A song," Mia had uttered, four days earlier. "You want us to put out a song."

Theo had gathered the others for a backyard conference: seven orphans and five Gothams, all skeptically watching him from lawn chairs. Mercy and Yvonne had missed the council meeting and had to be briefed on Theo's latest epiphany. He was still having trouble explaining it.

He paced the grass in a caffeinated tizzy, his shirttail flapping wildly. "The song is just the envelope. I'm talking about an invitation. It's like *Close Encounters*. Devil's Tower. You know, *doo*-doo-*doo*-doo-doo."

Even the orphans were blank-faced. Theo tried a new approach. "Okay, when Hannah first saw Jonathan at that nightclub, she didn't know him from Adam. It wasn't until he played . . . what was it? Zeppelin?"

"Pink Floyd," Hannah and Jonathan said in unison.

"It wasn't until he played Pink Floyd that he stood out like a beacon. She knew right then and there that he was one of us."

Theo saw Liam swapping a baffled look with Carrie. He shook a finger at them. "Right! See? You don't know who Pink Floyd is. You wouldn't know a Beatles song if it humped your leg. But I'd bet my life that anyone from our world—*anyone*—would recognize 'Come Together.' They'd know it at the first very *shoop*."

Heath opened his mouth to correct him. Theo waved him off. "I know. It's 'shoot me.' The point is that it's one of the most famous songs we have."

"We get the premise," Zack said. "We're just stuck on the details. You want to use this song as a bird call—"

"More than a bird call. A dog whistle. A *shibboleth*."

"So you want to blanket the world in this bird-dog shibboleth whistle—"

"Not the world," Theo said. "We'll have to find a different way to get the foreign orphans. But the ones within our borders? The Coppers, Irons, and Platinums? Oh yeah. We can reach them."

"How?" Amanda asked. "Even if we get all the right people to hear the song—"

"The Godzilla of *ifs*," David grumbled.

"—how does it bring us all together?"

Theo scanned the faces around him and laughed. He'd spent so much time being stressed and overwhelmed that his friends rarely saw this side of him. He'd been a certified genius once, a prodigy. Now after five years of alcoholism and ten months of transdimensional chaos, he was once again in top form.

He stuffed his hands in his pockets and smiled charmingly at Amanda.

"It's easy," he told her. "We give them a way to sing back."

The next day, while Jonathan and Heath began their rehearsals, Yvonne returned from town with a brand-new powerphone. The device weighed five pounds and fit in the hand like a clothes iron, but its signal strength was second to none. It was the only celestial mobile that was guaranteed to work in the underland.

Soon the handset was charged and the hotline was ready. The big challenge now was giving out the number to an entire nation without having it fall into the wrong hands.

Luckily, Theo had a solution. He gathered Amanda, Zack, and Mia around his laptop and showed them their new phone number. They squinted at it like it was an enigma, an answer just waiting for a question. #83-11-24800.

Mia smiled with fresh inspiration. "I got the three."

"I got the eight," said Zack.

"The eleven's a no-brainer," Amanda said.

Within an hour, the phone number was converted into esoteric hints: the number of letters in Luke Skywalker's saga, the number of points in a field goal, the day in September that the Towers fell, the number of World Wars, the number of Beatles, the old prefix for toll-free calls. Any breacher with a pen and two brain cells to rub together would have no trouble reassembling the number, while even the smartest Altamerican would choke at the first alien reference.

Zack and Mercy spent the next two days painting the clue cards on canvases, decorating each one with artistic flourishes. At Theo's request, they designed a final call-to-action, a three-card plea to all the orphans out there:

WE KNOW WHAT YOU'RE GOING THROUGH.

WE ARE YOU.

CALL US. LET US HELP EACH OTHER.

Mercy filmed the cards on her lumicam. Jonathan and Heath provided the soundtrack. By Saturday night, the group had a four-minute and ten-second music video—the ultimate bird-dog shibboleth whistle. Only one question remained.

"How do we get it out there?" Hannah asked.

The issue had initially stumped Theo. For a nation with flying cars and force fields, their Internet was straight out of 1994. There was no outlet, no bandwidth, no public demand for online movies. The very notion of viral videos was completely foreign.

That only left one option, a rather tricky one at that.

"Surpdog."

This time, only the Gothams in the group understood the reference. They stared at him with matching looks of doubt.

"That's crazy," Mercy said.

"It'll work."

Peter shook his head. "No one knows who this guy is. Even if we find him—"

"We'll find him," Theo insisted.

"—there's no guarantee he'll help us."

The orphans in the circle remained hopelessly lost. Hannah threw her hands up. "Who the hell are you talking about?"

To fully grasp the legend of Surpdog, one had to know a little about the late Dennis Dudley. The third and youngest son of President Irving Dudley was, by all accounts, an unbearable man. He was a narcissist, a nihilist, an unabashed racist, and a paranoid conspiracy theorist. He also happened to be one of the greatest inventors of his generation. In 1976, while working as a researcher at Edison Temporics, Dudley solved a riddle that had been vexing the scientific community for years. He discovered how to send two-dimensional lumic images through the air without electronic conversion. No binary switches. No blocky pixels. Just eye-popping visuals that looked as real as life itself.

His eponymous transceiver—a six-foot obelisk made of wire, glass, and copper—forever changed the face of broadcasting. It was the death of television and the dawn of the lumivision age.

By the time Dudley died in 1985, his invention blanketed the nation—a hundred thousand mini-towers on the street corners and rooftops, in the hills and fields, even floating on lakes. The dudleys worked in perfect harmony, each one routing a million images per second. The average lumivision signal passed through a hundred and twelve relays before bursting into color on someone's screen.

There was just one problem. Dudley had built a secret functionality into his constructs, a way to turn any tower into a guerrilla broadcast station. He'd wanted an emergency media system in place for when the blacks took over the country and had assumed his fellow white men would be smart enough to figure it out. The exploit was so well hidden that nobody discovered it until 1987, when a twelve-year-old prodigy named Kevin Thurber (a black kid) opened up a dudley and noticed some curious crosswires.

The next night, the sixty thousand viewers of Oklahoma-3 caught a strange flicker in the middle of *Laugh Riot*. Their lumivisions gave way to a crystal-clear image of a wide-eyed Kevin Thurber.

"Is it on? Did I do it?"

He did it. Thurber had hacked a dudley with little more than a lumicam and a homemade wire bridge, making him the first lumivision signal pirate. A glib local journalist called him "Thurber the Usurper," a name that led to the new slang term for his accomplishment: surping.

The next two years weren't kind to the lumivision networks. At least twice a week, some tech-savvy miscreant surped a broadcast for their own purposes, whether it was to vent their spleen, waggle their privates, or air a special message. A woman surped National-12 with a plea to find her missing sister (it worked). A man surped Cincinnati-4 to ask his girlfriend to marry him (it didn't work). The singer Tamara Tamley got her first big break by crooning a beautiful ballad in the middle of *Cop Cat*, one of the rare instances of a surpcast offering better-quality programming than the show it replaced.

In 1989, Edison Temporics completed its systematic overhaul of the dudleys, a slow and meticulous upgrade that made the transceivers inviolable, at least to the average tamperer. Surping soon became limited to the crackerjack elite, the technological ninjas who could bypass a tempic wall just as easily as a firewall. Thanks to a new monitoring system and the recent invention of the ghost drill, DP-9 was able to find and catch most of these criminals. The remaining surpers either scaled back their operations or hung up their toolkits entirely.

The lone exception was Surpdog.

The man was a phenom, even among the supersurpers. He'd commandeered more than six hundred broadcasts over twenty-three years, never lingering in one area, never hacking the same dudley twice. Even more frustrating for the Deps, he used a one-of-a-kind solic disruptor to stymie their ghost drills. They had no visuals on him, no witness accounts, no evidence at all except a smattering of dog tracks. His inexplicable paw prints earned him the second half of his nickname.

Surpdog's motives were just as baffling as his methods. Unlike the rest of his ilk, he never delivered any masked manifestos. His videos were merely fifty-four seconds of beautiful images from other parts of the world—the Highlands of Scotland, the desert sands of Egypt, the bamboo groves of Japan. The pictures kept changing but the theme remained the same. The best anyone could guess was that Surpdog was a worldly dog, one who didn't appreciate America's isolationist tendencies. It seemed an awfully strange cause to wrap a criminal career around, yet Surpdog persisted year after year, with no signs of slowing down.

Theo had learned about him last October, while he and Amanda were prisoners of DP-9. The West Virginia field office was a hub of the Broadcast Crimes division and had been littered with flyers about their number one target. When Theo had asked Melissa about Surpdog, she explained the case with shrugging indifference. He was a harmless man with an admirable message. She was in no hurry to see him caught.

Now, eight months later, Theo had become very intent on finding Surpdog. And he knew just the pair to do it.

On Friday morning, while Jonathan and Heath recorded their song, Peter took David on a covert trip to the surface. Tomkins Cove lay ten miles north of Quarter Hill, a small and wealthy suburb on the western bank of the Hudson. If outsiders knew the name, it was from the *Tomkins Cove* supernatural drama that was wildly popular in the 1980s. The show had been one of the very first casualties of the lumivision era, as the vampires looked pathetic in super-high-definition.

Peter had learned from local news archives that Surpdog had been to the area recently. The dudley he'd used to surp New York–5 stood right behind the local police station. Those who'd been hoping to catch the end of *Nina Shield, Private Eye* were infuriated to find the show preempted by fifty-four seconds of windmills and waterfalls.

Now Peter kept a watchful eye on the precinct while David scanned the dudley's past. As Theo had hoped, the boy wasn't burdened by the limits of ghost drills. He could easily see Surpdog through the solic haze, the curious trick that had stumped a nation for years.

David creased his brow, then broke out in laughter. Peter eyed him strangely. "What? Did you get him?"

He did, except there was no "him" to get. That was the trick. The great and mighty Surpdog wasn't a man at all.

If the police had bothered to look out their window three months ago, they would have seen it: a huge white Komondor, at least a hundred and eighty pounds, charging out of the woods like a woolly bear. The dog ran toward the station—tongue wagging, leash dragging—until he reached the dudley at the edge of the cruiser lot. There he stopped to do his canine business: sniff the grass, scratch his side, pee a little. Even if witnesses had been standing right next to him, they wouldn't have seen the ten-pound solic disruptor that was strapped to his stomach, tucked away behind the hanging ropes of fur.

In an invisible burst, the area became unghostable. The tempis melted away from the base of the dudley, revealing a small metal access door. The dog scratched at the panel, just as he'd been taught. An electronic passkey on his ankle popped an inner latch.

The dudley had been unlocked before the human half of Surpdog even appeared.

She came shuffling out of the forest, a small Polynesian woman in a tank top and running shorts. After reuniting with her Komondor in fake exasperation, she crouched to pick up his leash. Once safely hidden between the dog and the dudley, the woman activated her tempic gloves, pulled her tools from her water bottle, and hacked the console. Forty-four seconds, in and out. Surpdog walked away in perfect innocence, just another evening jogger and her pet.

David followed their ghosts for eight more blocks, until they entered a white camper aerovan. All Peter needed was the license plate number and a few well-placed phone calls to uncover her identity. She was a forty-five-year-old immigrant from the Hawaiian Republic, a field technician for Edison Temporics. Her name was Alamea Wilson but everyone called her Ally. The dog's name was Barney.

Two days later, in a Vermont forest clearing, Ally woke up to the sound of thunderous barks. It seemed her partner in crime was worked up about something—a deer, a snake, maybe even a chipmunk. Sadly, there was nothing she could do about it. Her employers had once again sent her on assignment to Bennington, a town without a single Komondor-friendly motel. That meant another week in the camplands, which meant another week of Barney yelling at nature.

Ally folded up her bed, threw on her robe, and grabbed a large bag of kibble from her storage bin. A little breakfast would shut Barney's barkhole, then she could decide her plans. The *Queen of America Pageant* was airing tonight, at least twelve million viewers in desperate need of perspective. Unfortunately, Edison had already logged her arrival. She'd have to fly at least a hundred miles out of Bennington if she wanted to hack a dudley.

Barney's barks grew louder, more insistent. Ally bumped the door open and brought his food bowl outside. "All right. All right. I'm—"

She looked up to find two men and a woman standing just inside her tempic fence. Her bowl fell to the ground. She reached for the handphone in her pocket.

"You have three seconds to leave before I call the—"

"Surpdog."

Ally's muscles hardened. Her eyes grew to circles. She stammered at the man who'd spoken to her, a disheveled Filipino who looked young in the face but old in the eyes.

"It's all right," Theo told her. "We're just here to talk."

It took twenty-two minutes for Ally's hands to stop shaking. She'd always feared the day would come when somebody sniffed her out, but she imagined they'd be from DP-9 or Edison Temporics. These people were something else entirely. They had no intention of bringing her to justice. All they had for her was an offer and a song.

Theo, Amanda, and Peter watched Ally from folding chairs as she screened their homemade video production, an indecipherable message set to bafflingly strange music.

The moment it ended, Ally closed her lapbook and blinked dazedly at her guests. "There wasn't a single part of that spoolie that made sense to me."

Peter smiled. "We told you it was cryptic."

"What the hell is it?"

"It's not meant for you," Theo told her. "It won't mean anything to anyone but a handful of people."

"And it'll mean everything to them," Amanda said.

Barney's tongue lolled blissfully as Amanda stroked his ear. The dog had already accepted the strangers as friends, which was more than Ally was willing to do. These people reeked of powerful secrets. Stranger still, the Irishman seemed the least foreign one among them. The other two kept using alien words like "video" and "prime time."

Ally ejected the spoolie and twirled it in her fingers. "This is crazy. I mean, for all I know, you guys are terrorists. This thing could wake up a hundred sleeper cells."

Peter smiled patiently. "Terrorists have telephones. They don't need surpers."

True. They also didn't go around offering satchels of cash to complete strangers. Ally could travel the world on what these people were offering, and that was just the advance payment. Maybe that was the problem. Maybe this was too good to be true.

She jerked her head at the disc. "It doesn't matter. This is a four-minute spool. Anything longer than fifty-four seconds gets shut down by the network. They always find the signal."

"You'll get around that," Theo assured her.

"How?"

"I have no idea. I just know that you will."

Ally wrung her hands, stymied. She supposed she could try a daring quintuple surp: five different dudleys set to a synchronized time release. It would be taxing as hell on her and Barney, but it would buy enough time to play the whole crazy message.

She took a wistful look at Barney. "C'mere, stupid."

He galloped to her side, wagging his tail in mindless bliss as Ally hugged his head. "He only has a year or two left. The vets say he can't handle another reversal."

"I'm sorry," Amanda said.

"Don't be. He's had a long, happy life. But once he's gone . . ." Ally shrugged miserably. "My surping days are already numbered. Once Edison rolls out their new magnivisions, the whole infrastructure's gonna change. Triple-encrypted signals sent directly from space. No more dudleys. No more hacks."

Theo shuddered. His foresight insisted, without a shred of uncertainty, that the magnivision age would never come.

It's either the end of the world or the end of the world as we know it, Merlin had told him.

"Then make this your swan song," Peter suggested to Ally. "Go out with a bang."

"I'd love to. I just . . ." She opened her mouth to say something, then censored herself. "I'm better with machines than I am with humans. I can read machines. You folks—"

"We're not looking to hurt anyone," Amanda assured her. "We just want to find our people."

"What people?"

"Immigrants," Peter delicately replied. "They're lost in this country and they need us."

"You'll be helping us save lives," Theo added. "A lot of them."

Ally mulled their words a moment, her gaze lingering on the treetops. "It's funny. I've spent half my life reminding Americans that there's a whole world out there. They're so goddamn insular. Anything foreign sends them right into their clamshell. I never understood that mind-set. Not until now."

She waved her finger between Theo and Amanda. "I get the hunch that 'immigrant' is a gentle word to describe you two. I think it would break my brain to find out where you come from. There's a part of me that desperately wants to know. The rest of me . . ." She shrugged. "I like my world the size it is."

Ally pinched the spoolie between her fingers and held it up to the sun. "Luckily for you, I love confusing the shit out of people. This is right up my flagpole."

She dropped the disc into her pocket, then fluffed the fur on Barney's neck.

"Give us a week," she said. "We'll get your message out to everyone."

On Sunday, June 5, as the East Coast clocks chimed the nine P.M. hour, a gentle hush swept across the nation. Families turned off their phones and gathered around their lumivisions. Bartenders switched their wall sets to National-1. It was the third and final hour of the *King of America Pageant*, the most exciting leg of the show. This was the part where contestants stopped flexing their oiled muscles and started beating the crap out of each other.

The pubs and casinos roared with excitement as the Prince of Oregon faced the Prince of Washington in final combat. They circled each other on a suspended platform, brandishing their sparstaffs while they struggled to avoid the air vents on the floor. Unlike last week's *Queen of America Pageant*, where the grates' only danger was an upblown skirt, these vents were set to hurricane blast. One ill-timed step could send a challenger flying into the water. The gamblers in Seattle bet extra money that the long-haired fop from Oregon would be the first to get galed.

Forty-one seconds into the match, an air geyser knocked the staff out of Washington's hand. Oregon charged at him with a guttural cry. Washington stood his ground at the edge of the platform. His only hope now was to dodge at just the right moment.

Just as the princes converged in the same frame, the image shuddered, then went completely black.

All across the country, viewers screamed in frustration. Some frantically checked their signal connections. Others cursed Surpdog's name. By now most Americans recognized the telltale signs of Ally's meddling, and had been conditioned to expect her usual nonsense: fifty-four seconds of international images, all pretty and pointless and *very* annoying. If they wanted to see Timbuktu or Fuck-a-doo, they'd go to a library and—

A guitar riff suddenly seized everyone's attention. The masses fell quiet. Twenty-five million brows knitted in unison as Heath's breathy hiss filled the air.

"Shoot me."

And then it began: a cryptic serenade, a song for all the orphans of America. For the next four minutes, the viewers of National-1 sat in total silence as they listened to the music of a dead sister Earth. While some were stuck on the impenetrable lyrics and others got tangled on the text of the clue cards, the majority kept their minds on the music. The notes moved through their consciousness like an alien paradox—both mellow and edgy, familiar and strange, unnerving yet utterly mesmerizing. A million people found themselves tapping their feet to the rhythm. The more sensitive listeners reeled at the grief in Heath's voice. His haunting cracks of sorrow left them thoroughly convinced that the song was an elegy. They weren't entirely wrong.

The Silvers and Golds watched from Hannah's living room, their faces quivering with emotion. For all their work and careful planning, none of them had anticipated the overwhelming power of their accomplishment. They'd brought a piece of their world back from the dead and hung it up in the sky for everyone to see. Two Earths had come together, right now, over them.

And for a brief spell, they were home.

Mia turned her teary eyes onto Theo. "You did it. You actually did it."

Theo shook his head. He wasn't the one who'd ripped a Beatles song out of his chest, or solved the mystery of Surpdog in less than an hour. It was too soon to be celebrating anyway. None of this would mean a damn thing if the message didn't get to the right people. That was entirely up to the wind now.

As expected, Ally's monumental surp became the week's biggest story. Radio stations played "Come Together" in its entirety. Newspapers printed the text of the clue cards on their front pages. Experts and pundits dissected every word of the lyrics (which John Lennon himself had called "gobbledygook"). From state to state, channel to channel, the same question lingered on everyone's lips. *What does it all mean?*

Only Merlin McGee, America's premier prophet, offered a semblance of a rational answer. "I don't know," he told a National-4 reporter, "but it's a damn fine song."

By the end of the week, there were no new angles to explore, no more trees to shake. The talking heads decided that Surpdog had gone barking mad and that was that. *Meanwhile, in other news . . .*

Theo turned off the lumivision and paced his room. He'd spent the last five days in jittery anticipation, never once letting the powerphone out of his earshot. It seemed impossible to exist in this country without hearing the message, yet the hotline hadn't rung once. No Coppers, no Platinums, not even a teasing congratulation from Evan.

"Shit."

Theo had no idea what to do. His faith had crumbled. His foresight was nothing but fog. He rushed to his laptop, opened his bitmail program, and furiously typed a new message.

I'm asking you again: please help me. You're the only augur I know who isn't crazy or broken. And I know you know Ioni. Just tell me what she wants. Talk to me!

He sent the message, for all the good it did. He'd bitmailed Merlin a dozen times this week, using the secure and anonymous address that Peter had given him. The man had yet to respond. Like the breachers of America, Merlin seemed determined to drive Theo crazy with his silence.

Fuming, Theo began a second message. **Screw this. I'm done. Next time you see your boss, tell her . . .**

The powerphone rang in a shrill, urgent chirp. Theo fumbled for the handset and checked the caller identification screen. All it said was "Calm Down."

He pressed the phone to his ear. "So that's what it takes to get you."

"I mean it. Relax. And stop writing Merlin. He's not going to answer you."

Theo was thrown by Ioni's phone voice, a high and youthful timbre that nearly robbed her of all mystique. She sounded more like an actress in an acne cream ad than the queen of all augurs.

He cradled the phone on his shoulder and resumed his fitful pacing. "You told him not to talk to me."

"I *asked* him not to talk to you. I'm not the bossy boss you think I am."

"You're not *any* kind of boss! You give me no information, no guidance. I have no idea what I'm doing!"

"Yes, you do," Ioni said.

"The song didn't work."

"Yes it did."

Theo heard a fizzy hiss on the other end of the line. Ioni had popped open a can of something carbonated and was pausing to take a sip.

"The Platinums will call you in twenty-two minutes," she said. "The Irons in fifty."

Theo stopped in his tracks and scanned the clock on the wall. "Bullshit."

"Well, half the Irons. The other half will call next week."

"I don't believe you."

"Care to put money on it?"

He didn't. Ioni's prescience was one of the few things he didn't doubt about her. But why couldn't he see these things for himself? How could he be so blind to the events of the next hour?

Theo climbed into bed and draped his arm over his eyes. "What about the Coppers?"

"I'm not sure about them," Ioni admitted. "They're a bit of a wild card."

"But they have the number."

"Oh yes." A smile lifted Ioni's voice. "Your plan was inspired, Theo. Your message reached them all."

A wave of euphoria washed over him. He wanted to laugh and cry and whoop like a madman. Only the thought of unfinished business kept him grounded.

"There are still five other groups out there," he reminded Ioni.

"Theo . . ."

"We won't be able to get them with a song."

"*Theo*. You just paved a brighter future for a whole lot of people. You saved your friends from some very dangerous missions, and you did it all without harming a soul. Victories like this don't come very often. Take a night to enjoy it."

Theo heard the rustling of sheets, the creaking of box springs. It seemed Ioni was also lying down in bed.

"I still don't entirely trust you," he admitted.

Ioni sighed. "That's okay. I don't entirely trust myself either."

"Can't you give me more information? I mean, with everything at stake—"

"That's *exactly* why I don't give you more. It's why I don't want you talking with Merlin."

"You're afraid I'll break the string."

"I'm afraid the string will break you."

Theo thought back to his conversation with Ally. Would she have done a better job if she knew about parallel worlds and Pelletiers, the four-year deadline that hung over everyone? Apparently not, because she did her work flawlessly. If anything, the extra baggage would have slowed her down.

A long moment passed before Theo spoke again. "I have dreams."

"I know."

"The night I met Merlin, I saw a city in the distance. It was weird and empty and it scared the living shit out of me. It was like looking at my grave."

Theo gave Ioni a moment to respond. She didn't.

"Merlin told me the fate of the world would be decided there," he said. "He said the city was falling either way and so were we. Except I don't think he was just talking about me and him. I think he was talking about all our kind. The

Gothams, the breachers, the Majee, the Pelletiers. All the timebending freaks. Even you."

Theo covered his eyes with his hand. "I think we all have to die to stop what's coming."

The line went silent for another five seconds. "Ioni?"

"I'm here."

Her voice was low now, somber. At long last Theo could hear her age.

"You've backed me into a hell of a corner," she said. "I can't tell you anything without risking everything."

"Then don't. I'm only saying it because . . . I don't know. If that's what it takes to save billions of lives, I'll do it. So will my friends. I just wish I knew."

"Why?"

Theo ruminated on it a moment. "I don't know. Maybe I'm a masochist. Maybe I'm tired of surprises. Or maybe I just want the comfort that my life and death will mean something." He chuckled. "I've already made more of a mark on this world than I ever did on the last one."

He heard the faint metal clack of Ioni's watches. He could only guess that she was checking the time.

"Theo, I want you to do something for me, all right? This is the easiest thing I'll ever ask of you."

Theo narrowed his eyes suspiciously. "What?"

"The minute you get off the phone with the Irons, I want you to share the good news with your friends. Bang the doors. Bring them out. Yell like Paul Revere. Tell them that this is just the start of something wonderful. The orphans of your world are coming together. There'll be a lot of new houses on Freak Street."

Theo tapped his jaw, his mind teeming with questions. "I'll tell them. But—"

"No buts. Just take a night off and have a good time. Can you do that for me? Please?"

Theo heard a foreboding sorrow in her voice, as if the party she wanted was a last hurrah for something—or someone.

Ioni picked up on his hesitation. "Theo . . ."

"I'll do it," he said. "Just answer me this one—"

"No."

"Why am I only seeing fog in the future? Are the Pelletiers jamming me again?"

"Goddamn it, Theo."

"What's coming? What do they not want me to see?"

"Just do what I say!"

Ioni hung up. Theo jumped out of bed and cursed a storm. His faith in her had never been shakier, yet he was already starting to sense the truth of her words. A warm wind tickled him from the near future—a pleasure, of *triumph*. Ioni wasn't lying. Theo and his friends would have a very good night.

Everything after that was shadows and fog.

He sat at his desk, twiddling his thumbs until the powerphone rang again. Theo didn't bother to check the caller ID. He cracked his neck, cleared his throat, and then, with a grin on his lips, he answered the call of the Platinums.

THIRTY-NINE

Zack bowed his head like a man in prayer, his eyes closed in a twitching wince. The Lee family elevator seemed almost deliberately designed to unnerve him. The rollers squeaked like dying mice while the car's sputtering lurches sent his stomach into somersaults. Most rattling of all were the interior embellishments: mirrors, mirrors on the walls, a full-length mirror on each door. Zack couldn't step inside without reliving his time in the Pelletier dungeon. He still felt a cold squeeze around his heart whenever he saw his reflection.

Mercy flanked his side and studied him closely. "What?"

"What, what?"

"Every time you ride this thing, you look like you're getting fisted."

Zack kept his head down. A different girlfriend might have simply asked him if he was okay, but then Mercurial Lee didn't hide her true nature. Most of the time, he appreciated her saltiness. Just not tonight.

"I'm fine," he insisted. "Just a little claustrophobic."

He didn't know why he lied to her. She knew him well enough by now to see through his bullshit. In a better state of mind, he might have told her not to take it personally. Even his closest friends didn't know about the mirror room.

Mercy finished the last of her cider punch, then crumpled the cup in her hand. A spontaneous party had broken out on Freak Street earlier, in celebration of Theo's news. The Platinums and half the Irons were making their way to Quarter Hill and would be here by Monday—twelve new orphans, an eighth of their world's remaining population. Theo strongly believed, from his brief but telling phone conversations, that they were all good people. He was particularly high on the leader of the Platinums, an eloquent young rabbi named Caleb.

It was a miraculous coup, yet Zack had barely cracked a smile all night. He'd spent most of the party sitting off to the side, nursing a beer while he mingled with Heath. Every time Mercy looked his way, she caught him staring at Amanda, watching her with heavy eyes as her fingers clasped Peter's. His grief had been so palpable that even David, no friend of Mercy's, gave her a sympathetic pat on the shoulder. *Give him time.*

The elevator made its final creaking moans. Mercy twisted the ring on her middle finger. "I like Mia."

"So do I," Zack said.

"You know that she and Carrie are a thing now, right?"

"She tell you that?"

"No. They're doing their damnedest to keep it hushed."

"So how do you know they're an item?"

"Because I have eyes, Zack. I see things."

At long last, the elevator reached the surface. The doors opened to the Lees' secret parlor, a miniature museum of figurines and priceless paintings. Zack once again marveled at the sight of *The Blue Boy.* He wondered what would happen if he reversed the canvas two and a half centuries, all the way to Gainsborough's earliest strokes. Maybe there was a second image hidden beneath the oils, a half-formed concept that lay buried inside the child like a parasitic twin.

Mercy led Zack through her family's long corridors. Her voice took on a bitter tone. "You know what impresses me most about Mia? She was in love with David for the longest time, but when it didn't work out, she got over it. She just brushed off her shoulder and moved on."

She tossed a pointed look over her shoulder. "Imagine that."

Zack met her scowl with a sneer. "Gee, if I didn't know any better—"

"You *don't* know better."

"—I'd say you were mad at me."

Mercy brought him into her bedroom and closed the door behind them. "I'm not mad, Zack. I'm tired. If you want to be with Amanda, then be with her. Find a way. But this constant moping—"

Zack chuckled disdainfully. "Moping."

"You think you're not? Do you even see yourself?"

The motion sensors activated, shining soft cones of light on Mercy's wall art. Zack approached her nearest painting, a two-tone image that was either a woman or a mockingbird, depending on which color you were looking at.

"Negative space," he muttered.

"What?"

"It's the name we had for this kind of illusion." He traced a finger down the canvas. "Some people only ever see one part of the picture. To them it's either a vase or two faces and that's all there is to it."

Mercy crossed her arms. "Your point?"

"You have eyes. You see things. How did Heath look tonight?"

"Miserable. Almost as bad as you."

"Good. So you did notice." Zack turned around to face her. "Now why do you think he was moping? Because he can't have Amanda?"

"Look—"

"Negative space," Zack repeated. "While everyone was celebrating the people who are coming, Heath and I were talking about the ones who aren't. A pair of sisters named Carina and Deanna. A bunch of guys named Sebastian, Drew, and Gavin."

He thumped his head sarcastically. "Shit. There was one more. I forget his name. No, no. Don't tell me. It'll come to me."

"Zack . . ."

"Trillinger!" He snapped his fingers. "Josh Trillinger. That's it."

Mercy sat down on the bed and stared at her fumbling fingers. "You goddamn turners. Always reversing yourselves."

"What's that supposed to mean?"

"You *said* you forgave me."

"And I do. That isn't about blame. It's about me missing my brother."

Mercy shook her head. "It's more than that."

"You're telling me how I feel?"

"You've been cold to me for days. I'm not the only one who sees it."

Zack moved to the window and peered up at the moon: the real one, not that flat white lie that hung above the underland. Seventeen countries had already staked their flags there, using aeris-powered spacecraft and tempis-coated pressure suits.

"It's not you," Zack assured Mercy. "I've been like this with everyone. Hannah called me a piss blizzard tonight."

"Why?"

"Because she sucks at metaphor."

"Why are you pulling away from your friends?"

Because one of them's Semerjean. "I don't know," Zack said. "I don't know what's going on with me. I just . . ."

"What?"

Zack opened his mouth to say something, then immediately thought better of it. He hadn't mentioned a word about the Pelletiers in two weeks, if only to spare the others from his stupid, half-baked theories. Except now the pieces were coming together. A sharp new picture was forming in the negative space. Zack wasn't sure if he was getting wise or going crazy. With the Pelletiers, one was as good as the other.

"Just give me a few days," he said. "Let me work it out on my own."

Mercy studied him through slitted eyes, then told him to take all the time he needed. Zack had no trouble reading the subtext from her tone. *Start now. Go.*

Soon he was back in that infernal elevator, avoiding his reflections as the car squeaked and tottered. Halfway down, he forced his eyes open and took a good hard look at himself. He was an even more wretched sight than he remembered—bleary-eyed, pale-skinned, a ghoul from any angle. Jesus. No wonder everyone was worried about him.

Evan snickered from the back of Zack's consciousness. *Look at you. The Zack-in-the-Box. The sad little jester. Shit, man. You couldn't even give your girlfriend a proper good-bye.*

Zack lowered his gaze and muttered under his breath. "It wasn't a good-bye."

Yeah, you just go on thinking that, Blue Boy. You know you're never going back to her. And it's not because of your brother and it's not because of Amanda.

"Shut up."

It's because the Pelletiers want you with Mercy.

Zack pressed his hands to his eyes, for all the good it did him. Evan continued to circle his thoughts, taunting him from every mirror.

They went out of their way to break up you and Amanda. They bent over backward not to kill Mercy. How many times have they spared her now? Three? Four? Gosh, it's almost as if they have a reason to keep her alive.

"Fuck you."

Come on, man. Think! You and Mercy, Amanda and Peter, David and Yvonne. It's all a big square dance, a breacher/Gotham mating game. That's the only reason they brought you here.

"Bullshit."

You're just their breeding mouse, Zacky.

"Go away!"

Squeak fucking squeak.

Zack's body screamed with temporis, a bright white flash that burst from every pore of his skin. His clothes became musty and threadbare with age. The mirrors all around him turned cloudy, brittle. He looked up just in time to see the glass succumb to the elevator's vibrations. Hairline cracks spread in furious branches.

"Shit . . ."

He crouched on the floor and covered himself as the mirrors came down in a thousand pieces. By the time the car settled, his jeans looked like they'd been dragged through a briar patch. Thin streams of blood dribbled from the holes.

He stepped out into the underland and focused his thoughts on the elevator. As always, the universe resisted and Zack insisted. *Just there*, he bargained. *Just look where I'm looking and break the rules there.*

The air inside the car rippled. The glass shards wobbled until, all at once, they began to move. They clacked together into larger fragments, then leapt back to their original places on the wall. Zack almost felt competent again as he watched the seams melt away, but something wasn't right. The mirrors were marred with hundreds of wrinkles, like used tinfoil. Any professional restorer could have told Zack that silver glass didn't reverse well. It was the silver, not the glass, that proved stubborn to manipulation.

Flustered, Zack cut a hurried path toward Freak Street. The underland was desolate this time of night. He didn't see another living soul until he crossed the village square and noticed a lanky figure hunched forward on a park bench. Even in the distance and the faint glow of the lampposts, Zack had no trouble recognizing him.

"David?"

The boy didn't look up at Zack's approach. He didn't move at all.

"David, are you okay?"

Clearly he wasn't. His skin was flushed. His brow was creased. He reminded Zack of the mirrors in the elevator—a smooth veneer, forever rumpled.

Zack sat down next to him. "Talk to me. What happened?"

A few seconds passed before David made eye contact. His voice came out in a croaking stammer. "I thought he was crazy."

"Who?"

"Rebel. I . . ."

David took a long look at the illusive moon before rising from the bench. "There's something I have to show you."

He led Zack through the shadows, to the corner of town that one could charitably call a business district. Between a volunteer library and a self-serve coffeehouse lay a narrow path of concrete, one of the underland's few alleys.

David conjured a floating orb of lumis and guided Zack down the passage. "I had an argument with Yvonne tonight," he explained. "Stupid stuff. Mostly my fault. She left on a bad note and I was feeling restless, so I went for a walk. That's when I saw something."

"Something," Zack echoed.

"Something in the recent past."

The alley ended in an L-shaped alcove, a sizable niche filled with bike wheels, broken chairs, and other dusty refuse. The Gothams seemed unwilling or unable to discard their old junk. It piled up in the hidden spaces. Out of sight, out of mind.

David set up a folding chair. "You're going to want to sit for this."

Warily, Zack obliged him. David closed his eyes and concentrated until a temporal ghost appeared in front of him, a waifish blonde in a boy's undershirt and jeans. She twirled among the clutter in wild delight, as if she'd just been freed of a soul-crushing burden. Zack couldn't recall ever seeing her before. She was peppy and pretty and she didn't take herself too seriously. That last part alone made her rare among the Gothams.

He turned to David. "Okay, I'm lost. Who is this?"

"You don't see them?"

"See what?"

"Look at her wrist."

Zack scanned her arm and caught a sharp glint of silver. Her wristwatch was a fancy antiquity, even more exquisite than David's. Next to it was a plain digital timepiece that looked cheap enough to come from a cereal box.

More telling than the quality was the quantity of her watches. Zack sat forward, dumbstruck. "Wait. Is that . . ."

"Yes." David's voice dropped an octave as he glared at the ghost. "I believe it is."

If Theo, Hannah, or Mia had been there, they could have confirmed it. They were the only ones in the group who'd met Ioni. The others merely knew her through anecdote.

"When was this?" Zack asked David.

"Last Tuesday. Around midnight."

"But what the hell was she doing here?"

A shimmering glow forced Zack to shield his eyes. He squinted and saw a ten-foot portal fill the air behind Ioni.

His throat closed. *Oh no . . .*

Two willowy figures emerged from the whiteness, their ghosts flecked with temporal static. They could have stepped right out of one of Georges Seurat's pointillist paintings—*Les Poseuses* or *A Sunday on La Grande Jatte*. Even with the image grain, Zack could easily recognize the man and woman from their features—his chalk-white hair, her coal-black eyes, their elegant clothes and menacing airs.

Zack shot to his feet and stumbled backward, as if Azral and Esis could turn real at any moment.

David held his arm. "It's okay. It's all right."

"You could have warned me!"

"That's why I told you to sit!"

Zack turned back to the three spectral figures. If Ioni was frightened by the sudden arrival of the Pelletiers, she did a good job hiding it. She hugged Azral with giddy exuberance and gave Esis a kiss on both cheeks.

"*Mou s'alla amn mienka!*" she said. "*Me'tse haas en n'affa?*"

Azral closed the portal behind it, then took a distasteful look at his surroundings. "*Kusu n'affa.*"

Zack felt as if someone had punched all the breath out of him. He had to press his temples just to hold his thoughts together.

"She's with them. She's been working with the Pelletiers."

David nodded bleakly. "I think she *is* a Pelletier."

Zack fell back in his seat. The one comfort he'd had about Ioni was her hatred for Azral and Esis, but now it seemed the whole thing was a sham. The bastards were playing everyone from both sides. And that wasn't even the worst part.

"The string," Zack said. "All that stuff she told Theo . . ."

His heart jumped in panic when Esis looked his way. She was scanning the alley for something. Or someone.

"*Hou sa macore e'ley?*" she asked Ioni.

"*Illy aun,*" the girl replied with breezy assurance.

A daft thought suddenly occurred to Zack, a theory both awful and reassuring.

"Semerjean," he uttered. "Holy shit. What if all this time—"

"No," said David.

"But if she wore enough tempis—"

"Zack, she isn't Semerjean."

"How do you know?"

Grim-faced, David pulled a second chair from the wall and hunkered down next to Zack. "He's coming."

A new portal opened in the mouth of the alley. A fourth ghost joined the others. He was six feet tall and broad in the shoulders, a formidable presence even without his tempic armor. Unlike Azral and Esis, Semerjean's image wasn't marred by static. Zack could see every speck of stubble on his face. He could count the wayward hairs on his ponytail.

"No. No, no, no . . ."

Jonathan closed the portal with a flick of his hand, then smiled at his brethren. While he was content to give Azral an affectionate squeeze of the shoulder, he greeted Esis far more intimately.

Zack felt a hot wave of nausea at the sight of their kiss. "Goddamn it. God fucking damn it."

"I know," David said. "He played us all for idiots. I never suspected. Not even for a moment."

"It doesn't make sense."

"Of course it does. We would have never found Jonathan if it wasn't for Ioni. She practically hand-delivered him to us."

Zack couldn't take his eyes off Semerjean. Aside from the fact that he was standing with enemies, he looked just like the Jonathan everyone knew and loved. Actually, no. He carried a hint of shrewd confidence that Zack had never seen before, even when he was playing guitar. It was all in the smile. The smile and the—

"—eyes. Why do his eyes look different?"

David crossed his arms and fumed at the ground. "Because they're blue now."

"Jesus . . ."

While the Pelletiers conversed in their native tongue, Zack noticed a folded square of cloth under Semerjean's arm, a royal blue fabric with a glossy sheen.

"What's that thing under his—"

"Shhh! Did you hear that?"

"Hear what?"

David rewound the scene ten seconds, then resumed playback. Now Zack could hear what he was talking about, a repeated word that was both strange and familiar. *Heh-NAH.*

"Hannah . . ."

David nodded uneasily. "I missed it the first time. They're talking about her."

Zack suddenly became very aware of the cuts on his legs, a dozen tiny eyes all weeping in trickles. He wanted to scream. He wanted to cry. He wanted to reverse the whole world until all of this was undone.

"Turn it off," he told David. "Put it away."

"Not yet."

"Why?"

"Because you haven't seen the worst part."

The conference wrapped up. Azral and Esis gave their affectionate goodbyes before summoning a new portal and disappearing to parts unknown.

Alone in the alcove, Ioni and Semerjean traded a muted look of displeasure. Zack couldn't tell if they were angry at each other or just tired.

Semerjean pulled the fabric from under his arm and held it out to Ioni. She pursed her lips in a juvenile pout.

"Come on. Please? Ten more minutes."

"*El'una chine na Hannah ho'kiesse,*" he told her. "You don't want her wondering."

She snatched the cloth. "Can't wait for this to be over."

"Soon," Semerjean promised.

Zack swallowed a scream as the fabric unfurled and revealed itself. It was a homemade New York Giants jersey with a crudely stitched "44" on the front and back, a shirt he'd seen a thousand times on someone else.

His face blanched. His arms went limp at his sides. "No . . ."

Ioni threw on the shirt, then pressed the face of her digital watch. Her timepieces merged into a single golden bracelet. Everything about her appearance began to change—her hair, her nose, the color of her skin. She was metamorphosing right in front of Zack's eyes like a sorceress. A werewolf.

Once the transformation finished, there was no Ioni to be found, just a small black boy who'd become quite precious to some.

"Heath," David growled. "He's been Ioni this whole time. They've been lying to us from the very start."

Zack sat in stunned silence while Semerjean and Ioni fell back into character. Soon "Jonathan" wore an innocuous expression while "Heath" reclaimed his nervous tics. The pair swapped a quick, knowing glance before walking side by side up the alley. Back to Freak Street. Back to Hannah.

David leaned against the brick and puffed a heavy breath. "I'm sorry, Zack. There was no good way to prepare you for this. It's been thirty minutes and I still can't wrap my mind around it. I mean . . ."

He paused a moment, deliberating his words.

"If there was ever a real Jonathan and Heath, then I don't think they got very far. I think all the Golds are dead. But then what do I know? I've been a complete fool."

He looked to his fellow Silver, still staring into space in a catatonic trance. "Zack, I don't need to tell you the trouble we're in. We have to handle this with extreme—"

A strange noise trickled out of Zack's throat. David couldn't tell if it was a cry or a laugh. "Zack?"

He chuckled again, louder this time. He followed it with another, then another, and then a staccato barrage. His laughter kept intensifying, higher and faster, until his eyes filled with tears and he could barely draw a breath.

David soundproofed the area and peeked down the alley. "For God's sake, get ahold of yourself."

Zack wanted to but he couldn't stop. From the minute Semerjean gave him his silver bracelet, he'd been racking his brain over the Pelletiers. He'd pondered them from every plane of reason, every angle of reality. He even expanded his mind to accommodate some truly wild notions. But the one thing he never considered, not until this very moment, was that the assholes had a sense of humor. They were funny. Oh God, they were funny, funny people.

He wiped his eyes and let out a winded moan. "Holy shit. That was brilliant. That was a work of art. They had me going right till the end."

"What are you talking about?"

Zack swept his hand around the alcove. "This whole thing, it was bullshit! A CGI prank. They planted it for you to find, just like that van and money."

David tapped his lip in contemplation. "I'm not sure you're right."

"Come on. You think the Pelletiers would let you ghost them? You think if they could meet anywhere by portal, they'd meet here?"

"They're not gods, Zack. And they're not infallible."

"I'll say." He laughed again. "Jesus, they must think we're dumb. Maybe we deserve it. I don't know."

Zack stood up and folded his chair. "In any case, they can take their games and shove them. I'm done playing along."

David jumped to his feet. "Wait. Where are you going?"

"Home."

"You're just going to *ignore* this?"

"Of course not. I'm going to warn Jonathan and Heath that the Pelletiers are trying to frame them."

David's face went slack. "You can't do that."

"Watch me."

"Damn it, Zack. *Wait.*"

Zack turned around. David threw his hands up, exasperated. "Look, you could be right. This could all be a hoax. But if it's not—"

"It is."

"If it's *not*, then you and I have some very dangerous information, something the Pelletiers don't want us knowing. We make one bad move and there'll be consequences. They could kill us. Or worse!"

"David—"

"Do you really want go back to the mirror room?"

The words froze Zack to his very soul. He stood in perfect stasis, wide-eyed, white-faced.

David raised his palms. "Look, I'm just saying that we need to think before we act. Now I have a plan, a more cautious one. Will you at least hear me out?"

Zack nodded his head from a million miles away, from a dark corner of the universe where he could see nothing, feel nothing, think nothing at all. Only a fragment of a thought hovered in the periphery. It flickered in the blackness like a distant star.

I never . . . I never . . .

"Jonathan and Heath are night owls," David said. "They don't go to sleep until three or four. I suggest we play it safe until then. Don't talk to anyone. Don't do anything suspicious. At first light, we'll start bringing the others into the fold. First Amanda and Peter, then Mia."

Zack nodded again, though David might as well have been talking from the far side of the moon. All he could hear was the sputtering voice in his head.

I never . . . I never told . . .

"We should leave Theo out of this for now," David added. "The Pelletiers put a ring in his brain and I don't trust it. For all we know, they can see and hear us through him."

He took a wary look at Zack. "Are you listening to me?"

I never told you . . .

"Zack?"

His paralysis broke. The blood came rushing back to his face. He forced himself to make eye contact with David, using every ounce of his willpower to keep his screams inside of him.

"Okay," Zack mumbled.

"Okay to what?"

"Your plan. You want to wait until morning, I'll wait. I . . ." Zack could feel his composure crumbling, a web of cracks snaking in all directions. "I'll try it your way."

David studied him suspiciously before nodding.

"I'm glad to hear that. I really am." He clasped Zack's shoulder. "The only way we'll get through this is if we work together."

A streak of light caught Zack's eye from above, a shooting star against the nightscape. Like nearly everything else down here, the meteor was an illusion, a façade, a parody of something real. But the scream in Zack's throat was all too genuine. He had to keep it down inside him if he wanted to survive. He had to play along with the joke, even though it wasn't funny. It wasn't even remotely funny anymore.

He turned to David and gave him a shaky nod, while his mind and soul continued to howl. *I never told you about the mirrors.*

Mia woke up at half past four, alert and unrested. She was a veteran insomniac by now and knew that nothing on Earth would help her fall back asleep. Her hungry id urged her to roll over and spoon Carrie, to caress her so tenderly that she'd wake up in a loving mood. But the poor girl had her power finals in the morning. She needed all the rest she could get.

Mia slipped out from under the covers and admired Carrie from the edge of the bed. She slept on her back, her hair spread across the pillows like molten gold. The sight of her evoked such powerful feelings that Mia almost felt like a stranger to herself. Luckily, she wasn't suffering her madness alone. Carrie was just as loopy as she was, just as clueless, just as frightened and delighted. If there was a more beautiful force in the universe than warm, reciprocal love, Mia couldn't think of it.

A noise from the living room made her heart jump—the unmistakable flitter of window blinds. She peeked out of the bedroom and saw a tall, shadowed figure keeping watch on the street through a crack in the slats. Mia's fists unclenched the moment she recognized him.

She hurried into the living room and closed the door behind her, her voice hissing out in a whisper. "Hey!"

Zack threw a desolate look over his shoulder before resuming his vigil. "Sorry."

"What are you doing here?"

She turned on a lamp and balked at the state of him. His clothes were ripped all over, his jeans mottled with blood.

"Oh my God. What *happened* to you?"

He released the blinds and turned around. Now Mia could see the full extent of his trauma. He looked shell-shocked, devastated, as if he'd lost another brother.

"You're scaring me, Zack. Talk to me."

He took a seat at the dining table, his fingers moving absently over the scars on his hand.

"When the Pelletiers took me, they put me in a room. They made it so that I never got hungry and I never needed sleep. I couldn't rip my clothes, pull my hair out, or do anything to change anything. It was like I was trapped in a moment, locked in a cage of pure consistency. And no matter where I looked, there I was. A single mirror image. There was always just one of me and he was always the same."

He snatched a ballpoint pen and clicked it over and over. "The mirrors were the worst part, and I can't even explain why. They turned my reflection into a thumbscrew and they just kept twisting it into me."

Mia sat down and held his arm. "God. Zack . . ."

"You didn't know any of that, did you?"

"No. How would I?"

"I don't know. I thought maybe Evan told you. At least about the mirrors."

Mia shook her head. "He didn't say a word."

Zack leaned forward and propped his head with his hands. "Neither did I. Not to anyone."

"I'm worried about you, Zack."

"Not me."

"What?"

"I'm not the one you need to worry about."

He tore a blank scrap of paper from Carrie's math book and scribbled furiously onto it. Mia tried to read it but he was too quick with the pen. Before she could make out the first words, he rolled the paper into a tight stick.

"What is that?" Mia asked. "What did you write?"

Zack stared at the message before holding it out to her.

"This is what the Pelletiers have been hiding from us," he said. "This is the note they keep burning."

Mia plucked the stick from his fingers, her stomach gurgling with stress. Her body went rigid as she read Zack's sloppy handwriting. Her voice turned low and cold.

"Get out."

"Mia . . ."

"Get out of this house right now."

"Mia, look at me."

She didn't have to look to know that he was crying. She could hear the tremors in his voice, a nebulous mixture of sorrow and rage.

"I'm not broken," he told her. "I'm cracked as hell but I am not broken. And I know what I know. Every word of that note is true."

"Fuck you."

"He screwed up tonight. When he mentioned the mirror room, he gave himself away." Zack wiped his eyes with his sleeve. "There was no possible way he could have known."

A savage scream welled up inside Mia. She wanted to flip the table over, throw everything in the kitchen at Zack. But even now, she knew her rage was misplaced. Her future selves knew exactly where it belonged, and had told her so a thousand times.

You're so stupid.

So stupid.

So blind.

You're so blind.

You're so blind you can't even see what's going on right in front of you.

Right under your nose.

Right under your fucking nose!

You can't even see that he's laughing at you.

He's laughing at you, Mia.

He is laughing at you.

Tears dribbled down her cheeks. She covered her face with her hands. "Goddamn you, Zack . . ."

"You can prove me right or wrong," he told her. "You know how."

"I *tried* that already."

"Mia . . ."

"I sent a warning with his name on it. It didn't burn."

"But you also sent a retraction."

Mia nodded uneasily. She'd felt so bad about abusing her past selves that she'd chased every fake warning with an apology. *Disregard that first note. I was just testing something.*

"You put out your own fire," Zack told her. "The Pelletiers didn't have to do a thing."

"How do you know?"

"Because I know them." He let out the bleakest of chuckles. "I understand them now."

Mia launched from her chair and paced around the kitchen island. She made three sloppy circuits before she returned to the table and snatched the note.

"If this doesn't work—"

"Just send it."

Mia once again looked at the warning in her hand, the nightmare that fit like a lock and key into her future.

There was never a David. There is only Semerjean.

Mia's breath whistled in her throat as she opened a tiny portal to last week. She dawdled at the rift, her mind stuck between moving forward and running away. A fatalistic voice in her head assured her that there was no choice left in the matter. This was the night the future caught up to her. This was the moment she joined all the billions of screaming Mias out there in the strings.

She pushed the note into the portal with a quivering hand, and then watched the paper burn.

PART FOUR

THE ACTOR

He flew like a hawk over the plains of Québec, his arms spread, his body sheathed in aeris. From the view at ground level, he was nearly imperceptible, just a glimmering speck against the cloudscape. Only an elderly birdwatcher on the outskirts of Granby managed to see him for the airborne anomaly that he was. Her eyes bulged behind her binoculars. Her voice trickled out in a stammer, *"Ça a pas..."*

Semerjean acknowledged her with a teasing wave, then vanished in a streak of light.

He de-shifted fifty miles to the west, a thousand feet above the center of Montréal. There in the Outremont district, on the upscale end of Boulevard Laplante, stood a four-story structure of marble and glass: an eight-hundred-seat performance hall that was just days away from opening. Like everything else on this terminal planet, the building was doomed to fall in four years' time. But in another string of history, the one that Semerjean remembered, the St. David Theater would abide through twenty-six hundred winters. It would survive countless recessions and regional makeovers, even a war or two, until it became the oldest, most distinguished playhouse in North America.

Semerjean lowered himself into a portal and apparated inside the building. Once his feet touched down on the wooden planks of the thrust stage, he melted away his aeris and took an astonished look around. The theater was nothing like he remembered. Everything was so different, so new, yet he was overwhelmed with nostalgia. It was here at St. David that a struggling Australian actor got his first big break. It was here that he learned the vaunted art of lumicraft, until he could perform all of Shakespeare's plays with nothing more than his will and his ensemble of ghosts. And it was right here onstage, during one of his most celebrated performances, that he first laid eyes on the love of his life: a brilliant young doctor who crackled with power. She didn't need augments or cybernetic implants. She was a child of the Cataclysm, a direct descendant of the world's first timebenders. She was a natural talent, just like him, and she was beautiful.

They'd made love on a bed of tempis, in a small dressing room just thirty yards from where Semerjean was currently standing. Esis had stroked his chest beneath his red silk blanket and confirmed his suspicions that this was no mere dalliance. She'd looked to the future and saw their lives together. Their strings were entwined as far as the eye could see.

"We will marry in short order," Esis had informed him. "We'll have one child and a house by a lake. Together we'll share a most joyous life, though your pride will be tested when I become more famous than you."

"Famous." Semerjean had smiled as if she were toying with him. "The only famous doctors are the ones who've cured something. There aren't many ailments left."

It was then that Esis put her lips to his ears and whispered the words that would eventually change everything.

"There is death," she said. "And I will cure it forever."

Now, Semerjean wandered aimlessly across the stage, his thoughts drifting back to their thirtieth year of marriage. The memories of an old argument circled his head like a swarm of gnats.

"You have to stop this, Esis. Your reputation—"

"You think I care what those fools say of me?"

"*I* care. You had a promising career once. Now you can scarcely find work because of this . . . preoccupation of yours."

"Preoccupation?"

"Do you even realize how mad you sound? You want to crossbreed our ancestors with people who don't even exist!"

"They exist."

"Even if you *had* the technology to visit this theoretical Earth of yours—"

"We'll have it," Esis assured him. "Our son will invent it."

"Azral doesn't share your optimism. He also believes that even in the best case, there would be untold devastation."

"That is . . . unavoidable."

"Two Earths, Esis. Billions of people."

"Our discovery will spread across the strings. Eternal life for *trillions* of people."

"Only if you succeed."

"We'll succeed," Esis assured him. "I see this future, clear as sky. I'm sorry that you can't."

Semerjean stopped at the edge of the stage. He'd come to St. David to unwind for a bit, to lose himself in better times. But all he seemed to be doing was dredging up old doubts.

"I'm not even sure why you need me," he'd once confessed to his wife and son. "You're both brilliant scientists. I'm just a tired old actor who plays with ghosts."

Esis had reminded him that he wasn't just any old actor. He was a legend, and he had a finesse with people that she and Azral lacked. That skill would become invaluable soon, as there was one group of subjects—the most difficult and promising of all the chosen ones—who required special attention. The Silvers needed a strong arm to protect them, a subtle hand to guide them. No one was better suited for the task.

Semerjean moved to the footlights and gazed out at the seats. Oh, to be a simple performer again, to work with the figments of his imagination instead of live, stubborn beings. He'd assumed these children would be easy to manipulate, but they surprised and defied him every step of the way, continually forcing him to improvise. He'd shed blood and lost fingers, suffered contusions and poisons and four-mile plummets. Now one of his charges was even coming dangerously close to uncovering his true identity. Semerjean had pulled a desperate trick on Zack last night. He still wasn't sure if it worked.

No, he assured himself, it'll be fine. All he had to do was remove Jonathan and Heath from the equation, create another ghost show to make it look like they fled. Those two had long outlived their usefulness anyway. Only a handful of people would miss them.

He flicked his finger at the audience, creating five familiar holograms in the middle of the tenth row. The Silvers stared back at him with vacant eyes—the actress, the widow, the augur, the cartoonist. Semerjean fixed his gaze on the youngest member of the group, his favorite one by far.

"*Jua non'na no searis denikala né a coeura,*" he said to Mia.

It had been a poetic expression in his native era, a slogan for all the rulebreakers and trailblazers, the ones who did questionable things for the greater good. *Some hearts must break for the sake of the future.*

Semerjean vanquished the spectral images, then drew a portal to New York. He'd dawdled enough in the Great White North. It was time to get back to work. This would be a heartbreaking day for the Silvers, he feared. It'd be even worse for the Golds.

He returned to the underland at half past six, in a thin and cluttered alley behind the lumic guild headquarters. Semerjean always hated coming back to this place. The processed air tasted awful in his mouth. The artificial sky, which was just now beginning to show the first hints of sunlight, looked as crude as a child's crayon sketch. How the Gothams took comfort in this fake, plastic world was a mystery to him. His forebears were even simpler than he'd imagined.

After ghostproofing the alley with a quick burst of solis, he closed his eyes and pressed the face of his wristwatch. A three-dimensional rendering of Freak Street appeared inside his eyelids: six translucent cottages, four of them filled with live human images. Zack continued to pace his kitchen in a state of distress while Theo dozed soundly in the bedroom. Most of the others were still fast asleep: Hannah and the Golds, Amanda and Liam. Clearly Zack had opted not to raise any alarms. He was biding his time, strategizing, just as Semerjean had hoped.

Only Mia was awake and flailing about. Her heart rate was elevated to a disturbing degree. She and Carrie were both anguished to the point of tears. Were the two girls having a love spat or did Zack say something to them? And where on Earth was—

"David?"

Semerjean turned around and saw Peter watching him from the alley's edge. Though his sweatshirt and jeans looked fresh out of the dresser, his hair was unwashed, his face unshaven. Something had abruptly pulled him out of bed, but his stress indicators were normal.

Peter looked around in mild confusion. "Huh. Thought I felt something back here. Guess not."

Semerjean cursed himself. He was usually much better about masking his power signatures. Peter shouldn't have been able to sense his portals at all.

"What are you doing up at this hour?" he asked David.

Semerjean scrambled to get back into character. His expression softened. His vocal cords tightened. He replied through a twenty-first-century Australian accent that by now had become second nature.

"Couldn't sleep. Figured I might as well go for a walk."

"Back here?" Peter shook a finger at him, chuckling. "I know what you're doing. You're snooping around through local history."

Semerjean shrugged with false admission. "Just trying to understand these people."

"I get that," Peter said. "And you have every reason to be nervous after what Gemma did. But listen to me . . ."

While Peter continued to drown him in assurances, Semerjean activated a silver ring in the front of his brain, a ten-gram device whose name had no translation in English. His thoughts traveled through the God's Eye, emerging twenty-two hundred miles to the southwest.

Sehcoeur? Sehgee?

Still nothing from Azral or Esis. The two of them had been offline for hours, tucked away in the Guadalajara facility while the Pearls gave birth to their hybrids. Semerjean prayed that at least one of the infants proved suitable for their purposes. Otherwise Esis would be in a foul mood for days.

"—so stay alert but don't let paranoia get the better of you," Peter said.

David nodded uncomfortably. "Good advice."

"You're probably wondering what *I'm* doing up at this hour."

He was, but a hindsight scan quickly answered that question. Peter was just coming back from the vivery, which meant that someone got hurt last night. Semerjean had to scroll back six hours to see who it was.

Journey . . .

"I was seeing Journey Tam," Peter said. "Poor girl tried to hang herself."

That was unsettling news to Semerjean, but David had no cause to know her. "I'm sorry. Who . . . ?"

"Augur," Peter explained. "One of the better ones. Something's been spooking her these past few days, and she's not alone. Boomer MacDougal's been saucing up again. Lori Orlowski's gone on a sudden vacation. And no one's seen Rebel in days."

Semerjean grumbled in his thoughts. He didn't need this problem. Not today. "Did Journey say anything specific? A warning or—"

Peter shook his head. "She won't talk about it. Neither will Boomer. I don't know what these folks are seeing, but it sure as hell can't be good."

Semerjean knew exactly what was stressing the augurs, and they were making far too much noise for his comfort.

"Strange," said David. "Theo seemed just fine last night."

"Yeah, that worries me more. If he can't see what's coming, that usually means one thing."

David nodded grimly. "Pelletiers."

"Afraid so."

That was sound reasoning for a man of Peter's limits. But as always, he was missing a crucial piece of the story. Semerjean hoped to keep it that way.

"So what now?" David asked. "You going to visit Prudent Lee?"

Peter smiled. "Smart boy you are."

Semerjean bristled at his patronizing tone, a perpetual annoyance over the last eight months. When the fool wasn't calling him "boy," "lad," or "son," he was dismissing David's counsel as the prattlings of a child. It was Peter more than anyone who tested the limits of Semerjean's patience. He longed for the day he could drive a spike through the man's skull, along with Rebel's heart, Melissa's eye, and Evan Rander's scrawny neck.

But Azral and Esis had looked at the strings and found all these people to be more useful alive. They held Peter in particularly high regard, especially now that he was copulating with Amanda.

Peter gulped the last of his coffee, then chucked the cup into a portal. "Well, I better get on with it. You doing all right?"

Semerjean blinked at him. "What?"

"Saw you and Yvonne had a tiff last night. She didn't look happy."

"Oh." Semerjean was such an old hand at playing David that his cues came reflexively. A hint of regret. A reticent pause. An awkward stammer, as the boy wasn't accustomed to talking about his feelings.

"I'm not entirely sure what happened, to be honest. You might have noticed I'm not very good at reading people."

Peter patted his back. "Not your fault. You had an unusual upbringing."

That was true. Everything David had shared about his past had been plucked straight from Semerjean's history: his early years in Perth, his mother's slow death, his brilliant father and their travels around the globe. He'd conveniently failed to mention that it had all occurred in a parallel timeline, more than two and a half millennia from now.

"You'll be all right," Peter said. "Love's a volatile thing, especially among the young. The fights come quick, but they go away quicker."

He started toward the elevator, then turned around.

"Just make sure you fix it, son. These are dire times, and life's too short for squabbling."

At long last, he and Semerjean agreed on something, though only one of them had hope that this world could be saved. That was the most annoying thing about Peter. He was wrong. He was always so wrong about everything.

Prudent hobbled across her kitchen on swollen red feet—a torturous journey, like walking on needles. Her over-reliance on sedatives had thickened her blood, leaving sporadic clots in her extremities. Her doctor warned her that she'd never reach sixty if she kept abusing the apasticine. He had no idea why that made her laugh.

She opened her juve with a fumbling hand and threw in a SmartFeast breakfast platter. Once the machine read the time code on the lip of the plate, it knew the food had to be reversed eight days, five hours, four minutes, and fifteen seconds to reach a state of piping hot freshness. Prudent adjusted the timer for a tiny bit of undercooking, then pressed the start button.

Her husband sat at the dinette table, as dull and moony as ever. His glazed eyes turned to the far wall of the kitchen, then sprang open in horror. He raised a trembling finger at Prudent.

"Aah. Aaaaah . . ."

"Patience," she told him. "It's cooking."

He pushed his chair back, panicked. Prudent looked to him. "Jun, what in the world—"

"I believe he's referring to me," said a voice behind her.

Prudent turned around and jumped at the sudden presence of Semerjean. He smiled at her charmingly, as if he was just a friendly neighbor stopping by on a whim.

"Prudent Lee! My favorite adverb. You're looking radiant this morning." He tossed a cordial nod at her husband. "Jun."

Semerjean loved visiting the elder Lees, the only two Gothams who knew his secret. He never had to play David around them and he never had to worry about them blowing his cover. They had enough foresight left in their drug-addled brains to know the consequences of crossing him.

Prudent stumbled backward, tripping over her heel. Semerjean caught her with a quick tempic hand before she could fall.

"Whoa. Easy. This is just a social call. I'll be gone before your, uh . . ."

He peeked through the juve window and winced at Jun's breakfast: four strips of hog flesh, two chicken ovulations, a chemical-laden biscuit, and a gelatinous fruit treat that looked like a child's failed science experiment.

Semerjean turned to the Lees in gawking revulsion. "How do any of you people live past forty?"

Prudent moved behind Jun, her fingers hooked into his shoulders. "Please. I've done everything you asked."

Technically, that was true. She'd done a bang-up job bringing Zack and Mercy together, and had kept an airtight lid on the augurs' guild. None of them shared a single prophecy without her permission, certainly nothing that would jeopardize Pelletier plans.

Unfortunately, Zack and Mercy had suffered a parting of the ways last night, a break that would almost surely become permanent if something wasn't done. As for the augurs . . .

"We have a problem, Prudently."

The security console on the wall beeped three times. Its lumic screen showed Peter standing just outside the base of the elevator. He waved up at the camera, his expression grave and somber.

Prudent looked at Semerjean quizzically. He flicked a curt hand. "Go on."

She hurried to the console and unlocked the lift for Peter. "I . . . I don't know why he's visiting."

"Really? Because I do."

"My people have been quiet," she insisted. "He must have heard something from Rebel or—"

Semerjean shook his head. Rebel and Theo were the only two augurs outside Prudent's purview. The Pelletiers managed them personally.

"Your people have been hanging themselves," Semerjean said. "Fleeing the village under mysterious circumstances. Even a clod like Peter is starting to ask questions. Do you see my concern?"

"Please. They're just scared."

They had good reason to be. Sometime in the next seventy-two hours, Integrity would burrow its way into the underland—more than two hundred soldiers, armed to the teeth with state-of-the-art weaponry. They'd have countermeasures ready for nearly every type of temporal power, and they wouldn't be shy about killing people. The prescient glimpses of the siege were horrific. Only the Pelletiers saw the long-term benefits.

"The invasion will change things," Semerjean admitted. "But when the dust settles, your people and mine will be in a stronger position than ever. You'll just have to trust me on that."

Prudent looked away, her voice barely a mutter. "People will die."

"People *always* die. The trick is keeping the right ones alive."

He summoned the life-size image of a tall, shaggy teenager. Sage Lee slouched in a leather recliner, watching European lumivision with a hopelessly bored expression.

Jun wept at the sight of him. Prudent covered her trembling mouth. Semerjean hadn't showed them a live image of their son in days. They were due for a carrot.

"P-please," Prudent begged. "Don't hurt him."

"Just a few more weeks and my work here will be done. After that, we'll have no reason to keep him. You'll get him back, alive and well."

"A-and the others?"

"I'll bring them all back." Semerjean leaned in closer, his voice low and severe. "But if you or any of your augurs breathe one word about Integrity—"

"No!" Prudent cried. "We won't! I promise!"

"So when Peter gets here, how will you handle him?"

The primarch bowed her head, sniffling. "Prudently."

"That's my girl."

His handphone vibrated. He pulled it out of his pocket and groaned at the message on-screen.

Are you awake?

Semerjean fumbled with the phone's archaic keyboard. **Just woke up.**

We need to talk, Yvonne texted. **Someplace private, away from your friends.**

He told her to meet him in the village theater, then closed the phone with a sigh. He had at least four assets to manage over the course of the next hour, and two Golds to kill. Events were moving faster, more erratically, but he was still in control.

Am I?

He could feel the growing anguish of his other selves, billions of Semerjeans in parallel timelines, all experiencing a slightly different version of the morning he was having. Some of them were getting flustered. Some were downright furious.

"You're tired," Prudent said.

He spun around to face her. "*Excuse* me?"

She balked at the sudden change in his eyes—lighter, bluer, fiercer. They were the same eyes his victims saw behind his tempic mask, the ones that had chilled Zack and Mia to the bone.

Prudent shrank from his glare. "I-I'm sorry. I know how hard you've been working. I was just—"

"—playing me," Semerjean said. "You were hoping to win me over with false sympathy. Do you think I'm naïve?"

"No!"

"Do you think I'm a child?"

"Please! I'm sorry!"

He looked at an image of Prudent's son, then defused himself with a sigh. "I suppose I can't fault you. You have your goals and I have mine. But if you paid more attention, you'd know that there are only a handful of people on this world who matter to me. The rest of you—"

He popped Sage's image with a snap of his fingers.

"—are just ghosts."

Peter's elevator arrived with a loud, hollow *ping.* The rejuvenator came to a beeping stop. The foul stench of bacon filled Semerjean's nostrils. If there was ever a cue to leave . . .

He waved a portal into the air, then shot a final look at Prudent. "Control your people. I won't warn you again."

———

He waited impatiently at the front of the amphitheater, yet another stage for him to pace. For all their flaws, the Gothams had built a surprisingly nice venue for themselves. Good design. Great acoustics. All they had to do was shut off that hideous undersky and this place would be ready for Shakespeare.

Semerjean tried to hail Esis again, then cursed out loud when she didn't respond. It was pathetic that he needed her help anyway. There was once a time, many years ago, when he saw the future as well as she did. Sadly, the neural degradation that inevitably afflicted all his people was starting to take its toll on him. He was getting old in a way that temporis couldn't fix.

Don't blame the age, his inner critic chided. *Prudent was right. You're tired. You've been playing this role for far too long, and now you're making mistakes.*

Semerjean walked faster, his lips pursed in a scowl.

You nearly died at the hands of a mentally ill child, the hard voice reminded him. *You've mismanaged your friends—*

Not my friends, Semerjean insisted.

You've mismanaged your assets. *Only two of the five Silvers are entwined with the right people.*

I'll fix it, he assured himself. *I just need more—*

"David!"

Semerjean looked up and saw Yvonne at the far end of the stage, her head tilted, her arms raised in confusion.

"I called your name three times," she said. "What are you doing?"

As always, the child had primped herself up like a runway model: teased hair, elegant makeup, a hint of perfume, a demurely enticing summer dress. She must have woken up at the crack of dawn to prepare for this encounter, not that Semerjean was surprised. Life had taught her from a very early age that appearances were everything, that society offered no prizes to the meek and unpoised. In some ways, Yvonne was just as much of an actor as he was. Maybe that was why he liked her.

He fell back into character. "I'm sorry. I've been out of sorts all morning."

"All morning?"

"And last night," he admitted. "I should have never snapped at you. I apologize."

His relationship with Yvonne had been nothing more than strategy, a way to goad the Silvers into finding their own Gotham love interests. Unfortunately, Yvonne was beginning to sense the limits of David's affection. The frustration was making her combative, and her combativeness was making him edgy. Sometime near the end of Theo's party, she'd asked him if she was just a fling to him. He'd told her to stop being so needy, yet another grave mistake in hindsight.

Yvonne sat down on the edge of the elders' stone table. Her high-heeled shoes dangled inches off the stage.

"I barely slept a minute," she said. "I was just so angry at you. Not just angry. Confused. I thought we had something good, David. I mean . . ."

While Yvonne spoke, a familiar voice flittered onto the neural link. *<Hello, sehfarr.>*

Semerjean clenched his jaw, struggling to look attentive while he mentally responded. *<Azral! I've been trying to reach you. What's happening? Where's your mother?>*

<She is . . . upset,> Azral told him. *<None of the children are viable.>*

Semerjean closed his eyes. The Pelletiers had put great hopes in the Pearls, only to be let down again. All this work, all this trouble, just for an elusive genetic mutation. If Semerjean had believed in anthropomorphic forces, he might start to think that nature was teasing them.

<I'm sorry,> he sent. *<I know how hard you and Esis—>*

<I'm afraid the news is worse, Father.>

<What do you mean?>

<The Silvers. They know.>

Semerjean's stomach dropped. He closed his eyes and checked the telemetry map of Freak Street. Much had changed in the last few minutes. The orphans had gathered in Jonathan's living room, their eyes filled with tears as Zack and Mia addressed them. Theo leapt to his feet and overturned the coffee table. Amanda's body broke out in razor-sharp spikes of tempis.

<No,> thought Semerjean. *<I can contain this. I'll reverse them.>*

Yvonne noticed his twitchy distraction. "David, are you even listening to m—"

He flicked his hand, enveloping her in a redshift field. The girl stood as still as a mannequin, her body suspended in a single moment of time.

<It's over,> Azral told Semerjean. <There's no undoing this.>

<There is! If I could just see where I went wrong—>

<Where you went wrong?>

Esis joined the neural conference. Her anger raked through Semerjean's thoughts like barbed wire.

<It was Trillinger,> she sent. <It's always Trillinger!>

Though Semerjean wanted to deny it, a thorough revisiting of last night's conversation quickly proved her right.

<The mirrors . . .>

<The mirrors,> Esis confirmed. <How could you be so careless?>

He sent a fragment of his consciousness back in time to amend all damage, a new branch of history where he never upset Yvonne, never revealed his true self to Zack. Indeed, the Semerjean of that timeline would have a much nicer morning. But here in this string, life continued. Here, Semerjean had no choice but to face the consequences of his errors.

Azral's calm thoughts soothed him like a warm, tender hand. <It's only a minor setback,> he assured his father. <The Silvers are still alive and fertile, still integrated with our ancestors. They can be manipulated from afar.>

Semerjean closed his eyes and sighed. Azral had grown up in the light of his mother's ambition, a lifelong obsession that blinded him to certain nuances. He thought the people of this era were as simple as cogs, and could be strong-armed into doing whatever the Pelletiers wanted. No. That might work for the Gothams, who only knew death through nibbles and pecks. But the Silvers were different. They had seen the universe at its absolute cruelest. They required a subtler hand.

Esis scoffed at her husband's gloom. <Enough of this. We come for you.>

"Wait!"

Semerjean de-shifted Yvonne. She stood up from the table, disoriented.

"W-what . . . what just happened? I feel—"

"Go home."

"What?"

He dropped his Australian accent and looked at her with Semerjean's eyes. "Leave this place. In thirty seconds, you won't want to be here."

Yvonne stared at him in shock. "David, what's wrong with you?"

"I'm telling you—"

"No! You can't talk to me like that. I thought we respected each other."

Semerjean sighed in surrender. It was already too late. His wife was looking for blood and she'd get it, if not from Yvonne, then from someone more important, like Zack or Mia.

"I never respected you," Semerjean confessed. "But I do like you. I enjoyed most of the time we spent together."

Yvonne took a horrified step back. "Who are you?"

To Semerjean's dismay, he was briefly stuck for an answer.

"I am the patriarch of a very ambitious family," he said. "I believe in what we're doing here. I believe that any harm we cause will be exponentially dwarfed by the benefits to humanity."

"What the hell are you talking about?"

"My name is Semerjean Pelletier," he said. "And I am sorry."

A ten-foot portal split the air behind Yvonne. She barely had a chance to feel the cool wind of the temporis before Esis arrived onstage. The two of them looked remarkably similar, with their dark eyes and supple beauty, their lissome builds and wavy hair. The resemblance wasn't entirely coincidence. In the Pelletiers' timeline, Yvonne Whitten had lived a full life and birthed many children. Her lineage stretched on and on through the centuries, until a distant descendant—a granddaughter of forty-eight greats—gave life to a perfect girl named Esis.

Unfortunately for Yvonne, the rules of time didn't work in her favor. A person could kill their direct ancestor without paradox or consequence. That was one advantage to living in a multistring paradigm.

Semerjean looked away as Esis stabbed Yvonne through the shoulder blade. The tempic sword pierced her heart so quickly that the girl didn't even have time to understand what was happening to her. Her head snapped back. She sucked a loud gasp. Then her body fell limp on the blade.

Esis whisked away the tempis. Yvonne crumpled face down onto the stage. Semerjean studied her corpse only briefly before glaring at his wife.

"You didn't have to kill her," he growled in English.

Esis responded in their native tongue, her eyes narrowed to slits. "Do you speak to me as my husband or the boy he portrays?"

"I'm speaking to *you*. She wasn't a threat to us!"

"Her death serves a purpose," Esis said. "In forty-eight hours—"

"I don't want to hear it."

"Don't be petulant."

"Petulant? I put *ten months* into the Silvers!"

<*And now you're free,*> Azral sent.

He stepped out of the portal and faced Semerjean from downstage. "You've suffered these fools long enough, Father. Rejoin us."

Semerjean closed his eyes and took another scan of Mia and the others. By now, their biometric readings were practically off the charts—all the grief, all the rage, all the regret and humiliation. He knew all along that this day would come, but he'd hoped—perhaps naïvely—that he would leave them under better circumstances. They'd scarcely have a day to recover before the next storm hit, before Integrity waged their final assault.

He supposed there was only one thing left to do.

"Give me a minute," he urged his wife and son. "I will follow."

Esis eyed him suspiciously a moment before exiting with Azral. Alone again, Semerjean walked to the elders' table and fumbled with the band of his wristwatch.

"This was a necessary evil," he began. He spoke for two more minutes before placing his watch on the table. The device had served him well these many months, but he didn't need it anymore. One of his former companions would get a better use out of it.

As the village clock chimed the top of the hour, Semerjean stepped halfway into the portal and took a final look around the theater. This had not been his best performance. Not by a long shot. Mistakes were made. People were hurt. All Semerjean could do was spare a sorrowful thought for the two young souls who'd died just now, right here on this very stage. On some small level, he'd miss Yvonne. He'd miss David even more.

FORTY-ONE

Forty-one minutes after Semerjean departed, an ear-splitting shriek tore through the underland. The noise was loud enough to turn every head in the village, shrill enough to shatter lightbulbs. Winnie Whitten had once again unleashed her banshee scream on her people, and with good cause. She'd gone looking for her sister and found her bloody corpse in the amphitheater.

Within minutes, everyone in the clan knew that Yvonne Whitten was dead.

The Mayor was the first to scan the past and view his daughter's final moments, an unfathomable betrayal that turned his legs to jelly and sent him weeping to the floor. Word spread fast about what he saw, until hundreds of panicked Gothams gathered in the village square. Soon the elders arrived to confirm the ugly rumors: a Pelletier had been living among them for weeks, hiding in plain sight as the breacher David Dormer.

Ten minutes later, another girl's scream pierced the windows of Freak Street. The residents hurried outside and saw a scuffling commotion through Carrie's window.

"Daddy, *no!*"

Stan Bloom stormed out the front door, his daughter thrashing and kicking in his grip. He didn't need his tempis to secure her. One beefy arm was more than enough to keep her slung over his shoulder.

"Daddy, please! You don't understand!"

"I understand plenty."

The orphans and Pendergens watched them from a distance, their eyes drooped, their faces racked with grief. David's bombshell treachery had reduced them all to smoking craters. They didn't have the strength of mind to handle this newest drama.

Carrie fixed her crying eyes on Peter. "Please! Tell him! Tell him I'm safe here!"

He stepped forward with a sigh. "Stan—"

"Shut up." Stan spun around and pointed at David's house. "Two doors. He was living *two doors* down from my daughter!"

"He had us all fooled."

"*All* of you?" He jerked his head at the Silvers. "Those people have been with him from the very beginning. They damn well knew what he was."

Amanda's teeth clenched. Her knuckles frosted over with tempis. "You're an idiot."

Peter held her arm. "Amanda . . ."

"You think we aren't hurting? He was like a *brother* to us!"

"Yeah," Stan said. "That's what worries me."

The back of his sweatshirt shredded apart as waxy white wings grew out of his shoulder blades. He secured his daughter with a tempic harness, then shot a dirty look at her friends.

"Stay away from us. All of you."

He took to the sky with a graceless leap. Mia lowered her head, wincing as Carrie screamed at her from above.

"Mia!"

The Blooms disappeared beyond the tree line, invisible but not inaudible. *"Mia!"*

The group dawdled on the street in dismal silence until Carrie's voice finally faded into the distance. One by one, the orphans returned to their houses. Peter followed Mia across the lawn.

"Look, Stan's just rattled. Once he calms down—"

"He's right."

"What?"

Mia turned around to face him, her brown eyes cracked with veins. "She's not safe with us."

"Mia—"

"Nobody is."

She waved a portal in the air, then charged headfirst into it. As the disc closed behind her, Peter stuffed his hands into his pockets and took a sullen look at the fourth-to-last cottage, the one that Semerjean had shared with the sisters. The bastard had done immeasurable damage, and the fallout was only just beginning. God only knew what kind of mess the Platinums and Irons would find when they got here next week—fractured people, fractured trust. They'd be lucky if this place didn't fall into war.

By noon, Mia had moved all her belongings back to Zack and Theo's house, to the rustic little bedroom with the cedar walls and the cherrywood desk. As she unpacked her shirts, she glanced out the window and saw a small gathering in the backyard. Hannah, Theo, Jonathan, and Liam sat scattered in a circle of twelve folding chairs, a remnant from last night's party. Mia recognized the complicated looks on their faces. They were trying to shape their grief into something manageable, as if such a thing were even possible. How do you mourn a boy who never existed? How do you miss a living lie?

You're such a marvel to me, David had once told Mia. *You never speak just to hear yourself talk and you always mean what you say. You're a truly genuine person. Just one of the many reasons I adore you.*

"Fuck!"

Mia threw her shirts to the floor. If anything, Semerjean had adored her gullibility, her predictability, her blind and fawning devotion to him. He'd probably shared a thousand laughs with Esis over that fat, smitten child. *If only the others were as easy as her.*

She rushed to the desk, tore a blank scrap from her journal, and began scribbling furiously. That piece of shit wouldn't laugh if she managed to warn a past Mia about him. Maybe she could make life that much harder for Semerjean in another string.

Don't trust David. He's not

Cursing, she crumpled up the paper. If she'd learned one thing today, it was that the Pelletier filters worked. She had to phrase her message carefully if she wanted it to get through.

Mia tore a new scrap and started again.

Don't trust the boy. Everything he says is a lie, even his name.

She opened a keyhole portal to last August and pushed the note through. The paper burned quickly enough to singe her fingers.

"Ow! Shit!"

Mia spent the next twenty minutes trying to work around the censors, using everything from code words to pictographs to esoteric song references. Some of her warnings were so cryptic that she feared even her younger self wouldn't understand them. But it was all moot. Even her most obscure messages burst into flames, just more flakes of ash on the beds of Past Mias.

She swept her journal to the floor and buried her face in her hands. She couldn't do a thing to save her other selves from this agony. They were all whistling toward the cliffside, smiling at David with hearts in their eyes while that horrible creature—

You're such a marvel to me.

—kept lying.

Mia jumped to her feet and rushed out of the bedroom. She couldn't spend one more second alone with her thoughts. They'd eat her alive like piranha.

The backyard chatter came to a stop as soon as Mia stepped outside. She hated the way the others looked at her, as if the wife of the deceased had just arrived at the wake. She wanted to tell them that she and David hadn't been all that close in the end. She'd fallen in love with a much better person, while that monster dug his claws into poor Yvonne.

"I'm glad you're here," Hannah said. "These guys don't believe me."

Liam frowned at her. "It was obviously a trick."

"How do you know? You weren't even there."

Mia was distracted by something in the neighboring yard. Heath sat on the grass in sulky repose, his whole body crawling with tempic tarantulas. Best Mia could guess, it was his own weird way of asking for space.

She looked at Hannah again. "Sorry. What are you talking about?"

"Back on that aerstraunt, when you and I met Semerjean. David was right there with us. They talked to each other. He cut David's hand."

Mia slumped in her chair. Hannah was clearly still clinging to hope that all of this was a frame-up, that the David she knew and loved was still out there somewhere.

"He was playing us," Mia told her. "That Semerjean we saw was nothing but a ghost."

Liam nodded. "That's what we've been saying."

Hannah threw her hands up. "It just doesn't make sense. Why didn't I feel him when he was shifting? Why didn't Heath and Amanda feel his tempis?"

"Because he's smart," Theo said. "He covered his tracks and kept a tight leash on anyone who could sniff him out. Me and Mia, Prudent Lee. He must have even had a way to keep Evan quiet."

Mia snorted derisively. Semerjean was a brute and Evan was a coward. The "trick" was probably nothing more than a physical threat.

Liam absently tugged at the fabric of his gloves. "He saved my life at Atropos."

"He saved all of us," Mia said. "It was just part of his job."

Jonathan polished his guitar, his glum eyes fixed on the distance. "I don't know what Heath and I did to get on his shit list."

"Yes you do," Hannah said.

"If this is about you and me 'entwining,' then why did David—"

"Semerjean," Mia corrected.

"—why did *Semerjean* try to frame Heath?"

Theo stroked his arm in vacant thought. "I don't think he was trying to frame Heath. I think he was trying to frame Ioni."

"What do you mean?" Jonathan asked.

"She's no friend of the Pelletiers, and she's smart enough to stay out of their reach. The only way for them to stop her is to discredit her. And the best way to do that is to make us think she's one of them."

Theo looked to Heath, still playing with spiders. "He just got caught up in that."

Hannah leaned forward and muttered at her lap. "She knew."

"What?" Theo asked. "About Semerjean?"

"Yeah. When I met her last year, she told me that I had to take care of you. Me and Amanda and Zack and Mia. She said we're your family now. I always . . ."

Hannah closed her eyes. Mia could see her fighting back tears.

"I always wondered why she didn't mention David."

Jonathan turned a knob on his guitar and then tested a C-minor chord. A black chuckle escaped him.

"What?" Liam asked.

"Just thinking about all the times I saw him gagging at us. Whenever we ate a sausage or a skeezy cheese."

Hannah fought a grin. "Or when I put on my skin cream."

"Or when we talked about science," Theo said. "You could see his lip quivering, like he just wanted to say 'No, you idiots! That's not how it works!'"

Jonathan laughed. "Man, we must have driven him crazy."

"Good," Mia said. "I hope he suffered every day."

"And I hope he's proud of himself now," Hannah said. "Wherever he is. The king of all liars. The world's greatest sleeper agent."

An old memory hit Mia like the tail of a whip, her very first conversation with David. They had just arrived at Sterling Quint's research facility when the scientists left them alone in the game room. Despite the fact that their world (*her* world) had come crashing down ninety minutes earlier, David seemed fine enough to putter around the pool table and make small talk. He'd asked Mia what "Farisi" meant. She told him she didn't know. Then, out of politeness more than anything, she asked him the meaning of his last name. The question had brought a ghost of a smile to his face.

Dormer, he replied. *French-Latin.*

Mia stood up fast enough to knock her chair over. Hannah reached for her. "Mia?"

It means "sleeper."

She covered her mouth and fled back into the house. There had been a moment this morning when she considered the notion that maybe, just maybe, Semerjean had developed some genuine fondness for her. Now she knew exactly where she stood in his esteem. He'd been mocking her relentlessly for ten months straight, brandishing his name like a middle finger.

Crying, Mia scooped her journal off the floor, ripped a blank page, and began a new missive.

I've been racking my brain trying to come up with a way to spare you from the pain I'm feeling. I don't even know why I'm bothering. The clues have been there from the very beginning. You're just too stupid to see them. You're so stupid and blind that you can't even see what's happening right under your nose.

You want some advice? Kill yourself. Just find a rope and end it. There's no hope for you, Mia. You deserve every bit of what's coming.

She rolled the note into a tight stick, then pushed it into a portal. The paper passed through time without interference, just like the ten thousand other hate letters that had reached her from the future. Clearly the Pelletiers approved of the message.

Mia tore a new scrap and immediately began another.

Zack woke up at sunset with a head full of cotton and a strong desire to break something. He'd had more time than anyone to process David's betrayal, yet he seemed to be moving backward on the Kübler-Ross stages of grief, from Depression to Bargaining to a shit-ton of Anger. His hatred for Azral, Esis, and Semerjean had reached an almost divine apotheosis, as if he could break out of his skin at any moment and become a holy spirit of vengeance. He imagined the looks on their faces when he brought the whole damn sky down on their heads, the screams on their lips when they woke up in Hell.

Great, an inner voice complained. *Now you're all the way back in Denial.*

Zack had barely brushed the grit from his eyes when a portal opened up on his wall. He shielded his eyes at the sudden rush of light.

"Jesus!"

Peter stepped through the opening and registered his surprise. "Good. You're awake."

"You know, doorknobs aren't complicated."

"Neither are portals."

"Just admit that you like freaking me out."

Peter shrugged. "It could've been worse."

"How?"

"I could've been Semerjean."

Zack saw his pointed expression and looked away. "I'm sorry about that, okay? I was an asshole for ever doubting you."

"Thank you."

"Is that why you're here? To get an apology?"

"No." He grabbed Zack's shirt from the foot of the bed and tossed it at him. "Get dressed."

Soon Peter and the orphans arrived at the amphitheater, where a teenage lumic awaited them. Ollie Orlowski was no one's idea of a handsome boy. His chin was weak, his eyes were uneven, and he had the worst acne of any kid in the clan. But he was universally well liked for his wit and intelligence, not to mention his kindness. He'd never said a bad word about the breachers, even when David stole the heart of his longtime crush, even now when half the Gothams suspected them all of being demons in disguise.

Peter led the others onto the stage, then gave Ollie a hearty handshake. "I really appreciate this."

"No problem," Ollie said, with a tone that suggested anything but. "Just play the part we talked about?"

"Yes."

"No," Zack said. "I want to see the whole thing."

"Zack . . ."

"Maybe they said more than they meant to. There might be something we can use."

"Listen to me." Peter pulled him close and lowered his voice. "That boy over there grew up with Yvonne. He loved her, and he's doing us a courtesy. We're not going to make him replay her death."

The others nodded in agreement. Half of them had already seen Esis kill people. The last thing they needed was to watch Yvonne's murder. Zack found it funny, in a not-so-funny way, that his old friend David would have taken his side on the issue. He always favored strategy over sentiment.

Grudgingly, Zack relented. Peter nodded at Ollie. "All right."

The boy raised his arm. A temporal ghost materialized onstage. The hearts of five Silvers broke at the sight of the golden-haired boy in front of them. Even now, with all their knowledge, he looked nothing like a Pelletier. He was still the dauntless young Australian who'd been part of their tribe from the very beginning.

He was still David.

His specter puttered at the edge of the elders' table before turning to face his audience. Half the group flinched at his direct eye contact. Clearly he knew they'd be watching him from the not-too-distant future. More jarring still, he knew exactly where they'd stand.

"This was a necessary evil," the ghost of Semerjean began. "My family and I went to great lengths to find you and bring you here. Though you were all—and I use the term politely—ordinary people where you came from, you each have a neurological mutation that's nothing short of miraculous. It . . ."

He looked away, chuckling. "I had to bite my tongue whenever one of you wondered why the Pelletiers gave you your temporal talents. We didn't. You've had the potential all along. The only thing you lacked was temporis. Here on this world, the energy flows freely. Here, you're all extraordinary. More than that, you have the potential to provide us with something of immeasurable value, a scientific breakthrough that'll usher in a new golden age for all of humanity."

Though Hannah tried to process his words, she kept getting caught on his wavering accent. It bounced back and forth from Australian to alien, as if he couldn't decide who he wanted to be.

He wasn't ready, she thought. *He didn't want to give up the act.*

Semerjean continued. "We selected ninety-nine of you from ten different cities, and we took a different approach with each group. Some, like the Golds of New York, were remarkably easy. Our work with them ended months ago. Others, like the Silvers of San Diego, present continual challenges, both strategic and ethical. Do we take what we want by force, or do we coax it from you through subtle manipulations? We followed our consciences, as well as the strings, and we chose the gentler path. We gave you freedom and free will."

Amanda closed her eyes, sickened. He'd deceived them for months, used Yvonne as a stage prop, and then stood by idly while Esis killed her. And he had the nerve to talk about ethics.

Semerjean pushed his hands into his pockets and rocked on his feet, a David-like gesture that hit the Silvers like a slap. "Our decision required a significant investment on our part, a full-time presence inside your group. My task was to protect and guide you, to keep you all together."

His expression turned grim. "And to keep some of you apart."

Everyone looked to Zack and Amanda. They kept their heads forward and their hard eyes locked on Semerjean.

"I don't expect you to believe me but . . ." He looked to his left and sighed at an empty part of the stage. "I'm well aware of the pain we've caused, and I don't blame you for hating us. I think back to the great minds of this age who cured terrible diseases, like polio and smallpox. If you judged them solely by their treatment of lab animals, you'd think they were monsters. But they had a vision and a purpose. They saved more lives than . . ."

Semerjean winced at his blunder. Hannah scoffed at him. "Yeah, that's right. You just compared us to rats."

"I must have really come to like you people," Semerjean said. "Here I am, talking to air, hoping that you'll think more kindly of me in the future. I can't imagine that'll happen. I've seen your notes, Mia, the ones that never got to you. It breaks my heart to break yours. I've been dreading this day for a very long time."

Mia covered her face, struggling to keep her screams inside of her. If she started now, she'd never stop. She'd scream herself into oblivion.

Semerjean looked down at his wristwatch, then unhooked the clasp. "Well, I suppose it's time for me to step off the stage—to give up the ghost, as one might say. I offer you all my deepest apologies, and I leave this device to anyone who wants it. It has many hidden functions that only work for me, but some of its perks are universal."

He placed the watch on the elders' table, merging its ghost with the real live object. None of the Gothams had dared to touch it. For all they knew, it would explode on contact.

Semerjean sidestepped into the invisible portal, his left arm disappearing inch by inch, as if God Himself was erasing him.

"I wish I could tell you, for your sake more than mine, that you'll never see me again. But you will. Not long from now, my family and I will have a . . . proposition for you, a new arrangement that'll save the lives of many people. When that time comes, I hope you'll put aside your resentment and hear us out."

He threw an ominous look at his former companions. "And for those who wish to sabotage our work here, out of some petty sense of vengeance, I have one last word of advice."

His sharp blue eyes narrowed at Zack. "Don't."

At last, Semerjean departed. Ollie lowered his arm with a tired sigh. Only

Peter had the strength of mind to thank him. The others dawdled onstage in frustration and depression, until Heath wandered off from the group.

Jonathan saw what he was moving toward. "Buddy, I wouldn't do that."

Hannah's eyes bulged. "Heath, no!"

Heath picked up Semerjean's wristwatch and dangled it in his fingers. He studied the face, then the back, and then pressed it to his ear.

"It ticks," he matter-of-factly informed the others. "It sounds just like the real thing."

After fifteen minutes of soft red dusk, the Heavensend transitioned to Night-scape Template 163: *Magical Alaska.* Five thousand stars twinkled down from the undersky while an aurora borealis bathed the town in fluorescent green ribbons of light.

Zack ambled his way down the narrow neck of Freak Street, the most un-derdeveloped part of the village. There were no structures, no lampposts, no benches or gardens, just scattered patches of baby elms on both sides of the street. Every couple of weeks, just as nature began to remind the Gothams that *Hey! Trees need sunlight!,* a turner came by to reverse all the saplings to a green and healthy state. Then the pitiful things would start to die all over again. Wither, rinse, repeat.

Their plight was so depressing that Zack was almost relieved to see the mini-apocalypse that Amanda had unleashed upon them. He followed the trail of broken trees until he saw moving figures off the side of the road: two large tempic hands that looked like misshapen creatures in the light of the borealis.

"Wow."

By now, Amanda had cleared a nice parcel of land, enough for at least six new orphan cottages. Zack could see from the healthy flush in her skin that she was venting just as much as she was landscaping.

He leaned against a tree and watched her tug at a sapling. "You plan to do this all night?"

Amanda ripped out the elm with a grunt, then tossed it onto the street. "I shared a house with him. I don't really feel like going back there."

"So stay with Peter."

She eyed him suspiciously. "Is that sarcasm?"

"No."

"Have you seen Mercy today?"

Zack picked up a twig and chucked it into the darkness. "No."

Amanda shrank away her tempis before taking a long swig from a bottle. She swished the water in her mouth for a couple of seconds.

"We gave him exactly what he wanted, didn't we? Me and Peter, you and Mercy. He's been angling for that all along."

Zack nodded dejectedly. "Afraid so."

"What about the others? Hannah? Theo?"

"I'm pretty sure he has people in mind for them too."

Amanda stared up at the fake moon with visible contempt, as if she was one beat away from punching it out of the sky. "Every time I came home, he was on the couch with Yvonne, kissing her and giggling and making me feel all uncomfortable. I got so annoyed, I started hiding out in Peter's house. It was . . ."

She threw her bottle to the ground. "That girl was nothing to him. Just a tool."

"That's all any of us are to them," Zack said. "Tools and breeders."

"It doesn't even make sense! We've been using . . ."

Amanda caught herself and looked at Zack awkwardly.

"Us too," he told her. "Condoms. Every time."

"You think he tampered with them?"

"He'd be stupid if he didn't."

"Goddamn it!"

Zack flinched. He'd seen her on some of the worst days of her life, but this was the first time he'd ever heard her take the Lord's name in vain.

"These are *our lives*," she yelled. "They have no right to do this!"

"That's not the way they see it."

"Why push us through all these hoops? I mean, they're scientists. They could just mix our genes up in test tubes and grow the babies they want."

Zack shrugged at the ground. "Maybe that's what they did with Jonathan's group. Maybe that's why they don't need them anymore."

"But not us," Amanda said. "We're supposed to make babies the old-fashioned way."

"Apparently."

Desolate, Amanda walked over to Zack and leaned against the other side of his tree. Her shoulder brushed against his.

"I can't stand the thought of you and Mercy," she confessed.

"I can't stand the thought of you and Peter."

"It's not serious." Amanda crossed her arms and sighed. "It's just . . . an arrangement."

"Yeah, well, Mercy and I aren't exactly ring-shopping. In fact, I'm pretty sure we broke up last night."

"What?" Amanda looped around to face him, her eyes wide with fear. "You can't."

"Didn't you just say—"

"It doesn't matter how I feel. You have to go back to her. Azral and Esis already hate you. If you give them one more reason—"

"I don't care."

"*I* care," Amanda said. "You're one of the most important people in my life, and I'm not going to watch them take you away. Not again."

Zack shook his head. "I'm not playing their game anymore."

"We don't have to play their game. We just have to play ours smarter."

She pulled out the crucifix on her necklace and showed it to him. "This is my last possession from the old world. I nearly pawned it last year when we were desperate for money. You remember that?"

"Of course."

"And do you remember who stopped me?"

Zack looked away. "I did."

"That's right. It had nothing to do with faith or Christ. You just knew that I needed one last keepsake from my old life, something to cling to when things got crazy. You were thinking ahead, and you were right. This necklace has held me together just as much as you have."

She cupped her hand against the side of his face. "I love you, Zack. They can stop me from being with you but they can't change the way I feel. And if they can hatch their long-term plans, then so can we."

He pursed his lips, skeptical. "You seriously think we have a chance against them."

"I forced Esis to save your life. You exposed Semerjean for the liar he is.

They're not unstoppable, but we'll never win just by making them mad. We have to bide our time and strategize."

Amanda let go of him. "So go back to Mercy. Be with her, but don't get too comfortable. Because the minute we beat those pieces of shit, I'm coming for you. We're going to spend the rest of our lives together."

She cast a dismal stare at her feet. "And we'll make lots of babies."

Thousands of miles away, in the penthouse suite of an Ibiza hotel, the man once known as David Dormer lay naked in bed while his wife slept beside him. He folded his arms behind his head, watching through stony eyes as a mouse-size Amanda loitered on his stomach, whispering sweet promises of victory to Zack. The woman, as usual, was acting steadfast and determined with only a quantum of facts at her disposal, though Semerjean had to give her credit for thinking strategically. Amanda was finally learning to channel her anger.

But Zack . . . oh, Zack. What a disappointment. Semerjean only had to read his tiny face to know that Esis was right yet again. He would not go back to Mercy Lee. He wouldn't even deign to pretend, even though he knew his life depended on it.

Semerjean watched him quietly, and for a moment it seemed that Zack was looking right back at him. How could a man be so clever yet so dense? Semerjean supposed it didn't matter. The die was cast. The future was set. Esis was coming for Zack tomorrow, and there wasn't a damn thing anyone could do about it.

FORTY-TWO

The Sunder family library was the most exquisite room in the manor, a two-story orgasm of mahogany and leather that had been photographed twice for *American Taste* magazine. The Victorian furniture alone cost a million dollars. The paintings had their own insurance policies. Peter couldn't even guess the value of the books, all first-edition classics that had been painstakingly acquired by auction. Irwin Sunder only brought people here when he wanted to impress or intimidate them, and he didn't seem keen on impressing Peter. The fact that they were meeting alone, without the other elders, was especially telling.

The two men faced each other from opposite sides of Sunder's desk, their eyes locked in contact as a young black servant prepared their tea. Sensing that she was impeding their business, she filled their cups with nimble haste, then removed the tray.

Sunder nodded at her. "Thank you, Dorothy. Close the door behind you."

Peter watched over his shoulder as she made for the exit, her ponytail swinging with each hurried step. "Working early on the Lord's day."

"I'm not a Christian," Sunder reminded him. "And my weekend maids earn double pay."

"You ever worry about them discovering your, uh . . ."

Sunder bristled at the mere suggestion. "My family has discipline. We never use our blessings on the surface."

It was lucky for Peter that the man wasn't a ghoster. He might have looked back twenty years and seen Peter and Ivy playing portal tag throughout the house. He wouldn't like what they did when they caught each other.

Peter lifted his teacup. "Very sorry about your granddaughter, by the way."

At 7:01 yesterday morning, just as Semerjean took his leave of the Silvers, Gemma Sunder had made a quiet exit of her own. The girl shuddered on her hospital bed, her first hint of movement in three and a half weeks. Then her vital signs dropped. Her monitors squealed. By the time the nurses got to her, there was nothing they could do. Gemma died just a few days short of her eleventh birthday.

Sunder fidgeted with his tie, his brown eyes filled with sorrow. "Thank you, Peter. I'm surprised you heard about it, what with all the other drama."

"I heard."

While Peter had come to the meeting in a button-down shirt and jeans, Sunder was dressed in a black three-piece suit, the same one he wore to Bug and Ivy's funeral. Yvonne's memorial service was starting in an hour and no one, not even the Sunders, wanted to add Gemma to the ceremony. They'd place her urn in the family mausoleum and then rarely speak of her again.

"She was a troubled child," Sunder admitted. "Her powers warped her in ways we'll never understand."

Peter looked away at a high and distant bookshelf. In a less polite mood, he might have suggested that it was lack of love, not the temporis, that made Gemma the way she was.

"I guess every flock has its black sheep," Sunder mused. "Yours especially."

Here it comes, Peter thought.

"This Semerjean business has us all turned around, Peter. Some of the house lords are threatening to leave. Others are demanding we investigate David's friends, you included."

"He had us all fooled."

"You lived with him for *months.*"

"He had us fooled for months."

Sunder stood up and toyed with a wooden globe, a rare and pricey relic from pre-Cataclysm New York. "I don't think you understand the gravity of the situation. Nobody trusts the breachers anymore. Everyone wants them gone."

Peter scowled. "Once again, you're blaming them for the sins of the Pelletiers."

"One of them *is* a Pelletier!"

"And that one is gone."

"Yeah? And how many other surprises did they leave for us? How many sleepers?"

"Don't be an idiot."

Sunder slapped the desk, his fingers white with tempis. "You listen to me very carefully now, because you only have two options."

Peter sat up in his chair, a sneer on his lips. "Money or exile."

"That's right. We'd like to avoid the hassle of an expulsion trial. Our people are tired. They've had enough drama. But if you and your friends leave willingly—"

"You'll make us all rich and happy fugitives."

Sunder frowned at his sarcasm. "Bring your son this time. Find those other breachers. You'll have strength in numbers and you'll have resources."

"Go to hell."

"Peter, think ahead for once."

"Think ahead?" He rose to his feet. "The sky's coming down in four years' time and I'm the only one who seems to remember. If you care about your family—"

"Don't you dare play that card with me."

"Fine. I'll play another."

He drew a portal on the surface of Sunder's desk and reached into it. After a few seconds of fumbling, he pulled out a large manila envelope.

"What are you doing?" Sunder asked him.

Peter slid the envelope across the desk. "Thinking ahead."

Sunder sat down and leafed through the contents: a full schematic of the underland, plus photographs, maps, and detailed access instructions. The packet also included the contact information of every elder, primarch, and head of house.

"I was a journalist for twelve years," Peter reminded Sunder. "Made a lot of friends on the outside. People I trust. This morning, three of them got copies of that package."

Sunder's mouth fell open. "You wouldn't dare."

"If they don't hear from me once a day, they've been instructed to send their documents to the National Integrity Commission. I was nice enough to include postage."

Sunder mulled the threat a moment before shaking his head. "No. You're bluffing. You wouldn't destroy the clan like this."

"Destroy?" Peter waved him off. "You'll be fine on the run. You'll have strength in numbers and you'll have resources."

"You vicious bastard."

Peter set down his teacup and walked toward the door. "We're staying right where we are. And if you harm a hair on any of my people—"

"*Your* people?"

"My people," Peter said. "I'm an orphan, just like them. I get to choose my family. There's only one of them I never liked and he's gone now."

He turned around at the door. "Oh, and you'll be building houses for those new breachers that are coming. We do want them to feel welcome."

"I swear to Christ, Pendergen—"

"You're not a Christian."

Peter closed the door behind him and breathed a heavy sigh. It would be just a matter of time before the elders called his bluff. He needed a backup plan, fast. Maybe he could take the orphans abroad, or seek shelter with the other clan of timebenders. The Majee had an entire skyscraper to themselves, more than enough room for a few dozen refugees. Would they be willing to help?

He took the stairs down to the wine cellar and opened the panel of a thermostat. After inserting his keycard and entering a twelve-digit code into a number pad, a wall of wine racks sank into the floor, exposing two safes and an elevator. The doors to the lift opened immediately.

Peter took a half step forward, then stopped. Something was troubling him from the base of his instincts, a sense that he was being watched. He looked around the cellar. There was nothing down here but bottles and dust.

Rattled, he backstepped into the elevator. The doors closed. The wine rack wall slid back into place.

Fifteen seconds after his departure, the weekend maid that everyone knew as Dorothy crept down the stairs and examined the fake thermostat. She'd been working for the Sunders for two weeks, and had suspected from the start that the cellar was an access point. Now, at last, she had confirmation. She thanked the stars for Peter Pendergen and thanked them twice that he hadn't recognized her.

She pulled up her sleeve and spoke into her bracelet, an encrypted-channel transmitter that Cedric Cain had given her.

"It's here," Melissa told him. "I found it."

———

By nine A.M., the Gothams had descended en masse to the underland. Lift by lift, portal by portal, eleven hundred people filed into the village and formed a tight crowd in the central square. The elders didn't like holding a memorial service from the steps of their municipal building, but they could hardly use the amphitheater after yesterday's tragedy. For the lumics of the clan, the ones who knew and loved Yvonne the most, it would only take a slip of thought to watch the girl die in hindsight. Just as the future tormented the augurs, the past could be horrendously cruel to ghosters.

With all the Sunders out of the house, Melissa returned to the cellar and changed into something more appropriate. Her sleek black speedsuit was a vast improvement over the clunky rig she wore at DP-9. Fiberweave armor girded her arms and legs like dragon hide while osplate panels made the rest of her nearly bulletproof. The shifter on her back had been jury-rigged for a maximum speed of 30x and her helmet visor allowed her to see both thermal and infrared. She carried a .38 pistol in her left holster, an electron chaser in her right, and four grenades on her belt.

She also had an elevator key, a clone of the access card that Rena Bloom-Sunder had left on her dresser. Bypassing the card slot was easy. The keycode, however, required a little extra wizardry.

Melissa pulled four candle-shaped devices from her shoulder bag and stuck them on the wall around the console. The technology had been invented two years before by an MIT dropout, a single mother with a ferocious IQ and a penchant for self-destruction. Cain had helped her straighten her life out before giving her a cushy job with Integrity. In gratitude, she made sure that no one else got their hands on her incredible machine. America wasn't ready for miniature ghost drills. The nation's computers and passlocks would never be safe again.

After a few moments of calibration, the hazy image of a hand appeared between the ghoststicks. Melissa sharpened the picture until she could see exactly which keys Peter had pressed, in which order. Once she repeated the sequence, the fake wine rack sank into the floor, and the elevator began its long return from the underland.

Melissa stashed her mini-drills. "How are we doing for time?"

Two hundred miles to the southwest, in a Capitol Hill parking lot, Cain closed the door of his Cameron Bullet and hurried toward a government security checkpoint. Though the D.C. weather was brisk enough to warrant a trench coat, his black fedora and gloves made him look conspicuously sinister. A passing tourist assumed the old man was either an assassin or a congressman.

"Lousy," Cain told Melissa. "Gingold's men are all in place. He's about to give the order."

"Damn it." She checked her watch. "You said you'd stall him."

"I said I'd *try*. I'm meeting the senator now but things are going to get worse before they get better. Stay focused on the mission. Don't go trying to save everyone."

"Cedric—"

"Get the orphans out of there."

The line went dead. Melissa could only assume that he'd discarded his transmitter, which meant she was officially on her own.

The elevator doors opened. She steeled herself with a breath. "All right, then."

Halfway into her descent, she activated a button on her belt. Her helmet and armor changed color to match her surroundings, a full-body lumiflage that adjusted itself in real time. Cain had invented that lovely feature himself. He might have even shared it with Integrity if they hadn't taken his Sci-Tech division away from him.

The doors opened. Melissa scanned the nearby environment, then made a high-speed dash for the trees. Her armor had barely changed color when she stopped to marvel at the underland.

"My God . . ."

She'd expected to find a large-scale bunker, all vault lights and metal walls. Instead it seemed the Gothams had created their own pocket universe down here. What an extraordinary feat of engineering. The fact that they'd built it all in secret—

"Hi there."

She turned around to find Hannah standing right behind her, close enough to allow her blue jeans and T-shirt to become incorporated into Melissa's lumiflage.

"What—"

Melissa stumbled backward. Hannah caught her arm before she could topple over.

"Whoa. Careful there."

Her words sounded perfectly normal. Hannah must have been shifted at Melissa's exact speed. Stranger still, she'd managed to recognize her through her stealthsuit.

"How on earth—"

"Come on," Hannah said. "Let's get you inside before the Gothams see you."

"How did you know I was . . ." The answer hit Melissa before she could even finish the question. "Theo."

"Saw you coming an hour ago," Hannah said. "He sent me to get you."

"He must see the rest of it, then."

"The rest of what?"

The air vents suddenly stopped humming. The Heavensend died, throwing the entire village into darkness. Even the lumic readout inside Melissa's visor went black.

"Oh no . . ."

The distant cries of a thousand Gothams filled the air. It had been easy to forget, with the lamps and the breeze and the illusion of sky, that the underland was nothing but a giant tomb. Worse, everyone could register the tingle of solis on their skin. This was more than a generator failure. The blackout was happening deep inside their bodies, too.

Hannah pushed her inner accelerator and felt absolutely nothing. "I'm blocked. I can't shift."

Neither could Melissa. She activated her infrared vision and scanned her suit's gauges. Her portable electronics were working just fine, but her temporic devices had been nullified.

"Damn it." She took off her helmet and pushed it into Hannah's hands. "Put that on and lead me to the others. Hurry!"

"What's happening?"

Melissa gripped Hannah's arm, her stomach twisting in knots. She thought she'd have a few more minutes to extract the orphans, but clearly time was up.

The invasion had already begun.

FORTY-THREE

Three and a half weeks earlier, mere hours after Gingold first heard the word "underland," a pair of kelly-green aerotrucks descended into Quarter Hill. The residents of Troy Street watched with quiet interest as a dozen exterminators from the Smite-a-Mite company disembarked and erected a tempic shell around the Ackerman house. The place was clearly being fumigated, though the neighbors couldn't fathom why so many men were needed for the job. They came in and out of the house at all hours, making jackhammer noises in the basement. Must have been one hell of a bug problem.

Soon the "exterminators" sent a high-powered wave scan through the crust of the earth, revealing a solic/electric power grid a thousand feet below the surface. By the end of the week, Integrity knew the exact size, shape, and location of the underland, and had set up four more digsites around town. Sixty-two agents and seventeen mole drones worked day and night to drill tunnel paths into the earth—down, down, down to the secret world of the Gothams.

On Saturday morning, twenty-six hours before the start of the invasion, an operative punched a one-inch hole through the ceiling of the dome and sent in a team of camera flies. While the tiny drones mapped every street and exit, directional mics picked up dozens of conversations. Integrity soon learned that the Gothams were burying one of their own on Sunday, a teenage girl named Yvonne. Every man, woman, and child would be down there at nine A.M., in a tightly enclosed space hidden far away from civilians.

Gingold couldn't have prayed for a better opportunity.

At 9:03, just moments after the lights went out, a thunderous explosion rocked the eastern wall of the dome. The Gothams in the village square fell into screaming disarray, prompting Irwin Sunder to climb the base of a support column and shine his handphone onto his face.

"People, just stay calm and stay where you are! Please!"

Hundreds of phone screens lit up the square, giving everyone a flickering view of the chaos. Parents hugged their children defensively while panicking kinsmen tried to push their way out of the crowd. Bruce Byers fell to the grass and was trampled into unconsciousness. Shauna Ryder was shoved against the guild directory. Her front teeth cracked against the stone.

"Please!" Sunder begged. "Calm down! You're only going to—"

"*Stop.*"

Harsh yellow lights hit the crowd from every angle. Fifty-six soldiers flanked the square from the rooftops. Between their high, scattered perches and their head-mounted targeting displays, the snipers had the whole clan covered. They could kill any one or fifty people at a moment's notice.

Gingold watched from the roof of the municipal building, his body covered in deep black osplate. Like the rest of his team, he'd swapped his light tempic armor for a clunkier metal suit. All his weapons and scanners were nontemporic. Gingold had known from the start that the only way to beat these freaks was to flood their home with solis. Integrity could get by without its timebending tricks. These folks, not so much.

He raised a bullhorn to his lips. "Ladies and gentlemen—"

While most of the crowd looked up, Ollie Orlowski made a fevered dash down an alley. Fifty Gothams screamed as a hissing gunshot sent the boy to the ground.

"That was a stun bolt," Gingold attested. "The next person who runs gets a bullet in the leg. The one after that gets a bullet in the head."

Frantic chatter filled the square. The sounds of heavy footsteps drew closer. While Gingold and his snipers had rappelled down from the ceiling, the infantry charged in through the blast hole in the eastern wall. Now at last they reached the center of the village: a hundred and forty armored soldiers, all spreading like oil around the Gothams. They dragged a handful of stragglers back into the cluster, then draped Ollie's limp body over a park bench.

Sunder stared up at the glass-eyed man with the megaphone. "Who are you?"

"I'm Oren Gingold, senior agent of the National Integrity Commission. You're all being detained as exceptional threats under Article Five, Section Two of the United States Security Code."

"You can't do this," Victoria yelled. "We're American citizens!"

Gingold magnified his view of the primarch until her personal information popped up as an overlay. "Don't play dumb, Chisholm. You people have been skirting the law for decades. Some of you have killed federal agents. All of you are guilty of harboring fugitives."

He scanned the frightened faces below. No sign yet of the people on his wish list. No Rebel Rosen. No Peter Pendergen. Not a single one of the otherworlders.

"Far as I'm concerned, each and every one of you is a threat to human life. I'd like nothing more than to bury you here." Gingold paused in momentary thought. "But Chisholm's right. You are Americans. That buys you one chance. Surrender peacefully and no one else gets hurt. That's the best offer you'll ever get from me."

The soldiers on the ground raised a dozen floodlights while another team set up an electric rope cordon around the Gothams.

Carrie held her father tight. "Daddy . . ."

"It's all right," Stan whispered. "Stay with me."

Gingold lowered the bullhorn and addressed his people through his transmitter. "Flyers, get the evacs ready. Thermals, fan out. I want every inch of this place searched."

He swept his electronic gaze around the Gothams, his lip curled in a scowl. "There are a lot of faces I'm not seeing."

In better times, when the lights worked, the perimeter park was the most vibrant part of the village. The two-mile path of Crimson Queen maple trees looped all around the base of the dome, providing endless color for the Gothams who walked it. The illusion of nature was broken every hundred feet or so by a doorway on the outer wall—an elevator here, a stairwell there, a long ladder tube to the surface. There was even a golf cart ramp that sloped all the way up to West Nyack. The underland didn't lack for exits.

Unfortunately for Melissa, Gingold had done his homework. His snipers kept their infrared sights on every manual escape hatch, while power grid blackouts, both above and below, kept the elevators out of commission. Even Peter Pendergen, a man who excelled at making his own exits, was trapped down here.

But he knew the underland better than Integrity, and he believed there was an escape route that Gingold had overlooked.

Melissa followed Peter through the perimeter park, their pathway lit by the ambient glow of the village square. From Freak Street, they'd fled to the lower east quadrant of the dome, a mere forty yards from Integrity's main entrance. Melissa magnified her infrared vision and saw dozens of soldiers moving back and forth through the blast hole. It was just a matter of time before one of them switched on their thermals and looked back.

"Are you sure this will work?" she asked Peter.

"I'm not sure of anything," he said. "I just know it's the only lift we have that's independently powered."

"Powered by what, exactly?"

"Gasoline."

Dear God, Melissa thought. Those combustion engines were all decades old. You couldn't even buy that kind of fuel anymore.

"Petrol has a shelf life," she told him. "If you don't change it—"

"It's all right. Our turners reverse the generator twice a year."

"Turners," Melissa echoed. "You mean the people who do what Zack does."

"Yes."

"I can only guess that they're your healers."

"And gardeners."

Melissa's face went slack. "My God. The world you have. The *society* . . ."

"Yeah." Peter took a glum look at the Integrity floodlights. "It was good while it lasted."

The trees broke again to reveal an elevator entrance, a much narrower one than the others.

"This is it," Peter told Melissa. "The emergency lift."

Melissa studied it skeptically. The door was covered in dust and blocked by trash bags. The generator hatch looked like it had been salvaged from an old British war submarine.

"I think your turners skipped a few visits," Melissa said.

"It'll work," Peter insisted.

He pressed the call button and breathed a sigh of relief when it lit up. Though the generator coughed and creaked, the motor still ran. The car was coming down from the surface.

Melissa took another thermal scan of the area, then flashed her penlight twice. Theo caught her signal and led the others out from behind a gazebo. Two by two, the orphans and Liam made a skulking procession down the park path.

"Where does this thing go?" Melissa asked Peter.

"Grade school. Not far from the southern gate."

"Will it fit all of us?"

Peter shook his head. "Maybe five or six if you squeeze."

"Damn it." Melissa looked back to the invaders at the eastern gate. "We don't have time for two trips."

"We *would* have had time—"

"Don't start that again."

"—if you'd been straight with me. You could have come to me at Sunder's house."

Melissa glared at him. They had drawn their guns on each other four minutes ago, when Hannah brought Melissa back to the cul-de-sac. She and Peter didn't exactly have a history of trust.

"You had my memory erased," she reminded him. "I didn't think for a minute you'd bring me down here."

"I wouldn't have." He tilted his head at the Silvers. "But I would have gotten them out."

Soon Theo, Amanda, and the rest of the group caught up with them. Melissa could see the trauma on their faces; something had shocked them well before the invasion. She only had to register the missing member of their group to get the gist of their misery. What on earth had happened to David?

Liam threw a frazzled look over his shoulder. "This isn't right. We can't just leave them."

"Liam . . ."

"They're still our people."

Peter held him by the shoulders. "Son, listen to me. We can't help them by staying. We need to get out."

"But what about them?"

"My associate's working on it," Melissa told Liam. "He's in Washington right now, trying to stop this siege at the highest levels."

Hannah eyed her jadedly. "A little late for that."

"All they need is a stand-down order. They'll be forced to leave immediately."

"And then what?" Amanda asked. "You think they'll just forget about us?"

"Forget? No. But under new management—"

"—nothing will change," Zack said. "We're timebending mutants from another planet. They're not going to rest till we're locked up or dead."

Theo nodded. "Especially after what the Pelletiers did to your people. That's all the justification they need."

Melissa turned her ear to the generator. The elevator seemed to be coming at a snail's pace. "We'll have plenty of time to argue about this. Our first priority's getting out of here."

Mia crouched down next to her, her jaw clenched tight. She looked ten years older than the child in Melissa's files. Something about her had changed dramatically. Something in the eyes.

"There's a girl back there who means everything to me. What'll they do to her?"

"She . . ." Melissa could feel the start of a dozen non-answers—evasions and platitudes, flimsy assurances of hope. But at the end of the day, this was an impossible situation. There was no good way to spin it.

"She'll be sedated," she told Mia. "Then transported to an aerial facility high above the Atlantic. From what I'm told, they've built hundreds of solic cells, enough to hold everyone in the village. They'll be kept there indefinitely, questioned and analyzed—"

"Analyzed," Jonathan mocked. "That's a nice way of putting it."

Mia jumped to her feet. "No. I can't let them do that. Not to Carrie."

"Not to any of them," Liam stressed. He grabbed his father's arm. "We have to do *something*."

Peter leaned against a tree, his face racked with conflict. Melissa knew his dilemma all too well, the horrible schism between idealism and realism, society and family. Sometimes you had to look out for the people you loved, and damn the rest of the world. Other times . . .

He sighed at Melissa. "How are they blocking our abilities?"

"You know how."

"Solis, yes. But where's it coming from?"

She pointed her finger at the dark upper reaches. "You can't see it, but there's a rather large disseminator at the top of the dome."

"Disseminator?" asked Amanda.

"A portable supergenerator, mostly used for military operations. It has the output of a hundred solic towers."

"That'd only be enough to stop a fraction of us," Peter said.

"In open air, yes. But in a hermetically sealed chamber, even one of this size . . ." Melissa shrugged. "It's like smoke in a jar. Gingold knew exactly what he was doing."

Hannah narrowed her eyes at the ceiling. She could faintly make out the shape of an upside-down obelisk hanging directly above the clock tower.

"It takes power to block power," she said. "Something must be giving it juice."

Melissa nodded. "Could be a solar converter. More likely they've tapped into the Quarter Hill electric grid. In either case, the energy's coming from the surface."

Zack paced the grass, his eyes dancing with thought. "So we find the plug and pull it. Our powers should work up there, right?"

"They should."

Everyone could hear the skepticism in Melissa's voice. Theo raised his eyebrows at her. "But?"

She tossed her hands up. "Say you succeed. Say you all get your abilities back and turn the tables on your oppressors. Then what?"

"What do you mean?"

"Integrity's a massive organization. You can't erase their knowledge. And if you should slaughter two hundred of their soldiers, it won't matter who runs the agency. They'll hunt you down to the ends of the Earth."

Melissa watched them closely as they processed her quandary. Her eyes drifted over to the watch on Heath's arm, a fancy silver antiquity that she'd seen before in countless photos and ghost images. It used to be David's.

"Two hundred soldiers," Liam said. "We have more people than that. Hell, we have more tempics than that."

Melissa turned to him. "Did you hear me, boy? I said—"

"He knows what you said," Mia snapped. "His point is that we can take them down without killing them."

Hannah nodded. "Blind them with lumis. Pin them to the ground with tempis."

"Heal the ones who get hurt," Theo said.

"And push them out through portals," Zack added. "Wouldn't that send a message?"

Melissa lifted her visor and traded an uncomfortable look with Peter. He knew as well as she did that it wouldn't be so easy. There'd be casualties on both sides. Consequences. But would it be any worse than this nightmare?

Amanda kneeled down in front of Melissa. "I knew from the day I met you that you were different than the other agents. You didn't just see me as a tempic freak. You treated me like a human being with human rights."

She jerked her head at the distant floodlights. "There are hundreds of people back there who've never hurt anyone. We can't just walk away and hope that everything will work out for them. I don't think you can either."

Hannah moved behind Heath and put her hands on his shoulders. "You know these pricks. You know their machines. If anyone can help us, it's you."

Melissa pulled off her helmet and held it against her chest. In fact, she'd already marked the global position of the disseminator. Its power source would be directly above. Same latitude and longitude.

The elevator finally arrived. The door squeaked open. Melissa groaned when she saw the interior. It was even smaller than Peter said it would be. Four passengers at the very most.

"Gingold's a cautious man," Melissa warned. "He'll expect resistance, which means the generator will be heavily guarded."

"I'll handle the goons," Hannah said.

"We both will," Amanda said.

Melissa frowned. "Don't be so confident. On the surface, they'll have tempic armor and probably speedsuits. I'll also need a fair bit of time to disable the generator."

"I can drop it," Jonathan told her. "Just lead the way."

Heath's eyes bulged in horror. "No!"

"I'll be all right, buddy. Just find a place to hide."

Melissa pulled a walkie-talkie from her belt and pressed it into Theo's hands. "This is set to an encrypted channel. Don't use it until you hear from me." She looked to Peter. "Do you have any vaults or bomb shelters here?"

"We've got both down below," Peter said.

"Good. The thick walls should hide you from their scanners."

A *boom* in the distance made Mia and Liam jump. Melissa assured them that it was just a warning shot. Integrity used the loud guns to keep people in line.

"You better go," she told Peter. "Be careful."

"You too." He looked at Amanda. "Stay safe."

As Melissa and the Givens stepped inside the elevator, Heath pulled at Jonathan's arm. "Wait!"

"Heath . . ."

"Don't go."

"I've got a job to do, buddy, and so do you. You gotta get to that shelter."

"Please!"

Jonathan kneeled in front of Heath and touched the rim of his golden bracelet. "It's been you and me from the beginning. It'll be you and me at the end. So keep your head down and don't get shot, okay?"

Smiling, he brushed the tip of Heath's nose. "We still have a lot of songs to do."

Melissa held the door impatiently. "Jonathan."

"I'm coming."

He joined Hannah at the back of the car. Their fingers clasped together.

Hannah looked at the billy club in Melissa's thigh holster. "I'm gonna need that beatstick."

The door closed. The elevator rose. From the slow, sputtering sounds of the generator, Melissa strongly doubted there'd be a return trip.

She tucked her helmet in the crook of her arm and passed her club back to Hannah. "How did he die?"

"Who?" Amanda asked.

Melissa eyed her guardedly, as if she was being deliberately obtuse. "David."

The elevator fell silent. While Amanda and Jonathan kept their eyes on the floor, Hannah tested the weight of her new weapon. "Horribly."

Peter led his group north through the perimeter park—a slow, looping path that took them all the way to the Memorial Garden. They heard the footsteps of passing soldiers and took quick refuge behind the Requiem Wall. Mia found it ironic, and more than a little prophetic, that they were hiding behind the names of a thousand dead Gothams. The thought of Carrie suffering in some secret government lab was more than she could bear. She'd be nothing but a lab rat to those scientists, a pin cushion. And if they were truly depraved . . .

"No."

Peter shushed her and peeked around the edge of the stone. The soldiers were barely visible except for the glints in their armor and the lights on their thermal scanners. Luckily, they seemed more interested in the nearby buildings than the graveyard.

Mia and the others waited breathlessly in the shadows until the soldiers kept moving. After a few more seconds, Peter waved Zack and Theo over.

"How well do you know Guild Street?" he whispered.

"Not at all," Theo said.

"I went there once with Mercy," Zack said.

Peter pointed to the north. "The travelers' hall is all the way at the end on the right side. It's the smallest building on the street. There's a hatch in back that'll take you down to the tunnels."

Liam furrowed his brow. "Dad, what are you doing?"

"The bomb shelter's nearby. Just follow the signs."

"Dad?"

Peter looked at his son with heavy eyes. "I'm gonna go join the others."

"You mean get yourself captured," Zack said.

"We have to be ready when the power comes back. The tempics, the swifters, all of them. If I join the pool, I can talk to the primarchs. We do this right and maybe no one will die."

Liam nodded. "I'll come with you."

"No."

"I'm coming too," Mia insisted.

"*No.* You get to that shelter, all of you."

Liam's cheeks burned red. He had to fight to keep his voice down. "God-damn it, Dad. *Think* for a second."

"Don't you talk to me like that."

"I *will* talk to you like that. You left me for seven months."

"I was keeping you safe."

"Yeah? How did that work out?"

Mia saw the agonized look on Peter's face and couldn't help but feel a bit forlorn. She'd always imagined herself to be like a daughter to him, but their bond was just a flicker compared to what he had with Liam. The boy held all the keys to the fortress, all the nuclear codes. He was the core and the axis of the world Peter fought to save.

And in this instance, he was right.

Liam held Mia's arm, his blue eyes locked sternly on his father. "You're a big, strong man. They're going to watch you closely. But Mia and I aren't threatening. We can move through the crowd, spread the word ten times faster than you can."

He jerked his head at Mia. "And when the power comes back, you're going to need every traveler you can get."

Mia could practically hear the gears in Peter's head turning. He stared at the grass for eight long seconds before gripping Zack's shoulder.

"You and Heath get Theo to that shelter. Do whatever it takes to keep him alive."

Theo glowered at him. "Peter, I told you—"

"Don't start." He pulled a .32 pistol from his belt and pushed it into Zack's hand. "Whatever it takes. You hear me?"

Zack studied the gun. "Travelers' guild. Hatch in the back."

"You got it." He clapped Zack's back. "Go."

Mia watched from behind the stone as Theo, Zack, and Heath crept out the gate. She barely had a moment to catch her breath before Peter turned her around and brushed her hair in front of her eyes.

"What are you doing?"

"Keep your head down," he told her. "Don't look at anyone. Don't say a word."

Hand in hand, he led Mia and Liam through the western gate of the garden. They barely made it half a block before the glowing red sights of sniper rifles danced across their chests.

Peter stopped in place and raised his hands high. "We're unarmed! We surrender!"

Within moments, a group of soldiers arrived and escorted the trio at gunpoint. As her stomach fluttered with stress and her legs threatened to buckle, Mia pictured Semerjean watching her from a cozy hotel room.

He knew this was coming, she realized. *He let this happen.*

After two more blocks, she heard the anxious chattering of hundreds. She looked up and reeled at the nightmare in the village square. Integrity had turned the whole place into an internment camp, with water stations on one side of the pen and toilet booths on the other. A line of canvas tents had been erected just outside the electric cordon.

Only Peter was tall enough to see the activity on the far side of the square. A phalanx of soldiers had formed a living gate, parting only to let six male prisoners through. From there, armed guards escorted the group down the street and out of sight. The transport process had already begun.

A guard deactivated a segment of the buzzrope and waved them inside. "Come on. Come on. Hurry."

"Hold it," yelled a voice in the distance.

Peter cursed under his breath. He'd been hoping to get into the pen without being recognized, but clearly someone was on the ball.

Gingold approached the trio of new prisoners, then scowled at their escorts. "Idiots. Did you even look at the files?"

"Sir?"

He lifted Mia's chin and brushed the bangs from her brow. Her heart dropped at the black glass discs that stood in place of his eyes.

"Well, well, well," he said. "Our little doormaker. They're still talking about you in Seattle."

Mia lowered her head and muttered something profane. Gingold smiled. "See? I knew I liked you for a reason. If you tell me where your friends are—"

"Fuck you," Mia repeated.

"It's all right. We have time." Gingold looked at her escort. "Put her in Tent One."

"Don't!" Peter yelled.

The nearby Gothams gasped as Gingold clocked him on the jaw. Peter fell to his knees, his mouth dripping blood.

"I know you," Gingold said. "I've studied your tactics, and I don't think for a moment that you would just surrender yourself. You've got a plan and I can't wait to find out what it is."

He turned back to the soldiers. "Tent Five."

Liam opened his mouth to say something. Peter quickly shook his head. *Don't.*

As Peter and Mia were carted away, Gingold scrutinized Liam thoroughly. He rolled up the boy's gloves, revealing six inches of burn scars.

"Rough hands," Gingold noted. "Some might call them warrior's hands. Are you a fighter like your dad? Have you been hardened like Farisi?"

Liam looked away, twin trails of tears running down his face. Gingold clucked his tongue. "Nah. You're just a boy."

He straightened Liam's gloves, then gestured to his escort. "Put him in."

The soldiers shoved Liam into the Gotham pen. A quick-handed lumic caught him before he could fall.

Mother Olga saw him and fought her way toward him. "Liam!"

The Gothams cleared a path. She pulled Liam into her heavy arms. "Oh, my sweetheart. You poor thing. Did they hurt you?"

Liam sniffled and shook his head. Though he didn't share his father's faith, it seemed like divine providence that the first kinsman he encountered was the most esteemed, beloved primarch of the clan. If anyone could get their people ready, it was Olga.

"You need to listen to me very carefully," Liam whispered. "We have a lot to do."

FORTY-FOUR

There had once been a place on the native world of the Silvers: a two-bedroom walk-up in the Jackson Heights neighborhood of Queens. Though the rooms were small, the walls were thin, the faucets spit brown water, and the heat rarely worked in the winter, Samara Bradshaw's apartment had been decorated with a brilliant eye for color. Every inch of the place—from the wall paint to the throw rugs to the hinges on the kitchen door—complemented each other in pleasing shades of blue.

Whenever a new boyfriend came home with Samara (and it had happened quite often, as she was a lovely young singer with an incurable weakness for charmers), he would immediately ask about her color obsession. That was when she introduced him to the apartment's true designer: her teenage son, Ahmad.

None of Samara's lovers ever knew what to do with the boy, this strange little mumbler with all the charm of a seizure. When he didn't prattle on about unsolicited topics—the principles of color theory, the musical evolution of the Beatles, the hunting habits of the arctic white wolf—he threw shrieking tantrums over everything and nothing.

Inevitably, Samara's boyfriends found convenient excuses to stop calling her. Some flat out told her that her boy was the deal-breaker. After being questioned about his facial mole, one man stood up at the dinner table and called Ahmad a retard. Samara chased him out the door with a kitchen knife.

She'd barely finished catching her breath before she gripped her son by the shoulders. "Don't you listen to him, okay? He doesn't know you. He doesn't know a goddamn thing."

Ahmad wasn't so sure. His classmates called him a retard all the time. His teachers constantly lost patience with him. He could barely count the number of times he heard his mother fighting in the principal's office, her strong voice bleeding through the door. *You see this letter? That's my doctor saying your doctor's full of shit. My boy's just fine. He's just different is all.*

On the last day of Ahmad's freshman year, the principal finally put her foot down and told Samara that the school could no longer accommodate him. He'd have to try his luck in another district or become enrolled in a program for high-functioning autistics.

Ahmad watched his mother on the bus ride home. She stared out the window with white-hot intensity, as if she were trying to melt the entire city with her mind.

"What's wrong with me?" he asked her.

Samara grimly shook her head. "Nothing. God gave you more than these people can handle. This is their problem. Not yours."

That summer, she'd found herself a new lover: a seven-foot mountain of muscle and bone who made the couch creak every time he sat on it. Though the man could have worn Ahmad like a scarf, he spoke to him in a soft voice and smiled at him even when Samara wasn't looking. Stranger still, he listened to every one of Ahmad's scholarly lectures, interrupting only to ask questions. *Why do TVs use a three-color system but printers use four? Why did the Beatles break up? What do the wolves do when their environment changes?*

On the third of July, the boyfriend surprised Ahmad with a birthday present: a New York Giants jersey with a 44 on the front and back. He explained that there was another Ahmad Bradshaw out there, a running back who'd recently scored the winning touchdown in the Super Bowl. It was a good name to have. A good shirt.

For Ahmad, who'd never cared a whit about names or sports, the jersey was a horror. The fabric felt weird, the sleeves were an odd length, and the royal blue color was all wrong for his skin tone.

"No. No no no . . ."

The boyfriend lowered his voice and gestured at the bedroom, where Samara was sleeping. "Son, listen to me. Your mother's a good woman. She'll fight for you till the day she dies. But you're fifteen now. It's time to step up."

Ahmad's eyes widened. "What do you mean?"

"The world isn't always gonna be your color," the boyfriend warned him. "Screaming and crying won't fix it."

Ahmad looked away, scowling. "What do you expect me to do?"

The man smiled knowingly. "What do the wolves do when their environment changes?"

Ahmad knew the answer, of course, but the comparison hardly seemed appropriate. Wolves had to adapt in order to survive. Ahmad was merely struggling to live a less aggravating life. Still, the man had made a good point about Samara. The strain of her battles was starting to show. Maybe it was time to take some of the weight off her shoulders.

Over the next few weeks, Ahmad began forcing himself out of his comfort zones, just to test his mettle. He sampled foods that were previously anathema to him, played music from artists that everyone but him seemed to love. He donned his hideous football jersey day after day, until the royal blue cloth became part of his personal color scheme.

He'd been wearing the shirt on July 24, when the sky took on a sickly light and a hundred different airplanes came crashing down onto New York City. The events of the morning played like a fever dream: the explosion, the fire, the panicked dash down a stairwell, the white-haired man in the lobby and the golden bracelet in his grip.

The next thing Ahmad remembered, he was standing on the street of an entirely different Queens, his wide eyes fixed on the flying traffic. He had tried—oh, Lord, he had tried—to roll with life's punches, to face the world like a grownup, or at least a grownup wolf. But this? This was too much for a fragile mind to handle. This would not do at all.

Ahmad retreated to a safe room in his mind while scientists from the Azral Group took him to their research complex in White Plains. He remained catatonic for twenty-two days, staring out the window of the second-floor day lounge, until he heard the start of a very familiar song. Someone in the room—a long-haired white guy who rarely talked much himself—was playing "Day Tripper" on an electric guitar. The notes were right but the tempo . . .

"Your timing's off," Ahmad calmly informed him. "You're rushing the twelve-bar. That's not how they played it."

The guitarist blinked at him in surprise, and then played the riff at a slower speed. He nodded, impressed. "Well, I'll be damned."

He put down the guitar and studied the boy cautiously. "It's good as hell to see you talking. I'm Jonathan. What's your name?"

Ahmad stammered, confounded. Though he could easily recall the details of his past, his name had become a vaporous thing. All he could recall was the name of his mother's last boyfriend, the only one he ever liked.

"*Heath.*"

Heath snapped out of his daze and looked around. Someone was calling him in the darkness—a stern, hissing whisper that cut through the air like an arrow. He peeked above a rose hedge and saw Theo and Zack at the edge of the lumics' guildhouse, both beckoning him with brusque gestures. He scrambled around the hedge and crept his way over to them.

"Keep up," Zack told him. "We don't have time to go looking for you."

Heath nodded, chiding himself for falling behind. Once again, the savior of the world needed him. He refused to fail Theo by getting hung up on personal distractions: his fear and nostalgia, his worry over Jonathan, his hatred for these soldiers and the blackness they brought. The glow from the center of town cast ominous shadows throughout the village, making Guild Street look like a sinister back alley. The stairs to the bomb shelter were still six blocks away.

Zack peeked around the corner of the lumics' building, then quickly pulled back.

"Soldiers?" Theo asked.

"Yeah. Four of them."

"How far?"

"About fifty yards. I can't tell if they're coming or going."

"They're moving away," Heath said.

Zack and Theo didn't have to ask him how he knew. The kid had the sharpest ears of anyone in the group. He could identify his friends by the sound of their footsteps, and knew all the doors on Freak Street by the distinct ways they creaked.

While Heath kept his ear on the soldiers' progress, Zack leaned against the wall and took an uneasy look at his arm. Heath's golden bracelet now had a sinister companion, an "antique" wristwatch that, until yesterday, had been the ornament of a traitor.

"I wish you wouldn't wear that," Zack muttered.

Theo nodded. "You don't know what it does."

Heath could only shrug in reply. If he had even the slightest ability to explain himself, he might have told them about a pledge he'd made to another

Heath, a promise to adapt to life's jarring changes. Instead of shrinking away from the unfamiliar, he would wrap those things around him and make them his own. It had worked with the football shirt. It had worked with Azral's bracelet. It would work again with Semerjean's wristwatch.

Theo peeked over the backyard gate and caught the distant silhouette of a rooftop sniper. "I didn't see this coming. Not a single bit of it."

"The Pelletiers," Zack guessed.

"Yeah. But what do they gain by jamming me? What do they gain by any of this?"

"I don't know. Semerjean said he'd have an offer for us soon. Maybe they're softening us up for the sales pitch." Zack frowned at Theo. "The real question is why Ioni didn't tell you."

Theo matched his frustrated look. "That's something I plan to ask her."

Heath heard a faint noise in the vicinity, the whimpering cry of a pre-adolescent. He traced the sound upward and saw a barred window on the second floor of the guildhouse: a prison cell. What on earth would the lumics be doing with a captive child? Unless . . .

Harold.

Peter had once mentioned something about the last surviving member of Gemma's disparates, that chubby blond kid who made spectral blue tigers. His crimes had been horrendous, but he was too young to exile and too crazy to be free. Locking him up was the only sane compromise.

But now the kid was a sitting duck where he was. It was just a matter of time before the soldiers found him.

You have to help him, said a wolf in Heath's head. *Get him to the shelter. It's the right thing to do.*

Screw that, said another wolf, the ornery creature that Heath had named Rose Tyler. *That little bastard tried to kill you. You gonna risk the savior's life just to be nice?*

Heath sighed in resignation. As much as he hated to admit it, Rose was right. Theo was the only priority. The tiger-boy would have to fend for himself.

"What do you hear?" Zack asked Heath. "Are the soldiers gone?"

Heath tuned out Harold's cries, then climbed back to his feet. "Yeah. Let's go."

They moved carefully through the shadows until they reached a flood-lit intersection. The village square was only three blocks away, close enough to provide a glimpse of the mayhem. Gunmen paced the grass and the roof-tops while the Gothams stood miserably behind a buzzrope. Zack and Theo peeked around the corner just in time to see a soldier pepper-spray a group of loud complainers. They clutched their eyes in screaming pain.

Zack shot a hateful look at the operative. "Asshole."

"He's not going to like it when the tables turn," Theo said.

"*If* they turn."

"They will," Theo said. "Melissa knows what she's doing."

Heath looked to the other end of Center Street, then cocked his head in confusion. Two blocks away, a dozen agents rushed to assemble some items: a pair of freestanding doorframes, each one as large as a school bus. Circuitry jutted out at strange and ugly angles. If these were machines, they were crude ones, the kind a crazy inventor would build in their garage.

Zack squinted curiously at the constructs. "What the hell are those things?"

"No idea," Theo said. "They almost look like tempic barriers."

"If we can't make tempis, neither can they. Even if they could—"

"*No!*"

Heath was the only one to see the jittery red dot on Zack's shirt. He barely had time to yell before a hissing bolt flew hundreds of feet through the darkness and impaled itself in Zack's shoulder blade.

Grimacing, Zack fell to the concrete, his body thrashing. Theo dropped to his knees and reflexively reached for the projectile in his back. If his foresight had been working, he might have known that he was grabbing a high-voltage stun bolt, and that it was still carrying a charge. Electric current shot through Theo's arm, just as a sniper's second bolt struck him deep in the thigh. He shuddered in place before collapsing on top of Zack.

Heath stumbled back, his thoughts screaming in alarm. He could already hear the clanking boots of soldiers. He didn't have the time to drag Theo out of here. His only choice now was to—

Fight, his inner wolves urged him. *Let us out!*

No. How could he? The underland was filled with solis. Everyone's powers were neutralized.

Yet here we are, the wolves reminded him. *Wide awake and ready to fight.*

The footsteps grew louder. Long shadows spilled into the intersection. Heath saw four soldiers—the same ones that had crossed his earshot earlier—approach Zack and Theo. One of them quickly spotted Heath.

"You! Stop right there!"

Heath's thoughts went blank. The cage of his consciousness opened wide. By the time the soldiers aimed their weapons, ten large tempic masses had shot out of his fingers. They transformed in midair, forming tails and claws and snarling muzzles.

"Holy—"

Only half the group managed to fire their rifles before the wolves pounced. The creatures pinned them all to the pavement, tearing at them through the soft parts of their armor. Heath could feel a wolf chomp the index finger off one man—a phantom taste of blood and bone that nearly made the boy retch.

Stop it, Heath ordered. *Just keep them where they are!*

A hundred yards away, at the edge of the square, the soldiers and Gothams all stopped to watch the violence. The snipers aimed their sights on the wolves.

"Hold your fire," yelled the voice in their headsets.

Gingold was well acquainted with Heath's menagerie, and he had the scars to prove it. He also knew from their last encounter that the boy was squeamish about killing. The soldiers were in little danger. The real problem was the kid. Making tempis in these conditions was scientifically impossible, like lighting a match underwater. How the hell was he doing it?

The answer, Heath suspected, was right there on his wrist.

Eight months prior, in a Battery Park office building, Mercy Lee had crippled Esis with a well-placed burst of solis. Her near-death experience prompted Azral to make sure that no one in the family got depowered again. He built a mechanical safeguard, no larger than a teardrop, and incorporated it into three accessories: his golden ring, his mother's diamond necklace, and his father's silver timepiece.

The moment Heath put on the wristwatch, he'd become completely immune to solis, a parting gift from Semerjean Pelletier.

Heath retreated into his thoughts, to the warm white room where his animals lived. They were all wolves at heart, and they fiercely resisted whenever he tried to make them into something else. But wolves couldn't carry Zack and Theo to safety. He needed something more versatile. He needed—

Men? a guttural voice asked him. *You want us to walk like you?*

No, Heath pleaded, *I need you to run.*

The snipers watched with puzzled brows as six of Heath's wolves began to evolve. They stood up on their hind legs and shook their bodies vigorously, as if someone had splashed water on them. By the time they stopped thrashing, the creatures had transformed into something else entirely—six tall and faceless humanoids with the sturdy build of weightlifters.

Gingold reached a rooftop just in time to watch the tempic men flee north up Guild Street. He replayed the image in his optic feed and studied it in still frame. Two of the hulks carried Zack and Theo in their arms. The other four moved in a tight diamond formation. Gingold had to magnify the picture to see a hint of the boy between them. They had clustered around their lord and creator, shielding him from weapons fire.

Unfortunately for Heath, Gingold already knew that trick. And he had the perfect countermeasure.

He looked to the six agents next to him, all crouched around a trio of mortar cannons. "Now."

Heath could hear the discharge from a hundred yards away, a chain of thick and hollow puffing sounds. *Thoop. Thoop. Thoop.*

The bombs flew a high arc over the village, then fell whistling onto Guild Street. The first one demolished the front wall of the turners' hall, eighty feet away from Heath. The second one tore up the street behind him, rattling his eardrums, pelting his men with chunks of rubble.

The third one hit like the end of the world.

Heath's tempic men vanished as the hot blast sent him tumbling through the air. Zack landed in a patch of azaleas. Theo came to a rolling stop on the concrete. Heath crashed against the door of the thermics' guild building, his legs smacking against the wood. He fell to the ground in a messy heap and blacked out for forty-four seconds.

By the time his eyes opened, he wasn't sure if he was alive or dead. His muscles ached. His skin bled in ten places. He couldn't hear anything but the ringing in his ears. It wasn't until he saw Theo's lifeless form that he remembered the task at hand.

Gotta . . . gotta get him to safety. Gotta . . .

He clambered to his knees and crawled his way toward Theo, until a harsh white glow froze him in place.

Three armored soldiers approached him, their rifle lights aimed squarely in his eyes. Frantic, Heath fled inside his head and called for his minions. No response. The explosion had done what the solis couldn't. He was powerless.

"Put him down," Gingold ordered the soldiers. "Don't take any chances."

Heath looked up, his eyes tearing. He imagined his mother weeping from Heaven, with God's hand on one shoulder and Big Heath's on the other.

I'm sorry, Heath told them. *I tried.*

One of the soldier's helmets cracked in a spray of red mist, a fresh new hole in his visor. Heath squinted in the light, baffled, as another gunman fell, then the third one. If Heath's ears had been working, he would have heard the booming gunshot that had accompanied each death. All three soldiers had taken a bullet to the eye.

Heath turned his head to see a muscular figure advancing through the wreckage, a .44 revolver in his hand. He wore at least six different ammunition pouches over his black leather armor, and carried enough weapons to take down a platoon.

He stepped into the light and held a mechanical hand out to Heath.

"Come on," Rebel said. "Let's get you out of here."

Heath scuttled away, panicked. "No. No, no, no . . ."

Rebel motioned impatiently. "I'm on your side, kid. I don't have time to convince you."

Mercy burst out of the turners' guild building, as armed and armored as Rebel. She had just finished dressing for Yvonne's memorial when her mother broke the news of the coming invasion.

Go with Rebel, Prudent had told her. *He has a crucial task for you and Zack.*

Mercy looked to her left and saw Zack lying face down in a flower bed. "Oh no . . ."

"He's all right," Rebel told her. "I'll take him. You get Maranan. Hurry."

Mercy rushed to Theo's side. Rebel turned back to Heath. The boy had climbed to his feet and was slowly retreating.

Rebel sighed at him. "Last chance, kid."

Mercy hoisted Theo into her arms, her nervous gaze fixed on Heath. "Come on. We'll take you to—"

Heath turned around and disappeared into the smoking ruins of Guild Street.

"Wait!"

"Forget it," Rebel told Mercy. "We have bigger things to worry about."

"He's just a boy."

Rebel slung Zack over his shoulder, scoffing at Mercy's assessment. The kid may have been young and a little bit daffy, but he was strong in all the ways that mattered. Rebel was sure that at the end of the day, when the village lay in tatters and the dead filled the streets, the boy and his wolves would be just fine.

FORTY-FIVE

Stores came and went in Quarter Hill, but no one had expected Manganiel's to close. The plant and garden megamart had been a staple of the town since 1980, winning numerous state "Shoppy" awards, including Best Nursery, Best Helpstaff, Best Inventory Design in a Large-Scale Floorspace, and Best Owner.

At least once a year, a developer from a major retail chain serenaded Kath Manganiel, offering her blinding amounts of money for her prime location in the commercial district. No one had been able to sway her until seventeen days ago, when Integrity operatives found her in her illegal tobacco garden and offered her an entirely different kind of bargain. She relinquished her store to the U.S. government, then promptly fled to Florida.

Now a bored young soldier prowled the aisles of the showroom, his field-boots flecked with shriveled leaves and petals. Here on the surface, far above the solic haze, he was free to wear his light and hardy tempic armor. He almost felt bad for his comrades down below, lumbering around in those black metal chokesuits. Then again, they were actually getting to do something while he was stuck in some plant shop, reluctantly learning the difference between hydrangeas and hypericums.

The soldier paused at the end of Aisle 9 (PARTIAL SHADE PERENNIALS), lifted his face mask, and took a swig from his water bottle. Every watt of the store's electricity was being funneled to the basement, killing all the fans and air conditioners. Worse, the sun was already starting to bleed in through the skyglass. Come noon, it was going to be a real ball-soaker in here.

A vibration tickled the soldier's torso. He looked down at his chestplate and saw it dancing with milky ripples.

"What . . ."

He reached for his radio, just as two lily white hands bloomed out of the tempis and covered his mouth and nostrils. His body crashed into a ceramic planter, then thrashed about on the floor. After a minute of kicks and muffled cries, he finally fell still.

Amanda peeked around the corner and reeled him in with a tendril. Jonathan studied him over her shoulder. "Is he dead?"

She leaned in to check his breathing. "He's alive."

"You say that like it's a bad thing."

"I might have overdone it," she admitted. "You can't deprive a brain of oxygen without risking—"

Amanda raised her head in alarm. She felt more tempis in the area: two armored figures behind the potted trees of Aisle 10.

She jumped in front of Jonathan. "Look out!"

The soldiers turned the corner and raised their rifles. Before they could shoot, they were hit by a pair of quick assailants. Hannah struck the back of their knees with a billy club while Melissa zapped their necks with a stun chaser. The soldiers slammed against the ground and stayed there.

The two women de-shifted, then dragged the soldiers up the aisle.

"You okay?" Jonathan asked them.

"We're fine." Melissa dropped her victim next to Amanda's. "Sorry for the close call."

"We had two more by the registers," Hannah said. "They weren't as easy."

Amanda looked around. "I can't feel any more of them."

Melissa scanned the aisles through her thermal visor. Though the tempic armor made the soldiers easy for Amanda to detect, it also masked their heat signatures. Melissa could barely see them. All she knew was that Manganiel's was located directly above the solic disseminator, which meant the power source was in here somewhere. Surely Gingold would have more than five men guarding it. Where were the rest?

She switched off her thermals and examined the suffocated soldier. "He's breathing," Amanda said. "I might have given him brain damage."

"It's all right. Whatever we do to these people can be reversed."

"Not everything," Jonathan reminded her.

"Yes, well . . ." Melissa eyed him guardedly. "Let's do what we can to avoid fatalities."

After one last thermal scan, she led Jonathan and the sisters down a stairwell. The basement stockroom had been completely redone since Integrity moved in, though "undone" might have been the better word for it. All the inventory had been shoved aside by bulldozers. Dirt and rubble lay scattered about in piles. Melissa looked to the center of the room and saw the fruits of the agency's labor: an excavated gorge, twelve feet deep and lined with wooden scaffolds. All the light in the cellar seemed to come from it.

Jonathan studied the big square hole from a distance. "Well, that's creepy as shit."

Melissa shushed him, then activated her lumiflage. Her armor became cloaked in ambient images.

"I'll be back," she whispered. "Stay down and keep quiet."

She crept her way to the gorge and peeked down over the edge. The place was filled with industrial equipment: substations, cooling towers, precipitators . . . but no generator. Six technicians in casual clothes flittered busily between consoles, a holstered gun at each of their hips.

Melissa traced a visual path along the maze of floor cables. The heaviest ones snaked to the north, into a wide scaffold tunnel at the farthest end of the pit. The device they were looking for must be in there, but how far did the passage go?

A glint in the distance caught Melissa's eye. She magnified her visor display and saw faint gray figures moving around behind the dirt mounds. There were soldiers in the upper cellar, and they were doing their best to stay hidden.

They're on high alert, Melissa realized. *They know we're—*

A bullet struck the small of her back. Her armor's battery exploded in a jet of sparks, killing her shifter as well as her chameleon cloak. Melissa barely had a moment to regain herself before three more soldiers fired at her. The first bullet missed. The second one careened off the side of her helmet. The third one hit her square in the chest.

Hannah peeked out of her hiding spot and saw Melissa fall backward into the gorge. A bullet whizzed past her head.

Jonathan pulled her back. "Get down!"

"They got Melissa!"

"How many are there?"

"I don't know. I can't see them!"

Amanda crouched behind a stack of debris, her eyes closed in concentration. She could only vaguely feel the tempis in the distance—eight, nine, maybe ten suits of armor, all scattered around the stockroom. They were moving so fast, they must have activated their shifters. And two of them were rushing toward—

"Hannah!"

The pair arrived before Hannah could even sense them. They skidded to a halt behind her and Jonathan, their rifle barrels raised mere inches behind their heads.

"No!"

Panicked, Amanda thrust her arms. If she'd had a split second more to formulate a strategy, she might have handled the soldiers more delicately. She could have paralyzed their trigger fingers, thrown them against a wall, crippled them or blinded them or closed up their airways.

But the moment she saw the gun at Hannah's head, her thoughts went blank and the tempis took over. She went to the cold white place where Esis lived.

The soldiers yelped as their armored limbs locked firmly in place, immobilizing them. Hannah had no idea what was happening to them until their suits constricted with violent force. The sounds that came next would haunt her for the rest of her life: a pair of shrieks, a spurting gurgle, the most sickening *crunch* she'd ever heard. The men fell to the floor in dull, wet heaps. Blood dribbled out of the fibrous parts of their armor.

Shaken, Hannah jumped into blueshift and closed her eyes. She sensed eight temporal auras, all moving in the same direction. The squad was regrouping at the northern end of the cellar, no doubt to call for backup and to deliberate a new plan of attack. Amanda had just crushed two of their own like beer cans. This was a full-blown crisis.

Hannah checked on her sister, still staring at her victims in a state of trembling shock. She wouldn't be snapping back into action anytime soon, and there was no way to bring Jonathan into the fight. The tempic armor made these enemies undroppable. They'd riddle him with bullets before he could even try.

She had to deal with the other eight soldiers herself.

Hannah traced her finger through the dirt on the floor, a quick and sloppy message for Jonathan: *Stay down.*

He had only just begun to look her way when she snatched a rifle from one of the dead soldiers and bolted into the darkness. Her targets were armed and armored and only slightly slower than her. Her only hope was to strike at them from the shadows, to keep them off-guard and guessing while she took them out one by one.

She hid behind a bulldozer and peeked through the hydraulics. A soldier crouched just thirty feet in front of her, back turned. Hannah's stomach fluttered as she raised her rifle and looked through the scope. The crosshairs dawdled around the wires of his backpack shifter.

Please let this work. Please . . .

She squeezed the trigger with all her strength, but the thing was hopelessly jammed. If Melissa had been with her, she would have told her that Integrity didn't like having their own weapons used against them. Every operative wore an electronic smartkey on their dominant hand, either as a ring or a subdermal implant. No agency gun would fire without one.

Cursing, Hannah searched the rifle for a safety switch, accidentally knocking the barrel against the bulldozer blade. A metallic *clang* echoed through the basement. The soldiers turned their heads in synch.

"Shit."

Hannah gritted her teeth and doubled her speed, ignoring the hard spikes of resistance from her brain. She escaped the bulldozer just before a hail of gunfire tore fifty new holes in the chassis. Its windows shattered. Metal shards flew through the air. Only one of the soldiers—the lone female in the group—looked beyond the wreckage and saw a trail of Hannah's dust.

She turned back to her teammates. "It's a fast one! We got a sw—"

Hannah lunged from the shadows and struck her legs with her billy club. The armor was nothing but fiberweave in the back of the knees, blade-resistant but vulnerable to blunt force. At the right speed and angle, a swifter could break a kneecap from the other side.

The woman had only just begun to fall when Hannah looped around and clubbed another soldier on the back of the hand. While the tempis kept his bones from breaking, the shock of impact was enough to get him to drop his weapon. Hannah caught it and chucked it before her six remaining enemies could turn their rifles on her. Even at 20x, they moved like drowsy old men in her perceptions.

Keep going, Hannah urged herself. Maintaining this speed hurt like hell, but it was her only advantage. She couldn't let up for a second.

She pivoted around the nearest soldier and yanked a pair of rubber cables from his shifter. His smoky aura dissipated. He froze like a statue in Hannah's vision. One more down. Five to go.

You can't keep this up, her higher functions warned her. *These are trained killers. You're just a washed-up actress.*

Shut up.

Hannah doubled back and disabled another shifter. A frustrated soldier swung his fist at her head. She dodged it by inches and slammed her club against his helmet. He stumbled backward, a thick web of cracks on his visor.

Three left. A trickle of blood ran down Hannah's nose, and she came dangerously close to smiling.

Washed-up actress, she scoffed. *I'm the wind behind these people's backs. I'm the whistling in their ears. I am a blade of steel and fire, and I will not be—*

A piercing agony suddenly struck her in the frontal lobe, a pain like none she'd ever felt before. The wound had been inflicted twenty-six days earlier, on the night that Theo got dropped through the clock tower. Hannah had pushed her powers beyond their natural limits to save him.

Now, at last, her powers were pushing back.

Hannah stumbled as she struggled to collect herself. She felt a shifted presence in the back of her thoughts. One of her enemies was rushing her from behind.

She jumped to the left, but not quickly enough. The soldier's nightstick slammed into her shoulder, the same one she'd dislocated on her very first day on this world. As the bone once again popped out of its socket, Hannah crashed to the ground and fell out of blueshift. She looked up at her assailants through a pained and teary wince. She'd been doing so well against them. Now it was all over.

"Fuck you," she hissed. "You can all go f—"

The soldiers dropped their guns in unison, then raised their arms in a perfect V. Hannah scuttled away from them, mystified.

"What?"

She turned her head and saw her sister in the near distance, her skin covered in a rocky sheath of tempis. The crags on her brow were so pro-nounced that Hannah could only see shadows where her eyes should have been.

"Amanda?"

The soldiers arched their heads back, yelping.

"Amanda, wait—"

A loud *crack* reverberated through the basement, followed by a soldier's scream. Hannah had no idea what her sister had done until it happened again: a violent twist of an enemy's hand, a splintering of bone.

Holy shit, Hannah thought. *She's breaking their arms.*

Amanda dropped the soldier to the floor, then snapped the wrists of the next one, and the next one, and the one after that. By the time she got to the eighth and last soldier, Hannah was sure she knew what Hell sounded like. The victims writhed atop each other, cursing and howling and swearing revenge.

"Shut up," Amanda said. "Just shut up."

She kneeled at Hannah's side and examined her shoulder. Even her gen-tlest touch made her sister flinch in pain.

"It's out of joint," she told Hannah. "I'll have to pop it back in."

"Not here." Hannah raised her good arm and ran her fingers down her sister's face. "Take this off."

Amanda dissolved the tempis and looked away. Hannah could see every bit of pain on her face, the thick streams of tears that rolled down her cheeks. She'd been crying nonstop since she'd crushed the two men, and Hannah didn't have the heart to tell her the awful truth: that it got easier. The grief, the guilt, it all went away. She barely even remembered what Naomi Byers looked like.

She pressed her forehead to Amanda's, while the soldiers behind them continued to writhe.

"It's all right," she said. "We're all right."

Melissa stood against the dirt wall, her hands raised, her sciatic nerve throb-bing. Falling twelve feet in metal armor wasn't especially good for her back, or the armor. But these were ancillary concerns, as there were currently six technicians holding her hostage. Three of them looked jittery enough to shoot at shadows. Two of them weren't even holding their guns properly.

"Look at me," said the oldest man in the group, a weak-chinned analyst with the beadiest eyes Melissa had ever seen. He reminded her of the old British caricatures of King George VII, with the two black dots in the middle of his face. Appropriate really, as this fellow seemed determined to play King of the Pit.

"I said *look at me*."

Melissa wearily made eye contact. "What's your name?"

"Shut up. I'm the one asking questions."

A soldier wailed from the upper reaches of the cellar. King George flinched at the man's agonized cry.

"What's happening up there?" he asked Melissa. "What are they doing?"

"They're breaking wrists, just as I advised them to do."

"How the hell do you live with yourself?"

"I could ask you the same question," Melissa said. "You're waging war on American soil, imprisoning people who've never once broken the law."

"You know damn well why we're doing this!"

"Yes." Melissa glared at him reproachfully. "Because you're frightened little men, afraid of change. Afraid of anything that threatens your delicate dominance."

King George stepped forward and pressed his gun to Melissa's temple. She could tell from his body language that he wasn't blustering. He was looking for an excuse to kill her.

"You think I'll stand here and get lectured by you? You're a goddamn traitor. If I plugged you right now, I bet—"

An electric substation disappeared into the dirt, tearing dozens of cables. Only Melissa and a technician saw it happen. The rest merely blinked at the glaring new gap in the console deck.

"What the hell—"

A computer fell next, then another one, then a cooling tower. The devices weren't sinking into the ground. They were plummeting through it, like ghosts.

"That's enough," Jonathan yelled from above. "Drop the guns or I drop you."

Melissa's heart skipped a beat. She didn't know Jonathan well enough to tell if he was bluffing. The man could obviously kill with a thought. But *would* he?

As another substation dropped through the earth, five of the technicians surrendered their sidearms. King George kept his gun against Melissa's head.

"One more and I shoot your friend!"

"Friend?" Jonathan chuckled. "Buddy, I barely know her."

"You're lying."

"I'm not."

"He's not," Melissa confirmed. "We've only met once before."

"But I like her well enough," Jonathan said. "And you're clearly a prick. So I'm giving you three seconds to throw down your gun before I make your arms fall off."

The others took a step back as, one by one, their surrendered weapons vanished into the earth.

King George stood his shaky ground. "You're lying."

Jonathan sighed. "One . . ."

"I'll shoot her! I mean it!"

"Two . . ."

Melissa grabbed George by the wrist and flipped him over her shoulder. He didn't have a chance to catch his breath before her hard metal boot pressed down on his chest.

"Forgive me," she said, "but I wasn't sure if he'd really maim you, and I didn't feel like finding out."

"Go on," George wheezed. "Kill me. That's the only way you'll—"

"Oh shut up." Melissa released her foot, then shot him in the neck with her stun chaser. "Prat."

She ordered the other techies against the wall, then bound their wrists with the bresin ties from her shoulder pack.

By the time she finished, Jonathan had reunited with the sisters. They made their way down the scaffold ramp. Melissa saw Hannah's arm wrapped in Amanda's jacket, an ad hoc sling.

"Is it broken?"

Hannah shook her head. "I'm fine."

Melissa studied Amanda's face. Clearly the older Given wasn't fine, and it was easy to guess why. "How many?"

Amanda lowered her head. Hannah stood in front of her defensively. "It doesn't matter."

"It'll matter very much to the agency. I assure you of that."

"Let's just find the generator," Jonathan said. "Before they send backup."

Melissa led the group to the far end of the pit, down a sloping tunnel of cables and lanterns that ended in a large chamber. A humming machine filled the majority of the space, a five-ton orb with gauges on one side and dozens of plugged cables on the other. Though the generator vibrated heavily enough to shake dirt from the walls, it didn't sound much louder than the average table fan.

Jonathan walked around the metal sphere, his finger brushing against the surface. "So this is it, huh? I would have expected—"

"Jonathan!" yelled Hannah.

He paused where he stood. He'd been so distracted, he nearly stepped into a pit at the base of the generator. It was four feet wide and unnaturally smooth, as if Integrity had drilled through the world with a laser. A cable as thick as a velvet rope extended from the generator and spilled deep into the abyss.

Jonathan stepped away from the edge. "Wow. Does that thing—"

"Yes," said Melissa. "All the way down to the solic disseminator."

"Can't I just drop the wire?"

She shook her head. "They could replace it in minutes. Best to be sure."

"Okay. Stand back."

Jonathan needed a full minute of concentration to turn the generator intangible. As the sphere fell through the earth, its severed wires flopped to the ground, hissing and crackling before going dormant. The disseminator cable retracted into the pit.

"Is that it?" Hannah asked Melissa. "Did we do it?"

"I'm not sure."

"What do you mean?"

Melissa pulled her transceiver out of her shoulder bag. "The generator was built by Dalton, a British manufacturer. They're for wartime use, which means they're loaded with contingencies. If the disseminator's also a Dalton, then it probably has a backup battery inside of it."

Hannah scowled at her. "So it's still pumping solis down there."

"If it has a battery, then yes. It would have enough power for at least forty more minutes of operation."

Jonathan smacked a wall. "Goddamn it!"

"That's too long," Amanda said. "We have to do something."

Melissa nodded. "I agree. But before we decide our next step, I need to know for sure."

She turned on her radio and raised it to her lips. "Theo, can you hear me?"

No response. She tested the device for damage before trying again. "Theo, are you there?"

The speaker came to life with a garbled hiss. "Who is this?"

The sisters and Jonathan looked at each other, baffled. The man on the line was most definitely not Theo, though his low, raspy voice was easy enough to recognize. They all had a long and tortured history with him.

Amanda plucked the radio out of Melissa's hand. "Rebel?"

"Oh, hey, Given. We were just talking about you."

"What are you doing? Where's Theo?"

Rebel puttered about the warrens, in a wide tunnel junction just fifteen feet below Freak Street. He cradled Theo's radio on his shoulder while placing a half pound of putty explosive in an air vent.

"He's fine," he assured Amanda. "We got him to the shelter."

"What about the others?"

Rebel looked over his shoulder. Zack sat against the wall, awake but only marginally lucid. Mercy grabbed a painkiller patch from her medkit and pressed it to his neck.

"Trillinger's in good hands," Rebel said. "Heath ran off. Haven't seen any of the others."

Jonathan snatched the radio from Amanda. "What do you mean, he ran off?"

"Is that Christie?"

"What'd you do to him?"

"Saved his ass is what I did. Kid wasn't grateful."

"I swear to God, if you hurt him—"

"It's not me you need to worry about, brother. You got bigger problems."

Melissa took her radio back. They didn't have time to trade banter with this fool.

"Rebel, listen to me. We just deactivated the power supply for the solic disseminator. Do you feel any change down there?"

Rebel looked to Mercy, the clan's foremost expert in solis. She grimly shook her head.

"Nope. Still swimming in it."

Melissa rubbed her brow. "Damn it."

Hannah leaned in to the radio. "Rebel, what were you talking about? Why does Jonathan have bigger problems?"

Rebel stuck a detonator onto the explosive charge. "I've seen the future, Given. These soldiers are just a temporary problem. When the Pelletiers get here, and you can bet your ass they will, the real pain begins. They're coming to clean house. All the folks who've wrenched up their plans, all the obstacles in their path. I'm on that list, and so's your boyfriend. Guess they really don't like the two of you together."

Hannah's face went pale. "You're lying."

"Believe what you want, but it's happening. If you see Azral coming, Christie, I only got one piece of advice."

Rebel lifted the air vent cover and secured it with a *click*. "Run."

Jonathan closed his eyes, cursing. "What about Zack?" Amanda asked Rebel.

A brief silence passed. Amanda raised the handset. "Rebel, *what about Zack?*"

Rebel took a long sip from a water bottle before answering. "Esis is coming for him."

"No!"

"It's all right," Rebel assured her. "We'll be ready for her."

"Wait. What are you talking about?"

"Gotta go."

"*Rebel!*"

Amanda dropped the radio and looked down at her hands. They were trembling and spotted with tempis.

"I have to get down there."

"Amanda . . ."

"I have to stop her."

Melissa held her by the shoulders. "Amanda, listen to me. Our work here isn't done. If we want to save those people down below, we have to finish what we started. I can't do it without you."

Hannah gestured at Jonathan. "What about us. What do we do?"

Melissa rummaged through her shoulder pack and pulled out three more items: a keycard, a scrap of paper, and a handheld computer. She loaded a map of Quarter Hill on the screen and marked a digital waypoint.

"You two need to leave as fast as you can. Follow this map to Irwin Sunder's house. You'll find a false thermostat in his wine cellar. The keycard and access code will get you back to the underland."

"Not if the power's still out," Jonathan said.

"We'll get it back," Melissa assured him. "Just be careful. There are soldiers all over town."

"What about you and Amanda?" Hannah asked.

Melissa jerked her head at the yawning pit. "That's our way back."

Jonathan stared down the hole, horrified. "Are you kidding me?"

"Someone has to destroy the disseminator. It's our only hope."

Hannah shook her head. "Uh-uh. You're not dragging my sister down that—"

"Hannah." Amanda squeezed her good arm. "She's right. We can't wait for the battery to die."

"What if your tempis craps out halfway? What if they drop a bomb?"

"We'll be all right," Amanda insisted. "Just go."

While Melissa shed her broken armor, Hannah steeled herself for another temporal shift. Her head and shoulder still ached like crazy, and she couldn't get Azral out of her mind. Still, the road ahead felt easy compared to Amanda's. The woman had already been through hell today, and now she had to go deeper.

She wrapped her sister in a one-armed hug. "Be careful. Please."

"I will," Amanda said. "Stay safe, both of you."

Hannah climbed onto Jonathan's back and launched them both into blueshift. Loose cables fluttered as they made a quick escape.

Amanda looked to Melissa. "How exactly are we going to destroy the disseminator? If we get too close—"

"We won't. We just have to get within dropping distance."

Melissa stripped down to her tights and shock padding. Amanda watched her closely as she grabbed her grenade belt.

"You can't be serious."

"You wanted to save everyone," Melissa said. "This is how we do it."

Amanda peered down the well with heavy eyes. She'd never made a tempic rappel before, much less an eight-hundred-foot one. If she lost her concentration, even for a moment . . .

"Two," she mumbled.

"What?"

"You asked me how many soldiers I killed back there. The answer is two."

Melissa clasped the grenade belt around her waist, expressionless. "I've killed four people in the line of duty."

"Criminals," Amanda guessed. "Not federal agents."

"These agents *are* criminals. Don't ever forget that."

Amanda nodded absently. "I'm just thinking about my people. Zack . . ."

"We'll help them," Melissa said. "Just get us down there."

Amanda grew a willowy white tendril from her palm, then pulled Melissa into an embrace. The tempis snaked around their bodies, binding them together.

"You believe in God?" Amanda asked.

Melissa thought about it a moment before answering. "Can't say I do. But then I didn't believe in chronokinesis either, so what do I know?"

Amanda formed a strong tempic clamp around the mouth of the well, then sighed over Melissa's shoulder.

"You're a good woman."

"So are you," Melissa said. "If the afterlife works like the Christians believe, then I have no doubt you're going where the good people go."

Amanda wasn't as sure about that. Her faith in God had become shakier than ever. She feared that one more trauma would send her into a dark place, where people like her became monsters like Esis.

Melissa tightened her grip on Amanda. "Okay. Let's do this before we lose our nerve."

She and Amanda drew a simultaneous breath before plunging into the pit. They disappeared into the murky depths, then began their long trip back to the underland.

FORTY-SIX

Theo had no idea where his mind had taken him this time. He staggered down the street of a vast and empty city, one that had been utterly ransacked. Cars lined the streets at haphazard angles. Half the store windows were broken. Stray cats prowled the wreckage of a pizzeria, jumping from table to table in search of scraps. Theo couldn't tell if he was having a dream or a premonition. If this was the future, then where was he? *When* was he?

He stopped in an intersection and looked up at the sky. The sun was bright enough to burn spots in his vision but the temperature was erratic—a warm breeze one moment, a cool one the next. Something very unnatural had happened here. Theo couldn't shake the fear that all of this was just prelude to something worse. A storm. A war.

An ending.

"I know this place," he muttered. "I've seen it in dreams but—"

"—always from a distance," said a familiar voice behind him.

Ioni sat on the hood of a taxi. Her blond hair was wet. Her body was wrapped in a thick white bath towel.

Theo turned around and shot her a black look. "You."

"Yup. There's that Maranan charm again."

"What is this? Why did you bring me here?"

"It's your brain, buddy. You brought me."

"From the shower?"

"What?" Ioni glanced down at her towel. "Oh. That's new."

"Why are you wearing that?"

"I don't know. You're the one in the driver's seat. Maybe it turns you on a little. Maybe I stank the last time we met."

Theo struggled to remember his last waking moments. There had been darkness and violence in the underland, dangerous men moving around in the shadows. Someone got hurt. Was it Zack?

"My power's gone," he remembered. "This can't be a vision."

Ioni shrugged. "The typical augur has a hundred premonitions in his sleep every night. They're all still there in your deepest layers of memory. Your subconscious is probably playing a golden oldie."

"A memory of a future."

"Something like that." Ioni studied her towel again. "Oh, I get it now. Wow. You're good."

"What are you talking about?"

She shook her head disconcertedly. "You'll find out next year."

A soiled scrap of newspaper blew past Theo's feet. He debated catching it and checking the date.

"Fourteen months," Ioni informed him. "Give or take."

"What?"

"You want to know where we are on the timeline. I'm telling you."

"We're fourteen months in the future."

"Give or take."

Theo examined a minivan parked halfway across the sidewalk, a five-door Bandolier. The license plate read "North California—The Gold Rush State." Most of the other vehicles were similarly tagged.

"What the hell happened here?" he asked Ioni. "Looks like war."

"And yet . . ."

Theo got her gist immediately. There were no bodies, no bloodstains or bullet holes. No signs of anything other than opportunistic looting.

"Evacuated," Theo guessed. "The whole city's been cleared out."

Ioni smiled proudly. "And then some."

"You did this."

"Not me. That would be our good friend Merlin McGee."

"That's why you made him famous? To scare everyone out of a city?"

"And save four million lives," Ioni said. "This isn't a prank, Theo. We have a damn good reason to get them out of here."

"Why? What's going to happen?"

Ioni stroked the bands of her watches, her fingers moving absently between the digital and the analog.

"This city will fall," she said. "Some good people will fall with it."

Theo nodded bleakly. "I'm pretty sure I'm one of them."

"Don't talk like that."

"Am I wrong?"

Ioni looked away. "It's not a given."

Theo turned his head and saw an abandoned police van down the street, with big silver letters on the side: SFPD.

"San Francisco," Theo said. "This is San Francisco."

Ioni swung her legs and dangled them off the side of the cab. "You're dwelling on a future far ahead of you—"

"Fourteen months isn't far!"

"—when you've got a whole mess of problems in the present."

Harsh memories came flooding back to him. The snipers had hit Zack with a stun dart. Theo foolishly went reaching for it. A painful shock. A stab in his leg.

They got me, he realized. *They shot me too.*

He raged at Ioni. "You knew this was coming and you didn't tell me."

"Theo—"

"You knew about *David* and you didn't tell me!"

She stared glumly down at her feet. "The knowledge would have killed you."

"I'm dying right now!"

"No, you're not. You've been moved to a safe place. You need to stay there."

"What about my friends?"

"They can take care of themselves."

"Goddamn it . . ."

"You have to *survive*, Theo. I'll need you here in fourteen months."

"Fuck you."

"Theo . . ."

A crackling hiss filled his ears. The air around him rippled. Theo couldn't tell if the world was ending or if he was simply waking up.

Ioni appeared right in front of him and grabbed him by the shoulders. Her expression was so urgent that he barely even noticed that her towel was gone. Her skin was nothing but white light.

"Look, tell Mia I'm sorry," Ioni said. "It's nothing personal. I like her."

"What?"

"It's just the way it has to be."

"What are you tal—"

A hot wind overtook him. Theo fumbled in blindness until his body stopped burning and he could finally breathe again. He opened one eye and saw a dim, naked lightbulb hanging six feet above him.

Theo sat up and took a groggy scan of his surroundings. He was lying on a cot in a large metal vault, one filled to the ceiling with supply tubs and emergency rations. He could only assume he'd reached the Gothams' bomb shelter, but where were—

A wrinkled hand gripped his arm from behind. "Careful. You're still weak."

Flinching, Theo turned to look at his new acquaintance: a middle-age man of Asian descent. His face was lined with premature wrinkles. His hair stuck out in messy cowlicks.

Theo struggled to focus his blurry vision. "Wait. I know you."

"Yes."

"I had dinner at your house. You're, uh . . ."

"Jun," the man genially replied. "Jun Lee."

Theo blinked at him, confounded. The man was usually doped to the gills, a doddering bobblehead. Now he seemed shockingly lucid.

It's the solis, Theo guessed. *He can only function when he can't see the apocalypse.*

"What are you doing here?" Theo asked. "Where are the others?"

Jun hobbled his way to a nearby table and poured steaming hot tea into a mug. "My wife's in the square with the rest of the clan. My daughter is . . . elsewhere."

"I meant *my* people. Where are Zack and Heath?"

"Zack was here just minutes ago. He left on important business."

"What business? What are you talking about?"

Jun's expression turned awkward. "It is . . . not your concern."

"He's my *friend*. If he's in trouble—"

"The best way you can help him is by staying alive." Jun held out the mug to Theo. "Here."

Theo knocked it to the floor. Everyone was so determined to treat him like a glass figurine, to pack him tight in bubble wrap while the people he loved kept risking their lives.

"What about Heath?"

Jun slowly shook his head. "We don't know where he is."

"You mean he's still out there? Alone?"

Theo jumped to his feet, teetering on wobbly knees. He looked down and noticed a strip of white gauze around the thickest part of his right thigh. Integrity got him good with their stun bolt. His bones ached with every step. The muscles in his leg felt like jelly.

He saw Peter's .32 pistol on the tea table and limped as quickly as he could toward it.

"Please," Jun begged. "If you leave this place, you won't be safe."

"If I let my friends die, I don't deserve to be safe."

"You have a crucial role to play. You know this."

"Oh, shut the hell up. You know goddamn well I'm not the savior."

"Even a false messiah has power."

"Right."

Theo moved to the vault door and studied the latches. He supposed getting out was just a matter of reversing the current settings.

Jun sighed disapprovingly. "You don't have much foresight for an augur."

"And you don't have much courage for a husband and father."

"I have faith in my family. Where's your faith in yours?"

Theo rushed to undo the latches. They slid to the right with hollow clicks. "Heath's saved my life three times now. Lack of faith isn't the issue."

"Please. Think about the future!"

The metal door swung open with a rumble. Theo shot a last dirty look at Jun. "Fuck the future."

He squeezed through the opening, into the dim and winding tunnels. His head pounded, his leg dragged, and his power remained locked behind a thick wall of solis. Worse, his friends had been scattered to the winds, each one lost in their own dire crisis. Theo couldn't help them all. He wasn't even sure he was doing the right thing by helping Heath first.

Tell Mia I'm sorry, Ioni had told him. *It's nothing personal. I like her.*

Furious, Theo closed the door behind him and shambled through the warrens. *Goddamn it*, he thought. *Goddamn it all.*

She sat perfectly still on a hard metal folding chair, her right hand chained to a table. The cuff was so tight, she could barely feel her fingers. The seat pressed like knuckles against her buttocks. A small electric Thermodell, the nation's number-one brand for space heaters and hellfans, blew stifling hot air into her face, making every breath a chore.

But all these problems were dwarfed by the glass-eyed bastard in front of her. Mia was trapped in this tent with the leader of the invasion, the eeriest man she'd encountered since Azral. Just looking into his black lenses—never once blinking or turning away—made her envy her past self. She wanted to go crawling back through time and space until she was safe at home in her daddy's arms.

Still, Mia would be damned if she let Gingold see her fear. She stashed all her discomfort behind a mask of stone—no cowering, no fidgeting, no flinching at noises. She could hear the sounds of violence through the walls of her enclosure, some poor man being brutalized in another tent. If those were Peter's cries, Mia didn't want to know. She'd do him no good by cracking.

Gingold watched from the other side of the table, his chair tilted back at an angle. In their six and a half minutes together, he'd barely said a word. He let the seven photographs on the table do the talking. They'd been taken from the wall of Mia's Brooklyn bedroom, snapshots of Amanda and Hannah, Theo and Zack, Jonathan and Heath. There was even a picture of David in the mix, a small form of torture in itself.

Fuck you, she thought but didn't dare say. *I'll never tell you where they are.*

Something tickled her skin with tiny legs. Mia looked down and gasped as a reddish brown spider skittered across her toes. She shook her leg frantically until both the spider and her sandal went flying off her foot.

Embarrassed, she searched Gingold's expression. If he took pleasure in the death of her bravada, he didn't show it. Mia supposed that entitled him to something.

She reached out with her free hand and brushed David's photo off the table. "He's dead, all right? There you go. That's one."

Gingold stared at her, expressionless. "You're lying."

"I'm telling you—"

"He's not dead. Just gone. He left after you and Trillinger exposed him as a Pelletier."

Try as she might, Mia couldn't hide her surprise. A hint of a smile lit Gingold's face. "We've had ears on your village for twenty-six hours. His name's come up quite a bit."

The spider climbed the leg of the table. Mia watched it bumble heedlessly onto the surface.

"You need to work on your guile," Gingold said. "You had four tells just now: two in your face, one in your voice, and one in your body language. I didn't need my intel to know you were rubbing me."

The spider skittered its way toward Gingold. Mia couldn't look away. Was the hot air messing with its senses? Was it tired of life? Why else would it throw itself into the path of a predator?

Why would you? asked a harsh voice in her psyche. *You volunteered to get captured, remember? You walked right into this.*

"I have all the time in the world for your horseshit," Gingold attested. "I have infinite patience."

Mia blinked at him distractedly. "What?"

"See, those were lies. I said them with confidence and with full control of my semblance."

He brought his armored glove down on the spider. Mia jumped in her seat.

"Look at me, Farisi."

Mia looked up and saw herself in his lenses. Her last shreds of courage were utterly gone. She was just a small, helpless thing, mottled in sweat.

"Playtime's over," said Gingold. "Now you're going to tell me—"

"Sir."

His second-in-command barged into the tent, the same operative who'd handcuffed Mia to the table. Tomlinson was easy for her to remember, as he was one of the few soldiers here who'd removed his face mask.

Tomlinson tossed her a brief, dismissive look before turning to his commander. "We have an issue on the surface. The Dalton—"

Gingold shushed him, then escorted him out of the tent.

Alone at last, she wiped the sweat from her brow and fluffed the collar of her shirt. Her gaze drifted over to the poor little spider at the edge of the table, still writhing in agony after being half crushed. If Mia had been just a few inches taller, or if her handcuff chain had another few links to it, she could have reached across the table and put it out of its misery.

Instead she counted its final seconds and wondered how long they felt in spider time. A week? A month? A *year*? Maybe the creature had suffered so long that it couldn't remember its life before Gingold. Maybe dying was all it knew.

After a long, quiet minute, the spider finally stopped kicking its legs. Gingold stormed through the tent flap and paced behind his chair. He seemed restless now. Edgy.

"Bring him over."

Mia tilted her head. "What?"

"Yes, *now*."

It took her a moment to realize that he was talking into his headset. He switched off the radio, cast an impenetrable look at Mia, then swept three more photos to the ground. Amanda, Hannah, and Jonathan were now officially off the table.

Mia's heart pounded. *Oh no* . . .

Gingold gripped the back of his chair, his lenses once again locked on her. "Sometime today, Melissa Masaad came back into your life. She had full awareness of our operation here, thanks to a high-ranking traitor in the agency, and she came up with a plan to stop us. Part of it involved sneaking to the surface with three of your friends and disabling our Dalton."

He didn't have to tell Mia that he was talking about the solic disseminator. Her stress burned like lava in the pit of her stomach. *Don't. Don't you dare tell me they're dead.*

Gingold opened the tent flap, giving Mia a peek at the village square. The Gothams remained penned behind a buzzrope—still helpless, still scared.

"All your friends did was switch us to battery power." Gingold closed the flap and resumed his fitful pacing. "We have enough spares and backups to run the Dalton for days."

He turned and shook a finger at her. "But you had hope, which is why you and Pendergen surrendered. You wanted to get caught so you could prep these people for a full-scale counterattack."

Gingold moved behind Mia and pressed his hands against the table. The weight of his chest forced her forward. She couldn't see anything now but the photos of Zack, Theo, and Heath.

"It all fits together," Gingold said. "Except for these three. What's their mission? Where are they going? How's the boy still able to make his tempis?"

He leaned in close enough for Mia to smell his breath, a noxious blend of coffee and menthol. "I don't have time to mutt around with you, Farisi. I want answers now."

Mia kept her eyes on the photos. Her voice creaked out in a tremulous whisper. "So do it already."

"Do what?"

"Hit me, cut me, whatever it is you do."

Gingold followed her gaze to the dead brown spider. "You think I like hurting small things."

"I know you do."

"You don't know shit." He retreated to the other side of the table. "I dealt with child soldiers in Palestine. Baby terrorists and insurrectionists. You'd think they'd be easier to crack, but no. Their minds work on a much purer level. They believe their own lies."

Mia heard the sounds of struggle outside the tent. A curse. A thump. A low grunt of pain.

"In my experience," said Gingold, "there's only one good way to get the truth out of kids."

Mia's face went white as Tomlinson and another soldier dragged Peter inside. His mouth dripped blood. His left eye was swollen shut. Both his hands had been cuffed behind his back. None of that stopped him from struggling as his captors tried to force him to his knees.

Tomlinson clubbed the backs of Peter's thighs. "Get down!"

Mia jumped to her feet, struggling against her chain. "Stop it! Stop!"

Gingold eyed her smugly. "I don't hurt children. I don't have to."

He pulled his sidearm from its holster and pressed the muzzle against Peter's temple.

"No!" Mia cried. "Please!"

Gingold jerked his head at the photos. "What's their mission? Where are they going? How's the boy still able to make his tempis?"

Peter fixed his good eye on Mia. "Not a word, hon."

Tomlinson struck him again. "Shut up."

"You know the stakes," Peter told her. "He has to live."

"I said *shut up.*"

Gingold caught Tomlinson's arm. "Let him talk. It doesn't matter."

"But sir—"

"Let him talk." He scanned his watch, then turned back to Mia. "In sixty seconds, you'll see something that'll haunt you for the rest of your life. Whenever you close your eyes, whenever you let your guard down, whenever your mind feels like torturing you, you'll see it. But you have the power to stop it from happening. It doesn't have to go this way."

"He's lying," Peter insisted. "He'll kill me either way."

Gingold shook his head. "He's trying to take the burden off you. It won't work. You know his fate's in your hands. You know exactly how to save him." He checked the time again. "You now have forty seconds."

Mia locked her teary eyes on Peter's. He gave her a weak smile. "You're gonna survive this, darlin'. You'll get out of this place and help finish the work we started. That's all that matters."

Gingold pursed his lips, as if Peter was merely singing her a lullaby. "Thirty seconds."

"Take care of Liam," Peter told her. "Don't let him die here. Keep honing your talents. And no matter what happens, sweetheart, no matter *what*—"

"Twenty seconds."

"—don't ever give up on the string."

Mia covered her mouth, weeping. She could barely hear a thing over the rushing blood in her head. "Peter!"

"Daughter of my heart. That's what you are to me."

"Twelve seconds," Gingold said. "He'll die for sure. Your friends might not. Your best bet is to talk to me. What's their mission? Where are they going? How's the boy still able to make his tempis?"

"Fuck you!"

Peter smiled proudly. "That's my girl."

Gingold scowled at Mia. "Five . . ."

She forced her words through choking sobs. "I swear to God, Gingold—"

"Four . . ."

"—if you kill Peter—"

"Three . . ."

"—I'll kill you myself."

"Two . . ."

"I'll make it my life's mission!"

"One . . ."

"It's the wristwatch! The wristwatch!"

Gingold stopped, puzzled. Mia fought to catch her breath. "If Heath's making tempis, it has to be the watch. It used to be Semerjean's. It has special powers."

Tomlinson swapped a dubious look with the other soldier. Mia kept her eyes on Gingold. "I'm not lying. Look at me. Do you see any tells? Do you see any—"

The sound of a gunshot made Mia scream. She opened one eye, expecting to find Peter dead on the floor. But he was very much alive and just as confused as she was. Gingold hadn't fired his weapon at all.

Before anyone could speak, another shot rang out. Then a third, then a fourth, and then a salvo of gunfire.

Gingold stormed out of the tent and looked around the square. The clamor was coming from the east.

He switched on his headset. "What the hell's happening? Hastings, report!"

His earpiece crackled with pops and hisses. Gingold could barely hear his sniper over the popcorn sounds of gunfire.

"They're attacking from all sides, sir! They're everywhere!"

"What's everywhere?"

"Animals!" yelled Hastings.

Gingold lowered his head and cursed. Every great warrior had a nemesis. He never expected his to be a scrawny black kid with mental problems. This was getting ridiculous. It was time to finish Heath once and for all.

He pushed through the soldiers at the edge of the square. Half of them had joined the snipers in frantic gunfire. The others merely stared in bewilderment.

Gingold shoved a dawdling soldier. "What are you doing? I *told* you those things aren't lethal! Just find the boy who . . ."

He turned his head and finally saw what everyone was gawking at. Hundreds of animals came rushing down Center Street, but they weren't wolves at all. They weren't even tempic. These were beasts of an entirely different color.

"You've got to be kidding me . . ."

Gingold and his men jumped out of the way as the stampede reached the square. They spilled in like water: fluorescent blue tigers, each of them graced with saber teeth and glowing yellow eyes.

The Gothams in the pen were equally baffled. There wasn't a soul in the clan who hadn't been startled, stunned, or stymied by the presence of Bo the Tiger. Now here he was in multitudes, throwing an entire army into disarray.

Elder Rubinek turned her wide eyes to the east, toward the source of the disruption. "Harold?"

A hundred yards away, on the concrete roof of the lumics' guild building, Harold Herrick watched the chaos through his coke-bottle glasses and laughed.

To call the boy a misfit would be an understatement. He was the black sheep of the Herricks, the embarrassment of the lumics, and a criminal of the clan. Under the misguided leadership of Gemma Sunder, he'd participated in a violent attack against the breachers that had backfired horribly, killing all of his teammates and forcing him to face the clan's judgment alone.

Harold thought he'd rot in his solic prison cell, until he was freed by an unlikely ally. Heath took Harold to the roof of the guildhall, gave him an antique silver wristwatch, and then told him to raise hell.

This just might have been the best day of Harold's life.

While the tigers continued to wreak havoc, Heath crouched down next to Harold and eyed the snipers on the distant rooftops.

"Take them out," he said.

"Who?"

While most of Gingold's marksmen kept their rifles on the tigers, a few were beginning to look beyond the square. One of them turned his sights to the southeast, toward Heath and Harold.

Heath pointed at the sniper. "The gunmen! The gunmen!"

"Oh."

Harold flicked his hand. The nearest sniper shrieked as his helmet lit up on the inside. Every crack, pore, and opening flared white needles of light. His visor cast a spotlight beam at the ceiling.

The sniper had barely fallen to his knees when Harold moved on to the next victim . . . and the next one, and the next. Wave by wave, their helmets lit up like jack-o'-lanterns. They stumbled around their perches, screaming and blind. One of them tripped over the edge of the building and fell three stories onto a rose garden.

"Good job," said the tiger at Harold's side.

"I missed you, Bo."

"Yeah, yeah. Don't get sappy."

The Gothams watched with wide-eyed marvel as the invaders continued to scramble. A soldier shot at a tiger and hit his partner in the knee joint. Another one shattered a lightpost, sending white-hot sparks onto the roof of an interrogation tent. While agents hurried to extinguish the fire, a second marksman stumbled off the roof and crashed into a portable generator. The machine imploded with a sizzling hiss, a momentary hiccup that caused the buzzrope to flicker.

Victoria Chisholm watched from a distance as an operative took out his hand console and wirelessly restored power to the rope.

"That's him," she whispered. "That's the one who controls the fence."

With Mother Olga's help, Liam had quietly approached a number of clan leaders and brought them to a distant corner of the pen. They convened in the shadow of the guild directory: four elders, three primarchs, two house lords, and a house lady. None of them were optimistic about Melissa Masaad's plan. The tigers were giving Victoria a bold idea of her own.

"Just wait until our powers come back," Mother Olga urged her. "It's our only chance."

"You put too much faith in this rogue agent."

"And the breachers," Irwin Sunder added.

Elder Kohl stroked her arm nervously. "Olga's right. If we attack now, it'll be suicide."

"What choice do we have?" Sunder asked. "How long are we supposed to wait for a miracle that's not coming?"

"It's coming," Liam insisted.

"They've already taken a hundred of us, boy. If we wait too long, we'll all be gone."

Victoria kept a watchful eye on the fence technician. "Debate all you want, but Harold Herrick just gave us an opportunity. It won't last forever."

She wasn't wrong. Gingold was already beginning to suspect the true nature of the tigers. For all their roars and threatening gestures, they had yet to maul a single soldier. And there was something about the way they moved . . .

He climbed atop a generator and studied the creatures through his bionic cameras. They didn't register at all in thermal scans, yet they glowed like fire in infrared. A still-frame analysis revealed that their paws were barely connecting with the grass beneath their feet. One of them had brushed seamlessly through a park bench, as if it was nothing but—

"—lumis."

Grumbling, Gingold switched his headset to the operation's all-channel.

"It's a ghost show, people. Hold your fire. Hold your fire."

His soldiers could barely hear him over the gunshots and shouting. Gingold raised his mic volume, then raised his hands high.

"Goddamn it, everyone, I said—"

His left lens shattered. The back of his head opened in a spray of blood. Tomlinson had just enough time to register the gaping hole in Gingold's skull before his body fell to the grass.

"Sir?"

Tomlinson dropped to his knees and checked Gingold's vitals, as if he'd somehow misread the situation, as if his stoic commander had suffered anything but a bullet through the brain.

"He's dead," said Tomlinson. "He's dead. Somebody—"

A second bullet tore through the generator, cutting Tomlinson's face with shrapnel. Frantic, he dove behind a supply crate and peeked over the lid. This wasn't friendly fire. There was a brand-new shooter in the square.

Winnie Whitten was the first to spot him. She looked up at the second floor and saw his round frame in the window. "Daddy?"

Sunder followed her gaze upward, then covered his gaping mouth. "Oh no . . ."

Daniel Whitten was an iconic figure in the clan. As primarch of the lumics, house lord of the Whittens, and primary executive in charge of underland operations, he carried even more responsibility than the elders. He wore his authority with such folksy charm that everyone in the village had a genial nickname for him.

"Mayor!"

Sixty-five seconds earlier, as Harold's tigers invaded the square, the Mayor opened a hatch near the base of the family directory. Only the snipers could have stopped him from escaping down the ladder, but they were blind now. The Mayor took the tunnels to the municipal building, then climbed the stairs to his office. There on the western wall, in a locked glass cabinet, lay one of his most precious possessions: an 1874 Colt single-action army revolver. Like most of the Mayor's valued possessions, the gun was strictly for show. But he kept it in mint condition, and fully loaded.

He saw no reason not to use it now.

Prudent Lee gasped as the Mayor fired on another solider. It missed the man's head by inches, but easily got his attention.

"Daniel, *stop*!"

His fourth bullet hit a soldier in the chestplate and sent him toppling into the electric rope. Now the gunmen in the square began to ignore the tigers around them. Some of them looked up.

Mother Olga kept her frantic gaze on the Mayor. "For God's sake, run!"

The Mayor fired his second-to-last bullet, another freakishly lucky shot that struck an enemy through the eye. *How ironic*, he thought. He'd lived such a charmed and easy life that he could only assume that the fates had divinely blessed him. Even in these dire times, when the shadow of apocalypse loomed over everything, the Mayor had every faith that the universe would provide for him and his loved ones.

But then his sixteen-year-old daughter, the light of his life, had her heart and neck broken by demons. He barely had the chance to mourn her before gunmen came storming into the village—*his* village—and turned Yvonne's memorial service into a horror show.

No, this would not do. This would not do at all. All his confidence, all his serenity, all his faith in the goodness of creation, it was all just smoke and mirrors. He'd been living a life of cheap illusion and now, at long last, he could see how the world truly worked.

As fifteen soldiers aimed their rifles, and twenty Whittens screamed his name, the Mayor looked down at his kinsmen with teary eyes. He raised his pistol one last time.

Integrity tore him down before he could fire his last bullet. His body toppled over the window ledge and crashed into a shrub.

In that moment, the Rosens spun around on their captors and wrestled with their guns. They were the six sturdiest women of Rebel's family and they were about to be taken to Integrity's remote facility. But the Mayor's death had triggered something inside of them. Screaming, the Rosens thrashed and kicked at their captors until half of them were disarmed. A dozen sharpshooters arrived from the transport area and plowed them all with electric bolts. Only two of them survived.

The fence technician watched from a distance, his eyes wide behind his face mask. He opened a channel to Central Command in Bethesda.

"Uh, we have a situation here. Local command's not responding. Are there new orders? Should we, uh—"

Victoria swept his legs from behind, sending him flat onto his back. While five of her tempics pinned him to the grass, she stole his fence console, then studied the controls.

"Don't!" Liam yelled. "We're not ready!"

"Quiet, boy. It's now or never."

"You'll get us all killed!"

Twenty yards away, Andrew Tomlinson took a frantic look around. The whole operation was going to shit. Gingold was dead. The snipers were blind. The locals were getting more violent by the minute. And those tigers—those goddamn tigers—were still raising hell everywhere.

Five soldiers ran to Tomlinson, confused and alarmed. "You're the secondary, man! What do we do?"

Tomlinson thumped his headset, struggling to make sense of the chatter in his earpiece. Central Command had gone into a tizzy and none of the directors could agree on how to proceed.

"Pull out. Get your men out of there!"

"Do not abort, soldier. Maintain control."

"Just kill them already!"

"Do not—repeat: do not—kill the subjects."

At last, Victoria pressed the right button on the fence technician's console.

The buzzrope around the square stopped humming. Fleeta Byers tested the cord before jumping it. Dozens of others followed her lead. The Gothams dispersed up the streets and down the stairwells, through doorways and alleys and hatches to God-knows-where.

A soldier grabbed Tomlinson by the shoulders. "Goddamn it, man! We're losing them! What do we do?"

Heart pounding, Tomlinson shut off the link to Central Command and hailed every soldier on the all-channel.

"Shoot them," he ordered. "Shoot them all."

FORTY-SEVEN

Amanda looked up in a futile attempt to gauge her progress. There was eight hundred feet of bedrock between Quarter Hill and the underland, and she had no idea how far she'd traveled. The generator room was just a tiny bead of light above her. She saw nothing but blackness down below.

She tightened her tempic hold on Melissa. "How close are we?"

"I'd say we're friends at the very least."

"You're making jokes now?"

"Trying to."

Amanda couldn't blame her for being nervous. They were descending like spiders on a line of pure tempis, kept alive solely by the force of Amanda's will. One bad thought, one shudder of fatigue, and gravity would take them the rest of the way down.

Melissa shined her penlight at the curved stone wall. The moledrones that had drilled this shaft were kind enough to draw marker lines.

"We're at three hundred feet."

"That's it?"

"It's all right. We're making good progress."

"No we're not. Hang on."

"Wait . . ."

Their stomachs lurched as Amanda tripled their drop speed. At a hundred feet, her tempic rope had become her longest creation ever. At two hundred feet, she'd broken all Gotham records. Now at three hundred feet and counting, Amanda reeled at the magnitude of her power. She was starting to wonder if she could touch the moon itself.

Melissa raised her penlight and saw the next marker whiz past.

"Three-fifty," she said. "The next one's our stop."

"What?"

"*Stop.*"

Amanda brought them to a dangling halt, just a few feet shy of the halfway mark. Melissa wriggled awkwardly in their tempic harness.

"What are you doing?" Amanda asked.

"Preparing the grenades."

"We're still four hundred feet up."

"This is as far as we can safely go," Melissa said. "If you get too close to the solis—"

"I know. But what if the grenades blow up before they reach the disseminator?"

"They'll reach it."

"How do you know?"

Melissa fumbled with her belt. "As an object falls, its speed increases nine-point-eight meters per second, squared. These grenades have a five-second timer. If my calculations are right, they should be a hundred and twenty-two meters below us when they explode."

Amanda didn't have the mental energy to check her math. She barely had the strength to do a metric conversion. "So that's—"

"—four hundred feet."

"—four hundred feet."

"And that's only if I drop them," Melissa said. "I'll get at least another eighty if I throw."

For all her intellect, she was having the damnedest time unhooking her grenade belt. "Let me," Amanda said.

"Your hands are already—"

"I don't need hands."

A spindly arm extended from the harness and manually explored the belt loop. Melissa gasped at the cool fingers on her stomach.

"Goodness. I guess we really are friends now."

"Don't make this weird."

"It's well past weird." Melissa aimed her light at Amanda's fumbling appendage. "After all this time, I still can't—"

"Hold it."

Amanda looked up in sudden alarm. She could feel strong hands on the most distant part of her tempis. Someone in the generator room was messing with her grapple.

"Shit. We're in trouble."

"What do you mean?"

The harness rippled in distress. Melissa hooked her arm around Amanda. "What's happening? Are you all right?"

"They're hurting me . . ."

"What?"

"They're hurting the tempis!"

Melissa craned her neck, cursing. Reinforcements must have reached the generator room. She hoped that Hannah and Jonathan got out in time.

The temperature rose. A flickering glow filled the pit from above, a bright blue fireball at the top of the shaft.

Melissa recognized it immediately. "Magnite."

"What?"

"They're sending a heat drone after us."

Four minutes before his untimely death, Oren Gingold had instructed his men to drop a torcher down the well. The remote-controlled flyer was the size of a vacuum cleaner, and packed enough magnesium thermite to burn a four-story building to the ground. Melissa had seen the British Army clear an entire cave of insurgents with just one of those things. Their screams still haunted her at night.

"You need to make a shield," she urged Amanda. "At least six feet thick."

"I'm doing everything I can just to keep us up!"

"Amanda, if that thing reaches us, we'll know a whole new world of pain. There's more than one reason they call it a torcher."

"I'm trying! I . . ."

Amanda winced in agony. Her rope and harness began to lose their shape.

"Amanda!"

Her support line vanished, sending both women into free fall. Panicked, Amanda raised her arm and shot a geyser of tempis up the shaft. The pit became corked with nine and a half feet of solid white force. But the rock walls were smooth and the tempis was smoother. It slid seamlessly down the pit.

Melissa's arm bumped painfully against the bedrock. She lost hold of the grenade belt.

"No!"

Amanda caught Melissa with her other hand's tempis, just as Melissa caught the grenades with her foot. They continued to drop with the stopper in tow, all the way past the 450-foot marker.

"Friction!" Melissa yelled. "We need friction!"

Screaming, Amanda popped a dozen blades from the sides of the tempis. They scraped, then carved, then burrowed into the stone, until the whole mass came to a slow and grinding halt. Amanda and Melissa dangled on the underside, their bodies swinging on a thin tempic strand.

Melissa smacked against the stone and dropped her penlight in the process. She saw it tumble down the shaft before her vision went black.

"Damn it."

"You still have the grenades?"

"Almost." She struggled to lift the belt back into her hand. "Got them."

She gripped their new harness and felt a strange softness to it, like clay. They must have reached the edge of the solic field.

"We have to stop here," Melissa said. "We go any lower, we die."

"Just throw the damn bombs already!"

A faint blue light filtered in through the tempic barrier. Amanda screamed in pain. The torcher had reached them in the lower depths of the pit. They couldn't go up or down now, and Melissa feared it was just a matter of moments before Amanda lost her tempis.

She pulled a grenade out of its holster and balanced it in her hand. For half a moment, Melissa envied Amanda for having someone to pray to. All she could do was close her eyes, kiss her fist, and hope for the very best.

Melissa yanked the pin with her teeth, then hurled her first grenade at the disseminator.

The massacre began at 9:55, with only fourteen soldiers shooting at Gothams. They were the rasher minds of the National Integrity Commission: the nervous, the jaded, the vengeful, and the vicious. They were the ones who believed that orders were orders, and that any excuse to kill was a good one. The moment they heard Tomlinson say, "Shoot them all," they aimed their rifles at the scattering crowd and they fired.

The rest of the gunmen simply froze, half of them staring at the children in the square.

Tomlinson raged at them through their headsets. "Goddamn it. Gingold's dead, and these freaks have their own armory. This is an 'us or them' situation. So sack up and *help us!*"

Wave by wave, the soldiers joined the action. The underland became drowned in the *rat-a-tat* of gunfire, and nine hundred Gothams ran screaming for cover. They fled in every direction, tripping and trampling each other as they desperately held on to their loved ones.

Stan Bloom scooped his daughter into his arms and made a fevered dash for the municipal building. He thought he'd been smart by keeping Carrie in the center of the crowd—invisible, unreachable—but then the shooting started. Now his kinsmen on the fringes were escaping in droves while he was forced to run through fifty yards of battlefield.

Carrie watched over her father's shoulder as gunmen cut down people she'd known since birth. Ripper Ballad, the only swifter in the guild she could even remotely tolerate, fell flat on his face and stayed there. Keiko Tam, Carrie's ninth-grade nemesis and occasional lust object, took a fatal shot through the neck.

Most devastating of all was Jessica Groom: the primarch of the subthermics, the woman who'd trained Carrie and her mother in the art of wintercraft. She was running for the tunnel hatch when a bullet ripped through her chest and sent her tumbling to the ground. Her teenage daughter fell weeping at her side, shaking her shoulders, begging her to get up.

Carrie's heart stopped as two armored soldiers closed in on the girl. "Oh God, Shell. Run. *Run.*"

Shoshanna Groom was a year older than Carrie. Everyone called her Shell because of the beautiful tempic skins that she made. She wore them so often, she almost looked naked without them.

The soldiers flanked her. Shell looked across the distance and locked her wet eyes with Carrie's—a look of overwhelming sorrow, as if she'd scoured every inch of the multiverse and found nothing worth saving.

Carrie buried her face in her father's shoulder as the soldiers gunned Shell down.

Several feet ahead of them, Elder Rubinek opened the front doors of the municipal building and waved a river of people inside.

"Hurry! Hurry! Stay close to your children! Don't—"

The people around her screamed as a bullet pierced her temple. Her eyes rolled back and she fell dead to the floor.

Panicked, Stan doubled back from the entry and took his daughter another direction.

"Where are we going?" asked Carrie.

"I don't know!" He held her close as more gunfire and shrieks erupted behind them. "I don't know."

Six seconds after the carnage started, Peter poked his head out of the interrogation tent and recoiled at the bloodshed in the square. His cuffed hands trembled behind his back.

"Butchers. Those goddamn butchers."

Mia eyed him warily. "Don't you dare go out there."

"But Liam . . ."

"Peter, *listen* to me."

A stray bullet tore through the tent wall, missing Mia by millimeters. She shrieked at the kiss of hot air on her thigh.

Mia watched with confusion as Peter kneeled to the ground and placed his shoulder under the front edge of the interrogation table.

"Wait. What are you doing?"

"Giving you cover," said Peter. "Get ready."

"Wait! Don't—"

Grunting, he pressed his weight against the table until it tilted toward Mia. She stepped back as far as she could. This metal beast was about to flip onto its side.

"Peter!"

The table fell, and Mia fell with it. She struggled her way to a kneeling crouch.

"Stay there," Peter told her. "Keep your head down."

Mia didn't have much choice in the matter. Her wrist was cuffed to the lowest part of the tabletop. She was practically chained to the floor.

"Please," she begged Peter. "Your hands are tied. You can barely walk."

"I'll be back with my son."

"No you won't! Peter!"

He disappeared through the tent flap, then limped his way into the war zone.

———————

Liam lay on his back in the northeast corner of the square, on a winding gravel walkway known as Founders' Path. He wasn't entirely sure how he got here. Last thing he remembered, he was hiding behind the guild directory with a whole bunch of clan leaders. Then a group of soldiers found them. A bright light flashed inside each of their helmets. Somebody—

Harold.

—had saved their lives. And then they all ran like hell. Yes. It was all coming back to him now. Everyone fled in different directions but Liam stayed with Mother Olga. She kept insisting that he leave her (*"I'm too old. Too fat. I'll just get you killed."*) but Liam refused to listen. He led her by the hand down Founders' Path, ignoring the nagging voice in his head that wondered if maybe she was right.

Then he heard something loud at the roof of the dome—an explosion, like thunder. He looked up and saw the solic disseminator wobbling.

"Liam!"

That was when someone tackled him to the ground. The sounds of gunshots nearly made his eardrums burst. Liam blacked out for the briefest of moments and now here he was—his body pinned to the walkway, his ears ringing miserably. His lifted his head to view the person on top of him and saw her wide blue eyes staring back at him.

"Olga?"

He freed a hand and jostled her shoulder. Once, twice, three times. She didn't respond. Liam couldn't even get her to blink.

"Oh, God. No. Somebody help her! Please!"

Liam twisted his head and screamed. *"Somebody help her!"*

He heard heavy boots on the gravel. A squat and burly soldier crossed into his view. Liam brushed the tears from his face and glared at him.

"She healed people. That's all she did and you *killed* her!"

The soldier stared at him inscrutably. Liam had no idea what was going on behind his face mask. He didn't even know the man was a woman until he heard her voice.

"My brother was a field medic," she told him. "He healed people too."

The soldier aimed her rifle at his head. "You bastards killed him at Atropos."

Another rumble of thunder. Liam looked up at the disseminator as it became engulfed in debris and yellow fire.

They did it, Liam realized. *They did it.*

Melissa had needed all four of her grenades. The first one cleared the hundreds of feet of electrical cable that had gathered at the bottom of the shaft. The second one destroyed the access hatch that separated the pit from the underland. The third one knocked the disseminator off five of its eight moorings, leaving it dangling from the ceiling like a loose baby tooth.

The last grenade finally set it free.

All the action in the village came to a stop as the Dalton crashed down into the clock tower. It tore through the roof, demolishing half the gearworks before breaking against a patch of hard wooden floor. Its dying sparks were bright enough to illuminate the two surviving clock faces. The glass shimmered with radiant waves of blue.

Within moments, the entire dome began to flicker. The undersky pulsated like a strobe light—black to white, black to white—until it finally settled on white. A thousand and six people looked up through shielded eyes as huge red letters flared down from the ceiling:

HEAVENSEND° II ELITE SKY LUMICASTER
(SYSTEM IV-454-211)
CONSOLE IS RESTARTING. PLEASE BE PATIENT . . .

In the center of the square, just a few yards away from the corpse of Oren Gingold, a young soldier exchanged a blank look with Winnie Whitten. He'd been just one rationalization away from shooting the girl when everything went crazy. Now all he could do was watch, bewildered, as she drew a comically deep breath.

"What—"

Winnie unleashed a mighty scream, one loud enough to crack his visor and send him flying off his feet. The sonic cry reverberated throughout the underland, shaking Gothams and soldiers alike out of their stupor.

Back on Founders' Path, the soldier who'd killed Mother Olga aimed her rifle at Liam. He raised a desperate hand at her. The woman thought he was pleading for mercy until the palm of his glove split open. In a span of a gasp, the temperature inside her armor quintupled. She shrieked and flailed for seven seconds before collapsing in a smoking heap.

One by one, the Gothams began to retaliate. A swifter yanked the hunting knife from a soldier's belt and jammed it straight into his visor. A turner waved his arm and aged Elder Rubinek's killer to a skeleton. A traveler opened a portal directly beneath the feet of two invaders. They reappeared a hundred and fifty feet in the air, then fell screaming back to earth.

Tomlinson tripped backward over his heels, stammering as a tempic hurled a soldier over the roof of a building. None of the Gothams were running anymore. Many were starting to come back from the alleys and side streets, a look of sheer hatred on their faces.

"Shit. Shit . . ."

He reached for his headset and opened a subchannel to the contingency team. "Open the gates," he told them. "Open the gates!"

Tomlinson caught movement in the corner of his eye. He had just enough time to turn his head and see the tempic fist of Victoria Chisholm. And then his whole world went from white to black.

FORTY-EIGHT

Heath paced the roof of the lumics' guild building, his eyes roving anxiously around the violence in the village square. Everything had gone topsy-turvy in the last thirty seconds. The sky had turned from black to white and the victims had become the aggressors. Everywhere Heath looked, Integrity was suffering the wrath of Gothams. It didn't matter if the soldiers fought or ran or raised their hands in surrender. They were all slaughtered. The situation hadn't righted itself. It just became a whole different shade of wrong.

"They're killing them," Heath said. "They can't do that."

Harold and Bo shared the same jaded look. "Of course they can," said the boy.

"Those dicklicks made their own bed," said the tiger.

Heath shook his head. "They'll just keep sending more people. They'll keep sending them and sending them and it'll never end."

Bo narrowed his yellow eyes at Heath. "Bit of a nutbird, aren't you?"

"Stop it," Harold said. "He saved us."

"Right. He also killed Squid."

Flustered, Heath moved to the other side of the roof and saw a small group of soldiers at the end of Center Street. He'd noticed them earlier when he was sneaking around with Zack and Theo. They were completely removed from the greater conflict, their attention fixed on a pair of mysterious-looking door-frames. Dozens of wires connected them to generators. They were machines of some kind, but what did they do?

"Heath!"

He peeked over the roof's edge and saw Theo at the intersection of Guild Street and Central, not far from where the snipers had shot him. His face was white and covered in sweat. He waved his hands frantically.

"Get off the roof! Get out of there!"

The doorframes came to life with a high-pitched hum. The air inside them crackled with static. Heath had no idea what was happening, but if the augur was panicked, then it was time to run.

Harold watched Heath as he bolted for the stairs. "Where are you—"

"We have to go!"

The hum grew louder. The doorframes pulsed with shimmering light. Every traveler in the village turned their head to the east. Something new and strange had appeared on the portal network: a cold, lifeless presence that none of them had ever felt before.

Peter took a few steps back and saw the two glowing doorframes in the distance. "You can't be serious."

Over the last four decades, as temporal technology gradually caught up to the Gothams, the teleporters of the clan had become increasingly smug. Unlike the turners, the lumics, the swifters, and the tempics, the travelers had no mechanical imitators. There wasn't a single machine on God's green Earth that could make a working portal.

Or so they believed.

In truth, spatial fold technology had already existed for five years, ever since Klaus and Edda Hilgendorf, a pair of middle-age physicists from the south German colonies, invented it by accident. They'd been working under contract for a European sex toy company, laboring night and day to develop a warm, pink version of tempis, when a miscalibration turned their homemade barrier into something else entirely. Without even trying, the siblings had created humanity's first machine-generated teleport field.

Two months and countless experiments later, Klaus and Edda succeeded in sending their cat Vivian on a wormhole journey across the laboratory. Gobsmacked, the Hilgendorfs looked beyond the wealth and plaudits of the immediate future and realized, with some trepidation, that they were about to change the world.

Unfortunately for them, the world had other notions. Within minutes of announcing their discovery on EuroNet, the Hilgendorfs were murdered in their home by British secret agents, who erased every trace of their handiwork and then convinced the public, quite easily, that these daffy German dildo-makers had not in fact invented a teleportation device.

Despite the Commonwealth's best efforts to eradicate the machine, a high-ranking spy in British Intelligence sneaked a copy of the schematics to his Russian employers, one of whom was a Chinese mole. The mole's mistress was a covert operative for the Republic of India, which Pakistan knew because it was tracking her every move. On and on the circus went, until twenty-nine countries had acquired step-by-step directions for building a Hilgendorf gate.

Eventually, the prime minister of England brokered a one-of-a-kind treaty between the industrialized nations of Earth, a secret agreement to suppress all forms of teleportation technology. Everyone in the room knew the machines were a game-changer, the kind that rendered borders obsolete and made national security a thing of the past. The world simply wasn't ready for portals.

But Integrity was.

Oren Gingold had always been a cautious man. When his advisors assured him that the solic disseminator was their one and only key to victory, Gingold reminded them of the teachings of Sun Tzu: never rely on just one tactic, and always have a backup plan. If the solis failed and the siege went poorly, Gingold wanted a way to beat the Gothams at their own game: a formidable army that could handle the freaks at full power.

Theo was the first to hear the reinforcements coming, a hair-dryer hum on the other side of the portals.

"Shit."

He shot the lock of the tempics' front door and fled into their guildhall, just as the cavalry came bursting out of the Hilgendorf gates.

Two by two, they flew into the underland. To the naked eye, they were nothing but red streaks. If Hannah had been there, and if she'd been shifted fast enough, she would have seen something that resembled a fleet of giant ladybugs. The drones were five feet in length, each one sheathed in a crimson dome of osplate. Nestled on the underside among its seven aeric liftplates were weapons and launchers of every kind. The machines shot solis, electricity, rockets, grenades, and five different types of bullets.

But their real specialty was the twenty pounds of magnite they kept beneath their shells, enough to set fire to a whole city block.

That was the reason Integrity called them "dragonettes."

From the moment Theo got his foresight back, he knew the metal beasts were coming and that Heath would be the first to suffer their wrath. But in the desperate quest to warn him, he'd dawdled too long in the open. Now the future had turned its angry eye on him.

A dragonette broke free from formation and hovered at the tempics' front window. Two hundred miles to the southeast, in the cubicle farm of a Washington, D.C., government office, a chubby young redhead in a sweatshirt and jeans sat forward at her computer terminal. She pressed a button on the keyboard, switching her dragonette to thermal view and exposing Theo's location. The target had ducked behind a thick stone wall, but that only earned him a spitter.

She pressed another button. Theo slid beneath a metal desk as a three-foot missile came crashing through the window. It bounced across the floor on weak aeric thrusters before opening its cone and shooting a dozen globs of sticky gel. Each one was as strong as half a stick of dynamite, and each one exploded on impact.

All at once, the whole world seemed to fold in on Theo. The floor ripped up. The ceiling came down. Blast heat singed the left side of his body while the collapsing desk broke seven bones on his right side. Were it not for the thick sheath of tempis that bloomed around his skull—a last-second gift from Ioni Deschane—he would have died instantly. Instead, he fell unconscious beneath six hundred pounds of plaster, steel, and wood.

Back in Washington, the drone pilot studied Theo's mangled silhouette on her thermal screen before pressing a button on her flightstick. The dragonette sprayed a cone of magfire through the window, dousing half the foyer in flames.

"First kill," the pilot bragged. She sneered at her coworkers, all hard at work in their own shifted cubicles. "Should I slow down for you fellas?"

Twenty yards south of Theo, and two floors up, Heath spun around at the base of the stairwell and gestured frantically at his companion. "Come on! Come on!"

Harold hurried down from the roof, conspicuously alone. One peek at the dragonettes was enough to wreck his concentration and send his tiger into the ether. "What *are* those things?"

"I don't know!"

"How did they even—"

Harold stopped on the stairwell, his eyes bulged in terror. Heath followed his gaze and saw a dragonette hovering right outside the window, its machine-gun turret pointed right at them.

"No . . ."

The window exploded in a hail of gunfire. Two of the rounds hit Heath in the stomach. Three hit Harold in his legs and chest, and sent him rolling down the stairs.

Many miles away, a supervisor passed the drone pilot's desk and nodded approvingly at his screen.

"Good work. Slag them down, then rejoin the others."

Scowling, the pilot waited for his boss to leave before flying his dragonette away from the window. He wasn't going to spray magfire on his targets. They were just kids, goddamn it. They were dead enough.

Mia couldn't tell what was going on from behind her fallen table. All she could hear was a cacophony of screams and weapon fire. She had no idea that a fleet of drones had come to kill every last timebender in the village. She did, however, feel the spatial presence of her fellow travelers. Her powers were back, which meant it was time to leave.

She opened a four-inch portal in the grass, then dipped her handcuff chain inside it. An ounce of thought closed the disc like a guillotine. Mia fell back against the ground, her severed chain dangling from her shackle.

She barely had a moment to enjoy her freedom when a swifter burst in through the tent flap and smashed his legs against the table. He flipped over the edge, snapped his neck, and came to a rolling stop on the grass next to her.

"Jesus!"

A few feet to the left and Mia would have been caught in his path. She jumped back, startled, and then cautiously checked on him. His green eyes were frozen wide in terror. His mouth hung open listlessly. He was dead, gone. The fool had been running blind at top speed.

Rattled, Mia hurried out of the tent and took a wide-eyed look around the square. Everything had changed in the last few minutes. The undersky was nothing but a giant restart message. Fires burned everywhere in patches. A multitude of corpses, both soldiers and Gothams, lay scattered about the grass. The stench of blood was overwhelming, enough to make Mia gag.

She looked through the smoke and saw survivors in the distance, dozens of them. The Gothams who weren't running remained clustered under a crude tempic canopy. They all looked as panicked as that poor dead swifter.

Mia only had to look up to see why.

Blurry red creatures flew through the air like missiles. They moved so fast that Mia didn't even know what she was seeing until one of them slowed down. It was a new kind of drone, even worse than the ones that had terrorized her at Atropos. It seemed Integrity had given up on herding their prisoners and were now killing everyone.

She looked around in panic. "Peter . . ."

A half-dead soldier staggered out of the smoke and raised his rifle at Mia. Before she could move, a long white tendril snaked around his leg. It hung him by the foot, then smashed him against the ground seven times. He spilled onto the grass like a rag doll.

Mia stumbled backward, terrified, as the tempic tendril came for her. "No, wait!"

It looped around her waist and yanked her thirty yards to the west, into a dark and narrow crevice between the municipal building and the recreation center. She rolled screaming into the passage. A strong pair of arms set her back on her feet.

"Pay attention, girl. It's a death zone out there."

Mia brushed the bangs from her eyes and immediately recognized the bearded man in front of her. She only knew Irwin Sunder as an elder and a blowhard. She had no idea he was a tempic.

She winced at her throbbing arm. "Why'd you *do* that?"

Sunder scoffed. "What, save your life? Good question. Can you still make portals?"

"Yes."

"Good. Go far away and take these children with you."

Mia looked past Sunder and saw nine kids huddled between boxes, all trembling in misery and fright.

"I'm not leaving," Mia told Sunder. "Not without my friends."

"Stay, go, I don't care. But you're making a portal and you're saving this lot."

"Look, Peter's still out there. If I don't find him—"

Sunder gripped her arm and spoke in a raspy growl. Mia could see that the man was at the end of his tether.

"I only had one traveler in my family," he reminded her. "You people killed her. So make things right—"

"Shut up."

Mia closed her eyes and concentrated until she formed a link with her exit point. A ten-foot portal materialized in the air.

"This'll take you to Brooklyn," she told the others. "Go."

The children hesitated. Half of them kept their nervous eyes on Sunder. He opened his wallet and gave all his cash to the oldest kid. "Go on. Keep moving. We'll find you when this is over."

One by one, the youngsters scrambled through the portal. Mia waved them on impatiently. Peter was still somewhere out on the battlefield, injured and bound. If she missed her chance to save him . . .

At long last, the children were gone. Mia closed the portal behind them and glared at Sunder. "We done?"

"No. There's an armory in the warrens—"

"Are you *kidding* me?"

"—and you're going to take me there."

"I've never even *been* to the w—"

A dragonette crashed onto the roof of the rec center, spilling flaming debris into the passageway. Sunder cast a tempic shield over himself and Mia.

"What the hell's happening?"

Mia had no idea. She followed Sunder back to the edge of the square and saw ten winged tempics engaging the dragonettes in combat. One of them looped a lightning-quick circle around a drone, then smashed it on the underside with a tempic hammer. The machine bled a torrent of circuitry and weapon fragments before spinning into the ground.

Sunder took a step forward, his fist shaking high in the air. "Yes. *Yes!*"

"What's going on?" Mia asked him.

"Victoria," he said. "She's way ahead of me."

The Gothams hadn't been entirely unprepared for invaders. Between the bomb shelters and the storehouses, they kept a sizable armory of rainy-day weapons: pistols and rifles, grenades, even a rocket launcher or two.

They also had speedsuits, and for very good reason. The only thing in the world more dangerous than a flying tempic was a shifted flying tempic.

Victoria swooped onto the back of a dragonette and stabbed it with a blade of her own making. The drone wobbled through the sky, belching smoke from two wounds. Victoria jumped off its carapace just before it crashed against the base of the clock tower.

Somewhere in Washington, a supervisor barked new orders. Half the dragonettes in the underland turned their glass eyes toward the center of town and rushed to join the fight.

Mia looked up and saw nine swifters take formation on the rooftops, their hands moving in blurs as they aimed their assault rifles. At their speed, the dragonettes moved like blimps. Their delicate undersides were easy to hit. Two of the drones exploded in midair. Another one lost half its lifters and fell spinning to the grass.

Sunder did a double-take at Mia as she hurried through the square. "Wait. Where are you going? I still need you."

"I'm looking for my people."

"We took you in. We *are* your people!"

Mia glared at him over her shoulder. "You never cared about us."

She ran deeper into the square, coughing. The smoke was making her eyes water. She could barely see ten feet in front of her.

"Peter?"

A grim voice in her head told her to start checking the corpses. She refused to listen. Peter wouldn't let himself die. Not here, not now, not when the people he loved were still in trouble.

Another dragonette came crashing down onto the grass, along with a flying tempic. The drone must have gotten in a good shot before it died. Mia only had to look at the victim's charred body to know that he was beyond saving.

She cupped her hands around her mouth. *"Peter!"*

"Mia?"

She saw a skinny blonde through the smoke. Her heartbeat doubled. "Oh my God . . ."

Carrie stumbled out of the haze, her hair matted, her black dress torn in a dozen places. She stared at Mia in trembling confusion, as if the lovely girl in front of her were just a mirage.

"Is that really . . . are you really . . . ?"

Mia ran toward her and held her tight. "Oh my God. Carrie . . ."

"I didn't . . . I didn't even know if you were alive or . . ."

"I'm alive." Mia couldn't stop her tears from spilling. "I'm here."

"Please. You have to help me."

"What?"

Mia pulled back and saw smears of blood on her shirt. The front of Carrie's dress was soaked in it.

"It's not mine," Carrie said. "It's my dad's. They shot him."

"What? Where is he?"

"Behind the library. He's too big to move and I can't find a turner. Please! You have to port him to a hospital!"

"Carrie . . ."

"He's dying!"

Mia closed her eyes, her thoughts spinning wildly. She'd been living so long in a tight, insular family that she forgot what it was like to be a part of a society. There were *her people* and there was the rest of the world. Peter Pendergen was one of her people. Stan Bloom was the rest of the world.

But then what kind of person would she be if she didn't help the girl she loved? How could she justify it, even in wartime?

Daughter of my heart, Peter had called her. *That's what you are.*

Carrie tugged her hand. "Mia, come on!"

That's what you are.

Crying, Mia struggled through the splinters and cracks of her concentration, until she drew a spatial link to the library. A six-foot portal opened up in the air.

She clutched Carrie's hand and sucked a deep breath. "Come on."

Melissa was six hundred feet down the disseminator shaft when she finally saw light at the bottom. At long last, the situation was starting to improve. There was no more darkness down below, no more solis, no more torcher breathing fire at her head. Her stalwart companion had obliterated the drone with a tempic tantrum, a great white mouth that chomped the machine to pieces. If Melissa didn't know it before, the wisdom was now thoroughly cemented: don't ever make Amanda Given angry.

But they weren't out of trouble yet. Though Amanda had staked a firm hold on the walls of the shaft, her exertions were finally taking their toll. Her head lolled drowsily to one side. Thin streams of blood dribbled from her nose. Even more alarming was the crude, tenuous appearance of their support line. The tempis looked less a rope now and more like overstretched putty.

As Amanda lowered them down past the 650-foot marker, Melissa reached out and wiped the sweat from her brow.

"Hang in there," she said. "You're doing great."

"Stop saying that."

"It's true."

"Doesn't matter." Amanda closed her eyes in a twitchy wince. Her voice fluttered wildly. "The more I think about it, the more it hurts."

"Well, if you're looking for distraction, there's a question I've always wanted to ask you."

"A question."

"Yeah. Why did you leave medical school?"

Their harness rippled. Amanda peeked at Melissa with a bloodshot eye. "How'd you know about that?"

"I chased you for months," Melissa reminded her. "Everywhere you went, I broke out the ghost drills and followed your old conversations."

"Spied on us."

Melissa shrugged. "It was my job to understand you people."

"I still never talked about that."

"No, but your sister did. She told Theo you quit school but she didn't say why."

Amanda sighed at her feet. The look on her face was miserable enough to make Melissa regret asking.

"Lost my baby," Amanda replied. "Lost my way."

"I'm so sorry."

She feebly shook her head. "He would have . . . he would've . . ."

"Amanda?"

"He would've died anyway . . ."

The rope quivered. Their bodies bounced erratically. Melissa looked up and saw the tempis withering into a long, frayed thread.

We're not going to make it, she realized. *She can't hold on.*

"Amanda, listen to me—"

"Please. No more pep talks . . ."

"I'm not familiar with that term. I just know you've suffered and lost more than I can possibly imagine. You have every excuse in the world to be jaded, yet here you are, fighting to save a clan of people who, historically speaking, haven't been very kind to you. You're an extraordinary woman. Whatever happens, you need to know that."

Amanda dipped her head. "Killed people . . ."

"So have I."

"Could've found a better way."

"That could be carved on anyone's epitaph."

"Been trying so hard to live up to her example."

"Whose example?"

"Hannah. She's gotten so strong."

Melissa checked the rope again. The tempis was melting before her eyes. "Amanda."

"Wish I . . . wish I'd told her that more often."

Amanda's eyelids fluttered. The rope disappeared. For the second time, she and Melissa went plummeting down the pit.

Melissa looked down at the expanding light below her. She didn't have the time or mind to sort her own regrets. All she could do was hold on to her friend and face the reaper with dignity.

"You did fine," she assured Amanda. "You did just fine."

Mia's portal opened two blocks north of the square, on a half-mile patch of sidewalk that ran east to west along Temperance Street. She was only halfway through when Carrie pushed past her and bolted toward the library.

"Careful!" Mia yelled.

"He's this way!"

"These portal edges are sharp. You could have hurt yourself!"

Carrie hooked around the corner, then disappeared down a filthy passageway.

Frowning, Mia closed the portal and chased after her. The alley was four feet wide at the very most, and didn't lead anywhere but a junk-filled alcove. Stan Bloom must have been desperate or delirious to bring Carrie this way. From the messy trail of blood on the pavement, Mia could only guess it was both.

Carrie turned around in the alcove. "Hurry!"

"I'm coming. I—"

Mia stopped short when a dragonette dropped down behind Carrie. The thing was so fast, it might as well have teleported there.

"Carrie!"

The girl only had time to twist halfway around before a short black nozzle popped out of the dragonette's shell. It spun toward her in blurry haste, then belched a bright blue geyser of flame.

"No!"

Everything inside Mia came to a screeching halt: her breath, her heart, her muscles, her mind. Even the outside world seemed to fall into still frame as she locked her screaming eyes on the magfire. The flame glimmered like crystal in the light of the undersky, an exquisite bouquet of sapphires and opals. Mia had enough time to think that Heath, that insatiable nut for all things blue, would have loved it.

After another staccato barrage of thoughts, it occurred to Mia that nothing was happening. The flame had yet to reach Carrie. It wasn't even . . .

"What?"

It wasn't moving at all. None of it. The drone, the fire, the girl in its path. They all dawdled like stone in Mia's vision.

She looked up and saw a winged tempic locked in motionless combat with another dragonette. Beyond them, two distant figures floated impossibly above the ruins of the clock tower. Everything in the village had come to a stop except for Mia. How was that even . . . ?

The silence was broken by footsteps behind her—the slow, *clopping* patter of loafers on concrete.

Oh, no. No . . .

"Hello, Mia."

Trembling, she turned around. He stood on the sidewalk of Temperance Street: the Australian boy who was actually neither, the demon who had broken her heart.

Semerjean stuffed his hands in his pockets and smiled glibly at Mia. "I suppose we should talk."

FORTY-NINE

There was a stubborn part of her mind that still called him David.

Even now, as her fingers clenched and her inner self screamed with fury, a dizzy little piece of herself remained lost in denial. It clapped its hands with childish glee, welcoming him home as if everything that had happened over the last thirty hours was just a big misunderstanding. *Oh, David. I knew you'd never betray us. I'm so glad you're back.*

But there was no mistake about the son of a bitch in front of her. He was Semerjean Pelletier. He'd been lying nonstop from the day they met.

Mia took a moment to process his new look, all the tiny bits of David he'd washed away like stage makeup. His long blond hair was now a short caramel brown. His teenage facial scruff, that fine sheen of fuzz that never quite grew or went away, had been shaved. He'd swapped his modest, rumpled, "can't be bothered to care" clothes for a sharp red oxford and khakis. Most jarring of all, he sported all ten of his fingers again. His maimed right hand had been completely healed.

Though Semerjean looked at least eight years older (and twice as handsome, Mia grudgingly noted), there was something viscerally repugnant about him, a hard new tightness in his mouth and jaw that vaguely reminded her of someone. Mia was too rattled at the moment to figure out who.

Semerjean's eyes hovered gravely around the blood on her shirt. "We've had better weekends, haven't we?"

"We?"

"Despite what you think—"

"You don't want to know what I think."

"—I haven't enjoyed a minute of this."

"Fuck you." Mia stepped forward, her brown eyes burning with rage. "Fuck you and your whole fucking family, you goddamn lying shitfuck!"

Semerjean blinked at her. "Wow. Mia . . ."

"Don't. Don't you dare say my name. You don't get to say my name, y-you . . ."

Try as she might, she couldn't hold back her tears. The events of the day had left her utterly demolished. She'd been chained up and terrorized, watched a soldier and two Gothams die right in front of her. She had no idea if the people she loved were alive or dead, any of them. Even Carrie—

Carrie!

Panicked, Mia turned around to check on her. Though the dragonette's flame had yet to reach her, thank God, it looked slightly larger than it did a minute ago. Time hadn't stopped. It had just slowed to a crawl.

Mia's stomach tightened. She shot a wary look at Semerjean. "You shifted us."

"And then some."

She finally noticed his accent, a slightly alien version of a cultured British twang. "Is that how you really talk?"

"In English, yes." He smiled softly. "I was raised in the theater. My mentors were very strict about—"

"I don't care." Mia surveyed her surroundings. "Why isn't everything blue and cold?"

Semerjean showed her his left hand. A two-inch disc of silver had been firmly affixed to the back.

"Stabilizer," he said. "I wanted you to be comfortable."

"Comfortable." She gestured at Carrie. "Can I move her?"

"You're shifted at a thousand times her temporal velocity. I wouldn't advise it."

"We can't just leave her like that."

"We?"

Mia squinted at him suspiciously. His expression had turned a few degrees cooler. His smile had become a little smug.

"I can move her with tempis," he said. "Or shield her. Or teleport her. Or I can simply destroy that metal monstrosity. There are a dozen ways to save her. I can even save her father, if you wish."

"If I wish?"

"I'm offering you a quid pro quo. You come with me for a couple of minutes, listen to what I have to say. As soon as we're done, we'll come back here and I'll save the lives of both Blooms. 'Easy peasy,' as Hannah would say."

Mia bristled at his casual mention of Hannah. He invoked her name as if they were still chummy, as if he hadn't betrayed her love and good nature.

"Where would you take me?" she asked him.

"Just around the village. I have some matters to attend to. We'll talk while I work."

"Work," Mia repeated. "You mean 'kill people.'"

Semerjean plucked a piece of lint from his shirtsleeve. "I have three names on my list. No one you'd know or particularly care about. I also have some people to save."

"Anyone I care about?"

"Pretty much everyone you care about."

"Jesus." She closed her eyes and turned away from him. "Why are you doing this?"

Semerjean sighed impatiently. "Mia, in eighteen minutes and forty-nine seconds, that magnesium fire will singe Carrie's skin. In nineteen minutes, she'll be in indescribable agony. In twenty minutes, she'll be dead."

"No! Please! Look, just save her and I'll come with you!"

"Come with me and I'll save her," Semerjean countered. "My work is quick. We'll be back with minutes to spare."

"Goddamn it." Mia bounced her anxious gaze between Carrie and the dragonette, then tossed her hands up in surrender. "Okay, fine. Fine!"

"Lovely."

With a graceful wave, Semerjean created a twelve-foot disc of solid white energy beneath him. Mia thought it was tempis until it lifted him a foot off the ground.

He extended his hand. "Shall we?"

Mia climbed aboard without touching him, then stood as far away as she could. "Go."

They floated away from Temperance Street, as calm and graceful as a cloud. While Semerjean steered with subtle hand gestures, Mia stood to his side and examined him. There it was again, that familiar tightness in his jaw. She knew exactly who it reminded her of now.

"Gingold," she muttered before she could stop herself.

Semerjean looked at her over his shoulder. "What?"

"Nothing." Mia hugged herself, her skin crawling with revulsion. "Just say what you have to say."

The first minute passed without a word being spoken. Semerjean seemed perfectly content to fly a leisurely path around the underland while Mia looked down at the suspended action. The battle had spread well beyond the village square, with Gothams fighting Integrity on nearly every street. Four different intersections had been overtaken by tempic domes. Mia could feel the portals inside all of them. The travelers and tempics were working together to set up evacuation stations, for all the good it did. Dragonettes were already beginning to melt three of the domes with their solic cannons.

Semerjean stood at the edge of his flying platform, his blue eyes fixed on the dragonettes. Every time he got within forty feet of one, he thrust a long tempic arm through the wall of his temporal bubble and touched the hull three times with his "finger." *Tap, tap, tap.* If his dainty touch had any effect on the drones, Mia couldn't see it. As far as she knew, he was playing his own weird version of freeze tag.

"What the hell are you doing?"

Semerjean smirked at her. "She speaks at last."

"You're the one who wanted to do the talking."

"I was hoping to have a dialogue."

"Fine. We're dialoguing. What the hell are you doing?"

He tagged another dragonette. "Can't speak for you, but I'm not a fan of these flying death turtles."

"You're destroying them."

"Thoroughly."

"They don't look destroyed."

"Patience, my dear."

"Fuck you. Don't patronize me." Mia watched a tendril retract into his skin. "All this time, you've been a tempic and a swifter."

Semerjean smiled immodestly. "And a turner. And a traveler. And a thermic. And a solic."

"And a traitor."

His humor faded. "A traitor works against his people. I was always on your side."

"You *lied* to us."

"I kept you and the others alive."

"Yeah, poorly."

"What are you talking about?"

"All those times we could have used another tempic," Mia said. "Or a traveler. Or an augur!"

Semerjean frowned at her. "I never said I was an augur."

"What?"

"As for my other talents, I used them all the time to help you."

"When?"

He reached out with a split tempic projection and tagged two dragonettes at once. "Last year, when Zack fell off that hotel balcony. You remember that?"

"Yeah. Amanda saved him."

Semerjean laughed. "She was an amateur at her talent. She didn't have a prayer of catching him. The moment the tempis came out of her hand, I took control of it and rescued him properly."

He saw a trio of drones in the sky above Freak Street and flew the platform toward them. "That same day, Hannah took a blow to the head. Her concussion would have killed her if I hadn't intervened."

"How?"

"I reversed her back to perfect health while the rest of you were sleeping."

Mia pinched her lip in thought, her eyes darting busily around the platform. She could vaguely remember David insisting that he stay in Hannah's room that night. Something about the bed being more comfortable.

"I also healed you," Semerjean told her. "When Rebel shot you in the chest."

"That was Zack!"

"It was *me*. Zack couldn't reverse a baby deer without killing it. So I manipulated his temporis. Cell by cell, I made sure that you were healed the right way, without permanent side effects. Are you starting to see now?"

He tapped the three dragonettes, then made a sharp left turn. "I had to work night and day to keep you Silvers alive. You could have made it easier."

Mia crossed her arms and looked away. "You only saved us because you need us."

"Yes, but you don't know why."

"Of course I do. You want us to make babies with the Gothams."

"That's the *what*. I'm talking about the *why*."

He lowered the platform to street level, near the scene of a brutal skirmish. Five turners and a tempic were locked in combat with a soldier and two dragonettes. By all appearances, the Gothams were winning. The turners had aged the drones, clouding each and every one of their camera lenses, while the tempic made short work of the soldier.

Semerjean touched each dragonette, then waved his hand at one of the turners.

Mia did a double-take. "Wait. Did you just do something to that guy?"

"Yes. I just ended his life."

Mia studied the victim, a bald and burly man she'd seen around the village. Like the dragonettes, he seemed no worse for the wear.

"That's Frank Godden," Semerjean explained. "One of the three people on my list."

"What did he do to you?"

"Personally? Nothing."

"So why are you killing him?"

Semerjean exhaled in Godden's direction. "In a few days' time, he would have taken Alma Rubinek's seat on the elder council. His particular brand of idiocy would have created unpleasant consequences for you and your friends. He was a storm cloud on the horizon. Now he's not."

"How do you know all that?" Mia asked. "I thought you weren't an augur."

"My wife and son see the strings just fine."

Hot blood rushed to Mia's face. For a moment, she wondered if she'd gone mad. The Pelletiers were fighting to save Mia and her friends from future problems, but they hadn't lifted a finger to stop this invasion. Nothing added up. Not a goddamn thing.

Semerjean turned the platform and flew it west toward the ruins of Guild Street.

"Speaking of augurs," he said, "I believe Theo needs our help."

Mia glanced over her shoulder at Frank Godden. He seemed a few inches shorter than he did a second ago. It took Mia a full moment to realize that the man wasn't shrinking, he was sinking. The concrete was swallowing him inch by inch.

Mia looked at Semerjean in horror. Now she knew exactly what he was doing to the drones and the human targets.

He's dropping them, she thought. *He's a dropper too.*

"Prepare yourself. This might be a little unsettling."

His words trickled like water around the edges of Mia's consciousness. She was barely listening. Her eyes and thoughts remained hopelessly stuck on Frank Godden. She didn't even notice when Semerjean thrust his hand and sprayed a cone of black mortis at the tempics' guild hall. It spread like a shadow across the southern face of the building, dissolving it brick by brick.

By the time Mia turned around, the mortis was gone, along with an entire wall of the structure.

"What just happened? What did you do?"

Semerjean smiled coyly. "Made an entrance for us."

He maneuvered the platform inside the building, where a violent struggle had taken place. The foyer looked like it had been torn apart by bazookas. Nearly half the second floor had come crashing down on the first. The entry was little more than rubble and burning wood.

Mia noticed a nearby fire and was immediately transfixed. At a thousandth-speed, the flame danced in a hypnotic rhythm, like aquatic weeds swaying in the tides.

She snapped out of her trance and looked at Semerjean. "How much time do we have?"

He shrugged with droll humor. "I don't know. I gave away my wristwatch."

"If Carrie dies—"

"Calm down. We still have fifteen minutes."

Six spindly tempic arms emerged from the edge of his flying disc. They stretched across the foyer, moving heavy pieces of wreckage to one side while smothering the occasional flame. Mia swallowed the urge to ask him what he was doing. She was sick of the question. Sick of his games.

"How old are you really?" Mia asked.

Semerjean kept his eyes on his work. "Depends how you mean it."

"I don't understand."

"Time's a lot more flexible where I come from. We can live a year in a day, spend a month in the God's Eye, jump back through the strings and relive a past decade. Our experiential age isn't tied to a calendar. Only the vainest among us try to put a number on it."

He stared down at his smooth hands. "If you want to know my physical age, that's easier. I'm just a month shy of seventeen."

Mia stared at him, dumbfounded. "How is that possible?"

"Reversal's come a long way in my era. We can keep all our memories, shed years from our age without losing a moment of experience. Our bodies aren't trapped in chronological degression. We can be as young or old as we want to be."

"God." Mia shook her head in astonishment. "You could live forever that way."

Semerjean chuckled. "You'd think so, but no."

"What do you mean?"

"Nature is stubborn," he said. "It doesn't much like the idea of immortality. So it gave us a new disease, one that only affects the exceptionally long-lived."

"What is it?"

"There's no name for it in English. The closest translation would be 'terminus.'"

Mia eyed him skeptically. "Terminus."

"It's humanity's last illness," he told her. "A neurological sickness that follows us through the strings. It can't be cured by any means we know of, and it takes great pleasure in killing us slowly. Some lose their memory. Some lose their sanity. Some, like me, lose their powers one by one."

Mia balked at his news. Lack of power seemed to be the least of Semerjean's problems. "You have terminus?"

"My whole family has it."

He stared at the rubble with an expression that Mia had never seen on him before, a deep and genuine mournfulness. All of David's grief about the old world and the coming apocalypse had never looked like that. Those were play acts. This was real.

"You're all dying."

Semerjean sneered at her. "Don't get your hopes up. Even if we fail, we still have decades."

"Fail what?"

"Isn't is obvious? We're here to cure terminus." He cast his steely gaze on a fire. "We have no intention of dying."

Mia's knees briefly buckled. She was just a hapless kid from La Presa, a ninth-grade dropout. Now here she was, talking immortality with a twisted cosmic demigod.

"You're probably wondering what all of this has to do with you," Semerjean mused.

Mia nodded absently. He conjured a ghost in the middle of the disc: a full-size hologram of a tall and lovely brunette. Mia could easily guess who she was looking at.

"Esis."

"The one and only," Semerjean said. "You haven't met her yet. If you're lucky, you won't meet her today."

"She's coming?"

"Yes. She . . . has her own business to take care of."

There it was again, that look of genuine sorrow. Mia was deathly afraid to ask him about it.

"She's a neurogenetic surgeon," Semerjean explained. "Decades ahead of her peers. Some time ago, she came to believe, to much derision, that the only way to end terminus is to genetically reengineer our brains."

Mia blinked at him. "You can do that?"

"Of course. Nearly everyone on my world has a designer enhancement of some sort. But what Esis proposed was much different. She suggested we fashion our brains to resemble those of our earliest chronokinetic ancestors, the so-called Gothams of Quarter Hill."

"What?"

"Yes, even I was skeptical." He gestured at the wall, at a grandiose photo of the tempic guild's current leaders. "We've spent two and a half millennia evolving from these idiots. Why would we choose to regress? But their brains do have an extraordinary resilience, something my people have lost over time. For Esis, that was a starting point."

The tempic arms continued to clear debris. Semerjean paced the edge of his platform.

"For many years, she tried to build a perfect brain from the Gotham template, one that would provide full immunity to terminus without compromising our abilities. But nature proved stubborn once again. Eventually Esis realized that a new genetic element had to be introduced, something that only existed in theory."

Mia didn't like where this was going. "You're talking about—"

"You," Semerjean said. "You, your friends, and all the other so-called breachers. You all grew up on a world without temporis, yet your brains developed the very same mechanism that allows for chronokinesis. It truly is a wonder. My people were made from the Cataclysm, but you developed naturally. You have no idea how special you are."

An oily nausea washed over Mia. "That's why you picked siblings."

"Yes. The mutation runs strong in certain families, like the Trillingers and the Givens."

"But not mine."

His morbid look was all the answer she needed. All this time, she'd been holding on to a tiny flicker of hope that at least one of her brothers had survived. Another pipe dream. Another delusion.

She cleared the choke from her throat. "How did you find us? How'd you even get to us?"

"I won't bore you with the details. Suffice it to say that what we did was unprecedented, the first lateral jump across worldstrings. My son had to invent an entirely new form of temporis to—"

The tempic arms stopped moving. Semerjean peered down over the edge of the platform. "Damn. It's worse than I thought."

Mia followed his gaze and gasped at the bloody sight below. "Oh no!"

Theo already looked like one of the dead. The left side of his body was covered in burns. His right arm and leg had been crushed by debris. His eyes were wide open, unblinking. Mia prayed that was just an effect of the temporal shift.

"He's alive," Semerjean assured her. "Barely, but . . ."

Puzzled, he tilted his head. Mia recognized the look on his face, the same thousand-yard-stare that David used to get when he was scanning the past.

"What?"

Semerjean blinked at her a moment, then tensely shook his head. "Nothing. Let's see what we can do for him."

He pulled a golden coin out of his shirt pocket and tossed it off the platform. It swerved toward Theo with deliberate insistence, impervious to the slowdown that affected everything around him. Mia watched with fascination as the disc landed on Theo's chest and began burning through his sweatshirt.

"He'll be all right," said Semerjean. "Let's move on."

"Wait."

"I thought you were worried about Carrie."

"Now I'm worried about Theo."

"He's healing," Semerjean insisted. "We want him alive just as much as you do."

"Then why did you let this happen?"

"You think I control the universe?"

"I think you control his visions. He could have seen this war coming weeks ago, but you stopped him. You *wanted* it to happen because it helps your plans somehow."

Semerjean sighed. "Mia . . ."

"All this pain, all this death, and for what? So you and your family can live forever?"

"My *family*?" A flush rose in his cheeks. "This is for everyone. The minute we get home, we'll make our discovery available to any living soul who wants it, at no cost or condition. Our gift will spread across the strings, *trillions* of people given infinite life. Can you understand a feat of that magnitude, Mia? Can you even begin to wrap your mind around the scope of our mission?"

Mia recoiled at his anger. *Stupid girl,* she thought. *You'll get Carrie killed!*

"I'm sorry," she said. "I shouldn't have assumed."

Semerjean's expression softened. He flashed his palms in gentle accord. "It's all right. You're under a lot of stress. I suppose I'm partly responsible for that."

Her stomach churned. She fought the urge to scream. "Who are you saving next?"

"Well, that depends."

"On what?"

Semerjean looked through the missing wall, at the lumic guildhall across the street. "On how you feel about Heath."

They had barely pulled out of the guildhouse when Mia closed her eyes and muttered something. Semerjean looked at her confusedly, as if she'd just yipped at him in the secret language of poodles.

"I'm sorry. What?"

"I said *stop.*"

The disc froze in midair, twelve feet above the asphalt of Center Street. Mia crouched at the edge of the circle, her face racked with sickness and misery.

Semerjean backed away from her. "Are you about to, uh . . ."

Mia shook her head, even as her breakfast threatened to surge back up. He had placed Heath's life in her hands as if it were a cheap trinket, as if letting him die was even an option. Even more horrific than Semerjean's "dilemma" was his shrugging explanation. *I don't know,* he'd told her. *I've just seen the way he grates on you.*

If there had been any hope left that her good friend David still existed in some form, it was gone now. There wasn't a trace of him left. No warmth, no charm, no morality she could even remotely comprehend. He'd been an alien this whole time. The parts of him she'd loved were just fiction.

Semerjean looked at the Hilgendorf gates in the distance, then tapped them with a long tempic finger. The portals flickered out of existence. The machines began to sink into the concrete.

Mia climbed to her feet and turned away from him. "Why are we even doing this? What do you want from me?"

"I don't know," he admitted. "I guess I was hoping I could explain myself, give you a better sense of who I am."

"I know who you are. You're a goddamn scientist—"

"I'm nothing of the sort."

"—who manipulated us for his own bullshit reasons."

"It's not that simple."

"If you just wanted babies, there are a million easier ways to get them."

Semerjean laughed. "You have no idea how true that is."

"So then why all these games? Why not try something else?"

"We're trying everything," Semerjean assured her. "With every group and every timeline, we're doing something different. This is admittedly one of our more complex efforts."

"It makes no sense!"

"That's because you're thinking in linear terms," he said. "A to B, B to C. The straightest path isn't always the best one, especially when it comes to nature."

Semerjean waved a colorful image into the air: a three-dimensional rendering of a human brain. A yellow bead of light glowed at the base.

"If you want to know why my wife has a bad temper . . ." He pointed at the dot. "It's this. All we need is one mutation, one tiny twist of evolution right here in the temporal lobe, for humans to achieve immortality. But nothing has worked. The future teases us with glimpses of victory, but it doesn't show us how to get it. So we experiment. We try a multitude of approaches in the hope that one of them, *one* of them, will finally bear fruit."

The image changed to ten floating bracelets, each one a different color. To Mia's surprise, they weren't all metal. She saw ruby and jade, multicolored opal, even a plastic-looking purple one.

"In this string, we've taken a segmented approach with our subjects. For the Pearls, it's embryonic engineering. For the Violets, germline editing. For the Golds? A multistage trial of controlled cellular parthenogenesis."

"What?"

"Cloning," Semerjean explained. "They're our clone group."

A shiver ran up Mia's spine. She imagined a lab somewhere with hundred copies of Jonathan, Heath, and Zack's brother. No wonder Semerjean didn't care about the originals. They were nothing but redundant spares.

Semerjean vanquished all the bracelets but one. It expanded to the size of a truck tire, then rotated in the air.

"Now the Silvers . . . oh, you were a challenge. We knew from the start that we needed to trust one group to the hands of nature—a natural conception, a natural mutation, a natural immunity to terminus. My wife and son looked to the strings and were very encouraged by what they saw. If their forecasts are right, then you represent our best chance for success. The sisters especially."

Mia felt queasy again. Semerjean eyed her worriedly. She wound her hand, urging him to continue.

"The question was how to get you all to breed with the right partners," he said. "Azral's original plan was . . . distasteful, and not particularly effective. Esis and I came up with a much more humane approach, though it involved some deception. It also required a full-time presence in your group."

He lowered his head with a look of soft contrition. "So I opted to join you as one of your own. I developed a persona that would complement your personalities while masking my cultural differences."

Mia closed her eyes. "This was all just a game to you."

"No."

"That whole trip across the country—"

"No, no, no. That was never part of the plan. If things had gone my way, you'd still be in San Diego, living in comfort in Sterling Quint's facility. I would have eventually . . . encouraged some Gothams to join us there: Peter and Liam, Mercy Lee, a few potential partners for Theo and Hannah, even one for me. You know, for appearances."

Mia stared at him, hang-jawed. "Are you insane?"

"Look—"

"You think putting us all together would have gotten us to screw?"

"Well, obviously, my plan was a lot more—"

"You really do think we're animals, don't you?"

"I do *not*," Semerjean insisted. "I've given you credit from the very beginning. Please do me the same courtesy."

The wrath in his voice made Mia's heart skip. He took a deep breath, then spoke in a calmer tone.

"All I had to do was convince you that the fate of the world hinged on making children with each other. You would have questioned it, you would have complained about it, but in the end you would have done it. All of you."

He cast a heavy gaze at the frozen smoke plumes in the distance. "And life would have been so much easier for everyone."

Mia waited for her nerves to settle before speaking again. "So what happened?"

Semerjean frowned. "You know what happened. Rebel attacked us. Ruined all my plans and forced me to improvise."

"How did you not see him coming?"

"He had help."

"You people live off predictions. How—"

"He had *help*. Ioni guided him through the cracks in our foresight. That fool would be nothing without her."

Mia wanted to ask him about Ioni, but she suddenly became very conscious of the time. Heath was dying, and there were still plenty other people to save.

"Maybe we should—"

"Yes."

Semerjean flew their platform to the lumics' guild building and peeked inside a third-floor window.

"Well, there he is."

Hesitantly, Mia moved to his side. She could see Heath collapsed at the base of a stairwell, clutching his stomach with bloody hands. Another boy, one Mia had never seen before, lay crumpled next to him.

"Oh my God."

"Barbaric, isn't it?" Semerjean dug into his shirt pocket and retrieved more golden discs. "Two unarmed boys, shot by their own government. There's a reason we call this the Pre-Enlightenment Age."

"Who's that other kid?"

"Harold Herrick," said Semerjean. "The last of Gemma's disparates. It was rather intrepid of Heath to give him my wristwatch. He's not usually that bold."

Mia saw the double coins in Semerjean's fingers. "You're healing both of them."

"Yes. Should I not?"

"Of course you should! I just don't understand you. I don't know who you're here to kill and who you're here to save."

Semerjean hurled the discs through the broken window. They curved through the air like guided missiles before landing on the chests of their targets.

"I'm not sure why I'm healing Harold, to be honest."

He smiled slyly at Mia. "I guess I have a soft spot for lumics."

Her stomach flipped. If he hadn't just made a cruel joke about Yvonne, then he was in complete denial about what he'd done to her. Both scenarios were equally frightening. Semerjean had brought Mia on this journey to get to know the real him. It was working, but not in the way he'd hoped.

She threw a nervous look down the street. "Who's next?"

She stood perfectly still at the edge of the platform, her hands dangling limply at her sides. Mia knew from the moment she returned to the village square that she would see some awful sights, things she'd missed the first time around.

But nothing could have prepared her for the scene at Founders' Path.

A solider lay dead among the flowers, her armor scorched from head to toe. Somcone had cooked her alive inside her tactical gear, but that was nothing compared to what happened to her comrade. The other soldier had been bisected diagonally across the abdomen, a slanted half corpse. Where his lower parts went, Mia had no idea. He'd been cut in two by a closing portal. His legs could have been anywhere within a hundred miles of here.

Semerjean scanned Mia's face as she processed the carnage. She kept so still that she might as well have stepped outside the temporal field, just another casualty of war trapped in still-frame.

"Mia . . ."

"Shut up."

"They'll be fine. They're healing as we speak."

Semerjean wasn't talking about the soldiers, who were far beyond saving. Nor was he referring to Mother Olga, who'd taken a bullet to the back and had perished just a few yards up the path. He was only assuring Mia about the two Gothams next to Olga, a father and son who lay crumpled on top of each other, the blood of their wounds converging in a puddle.

At long last, Mia had caught up with the Pendergens.

Semerjean gestured at the gruesome half soldier. "That's the one who shot them. Managed to put two bullets into each of them before Peter finally retaliated. If he'd been a little more attentive—"

"Go to hell."

"I'm not the one who did this."

"You let it all happen."

Semerjean looked away. "I had to."

"Bullshit!"

"The government was coming for you one way or another," he said. "We did everything we could to throw them off your scent."

"Like *what*?"

"Those bodies they found in that Staten Island movie theater. Who do you think did that?"

Mia glowered at him. "What'd you do, kill us in another timeline?"

Semerjean shook his head. "They were just lab clones. Mindless. Esis grew them all in a day."

Mia looked around at the bodies in the square—men, women, and children, more than she could count. At her accelerated speed, she could barely tell the living from the dead. For all she knew, half of them were still alive and flailing in agony, like that sad little spider that Gingold had crushed.

Semerjean eyed her cautiously. "You want to know why I let it happen? The answer's right there."

Mia's whole body tensed as Semerjean gripped the back of her head. He turned her gaze westward, to the second floor of the recreation center.

She wriggled out of his grip. "I have no idea what—"

"Just look."

With a flick of his finger, the front wall of the building became transparent. Mia saw an armored solider on the second floor, a man who had yet to suffer the Gothams' wrath. He aimed a long round device at the battlefield, like the mechanical offspring of a spyglass and an airhorn. Mia had been around long enough to know what she was looking at.

"A video camera."

"And transmitter." Semerjean pointed at the soldier. "He only pretends to work for Gingold. His real employer is Cedric Cain."

"Who?"

"You'll meet him soon enough. Suffice it to say that he doesn't like what Integrity's become and, unlike us, he has the power to fix it. He's with the president of the United States right this minute, showing him live images from that camera. As one would hope, the president's outraged by the wholesale slaughter of American citizens. By sunset, every top-ranking official in the agency will be removed from power and an interim director will be named. That man?"

"Cedric Cain," Mia cynically guessed.

Semerjean smiled. "He's a long-term thinker. He understands the benefits of a cooperative partnership. He'll immediately extend an olive branch to you and the Gothams. By this time tomorrow, everyone here will be a friend and asset of the United States government."

He swept his arm around the square. "None of that could have happened without this. It's unfortunate—"

"*Unfortunate?*"

"—but that's just the nature of causality. Sometimes you have to step back to move forward. Sometimes you have to make war to create a lasting peace."

Mia gritted her teeth. The Pelletiers had done the exact same thing at Atropos, forced a bloody battle between the orphans and Gothams for the sake of the greater good. *Their* good.

Semerjean read the anger in her eyes. "You still don't get it."

"No, I get it. You want to bring eternal life to your people, no matter who it kills." She jerked her thumb at Mother Olga. "I'm sure she'd understand."

Semerjean closed his eyes, exasperated. "*Shie'tta ju-né.* This was always the hardest part of living with you."

"Me?"

"All of you. I could tolerate your meats and chemicals, your rock-hard mattresses and inane conversations. But what I could not handle, what I still can't bear, is your linear way of looking at things. You people are myopic to the point of blindness. Even your augur can't see the big picture."

Mia scowled at her feet. If she didn't fear for Carrie's life, she might have reminded him that Gemma Sunder almost killed him. The mighty Semerjean, felled by a child and her poison fruit.

He thrust a hand at Peter. "Nobody encapsulates that mindlessness more than that man. Look at him. He rushed into a battlefield with two bound arms and a wounded leg. What was he hoping to accomplish?"

"He was trying to save Liam."

"Yes, and look how well that turned out." He scoffed. "I should have never brought you to him. Every time I tried to advise him, he brushed me aside. 'Don't worry, son, I've got this.' 'Relax, boy. I know what I'm doing.' 'Quiet, lad. You don't know the full story.'"

Mia was neither impressed nor amused by his pitch-perfect impression. "He thought you were a kid. We all did."

"That shouldn't have mattered."

"Well, it did, and it was your own damn fault. You could have come to us at any age. You could have been our leader."

Semerjean hung his head. His voice fell to a mutter. "It was a . . . strategic decision."

"What do you mean?"

He shook his head. "It's not important."

"Just tell me!"

"I didn't want to be an adult around Hannah. I was afraid that . . ."

"What?"

"I was afraid she'd fall in love with me."

Mia's body went rigid. She kept her wide round eyes on the battlefield. Semerjean sighed at her. "Look—"

"Don't."

"I never meant for you to—"

"*Semerjean.*"

Mia closed her eyes in a sickly wince. She'd never called him by his real name before. The feeling was hideous, like she'd cast a dark spell in an old demonic tongue.

She forced herself to make eye contact. "Just finish your damn work already so we can save Carrie."

Semerjean stared at her blankly before nodding. "As you wish."

The platform rose off the grass. Mia studied Semerjean through a hateful squint. She wondered what would happen if she opened up a portal inside his cold, black heart. Would it work? Would it kill him? Or would it only make him mad? Mia pondered the question over and over as they continued through the underland, toward the second name on his kill list.

They were fifty feet above the square when he claimed his next victim. Mia had no idea who Semerjean was dropping. The woman was locked in flying combat with a dragonette, her face concealed behind a shaded black face mask. The moment Semerjean touched her with his long tempic finger, the lights on her speedsuit flickered. Her aeric wings began to lose shape.

Semerjean tapped the drone three times, then retracted his tempis. "Victoria Chisholm."

Mia looked at him. "Huh?"

He pointed a thumb at his target. "That was Victoria Chisholm. In case you were wondering."

Mia had indeed wondered, but she didn't want to ask. She was tired of being horrified by this creature in front of her, with his warped sense of ethics and his unbearable air of supremacy. Were the people of his world just like him? Did their four-dimensional perceptions kill the last of their humanity?

He eyed Mia curiously. "You're not going to ask me why?"

"I know why. She either got in your way or she'll get in your way in the future."

"It's not that simple."

"Yeah. You love saying that."

The platform ascended past the broken face of the clock tower. Semerjean studied the cracks in the glass, a branching array of hard, angry angles that looked like frozen lightning.

"Life will soon be very different here," he told Mia. "There'll be new orphans, new scientists, new government administrators. Some of the Gothams won't be able to handle the change. Some, like Victoria Chisholm, would have upset the delicate balance we've worked so hard to achieve."

Mia looked down at her feet. "You want this place to be a big breeding farm."

"A *volunteer* breeding farm. Everything we'd hoped to achieve in Terra Vista will be done here on a grander scale. We've been building toward this for months."

"So who's your third, then?"

"I'm sorry?"

"You said you had three people to kill. Who's the third one? Rebel? Mercy? Jonathan?"

"No."

"Zack?"

Semerjean's eyes narrowed to slits. "You have no idea what I've gone through to keep Zack alive."

"That's not an answer."

"No, I am not killing Zack. Or Jonathan. Or Rebel. Or Mercy."

"What about Azral and Esis?"

"I'm not killing them either."

Mia shot him a dirty look. "You know what I mean. Do they have their own kill lists? Are they coming after anyone I know?"

Semerjean looked away. "My wife and son are their own people."

"What's that supposed to mean?"

The disc came to a stop in the upper reaches of the underland, all air vents and roof panels. Mia couldn't help but wonder if there was some nefarious reason Semerjean brought her here. What if *she* was the third name on his list?

"What . . . what are we doing here?"

Semerjean sighed with haughty disappointment, as if he had to explain why the Earth wasn't flat.

"See, this is a perfect illustration of what I'm talking about. You look, you analyze, but you never see the whole picture."

"What do you mean?"

"Turn around."

Mia turned around and gasped at the two figures floating behind her. Amanda and Melissa dawdled helplessly above the clock tower, a mere ten yards from impact. Even at 1000x speed, Mia could see the pull of gravity on their bodies. They sank through the air as if it were made of molasses. Their limbs flailed as slowly as minute hands.

"Oh my God!"

Semerjean lowered the platform in measure with their fall. "Yes. They didn't think their cunning plan all the way through."

Mia studied them from the edge of the platform. Their skin was scraped all over. Their clothes were a jumble of rips and bloodstains. While Melissa's eyes screamed in alarm, Amanda's were closed in pain and exhaustion. She must have pushed her tempis to the limit and then some.

Semerjean scrutinized Amanda with a casual look of intrigue. "Huh."

"What?"

"Come see this. It's fascinating."

Grudgingly, Mia joined him. Her heart jumped in fright when Semerjean flicked his hand at Amanda, but all he did was turn the back of her shirt transparent. Now Mia could see what he was talking about: two scaly white formations on her shoulder blades.

"It's tempis," Mia said. "So what?"

"Look again."

Mia took a closer look. On second glance, they seemed more deliberate in design, as if Amanda's subconscious was crudely trying to fashion something. The scales weren't actually scales at all, just a weak attempt at—

"—feathers." Mia gaped. "She's trying to make wings. Does that mean—"

"Oh, yes." Semerjean grinned brightly. For a brief and painful moment, he looked just like David again. "Only ten percent of tempics can biologically generate aeris. Amanda just became one of them."

Mia reeled at the thought of Amanda soaring through the sky like a swan. It seemed so alien, and yet so fitting.

"Can those save her?"

Semerjean chuckled. "They'll barely slow her fall."

"So help her already!"

"I have just the thing."

He pulled a tarnished bronze disc from his shirt pocket and flung it at Amanda. It affixed itself to the back of her neck, then coated every inch of her in a skin-tight sheath of tempis.

Mia shuddered at her eerie new state. She looked completely inanimate now, *lifeless*, like an unfinished statue. "Will that keep her from falling?"

"No," said Semerjean. "It'll keep her from breaking."

He studied his handiwork approvingly, then clapped his hands together. "And now at last my work is done."

The platform descended. Mia looked up at the floating bodies. "Wait! What about Melissa?"

"What about her?"

"Aren't you going to save her?"

"Why would I? Her situation solves itself."

"What do you mean?"

"What do you think I mean?" He motioned to her. "She's the third name on my list."

The flying disc sank eighteen feet before Mia found her voice again. "Why?"

Semerjean pursed his lips. "I've explained it twice now. There are those who have the potential to cause great harm."

"But she saved us. She's a good person!"

"You think this is about good and evil?"

"Yes! She knew there was something wrong with you. She saw it from the moment she met you. We should have listened to her."

Semerjean snorted dismissively. "It's listening to her that gets you killed in the future."

"You're a liar."

"Yell all you want, but consider this: if an 'evil' man like me can fly around saving lives today, then is it not inconceivable that a good woman with good intentions could destroy many lives in the future? Have I not explained how the strings work?"

Mia fought to suppress her rage. The girl she loved was still in need of rescue. If she pushed Semerjean too hard, it'd be all over for Carrie. He'd probably kill her himself and make Mia watch.

But a voice in her head had been haranguing her for minutes, faulting her for letting Semerjean kill *anyone* today.

You still have some influence over him, it insisted. *He cares what you think. He practically admitted it himself.*

"No!"

Semerjean turned to face her. "Excuse me?"

Mia shook a finger at him. "I was there when you first met Melissa. She really got under your skin that night, made you angrier than I'd ever seen you. I don't think that was an act."

Semerjean smiled patiently. "Do tell."

"You lost your cool and then you lost two fingers. You've been mad at her ever since. Nobody loses fingers where you come from."

"Mia . . ."

"They probably don't even have pain."

The platform stopped in front of the clock tower. Semerjean stepped forward, his mouth turned down. The lightning cracks of glass loomed behind him.

"You've spent eleven months with David and only eleven minutes with me. What makes you think you know me?"

"Because it's been a long eleven minutes. And I've been paying attention."

Semerjean laughed. "A fourteen-year-old trying to gauge the mind of a three-hundred-and-fourteen-year-old."

"I thought only vain people put a number on it."

"I'm plenty vain."

"I think you are too," Mia said. "You can lie to me but you can't lie to yourself. There's no strategy behind killing Melissa. You just don't like her."

Time seemed to stop all over again as Semerjean stared at Mia. While a vengeful part of her took pleasure in his displeasure, the rest of her fell into panic.

This is it, she convinced herself. *This is where he kills me.*

After a seemingly endless silence, Semerjean fished into his shirt pocket and removed another bronze disc. He threw the object high into the air, his cool blue eyes never leaving Mia.

By the time she dared look up, a smooth skin of tempis had formed around both women. Amanda and Melissa were nearly indistinguishable from each other in their hard white shells. They looked more like sisters than the Givens ever did.

Mia turned to Semerjean, thunderstruck. "You saved her."

"For now."

"But . . ." Her inner voices screamed at her, begging her not to push her luck. "Why?"

Semerjean mulled the question, his gaze darting around the clamshell hood of the amphitheater. "It's not because you were right about me. You weren't. Furthermore, should you ever be in a position to analyze my wife and son, I strongly advise you don't. I'm the 'people person' in our family. They don't share my tolerance for fools."

He paced the platform with a contemplative expression. "But you made a good point. There's a word that you and the others continually used to describe David, a compliment that never sat well with me. Do you know which one I'm talking about?"

Mia tensely shook her head. She was done making guesses for the day.

"'Brave,'" he answered. "You thought I was courageous in the face of danger, but can it really be called bravery when I was never truly at risk? I have more strength, more power, more insight than all our enemies combined. You all saw me as David, when I was secretly Goliath."

He wagged a finger at her. "But *you*, you risked my wrath over a woman you barely know. You took me on knowing full well what I could do to you."

A genial laugh escaped him. "If that isn't bravery, I don't know what is."

Mia had no idea whether to be flattered or insulted. She kept an eye on Melissa, half afraid that Semerjean would suddenly change his mind again.

"It's all right," he assured her. "You've inspired me to take a less drastic approach with Melissa. I will 'sack up,' as the men here say, and face her on a more level battlefield."

Semerjean tapped his chin in thought. "It's funny. They say what doesn't kill you makes you stronger. You're living proof of that. But where I come from, my people only have one last mortal threat. What will happen when we destroy it entirely? What will we become?"

Mia's shoulders drooped with exhaustion. She had finally reached the limits of her tolerance.

"Look, I gave you my time. I listened to what you had to say."

"Well, that second part's debatable but—"

"Will you *please* save Carrie now?"

Semerjean put his hands in his pockets and flashed her a boyish grin. "I already did."

The platform descended on a quick, slanted path, fast enough to turn Mia's stomach. The moment it stopped, she moved to the edge and looked down. They were just thirty feet above Temperance Street, right where their journey had begun. Stan Bloom lay miserably on the floor of the alcove, his bloody chest lit with a bright, golden healing disc. Ten feet to his right, Carrie remained petrified at the mouth of the alley. There wasn't any trace left of the dragonette or its flame.

Mia looked at Semerjean, stammering. "When—"

"Eleven minutes ago. Right after we started."

"Why?"

He shrugged. "I'd tell you I did it because I care about you, but you wouldn't believe me. So let's just say there's more to gain by keeping her alive."

Mia felt like crying all over again—tears of relief, tears of rage, tears of exhaustion and lament. A hundred new questions piled up on her tongue. They all cleared a path for the king of the lot.

"What do you want with me?"

"I want you to make a child with Liam."

"I *know* that. I'm talking right here, right now. What do you want?"

Semerjean took a lingering look at the tower. "By external clocks, we've now officially spent one second together."

"So?"

He turned his gaze back to Mia. "I want one more."

While the war beneath them continued to rage in microscopic increments, Semerjean and Mia sat quietly on the edge of the disc, their feet dangling high above Temperance Street. By now, Mia had become so numb that she almost found this relaxing. She could have been kicking her legs off an old country bridge, spending a mindless Sunday morning with her old friend David.

"Who's Ioni?" she asked without thinking.

Semerjean leaned back on his elbows, an evincible contempt in his eyes. "Even we don't know for sure. Her powers and technology are alien to us. She's been on this world for more than a hundred years. She arrived with the Cataclysm."

He stared out at the perimeter park. "My son believes she *was* the Cataclysm."

Mia didn't even know how to begin processing that. Her mind fumbled for the next question. "Why Liam?"

Semerjean took a deep breath before answering. "He's a good kid. Smarter than his father. I thought he'd be a good match for you."

He eyed her carefully. "You could always pick someone else."

"I *did* pick someone else."

"Someone who could get you pregnant."

"I don't want to be pregnant."

"That's your choice," Semerjean said. The chill in his voice nearly made her heart drop.

Her fingers tapped a rapid beat on the aeris. "Did you even like us, Semerjean?"

"I like you and Zack very much."

"But not the others."

He flipped his hand in a lazy shrug. "The only one of you I actively dislike is Peter."

"He's done more for me than you ever have."

"Perhaps, but I wouldn't put too much stock in his string theory."

"Fuck you."

"There's no saving this world, Mia, but you can save yourselves."

"Just leave me alone already!"

Semerjean climbed back to his feet. He flanked Mia's side and watched the slow, silent action in the village square.

"As I said, things will be different after today. You'll have peace with the Gothams, peace with the government. And just a few minutes from now, my family and I will make our own peace offering. If you do the smart thing—"

"The smart thing," Mia mocked.

"—you'll have a long and happy future."

Hot blood coursed through Mia's face. She felt another wave of nausea coming on.

"We're not asking for anything untoward," Semerjean said. "Just the opposite. We want to create life to preserve it. That's all this is about."

"I *told* you—"

"I know what you said, and I understand why. But you're the smartest one of the Silvers, Mia. When all the dust settles and all your wounds heal, you'll think about everything I told you today and you'll come to see things my way."

"Why the hell would I do that?"

"Because you've met the real me now. You've seen me at work. There are people I need and people I don't, and you've seen firsthand how I handle both."

Semerjean leaned in closer and gripped her by the shoulders. "Think about the future. Be someone I need."

He walked to the other end of the platform, then brushed the silver disc on the back of his hand. The clock of the world suddenly came unstuck. The underland reverted to normal speed.

Smiling, Semerjean turned to Mia and made a sweeping gesture at the dragonettes, right as they all lost power. They spun toward the ground in whistling synch and then passed harmlessly through the floor of the village.

While the townspeople gasped and whooped in surprise, Semerjean kept his blithe blue eyes on Mia.

"Invasion's over," he told her. "We won."

FIFTY

The Heaven's Gate district of Quarter Hill was the wealthiest development in Rockland County—forty-four mansions on thirty-nine estates, each one owned by a billionaire investor. The place was so lush and ridiculously pretty that Hannah almost felt like she was violating it with her haggard presence. She and Jonathan clearly didn't belong here, but there was no one around to notice. Every resident of Heaven's Gate was a secret member of the Gotham clan, and they were all currently trapped in hell.

Hand in hand, she fled with Jonathan down Ashwin Street, past an endless variety of rose plants and property gates. They had barely made it out of Manganiel's before Integrity reinforcements arrived in dropships. Did the soldiers see them leave? Were they tracking them from a distance? Hannah had no idea. She just knew she had to get back to the underland before the people she loved were murdered.

She stopped at the edge of the Whitten estate and took a deep breath through her nose. "Okay. I'm ready."

"For what?"

"More shifting. Come on."

Jonathan looked into her bloodshot eyes. "You're not ready."

"I'm fine, all right? The headache's gone."

"Bullshit. You look like you just had a baby through your ear."

He checked the map on Melissa's handheld console, then eyed the palatial mansion across the street. "Moot point anyway. That's our stop."

Hannah was hardly surprised to learn that the estate in question was Irwin Sunder's. It was the most expansive lot on the block, with the biggest house, the tallest hedges, and the wroughtiest of wrought-iron fences. Each segment formed a twisting array of metal vines, all ending with flowers and looping around a calligraphic "S."

"God," Hannah muttered.

"Yeah. He's a tool." Jonathan frowned at her. "And to think you gave up your singing for him."

"I didn't do it *for* him."

"No, you did it to spite him. Except he doesn't give a shit, and Heath and I miss your voice."

"Are we really getting into this now?"

"I'm just saying."

He hurried across the street. Hannah scrambled to keep up with him. It was probably a good thing she hadn't shifted again. Her brain was still a ball of fire, and the pain that had begun in her dislocated shoulder had spread like a current across the right side of her body. The only relief she got was from the warm breeze that flowed through Heaven's Gate. She'd been underground so long that she had almost forgotten how good the sun and wind felt.

Hannah studied Jonathan anxiously as he stopped at Sunder's fence. "I'm still freaking out about what Rebel said. If Azral's coming for you—"

Jonathan scoffed. "When has Rebel ever been right about anything?"

"He was right about Semerjean."

"He thought *Peter* was Semerjean."

Jonathan dropped a three-foot section of iron gate, then passed through the opening. Hannah took a last look around before following him onto Sunder's lot.

"Look, if the Pelletiers want us to breed with Gothams—"

"*If*," Jonathan stressed.

"—then you and I are a problem." She toyed with the folds of her makeshift sling. "Maybe we should . . . I don't know . . ."

"Don't."

Jonathan led her through a copse of trees, onto Sunder's vast green lawn. "I'm having a bad enough weekend. I don't need to get dumped."

"You think I want that?"

"No."

"Good," Hannah said. "Because I'm in love with you. You're the first guy in my life who has me thinking long term."

"Then why cut us short?"

"Because I don't want you to die!"

She noticed a tall wooden box in the middle of the yard—a wireless speaker, from the looks of it. Maybe the Sunders had a lot of lawn parties. Maybe Irwin liked to gather up his servants and make them dance for his amusement.

Jonathan threw the speaker a cursory glance before stuffing his hands in his pockets. "So, what's the plan, then? You keep me alive in a big glass jar? What will that get us?"

"Time," Hannah said. "You think I'm the only one who loves and needs you?"

Jonathan closed his eyes. "No."

"Then why risk it?"

"Because I'm tired," he told her. "I'm tired of running, tired of worrying, tired of all the ticking clocks. I'm tired of assholes trying to kill us and I'm tired of making sacrifices."

They crossed the lawn to Sunder's driveway, a winding lane of tumbled white brick. Jonathan fished through his pocket and retrieved the elevator card and access code that Melissa had given him.

"I can't be like them," he said to Hannah.

"Like who?"

"Amanda and Zack. I see the way they look at each other and I know it won't get better. No matter what they do, no matter who they're with, they'll spend the rest of their lives making sad eyes at each other. At some point, you have to wonder what the point is. I mean, are we fighting for long lives here or are we fighting for good ones?"

Jonathan stared up at the sky. "I don't know. Maybe I'm just being selfish. All I know is that I can't give you up, Hannah. Not when I know how you feel. You're the only one who gets to say 'stop.' Not them."

He shook his head bitterly. "Not them."

Hannah bit her lip to keep from crying. All her pains and frustrations were spinning around her mind in a vortex. She could barely form a coherent thought.

"Jonathan—"

"There's another one."

"What?"

He pointed to the music speaker on the far side of the driveway. "Those things must be weatherproof."

Hannah opened her mouth to say something, then felt a sharp twinge in her senses. There was a smoky aura crossing fast into her airspace. It was coming in high and it was big.

"Jonathan!"

An Integrity dropship de-shifted above them, one of the four flying carriers that Hannah had seen outside Manganiel's. The vehicle looked like a stripped-down helicopter—no rotors, no skids, no passenger doors or windows. Just a large open hatch on each side of the chassis.

Hannah barely had a chance to grab Jonathan's arm before six armored soldiers popped out on tethers. She didn't have to look to know that they were shifted, and there was no way to fight them while they were out of reach. She couldn't even run. There was no time to jump on Jonathan's back and accelerate him before the gunmen—

"Now!" yelled the pilot.

Hannah and Jonathan dropped to the lawn and covered their heads while the deafening sounds of gunfire filled the yard.

After eight long seconds, the barrage finally stopped. Jonathan opened his eyes and saw Hannah lying face down on the grass.

"Hannah!"

She raised her head and looked him up and down. He didn't seem to have a scratch on him. "Are you . . . did they . . . ?"

"I don't think so. You?"

"I . . ." Hannah checked herself for bullet holes but couldn't find any. Everything around her looked just as healthy as it ever did—the lawn, the driveway, the music speaker.

"What the hell just happened?"

The soldiers urgently checked their rifle clips, as if some practical joker had replaced their ammunition with stage blanks. If Peter or Mia had been there, they could have told them that their bullets had worked just fine. They simply got swallowed into dozens of portals.

A horizontal disc opened directly above the dropship, fifty feet wide and bright as a moon. Hannah had seen countless portals before, but this one was . . . different. The surface swirled like hurricane clouds, its bright folds turning counterclockwise. It sucked in air with enough force to pull the dropship upward.

The soldiers clutched their tethers while the pilot fought against the vacuum. Even at full throttle, she could only hold the ship in jittery equilibrium: a thrashing tug-of-war between the engines and the portal.

Hannah and Jonathan scuttled backward from the rift as an upward breeze nipped at them. Loose clumps of dirt and grass went flying into the air, as if the gravity of tiny objects had suddenly reversed itself.

"What *is* that?" Jonathan yelled.

"I don't know! I never—"

Hannah suddenly remembered something she'd overheard Peter telling Mia, a warning about time portals. *They may be good for passing notes, but you never want to make one at full size. They'll draw you in and kill you. You and everyone around you.*

"Oh my God . . ."

Hannah frantically looked around. She was hoping that Peter had swung by for a timely rescue, but he'd never be so brutal. There was, however, another man who would.

No . . .

The dropship's engine died a sputtering death. Its liftplates all went dark. Hannah could hear the soldiers' screams as the portal swallowed their ship whole. Its landing wheels had barely vanished before the disc closed shut and the whistling wind came to a stop.

Jonathan clambered back to his feet and brushed the hair from his eyes. A smattering of grass blades fluttered back down to earth like snow.

"Holy crap."

Hannah lost her breath when she saw someone watching them. She fought to speak through trembling lips. "Jonathan, get out of here."

"What?"

He turned his head and saw the source of her terror: a white-haired man at the far end of the driveway.

"Oh." Jonathan's face went slack. "Shit."

He was the only one in the group who had yet to see Azral Pelletier, though he'd certainly heard enough about him. Even Heath, who'd watched Azral choke Melissa in the skies above Atropos, had expounded at length about the man's calm ferocity. If anything, the kid had undersold it.

Hannah rose to her feet and took a defensive stance in front of Jonathan. "Go."

"Hannah . . ."

"Run!"

He shook his head slowly. "That won't do a thing."

Azral floated six inches above the driveway on a thin golden disc, his hands casually tucked into his pockets. As ever, he'd come dressed in a stylish gray business suit, neatly buttoned over a tieless white oxford. And as ever, he wore a cold and haughty look on his face, as if the universe existed solely to annoy him.

Hannah's throat tightened. She took a shaky step forward. "No. Don't you dare."

Azral continued to glide his way toward them, his sapphire eyes locked on Jonathan.

"You never warned me," Hannah said. "You never told me not to entwine with him!"

If Azral heard her, he didn't show it. He had yet to acknowledge her existence at all.

Jonathan pushed the elevator card and passcode into her hand. "Sweetheart, listen to me—"

"No."

"He's giving you the chance to leave."

"No!"

"I don't want you seeing this!"

She ran toward Azral, blocking his path until he was forced to stop. At last, he met her gaze. Hannah had to crane her neck just to make eye contact with him.

"Okay, look. Look. Listen to me . . ."

Hannah stumbled on her words, momentarily thrown. She hadn't stood this close to him since the day her world ended. Once again, he walked the razor-thin space between beautiful and monstrous, like a hungry white tiger, like a holy angel come to deliver God's vengeance.

But there was something else in his expression that she hadn't noticed until now: a howling emptiness behind his eyes. If Azral was human, then he must have been a fanatic of the highest order. For all Hannah knew, he'd been born and raised for just one purpose—the very cause that she and Jonathan threatened. There was no use pleading with a man that obsessed. The only way to sway him was to work within his narrow scope.

"I'll give you what you want," Hannah offered. "You don't have to kill him. I'll give you a baby."

Azral raised a thin white eyebrow. Either he didn't believe her or, worse, she was offering him something he already considered to be his.

Hannah sniffed and wiped her eyes. Her breath came out in frantic wheezes.

"I've been a train wreck all my life," she told him. "But I've never once broken a promise. If you let Jonathan live, I *swear* to you from the bottom of my heart that I won't touch him again. We won't be a problem for you. I'll make a kid with whoever you want."

Jonathan shook his head frantically. "Hannah, *no!*"

She kept her unblinking gaze on Azral. "Read my eyes."

His head tilted five degrees. She finally piqued his curiosity.

"Read my *future*," she stressed.

Her whole inner world seemed to come to a stop as she waited for Azral to respond. No breath, no thought, not even a blink of the eyes. She might as well have turned to plastic in front of him. All she could feel was the prick of goosebumps on her skin, an anticipation of his cold honey monotone.

But Azral didn't speak. He merely turned his head toward the tennis courts for a moment, then retreated down the driveway on his flying disc.

Hannah chased after him. "Wait. Does that mean—"

He disappeared in a globe of light, one bright enough to make her wince. Hannah scanned the front yard through the spots in her vision. All that remained of Azral's portal was a smooth round crater in the surface of the driveway.

"What . . . ?"

She turned around to check on Jonathan, half expecting to see a mangled corpse. Yet there he was: still alive, still standing.

Jonathan closed the space between them, his mouth slack and trembling. His voice creaked out in a broken half whisper. "Why'd you do that?"

"I had to."

"Why?"

"I had to! I love you. I couldn't just let him kill you."

His eyes filled with tears. He turned his head and wiped them with his sleeve. "Goddamn it. I didn't ask you to do that for me."

"Jonathan—"

"You gave your whole life away!"

"Not my life. Just . . ." Hannah wrung her hands, stymied. Her heart was still hammering from her encounter with Azral, and her mind couldn't see past the immediate goal. He was alive. He was *alive*. What the hell else mattered?

"I don't care what you say about living a good life," she told him. "You'd give up your arms and legs to save me. You'd do it for me and Heath and everyone you love."

Jonathan closed his eyes. Hannah gripped the cloth of his sleeve, convincing herself that Azral wouldn't mind. Her inner Amanda grimly shook her head at her. *That's how it starts.*

"We'll find a way past this," Hannah promised. "You and me, together."

"Together?"

"We may not be a couple anymore, but we still get to be together. We still get to be the people we are."

Jonathan chuckled bleakly. "Two lost souls swimming in a fishbowl."

"Exactly."

They stared at each other for a tense and awkward moment before Jonathan looked away. He smacked his fist into his hand. "No. This is bullshit. I'm not going to stand by while you play breeding horse for that piece of shit. He has no right."

"Jonathan . . ."

"He has no right! I'll find a way out of this. I don't care what—"

A sudden *crack* filled the air, like the tail of a whip. Hannah looked around in alarm. It had sounded like someone had popped something—a tire or a balloon or a big fat cherry bomb. Maybe . . .

Hannah spun around to face Jonathan again. He stared at her vacantly, his skin freshly pale, his body teetering on wobbly legs.

"Jonathan?"

Hannah moved in closer and saw a trickle of blood run down the side of his face.

"Jonathan!"

She moved to catch him, but gravity was quicker. He fell to his knees, then collapsed on the driveway. A pool of blood formed around his skull.

"Oh, God. No . . ."

Frantic, Hannah crouched at his side and struggled to turn him over. The moment he flipped, she ran her fingers along his scalp until she felt a warm wetness. The blood seemed to be coming from behind his left ear.

The fragments of Hannah's mind abruptly snapped together. The voices in her head became united in panic. *Somebody somebody somebody shot him. Somebody shot him right in the head.*

She unwrapped her arm sling her sister had fashioned for her and bunched it against Jonathan's wound. She could already feel his blood seeping through the nylon.

"Oh God. Jonathan, hang on. Please!"

Jonathan kept his wide eyes on the sky. His breath came out in shallow gulps. Hannah didn't need Amanda to tell her that he'd gone into shock, or that people with bullets in their heads usually had seconds to live.

"No . . ."

She pressed the jacket harder, her eyes streaming tears as Jonathan began muttering.

"He's not gonna play. He's not gonna play. He doesn't like the feel of it."

Hannah wiped her eyes, smearing fat streaks of blood across her face. "Just hang on. I've got you."

"He doesn't like the feel of the strings. You have to learn. You'll have to . . ."

Jonathan looked at Hannah and for a moment, he seemed to recognize her. His pupils dilated. He clutched her wrist.

"Hannah, please . . ."

"Just hold on!"

"He's not gonna play. You have to learn. You gotta . . . you gotta . . ."

"Jonathan . . ."

"You gotta keep the song going."

His eyelids fluttered. His body seized. Hannah fell backward, then climbed to her feet. There was only one last hope for Jonathan. If she could envelop him in a redshift field . . . yes! She'd saved his life that way before. All she had to do was preserve him in a single moment, keep him in stasis until a turner could come heal him.

She'd just begun to channel her thoughts when Jonathan stopped writhing. His head rolled to the side, he let out a groan and then, with his last shudder of life, he brushed the trigger to his power.

Hannah stood there, paralyzed, as Jonathan dropped like a ghost through the bricks of Irwin Sunder's driveway. His body fell peacefully through the soil and bedrock, past the northern lip of the underland, and straight on through to the heart of the world.

"Hannah?"

She kneeled on the pavement with an empty stare, her arms hanging limp at her sides. Though her mouth was open, she couldn't seem to draw a breath or make a sound. It was as if her throat had been packed with wet cement.

No, not just her throat. All of her. She felt like she'd been hollowed out and filled with something vile.

"Hannah Given."

She only vaguely registered the fact that someone was calling her name, a very familiar voice at that. The man sounded close and disturbingly clear, even though Hannah couldn't see anyone around her. Maybe this was what madness felt like. Maybe her mind had finally cracked for good.

"Come on, Hannah. I know you can hear me."

A pencil-thin passageway opened up in her esophagus. She fell onto her hands and breathed in gasps. As fresh oxygen flooded into her brain, a stray thought came loose from the wreckage. The hole in Jonathan's head had been small, *too* small. Integrity would never use a gun of such weak caliber—nor would they leave Hannah alive. As for Azral, the man needed a gun like a shark needed a switchblade. He hadn't shot Jonathan either.

There was, however, another bastard out there in the world, one who had every motive and opportunity to kill the man she loved.

"Oh, Hannah Banana . . ."

She looked at the music speaker and saw a green light blinking at the base.

"Aah . . ." Hannah tried to speak but her tongue was still twisted. She couldn't seem to remember how to put words together.

Her tormentor snickered at her through the speaker. *"Oh good. You're making ape sounds. That's a big improvement from last time."*

Hannah shot to her feet and took a spinning look around the premises. If there was one thing she knew about Evan Fucking Rander, it was that he always came prepared. He'd be somewhere within eyeshot but not within reach. That meant . . .

She raised her head and saw a two-wheeled Pegasus hovering thirty feet above the tennis court. The aerocycle was one of Harley-Davidson's most illustrious models: the same high-handled, loud-engined, twin-exhaust hopper that movie stars used whenever they wanted to make a showy entrance.

Evan holstered his pistol and raised a microphone to his smiling lips. "And here we go. Helloooo, Saint Louis! Are you ready to *rock*?"

At long last, Hannah screamed. Her voice came out in a high, vengeful roar, one loud enough to scrape her windpipe.

Evan held up his handphone and played her cry back for her. "Perfect! Thank you. I was looking for a new ringtone. There are only so many times you can hear 'Funkytown.'"

Hannah sped toward the court in a shifted blur, her billy club clutched in her hand. She couldn't reach Evan, but maybe she could knock him off that bike of his. She could only pray that he'd survive the fall. She wanted him to be fully conscious when she jammed her thumbs into his eyes.

Evan sighed patiently as Hannah hurled the club. It barely flew ten feet before she doubled over in pain.

"Oops. Looks like someone wrenched her throwing arm." He clucked his tongue. "What happened? You hurt your shoulder again? Did Sister Christian pop it back in?"

Panting, Hannah backed up and faced Evan from the foot of the tennis court. He was dressed in a black leather motorcycle suit, his face half obscured by a carnival mask. He wanted her to see as much of him as possible without letting Integrity get a full look in their ghost drills.

"Come down here!" Hannah yelled. "Face me like a man!"

"Mmm. Yeah. I've been thinking about it and . . . no. But hey, it's nice to see you. Have you put on weight?"

"I'll kill you!"

"Whoa, whoa, hey. I didn't say it was bad weight."

His mocking voice hit her from every direction. He'd set five different speakers just around the tennis court.

"I can't lie," Evan said. "I've been waiting a long time for this. I don't just mean killing Jonathan, which is always a treat—"

Hannah shrieked at him again.

"—I mean *Semerjean*." Evan whooped with exaggerated relief. "I'm so glad I can finally talk about that now. The secret was killing me."

"*They'll* kill you!"

"Who, the Freaky Three?"

"You were supposed to leave us alone!"

"What? No, no, no. You're very confused. I had a talk with Davidjean the other day and he said 'Dude, no more killing Silvers.' And I said 'Dude, what about Golds?' And he said 'Them? Pffft. You'd be doing us a favor.'"

"You're lying!"

"Sweetheart, why do you think Azral left? He saw me in the wings, just waiting to do his dirty work for him."

"We had a deal!"

"A *deal*?" Evan bellowed with laughter. "He didn't buy your act for a second. He took one look at the future and saw you and Jonathan banging all over Freak Street."

"Bullshit! I would have kept my word!"

"Sweet Mother Jesus. It's like you don't even know yourself."

"I know what I'll do when I get my hands on you!"

"You should get your hands on a lozenge first. You sound like Batman."

Hannah ran to the billy club and shifted back into high-speed. Evan rolled his eyes as she smashed one of his speakers to bits. "Hannah . . ."

If she couldn't kill him, the least she could do was shut him up. Unfortunately—

"Hannah, dearest . . ."

—her powers were still strained. A sharp agony flooded her, like ice and barbed wire. She de-shifted on the tennis court and clutched her temples.

Evan shook his head. "Oh, this is just sad. I'm feeling for you. I really am."

Hannah chucked the club with her left arm. It missed the Pegasus by yards.

"Come on, Hannah. This is your *Empire Strikes Back*. You don't get to win this time. Take it like a Jedi."

She suddenly realized that there was no way he could hear her over the growl of his engine, and there was no way he'd miss the chance to delight in her cries. That meant . . .

Hannah ran to another speaker and saw a wireless microphone taped to the back. Of course.

She peeled the mic off the speaker, then held it up to her lips. There was no reason to use a billy club when she could throw her words at him.

"So this is what you do?" she asked him. "Kill every man in the world who's better than you?"

Evan rolled his eyes. "Here we go . . ."

"You've got your work cut out for you."

"You're wasting your time."

"You could murder every last man, woman, and child on this planet—"

"She sets up the zinger . . ."

"—I still won't fuck you."

"And . . . scene."

Hannah gritted her teeth as Evan applauded her from above.

"Not bad, not bad," he said. "Not as good as your last one, obviously. That one . . . yeah. You most definitely got under my skin. It made me careless and it got me in trouble. I . . ."

His smile faded. He stared at the horizon with a tortured expression before abruptly becoming chipper again.

"Anyway, it's all good now. I'm stronger, I'm wiser, and unlike you"—Evan's face lit up in a nasty smile—"I'm having a very good day."

Hannah's face tightened. She could feel her grief overtaking her rage, threatening to send her to the ground and reduce her to a sobbing wreck. But she couldn't fall apart. Not here. Not in front of this worm.

Evan brandished his pistol for Hannah to see: a long-barreled .22 with a targeting scope. "Took me ten rewinds to shoot him in the right part of the brain. My only plan was to get him to drop himself but *Jesus*, the babbling. That was unexpected. 'He's not gonna play. He's not gonna play. You gotta keep the song going.' God. What was that about?"

Hannah stood perfectly still, stone-faced, while Evan went on.

"At some point, someone's gonna ask you about Jonathan's last words. If I were you, I'd lie. Just make up something. Because the truth is just . . . yeesh."

Hannah kept quiet, her mind fumbling desperately. There had to be some way to kill him, something he overlooked.

Evan shrugged. "Hey, look on the bright side: if your next boyfriend's a Gotham, I can't kill him. At least not until—"

A sudden loud noise cut him off, an otherworldly hiss from the front of the estate. Hannah and Evan turned their heads just in time to see a huge portal open forty feet above Sunder's lawn. A metal monstrosity came spilling out the underside: a vehicle. A dropship. It fell to the grass with a clamorous din.

Evan tapped his jaw in nervous thought. "Well, shit."

Hannah didn't have to look too hard to see that it was the very same ship that had nearly killed her and Jonathan. She spied six armored soldiers dangling lifelessly from their tethers. The pilot sat slumped forward in her chair, her skin warped beyond all recognition. She looked like she'd been deep-fried and flash-frozen at the same time.

The implications sent a shudder up Hannah's back. Is that what time travel did to a body? Was that Azral's preferred method of execution—to send his victims screaming four minutes into the future?

The future . . .

Hannah turned around and squinted at Evan. The goddamn bastard was a looper. He knew all of her moves before she did, and had well-prepared comebacks for everything she said. Yet the arrival of the dropship had clearly taken him by surprise.

Evan forced a breezy smile. "Well, if that isn't a metaphor for your love life—"

Hannah ran toward the ship at 9x, the fastest speed she could muster without getting a headache, then disappeared inside. Evan leaned to his left to get a better look.

"Not sure what you're doing, hon, but—"

Hannah burst out of the dropship and rushed back to the tennis court, a dead soldier's rifle in her hands.

Evan looked down the barrel and laughed. "Oh, I get it now. Very nice. Quick thinking. There's just one problem, Boopsie: that's a government-issue rifle. It won't work without—"

His head snapped back as if he'd woken up from a nightmare. He screamed and floored his aerocycle, just as Hannah's new weapon exploded in gunfire.

She already knew damn well that civilians couldn't fire Integrity weapons. She'd learned it the hard way in the basement of Manganiel's. At the time, Hannah chalked it up to her own inexperience. But no, there had to be another trick.

While Hannah was shifted inside the dropship, she'd peeled the glove from a dead soldier's hand and found an interesting-looking ring, an electronic smartkey that would hopefully, God willing, help her rid the world of Evan Rander.

Sadly, the odds still weren't in Hannah's favor. Her right arm was injured, she had no experience with rifles, and her victim had a talent for correcting past oversights. Evan had already fled a hundred yards by the time Hannah got control of the weapon's recoil. With a savage howl, she sent a dozen bullets his way. None of them seemed to hit.

"Fuck!"

"Fuck!" Evan yelled. This was a horrible note to end on, but he was far too rattled to rewind and try again. It was a moot issue anyway, as the dropship was clearly Azral's way of saying "enough."

Evan had just passed the top of the Quarter Hill bulwark when he heard Hannah in his earpiece.

"You were wrong about Jonathan," she told him. "He wasn't babbling. He was telling me to learn guitar so I could play it for Heath, so he can keep bringing back the songs from our world. He knew exactly what he was saying."

Hannah looked at the pool of blood on the driveway, her eyes filled with tears. "His last words were beautiful."

Her voice dropped an octave. "Yours won't be."

She threw the mic to the pavement and crushed it beneath her sneaker. A high-pitched squeal filled Evan's ear. He pulled out the receiver and threw it away.

"Fuck."

Hannah hobbled her way to the bloodstain, then fell back to her knees. She knew that the underland was still in a state of emergency, but she was in no condition to help. All the wrath in her heart had fizzled to smoke, and there was nothing left but sorrow. She could see Jonathan standing on this very spot of the driveway, a wistful smile on his lips.

Two lost souls swimming in a fishbowl.

She buried her face in her bloody hands and screamed until she had no voice left.

A half mile to the south, far outside Hannah's view, a portal opened above the rooftop of Manganiel's. A fiery white figure crashed through the glass, then broke through the floor of the showroom. It continued on its blazing path—through the basement, down the shaft, and all the way to the underland.

The survivors in the village looked up as a streak of light burst in through the ceiling and barreled into the ground like a meteor. The rumble shook every wall and window in the village.

"What was that?" asked a Gotham.

"What was that?" asked a soldier.

"What the hell was that?" Mia asked from her floating aeric platform.

Semerjean peered down at the fresh new crater in Temperance Street, twenty feet wide and deep enough to cut into the tunnels. He closed his eyes with a maudlin sigh, then turned his back on Mia.

"That was my wife."

Fifteen feet below the thermics' guild building, in a long and narrow corridor of storerooms, Zack stood alone under a naked filament bulb. His back was still aching from the stun bolt he'd taken. His whole body moved like he was neck-deep in snow. Even under optimal circumstances, he knew the .38 in his hands wouldn't do a thing to stop the creature that was coming for him.

The walls shook. Dust fell in clumps. Zack saw a bright, flickering glow at the end of the tunnel. Esis had turned a sharp corner, and was now headed his way.

"Here she comes," Rebel said into Zack's earpiece. "Get ready."

FIFTY-ONE

She came floating down the tunnel in a globe of yellow light, her high-heeled boots hovering six inches off the concrete. Gusty winds blew all around her, ruffling her hair, her slacks, her surplice blouse and longline jacket. Without the supernatural embellishments, Esis would have blended in perfectly among the glitterati of this era: a tall and stylish business executive, an aloof but lovely art dealer, the intimidating head of a lumivision network, the uptown socialite whom everyone admired but no one liked.

But all a person had to do was look into her eyes—those pitch-black eyes with the wild, dancing spark in them—to know that Esis Pelletier was . . . different. For Zack, who'd already seen her at her worst, one glimpse was all it took to realize that Rebel was right. She hadn't come here today to save any Silvers. Quite the opposite.

"Hold your position," said the voice in Zack's earpiece. "If you run, she'll teleport. And we need her to cross that corridor."

No one knew what Rebel had been up to these past few days. He'd spent most of the time in the cellar tunnels, preparing for a battle that only a handful of augurs saw coming. The Integrity invasion was just a sideshow. The real threat, he knew, was arriving right on its heels. He saw Pelletiers in his foresight, clear as ice.

More than that, he saw a way to hurt them.

"Esis is the heart and soul of their mission," he'd explained to Zack, a mere two minutes before her arrival. "They can't finish their work without her. If she dies, then Azral and Semerjean have no reason to stay on this world."

"Except to kill us," Zack had said.

Mercy had been stuck on that point as well. Rebel shrugged it off.

"The three of us are on her kill list," he'd insisted. "We're all dead anyway. The best thing we can do is take that bitch down with us."

Esis was a hundred feet away from Zack when she passed the first motion sensor. A vault door next to her retracted on shifted wheels, springing open as quickly as an eyelid. She barely had time to turn her head before an automated turret came to life at 24x and sprayed her with .50-caliber rounds.

Zack watched her, cursing, as the bullets bounced harmlessly off her light enclosure. He had hoped at the very least that she'd throw up a tempic shield and suffer a few hundred psychic stings. But, as always, the woman had come prepared.

The turret ran out of ammunition. Esis looked to Zack with haughty bemusement, as if he'd just tried to kill her with a squirt gun.

"Don't worry," Rebel told Zack. "There's more coming."

"You're an idiot."

"Just stand your ground."

"How about *you* stand here?"

"She'll be seeing me soon enough."

While Rebel and Mercy had both armored up, Zack was stuck facing Esis in a T-shirt and sweatpants. His body was still reeling from Integrity's stun bolt, and the temporis inside him felt as slippery as mud. He had no hope of rifting Esis, nor did he put much faith in the crusty old weapon that Rebel had given him, a .38 revolver that looked more likely to explode than fire.

As Esis continued her gliding approach, a putty bomb went off behind a wall vent, sending flame and debris all around the edges of her lightshield. Another vent blew up, then another, then four others. For six loud seconds, that fifty-foot stretch of tunnel had become hell on Earth, yet Esis passed through all of it like she was drifting through a pleasant dream.

Zack suddenly recognized the yellow glow of her force field, the first form of temporis he'd ever seen. It had emanated from his silver bracelet eleven months ago, just as the sky came down on his native Earth. Whatever that stuff was, it was strong. Strong enough to withstand an apocalypse.

"This won't work," Zack muttered into his collar mic.

"Yes it will," Rebel told him. "Just keep your gun ready."

Esis was forty feet away now, close enough for Zack to see the wrath in her eyes. Another vault popped open next to her. Another cannon came to life. This one looked more like a giant gas nozzle than a conventional weapon. Whatever it fired was invisible to Zack.

"Solis," Rebel said. "Refashioned it from a government drone."

"It didn't do shit."

Rebel studied Esis on his monitor. Her force field continued to operate at full strength. It didn't even flicker. "Huh."

Mercy grabbed the microphone from him. "Zack, get out of there."

"No," said Rebel.

"That was our last trick! Go!"

"Do *not* leave," Rebel ordered. "Wait till she gets closer."

"And do *what*?" Zack asked.

Esis stopped ten feet in front of him and lowered herself to the ground. If anything, Rebel's buffoonery had turned her rage to amusement. She regarded Zack with idle curiosity.

"Why?"

The .38 dangled at Zack's side. He had to fight to keep from firing it at her. All he'd do was embarrass himself.

"Why what?" he asked.

"Why put your trust in that insipid ape? He's caused you nothing but pain."

Zack scoffed. "He's still better than you."

"Better," Esis mocked. "What a strange perspective you have."

"She takes one more step, you shoot her," Rebel growled.

"I've given Richard more than enough reason to hate me," Esis said. "But what drives you?"

"You're seriously asking?"

"I could have locked you all in prison cells, forced you to copulate with people of my choosing. You would have never seen the sky of this world, and yet *I* was the one who gave you freedom. I gave you *life*, Trillinger. And what do I get for my generosity?"

Zack gaped at her. "Holy shit. You really are crazy."

"*Why?*" Esis stepped forward. A thick vein pulsed on her temple. "Why must you make my work so difficult?"

"Now, Trillinger! *Shoot* her!"

"Run!" Mercy yelled.

Zack aimed the revolver, his eyes moist with tears. Both Rebel and Esis had lost their minds, and Mercy's advice was . . . impractical. He had no hope of escape, no hope of surviving. All he could do was steal the last word of the argument.

"Because you destroyed my world," he said in a choked voice.

He pulled the gun back and pressed it to his temple. "That's why."

Mercy screamed. Esis lunged forward. Zack closed his eyes, cast a silent apology to Amanda, and then pulled the trigger.

Esis tilted her head, confounded, as the weapon made an unexpected noise: a high-frequency hum that only she could hear. The soundwaves passed harmlessly through her energy bubble, then sent her nervous system into discord. Her shriek forced Zack to open his eyes again. The gun hadn't even clicked. Yet somehow, despite all logic and reason, it had caused Esis immeasurable pain.

He popped open the gun chamber and saw complicated circuitry where bullets should have been.

"What the hell's going on?"

A gritty laugh filled his earpiece. Rebel had acquired the weapon four days ago, an apology gift from a cagey old friend. Though he would sooner kill her than trust her again, this Ioni Anata T'llari Deschane, Rebel was an angry man in a desperate situation. He'd put his last ounce of faith in her, and was duly rewarded.

Rebel watched Esis through his monitor, still laughing as she writhed and howled inside her force field.

"What did you do to her?" Mercy asked.

Rebel wasn't entirely sure. Ioni had spouted off some garble about a disease called terminus and its many effects on Esis. One of them was an aversion to a very specific sound frequency.

The noise won't kill her, Ioni had warned. *It'll just weaken her. The rest is up to you.*

Rebel wouldn't have it any other way.

The shield around Esis flickered out of existence. Rebel kicked his door open and burst into the corridor, a Remington MP in his hands. The pump-action shotgun was nowhere near as elaborate as Zack's weapon, but it fired a hell of a lot more than soundwaves.

Frantic, Esis covered herself in tempis just as Rebel's first slug exploded against her chest. She screamed and flew back into a wall.

Rebel pumped his gun and shot her again. "Rift her."

"What?"

Zack could barely hear him over the thunder of the Remington. Between his near-death trauma and his screaming tinnitus, his mind was stuck in painful stasis. He couldn't shake the feeling that killing Esis was a mistake—not morally, but strategically. They had a rare and golden chance to sway the minds of all three Pelletiers, and Rebel was squandering it on a vendetta.

"Goddamn it, Trillinger. *Rift* her!"

Mercy charged into the tunnel, her brow flecked with sweat. Though she fired enough solis to melt a hundred tempic skins, it didn't do a thing against Esis. Her necklace, like Semerjean's wristwatch, provided complete immunity to Mercy's power.

Rebel shot another slug at Esis before she could get up. "Your gun," he yelled at Mercy. "Keep pounding away at her shell!"

Esis thrust her hand and cast a barbed tempic whip. It tore off a slice of Rebel's leg armor, along with a patch of his thigh.

He pumped his rifle and moved in closer. "That's all you got?" He shot her again. *"That's all you got?"*

"M'itta-ke né!"

Esis shifted into high speed and disappeared in a blink. The others looked up and down the tunnel.

"She's still here," Rebel said. "She's lumiflaged. She can't—"

A tempic blade cut the back of his neck. Rebel bellowed and spun around. Between him and Mercy stood a barely visible entity, a shimmering patch of air with a womanly shape.

Zack's face went white as Rebel aimed his Remington at the blur. "Wait!"

"Don't!" Mercy yelled.

Esis ducked out of range, just as Rebel fired. The slug tore through Mercy's armor and shredded half her chest.

"No!"

While Zack rushed to catch her, Rebel turned around and fired again. He didn't need to see his targets to hit them. When his foresight worked, it guided his arm through the spectrum of future possibilities. It told him exactly where to aim when he wanted to draw blood, even from an invisible swifter.

Esis shrieked as the slug hit her square in the chest, in the flimsiest part of her tempis. Her sternum cracked. She spit up blood. Her lumiflage and armor withered away.

Rebel pumped his gun for a kill shot, but it was out of ammo. Esis hobbled down the corridor at 15x.

Cursing, Rebel threw down the Remington and unholstered his .44. By the time he aimed it, Esis had already disappeared around a corner.

"Goddamn it!" He kicked Mercy's gun over to Zack. "Come on. We can still catch her."

Zack peeled off his tattered T-shirt and pressed it against Mercy's wound. She stared up at the ceiling in trembling shock, wheezing.

"I can heal her."

"Forget it. There's no point."

"She's not dead!"

"We're *all* dead," Rebel shouted. "You're just wasting time."

"Oh, shut up already! Just shut up! You're just as bad as Esis."

"Coward." Rebel ran after his quarry, his gruff voice trailing behind him. "You're fucking useless."

Zack threw him the briefest of glares as he disappeared into the tunnels. "Asshole."

Mercy's gasps became louder, coarser. Zack could see that she was slipping. There was no time to stabilize her. If he didn't heal her right here, right now, she was lost.

She's lost anyway, said a grim voice in his head. *Rebel was right. None of you are getting out of here. You could have at least tried to fight.*

Zack gritted his teeth and focused. Maybe he *was* a coward, or maybe he was just being stubborn. If the universe had driven any point into his head, it was that human existence was a brief and fragile thing. Every life mattered. Every moment mattered. And that went double for Mercurial Lee.

"Hang on," Zack told her. "I got you."

He jumped to his feet and waved his bloody hands over Mercy, until her body glowed and the wheels of time began to turn the other way.

"I got you."

FIFTY-TWO

A portal swirled open on the black granite face of the guild directory. Peter emerged from the stone and took a nervous look around. He'd only been gone for forty-one seconds, yet sometime during his absence, an overwhelming hush had washed over the square. Everywhere he turned, his people walked dazedly through the smoke, staring or crying or searching for loved ones. Tempics gathered dead soldiers into a big, messy pile. Turners moved between the bodies of their kinsmen, checking to see if there was someone, anyone, who still had a pulse.

Under different circumstances, Peter would have been one of the many corpses here. But his bullet wounds had healed. He could feel his blood replenishing itself—an unpleasant sensation, like ants beneath his skin. He only had to touch the golden disc on his chest to know why he and his son were still alive, why all the drones had vanished. The Pelletiers had ended the invasion, but not before dozens of innocent people were killed. As far as saviors went, Semerjean and company stood on a par with the Old Testament God— petty, selective, and utterly inscrutable. Peter didn't take much comfort in the fact that he and Liam were on their good side, especially if Zack was right about what they wanted.

A young voice filtered out of the portal. "Dad, please! I can help you!"

"I'll be all right," Peter told Liam. "You just rest, love. I'll be back in a bit."

"But—"

Peter closed the portal behind him, then moved deeper into the square. The first thing he'd done upon regaining consciousness was teleport Liam to Montauk, Long Island, to the opulent beach house where the Varnovs spent their summers. He'd already watched his son take two bullets to the chest. He'd be damned if he exposed Liam to any more danger.

"Goddamn it!" yelled a woman in the distance. "I said *help* her!"

Peter looked to his left and saw Shauna Ryder chasing after a turner, her twin sister dangling in her arms. Sadly, there was nothing to be done for poor Angela. The girl was a nonentity on the portal network. Her traveler's light had been permanently extinguished.

Clearly Shauna could sense it as well, yet she persisted in haranguing the healer. "Bastard! Why won't you save her? Why—"

A dozen Gothams gasped when an armored soldier, one of the many rooftop marksmen that Harold Herrick had blinded, fell screaming off the top of the municipal building. Peter looked up and saw a young blond swifter at the edge of the roof.

"Stop that!" he shouted. "They're not a threat anymore!"

The swifter gave him an obscene gesture, then disappeared in a blur.

Another howl turned Peter's head. Twenty yards to the south, an Integrity operative struggled in Sunder's tempic grip. A crowd of angry Gothams quickly gathered around him.

"Please," said the soldier. "I'm on your side!"

Sunder scoffed at him. "*Our* side?"

"I work for a man named Cedric Cain. He wanted me to film the invasion so he could show it to the president. We're trying to *save* you!"

"You think we're idiots?"

"No, I swear!"

Shauna dropped Angela's body, then lunged at the captive soldier. Her fingernails dug into his cheek. "Monster! You killed my sister! You *killed* her!"

"I didn't kill anyone!"

"Stop it," Peter barked. "All of you."

He could feel the hot stares of everyone around him, and he had a good guess why. He wore the clothes of a man who'd been riddled with bullets, yet he didn't have a visible scratch.

Sunder was the first to notice the shiny disc on Peter's chest, the unmistakable magic of the Pelletier family. "They healed you. What are you to them?"

Peter winced. "Irwin—"

"Have you been one of them all this time?"

Shauna Ryder attacked the soldier again. Another sniper was pushed off a roof. The crowd around Peter became restless, angry. Only Prudent Lee kept a level head.

"Please! If everyone would just—"

"*Stop.*"

The voice seemed to come from all directions. A heavy black shadow washed over the square. Everyone looked up to see a huge floating head near the top of the dome, a lumic image of someone they all recognized. He was more than a celebrity to the clan. He was something of a messiah.

Theo stood on the roof of the lumics' guild building, with Heath and Harold at his side. Like Peter, the three of them had been brought back from the brink of death by Pelletier wizardry, and it showed. Their faces were jaundiced and they could barely stand straight. But the moment Theo found the boys, he put them to work. While Harold projected Theo's image, Heath directed eight tempic men toward a group of wounded soldiers. One by one, they picked them up and carried them down Center Street.

"I understand that you're angry," Theo told the Gothams. "You have every reason to be. I can't even give you a moral argument for saving these people. All I can tell you is that Integrity isn't going away. A door's been opened that can't be closed, and we're all going to have to live with them."

Theo looked up and grimaced at the sickly sight of his doppelgänger. Of all the days to become a big floating head . . .

"I've looked to the future and I see good things," he said. "Everyone behind this invasion will be held responsible for their actions, and the agency will fall under new management. *Better* management. We'll have a new arrangement with the U.S. government that'll give us full freedom and protection. More than that, Integrity will help us with our biggest problem, the one that affects every life on this planet. They'll work day and night to help us stop what's coming. We *need* them."

Twenty feet below his specter, in the half-wrecked crest of the clock tower, Amanda and Melissa fluttered back into consciousness. They stared up at Theo in a moony haze, unsure if he had grown or they had shrunk.

"But if we kill anyone else, it'll all come undone," Theo cautioned. "So we have to find each and every one of these people, heal the ones who are hurt, and then send them out through portals. I know you don't like it, but it's the only way forward. Our future depends on it. Please."

Theo gestured at Harold. The lumic transmission ended. He watched from the roof with bated breath as Heath's tempic men brought the wounded soldiers into the square. Theo half expected the Gothams to ignore him and start hacking the men to pieces.

But no one made a single move against them. The healers in the square traded nervous looks, then began relieving the soldiers from Heath's men.

Holy shit, Theo thought. *They're doing it. They listened to me.*

Jun Lee had told him just minutes before that even a false messiah had power. He was right.

Two hundred yards away, in a narrow alley off Temperance Street, Mia and Carrie stared up at the sky. They had just reunited when Theo began his Wizard of Oz impression. The moment he vanished, Carrie pulled Mia into a hug.

"Thank you."

"For what?"

Carrie looked at the alcove at the end of the alley. Though her father remained unconscious, a healthy color had returned to his skin. His chest rose and fell steadily.

"Semerjean," Carrie said. "He wouldn't just save my dad like that. You made him do it."

Mia lowered her head with a maudlin expression.

"What happened?" Carrie asked. "Did he hurt you?"

"No. I just . . ."

She was so upset, she could barely speak. Hardly a minute had passed since Semerjean left her. His very last words had left her thoroughly wrecked.

"It's Zack," Mia said. "Esis is gonna kill him."

Carrie gasped. "Oh no!"

"He's down below somewhere. I have to find him!"

"Mia . . ." Carrie grabbed her by the shoulders. "Listen to me. I know those tunnels inside and out. There's a hatch right here in the library."

Mia wiped her eyes. "You should stay with your dad."

"You already helped him. This is where I help you."

"Carrie—"

"Look, I'm not just doing it because I owe you. I like Zack."

She cupped the side of Mia's face. "And I love you."

It felt like the guiltiest indulgence of Mia's life, to share a kiss with her girlfriend while Zack was in trouble. But she was fourteen, she was in love, and the day hadn't destroyed her yet. She was alive. She was alive and Carrie was alive, and for a single moment, everything in the universe felt right again. Even the Pelletiers had their place in the great cosmic scheme, and Mia was okay with that. More than okay, actually. She knew in her heart that Semerjean was the only one who could save Zack from Esis. All Mia had to do was convince him.

She stroked Carrie's hair, then flicked a finger at the wall. "I love you too."

A six-foot portal opened up on the brickface. Mia clasped Carrie's hand. "Let's go."

FIFTY-THREE

There were a hundred and fifteen storage vaults in the tunnels, most of them filled with emergency supplies. Some had been converted into special purpose rooms. Others had devolved into miniature junkyards. The Gothams were free to leave their unwanted items anywhere. There was no mayor of the under-underland.

Deep in the northeast corner, directly below the vivery, was a storage room filled exclusively with mirrors. They'd been stashed there by the hundreds: wall mirrors, door mirrors, hand mirrors, car mirrors, antique mirrors with gilded frames, cheap novelty mirrors with funny messages on them. They leaned against the walls in dusty stacks, every one of them cracked or deformed in some fashion.

If Mercy had been awake, and if she'd cared enough to explain it, she would have told Zack that the turners once used those mirrors for reversal practice, as silver glass was notoriously difficult to rejuvenate. The guildhall had become so cluttered with warped mirrors that they were forced to move them to the undercellar. No one had set foot in the vault since 1998, when Lucas Rall and Shelby Tam came down there for an art project and ended up conceiving their son Duncan.

For Zack, who'd spent more than enough time being surrounded by mirrors, there was no worse place to stop. But he was lost in the tunnels and the woman in his arms was only getting heavier. He had little choice but to set Mercy down until she woke up.

If she woke up.

Zack lifted her arm and checked her pulse again. It had been two minutes since he healed her dying body. Though her shotgun wound had become nothing but a memory, her breathing was still labored. Her eyelids fluttered like she was lost in a bad dream. Was this a temporary side effect, or did he completely botch the job?

Doesn't matter, he supposed. *Esis will be here any second.*

He sat against a mirror and held Mercy's hand. It seemed a perfectly awful time to realize what a good thing he had going with her. She was funny and clever and strange in all the right ways, and she had genuine feelings for him. But he couldn't let go of Amanda and he couldn't let go of his pride. He had to live his life on his own terms, or at least pretend that he was. And what did he get for his bold defiance? What the hell did it earn him?

Every mirror in the room flickered as a glowing white portal opened up in midair. Zack jumped to his feet, his wide eyes fixed on Esis as she stepped through the surface.

She had clearly done some healing over the last few minutes. Her cuts and contusions had all but vanished, and she once again walked like a healthy woman. The only lingering sign of damage was a shuddering twitch in her eyes, as if the wires in her brain were still being mended. Rebel had certainly done a number on her. Zack could see from the wet, dripping blood on her fingers that she'd already paid him back in spades.

"Damn," Zack said. "Guess you won."

Esis crossed the gap between them, uncomplacent, unamused. From the looks of her, she was done gloating, done bantering, done toying with her prey. She was done with Zack Trillinger and all his smarmy back talk.

But if he could trouble her just one last time . . .

"*L'ua tolla shii hoh-no kiesse,*" he said.

Esis stopped in place, confused. "What?"

Zack had no idea what he'd said to her. He'd heard Esis yell it at Azral once, and he remembered all the syllables. He knew he only had one shot at surviving: to distract the hell out of Esis, and then rift her twisted heart.

He channeled all of his temporis into his right hand, then thrust it at her chest. It had been a Hail Mary move on his part, a rather futile one at that. He could feel his energy bouncing off of her, like water against a wall. Esis had come here with the express purpose of killing him. Of course she'd be prepared for his power.

Zack's heart hammered as she moved within arm's length. A part of him wanted to beg for Mercy, but he knew that would go as well as his temporal attack. His stubborn ego demanded he go out with a zinger, but he couldn't find anything even remotely funny to say.

"You'll never get what you're looking for," Zack told her. "You'll die on this world."

If Esis was thrown or even bothered by his insolence, she didn't show it. She merely pressed a finger to his neck. He winced in anticipation of the cool, hard tempis that would be tearing through his throat.

"*Ma'nétta*," Esis hissed. "And good riddance."

"Wait."

Zack opened his eyes to see Semerjean emerge from the portal, a large armored figure slung over his shoulder.

Rebel, Zack realized. *Is he still alive?*

Esis turned around and eyed her husband balefully. "Don't try to dissuade me. That time is long past."

"I just want a minute," Semerjean insisted. "After that, he's all yours."

Rebel woke up on Semerjean's shoulder, then began thrashing in protest. His skin was covered in welts and gashes. Blood seeped from his shattered nose. The man had been out of his depth against one Pelletier. He'd never stood a chance against two.

The moment Semerjean threw him to the ground, Rebel rolled onto his back and pulled a .44 pistol out of his holster. Semerjean lashed out with a tempic tendril, knocking the gun into the hallway and breaking two of Rebel's fingers in the process.

"All right, Richard."

He lifted Rebel by the neck, then shoved him against a wall. A thick stack of mirrors came crashing to the floor.

"That's quite enough."

He ran a tempic spike through Rebel's shoulder, pinning him to the wall.

"Stay there, please. I'll deal with you in a moment."

Semerjean closed the portal behind him, then took a somber look at Zack. "So here we are."

"Here we are," Zack echoed. "You fucking asshole."

"Yes. I've already received my fair share of invective from Mia."

"Is she okay?"

"She's fine. The danger has passed."

"Good." Zack gestured at Mercy. "I suppose I can't convince you—"

"No." Semerjean stooped to examine her. "Without you, she has no value to us. Quite the opposite. She's disrupted our work one too many times, and would disrupt it again in the future."

He looked to Zack with a softer expression. "But I'll give her a quick death and I'll wait until after you're gone. I owe you that much."

Zack balled his hands into trembling fists. He had to fight to keep from screaming.

"I warned you," Semerjean said. "I'd told you for months that you were on a fatal course, but you didn't listen."

Esis frowned at her husband. "Nor did you, when I told you this was inevitable."

Semerjean scoffed. "As you can see, Zack, your situation has caused some friction in our marriage. When it comes to you Silvers, we rarely agree. I want Evan dead. She prefers him alive. She wants you dead. I still think you can be useful to us."

He shrugged his shoulders before pacing the floor. "But there are only so many times I can plead your case, and so many times you can undermine my faith in you."

"*L'ua tolla shii hoh-no kiesse*," Esis said with droll humor.

Semerjean nodded glumly. "You threw those words at my wife without knowing what they mean. Would you like me to tell you?"

Zack crossed his arms and turned away. "I really don't give a flying—"

"It means 'The time has come to mourn his passing.'"

"Christ." Zack chuckled bitterly. "That's even dumber than I'd thought it would be."

"You brought this on yourself."

"*You* brought this on me! If you didn't want us 'entwining' with each other, you shouldn't have made us coed. You shouldn't have put me with Amanda at all! Where's your goddamn foresight?"

Esis snorted vindictively at her husband. "At last, he speaks sense."

Semerjean ignored her. "You remember the first words I ever said to you?"

"Which you?"

"The day I gave you your bracelet."

Zack lowered his head, indignant. He had moments to live. He didn't need to go delving through old traumatic memories. "'Any other weekend, you'd be one of the Golds.'"

Semerjean nodded. "That's right. It was always our plan to put you with the New York group. But the crucial day came and we were faced with a last-minute vacancy in the Silvers. You just happened to be in San Diego, attending that silly convention." He threw his hands up. "My wife foresaw the conflict. I promised her I'd keep you and Amanda under control."

He walked the floor in circles, crunching mirror shards beneath his shoes. "I've made mistakes, Zack, but you can't say I didn't warn you. You charged into this with your eyes wide open."

Zack followed him with fierce gray eyes. "'The time has come to mourn his passing.'"

"I'm afraid so."

"How do you say it for seven billion people?" Zack asked. "How did you say it when you destroyed my world?"

"*Zhii-tah no-ma!*" Furious, Esis thrust a tempic tendril at him. Semerjean stopped it before the bladed tip could impale him.

She eyed her husband hotly. "*Se'tel nu'hassa mé?*"

"*Mei'tel la'dassa nüe.*" Semerjean looked to Zack with downcast eyes. "That was an unintended consequence."

"But not unforeseen," Zack guessed. "You damn well knew that people would die."

"The technology we used was brand-new. Unprecedented. If Azral had two or three more decades to perfect it, our travels would have been gentler. But we didn't have that kind of time."

Zack shook his head, his voice cracked with strain. "Two whole worlds. Billions of futures thrown away, and for what? So you could make a couple of mutant babies?"

"You know nothing," Esis snapped. "Two Earths are *nothing* in the infinite spectrum. A minuscule sacrifice."

"Yeah, well, they're everything to us."

Zack peeked into a mirror and saw Rebel struggling against the wall. He was using his prosthetic hand to fumble for something on his vest: a black metal tube with a pull pin at the top.

Amazing, Zack thought. *He never gives up. Never stops fighting.*

He turned back to his captors. "Guess I'll die without ever understanding you people."

Semerjean sighed at the floor. "I tried explaining to Mia. She didn't understand."

"Of course not," Zack said. "You broke her heart."

"I never meant to."

"That's because you don't understand us. You've been so focused on the big picture that you can't even see what you did to us. You destroyed our world, changed the rules of the universe, and then put us in constant danger. And you have the nerve—"

"Zack . . ."

"You have the *nerve* to act surprised when we got too close to each other. *You* did that!"

Semerjean rolled his eyes. "For Heaven's sake . . ."

"You made us a family when you took away everything!"

"Just stop."

"Stop *what*?"

"I'm not talking to you."

Semerjean threw a tendril over his shoulder and snatched Rebel's grenade. He dissolved it in a fist of mortis.

"Richard, Richard, Richard. Why do you persist?"

"Because you killed everyone he ever loved," Zack said. "What did you think he'd do?"

The Pelletiers ignored Zack and approached Rebel in unison. Semerjean grabbed him by the scalp and lifted his head into eye contact.

"Zack may be annoying, but I respect him. When Amanda's not around, he thinks very clearly. He adapts to his circumstances, puts aside his vendettas for the greater good. How else could you have gotten him to cooperate with you?"

"But *you*," Esis said, "you're incorrigible. You show no more thought than an avalanche."

Though Rebel shot a murderous look at his enemies, he didn't make a sound. Zack could only guess from the skewed alignment of his mouth that his jaw had been shattered.

Semerjean yanked Rebel from the wall and dangled him by the nape of his neck. "I can't lie. I was really looking forward to killing you today. But then you went and did something interesting."

Esis conjured an image of an old, rusty revolver, the same one Zack had used to break her force field. "There's advanced machinery inside this weapon, alien to us. I can only assume that the Lady Deschane is still aiding you in your struggle."

"No doubt," Semerjean said. "And that's bad news for you, Richard, because we have plans for that woman. You're going to help us draw her out of hiding."

Rebel made a guttural sound, the closest he could come to cursing.

"Oh, don't worry," Semerjean said. "We don't need your cooperation. We only need you to stay alive and suffer. She'll do the rest."

"If she cares," Esis added.

"If she cares," Semerjean repeated. "There's only one way to find out."

He opened a new portal in the middle of the room.

"We already have a cell for you. I'm afraid it won't be very comfortable."

Esis gave him a crooked smile. "But you will have time to reflect."

Zack's stomach dropped. He struggled to channel his power. Esis and Semerjean were immune to his temporis, but Rebel wasn't. All it would take was a rifted heart to spare him the torture of the mirror room. The man had suffered enough already. It was time for him to rest.

Zack's concentration was thrown by a sudden noise—a low, gurgling chuckle. Esis and Semerjean looked at Rebel with furrowed brows. Despite his broken mouth and horrid future, he'd somehow managed to smile. His mechanical hand contracted with a *whirr*, until only his middle finger was extended.

Semerjean looked to his wife with groaning eyes. "Even now, the idiot—"

"Sehcouer!"

Zack had already noticed the sluggishness of Rebel's prosthetic, as if something was gumming up the hydraulics. What he didn't know was that Rebel had stuffed ten ounces of Wild-9 explosive into his wrist, then set a detonation pulse to a very specific hand gesture.

It was the very last trick Rebel had up his sleeve, and it was a good one.

His arm exploded with a fiery roar. Half the mirrors in the vault fell crashing to the ground, along with Semerjean and Esis.

The shock of the explosion nearly stopped Zack's heart. Gasping, he studied the casualties on the floor. Rebel lay near the entrance in a motionless heap, his body twisted and blackened beyond recognition.

Esis was in much better shape. Though her clothes were torn and splattered with blood, the rest of her seemed perfectly fine. Her foresight had only given her a half-second notice of the hell that was coming, enough for her to grow a tempic skin.

She melted her armor away, then grimaced at the mess.

"Ju'a nonné-se . . ." She looked to Semerjean. *"Amora?"*

Semerjean cursed in perfect English as he clambered to his knees. Unlike Esis, he'd lost nearly all his precognition to terminus. He had no idea what was happening until he heard his wife scream.

Esis looked at him in horror. "My love!"

"Huh?"

He cast a mirror image of himself, then let out a cry. His face and chest had been cut up by metal shards. His right arm had been burned on one side and shredded on the other.

Semerjean raised his hand and eyed the stumps of his three missing fingers. "No! *No!*"

Screaming, he jumped to his feet and reversed Rebel an hour. Though the temporis was more than enough to restore Rebel's body, his mind and soul—the very parts of him that Semerjean wanted to hurt—were irretrievably lost. He'd gone to a place where even the Pelletiers couldn't reach him. He had escaped them for good.

Semerjean smashed a mirror in rage. *"Zhii-tah no-ma béyoe nüa!"*

Esis tried to examine his wounds, only to get pushed away. *"No gu'e eillá na-ho-niel!"* she yelled.

"Li'zhii t'ua ha-já! Ellon-è! Ellon!"

Just when Zack thought (or hoped, at the very least) that the two of them would come to blows, they suddenly remembered his presence.

"Don't," Semerjean warned him. "Don't you *dare* say a word!"

Esis waved her hand in a taut circle. A ball of light enveloped her and

Semerjean. By the time Zack unshielded his eyes, they were both gone, along with a big round chunk of the floor.

"God . . ."

He looked at Rebel, resting peacefully on the concrete. His lips had formed a hint of a smile, as if he'd planned all this from the very beginning.

"You crazy shit," Zack mumbled. "That was one hell of a stunt. Wherever you are, I hope you saw their reaction."

He sank to the floor and breathed a tired sigh. "Hope you and Ivy are having a good laugh about it."

Zack reached out to Mercy and checked her pulse again. She was still alive, thank God, but he couldn't imagine for one minute that—

A spherical portal filled the center of the room. Semerjean and Esis returned in a flash. Their clothes had changed. Their wounds were healed. They even looked well rested, as if they'd spent two weeks recovering from Rebel's bomb.

In point of fact, they'd taken five.

Semerjean plucked some lint from his sleeve, then bathed Zack in a charming smile. "Let's try this again."

Four hundred feet away, in a dank and narrow passage beneath the cottages of Freak Street, Mia and Carrie abruptly changed direction. They'd been wandering aimlessly through the tunnels when Rebel's bomb went off. The thunderous noise was all the compass Mia needed.

"Are we sure we're going the right way?" Carrie asked Mia. "That sounded like government stuff, not Esis stuff."

Mia clasped her hand and kept running. She could feel the powerful presence of a three-dimensional portal in the distance. There was no doubt about it. The Pelletiers were up ahead, and so was Zack.

Hang on, Mia pleaded. *Just hang on.*

"Zack, I don't think you're listening to me."

He wasn't listening at all. Between the ringing in his ears and his many scattered thoughts, Zack didn't have the space to process Semerjean's blather.

Half the voices in his head howled madly in panic. The other half shouted ill-advised strategies. *Rift them! Hurt them! Sweep them in the legs! Run out to the hallway and grab Rebel's gun!*

"Zack!"

He stared up at Semerjean from his perch on the floor. *"What?"*

"I said you made a good point. We've had some time to think about it and we realize you were right. We *don't* understand you."

"Jesus Christ." Zack closed his eyes, exasperated. "Just shut up and kill me already."

Esis looked at her husband skeptically. *"Ju'a no-ecù."*

"It's all right," Semerjean said. "He has yet to see, but he will."

Zack took a quick moment to study Esis, all the curious new aspects of her appearance. Her hair had been straightened. Her skin bore a healthy tan. Most jarring of all was the change in her expression: a new peace of mind, a *sanity*. Wherever she went on her twelve-second vacation, it had done her a world of good.

Semerjean created an elaborate tempic bench, then sat down in front of Zack. "Where Esis and I come from, they call this age the *Gel'lebrantia*: the Pre-Enlightenment Era. It began in 1912 with the introduction of temporis and ended four hundred years later, when humanity finally abandoned its linear perceptions and became true multidimensional beings."

Zack snorted derisively. Semerjean cocked his head. "What?"

"'Two Earths are nothing in the infinite spectrum,'" Zack echoed. "'A minuscule sacrifice.'"

"Those were my wife's words to you."

"Yeah." Zack shot a seething look at Esis. "That's 'enlightenment.'"

Esis paced behind Semerjean, her face a stoic mask. *"G'hie ma'tta no-lün."*

"Did she forget how to speak English?"

"I respectfully asked her not to engage you," Semerjean said. "If you have any sense of self-preservation—"

"Self-preservation?"

"—you'll keep a civil tongue."

"Fuck civil. I already know you're going to kill me."

"Perhaps not."

"What?"

Semerjean smiled teasingly. "Do I have your attention now?"

He created a second tempic bench out of thin air. Zack climbed off the floor and warily faced him from the other seat.

"I was wrong," Semerjean confessed. "I thought I understood you people, but I was just fooling myself. I don't know what it's like to have your limited perceptions, to live life one string at a time. I don't know how it feels to have my world destroyed, or to worry that each day is my last. I used to get so angry at you and the others for not thinking logically, but I realize now that I was putting an unfair burden on you. I was expecting you to act like rational beings when your circumstances have given you every reason not to."

Zack looked away, scowling. A less civil man might have told "David" where to stick his condescending apology.

Semerjean crossed his legs and took a casual gander at Mercy. "You did a remarkable job, by the way."

"What?"

"Your girlfriend. Your healed her beautifully. No rifting. No over-reversing. No long-term side effects at all that I can see. You've really evolved with your power." He turned to his wife. "Isn't that impressive?"

Esis pursed her lips with grudging politeness, as if she was being asked to praise the drawing of a dear friend's toddler. "Yes. Very nice."

Zack rubbed his aching temples. "What do you *want* from me?"

"We want you to make a child with Mercy," Semerjean told him. "That's all we ever wanted from you."

"So take our goddamn DNA and—"

Semerjean flipped his hand. "I already went over this extensively with Mia. I'm not explaining it again. Suffice it to say we want a natural conception."

"Except you gave up on us."

"*You* gave up," Semerjean said. "The moment you figured out what we wanted, the strings changed for the worse. There was almost no chance of you and Mercy cooperating with us. This is why we were discreet about our plans. This is why David existed at all."

He waved his finger and summoned four images into the air, the hazy ghosts of Zack, Amanda, Mercy, and Peter. "Fortunately, I've had time to rethink my strategy. I came up with a solution that even Esis accepts, a formal arrangement with no hidden caveats."

Zack didn't like where this was going. "What are you talking about?"

Semerjean enlarged the lumic images of Zack and Amanda. "I'll be honest. I don't understand this obsession you two have for each other. But since these feelings of yours keep hindering our plans, and since our current approach has proven ineffective, the best we can offer is incentive."

"Incentive," Zack parroted. "You mean we get to keep living."

"Better," Semerjean said. "You get to keep each other."

He smiled at Zack's blinking disbelief. "I understand that you're—"

"Bullshit."

"—skeptical. But it's really quite simple." Semerjean pointed at Mercy. "Two nights a month, when she's at peak ovulation, you try to conceive a child with her. And two nights a month, when Amanda's at peak ovulation, she tries to conceive a child with Peter. The rest of the time, the two of you can be together. You can live together, sleep together, entwine to your heart's content—"

"As long as you're careful," Esis stipulated.

"As long as you're *very* careful," Semerjean stressed. "We would be extremely displeased if you got Amanda pregnant."

Zack leaned back and examined Semerjean's benches, these elaborate constructs with slats and bolts and lavish Gothic "ironwork." Amanda had once joked about the ridiculously ornate things David would make if he were a tempic. She had him pegged. Even now, she had the son of a bitch pegged.

"This is the offer we should have made to you weeks ago," Semerjean said to Zack. "It's the best course for all of us. If you agree—"

"Fine."

"What?"

"I'll do it," Zack said. "I can't speak for the others, but I'm in."

The room fell quiet. Esis narrowed her eyes suspiciously. "He lies."

"I'm not lying."

"He has no intention of honoring the agreement."

Semerjean stood up. "Love—"

"He accepts too quickly!"

Zack threw his hands up. "You're giving me the choice between death and two girlfriends. How much time do you think I need?"

The Pelletiers stared at him inscrutably a moment before Semerjean roared with laughter. Even Esis couldn't escape the humor of Zack's retort. A slanted smile curled her lip and, before she knew it, she was guffawing with her husband.

Mia crept down the tunnel, baffled by the nearby sounds of laughter. She was just about to peek into the mirror vault when Carrie clutched her arm.

What? Mia mouthed.

Carrie pulled a cracked hand mirror from the wall and gave it to her. Breathless, she kneeled on the ground and aimed the glass by the doorway. Her heart lurched when she saw Rebel's corpse in the reflection, just six feet inside the room. A twist to the left revealed Semerjean, Esis, and Zack. Only the Pelletiers were having a mighty laugh. Zack looked ready to stab them both.

"You see?" Semerjean said to Esis. "I told you he was funny."

Zack gritted his teeth. "Fuck you. How would you like it if I forced you into an open marriage?"

"We already have one," Semerjean said. "And you should be more grateful. A minute ago, your death was assured. Now you have your life *and* Amanda."

Mia had barely had a breath to process their conversation before a woman's voice hailed her from the periphery of her senses.

"*Mia . . .*"

Puzzled, she looked to Carrie and whispered. "Did you hear that?"

"Hear what?" Carrie whispered back.

Zack rose from the bench and furiously paced the floor. "I don't even know if Amanda and Mercy will go for it. I wouldn't blame them if they didn't. It's their bodies. Their sacrifice."

Semerjean sighed. "Zack . . ."

"And what about Hannah?" Zack asked. "You gonna make the same offer to her and Jonathan?"

Semerjean's expression turned glum. "I would if I could."

"Why can't you?"

"Because Jonathan's dead," Semerjean told him. "He died seven minutes ago."

Carrie covered her mouth with a quivering hand. Mia had to fight the urge to run screaming into the room, clawing and punching at Semerjean's face. *Asshole! You knew he would die! You knew it the whole time you were talking to me!*

"Mia, listen to me . . ."

There it was again, that woman's voice that came out of nowhere. Mia looked to Carrie a second time.

"She can't hear me," the stranger told Mia. *"None of them can. You have to listen very carefully or more people will die."*

Zack grabbed a car mirror and threw it to the floor. Glass shards spilled across the concrete.

"Why?"

"I didn't kill him," Semerjean insisted.

"You *chose* him! You brought him into our lives!"

"*Ioni* brought him into your lives. If we had our way, you would have never met him."

"Fuck you!"

"It's Evan you should be angry at. He's the one who killed Jonathan."

"With *your* blessing."

Semerjean shook his head. "I sanctioned no such thing."

"Well then, it was your wife or your freak of a son."

Semerjean raised a stern finger. "Careful."

Esis's hands frosted over with tempis. "You will *not* disparage Azral."

Mia tried to follow the action through her mirror, but the reflection was . . . changing. Soon the glass became filled with an entirely different image: a pretty young face that Mia had seen once before. They had met briefly last September in an Ohio public library, this strange and chatty girl with two watches on her wrist.

Ioni met her baffled stare with a look of nervous urgency. *"Mia, listen. We don't have much time. An opportunity has come up and we have to take it."*

Carrie eyed Mia anxiously as she raised the mirror to her face. "What are you—"

"Shhhh!"

"It's all right," Ioni told Mia. *"I'm shielding you and Carrie from the Pelletiers' senses. But it won't last long. You have to work fast."*

Despite Ioni's assurance, Mia couldn't bring herself to speak. All she could do was stammer silently.

"Look to your left," Ioni told her.

Flustered, Mia looked to the wall. Ioni winced. *"Sorry. I mean your right. My view's all backward."*

Mia turned her head and saw what Ioni was referring to: a .44 revolver, the one that Semerjean had knocked out of Rebel's hand.

"You need to take that gun right now," Ioni said.

"And do what?" Mia asked.

"What?" Carrie asked.

"I know this is hard, sweetie, but you have to believe me. Inside that gun is the bullet that kills Esis Pelletier. I was hoping that Rebel would be the one to fire it, but he's gone now. It has to be you."

Somewhere, a million miles away, Zack continued to argue with Esis and Semerjean. A fat bead of sweat rolled down Mia's back, and she couldn't stop thinking about Jonathan. Like a phantom in her head, he warned her that there would be consequences to shooting Esis. Even if Mia somehow succeeded, she'd still have the wrath of Semerjean to deal with. And if she missed . . .

"There'll be blowback," Ioni admitted. *"But I have the power to protect you. The moment you fire that gun, I'll teleport you and Carrie and everyone else you care about to a safe location. The game will change, but it won't end today. You have to trust me, Mia. Please!"*

Esis raised her voice. Mia could tell right away that Zack was infuriating her again.

"The window's closing!" Ioni said. *"Do it!"*

Carrie's bright eyes went perfectly round as Mia reached for the .44. "What are you doing? Are you crazy?"

"Aim it," Ioni yelled. *"Aim it and shoot!"*

No one noticed Mia as she stepped in front of the doorway and raised the gun in both hands. Ioni had masked everything: Zack's eyesight, Esis's foresight, Semerjean's razor-keen senses. For a brief, hot moment, Mia existed outside the rules of continuity, a glitch in the software. Time itself seemed to hold its breath as she fixed the trembling gunsight on Esis.

"*Higher,*" Ioni urged. "*It has to go through her brain.*"

"I can't do this . . ."

"*You have to.*"

"He'll spend the rest of his life hunting me."

"*No he won't. You're only killing Esis in one string. And it's through this string that we'll save everyone.*"

"I . . ."

"*Mia, in four seconds, all hope will be lost. For you and Carrie and everyone else in the world.*"

"But how do you know?"

"*Three . . .*"

"This feels wrong!"

"*Two . . .*"

"Please!"

"*One . . .*"

"Goddamn it!"

Mia closed her eyes. She thought about Jonathan. And she fired.

All at once the universe seemed to come apart. The noise of the gunshot shattered her hearing. The recoil sent her tumbling backward. She bit her tongue so hard that she nearly forgot everything else that was happening around her. She was blind, deaf, senseless, helpless.

"Mia?"

She forced an eye open and looked up from the floor. Zack and Semerjean stood perfectly still, both equally shocked by her sudden presence. Mia swiveled her gaze to the right, toward her designated target. It had been just minutes since she'd gotten her first look at Esis. She'd been nothing but a harmless ghost then, a visual aid that Semerjean had created.

Now the real thing was standing right in front of her: surprised, unharmed, and very, very angry. Mia thought she'd missed her mark until she saw a two-inch portal hovering closely in front of Esis's head.

She caught it, Mia realized. *She caught the bullet. She—*

Something big and hard crashed into Mia—lifting her off her feet before shoving her against a wall. She looked down and saw Semerjean staring up at her. He held her high against the concrete, his blue eyes cutting into her like lasers.

"*What have you done?*"

"Mia!" Zack ran for her, but was held in place by Esis's tempic hand. A long white blade hovered menacingly in front of his heart.

"What were you *thinking*?" Semerjean asked Mia. "What on earth possessed you to—"

"*S'ua tolla shii hoh-no kiesse,*" Esis snapped.

"No!" Zack yelled.

"No," Semerjean said. "Not her. Not now. Not until I understand why."

He saw the broken hand mirror in the corridor, then winced in revelation. "Oh, Mia. Mia, Mia, Mia. You were supposed to be the smart one."

"Stop it!"

The temperature dropped fifty degrees. Carrie stumbled into the vault, her hands raised high, her breath coming out in puffs of mist. Semerjean depowered her with a quick wave of solis, then turned his furious attention back onto Mia.

"You were misled. Ioni played you for a fool, and now . . ." He chuckled in surprise. "You were my favorite. I didn't think there was anything you could ever do to make me angry."

His smile faded. His voice dropped to a guttural growl. "But you just found a way."

Blood trickled from Mia's mouth. She fought to speak through quivering lips. "Go on. Do it."

"Don't!" said Zack. "If you kill her, you'll never get anything out of us! We'll never c—"

Esis covered Zack's mouth with tempis. Semerjean kept his hot stare on Mia. "He makes a good point. We've been relying too much on violence as a corrective tool. It doesn't seem to help us. It only provokes more foolish acts of vengeance."

Tears blurred Mia's vision. She'd stumbled her way into a whole new nightmare and she wanted to take it all back. She wanted to roll herself up in a stick and mail herself back to the past.

"You disappoint me," Semerjean continued. "But then it's my own fault for being surprised. You're just a child. All this time, that's all you've ever been."

Semerjean dropped her back to the ground, then tossed a somber look at his wife. *"La'beho no-mé."*

Esis freed Zack, but not before slicing a superficial wound across his chest. He yelled in pain and tumbled backward to the floor.

Semerjean joined her side. "Our son requests our presence up above," he told the others. "So we take our leave. But before we go, I need to make something perfectly clear."

He flicked his hand at Carrie, enveloping her in a gossamer glow.

Shrieking, Mia ran for her. *"No!"*

Semerjean held her back with a tempic tendril. Mia could only watch through teary eyes as the temporis reduced her girlfriend to a fuzzy silhouette. Carrie twisted and writhed inside her bubble of light, her limbs flailing so fast that they barely looked human. If she was screaming, Mia couldn't hear it. She couldn't hear anything over the sound of her own cries.

"Carrie!"

The glow dissipated. Carrie fell to her hands and knees. Thin wisps of steam rose up from her back. She moaned in discomfort, but there wasn't a scratch or blemish on her. Against all of Mia's expectations, the girl was still very much alive.

But something wasn't right. Carrie's hair was twelve inches longer now, and tied in a ponytail. Her funeral dress had been replaced with a pink T-shirt and summer shorts. More than that, she was . . . smaller. Mia had spent many hours wrapped in the arms of Carrie Bloom, and those were not hers.

She struggled to break out of her restraint. "Carrie?"

Carrie rose to her knees on her circle of carpet, then looked around in confusion. Her voice was an octave higher than usual. Her teeth were lined with metal straighteners.

"Who . . . who are you people? Where's my mom?"

"Carrie, it's me!"

She looked to Mia with the eyes of a stranger, then shrank away from the blood on her shirt. "What am I doing here? What—"

Carrie saw Rebel's corpse and fled the room in a panic. Her shrill screams echoed all the way down the corridor.

"Carrie, *wait!*"

"Stop," Zack said. He'd known what was happening from the very beginning. He had felt the temporis work its cruel magic on Carrie, erasing away the last two years of her life. Every spark of growth. Every hard-earned memory.

"There's no point chasing her," Semerjean told Mia. "She's twelve years old. She doesn't know you anymore."

Zack looked away with sorrow and disgust. "Bastard."

"Bastard? I could have taken her life instead of just a fraction of it. It would have been no less than Mia deserved."

Semerjean moved to her in a shifted blur. His fingers clamped around her chin, forcing her to look up at him.

"Every time you see that girl, I want you to remember the kindness I showed here today. Next time you cross me, I won't be so generous."

He pointed a stern finger at Zack. "That goes double for you and Amanda."

Esis waved a flat portal on the far side of the room. As she accompanied Semerjean toward the light, her voice filtered into Mia's ear like a spectral hiss.

"Fair warning, child. That bullet you fired at me will return one day." She turned around at the portal and smiled teasingly at Mia. *"You won't like where it goes."*

Hand in hand, the Pelletiers vanished into the disc. Zack waited for it to close before he finally exhaled.

"Jesus."

Mia stood motionless among the mirrors, her body so rigid that Zack had to look twice to make sure she was still breathing. He wanted to ask her if she was okay, but the question seemed moot at the moment, even cruel.

Exhausted, he sat on the floor and rested his head in his hands. Soon Mia joined him in his repose. They stayed that way for several minutes, never speaking or moving until a stuttered cough broke the silence.

Mia watched with dead eyes as Zack tended to the other survivor in the room, a woman of some importance to him. Mercy was coming back to the world, and Mia didn't care at all.

FIFTY-FOUR

Sixty-eight minutes after the invasion began, the Gothams formally took back the village. The surviving soldiers were herded into the square, where they were stripped of their armor, healed of their injuries, and then thrown screaming into a portal. One shove was all it took to send them thirty miles north, to a huge, empty parking lot on the eastern side of the Hudson. As the soldiers recovered from the pain and shock of their first spatial jump, they looked around and found themselves standing outside a half-wrecked megadome, the aerport that had once been known as Atropos.

Once the living invaders were removed, the Gothams began disposing of their less fortunate enemies: a hundred and twenty armored corpses, including the mastermind behind the attack.

Melissa emerged from the municipal building in time to watch Gingold tumble lifelessly into a portal. The tempics had gathered the bodies into a pile and were shoveling them like coal into the breach. *Barbaric*, she thought. But was it any more detestable than what Integrity had done to them? How on earth did Cain ever expect to make peace with these people?

Amanda joined her on the front steps and took a gawking look around the square. By now, every dead Gotham had been covered with something: a sheet, a blanket, a crumpled black blazer. She could see at least forty casualties, and this was just one part of the village.

"God . . ." She studied the nearest draped cadaver, a woman she would have recognized as Elder Rubinek. "We were too slow to save them."

Melissa shook her head grimly. "We couldn't have done it any faster."

Amanda scanned the faces of the nearest survivors. The only two she recognized were Irwin Sunder and Prudent Lee, and she had no interest in talking to either of them.

"We have to find the others," she told Melissa. "Zack—"

"Hey!"

A middle-age Gotham made a beeline for them, her wrathful attention fixed on Melissa. "You don't belong here!"

She was a tall brunette of Asian and Irish descent, a striking woman under normal circumstances. But now her hair was a mess and her black gown hung in tatters. Amanda had never laid eyes on her before. All she could tell from her immediate senses was that she was a tempic and she was hysterical with grief. That was never a good combination.

Amanda stepped forward. "Okay, calm down."

"Calm down? My husband's dead!" The woman pointed at Melissa. "These monsters shot him right in front of me!"

"Melissa had nothing to do with that," Amanda said. "She risked her life to save you all."

"Says who, the *breacher*? You think I trust you after everything you've done?"

Amanda gritted her teeth. "Look—"

"You people walk with Pelletiers. You destroy everything you touch!"

A spiky skin of tempis grew over Amanda's hands. The woman matched her glove for glove. "Just try it. *Try* it. Give me an excu—"

She froze in horror at something behind Amanda and Melissa. They turned around and saw exactly what she was staring at: a white-haired man hovering thirty feet above the ground, his feet planted firmly on a floating disc of gold.

Amanda had no trouble recognizing him. "Oh no . . ."

The last time she'd laid eyes on Azral Pelletier, they'd been four miles up in the sky. Now here he was below the Earth's surface, looking as cold and ominous as ever. Though his entrance was far less dramatic this time, it was clear from the way he hovered over the square that he wanted to be seen. He dawdled on his disc with his arms crossed patiently, as if he had all the time in the world.

One by one, the survivors looked up. Theo and Heath paused at the East Street junction. Prudent Lee cringed at the base of the fountain. Peter watched from the edge of the southwest gardens, his body crouched at the side of a half-covered corpse. From a distance, the poor dead girl had looked exactly like Mia. Luckily, she was someone else's tragedy. He'd barely had a chance to feel guilty about his relief when Azral arrived and broke his train of thought.

Heath grabbed Theo's arm and pulled him back a step, as if that would somehow protect him from the tall, scary man. "What's he doing here?"

"I don't know."

"Is he gonna kill someone?"

Theo had no idea. As ever, the Pelletiers moved through the blind spots in his foresight—invisible, unpredictable. All he could feel was a sharp and painful absence, as if a face had been cut out of all his family photos. He only had to do a cursory scan of the future to see who was missing from it.

Oh God. Jonathan . . .

Theo looked at Heath with round, trembling eyes. There'd be hell to pay when the boy found out. Theo couldn't tell him. Not here. Not now. Not until Azral did whatever it was he came here to do.

A portal opened above the guild directory. The Gothams in the square let out a collective gasp as Semerjean and Esis emerged. They drifted through the air on small aeric platforms, then flanked their son on either side. A faint smile curled Azral's lip—a *proud* smile, as if there was no greater sight in creation than the three united Pelletiers.

Melissa stared up at Semerjean, stupefied. She suddenly figured out what everyone hadn't told her about David. "You're kidding me . . ."

Amanda locked her hard gaze on Esis. "Where's Zack?" she growled. "I know you can hear me. If you killed him—"

"He lives," Esis assured her. *"You'll see him soon enough."*

Once again, the woman spoke in echoes, a temporal whisper sent directly into Amanda's ears.

Semerjean joined their quiet conference. *"In a moment, my son will speak. You may feel the urge to interrupt him with one of your sanctimonious tirades. I wouldn't advise it."*

Amanda's back frosted over with spiky tempis. She thought of Yvonne, then hissed a curse she hadn't used in sixteen years. "Fuck you."

"Careful," said Semerjean. *"I'm in a bad mood and I never much liked you."*

"Yeah?" Amanda's voice quavered. "Well, I loved you."

Semerjean looked away with an uncomfortable expression. *"Just be quiet and there'll be no more deaths today."*

The trio hovered silently for another minute, allowing their audience more time to gather. Most of the Gothams had already left the village by now, leaving their strongest ten dozen to deal with the aftermath. They trickled in from the outer streets, their anxious eyes locked on the Pelletiers. Only a handful fled in mindless panic. The rest were either too tired, too angry, or too curious to leave.

Soon nearly every survivor in the village had assembled in the square—a hundred and fifteen Gothams, two Silvers, one Gold, and a former federal agent. They looked up at Azral with rapt, anxious attention as he raised his hand high.

A fluorescent glow enveloped the broken clock tower. The minute hands turned backward with eerie speed. Glass, wood, and metal fragments flew out of nowhere and melded into the framework. By the time Azral finished, the structure had been restored to full health. He'd even set the clocks.

The crowd was still looking up when Esis swept her hand and teleported something onto the grass: a shiny silver satchel at Amanda's and Melissa's feet. Puzzled, they stooped to examine it. The case sprang open before they could even touch the latch.

Melissa jumped back. "Goodness."

Curious onlookers formed around the two women as they examined the satchel's contents: reflective silver discs, at least a hundred of them. They were all the size of dollar coins, completely featureless except for their varying inscriptions.

Melissa pulled one from the top and furrowed her brow at its small engraving. "'Heart failure.' What is this?"

Amanda had a strong guess. She'd been the first of the Silvers to experience a Pelletier healing disc. Now it seemed she had a whole case of them at her disposal. If the inscriptions were accurate, then there were cures for every kind of malady, from blunt force trauma to temporal rift damage. Amanda even found a disc that purported to cure cancer.

Esis stared down at her with a sly half grin. "Those devices will work on anyone, but only you can activate them."

"Use them wisely," Semerjean told Amanda. "There will be no replacements."

With a thrust of his hand, he delivered the third and final blessing. Everyone turned their heads and squinted as an interrogation tent became enveloped in a blazing dome of light. Four seconds after it began, the glow dissipated, revealing thirty people standing on a smoldering circle of dirt. They were all dazed-looking youths in white silk loungewear, all thoroughly unfamiliar to Melissa and the orphans.

The Gothams, however, recognized them immediately. They'd been snatched away by Pelletiers in the middle of last August, as leverage against the clan's surviving prophets. No one expected to see them again except for Prudent Lee. She'd been waiting for this moment for a very long time.

She staggered toward the abductees, her glistening eyes locked on one of them. "Sage!"

A dark-haired teenager turned around and eyed her warily, as if she were just a cruel illusion. "Mom?"

She pulled him into a weeping hug. "Oh, my boy. My boy . . ."

Sage brushed the tears from his eyes, then reeled at the state of the village. "God, what happened? Where's Dad? Where's Mercy?"

Prudent held him tight. "They're fine. They're fine. I'll explain everything."

The other freed prisoners slowly staggered through the crowd, like sleepwalkers, until each of them was found by a weeping spouse or relative.

Theo watched the reunions from a distance, suspicious. The Pelletiers never did anything out of the goodness of their hearts. They were buttering up their audience, smothering them with kindness when they were weakest and most vulnerable. Theo didn't need his foresight to know that a soft sell was coming.

A gentle hum filled the square from above, loud enough to turn everyone's attention back on Azral. He straightened his collar, cleared his throat, and then at long last addressed the people.

"We give these gifts unconditionally."

Though he spoke at conversational volume, his voice reached every ear in the village. Carrie Bloom paused at the front of the vivery, confounded, while her father cocked his head on Temperance Street. Harold Herrick listened from the stall of a lumic guild bathroom. Even the four living souls in the tunnels—Zack and Mia, Mercy and Jun Lee—heard him loud and clear. They all looked up in muddled perplexity.

"You've all suffered greatly today," Azral continued. "We sincerely regret your pain. The United States government has forced us all into an intolerable situation, but now the conflict is over. Though their soldiers and scientists will continue to be a part of your lives, there'll be no more oppression. No more violence. A bright new day begins for all of us."

While Azral spoke, Peter saw Amanda in the distance and teleported to her side. They hugged like they'd been apart for months.

"Where's Liam?" Amanda whispered.

"He's safe. You see any of the others? Mia?"

"No."

Peter frowned at Azral. "Maybe we should go looking instead of listening to this gobshite."

Amanda shook her head. She knew the best thing they could do for Zack and the others was stay right here where the Pelletiers wanted them. The bastards were determined to put on a show, and they wouldn't take kindly to walkouts.

Azral waved an image into the air, a rotating hologram of a planet that only vaguely resembled Earth. Though its seven continents were easily recognizable, the oceans were filled with thousands of tiny land masses. Black dots peppered the cloudscape over North America and Europe.

"There are fourteen trillion people on the Earth of our era," Azral said. "Technological advances have provided us with unlimited resources, as well as endless options for habitation. We have cities in the sky, cities on the water, cities at the highest mountaintops, cities on the ocean floor."

He glanced up at the dome, still flaring the Heavensend's restart message. "We have thousands of cities buried deep below the earth, ones far more sophisticated than this."

His expression turned solemn. "It's a wondrous age my family and I live in. It saddens us that this world will never see it. The damage that's been done here is . . . irreversible. Even we don't have the power to heal it."

Testy mutters coursed through the crowd. Melissa gripped Amanda's arm. "Did he just . . . did he just say what I think he said?"

Amanda and Peter closed their eyes. More telling than their gloomy expressions was their complete lack of surprise. Melissa looked around and saw that she was the only one here who'd been blindsided by the news.

"How long?" she asked.

"We'll explain it after—"

"How long do we have?"

"Four years," Azral informed her. "Approximately."

Melissa turned around to find him staring right at her. A shiver ran down her back. Though she'd lost all memory of their last encounter, high in the skies above Atropos, she'd watched the dash-cam footage that Cain had recorded. She saw the look on her face when Azral choked the life out of her.

He turned back to the crowd. "We don't know the exact day this string will fold. There are endless variables that affect the timing. All we can say with certainty is that the end is coming and there's no way to stop it. In four years' time, this Earth will perish."

He flashed a coy grin at the people down below. "But that doesn't mean you have to."

While the audience mumbled in tense discord, Semerjean caught movement out of the corner of his eye. He looked to the north and saw a lone figure emerge from the Sunder family elevator.

The last of the Silvers had finally returned to the underland.

Hannah shambled down the walkway like one of the living dead. Her hair hung down in matted clumps, shrouding her eyes and making her oblivious to her surroundings. If there were still snipers terrorizing the village, she didn't know and she didn't care. She was in no condition to fight.

Azral studied Hannah briefly before continuing. "We have the means to bring a thousand people back to our homeland, and more than enough space to shelter you. There's a city buried deep below the Mantiqueira Mountains of Brazil that's gone unused for decades. Though its infrastructure is antiquated by our standards, it would be a self-sustaining paradise for you and your people. You'll have privacy and independence, limitless provisions, and full control of your environment. Your society could thrive there for generations to come."

Theo crossed his arms skeptically. *Here it comes.*

"This is no small gift we offer you," Azral said. "And we do not give it freely. There are conditions. To the natives of your clan, you must accept and embrace the people we've brought to your world, the ones you call 'breachers.' It's of the utmost importance that you keep them in your community. Your very survival depends on it."

All Gothams near Amanda turned their leery eyes onto her, while another twenty stared at Theo and Heath.

Semerjean's voice filtered into Theo's head like a second set of thoughts. *<Sorry,>* he teased. *<Didn't mean to ruin the whole messiah thing you had going on.>*

Theo seethed at him from the back of the crowd, disturbed but not surprised that the Pelletiers had a neural connection with him. They'd been pirating his premonitions from the very beginning, using his power to see the future from a different angle.

<You ruined a lot more than that,> Theo sent back.

Semerjean's smile deflated. *<Our offer's genuine. If you want to be a real savior, you'll convince these people to accept it.>*

<I would . . .>

<But?>

<But you're a piece-of-shit liar and I'll never trust you again.>

Semerjean hunched his shoulders in a surly shrug. *<Go on, then. Put all your faith in Ioni. I only hope it works out better for you than it did for Mia.>*

Theo's heart lurched. *<What are you talking about?>*

Fifty yards away, outside everyone's notice, Hannah stopped at the north edge of the square. The last time she was here, Integrity had the whole place under siege. Now the goons were gone and the Pelletier family, whom she hadn't seen together since she was five years old, floated serenely above the center of town. None of this made sense, but who knew? Maybe it was all just part of the same long nightmare. Maybe she would wake up any second now and find Jonathan sleeping next to her.

"What we ask is very simple," Azral declared. "We want you to conceive children with these breachers among you, the ones who are here and the ones who'll arrive shortly."

Heath looked to the north and saw Hannah at the mouth of an alley. His mouth fell open as he processed her appearance: the blood on her clothes, the grief in her eyes, the empty space all around her. She was alone. She'd gone to war with a good man at her side and she came back alone.

"No . . ."

Hannah caught his gaze, weeping, as Heath fell to his knees. He hid his face behind his wrists and turned his head violently back and forth, back and forth, as if he could shake the news away. Just shake it, shake it, shake it until the whole story changed. Shake it until Jonathan Christie came marching back into town, a guitar on his back and a grin on his face.

Heath gripped his hair and let out a whimpering moan, the saddest sound that Theo had ever heard in his life. He snapped out of his neural trance and followed Heath's vacant stare to Hannah. One look at her face was enough to crack his heart to pieces. He'd never seen her so devastated, and he'd met her seventeen minutes after the world ended.

Azral continued to explain the terms and benefits of his proposal, only marginally aware of the disruption at the back of the crowd.

"The children you produce for us will come to no harm," he assured everyone. "They will not be used for unscrupulous purposes. Quite the opposite. Your help will ensure—"

"No, no, no, no . . ."

Esis raised her aeric platform until she could see the sobbing boy in the distance, the last of the Golds.

<Ahmad,> she told her husband and son. *<I'll silence him.>*

Semerjean's eyes bulged as an old mistake suddenly caught up with him. He looked at Heath's wrist, then raised a hand at Esis. *<Wait—>*

"*No!*"

Every heart in the crowd jumped at Heath's bloodcurdling shriek. He'd done everything in his power to be strong and resilient—to face the world like a man, not a boy. But now his pain and his rage were too much to hold back. They had to come out.

She had to come out.

Heath thrust his arms and launched a mass of tempis over the crowd, a shapeless glob the size of a whale. It transformed in midair, forming limbs and paws and snarling white teeth.

In the span of a breath, the tempis had turned into a giant wolf, the most vicious one in Heath's pack. He'd named her Rose Tyler, and he feared her more than he loved her.

The Pelletiers were about to find out why.

Frowning, Esis flicked her hand, immersing the beast in an invisible cloud of solis. The energy should have been enough to pop it like a balloon, but the tempis endured without a ripple of strain.

<The watch,> Semerjean sent to her. *<He's wearing my watch!>*

Heath had taken the wristwatch back from Harold earlier, and he hadn't been nice about it. It was his trophy, his magic, his protection against future enemies. The wolves had become a crucial part of his life, and he never wanted to be separated from them again.

Unfortunately for the Pelletiers, the same device that made Heath immune to solis also rendered his tempis impervious to manipulation. They had no control over the great white beast that was lunging at them.

The spectators watched with wide-eyed fascination as the Pelletiers showed their first hint of worry. Semerjean and Esis cut through the air like missiles, throwing themselves in front of Azral before the wolf could reach him. Their hands exploded in jets of mortis, a dozen gooey black tendrils that wrapped around Heath's creature and bound it in the air.

Semerjean clenched his teeth, grunting, as he and Esis fought to contain the animal. The corrosive vines should have burned right through its hide, but tempis was a force of will, and so was Rose Tyler. She was the totality of Heath's rage, the middle finger his mother had always taught him to suppress, the scream he wanted to hurl at God for letting bad things happen to good people. She was the voice that cried for Jonathan Christie. And she was mighty.

Sweat dribbled down Esis's brow as Rose snapped and thrashed in her tendrils. Amanda nearly laughed at the panicked look she threw over her shoulder.

<Sehgee!>

Azral hovered behind her, his hands cutting through the air in quick, erratic motions. To the people down below, he looked he like was panicking in sign language. In truth, he was scrambling to disable the protections in Heath's wristwatch, a device he'd built out of spare silver bracelets.

At last, Azral found the remote kill switch, reducing the watch to a useless bauble. Esis vanquished Rose Tyler with a second burst of solis, then turned to Heath with a look of smoldering fury.

<Don't kill him,> Semerjean warned. *<The others will revolt.>*

Azral nodded in agreement. *<The boy is no longer a threat.>*

The Pelletiers returned to their floating formation, then took an anxious look at the crowd. The effects of Heath's disruption could be seen on each and every one of their faces: a nascent skepticism, a hint of derision. All the majesty and awe of Azral's offer had been thoroughly undermined.

Semerjean pursed his lips at the many doubtful faces below. "Look—"

As soon as he opened his mouth, a handful of Gothams began hissing at him. Even now, after all their traumas and ordeals, they couldn't forget the original reason they'd assembled down here: to say good-bye to their beloved Yvonne Whitten.

"Just go!" yelled Eddie Ballad, the brother of a boy whom Semerjean had murdered last year.

"Get out of here!" yelled Anna Bloom-Sunder, widow of Bug, mother of Gemma.

Semerjean raised his palms. "We'll be gone in a moment. I just—"

"Shut up."

The third interruption came from the northern edge of the crowd, from one of Semerjean's least favorite Gothams.

Peter stepped forward and glared at him reproachfully. "I can't speak for the others, *boy*, but I've had enough of your lip for one lifetime."

Hoots and applause rose up all around him. Azral glowered at the increasingly unruly mob. "We're offering a future for you and your children."

"That may be," Peter said, "but your timing's for shit. There isn't a single person here who hasn't lost someone today. We're in no state of mind to hear your devil's bargain."

Elder Tam wagged a stern finger at Semerjean. "'Devil' is right. I'd sooner die than trust you!"

"Nor should we," Irwin Sunder bellowed. "Those creatures murdered half my family!"

"They held me captive for *months*," yelled Sage Lee.

"*They killed my sister!*" Winnie Whitten shrieked at top volume.

The square fell into chaos as a hundred Gothams jeered at Azral, Esis, and Semerjean. The lumics filled the air with spectral noises—hisses and crackles and animal growls—enough to render all conversation impossible.

The Pelletiers turned to face each other, and communicated telepathically in their native tongue.

<*It's over,*> Esis said. <*They'll never cooperate.*>

<*Not today,*> Semerjean countered. <*Pendergen is right.*>

Esis looked at him askance. <*The man's a fool. You say so all the time.*>

<*He is a fool,*> said Semerjean. <*And I'd love nothing more than to crack his skull open. But in this instance, he makes a good point. They need time to lick their wounds and bury their dead.*>

Esis glanced at the fractious crowd. <*We should bury them all in this wretched tomb.*>

<*And we may one day,*> Azral said. <*But for now, let them rest. We'll see where they stand when cooler heads prevail.*>

He waved a twenty-foot portal into the air. <*Come.*>

The Gothams cried with delirious relief as Esis and Semerjean departed through the gateway. Azral drifted halfway into the portal, then turned around to take one last look around the square. In a distant corner, far beyond the rabble, Hannah caught his gaze and held it. There was something new and troubling in her expression, a look of calm hatred that went well beyond her years. For a moment, Azral caught a glimpse of something dark in the future, then just as quickly lost it.

Scowling, he vanished into the whiteness, then closed the portal behind him.

An addled hush fell over the survivors. Slowly, quietly, the scattered families began to come together. Peter brought Liam back from Long Island while, two blocks north, Stan Bloom found his way to Carrie. Amanda saw Hannah and hurried across the grass. They converged near the guild directory and hugged each other tight.

Thirty feet away, a soft hand squeezed Theo's shoulder. He turned around and saw Melissa, and fought the mad urge to embrace her.

"I know Azral's weakness," he uttered instead.

"What?"

A half-formed notion had been cooking in his head, ever since Semerjean and Esis rushed to save Azral from Heath's tempic wolf. It seemed a strange thing to do, as the man was more than capable of taking care of himself. Theo had watched him destroy a whole fleet of Integrity attack ships, using every temporal trick in the playbook—except one.

"Tempis," Theo told Melissa. "He's weak with tempis."

A stair hatch opened on the far side of the square. Zack and Mia emerged from the tunnels just in time to see the sky take on a whole new color. Everyone in the village raised their heads and looked up at the dome.

At long last, the Heavensend had completed its reboot. It remembered the gorgeous summer weather that was scheduled for the day, then brought it to life in vibrant color. By late afternoon, the four surviving elders would vote to lock the machine on its current setting, variety be damned. There would be nothing but clear blue skies and sunshine from now on, or at least the illusion of them.

FIFTY-FIVE

The local news was sedate that evening, with little to offer beyond the usual Sunday fanfare. A hit-and-run driver killed a child in Brooklyn. A Yonkers man died in an aerogliding mishap. The New York Furies scored a last-inning victory over the Cincinnati Robins, securing their place in the Women's League Championship. Residents of Quarter Hill were briefly disrupted by the sound of gunfire in the Heaven's Gate district. No casualties were reported.

As the last strips of daylight disappeared behind Irwin Sunder's mansion, Melissa waited impatiently by the front door. By now, Integrity had cleaned up and catalogued every last trace of the battle that had taken place here: the crashed dropship, the spent bullet casings, the large pool of blood on the driveway. It broke Melissa's heart to watch the last earthly remains of Jonathan Christie get siphoned into tubes. He'd lived a short and tumultuous life on this world, but he'd be remembered. The people who knew and loved him would be cherishing his memory for the rest of their lives.

The rest of their lives, Melissa thought with a scoff. That term used to mean something. Now all she could hear was Azral's flat, chilling voice.

Four years. Approximately.

An aerojet de-shifted and descended gracefully onto the lawn. Melissa watched, stone-faced, as a dozen well-dressed men and women came marching down the exit plank, all talking over each other like excited children. Until today, they were the misfits of Integrity: the idealists, the pacifists, the malcontents and rabble-rousers. Cedric Cain had carefully courted each and every one of them over the last several years, grooming them in secret and promising them a bright new future for the agency.

At long last, that future had arrived. And all it took was two hundred and fifty deaths.

Cain trailed his associates down the plank, his lanky frame towering over each and every one of them. Melissa credited him for not smiling in the wake of his triumph. This was not a good day for the National Integrity Commission, and she had no patience for anyone who thought otherwise.

The moment Cain spotted her, he broke away from his entourage and joined her on the front porch. Melissa gave him a deferential nod. "Director."

"*Acting* director," he stressed. "The heads haven't even finished rolling."

"You think there'll be prosecutions?"

He shook his head. "President's already starting to waffle. He just wants to bury this mess and move on."

Melissa closed her eyes in exasperation. "This is exactly why I left England."

"Yeah, well, if I've learned one thing in my career, it's that people are the same, no matter where you go."

He took an uneasy look around Sunder's property. "With some exceptions."

Melissa arched her back, grimacing. Cain noticed the many new scrapes and bruises on her skin, all souvenirs from her ordeal in the disseminator pit. "How you holding up?"

"I'm in somewhat dire need of a smoke."

Cain reached into his trench coat and retrieved a small container of hand-rolled cigarettes, pure Virginia tobacco. Cain always had access to the very best contraband.

He struck a match and lit her cigarette for her. "Probably goes without saying that you can write your own ticket in the agency. Any job you want. Any part of the world."

Melissa took a deep drag and exhaled with pleasure. "You know what I want."

"Oh yes. I figured as much. Just thought I'd give you the option."

Another aership appeared above Sunder's estate, a much larger vessel than the one Cain had arrived in. Melissa had already been briefed on who was inside: a hundred and two Gothams, the ones who'd been forcibly sedated by Gingold's soldiers and transported out of the underland. Cain had to move heaven and earth to get them back from the Sci-Tech facility. As expected, they were all in good health and perfectly wretched spirit.

Cain sighed at the hovering aership. "Hope that'll smooth things over with the clan chiefs."

"Not by much," said Melissa.

"Figures." He looked to his subordinates and waved them over. "Anything else I should know before I finally meet these Gothams?"

"Yes." Melissa took a final drag of her cigarette, then crushed it under her sneaker. "They hate being called that."

A hundred eyes followed Melissa and Cain as they led the procession into the heart of the village. By now, the underland was starting to look decent again. The dead had been identified and returned to their families. The blood and gore had been reversed away. The ghastly remains of Gingold's equipment—the guns and tents, the generators and spotlights—had been gathered into a sloppy pile and flushed by portal into the sea.

But the damage lingered on the faces of the people. Melissa could see it everywhere. Some of the locals looked angry enough to make her fear for her safety. All it would take was one vengeful tempic, one traumatized swifter, to kill her and Cain and the whole delegation. Luckily, the Gothams were painfully aware of the importance of this parley. If the peace talks failed, the clan would have to go on the run or brace themselves for another invasion. Neither option was very palatable.

By eight o'clock, the interim heads of Integrity were seated in the council chamber, along with all the surviving clan leaders. Luckily, Cain proved to be a much better diplomat than Azral. He absorbed every ounce of the Gothams' wrath, then laid out his plans in straight and humble plainspeak.

"This is a partnership," he told them. "You work with us, we'll work with you. You tell us your secrets, we'll help you keep them."

Ninety minutes after it began, the meeting ended with handshakes and guarded optimism. Cain formally introduced everyone to Leticia Gutiérrez, a small and affable woman who'd spent eight years running Integrity's field office in Madrid. As of Monday, she'd serve as the full-time, on-site coordinator for all of the agency's operations in the underland. To the Gothams, she was their new best friend. To the administrators and scientists who'd soon be populating the village, she was the new mayor.

At 9:45, Melissa escorted Cain's group back to the elevator, bristling at their giddy plans for the underland. An administration building over here, a research building over there, a new access tunnel for vehicles, a solic jail for the more belligerent timebenders. Gutiérrez even suggested they reinstall Gingold's disseminator, in case the natives really got restless.

Cain ushered his people onto the lift, then stayed behind with Melissa. "Don't worry," he said to her. "I'll keep them in line."

"If I see one constitutional violation—"

"That's not going to happen."

"—I will be the least of your problems."

"Melissa . . ." Cain held her by her shoulders. "Nine months ago, I asked you to take a leap of faith in me and you did. This is the part where it pays off. Just have a little more patience, okay? We'll make this work."

Melissa rubbed her throbbing temples. "I'm sorry, Cedric. After everything that's happened, it's just a little jarring to see."

"See what?"

"That Integrity won."

Cain lit up another cigarette, then took a somber look to the south. "I think it's time I meet the orphans."

The battle had barely left a mark on Freak Street. A small piece of dragonette had crashed against the side of Amanda's cottage. A wounded Gotham took refuge in Peter's house and bled on the carpet. Zack had only needed ten minutes to reverse away the damage. All that remained were the holes in their spirits, the yawning black space where Jonathan and David used to be.

Melissa summoned the remaining residents to Zack and Theo's backyard, then brought Cain into their circle of folding chairs. Only Peter and Amanda even bothered to make eye contact with him. Hannah and Theo stared down at their wringing hands. Zack and Liam doodled in their sketchbooks. Heath and Mia sat forward in their seats with miserable expressions, their heads buried in their hands. Melissa feared those two would need extreme psychological counseling, assuming there was someone even remotely qualified to handle their issues.

Cain crossed his legs and took a good, hard look at the orphans. "I hear you lost a good man today, and a not-so-good one yesterday. I'm sorry for both. On behalf of the United States government, I sincerely apologize for everything you suffered at the hands of my agency. It was a despicable act and it'll never happen again."

His left hand dawdled anxiously around a bulge in his coat pocket. Only Melissa knew that he was touching his cigarette case.

"It may be small comfort," Cain said, "but your faces have been removed from our criminal codex. Your records have been expunged. From this day forward, you're no longer fugitives. You can go where you like, though we humbly request that you continue to show discretion in public. The less news you make, the better for all of us."

Peter nodded with faint approval. Cain studied the gloves on Liam's hands before continuing.

"Additionally, I'm declaring you all to be special assets under Article Nine, Section Four of the United States Security Code. That gives you formal identification, a paycheck, and a whole mess of legal protections. You'll also have your own full-time dedicated liaison to the agency. I don't need to tell you her name."

Melissa smiled softly. Cain hadn't said a word about the position. He didn't have to. It was the only job she wanted and he damn well knew it.

"She's your den mother now," he told the others. "So keep her informed. And if the six of you—"

"Eight," Zack said.

"I'm sorry?"

He gestured at Peter and Liam. "They may not be orphans, but they're part of our group. Whatever we get, they get."

Cain scrutinized the Pendergens, expressionless. "You'll get no quarrel from me. I was about to say that we can house you up wherever you want. It doesn't have to be—"

"We're fine here," Peter said.

"Okay. But should you change your mind—"

"We won't," Peter insisted. "This is exactly where we need to be."

Melissa turned toward him, curious. The man was stubborn in all the same ways she was, but nowhere near as adaptive. She girded herself for many more clashes in the future, a perpetual tug-of-war between den mother and den father.

The yard fell into awkward silence. Amanda leaned back and took a wary look at Cain. "Question."

"Yes?"

"There's a man out there named Evan Rander. He killed someone very close to us, and we have every intention of finding him."

"We can help you," Cain told her.

Amanda shook her head. "We don't need your help. We just want to make sure you won't get in our way when we do what needs to be done."

Mia's bouncing legs came to a halt. Heath looked up for the first time since the meeting started.

"Maybe we should table this discussion for another time," Melissa suggested.

"It's all right," Cain said. He turned back to Amanda. "I appreciate you being up front with me. And I've seen Melissa's files on Rander. I won't cry in my soup if he meets a grim fate, but I can tell you from experience that vengeance doesn't always go the way you want it to. That's my chief concern."

Amanda's expression softened. "Fair point."

Hannah remained perfectly still, her dark eyes fixed on the grass. Melissa feared from the hard twist in her mouth that she had no interest in or use for Cain's wisdom. She wanted revenge, plain and simple. Melissa would have to watch her closely.

"We'll also have to talk about the Pelletiers," Cain said, "but it doesn't—"

Mia cut him off with a pitch-black chuckle.

"It doesn't have to be tonight," he finished.

The backyard fell into another long silence. Cain opened his mouth to say something, then stopped himself. Melissa knew exactly what was going on behind those shrewd blue eyes of his. This was the worst possible time to ask the question on his mind. But it couldn't wait. He had to know.

"Is it true?"

The orphans and Pendergens gave him their full attention again. Cain looked at each Silver in turn. "Is this world ending in four years?"

Peter took a deep breath through his nose. "That's not necessarily—"

"Yes," Mia interjected.

"We're working hard to make sure—"

"*Yes,*" Mia emphatically repeated. "Four years."

She rose to her feet and stood directly in front of Cain. "But you don't have to worry."

His eyes opened wide as Mia waved a portal into the air.

"The Pelletiers will kill you long before it happens," she assured him.

She whisked herself away, then closed the disc behind her. Melissa made a note to start vetting therapists.

Cain pulled out his cigarette tin. "Anyone mind if I, uh . . . ?"

"No," Peter and Amanda said.

"Thank you."

Cain popped a cigarette between his lips, passed a second one to Melissa, and then lit up both. He took two long drags before speaking again.

"Well, I guess the agency has a new secret to keep." He turned to Peter. "You say there's a chance to stop it?"

"I know there is."

"Okay, then. You have the full and unconditional support of the United States government. For what it's worth."

He blew a fat puff of smoke into the air. "If there's anything you people need—"

"Yes."

Theo hadn't said a word in hours. He'd been walking around with a troubled expression, as if he were trying to solve a complicated math problem. Now, at last, the numbers had come together. He looked at Hannah with a flash of guilt before locking his eyes on Cain.

"I need to leave."

FIFTY-SIX

He arrived at Alcatraz in a state of discord, a temporal jet lag that left him thoroughly discombobulated. The Transonic G-9 aerodart had been shifted at 18x, traveling from East Coast to West in just forty-eight minutes of standard time. Yet thirteen and a half hours had passed inside the cabin, with little for Theo to do but fidget and twist in his Elite Class seat. If the other passengers resented the interminable journey, they certainly hadn't shown it. They were all businesspeople from the looks of them. They probably relished the chance to sit back and relax while the outside world only barely creaked forward.

The courtesy shuttle pilot, a middle-age blonde with the arms of a weight-lifter, caught Theo's muddled expression as she flew him to the terminal gate.

"I know that look," she teased. "Your inner clock's gone cuckoo and you're trying to orientate."

Theo nodded. Thanks to temporis and time zones, his plane managed to land two hours and twelve minutes before it took off.

The pilot tapped his wrist. "You should get yourself a duochron watch. They self-adjust."

"So do I," Theo said. "Eventually."

The woman smiled politely. She was already aware of his federal VIP status, a badge that entitled him to priority service everywhere. Theo could only guess that he was the scruffiest-looking dignitary she'd ever seen—a wild prince of the Philippines, perhaps, or an eccentric scientist. If he told her the truth, she wouldn't believe him. If he showed her the balance on his government cash card, she'd probably cry.

"Well, whatever you're here for, you should take the time to look around," she told him. "There's no place on Earth like San Francisco."

"Yeah." Theo fixed his vacant stare out the window. "I've seen it."

The shuttle arrived at the terminal. The pilot thanked Theo for flying Transonic and wished him a pleasant stay.

He only had a few moments to marvel at the splendor of the aerport before his handphone vibrated. Theo frowned at the name of the caller, then answered the phone.

"You spying on me already?"

Melissa scoffed. "Can't you ever just say hello?"

"I literally just got here. How did you know?"

"I checked your flight status. It's not hard to do."

He threw a nervous look over his shoulder. "I told you I don't want anyone following me."

"There's no one following you, Theo. I kept my word."

He peeked over the guardrail and nearly buckled from vertigo. From the outside, Alcatraz National Aerport wasn't that impressive, just a squat concrete ziggurat on the northern side of the island. Inside, however, the place was surreal—a massive gorge of mezzanines and escalators that seemed to go all the way down to Hades. Flying platforms ferried passengers back and forth across the chasm while subterranean shuttles provided quick and easy passage around the Bay Area. Once upon a time, this rock had been impossible to escape. Now . . .

"You still there?" Melissa asked him.

"I'm here."

Melissa cradled her phone on her shoulder while she tinkered with her new computer. Integrity had installed a two-story housepod at the front end of Freak Street, a modular dwelling that would serve as both home and office. While her upstairs bedroom was still a jungle of boxes, her workspace was fully organized. All she needed was a lumbar cushion for her desk chair and she was ready for business.

She watched Theo on her monitor as he bumbled his way through Alcatraz. She'd only promised not to send spies after him. He didn't say anything about electronic snooping.

"Still wish I knew what were you doing there," she complained.

Theo shrugged. He felt awful leaving his friends after everything that had happened, but he desperately needed to be here. Something big was coming to San Francisco: a cataclysmic event that would either save the world or kill it sooner. The pivot point would occur in fourteen months, and Theo wanted to make damn sure he was ready for it.

He sighed into the phone. "I'm sorry, Melissa. I wish I could explain it better."

"If you need help finding Ioni—"

"No." Theo retrieved a granola bar from his shoulder bag. "Nobody can find her unless she wants to be found. And she'll be steering clear of me for a while."

"How do you know?"

Theo's face tightened as he chewed on his snack. "Because she screwed over Mia. That puts her right back on my shit list."

Melissa frowned at his image. "You have an entire government agency at your disposal. There has to be something we can do for you."

"Just be there for my friends. They'll need you now more than ever. Especially Hannah."

"You make it sound like you're not coming back."

"I'll be back," he said. "I just . . ."

Melissa tilted her head. "What?"

Theo mulled his words a moment before shrugging again. He could see the future clearer than ever, the long and twisting road that he was forced to walk alone. Though he'd return to the underland on many occasions, the place would never be home again. Not for him.

"Just have faith in me," he said. "If there's a way to save this world, I'm gonna find it."

Melissa opened a new window on her computer screen and opened the data file for Michael Pendergen, a.k.a. Merlin McGee. Theo had mentioned that he was an important player in events to come. Maybe she could find him and get her own answers.

"Just promise you'll check in as often as you can," she said.

"I will."

He saw a glowing sign for Golden Gate Aerocabs, then changed direction. "All right. I should go."

"Why?"

"What do you mean 'why'?"

"I mean why hang up?" Melissa said. "You're perfectly capable of walking and talking."

"I don't know. I figured you were busy."

"Not particularly."

"Okay." Theo shifted his phone to his other ear, then made his way for the cab stand. "What do you want to talk about?"

"Anything but the future."

Melissa leaned back, kicked off her shoes, and propped her feet up on the desk.

"Tell me your story, Theo." She turned off her monitor and plucked a cigarette from her desk. "Start at the beginning."

Peter leaned against the kitchen island, his dull eyes locked on a heat crisper. He wasn't in the habit of making toast for lunch, but he didn't have the mind to cook much else. A tenth of his clan had died violently on Sunday, and the agency that killed them was now calling the shots. His one hope for the future had left for San Francisco on a fool's errand. And just last night, before he even had a chance to get his bearings, his girlfriend broke up with him while also asking him to impregnate her.

I'm sorry, Amanda told him. *The Pelletiers have made this complicated. But with me and Zack, it's very simple. He's mine and I'm his. The rest of it . . . please forgive me.*

At the time, Peter had been too tired, too muddled, too shell-shocked to protest. Even now in the light of day, he could hardly fault her. But the thought of giving a child to Semerjean and company? No. That didn't sit well. That didn't sit well with him at all.

The toast rolled off the crisper belt, tumbling onto a paper plate. Peter spent five seconds looking for a bread knife before cutting his lunch in half with a portal. It only vaguely occurred to him that he'd done the exact same thing to a soldier recently.

"Dad . . ."

Liam stood in the doorway, looking pale and unrested. He'd woken up twice in the middle of the night screaming Mother Olga's name. Peter feared the horrors of Sunday would haunt him for the rest of his life. He was just one of several people to worry about.

"It's Mia," Liam said. "She's out back. I . . . think you should check on her."

Peter stepped out onto the patio and saw Mia in the next yard. She'd spent the last forty minutes rummaging through Carrie's house, dropping all their sentimental keepsakes on the grass: photos and love notes, cups and plates, movie spools, music spins, anything that even vaguely reminded Mia of better times.

"Sweetheart . . ."

Mia shot Peter a black look before disappearing into the cottage. She came back outside with an electric whirlet, the one she and Carrie had used every day to make frozen drinks.

"Look, I know you're upset," Peter said. "But Carrie's still with us. Anything you lost, you can get back."

"Get back?" Mia threw the mixer onto the pile. "She doesn't even recognize me!"

"Then introduce yourself. Start over."

Mia stared at him in disbelief, as if he'd told her to build a new Carrie out of mud and straw.

"You don't get it, Peter. You have no idea."

"About you and her?"

"Yes."

Peter listlessly kicked the grass. "I knew what you had. I'm not blind."

"Then how can you tell me to start over?"

"Because you can," he said. "There are people here who just buried their loved ones. You think Hannah wouldn't jump at the chance to start over with Jonathan?"

Mia fumed at the comparison. "That was low, Peter."

"I'm not trying to guilt you. I'm just saying—"

"Leave me alone!"

She pulled her journal from the crook of her arm and began tearing out pages. They fluttered chaotically onto the pile, like dead leaves.

"You still don't get it," she told Peter. "I'm his enemy now. If I get close to Carrie again, he'll just come back for her. He'll probably kill her next time."

"You don't know that."

Mia narrowed her eyes at him. "I know Semerjean."

Peter watched her worriedly as she tore up the rest of her journal, all the thoughts she'd written on the road, all the notes and intel from her future selves. She wasn't just throwing Carrie on the pyre, she was throwing herself.

"You can't torch that stuff," Peter cautioned.

"I'm not."

"You'll burn down the whole—"

"I'm not starting a fire!"

"Then what . . ." Peter's eyes bulged. "Oh, no. Don't you dare."

Mia moved to the edge of the yard, closed her eyes, and then raised her arms. A high-pitched hum filled the yard. Peter felt a rippling distortion in his senses.

"Mia, no!"

A temporal portal opened horizontally above the lawn, six feet wide and crackling with energy. Peter never had to teach Mia how to rip a hole in time. She'd been doing it from her very first day on this world.

But she'd never made a rift this big before. A sucking wind swirled around the pile, pulling all the loose papers into the portal. Mia increased its size until the larger items began to shake loose and tumble upward.

Peter struggled his way around the edge of the vortex. "Mia, close it! *Close it!*"

She kept widening the door until the heaviest of the keepsakes—that damn frozen drink mixer—went sailing into the past. It traveled eleven months backward, crashing hard at the feet of a thirteen-year-old Mia. Let the youngest of her past selves deal with the baggage. Let the "David" of the era try to explain it.

A lawn chair snapped shut and flew spinning into the portal. Mia struggled to close her gate, but was struck from behind by a loose piece of fence. She stumbled forward, shrieking, as the portal's wind took hold of her.

"*No!*"

Peter barged his way into her thoughts, clamping them down with sheer force of will. Unfortunately, he had no time to be gentle about it. Mia screamed in agony, as if her head had been crushed in an iron vise.

The portal vanished in an instant. The gushing wind stopped. Two uprooted lawn chairs came crashing down to the grass, along with Mia.

Peter hopped over the fence and kneeled at her side. "Goddamn it! Have you lost your mind?"

She lay flat on her back with her arm draped over her eyes. A thin stream of blood dribbled out of each ear. "Just go away."

"Do you *want* to die?"

"Yes!"

Her lips trembled. She wept into her hands. It wasn't until Peter touched her thoughts that he'd felt the full extent of her damage. All the traumas and sorrows of the last eleven months were spinning inside her head like knives, cutting her over and over and over again. She had no defense.

Peter pulled her into his arms and held her tight, his mind spitting curses at Semerjean.

"It's all right," he told Mia. "It's gonna be okay."

By the time he carried her back to his bedroom, she was already half asleep. Peter closed the blinds, tucked her into his bed, then watched her from an easy chair.

Liam peeked in through the door crack, whispering, "She okay?"

"No." Peter kept his glum stare on Mia. "She's gonna stay with us awhile, if that's all right."

"Yeah. Of course. She can have my room."

Peter squeezed his wrist and smiled. "You're a good soul, Liam. You always have been."

The boy lowered his head with a guilty expression. "I see it now."

"See what?"

"Why you left to help the breachers. They're good people."

Peter's expression darkened. He wouldn't have lifted a finger for them if he didn't think they could help him. It had always been about saving the world, about saving *Liam*. In many ways, it still was.

Soon Liam left and Peter resumed his quiet vigil. By two o'clock, he could hear Mia's gentle snores. He figured it was just a matter of moments before the air became bright with the light of a hundred mini-portals.

But surprisingly, it didn't happen. At long last, the Future Mias had nothing left to say. No notes of warning. No scathing rebukes. Not a single word until four o'clock, when a buttonhole portal opened up near the ceiling. A tight stick of paper hit the ground near Peter's feet.

Hesitantly, he picked it up and twirled it in his fingers. Though he had no way of knowing it, he was holding the second-to-last message that Mia would ever receive from her future selves. And it wasn't even for her.

He unrolled the stick and read her familiar scribble.

Don't worry, Peter. She has some hard months ahead of her, and she'll never again be the girl you remember. But she'll get through this. She'll come out the other side and she'll be stronger than ever.

Don't give in to the Pelletiers. Don't give up on the string. And whatever happens, whatever she says, don't ever forget what you mean to her. You're the father of the hearts of a billion Mias. And we love you.

Peter read the note five more times before stuffing it into his pocket. He leaned back in his chair, wiped the tears from his eyes, and smiled at Mia's sleeping form.

"Daughter of my heart," he whispered. "That's what you are."

He folded his hands on his chest and closed his eyes contentedly. "That's what you are."

A thin white tendril emerged from beneath the covers of Amanda's bed. It forged a blind, snaking path across the floor of the cottage: through the five-inch crack in the bedroom door, down the hallway, between the chairs of the living room, and up the wooden drawers of a kitchen cabinet. The tempis fumbled around the countertop until it found a fruit bowl, then took a firm pincer grip on an apple.

Zack watched from the other side of the bed as the fruit retracted all the way into Amanda's hand. "That was an astonishing act of laziness."

Amanda laughed. "I did that once when Hannah was in the kitchen. She almost hit the ceiling."

"I'd be more impressed if your tempis made an omelet."

"How about *you* make an omelet?"

"From here?"

"Forget it." She cut up the apple with a tempic blade, then split the wedges with Zack. "You're just as lazy as me."

By the time they finished, their humor was gone. They sat against the headboard, their hands clasped, their eyes busy with thought.

"He never liked me," Amanda said. "All that time I loved him like a brother, and he just barely tolerated me."

Zack scoffed. "Look at the people he does love. You really want to be in that company?"

"No. They make me sick." Amanda closed her eyes. "The thought of giving them a baby makes me sick."

"Yeah. Mercy's already looking for a way out."

"They'll kill her."

"She knows." He lay on his back and fixed his heavy eyes on the ceiling. "She just needs time."

Amanda nestled against him. "Do whatever you can to make it easier for her. I won't . . ."

"Amanda."

"I won't be possessive."

Zack turned to face her. "That's not how this works. It's you and me. We're the couple. Everything else is just—"

"—fine print."

"I was going to say 'temporary.'"

Amanda nodded tensely. "You're right. This is just a means to an end."

"A means to a beginning," Zack corrected. "The moment we get those assholes out of our lives, we're free."

"*If* we get them out."

Zack stroked her shoulder. "I watched Rebel knock them down with just his middle finger. You saw Heath put all three of them on the defensive. They can be surprised and they can be hurt. We just have to find their weaknesses."

Amanda looked to the satchel on her dresser, all the shiny new healing discs that Esis had given her. "Death."

"What?"

"They're afraid of death," she said. "That's the reason they're doing all this. They want to live forever because they're scared of what's on the other side."

She raised her hand to eye level and grew a small sphere of tempis. Zack watched it intently as it morphed into a human skull.

"My problem," said Amanda, "is that I'm more afraid of losing the people

I love, and the Pelletiers know it. They've been using it against me. That's *my* weakness."

"Not much you can do about that."

"Yes there is."

"Like what? Caring less?"

"Living more." Amanda sat up and stared into the empty sockets of her sculpture. "We're all going to die, Zack. Even if the Pelletiers don't kill us, even if the sky never comes down, time will catch up with us one day. And if we can't win on quantity, then maybe we should win on quality."

She looked to Zack. "I want to enjoy single every moment I have with you. I want to make love and make jokes and make the most out of this situation with Peter and Mercy. Every second we spend on this world will count for something. And when we finally face the Pelletiers, I will not fear death, yours or mine. I won't be afraid because I'll know that we lived good lives. We took the hand we were dealt and we played it beautifully."

The tempic skull melted back into her hand. "This is how we beat them."

Zack smiled at her from the mattress. "I knew I liked you for a reason."

"*Liked* me?"

"Maybe not the strongest word I could have used."

"Try another."

"I value you?"

"You know I can hurt you, right?"

She threw herself on top on him, then pressed her lips against his. They barely had a moment to enjoy their kiss before a shadow darkened the window. A hand knocked gently on the glass.

Amanda covered herself with a pillow and took a puzzled look through the blinds. Melissa stood in the side yard, a clipboard in her hands and an urgency in her expression.

"Get dressed," she said. "Both of you."

She led Amanda and Zack to the south edge of town, to one of the five community elevators that Integrity had claimed for their own. Fifteen soldiers stood guard at the doors while a small crowd of Gothams rubbernecked from the perimeter park.

Amanda struggled to see through the mass of bobbing heads. "They were asking for Theo?"

"By name," Melissa said. "Do you know how many people he reached out to?"

"Two groups. But I don't—"

The soldiers parted for Melissa, Zack, and Amanda, revealing twelve weary-looking strangers in weather-beaten clothes. They stood clustered in front of the elevator doors, their nervous eyes roving in all directions. Amanda's heart jumped when she saw a Pelletier bracelet on one of their wrists: a dark iron version of her old silver bangle.

The leader of the contingent, a muscular man with curly brown hair, stepped forward at the sight of Zack. "Are you Theo?"

"No. He had to leave on business." Zack extended a hand. "I'm Zack Trillinger. This is Amanda Given. If you are who we think you are—"

"We are," said the leader.

"—then we're from your world."

None of the orphans seemed convinced. Amanda could hardly blame them. They'd come here expecting Theo and got a whole mess of government soldiers instead.

Before anyone could ask, Zack buried the group in a barrage of old-Earth references: Obama, Madonna, iPhones, *Home Alone*, Fozzie Bear, Linda Blair, diet peach Snapple, Google Earth, Mr. Burns, unobtainium, and retweets. Melissa feared for a moment that Zack was having some kind of neurological episode, yet the orphans looked at him like he'd just grown wings and a halo.

The leader eagerly shook Zack's hand. "Wow. Okay. You weren't kidding. I'm Caleb Brooks, from the Tampa group."

The Platinums, Amanda thought but didn't say. If he was anything like her, he wouldn't like being called by his Pelletier handle.

Caleb motioned to the quartet to his left, the ones with iron bracelets. "These fine folks are from the Austin group. We found each other along the way."

Zack beamed at his twelve fellow survivors, more than he'd ever seen in one place. "You have no idea how glad I am to meet you."

"Just wait."

"What do you mean?"

"We're not all here yet," Caleb told him. "There wasn't enough room on the—"

The elevator returned with a hollow *ping*. The doors slid open to reveal a tall black woman and six filthy adolescents.

Mother stepped off the elevator and smiled coyly at Zack. "Hello again."

He blinked at her dazedly. Though he'd lost all memory of their scuffle in Seattle, Mia had told him everything he needed to know about the Coppers.

"Holy shit." He shook Mother's hand. "You're here. You came. What made you—"

"Change my mind?" She wrapped her arm around a honey-skinned girl, the twelve-year-old augur known only as See. "This one has never steered us wrong. If she says this is where we need to be, then this is where we need to be."

See turned her large hazel eyes onto Amanda. "I know you. I've seen you in visions."

"Really?"

"Yeah. You're always flying on your pretty wings."

"What?"

Caleb patted See's back. "This clever girl knew just where to find us. We've been traveling together for two days now."

"That's fantastic," Zack said.

The Platinums and Irons didn't share Zack's enthusiasm. Amanda could see from their tense, rigid postures that they weren't entirely fond of the Coppers.

Caleb smiled with forced politeness. "Yeah. It all worked out nicely."

Melissa scanned the faces of the nearby Gothams. More than fifty of them had gathered by now, and not a single one looked pleased. It seemed the orphans were about as welcome here as the U.S. government. Another issue to monitor.

Amanda looked to Caleb. "You've come a long way. Is there anything we can get you?"

"We're a little tired," he admitted. "We could use some beds."

Zack clapped his back. "We'll do better than that. We'll get you some houses."

"It's not far," Amanda said. "Just follow us."

Two by two, the orphans moved north. As Zack and Amanda led the procession, they kept looking over their shoulders and marveling at the many new faces behind them.

"Holy shit," Zack said. "That's nineteen people. *Our* people."

Amanda clasped his hand, her euphoria mixed with a touch of lament. She wished Theo was here to see the fruits of his labor. She wished Jonathan was here to play them a song from the old world. She even found herself missing David, at least the illusion of him. The heart was a strong and stubborn muscle, but sometimes that worked in her favor.

"Hey."

Amanda snapped out of her daze and saw Zack smiling at her. "Did I forget to say 'I love you'?"

"It might have slipped your mind."

"I love you."

Amanda squeezed his fingers, then looked ahead at all the new housepods on Freak Street. "Damn right you do."

The Memorial Garden had been closed since sunrise. The gates were shrouded with thick red curtains, blocking all view of the tribute committee as they carved new names onto the Requiem Wall. They'd never been faced with such a devastating update: a hundred and eleven kinsmen who'd been alive as of Sunday morning. Now they were all just etchings in stone. The laser engravers were so overworked, the committee had to unplug the machines and let them cool for an hour.

By late afternoon, the job was finally done. The curtains came down and the garden was reopened. Four dozen mourners came trickling in through the front gate, bearing roses and candles and photos of the deceased. One swifter brought a holographic bust of her dear, departed son. She placed it down near her family marker and set it to an endless loop.

Hannah moved invisibly among the crowd, her head dipped, her eyes hidden behind a pair of sunglasses. If it was gauche to come here wearing a leather jacket over a short black dress, she didn't care. The clothes fit her mood like nothing else in the closet. She wanted to drape everything around her in dark satin and leather. Wrap the world in black until it was nothing but a gap in the stars.

While half the mourners flocked to their family monuments, Hannah joined the rest at the Wall. There were enough new names to warrant five columns, with a special plaque for the elite deceased: the Mayor, Mother Olga, Elder Rubinek, Victoria Chisholm. Even Rebel got his own commendation for taking on the Pelletiers directly.

But someone very important was missing from the roster, the only name Hannah cared about.

She pushed her way forward and scanned the rest of the tally. There was no mention of Jonathan anywhere.

"What the fuck?"

A middle-age turner eyed her distastefully. Hannah glared at him through her shades. "He helped save you people. You'd be *dead* if it wasn't for him!"

"Hannah."

She turned around and saw Mercy beckoning her from the corner, her work clothes mottled with sweat and stone dust. She must have been one of the artisans on the tribute committee. Did she even know that Jonathan died? Did she care?

Hannah hurried toward her, only vaguely taking notice of the teenage boy behind her. Sage leaned against the gate with a bored and testy expression, as if his sister had harangued him into being here.

"Where is he?" Hannah demanded.

"You have every reason to be pissed," Mercy said. "I tried to get his name on the wall but some people—"

"Who?"

"—thought the breachers should have a separate marker."

"*Who?*"

Mercy gestured to the south, where Irwin Sunder stood with a cluster of his relatives. Hannah narrowed her eyes at him. "Son of a bitch."

"Yeah, he's a knob, but he's not worth your trouble. It doesn't matter anyway. Look . . ."

She drew Hannah's gaze to a monument by the wall, a ten-foot obelisk of bonded white marble. It featured a shiny brass plaque that, to Hannah's surprise, already had seven engravings. A woman named Carina, a man named Sebastian, a couple of guys named Drew and Gavin. It wasn't until she saw Josh Trillinger's name, right below Jonathan's, that she figured it out. They were the New York orphans, the ones with gold bracelets. The ones who died at the hands of Gothams.

Hannah turned to Mercy, the last surviving member of Rebel and Ivy's kill squad. "You knew their names."

Mercy threw a quick peek at her brother before looking away in shame. "Rebel knew them."

Hannah gently stroked the letters of Jonathan's name, and suddenly realized the folly of her outrage. The Gothams could have erected a statue of him in the center of town and it wouldn't have mattered. He was gone. He was gone and nothing on Earth would bring him back.

"I . . ." Hannah tried to work up the nerve to thank Mercy but she was distracted by the blank space on the plaque. There was room for at least thirty more names, everyone she knew and cared about on this world.

Sage crossed his arms and mumbled at the grass. "There are more."

Hannah turned to him. "What?"

"There are more of your people," he said. "I met some in captivity. Three Brits, an American, and a Frenchwoman. They had purple bracelets on their wrists and they kept talking about stuff I couldn't understand. There used to be nine of them but . . . I don't know. I don't know what happened to the rest."

Hannah approached him, fascinated. "Where was this?"

Sage shrugged. "No idea. We didn't have any windows. But one of the Brits swore back and forth that he heard the chime of Big Ben."

Hannah's heart pounded. It seemed she and her friends were due for a trip to London.

"Is there anything else you can tell me? Any signs or—"

A stuttered hush fell over the mourners. Hannah looked around and saw half the Gothams staring anxiously at the front gate, at the newest arrival in the garden.

She took off her sunglasses. "Heath?"

The boy shambled toward her, cringing at all the attention. He'd become something of a legend since Sunday, when his great white wolf threw the Pelletiers into disarray. If the Gothams hadn't seen it with their own eyes, they wouldn't have believed it. The breacher was strong, and he was no friend of the demons. Even Sunder regarded him with a grudging amount of respect.

The moment Heath reached Hannah, the others went back to their business. Mercy took Sage by the hand and let the orphans have their privacy.

Hannah squeezed Heath's shoulder. "I thought you were sleeping."

He shook his head, his moony eyes fixed on the obelisk. "What is this?"

"They made it for us," Hannah said. "For the ones we lost."

Now that she mentioned it, she realized she'd have to add Jury Curado to the list. Another dead lover. Another one of Evan's victims.

Heath ran a finger across Jonathan's name, tracing every curve and contour until his eyes glistened.

"Why did he have to die?"

Because he loved me, Hannah thought.

"Because . . ." She sucked a deep breath and repressed all her grief. If she started crying now, she wouldn't stop. And she refused to fall apart in front of Irwin Fucking Sunder.

"Because some people are cruel," Hannah said. "They don't know how to create anything. They only know how to destroy."

A long silence passed, interrupted only by the sounds of Heath's sniffles. Hannah moved behind him and stroked his hair.

"I'm going to take care of you from now on," she told him. "And you're going to take care of me. It's the only way he would have wanted it. It's what *I* want. Okay, Heath?"

Heath stared intently at the names of his fellow Golds, then muttered something under his breath. For a moment, she thought he said, "I'm odd," which, despite its truth, made no sense in context. It would take her a full day to realize that he was saying "Ahmad," and then another week to work up the nerve to ask him about it.

Hannah rested her chin on his head. "We're also going to keep working on the music project, you and me. We gotta keep bringing those songs back. Jonathan was very clear about that."

Heath shook his head. "We need a guitarist."

"I'll be the guitarist."

"You can't play."

"I'll learn," Hannah insisted. "I can be a really fast learner when I want to be."

The light of the undersky was starting to give her a headache. She put her shades back on and stood quietly at Heath's side. Soon she heard a soft noise from him—a coarse grunt, like he was clearing his throat. Hannah knew exactly what that meant.

"Wait, what—"

Heath kept his eyes on the breachers' stone. Then, in a high, clear voice, he began to sing.

> *Words are flowing out like endless rain into a paper cup*
> *They slither while they pass, they slip away across the universe*

Again, the Gothams stopped what they were doing and threw their rapt attention onto Heath. Hannah was the only one here who even remotely recognized the song he was singing. She knew it so well that she couldn't keep her lips from mouthing the words as Heath continued.

> *Pools of sorrow, waves of joy are drifting through my opened mind*
> *Possessing and caressing me*
> *Jai guru deva om.*
> *Nothing's gonna change my world*
> *Nothing's gonna change my world*

The Integrity agents just outside the perimeter fence moved in closer to listen, just as fifty Gothams clustered together in the garden. By now, everyone in Altamerica had become acquainted with the Beatles, though none of them had ever heard this particular song.

Hannah stayed perfectly still behind Heath, her brown eyes locked on Sunder's. She thought about the vow she'd made to him and the entire clan: a promise not to sing ever again. In hindsight, she couldn't even remember why she chose to honor that stupid pledge. There was no benefit to keeping it, no punishment for breaking it, no satisfaction at all in proving Sunder wrong. In the grand scheme of things, the man was nothing.

And she had sacrificed enough.

By the time Heath reached the second refrain, Hannah took a deep breath and accompanied him. A hundred people gathered around the pair as they channeled the music of their late, great Earth. Even the government agents in the audience reeled at the sorrow in their voices, the overwhelming beauty of their duet. The orphans sang in perfect harmony. They kept perfect time.

ACKNOWLEDGMENTS

Well, this was another huge book that took me way too long to write. Thank you, readers, for your extreme patience. I've met many, many wonderful people through *The Flight of the Silvers*. It drove me nuts to keep you all waiting. But you were all very nice about it, and your continued enthusiasm really kept me going on those difficult days. I thank you for that too.

There's no way in hell I could have finished this beast without my personal brain trust, the alpha readers who were given *The Song of the Orphans* in half-baked dribs and drabs: Mark Harvey, Leni Fleming, Jen Gennaco, Gretchen Smith, Ricki Bar-Zeev (aka my mother), and Nancy Price, who I'll mention again in just a bit.

Much gratitude to my beta readers, whose insightful comments helped me make tons of improvements to the narrative: Angela Ferrigno, Shauna Pittman, Ysabelle Pelletier, Craig Aikin, Mick Soth, Dave Bledsoe, Craig Mertens, Huan Nghiem, William McDermott, Krista Stein, Erin Anderson, Terry Minogue, Laurie Barnett, Susie Hancock, Kerri Rifkin, Dustin Shaffer, Mike Tunison, Laura Helseth, Kenja Purkey, Carey Gibbons, Sarah Brehm, Tara McDonough, Jason Cole, and the incomparable Stitch Mayo.

Special thanks to my fellow authors Kelly Jensen and K. M. Alexander for their invaluable feedback. Find them both on Amazon and then buy their books. You won't be sorry.

Extra special thanks to Michael Farmer for getting me those Beatles and Pink Floyd song rights for an insanely good price. Holy crap.

Super-mucho extra gratitude to the people who toiled behind the scenes to make this book happen, including Stuart M. Miller (my longtime agent), Marie Finamore (my production editor), Dorian Hastings (my copyeditor), David Rosenthal (my patron saint), and my incredible editor, Nina Shield, who probably put as many hours into *The Song of the Orphans* as I have. Huge thanks also to the dauntless *Orphans* marketing team: Marian Brown, Alison Coolidge, and Kayleigh George.

And then there's a whole mess of Bar-Zeevs to thank, most of whom share my DNA and all of whom kept me afloat in one way or another: Avi, Sara, Yona, Joan, and that aforementioned mother of mine, who'd convinced me to write the Silvers series in the first place.

Finally, once again, there's Nancy Price: my partner in all things. She tweeted me in 2015 to tell me how much she enjoyed *The Flight of the Silvers*. Next thing I know, I'm finishing the sequel in her house. I don't always move in with the readers who tweet me. But when I do, it works out nicely.

Thank you, Nancy, for everything you are and everything you do.